LANCE PARKIN

AHISTORY

with additional material by
LARS PEARSON

Also Available from Mad Norwegian Press...

Copyright © 2006 Mad Norwegian Press.
www.madnorwegian.com

Cover art by Sandy Gardner.
www.sandygardner.co.uk
Cover & interior design by Christa Dickson.
www.christadickson.com

ISBN: 0-9725959-9-6
Printed in the United States of America.
First Edition: January 2006.

mad norwegian press | des moines

'I loathe and detest people who produce these elaborate histories. As a writer you have to memorise this but it's gobbledygook.'

Gerry Davis,
Doctor Who story editor, writer
and co-creator of the Cybermen

TABLE OF CONTENTS

The following *only* catalogs main story entries for each adventure; some stories occur in muliple time zones, and hence have more than one page number listed. For a complete listing of *all* story references, consult the Index.

Some stories proved undatable and lack main entries; for a list of these, consult the None of the Above section (page 294).

TABLE OF CONTENTS

5

TABLE OF CONTENTS

TABLE OF CONTENTS

TABLE OF CONTENTS

TABLE OF CONTENTS

TABLE OF CONTENTS

Footnote Features

A great many people have been involved with this book. This is the third version. The first - *The Doctor Who Chronology* - was produced by Seventh Door Fanzines. It covered the television series. The second - *A History of the Universe* - was published by Virgin in 1996, and covered the television series plus the New and Missing Adventures up to *Happy Endings* and *The Sands of Time* respectively. It proved very popular. Nearly ten years on, this latest version covers roughly twice as many stories as the last one.

Thanks first and foremost to my editors - Mark Jones, Rebecca Levene and Simon Winstone, and for this latest version, Lars Pearson.

Thanks to the many other people who have offered information, comments, help, material, corrections or just said nice things. In alphabetical order, these are: Ben Aaronovitch, Nadir Ahmed, Keith Ansell, John Binns, Jon Blum, David Brunt, Graeme Burk, Andy Campbell, Andrew Cartmel, Shaun Chmara, Mark Clapham, Paul Cornell, Alex Dante, Jeremy Daw, Martin Day, Zoltan Dery, Jonathan Evans, Michael Evans, Simon Forward, Martin Foster, Gary Gillatt, Donald and Patricia Gillikin, Craig Hinton, David Howe, Edward Hutchinson, Alison Jacobs, William Keith, Andy Lane, Paul Lee, Daniel O'Mahony, Steven Manfred, April McKenna, Iain McLaughlin, Adrian Middleton, Lawrence Miles, Kate Orman, David Owen, David Pitcher, Andrew Pixley, Marc Platt, Jon Preddle, Gareth Roberts, Trevor Ruppe, Gary Russell, Justin Richards, Jim Smith, Shannon Sullivan, Richard Thacker, Steve Traylen, Stephen James Walker, Peter Ware, Martin Wiggins, Gareth Wigmore, Guy Wigmore and Alex Wilcock. I'm genuinely sorry if I missed anyone.

Thanks most of all to the innumerable people involved with the production of *Doctor Who*, in any and every form ... past, present and future.

This book seeks to place every event referred to in *Doctor Who* into a consistent timeline. Yet this is *a* history of the *Doctor Who* universe, not the "definitive" or "official" version.

Doctor Who has had hundreds of creators, all pulling in slightly different directions, all with their own vision of what *Doctor Who* was about. Without that diversity, the *Doctor Who* universe would no doubt be more internally consistent, but it would also be a much smaller and less interesting place. Nowadays, fans are part of the creative process. Ultimately, we control the heritage of the show that we love. I hope people will enjoy this book, and I know that they will challenge it.

A total adherence to continuity has always been rather less important to the successive *Doctor Who* production teams than the main order of business: writing exciting stories, telling good jokes and scaring small children with big monsters. This, as most people will tell you, is just how it should be.

Much of *Doctor Who* was created using a method known as 'making it up as they went along'. The series gloried in its invention and throwaway lines. When the TV series was first in production, no-one was keeping the sort of detailed notes that would prevent canonical 'mistakes', and even the same writer could contradict their earlier work. It's doubtful the writer of *The Mysterious Planet* had a single passing thought about how the story fitted in with *The Sun Makers* ... even though they were both authored by Robert Holmes.

Now, with dozens of new books, audios, comic strips, short stories and a new TV series, not to mention spin-offs, it is almost certainly impossible to keep track of every new *Doctor Who* story, let alone put them all in a coherent - never mind consistent - framework. References can contradict other references in the same story, let alone ones in stories written forty years later for a different medium by someone who wasn't even born the year the original writer died.

It is, in any case, impossible to come up with a consistent view of history according to *Doctor Who*. Strictly speaking, the Brigadier retires three years before the first UNIT story is set. The Daleks and Atlantis are both utterly destroyed, once and for all, several times that we know about. Characters 'remember' scenes, or sometimes entire stories, that they weren't present to witness.

'Continuity' has always been flexible, even on the fundamentals of the show's mythology - *The Dalek Invasion of Earth*, *The War Games*, *Genesis of the Daleks* and *The Deadly Assassin* all shamelessly threw out the show's established history in the name of a good story. Their version of events (the Daleks are galactic conquerors; the Doctor is a Time Lord who stole his TARDIS and fled his home planet; the Daleks were created by the Kaled scientist, Davros; Gallifreyan society is far from perfect and Time Lords are limited to twelve regenerations) is now taken to be the 'truth'. The previous versions (the Daleks are confined to one city; the Doctor invented the 'ship' and his granddaughter named it before their exile; the Daleks are descendants of the squat humanoid Dals, mutated by radiation; the Time Lords are godlike and immortal) have quietly been forgotten.

However, I don't want to write a book so vague that it becomes useless. I have to make firm decisions about where stories are placed, so I show my working. Each story has a paragraph explaining why I placed it where I did.

In some cases, this is simply a matter of reporting an exact date spoken by one of the characters in the story (*Black Orchid*, for example). In others, no firm date is given. I attempt to look at internal evidence given on screen, then evidence from the production team at the time (from the script, say, or from contemporary publicity material), then I branch out to cross referencing it with other stories, noting where other people who've come up with *Doctor Who* chronologies have placed it. What I'm attempting to do is accurately list all the evidence given for dating the stories and other references in as an objective way as possible, then weigh it up to reach a conclusion.

For a good example of this process at its most complicated, look for *The Seeds of Death* or *The Wheel in Space*. You may not agree with the date I've assigned them, but I hope you can see how I've reached it.

This book is one attempt, then, to *retroactively* create a consistent framework for the history of the *Doctor Who* universe. It is essentially a game, not a scientific endeavour to discover 'the right answer'.

All games have to follow a consistent set of rules, and anyone attempting to fit all the pieces of information we are given has to lay some groundwork and prioritise the information. If a line of dialogue from a story broadcast in 1983 flatly contradicts what was said in one from 1968, which is 'right'? Some people would suggest that the newer story 'got it wrong', that the later production team didn't pay enough attention to what came before. Others might argue that the new information 'corrects' what we were told before. In practice, most fans are inconsistent, choosing the facts that best support their arguments or preferences. *The Discontinuity Guide* has some very healthy advice regarding continuity: "Take what you want and ignore what you don't. Future continuity cops will just have to adapt to your version".

BASIC PRINCIPLES

For the purposes of this book I work from the following assumptions:

• Every *Doctor Who* story takes place in the same universe, unless explicitly stated otherwise. The same individual fought the Daleks with Jo on Spiridon, the Ice Warriors with Benny in London, became Zagreus in the Antiverse, blew up Gallifrey to prevent Faction Paradox taking over the universe and saved Rose from the Autons.

For legal, marketing or artistic reasons, it should be noted that some of the people making *Doctor Who* have occasionally stated that they don't feel this to be the case. However there are innumerable cross references (say, Romana being president of Gallifrey in both the books and the audios) and in-jokes that suggest very strongly that, for example, the eighth Doctor of the books is the same individual as the eighth Doctor of the Big Finish audios - or at the very least they've both got almost-identical histories.

• The universe has one, true 'established history'. Nothing (short of a being with godlike powers) can significantly change the course of history with any degree of permanency within that universe. The Mars attacked by the Fendahl is the Mars of the Ice Warriors.

• I have noted where each date I have assigned comes from. Usually it is from dialogue (in which case I quote it), but often it comes from behind-the-scenes sources such as scripts, publicity material and the like. It is up to the individual reader whether a date from a BBC Press release or draft script is as 'valid' as one given on-screen.

• In many cases, no date was ever given for a story. In such instances, I pick a year and explain my reasons. Often I will assign a date that is consistent with information given in other stories. (So, I suggest that the Cyber War mentioned in *Revenge Of The Cybermen* must take place after *The Tomb of the Cybermen*, and probably after *Earthshock* because of what is said in those other stories.) These dates are marked as arbitrary and the reasoning behind them is explained in the footnotes.

• Where a date isn't established on-screen I have also included the dates suggested by others who have compiled timelines or listed dates given in the series. Several similar works to this have been attempted, and I have listed the most relevant in the Bibliography at the end of this section.

• I have assumed that historical events take place at the same time and for the same reasons as they did in 'real history', unless specifically contradicted by the television series. I assume that the Doctor is telling the truth about meeting historical figures, and that his historical analysis is correct. (It has, however, been established that the Doctor is fallible and / or an incorrigible name-dropper.). When there's a reference to 'science', 'scientists', 'history' or 'historians', unless stated otherwise it means scholars and academics from the real world, not the *Doctor Who* universe (they are usually invoked when *Doctor Who's* version of science or events strays a distance from ours).

• Information given is taken literally and at face value, unless it's explicitly said that the person giving it is lying or mistaken. Clearly, if an expert like the Doctor is talking about something he knows a great deal about, we can probably trust the information more than some bystander's vague remark.

• My version of Earth's future history is generally one of steady progress, and as such I tend to lump together stories featuring similar themes and concepts - say, intergalactic travel, isolated colonies, humanoid robots and so on. If the technology, transportation or weaponry seen in story A is more advanced than in story B, then I suggest that story A is set in the future of story B. I also assume that throughout the centuries humans age at the same rate, so their life spans don't alter too dramatically, etc. A 'lifetime' in the year 4000 is still about 100 years.

• All dates, again unless specifically stated otherwise, work from our Gregorian calendar, and all are 'AD'. It is assumed that the system of Leap Years will remain the same in the future. For convenience, all documents use our system of dating, even those of alien civilisations. The 'present' of the narrative is now, so if an event happened "two hundred years ago" it happened in the early nineteenth century. On a number of occasions we are told that a specific date takes place on the wrong day: in *The War Machines*, 16th July, 1966, is a Monday, but it really occurred on a Saturday.

• I assume that a "year" is an Earth year of 365 days, even when an alien is speaking, unless this is specifically contradicted. This also applies to terms such as "Space Year" (*Genesis of the Daleks*), "light year" (which is used as a unit of time in *The Savages* and possibly *Terror of the Autons*) and "cycle" (e.g. *Zamper*).

• If an event is said to take place "fifty years ago" I take it to mean exactly fifty years ago, unless a more precise date is given elsewhere or it refers to a known historical event. If an event occurs in the distant past or the far future, I tend to round up: *Image of the Fendahl* is set in about 1977, the Fifth Planet was destroyed "twelve million years" before. I say this happened in "12,000,000 BC", not "11,998,023 BC". When an event takes place an undefined number of "centuries", "millennia" or "millions of years" before or after a story, I arbitrarily set a date.

A "generation" is assumed to be twnety-five years, as per the Doctor's definition in *Four to Doomsday*. A 'couple' of years is always two years, a 'few' is generally three to five, 'several' six to nine, 'many' more than ten, with 'some' taken to be an arbitrary or unknown number. A 'billion' is generally the American and modern British unit (a thousand million) rather than the old British definition (a million million).

THE STORIES

This book restricts itself to events described in the BBC television series *Doctor Who*, the original full-length fiction and the audio plays. This is not an attempt to enter the debate about which *Doctor Who* stories are 'canon', it is simply an attempt to limit the length and scale of this book. There are two types of information in this book, and these are distinguished by different typefaces.

1) The Television Series. Included are the episodes and on-screen credits of the BBC television series *Doctor Who* as first broadcast; the spin-off *K9 and Company* episode; and extended or unbroadcast versions that have since been commercially released or broadcast anywhere in the world - there are few cases of "extended" material contradicting the original story.

Priority is given to sources closest to the finished product or the production team of the time the story was made. In descending order of authority are the following: the programme as broadcast; the *Radio Times* and other contemporary BBC publicity material (which was often written by the producer or script editor; the camera script; the novelisation of a story by the original author or an author working closely from the camera script; contemporary interviews with members of the production team; televised trailers; rehearsal and draft scripts; novelisations by people other than the original author; storylines and writers' guides (which often contradict on-screen information); interviews with members of the production team after the story was broadcast; and finally any other material, such as fan speculation.

Scenes cut from broadcast were considered if they were incorporated back into a story at a later time (as with those in *The Curse of Fenric* VHS and DVD). I have not included information from unreleased material that exists (for example, the extended footage from *Invasion of the Dinosaurs* or *Kinda*), is in release but was kept separate from the story (for instance, the extra scenes on the *Vengeance on Varos* and *Ghost Light* DVDs) or that no longer exists (such as with *Terror of the Autons*, *Terror of the Zygons* and *The Hand of Fear*). Neither does the first version of *An Unearthly Child* to be filmed

(the so-called 'pilot episode') count, nor 'In character' appearances by the Doctor on other programmes (e.g.: on *Animal Magic*, *Children in Need*, *Blue Peter* etc.).

2. The books, audios and webcasts. This present volume encompasses the New and Missing Adventures published by Virgin, the BBC's Eighth Doctor Adventures (up to *The Gallifrey Chronicles*), the BBC's Past Doctor Adventures (up to *The Indestructible Man*), all of the Telos novellas and a number of one-off novels: *Harry Sullivan's War*, *Turlough and the Earthlink Dilemma* and *Who Killed Kennedy*.

The audios covered include *The Pescatons*, *Slipback*, *The Paradise of Death* and *The Ghosts of N-Space*, as well as the Big Finish *Doctor Who* range (that is, specifically, the ones with the Doctor in) up to *Terror Firma*.

The BBC webcasts *Real Time*, *Shada*, *Death Comes to Time*, and *Scream of the Shalka* (the last two somewhat controversially) are included.

A handful of stories were available in another form - *Shakedown* and *Downtime* were originally direct-to-video spin-offs, some Big Finish stories like *Minuet in Hell* and *The Mutant Phase* are (often radically different) adaptations of stories made by Audio Visuals. This book deals with the 'official' versions, as opposed to the fan-produced ones.

On the whole, the television series takes priority over what is said in the books, audios and webcasts, and where a detail or reference in one of the books appears to contradict what was established on television, I have noted as much and attempted to rationalise the 'mistake' away.

The NA/MAs built up a broadly consistent 'future history' of the universe. This was, in part, based on the 'History of Mankind' in Jean-Marc Lofficier's *The Terrestrial Index*, which mixes information from the series with facts from the novelisations and the author's own speculation. Many authors, though, have contradicted or ignored Lofficier's version of events. For the purposes of this book, *The Terrestrial Index* itself is non-canonical, and I've noted, but ultimately ignored, whenever a New Adventure recounts information solely using Lofficier as reference.

Useful information appears in writers' guides, discussion documents and the authors' original submissions and storylines. Where possible, I have referred to this material.

Despite this volume's efforts to be inclusive whenever possible, there are also some significant omissions:

The book *doesn't* cover short stories, whether they first appeared in annuals, *Doctor Who Magazine*, the *Decalog* and *Short Trips* anthologies or any of the innumerable other places they have cropped up. It also doesn't include any comic strips, even the venerable *Doctor Who Magazine* strip which has now run for almost exactly as long as the original TV series did.

It also doesn't include proposed stories that were never

made. These primarily include the trio of sixth Doctor stories abandoned after the Season Twenty-Two hiatus - namely, *The Nightmare Fair*, *Mission to Magnus* and *The Ultimate Evil*, all of which were later novelised. The unmade *The Masters of Luxor*, published as a scriptbook, was excluded for the same reasons.

Nor does it cover spin-off series (other than *K9 and Company*, which is a direct descendant of the television show). Since the last edition of this book there has been a proliferation of spin-off series that have featured characters from *Doctor Who*. These include:

• Bernice Summerfield (books, short stories and audios from Virgin, then Big Finish. Featuring the Doctor's companion who was first seen in *Love and War*).

• Big Finish spin-off series (*Dalek Empire*, *UNIT*, *Gallifrey*, *Sarah Jane Smith*, the *Unbound* stories etc).

• Faction Paradox (books, audios and a comic, featuring characters and concepts seen in the EDA *Alien Bodies* etc.).

• Iris Wildthyme (books, audios and short stories. A character seen in the original fiction of Paul Magrs, and who first appeared in *Doctor Who* in the *Short Trips* story "Old Flames" and the EDA *The Scarlet Empress*).

• Kaldor City (audios, spun off from *The Robots of Death* and the PDA *Corpse Marker*).

• Miranda (comic, from the character seen in the EDA *Father Time*).

• Time Hunter (novellas, featuring characters from the Telos novella *The Cabinet of Light*).

I have included information from these when it sheds light on an otherwise unclear aspect of *Doctor Who* continuity. The Benny audio *The Plague Herds of Excelis*, for instance, is helpful in dating the "Excelis Trilogy" in the *Doctor Who* audios.

KEY

The following abbreviations are used in the text:
TV - The TV series
NA - New Adventure (the ongoing novels published by Virgin)
MA - Missing Adventure (the past Doctor novels published by Virgin)
EDA - Eighth Doctor Adventure (the ongoing novels published by the BBC)
PDA - Past Doctor Adventure (the past Doctor novels published by the BBC)
BF - The Big Finish audio adventures.

In the text of the book, the following marker appears to indicate when the action of specific stories take place:

c 2005 - THE REPETITION OF THE CLICHE ->

The title is exactly as it appeared on-screen or on the cover. For the Hartnell stories without an overall title given on-screen, I have generally used the titles that appear on the BBC's product.

The letter before the date, the 'code', indicates how accurately we know the date. If there is no code, then that date is precisely established in the story itself (e.g. *The Daleks' Master Plan* is set in the year 4000 exactly).

"**c**" means that the story is set circa that year (e.g. *The Dalek Invasion of Earth* is set "c 2167")

"**?**" indicates a guess, and my reasons are given in the footnotes (e.g. we don't know what year *Destiny of the Daleks* is set in, but it must be "centuries" after *The Daleks' Master Plan*, so I set it in "? 4600").

"**&**" means that the story is dated relative another story that we lack a date for (e.g.: we know that *Resurrection of the Daleks* is set "ninety years" after *Destiny of the Daleks*, so I set *Resurrection of the Daleks* in "& 4690"). If one story moves, the linked one also has to.

"**u**" means that the story featured UNIT. There is, to put it mildly, some discussion about exactly when the UNIT stories are set. For the purposes of this guidebook, see the introduction to the UNIT Section.

"**=**" indicates action that takes place in a parallel universe or a divergent timestream that's later annulled. This information is set apart by boxes with dashed lines.

"**@**" is a story set during the eighth Doctor's period on Earth between the books *The Ancestor Cell* and *Escape Velocity*. During this period he was without a working TARDIS or his memories.

"**w**" refers to an event that took place during the future War timeline in the eighth Doctor books. Events in *The Ancestor Cell* annulled this timeline, but remnants of it 'still happened' in the real *Doctor Who* timeline, just as *Day of the Daleks* 'still happened' even though the future it depicted was averted.

I've attempted to weed out references that just aren't very telling, relevant or interesting. Clearly, there's a balance to be had, as half the fun of a book like this is in it listing trivia and strange juxtapositions, but a timeline could easily go to absurd extremes. If a novel set in 1980 said that a minor character was sixty-five, lived in a turn-of-the-century terraced house and bought the Beatles album *Rubber Soul* when it first came out, then it could generate entries for c 1900, 1915 and 1965. I would only list these if they were relevant to the story or made for particularly interesting reading.

I haven't listed birthdates of characters, except the Doctor's companions or other major recurring figures, again unless it represents an important story point.

Before our universe, others existed with different physical laws. The universe immediately prior to our own had its own Time Lords, and as their universe reached the point of collapse, they shunted themselves into a parallel universe and discovered that they now possessed almost infinite power.[1]

Rassilon speculated that the beings Raag, Nah and Rok had created and destroyed many universes.[2]

The Dawn of Time

The universe was created in a huge explosion known as the Big Bang. As this was the very first thing to happen, scientists sometimes refer to it as "Event One".

"Among the adherents of Scientific Mythology [q.v.] the element (Hydrogen) is widely believed to be the basic constituent out of which the Galaxy was first formed [see EVENT ONE] and evidence in support of this hypothesis includes its supposed appearance in spectroscopic analysis of massive star bodies." [3]

The Time Lords of Gallifrey monitored the Big Bang, and precisely determined the date of Event One.[4] **The Doctor claimed to have been an eye-witness at the origins of the universe.**[5]

"The dawn of time. The beginning of all beginnings. Two forces only: Good and Evil. Then chaos. Time is born: matter, space. The universe cries out like a newborn. The forces *shatter* as the Universe explodes outwards. Only echoes remain, and yet somehow, *somehow* the evil force survives. An intelligence. Pure *evil*."

The evil force retained its sentience and spread its influence throughout time and space. It became the entity that the Vikings would call Fenric.[6]

One ship managed to travel to the dawn of creation, albeit by accident. Terminus was a vast spaceship built by an infinitely advanced, ancient race capable of time travel. The ship developed a fault, and the pilot was forced to eject some of its unstable fuel into the void before making a time jump. The explosion that resulted was the Big Bang. Terminus was thrown billions of years into the future, where it came to settle in the exact centre of the universe.[7] The universe was created when the time-travelling starship *Vipod Mor* arrived at this point and exploded.[8]

The Urbankan Monarch believed that if his ship could travel faster than light, it would move backwards in time to the Big Bang and beyond. Monarch believed that he was God and that he would meet himself at the Creation of the Universe.[9]

TIMELESS[10] **->** The eighth Doctor piloted the TARDIS back to before the Big Bang, hoping to avoid a myriad of parallel realities by entering the correct history from the very start. Chloe, a small girl from a devastated planet, arrived onhand with Jamais, her time travelling dog. Jamais aided the overstrained TARDIS in reaching London, 2003. The Doctor's party again visited this era when Sabbath and Kalicum, an agent of the Council of Eight, attempted to seed an intelligence gestated within a heap of diamonds into the start of history. They succeeded, and the intelligence became part of the fabric of the universe.

The diamonds allowed the Council of Eight to map out events throughout the whole of history.[11]

Eleven physical dimensions existed at first, quickly col-

---

1 *All-Consuming Fire, Millennial Rites, The Taking of Planet 5.*
2 *Divided Loyalties.* These are the Gods of Ragnarok seen in *The Greatest Show in the Galaxy.*
3 This appears on the console screen in *Castrovalva.*
4 *Transit.*
  THE AGE OF THE UNIVERSE: The date of the creation of the universe is not clearly established on-screen, although we are told it took place "billions of years" before *Terminus.* Modern scientific consensus is that the universe is about fifteen billion years old, and books that address the issue, like *Timewyrm: Apocalypse* and *Falls the Shadow,* concur with this date. In *Transit,* the Doctor drunkenly celebrates the universe's 13,500,020,012th birthday (meaning the Big Bang took place in 13,500,017,903 BC). *The Infinity Doctors* estab-

lishes that the Time Lords refer to the end of the universe as Event Two.
5 The Doctor reads the book *The Origins of the Universe* in *Destiny of the Daleks,* and remarks that the author "got it wrong on the first line. Why didn't he ask someone who saw it happen?".
6 *The Curse of Fenric*
7 *Terminus*
8 *Slipback.* This is a clear continuity clash with *Terminus,* and a discrepancy made all the more obvious as *Slipback* was broadcast within two years of *Terminus* and was written by its script editor, Eric Saward. If we wanted to reconcile the two accounts, we could speculate that the *Vipod Mor* explosion was the spark that ignited the fuel jettisoned in *Terminus.*
9 *Four to Doomsday.* Monarch never achieves this goal.

lapsing down to the five dimensions familiar to us. The other dimensions came to exist only at the subatomic level.[12] Beings named the Quoth evolved inside atoms and were the size of quarks.[13] The Sidhe came to exist in all eleven dimensions.[14] The remaining six dimensions became the Six-Fold Realm, and each of the six Guardians represented one such dimension.[15]

As the universe was formed, an eight-dimensional 'radiating blackness' infused space and time. Eventually, the Unity of the Scourge evolved in this darkness.[16]

The first few chaotic microseconds of the universe saw extreme temperatures and the forging of bizarre elements that would be unable to exist later. This was the Leptonic Era, and one of the bizarre elements created was Helium 2. The Rani would later attempt to recreate this on Lakertya.[17]

Time and Space as we understand them began as these bizarre elements reacted with each other and cooled.

The Shadow, an agent of the Black Guardian, claimed to have been waiting since eternity began in the hopes of obtaining the Key to Time.[18] The Master attempted to kill the newly-regenerated fifth Doctor by sending him backwards in time to a Hydrogen Inrush early in the universe's history.[19] Matter coalesced, elements formed.[20]

The Dark Time, The Time of Chaos

The Time Lords from the pre-universe entered our universe, and discovered that they had undreamt-of powers. They became known as the Great Old Ones: Hastur the Unspeakable became Fenric; Yog-Sothoth, also known as the Intelligence, began billennia of conquests; The Lloigor, or Animus, dominated Vortis; Shub-Niggurath conquered Polymos and colonised it with her offspring, the Nestene Consciousness; Dagon was worshipped by the Sea Devils. Other Great Old Ones included Cthulhu, Nyarlathotep, the Gods of Ragnarok; Gog, Magog, Malefescent, and Tor-Gasukk. Across the universe, the earliest civilisations worshipped the Great Old Ones.[21] Not even the Time Lords knew much about them.[22]

Six almost-omnipotent beings, **the Guardians, existed from the beginning of time. They were the White Guardian of Order and the Black Guardian of Chaos,** the Red Guardian of Justice, the Crystal Guardian of Thought and Dreams; the twins, the Azure Guardians of Mortality and Imagination; and the Gold Guardian of Life. They formed the upper pantheon of the Great Old Ones.[23]

The Guardians created The Key to Time to maintain

10 Dating *Timeless* - This occurs at the universe's start.
11 *Sometime Never*
12 In *An Unearthly Child*, Susan defines the fifth dimension as "space".
13 *The Death of Art*
14 *Autumn Mist*
15 *The Quantum Archangel*
16 *The Shadow of the Scourge*
17 *Time and the Rani*
18 *The Armageddon Factor*. It's possible this is just hyperbole on the Shadow's part.
19 *Castrovalva*.
 EVENT ONE: The term "Event One" is first used in *Castrovalva* to mean the creation of "the Galaxy", but in *Terminus* the Doctor talks of "the biggest explosion in history: Event One", which he confirms is "the Big Bang" which "created the universe". There are a number of stories where the writers definitely confuse the term 'galaxy' and 'universe', and a number of others where they seem to. This book will list what was said in the stories, noting the more egregious examples, rather than ignoring them or trying to rationalise them away.
20 *The Curse of Fenric*
21 *All-Consuming Fire, Millennial Rites, Business Unusual, The Quantum Archangel, Divided Loyalties.*
22 *White Darkness*
 THE GREAT OLD ONES: The novels *All-Consuming Fire, Millennial Rites, Business Unusual, Divided Loyalties* and *The Quantum Archangel* state that many of the godlike beings seen in *Doctor Who* have a common ori-

gin. The Great Old Ones were a pantheon of ancient, incomprehensible forces created by horror writer H P Lovecraft, and adopted by the novels for this purpose. Perhaps the most well-known of Lovecraft's creations, Cthulhu, had already made an appearance in *White Darkness*.

Other *Doctor Who* entities explicitly referred to in the books as Great Old Ones are Fenric (*The Curse of Fenric*), the Intelligence (*The Abominable Snowmen, The Web of Fear, Millennial Rites* and *Downtime*), the Animus (*The Web Planet, Twilight of the Gods*), the Nestene Consciousness (*Spearhead from Space, Terror of the Autons, Business Unusual, Synthespians™* and *Rose*) and the Gods of Ragnarok (*The Greatest Show in the Galaxy, Divided Loyalties*). Gog and Magog - or at least beings with the same name - appeared in the 'Iron Legion' comic strip in *Doctor Who Weekly*.

The Doctor claims at the end of *Ghost Light* that Light is "an evil older than time itself". From the context, this appears to mean that Light arrived on Earth before human history started, not that he existed before the universe's creation, but he might also be a Great Old One. The Great Old Ones in the audio story *The Roof of the World* don't seem to be connected to this grouping.
23 The White and Black Guardians are first referred to in *The Ribos Operation. Divided Loyalties* says there are six Guardians, adding Justice, Crystal and unnamed twins to the two from the television series. *Divided Loyalties* also states that the Guardian of Dreams is the Celestial Toymaker. *The Quantum Archangel* assigns

the balance between Order and Chaos. It was composed of six segments that were scattered throughout time and space to prevent it falling into the wrong hands.[24] Each segment of the Key to Time represented a particular Guardian.[25]

Shug-Niggurath was pregnant, and died giving birth to the Nestene Consciousness on the planet Polymos, causing the whole planet to absorb the Consciousness. The Nestene Consciousness went on to colonise many planets, including Cramodar, Plovak 6 and the Reverent Pentiarchs of Loorn.[26]

The Chronovores existed outside the space-time continuum, consuming flaws in its structure. They too weren't constrained by the laws of physics.[27]

The first of our universe's native entities - such as the Mandragora Helix, the Eternals and the grey man's race - **sprang into being.**[28] The Time Lords come to worship some of the more powerful Eternals, such as Death, Pain, Vain Beauty, Life and Time. Certain Time Lords entered a mysterious arrangement to serve as the "champion" of one or more of these Eternals.[29]

Over the first few billion years, the first stars were born. Planets and galaxies formed. **On many of these worlds, sugars, proteins and amino acids combined to become primordial soup, "the most precious substance in the Universe, from which all life springs".** Hundreds of millions of years later, the first civilisations began to rise and fall.[30]

Jelloids from the binary quasars of Bendalos were the longest-lived race in the universe, and many think they were the first living creatures.[31]

Thirty thousand million light years from our Solar System, the first civilisation came into being. The beings were humanoid, and developed for ten thousand years before wiping themselves out in a bacteriological war. The grey man and his race saw all this, and he constructed the Cathedral, a machine "designed to alter the structure of reality". The grey man's race had been extremely dualistic, but Cathedral formed ambiguities and chaotic forces that ran throughout the universe, breaking down certainty. Its interface with physical reality was the Metahedron, a device that moved from world to world every eighty thousand years, remaining hidden.[32]

What remains of the ancient races suggests awesome power - many had great psychic ability and matter-transmutation powers that were almost indistinguishable from magic. All considered it their right to intervene in the development of whole planets - and to destroy such worlds if they failed to match up to their expectations. Immortal beings such as Light and the Daemons of Damos were worshipped as gods by more primitive races. The legends and race memories of many planets still contain traces of these ancient civilisations. Horns have been a symbol of power on Earth since man began, and beings of light have been worshipped. Nothing lasts forever, though, and these great races gradually disappeared from the universe.[33]

New societies sprang up to replace them, and soon the universe was teeming with life. In the late twentieth century, the Institute of Space Studies at Baltimore estimated that there were over five hundred planets capable of supporting life in Earth's section of the galaxy alone.[34]

The Time Lords

The first humanoid civilisation in the universe evolved on the planet Gallifrey, and mastered the principles of transmat technology while the universe was half its present size. They became the first race to master Time. Some legends said the Time Lords existed far in the past; there was some evidence that they lived in the

---

them their colours and adds the Gold Guardian (counting the twin Azure Guardians as one entity). *Divided Loyalties* says they are members of the Great Old Ones.
24 *The Ribos Operation*
25 *Divided Loyalties*
26 *Synthespians*™
27 The Chronovores first appear in *The Time Monster*, but their role is clarified in *No Future* and *The Quantum Archangel*.
28 *The Masque of the Mandragora, Enlightenment, Falls the Shadow.*
29 The Time Lords' gods were mentioned or seen in a number of New Adventures such as *No Future, Set Piece* and *Human Nature*. The seventh Doctor was often referred to as "Time's Champion". Mortimus (the Meddling Monk) is "Death's Champion" in *No Future*, and the Master is hinted as the same in the audio *Master*. *Vampire Science* has the eighth Doctor as "Life's

Champion", and in *The Dying Days* he declares himself to be "the Champion of Life and Time".
30 The prologue to *Timewyrm: Apocalypse* is a brief history of the formation of the universe, and it follows the modern scientific consensus. Primordial soup appears in *City of Death* and *Ghost Light*, and the quotation comes from the second of those stories.
31 *The One Doctor*
32 *Falls the Shadow*
33 *The Daemons*. Light appears in *Ghost Light*.
34 *Spearhead from Space*
35 'WHEN THE UNIVERSE WAS HALF ITS PRESENT SIZE': The phrase, uttered by a Time Lord in *Genesis of the Daleks*, has no clear scientific meaning and should probably be considered a figure of speech, the Time Lord equivalent of 'as old as the hills'. Then again, the universe at various points is referred to as having edges, a centre and corners, which suggests a discern-

present, and some say they come from the future.[35]

See the section on Gallifreyan History for more detail.

As the Gallifreyans were the first sentient race to evolve, they established a morphic field for humanoids, making it more probable that races evolving later would also be bipedal and binocular. Non-humanoid races only evolved in environments that would be hostile to humanoids.[36] Rassilon ensured that only humanoid lifeforms survived on many planets, primarily to prevent the Divergents from existing. He used biogenic molecules to restructure the dominant species of sixty-nine thousand worlds.[37]

Evolution on Gallifrey, as on many other worlds, had been accelerated by the mysterious Constructors of Destiny.[38]

A civilisation devoted entirely to war developed the Raston Warrior Robot, then vanished without trace.[39]

The Time Lords explored space and time, making contact with many worlds and becoming legends on many others. Rassilon's experiments created holes in the fabric of space and time, which unleashed monsters from another universe, including the Yssgaroth.[40]

The Time Lords unwittingly loosed the vampires on the universe. Until the Time Lords hunted them, vampires fed off mindless animals to service their needs. They later resorted to feeding off other beings.[41] **Seventeen known worlds, including Earth, have stories of vampires.**[42]

The vampires enslaved whole worlds until the Time Lords defeated them.[43] **The vampires were immune to energy weapons, but Rassilon constructed fleets of bowships that fired mighty bolts of steel and staked the beings through the heart. The Vampire Army was defeated, and only its leader, the Great Vampire, survived by escaping through a CVE into the pocket universe of E-Space.**[44]

The origins of the Time Lords are obscure, but in the distant past they fought the Eternal War against the Great Old Ones and other invaders from outside our universe, beating them back and imposing Order. Science and Order supplanted Magic and Chaos as the Time Lords mapped, and so defined, the universe.[45] The last form of magic to survive was psionics.[46]

During this war, the great Gallifreyan general Kopyion Liall a Mahajetsu was believed to have died. He actually survived, and vigilantly watched in secret for signs of the Yssgaroth's return. He would deal with the threat of such an incursion in 2400.[47]

This war may or may not be the same conflict as the Time War, in which Time Lords from a generation after Rassilon fought against other races developing time travel. The conflict lasted thirty thousand years. The Time Lords wiped out many races during this time.[48]

One such race was the Charon, who were capable of warping space, and whom the Time Lords destroyed before they ever existed. One Charon survived this and created its own clockwork mini-universe. Another

---

36 *Lucifer Rising*

37 *Zagreus*

38 *The Quantum Archangel*

39 The robot is seen in *The Five Doctors*, and according to *The Eight Doctors* it comes from a time when "the Time Lords were young". *Alien Bodies* mentions a Raston Dancing Robot, and Qixotl claims that the ancient legend is just the manufacturer's marketing ploy.

40 *The Pit*

41 According to a highly suspect account from the vampire Tepesh, part of a historical simulation in *Zagreus*.

42 *State of Decay*. Vampires appear in that story, *Blood Harvest, Goth Opera, The Eight Doctors, Vampire Science, Death Comes to Time, Project: Twilight* and *Project: Lazarus*. Some also appear as a part of the holographic record in *Zagreus*.

43 *Project: Twilight*

44 *State of Decay*

45 *Cat's Cradle: Time's Crucible*

46 *So Vile a Sin*

THE ETERNAL WAR: On-screen, we learn that the Time Lords fought campaigns against the Great Vampires (*State of Decay*), that they destroyed the Fendahl (*Image of Fendahl*), that they protected other

races from invaders (*The Hand of Fear*) and that they maintained a prison planet that contained alien species (*Shada*). In the New Adventures, particularly *Cat's Cradle: Time's Crucible, The Pit* and *Christmas on a Rational Planet*, this was the Eternal War in which the forces of rationality and science defeated the forces of superstition and magic.

47 *The Pit*

48 *Sky Pirates!, The Infinity Doctors.*

THE THREE TIME WARS: This is not the Last Great Time War between the Time Lords and the Daleks that's the backdrop to the 2005 television series. In the *Doctor Who Annual 2006*, Russell T Davies states 'There had been two Time Wars before this - the skirmish between the Halldons and the Eternals, and then the brutal slaughter of the Omnicraven Uprising, and on both occasions, the Doctor's people had stepped in to settle the matter'. Although they don't mention those specific incidents, the books concur that there were indeed two previous Time Wars - one in the ancient past (which, to avoid confusion, we might term the Ancient Time War) and the War against the Enemy in the eighth Doctor's future (which has become known in the *Faction Paradox* range as the War in Heaven).

unnamed race used Reality Bombs to disrupt the control systems of time machines. A few of these weapons survived hidden for billions of years.[49]

The Doctor witnessed the horrors of the Time War. At one point, the Time Lords were themselves attacked by an unnamed race in retaliation for something they hadn't yet done.[50]

The Time War ended with all threats to Gallifrey contained, or so completely destroyed that no evidence remained to suggest they even existed. Time Lords were encoded with genetic memories of their ancient enemies and were compelled to destroy any survivors. The Time Lords were ashamed of the Time War, to the point that they deny it ever happened.[51]

Mr Saldaamir, who would become a friend of the Doctor's father, was the last survivor of the Time War.[52] There was a Celestial War in which the Ooolatrii captured at least one primitive TARDIS.[53]

The Sontarans and Rutans were involved in 'eternal war'.[54] The origins of the conflict between them was lost in the mists of time and was the subject of much propaganda. Much later, the Rutans blamed the war on the Sontarans for attacking the Constellation of Zyt, which the Sontarans claimed was retaliation for a Rutan attack on Holfactur, which the Rutans said had been the base for attacks on the Purple Areas of Rutan Space, which in turn was revenge for an attack on Mancastovon. The war quickly escalated, and it would rage, ebb and flow across the entire galaxy for many millions of years.

Around the time the war started, the Sontarans became a clone race. Their greatest warrior, Sontar, had defeated the Isari. He was the model for all future Sontarans. To increase efficiency, the Sontaran body was simplified. All non-clones soon died. The leader of the Sontarans, always called General Sontar, had the memories of all previous General Sontars.[55]

The Time Lords colonised planets such as Dronid and Trion. Sharing their secrets with lesser races, though, led to disaster. Evolution on Klist was reversed, and the civilisation on Plastrodus 14 went insane.[56] **Eventually the Time Lords recognised the dangers of intervention when their attempts to help the Minyans resulted in the destruction of Minyos.**[57]

The Time Lords interfered on Micen Island, resulting in chemical and biological warfare and the destruction of the entire civilisation. The Time Lords built the Temple of the Fourth on the ruins, and codified the Oath of the Faction. They scattered in repentance for what they had done.[58]

The Time Lords remained content to observe, but monitored the universe and tried to prevent other, less principled races from discovering the secrets of time travel.[59] **They occasionally sent out ambassadors and official observers.**[60] **They also attempted to enforce bans on dangerous technology.**[61]

For more information on the history of the Doctor's people, see the Gallifrey section at the end of this book.

The Ancient Past

Before life evolved on other planets, the Exxilon civilisation was already old.[62] Other races such as the Raab of Odonoto Ceti, a race on Benelisa and the Cthalctose of 16 Alpha Leonis One evolved.[63]

c 6,000,000,000 BC - ETERNITY WEEPS[64] **->** Jason Kane used a Time Ring to reach 16 Alpha Leonis One, the home of the Cthalctose, from Earth in the year 2003. He met the Astronomer Royal, who had detected a black hole in the solar system and provided force field technology. Jason was placed in a stasis field and watched the Cthalctose civilisation develop for five hundred years. The Cthalctose attempted to contain the black hole, but eventually could no longer power the force fields.

Unable to save themselves, they built a device - "the Museum" - that could convert another world to resemble their own. This entailed using a terraforming virus that would generate sulphuric acid, which was present in the seas on their homeworld. The Cthalctose launched the Museum out of their solar system, and the forces of the black hole destroyed 16 Alpha Leonis One. Jason Kane's stasis field failed and he returned to 2003.

49 *Sky Pirates!*
50 *Heart of TARDIS*
51 *Sky Pirates!, The Infinity Doctors, Heart of TARDIS.*
52 *The Gallifrey Chronicles*
53 *The Crystal Bucephalus*
54 *The Time Warrior, Horror of Fang Rock*
55 *The Infinity Doctors.* The war has lasted as long as the Time Lord civilisation.
56 *The Quantum Archangel*
57 *Underworld*

58 *Death Comes to Time*
59 *The War Games*
60 *The Two Doctors, The Empire of Glass*
61 *Carnival of Monsters, The Empire of Glass*
62 *Death to the Daleks*
63 *Frontier Worlds, The Taint, Eternity Weeps.*
64 Dating *Eternity Weeps* - It is 'six billion years ago' (p3).
65 *Inferno*
66 *Love and War*
67 *Genocide* (p279).

Earth formed billions of years ago.[65] While the Earth was still forming, the Time Lords were in negotiations with the Tranmetgurans, trying to organise a planetary government and end the war that was ravaging the planet. The Hoothi - a fungoid group-mind that lived off dead matter and farmed entire sentient species - attacked Tranmetgura, introducing their dead soldiers into the battle. War broke out, and two thirds of the population were killed. The Hoothi harvested the dead, taking them aboard their silent gas dirigibles. When the Time Lords sent an ambassador to the Hoothi worlds, the Hoothi used him as a host and attempted to conquer Gallifrey. The Time Lords launched a counter-attack, forcing the Hoothi to flee into hyperspace. The Hoothi vanished from the universe.[66]

As Earth's solar system formed from dust, the Tractite named Kitig arrived through time via a time tree. As Kitig intended, this destroyed the time tree at the cost of his own life.[67]

The universe passed the point when it would naturally collapse. It was sustained by the people of Logopolis, who opened CVEs into other universes.[68]

The Great Provider began its intergalactic conquests four billion years ago.[69] Three billion years ago, carvings were made of the Great Old Ones on the planet Veltroch.[70]

c 3,000,000,000 BC - VENUSIAN LULLABY[71] -> The
Venusians were an advanced race, surprisingly so since all metals were poisonous to them with the exception of gold, platinum and titanium. Their cities were crude, with the buildings in cities such as Cracdhalltar and Bikugih resembling soap-bubbles made from mud and crude stone, but the civilisation lasted for three million years.

By measuring the day, which got steadily longer, the Venusians calculated that their planet was dying. For tens of thousands of years, most of the Venusians were resigned to their fate. Most of the Venusian animal species had become extinct: the shanghorn, the klak-kluk and the pattifangs. To conserve resources, Death Inspectors killed Venusians who had outlived their useful lives. Anti-Acceptancer factions such as the Rocketeers, the Below the

Sun Believers, the Magnetologists, the Water-breathers, the Volcano People and the Cave-Makers believed that they could escape their fate, but the majority saw them as cranks.

The Doctor, Ian and Barbara visited Venus at this time, just as the Sou(ou)shi arrived to offer the Venusians a place within their spacecraft. The Sou(ou)shi were vampires, and merely wanted to consume the entire Venusian race as they did the Aveletians and the Signortiyu. The Venusians discovered this with the Doctor's help and destroyed the Sou(ou)shi craft. The debris from the ship entered the Venusian atmosphere, blocking some of the sun's rays and lowering the planet's temperature. This prolonged the Venusians' existence for another one hundred generations. The consciousness of the Sou(ou)shi survived and travelled to primeval Earth.

w - Time Lords from the future launched an unmanned warship to destroy Earth, the original homeworld of the Enemy. The ship travelled at sublight speeds, and three billion years would elapse before it arrived there in 1996.[72]

The Nestene, a race of pure energy, began their conquests a billion years ago.[73] Around this time, the last seas dried up on Androzani Minor in the Sirius system.[74]

Life On Earth

c 400,000,000 BC - CITY OF DEATH[75] -> Four hundred million years ago, an advanced race - the callous Jagaroth - wiped themselves out in a huge war. The last of the Jagaroth limped to primeval Earth in an advanced spaceship. The pilot of the ship, Scaroth, attempted to take his vessel to power three - warp thrust - too close to the Earth's surface and the spacecraft detonated over what would later become the Atlantic Ocean.

Scaroth was splintered into twelve fragments and materialised at various points in human history. He

---

68 *Logopolis*. It's unclear when this happened, but there have been 'aeons of constraint', and an aeon is a billion years.
69 '4x10(2d8) yrs' ago, according to *The Gallifrey Chronicles*.
70 *White Darkness*
71 Dating *Venusian Lullaby* - The Doctor tells Ian and Barbara that they have travelled back "oh, about three billion years I should think".
72 *Interference*
73 "A thousand million years" before *Spearhead from Space*.
74 "A billion years" before *The Caves of Androzani*.

75 Dating *City of Death* - Scaroth and the Doctor both state that the Jagaroth ship came to Earth "four hundred million years ago". Contemporary science has a number of estimates of when life on Earth started, but all are much earlier than that. *The Terrestrial Index* takes that as a cue to set this story three and a half billion years ago.
SCAROTH OF THE JAGAROTH: All twelve splinters of Scaroth are accounted for in *City of Death*, assuming that none of them live for more than a century. One demonstrates "the true use of fire", a second gives mankind the wheel, a third "caused the pyramids to be built" as an Egyptian Pharoah or God, a fourth "the

would influence humanity's development for tens of thousands of years. This culminated in the building of a time machine in 1979, which he used to return to the past in an attempt to prevent his ship exploding. The Doctor, Romana and their ally Duggan prevented Scaroth from changing history.

Earth at this time was a barren volcanic world, but it had already produced Primordial Soup, and the anti-matter explosion acted as a catalyst. Life on Earth began.

The explosion of the Jagaroth ship left a radiation trace that the Euterpians detected many millions of years later.[76]

Life evolved much as palaeontologists and geologists think that it did.

Werewolves were among the oldest races on Earth. The werewolf Stubbe claimed to have been around at the Earth's creation.[77]

Around two hundred and sixty million years ago, the Permians - skeletal, lizard-hipped carnivores, bound together by a bio-electric field - were top of the food chain on Earth. They had a degree of intelligence, and the ability to mentally guide other creatures. They consumed electrical energy from living things, and were so efficient as predators that they wiped out 96% of life on Earth. With food becoming scarce, the Permians fed off each other. The last few of them went dormant and became fossils.[78]

In the 1970s, Dr Quinn discovered a colony of reptile people living below Wenley Moor in Derbyshire. They were the remnants of an advanced lost civilisation, and had spent many million years in hibernation. Quinn mistakenly believed that they came from the Silurian Period, and had a globe showing the Earth as it was before the great continental drift, two hundred million years ago.[79]

The Doctor watched the first Lungfish walk on a Devonian beach.[80]

The Age of the Dinosaurs

One hundred and sixty five million years ago, dinosaurs started to emerge on Earth.[81] In a different galaxy from Earth, which had become known as Home Galaxy, a number of advanced races made contact and reengineered themselves so that they could interbreed. They developed advanced artificial intelligence technology. The People and Also People constructed the Worldsphere, a Dyson sphere that completely enclosed the star Whynot, with a surface area six hundred million times larger than that of Earth. The regulating intelligence of the Worldsphere became known as God.[82]

An unnamed race created the Omnethoth, a sentient weapon that could control and alter its physical state, to conquer the universe. The Omnethoth wiped out its creators, seeded the universe with colonisation clouds and then went dormant.[83]

While dinosaurs walked the Earth, the Millennium War was fought across the galaxy. The Constructors of Destiny had created the Mind of Bophemeral - the ultimate computer and the most massive object ever built - from black holes, blue dwarfs and strange matter. Bophemeral, though, went insane within instants and destroyed the Constructors. A thousand races, including the Time Lords, Greld, Grey Hegemony, Kastrians, Ministers of Grace, Nimon, Omnethoth, Osirians, People of the Worldsphere, Rutans and Sontarans fought the Mind of Bophemeral and its drones. Kastria and Xeraphas were devastated in the war, but Bophemeral was defeated. The Time Lords time-looped Bophemeral and the Guardians intervened, using the Key to Time to erase all knowledge of this War.[84]

c 150,000,000 BC - THE HAND OF FEAR[85] -> On Kastria, the scientist Eldrad built spacial barriers to keep out the solar winds that ravaged the planet. He also devised a crystalline silicone form for his race,

---

heavens to be mapped", the fifth is an ancient Greek, the sixth is an unnamed Roman Emperor, the seventh is a Crusader, the eighth gives mankind the printing press, the ninth is Captain Tancredi, the tenth is an Elizabethan nobleman, the eleventh lives at the time of Louis XV (he is named as Cardinal Scarlatt in *Christmas on a Rational Planet*), and the twelfth is Carlos Scarlioni.
76 *Invasion of the Cat People*
77 *Loups-Garoux*
78 *The Land of the Dead*
79 *Doctor Who and the Silurians*
   CONTINENTAL DRIFT: According to scientists, continental drift is a continuing process. In *Doctor Who*, there's evidence that it was a single event. The Doctor talks of 'the great continental drift, two hundred million years ago' in *Doctor Who and the Silurians*. In the broad-

cast version of *Earthshock*, the Earth of sixty-five million years ago looks like it does today. Continental drift was a reality according to *Invasion of the Cat-People*. In *The Ark*, the Earth of ten million years hence also looks exactly like contemporary Earth, although we saw the continents devastated in *The Parting of the Ways*, and *The End of the World* acknowledges that technology was used to arrest continental drift.
80 *Transit*. This may be a dream sequence or an allegory.
81 In *Earthshock*, the Doctor states that the dinosaurs existed for "a hundred million years or so" and died out "sixty five million years ago", which is in tune with scientific consensus.
82 *The Also People*. No date is given, but the People fight in the Millennium War in *The Quantum Archangel*.

and built machines to replenish the earth and the atmosphere. Once this was done, he threatened to usurp King Rokon.

The Kastrians did not share Eldrad's dreams of galactic conquest, and so Eldrad destroyed the barriers. The Kastrians sentenced Eldrad to death. As killing a silicon lifeform was almost impossible, they constructed an Obliteration Module and sent it out into space, beyond all solar systems. The Module was detonated early at nineteen spans, while there was still a one-in-three-million chance that Eldrad might survive. The Kastrians elected to destroy themselves and their race banks rather than lead a subterranean existence. Eldrad's hand eventually reached Earth in the Jurassic Period, where it became buried in a stratum of Blackstone Dolomite.[85]

The Vardon-Kosnax War was meant to run fifty years, but disruption to history meant that it lasted three hundred.[86]

140,000,000 BC - TIME-FLIGHT[87] **->** The planet Xeraphas was the home of the Xeraphin, a legendary race with immense mental powers. It was rendered uninhabitable when it was caught in the Vardon-Kosnax War. The surviving Xeraphin came to Earth, hoping to colonise the planet, but they suffered from radiation sickness. They abandoned their physical forms, and became a psychic gestalt of bioplasmic energy until they were able to regenerate. The Master became trapped on Earth five hundred years after this and attempted to harness the power of the Xeraphin Consciousness.

Building a Time Contour Generator, the Master kidnapped a Concorde from the nineteen-eighties, and used the passengers as slaves in an attempt to penetrate the Xeraphin citadel. He was defeated when the Doctor followed him back through time and broke the slaves' conditioning.

About one hundred and thirty million years ago, the Plesiosaurus became extinct. Before this, the owner of a miniscope had kidnapped an example of the species. Miniscopes were built from molecular-bonded disillium by the Eternity Perpetual Company, and would literally last forever - as a result, the company went bankrupt. Concerned that many miniscopes contained sentient specimens, the Doctor successfully lobbied the High Council of the Time Lords and had miniscopes banned. Many years later, though, the Lurman showman Vorg travelled the Acteon Group with one of the few surviving miniscopes, which he had won at the Great Wallarian Exhibition in a game of chance.[88]

The Doctor visited Earth at the time of the dinosaurs. He reckoned the Cretaceous Era was "a very good time for dinosaurs".[89] Professor Whitaker kidnapped various dinosaurs using his Timescoop.[90] The Rani visited this period and collected Tyrannosaur embryos, one of which almost killed her later. She also expressed an interest in reviving the era with a Time Manipulator.[91]

= The paleontologist George Williamson tested his newfound time travel abilities by observing dinosaurs first-hand. Williamson's mere presence encouraged some saurian lizards to start walking upright and gain an evolutionary advantage, creating a parallel timeline. A dimensional doorway from this timeline

---

83 'Millions of years' before *The Fall of Yquatine*. The Omnethoth also fight in the Millennium War according to *The Quantum Archangel*.
84 *The Quantum Archangel*. The Millenium Wars (consistently misspelled with one 'n') were a feature of the early *Doctor Who Weekly/Monthly* comic strips.
85 Dating *The Hand of Fear* - The Doctor identifies the rock in which Eldrad's hand was discovered, and twice tells Eldrad that he has been away from Kastria for "a hundred and fifty million years".
86 *Neverland*. The war is referred to as over by *Time-Flight*. The Vardons are probably not the Vardans seen in *The Invasion of Time*. A Kosnax appears in *Cold Fusion*.
87 Dating *Time-Flight* - The Doctor informs the flight crew of the second Concorde that they have landed at Heathrow "one hundred and forty million years ago". He states, correctly, that this is the "Jurassic" era, but then suggests that they "can't be far off from the Pleistocene era", which actually took place a mere 1,800,000 -10,000

years ago. *The Seeds of Doom* gives a more accurate date for the Pleistocene.
88 *Carnival of Monsters*. The Doctor states that the Pleisosaurus "has been extinct for one hundred and thirty million years". The miniscope presumably captures its specimens in a time scoop like those seen in *Invasion of the Dinosaurs* and *The Five Doctors*. Vorg's Scope contains both a Plesiosaurus and humans from 1926, specimens taken from eras over a hundred and thirty million years apart.
89 *Doctor Who and the Silurians, The Happiness Patrol*.
90 *Invasion of the Dinosaurs*. Whitaker tries to take Earth back to a "Golden Age," but there's no indication that this is the age of the dinosaurs, which would hardly be an Earthly paradise for humans. He uses dinosaurs to scare people out of London.
91 *The Mark of the Rani, Time and the Rani*

would open in Siberia, 1894, and some advanced saurians went through it. The timeline was erased due to the Doctor and Williamson's actions in 1894.[92]

c 65,000,000 BC - EARTHSHOCK[93] -> Sixty five million years ago, the dinosaurs became extinct when the anti-matter engines of a space freighter that had spiralled back through time from 2526 exploded in Earth's atmosphere.

A hundred thousand years before the Silurians, the Earth had been ruled by "gargantuan entities".[94]

The Age of the Reptile People

On Earth, some reptiles had evolved into intelligent bipeds. There were two distinct species: the land-based Silurians, who built a great civilisation in areas of extreme heat; and their amphibious cousins, the Sea Devils.[95]

Silurian civilisation started as scattered clans, which were eventually united by Panun E'Ni of the Southern Clan, whose deeds were recorded in the Hall of Heroes. Panun E'Ni was deposed by Tun W'lzz, who freed the enslaved tribes to create a united Silurian civilisation.[96]

Silurians had advanced psychic powers, which seemed to be concentrated through their third 'eye'. They had telekinetic and hypnotic abilities, could project lethal blasts of energy and establish invisible force fields. Much of their equipment was operated by mental commands, although the Silurians were also known to use an almost-musical summoning device. Much of Silurian technology appears to have been organic. The Silurians domesticated dinosaurs, using a tyrannosaur species as watchdogs. They constructed the Disperser, a device capable of dispersing the Van Allen Belts.[97]

They used brontosaurs to lift heavy loads, and dilophosaurs as mounts. They communicated using a sophisticated language that was a combination of telepathy, speech and gesture. They had Gravitron technology which allowed a sophisticated degree of weather control. They travelled in vast airships.[98]

Their science was more advanced than human technology of the late twenty-first century, with particle suppressers and advanced genetic engineering. They also created creatures such as the Myrka, a ferocious armoured sea monster. Silurian Law prevented all but defensive wars, but the Sea Devils had elite army units and hand-held weaponry, and the Silurians built submarine battlecruisers.[99]

The Silurians lived in vast crystalline cities with imposing architecture.[100] One estimate is that their technology was three or four hundred years more advanced than Earth in the twentieth century. A provision of Silurian law was to execute members of different castes who mated. Strict laws also prevented experiments into genetic engineering and nuclear fission.[101]

The Silurians worshipped the Great Old Ones, with the Sea Devils venerating Dagon in particular.[102] They also worshipped a lizard "devil god", Urmungstandra.[103]

The Silurians saw apes as pests who raided their crops, and developed a virus to cull them.[104] Silurians also ate the apes, using Myrkas to hunt them.[105] Apes were caged and tortured.[106]

A rogue planetoid was detected by Silurian scientists, who calculated that as it passed by Earth, it would cause extensive natural disasters. The Silurians built hibernation shelters deep underground to survive the catastrophe.[107] The Silurians' preparations took twelve years. Silurian hybrids were sent to Shelter 429.[108]

---

92 "Several million years" before *Time Zero*.
93 Dating *Earthshock* - The Doctor dates the extinction of the dinosaurs, and confirms that the freighter has travelled to that era, back "sixty five million years". In the original TV version, the pattern of prehistoric Earth's continents are those of modern-day Earth. A correction was attempted for the DVD release, where an effects option allows the viewer to see an updated special effect. However, the correction itself is historically awry, as it features the super-continent Pangea, when the proper configuration should be somewhere between Pangea and the present day.
94 *All Consuming Fire*
95 *Doctor Who and the Silurians, The Sea Devils*. See "A Complete Misnomer" sidebar.
96 *The Scales of Injustice*
97 *Doctor Who and the Silurians*

98 *Blood Heat*
99 *Warriors of the Deep*
100 *Blood Heat, The Scales of Injustice, Bloodtide*
101 *The Scales of Injustice*
102 *All-Consuming Fire*
103 *The Crystal Bucephalus*, named in *The Taking of Planet 5*. The name was spelled Urgmundasatra in the Benny New Adventure *Twilight of the Gods*.
104 *Doctor Who and the Silurians*
105 *Bloodtide*
106 *The Scales of Injustice*
107 *Doctor Who and the Silurians*
108 *The Scales of Injustice*

"A COMPLETE MISNOMER": There are a number of contradictory accounts in the TV series, the books and the audios of when the Silurian civilisation existed, and it is impossible to reconcile them with each other, let alone against established scientific fact.

A lot of the dating references are very vague: *Doctor Who and the Silurians* says the Silurians "ruled the planet millions of years ago". *The Scales of Injustice* states the Silurians existed "millions of years" and "a few million years" ago, but also uses the term "millennia". *Bloodtide* says it was "many hundreds of thousands of years ago" and "over a million years ago". *Eternity Weeps* features the Silurians and shows the arrival of the Moon in Earth orbit. However, it's inconsistent with its dating, stating that this happened both "twenty million" (p127) and "200 million" (p117) years ago.

Ironically, the one thing we can safely rule out is that the Silurians are from the actual Silurian Era, around 438 to 408 million years ago. Life on Earth's surface was limited to the first plants, and the dominant species were coral reefs. The first jawed fishes evolved during this era. If nothing else, in terms of *Doctor Who* continuity (according to *City of Death*), this is before life on Earth starts. It's Dr. Quinn who coins the name "Silurian" in *Doctor Who and the Silurians*. Despite the name being scientifically inaccurate, everyone at Wenley Moor - including the Doctor - uses it. We don't learn what the reptile people call themselves, but the Doctor calls them "Silurians" to their face and they don't correct him. The on-screen credits also use the term.

In *The Sea Devils*, when Jo calls the reptile people "Silurians", the Doctor replies, "That's a complete misnomer. The chap that discovered them must have got the period wrong. Properly speaking, they should have been called the Eocenes". Yet the Doctor never uses the "correct" term in practice. The novelisation of *Doctor Who and the Silurians* (called *The Cave Monsters* on its first release) called them "reptile people", and the word "silurian" only appears as a UNIT password. The description "sea devil" is coined by Clark, the terrified sea fort worker in *The Sea Devils*, and the term appears in the on-screen credits for all six episodes. Captain Hart refers to them as "Sea Devils" as though that's their name. For the rest of the story the humans tend to call them "creatures" while the Doctor and Master refer to them as "the people".

By *Warriors of the Deep* and *Blood Heat*, however, the reptiles have adopted the inaccurate human terms for their people. *Bloodtide* starts with a flashback where Silurians refer to themselves by that name in their own era. In *Love and War*, we learn that the Silurians of the future "liked to be called Earth Reptiles now", and that term is also used in a number of other novels. The designation 'homo reptilia' that crops up in a number of places is scientifically illiterate. In *Blood Heat* the Doctor uses the term "psionsauropodomorpha".

In *Doctor Who and the Silurians*, Quinn has a globe of the Earth showing the continents forming one huge land mass, the implication being that it's the world the Silurians would have known. *The Scales of Injustice* follows this cue. Scientists call this supercontinent Pangea, and date it to 250 to 200 million years ago. Again, this seems too early, as it predates the time of the dinosaurs.

That said, while most fans have assumed - and the novels and audios have often stated - that the Silurians come from the same time as the dinosaurs (around 165 to 65 million years ago, according to both science and the Doctor in *Earthshock*), there is no evidence on-screen that the Silurians were contemporaries of any known dinosaur species. In *Doctor Who and the Silurians* the Silurians have a 'guard dog' that's a mutant, five-fingered species of tyrannosaur that the Doctor can't identify, and in *Warriors of the Deep* we see the lumbering Myrka. Likewise, while it seems obvious to cite the extinction of the dinosaurs and the fall of Silurian civilisation as owing to the same events, it's not a connection that's ever made on-screen. Indeed, we know from *Earthshock* that the dinosaurs were wiped out in completely different circumstances than the catastrophe that made the Silurians enter hibernation.

The key plot point with the Silurians' story is not that they existed at the time of the dinosaurs, it's that as their civilisation thrived, the apes who were humanity's ancestors were mere pests. The Sea Devil leader in *The Sea Devils* says "my people ruled the Earth when man was only an ape". *Bloodtide* says the Silurians ruled "while humanity was still in its infancy", and goes on to specify that the apes at the time were Australopithecus. The earliest evidence for that genus is around four million years ago - which ties in with the date for the earliest humans known to science in *Image of the Fendahl*. Although *Doctor Who* continuity has established humanity dates back millions of years more than scientists would accept, it doesn't seem to stretch anything like as far as the Eocene, 55 to 38 million years ago.

We don't know how long Silurian civilisation stood. One solution to the dating problem might be to say that it lasted for tens of millions or even hundreds of millions of years, from before the time of the dinosaurs (and surviving their extinction somehow) through to the time of the apemen. However, all accounts have the reptile people as a technologically-advanced, innovative, stable and centrally-controlled civilisation. At the time of their going into hibernation, they were merely "centuries" in advance of the human race in the twentieth century. This would seem to point to a civilisation lasting thousands of years rather than millions.

We have to conclude that the Silurians and apelike human ancestors were contemporaries, and that the end of Silurian civilisation was long after the time of the dinosaurs. There are more than sixty million years to fit the Silurians in, then, including the Eocene period favoured by the Doctor in *The Sea Devils*. It seems most likely, though, that the Silurian civilisation flourished for a few millennia at some point in the last five to ten million years.

BLOODTIDE[109] -> The surface of the Earth became a freezing wasteland. The Silurian scientist Tulok genetically augmented some of the apes to improve their flavour, and as a side-effect they also become sentient. As the Silurian Triad entered hibernation, Tulok was banished to the surface for the crime of illicit experimentation. He was rescued by his friend Sh'vak. They headed to the hibernation chambers, sabotaging the controls so that most of the species would not revive when planned.

The Silurians retired to vast subterranean hibernation chambers, but the rogue planetoid settled into orbit around Earth, becoming the Moon. After the Moon's arrival, the Van Allen Belt developed, filtering out much of the sun's radiation and cooling the Earth. The climate quickly stabilised at a lower temperature than the reptile people had predicted, and so they failed to revive as planned. The apes slowly began to evolve a greater degree of intelligence. Before long, the only trace remaining of the reptile people were the race memories of these first hominids, the ancestors of mankind.[110]

The planetoid was the moon containing the Museum of the Cthalctose. The gravitational forces wrecked havoc on Earth, destroying many Silurian shelters. Race memories of this event survived in human mythology as a great flood.[111]

The Birth of the Cybermen

Millions of years ago, a twin planet to Earth - Mondas - was home to a race identical to humanity (indeed, Mondas was an old name for Earth). Mondas started to drift out to the edge of space.[112] Mondas had been created by the Constructors of Destiny to research collective intelligence.[113]

It soon became clear that the Mondasian race was becoming more sickly. Their life spans were shortening dramatically and they could only survive by replacing diseased organs and wasted limbs with metal and plastic substitutes. These Primitive Cybermen gradually evolved to incorporate breathing apparatus that allowed them to return to the surface of Mondas, easing the pressures on the underground cities. Fewer and fewer children were being born, and it gradually became apparent that only Cybertisation could save the race. It was several more centuries before they bowed to the inevitable and the Mondasians became full Cybermen. A new race was born.[114]

> "Mondas had a propulsion unit, a tribute to Cyber-engineering - though why they should want to push a planet through space, I have no idea."[115]

---

109 Dating *Bloodtide* - It's set at the time the Silurians are going into hibernation, "over a million years ago", and "ten years" after Earth's surface has become uninhabitable. In *Doctor Who and the Silurians* and *The Scales of Injustice*, it's stated that the Silurians don't revive because Earth's climate stabilises below the levels the Silurians set. In *Bloodtide*, Tulok claims he prevented the reactivation, and the Doctor in Part Three finds evidence of his sabotage.
110 *Doctor Who and the Silurians*
111 "Twenty million years, give or take" before *Eternity Weeps*, according to Benny.
112 *The Tenth Planet*. It's unclear when Mondas leaves the solar system. The Doctor says it was "millions of years" ago. The Cyberman Krang says it was "aeons", and an aeon is a billion years. But the Mondasians were "exactly like" humans when Mondas started to drift away. As the land masses of the "twin" planets of Earth and Mondas are identical, it seems logical that life evolved in the same way and at the same rate on both worlds.

David Banks, in both his *Cybermen* book and his novel *Iceberg*, dated Mondas' departure to 10,000 BC. *The Terrestrial Index* concurred. Banks suggested that the "edge of space" was the Oort Cloud surrounding the Solar System. The audio *Spare Parts* contradicts that, saying that Mondas reaches the Cherrybowl Nebula, and states that Mondas left orbit because of

the Moon's arrival. *Real Time* says Mondas left "millennia" ago. In a story outline for a proposed sixth Doctor story, *Genesis of the Cybermen*, Gerry Davis set the date of the Cybermen's creation at "several hundred years BC". *Timelink* notes that as the Fendahl planet was the 'fifth' twelve million years ago, Mondas must have already left its orbit by that point.

Over the years, a number of fans - including myself in the first two versions of this timeline - have speculated that the Mondasians and the Silurians were contemporaries, linking the disaster that put the Silurians into hibernation with the one that threw Mondas out of its orbit. There's little to either support or contradict this in the stories themselves.

In the Virgin edition of this book, I suggested that Mondas was subject to time dilation, explaining why the Cybermen weren't more advanced. *Timelink* and *The Death of Art* reached the same conclusion. However, the continents on Mondas are exactly like those on Earth, so this theory doesn't account for the identical continental drift, if such a thing affected the ancient Earth in the *Doctor Who* universe.
113 *The Quantum Archangel*
114 *The Tenth Planet*
115 According to the sixth Doctor in *Attack of the Cybermen*. The implication seems to be that Mondas left the solar system deliberately and under its own power. However, *Spare Parts* shows the propulsion unit

? - SPARE PARTS[116] -> The Doctor and Nyssa arrived on Mondas when it was at the furthest point in its journey away from the Sun, on the edge of the Cherrybowl Nebula, 'a crucible of unstable energy'. Mondas was rife with diseases like TB, and 'heartboxes' were common for cardio-vascular problems. Mondas was ruled by a bionic group mind, the Committee. A scan of a tertiary lobe in the Doctor's brain suggested solutions to various organ rejection problems that had plagued the planet's Cyber-program, and the Cyber-templates were augmented with this new design. The Doctor realised he could do little to prevent history from unfurling as planned.

During the Miocene Era, around twenty five million years ago, the rocks on which Atlantis would later be built were formed.[117]

The Origins of Man

It's unclear when humanity evolved, and it depends on one's definition of humanity. Some estimates have men walking the Earth as early as six million years ago. The scientific consensus in the 1970s was about four million.[118]

The evolution of mankind received a boost when the Fendahl skull arrived on Earth twelve million years ago. On a nameless planet in our solar system that no longer exists, evolution went up a blind alley. Natural selection turned back on itself, and a creature - the Fendahl - evolved which prospered by absorbing the energy wavelengths of life itself. It consumed all life, including that of its own kind.

Then the Time Lords decided to destroy the entire planet, and hid the fact from posterity. But when the Time Lords acted it was too late, as the Fendahl had already reached Earth, probably taking in Mars on its way through. The Fendahl was buried, not killed. The energy amassed by the Fendahl was stored in a fossilised skull, and dissipated slowly as a biological transmutation field. Any appropriate life form that came within the field was altered so it ultimately evolved into something suitable for the Fendahl to use. The skull did not create man, but it may have affected his evolution. This would explain the dark side of man's nature.[119]

The Doctor visited Mars before it became a dead world.[120]

c 12,000,000 BC - THE TAKING OF PLANET 5[121] -> A Celestis outcast became concerned that the Celestis base of Mictlan might attract the Swimmers - phenominal beings large enough to crush the universe. The outcast hoped to destroy Mictlan before this occurred.

Using a Fictional Generator, the outcast brought the Elder Things from HP Lovecraft's work to life in Antarctica. This attracted Time Lord shock troops from the future, who slaughtered the Elder Things and subsequently read-

---

coming into operation at the far end of Mondas' journey ... and the fifth Doctor learning why.

116 Dating *Spare Parts* - There is no dating evidence in the story itself. It takes place when Mondas is at its farthest point from Earth and the implication is that the return journey to Earth will be much faster than the outward one, as it will be powered. *Spare Parts* could, then, take place a matter of decades before *The Tenth Planet* (and further evidence for this might be the Mondasian society of *Spare Parts* resembles Earth's in the mid twentieth century).

That said, while it's never quite stated, Mondas seems to have left the Solar System within the lifetimes of the older characters, not the 'millions of years' the Doctor spoke of in *The Tenth Planet*. There's no indication that Mondas immediately set course for a return to the solar system. We know that the Cybermen didn't attend the Armageddon Convention (*Revenge of the Cybermen*) and that the Convention was signed in 1609 (*The Empire of Glass*), so that they were a force to be reckoned with by the seventeenth century.

I would therefore speculate that the Cybermen piloted Mondas around the galaxy for a long time (certainly millennia) before finally returning to their native solar system.

117 *The Underwater Menace*

118 When asked in *Autumn Mist* when humanity evolved, the Doctor says 'the accepted figure's about half a million years, though its really nearer six'. It's only one suggestion that human origins in the *Doctor Who* universe stretch further than conventional scientific wisdom would have you think. According to *Image of the Fendahl*, the Fendahl skull arrived on Earth twelve million years ago, just as the first humanoid bipeds evolved - this is eight million years before Dr. Fendelman had believed.

119 *Image of the Fendahl*

120 *The Creed of the Kromon*

LIFE ON MARS: The Fendahl couldn't have wiped out all life on Mars, as the Ice Warriors come from Mars and lived there at least from the time of the Ice Age on Earth (*The Ice Warriors*) until the twenty-first century (*The Seeds of Death*). It should be noted that in *Image of the Fendahl*, the Doctor only speculates that the Fendahl attacked Mars.

121 Dating *The Taking of Planet 5* - It is 'about 12 million years ago' (p71). The Elder Things aren't the same as the Great Old Ones seen in Lovecraft's work, so there's no direct clash with this story and the appearance of the Great Old Ones elsewhere in the *Doctor Who* novels.

Delphon was mentioned in *Spearhead from Space*, Tersurus got a mention in *The Deadly Assassin* but didied a fleet of War-TARDISes. They intended to break the time-loop around Planet Five, hoping to use the Fendahl trapped within against the Time Lords' future Enemy.

A wounded TARDIS created a time fissure that would later be exploited by Professor Fendelman. The time-loop was breached, but this actually released the hyper-evolved Fendahl Predator: a Memovore, capable of consuming conceptual thought. The Memovore consumed Mictlan, and thus destroyed the Celestis, before the Doctor banished it to the outer voids.

By now, the planets Delphon and Tersurus had developed their unique forms of communication.

The first true human became aware of herself and immediately developed a sense of self-doubt. The Scourge had established themselves in our universe.[122] The owl evolved on Earth around this time.[123]

Ten million years ago, a derelict primitive TARDIS from the war against the Vampires began orbiting the planet Clytemnestra. Human colonists from the Earth Empire of the thirtieth century would mistake it for a moon, and name it Cassandra.[124]

Five million years ago on Earth, the climate of Antarctica was tropical.[125] Millions of years ago, an advanced civilization on Betrushia built an organic catalyzer to test species for survival traits. The catalyzer exceeded its design and threatened all life it encountered, causing the inhabitants to build an artificial ring system that constrained the creature to Betrushia.[126]

Millions of years ago, the neighbouring worlds of Janus Prime and Menda - respectively inhabited by giant spiders and a race of humanoids - ended a war. They agreed to build a doomsday device as a deterrent against further hostilities, and constructed a device that, if needed, would move a moon of Janus Prime and a moon of Menda into parallel orbit around the Janus System's sun. A hyperspace link between the two moons would then turn the sun into a black hole. The spiders later wiped out the Menda humanoids anyway, but not before the Mendans seeded Janus Prime with isotope decay bombs. This made the spiders devolve into savagery, leaving the doomsday device

untouched until 2211.[127]

By the time of the Pliocene on Earth, the Martian civilisation equivalent of the Industrial Revolution had already taken place.[128]

Around 3,639,878 BC, a group of Tractites arrived from the future using a time tree. They established a colony on Earth, which threatened to wipe out humanity and give rise to a future where the Tractites controlled the planet. The Doctor, aided by Jo Grant and Samantha Jones, arrived through time to try and prevent this. Jo obliterated the Tractites and their colony with a laser cannon, which prevented the aberrant future. The Doctor's Tractite ally Kitig stayed in this period to carve messages in rock for Jo and Sam to find 1.07 million years hence. At the end of his life, Kitig travelled back in time to destroy the time tree.[129]

Three million years ago, civilisation had started on Veltroch.[130]

2,579,868 BC - GENOCIDE[131] -> Captain Jacob Hynes, a genocidal UNIT member, arrived through time with a virus intended eliminate all mammalian life on Earth. Jo Grant and Sam Jones prevented him from releasing a deadly prion, and some primitive humans killed Hynes. A message from the Doctor's Tractite ally, Kitig, enabled Jo and Sam to find the buried TARDIS and locate the Doctor 1.07 million years previous.

A humanoid race sent probes out into the galaxy to build transference pylons, capable of teleporting people between solar systems at the speed of light. Ninety nine percent of the probe ships failed, but the remaining one percent allowed the Slow Empire to be established.[132]

A million years ago, the Mastons of Centimminus Virgo became extinct.[133] The Hoothi made the first moves in their plan to conquer Gallifrey. They enslaved the Heavenites, keeping them as a slave race and turning their planet into a beautiful garden world.[134] The Tralsammavarians died out.[135]

The Ice Warriors of Mars had space travel a million years ago.[136] Around the same time, diamonds were formed in the remnants of a Jovian planet in the

---

n't appear until the Comic Relief sketch *The Curse of Fatal Death*. According to *Alien Bodies*, the Raston robots are built on Tersurus.
122 *The Shadow of the Scourge*
123 *Just War*
124 *So Vile a Sin*
125 *The Seeds of Doom*
126 *St. Anthony's Fire*
127 *The Janus Conjunction*
128 *The Dying Days*
129 *Genocide*. It's 1.07 million years before 2,569,868 BC.

130 *The Dark Path*
131 Dating *Genocide* - The precise date is given (p260).
132 'Millions of years' before *The Slow Empire*. The Empire lasts 'two million years' once it has been set up.
133 *Slipback*
134 *Love and War*
135 *A Device of Death*
136 *The Dying Days*. They would send an expedition to Earth, as seen in *The Ice Warriors*. Its loss presumably convinced them to use their scarce resources another way, and put them off conquering our planet.
137 *Synthespians™*

Caledonian Reef.[137] **The earliest splinter of Scaroth gave mankind the secret of fire in his efforts to accelerate human development.**[138]

The Thal civilisation had begun half a million years ago on Skaro, and writings survive from this time.[139] A quarter of a million years ago, the Monks of Felsecar began collecting objects and information.[140] **Two hundred thousand years ago, homo sapiens - "the most vicious species of all" - began killing one another.**[141]

The planet Hitchemus was 7/8 covered by ocean, and the shifting climate there threw the genetics of the indigenous species of tigers into flux. A generation of tigers was born hyper-intelligent and built a weather control system. However, the tigers' progeny lacked the increased intelligence of their parents - presumably as a survival mechanism to prevent the tigers from over-developing their limited resources. Before passing on, the intelligent tigers built a hidden storehouse to preserve something of their developments. Intelligent tigers would sporadically be born in future, with multiple generations of instinctive tigers in-between.[142]

The First Ice Age

A Martian ship crashed on Earth, and became encased at the foot of an ice mountain.[143] Ice Warrior spaceship designs changed little after this time.[144]

One hundred thousand years ago on Earth, the First Ice Age began. By this time, two rival groups of intelli-

gent primates had developed: Neanderthals and homo sapiens.[145] Another group, the Titanthropes became an evolutionary dead end. They possessed more intelligence than Neanderthals, but their innate hostility made them kill themselves off before the emergence of Homo-sapiens.[146]

The being named Light surveyed life on Earth for several centuries during the Ice Age. Ichthyosaurs were included in Light's catalogue, as were the Neanderthals. Around this time, the Doctor visited a Neanderthal tribe and acquired the fang of a cave bear.[147]

The Daemon Azal wiped out the Neanderthals. Race memories of beings with horns and their science survived in human rituals. Light had preserved a single specimen - Nimrod - and a few individual examples of the race survived for tens of thousands of years.[148]

c 100,000 BC - AN UNEARTHLY CHILD[149] -> The Doctor, Ian, Barbara and Susan met a prehistoric tribe which was struggling to survive 'the great cold' and was in the throes of a leadership struggle between Kal and Za. Ian made fire, and the leadership dispute was settled in Za's favour when Kal was exposed as a murderer.

c 100,000 BC - THE EIGHT DOCTORS[149] -> The eighth Doctor observed his earlier self.

---

138 *City of Death.* The earliest known use of fire was around 700,000 BC.

139 Measured from the time of *The Daleks*, which I place around 2263. The Doctor says that the Thal records "must go back nearly a half a million years".

140 *Love and War*

141 *The War Games*

142 "Hundreds of thousands of years" before *The Year of Intelligent Tigers.*

143 *The Ice Warriors.* Arden states that the Ice Warrior Varga comes from ice dating from "prehistoric times, before the first Ice Age". Arden's team have discovered the remains of mastadons and fossils in the ice before this time. In *Legacy*, the Doctor states that Varga "crashed on Earth millions of years ago".

144 According to Benny in *The Dying Days.*

145 *An Unearthly Child, Ghost Light*

THE FIRST ICE AGE: According to *Doctor Who*, the Ice Age was a single event around one hundred thousand years ago. In reality there were waves of ice ages that lasted for hundreds of thousands of years as the ice advanced and retreated. We may now be living in an interglacial period. *An Unearthly Child* seems to take place at the end of the Ice Age: the caveman Za speaks of "the great cold" - although this might simply mean a

particularly harsh winter. Similarly, the butler Nimrod talks of "ice floods" and "mammoths" in *Ghost Light*, and he's one of the last generation of Neanderthals. In *The Daemons*, the Doctor says that Azal arrived on Earth "to help Homo Sapiens take out Neanderthal man", and Miss Hawthorne immediately states that this was "one hundred thousand years" ago.

146 *Last of the Titans*

147 *Ghost Light*

148 *The Daemons, Ghost Light.* Science tells us that the Ichthyosaurs actually died out at the time of the dinosaurs. In *Timewyrm: Genesys*, Enkidu is one of the last Neanderthals. In reality, Neanderthals only evolved about one hundred thousand years ago and survived for about sixty thousand years, until the Cro-Magnon Period.

149 Dating *An Unearthly Child* and *The Eight Doctors* - Ian confirms in *The Sensorites* that the story is set "in prehistoric times". (*An Unearthly Child* itself never explicitly states that it's set on Earth, rather than another primitive planet.) Now that we know that the production team called the first televised story *100,000 BC* at the time it was made (the title appears on a press release dated 1st November, 1963), dating the story has become a lot less problematical. Anthony Coburn's

The Cold, a form of intelligence, evolved in the Siberian ice. It became dormant as the planet warmed.[150]

The Galyari evolved as an intelligent lizard race that was descended from avians.[151] They sought to overrun the homeworld of the Cuscaru, but the Doctor came into possession of the Galyari's Srushkubr, the "memory egg" deposited on every colony world. He destroyed it when General Voshkar of the Galyari refused to withdraw. This released a dose of neural energy that would taint the descendants of the Galyari present for generations. The Galyari departed the planet, and their race later became nomads aboard a fleet of ships named the Clutch.

The Doctor's role in this affair made the Galyari regard him as "the Sandman," a legendary killer of Galyari children. The threat of the Sandman's return helped to keep the Galyari's aggression in check.[152]

Scaroth, the Fendahl and the Daemons all continued to influence human development until the late twentieth century.[153] At some point mankind will become embroiled in a conflict with the Leannain Sidhe, an energy-based race dimensionally out of phase with humanity, existing in all eleven dimensions rather than the 'visible' four but sharing the same planet. A truce between the two races will eventually be reached.[154]

The Gubbage Cones were the dominant empire in the galaxy.[155]

original synopsis of the story also gives the date as "100,000 BC".

The first edition of *The Making of Doctor Who* placed the story in "33,000 BC" (which is more historically accurate), but the second edition corrected this to "100,000 BC". *The Programme Guide* claimed a date of "500,000 BC", *The Terrestrial Index* settled on "c100,000 BC". *The Doctor Who File* suggested "200,000 BC". *The TARDIS Special* claimed a date of "50,000 BC", *The Discontinuity Guide* "500,000 BC - 30,000 BC". *Timelink* says 100,000 BC.

150 *Time and Relative*
151 *Dreamtime*
152 More than a hundred thousand years before *The Sandman*.
153 *City of Death, Image of the Fendahl, The Daemons*.
154 *Autumn Mist*
155 "Seventy thousand years" before *The Crystal Bucephalus* (p34). The fungoids on Mechonous in *The Chase* were named "Gubbage Cones" in the script but not on-screen.

Antiquity

The ozone layer of Urbanka collapsed around 55,500 BC. The Monarch of the planet stored the memories of his population, some three billion, on computer chips which could be housed in android bodies. Monarch built a vast spacecraft and set out for Earth. The ship doubled its speed on each round trip, and the Urbankans landed and kidnapped human specimens.[1]

Cave paintings on one Mediterranean island date from the Cro-Magnon period, forty thousand years ago, demonstrating that a primitive human culture had developed by this time.[2] Around 35,500 BC, the Urbankans kidnapped the Australian aboriginal Kurkurtji and other members of his race.[3] An Onihr captain took command of a vast Onihr ship thirty thousand years ago. In the twenty-first century, the same Onihr captain would seek to acquire time-travel technology on Earth.[4]

The T'Zun began space conquests around 23,000 BC. They defeated the fungoid Darkings of Yuggoth, but their genetic structure became corrupted and they mutated into three subspecies.[5] The energy fields of the dormant Permians influenced the early Inuit legends.[6]

Two Krynoid pods landed in Antarctica in the Late Pleistocene Period, twenty to thirty thousand years ago. They remained dormant in the Antarctic permafrost until the twentieth century.[7] Around 16,000 BC, Sancreda, a scout of the Tregannon - an alien race with great mental powers - was marooned on Neolithic Earth.[8]

Around 15,000 BC, the Urbankans returned to Earth. They kidnapped the princess Villagra.[9] Circa 13,000 BC, the Canavitchi of the Pleiades begin conquering neighbouring star systems, building an empire that would eventually stretch over seven galaxies.[10]

The being named Martin was born on Frantige Two, a dull planet and home to a species with an extraordinarily long lifespan. He would live fourteen thousand years into the twenty-first century.[11]

Circa 9000 BC, Traken outgrew its dependency on robots.[12] Around 8000 BC, the Euterpian civilisation died out.[13] Around the same time, the Jex from Cassiopeia start-

---

1 *Four to Doomsday*
MONARCH'S JOURNEY: There is a great deal of confusion about the dates of Monarch's visits to Earth, as recorded in *Four to Doomsday*. The story is set in 1981. The Greek named Bigon says he was abducted "one hundred generations ago [c.500 BC], and this is confirmed by Monarch's aide Enlightenment - she goes on to say that the visit to ancient Greece was the last time the Urbankans had visited Earth. Bigon says that the ship last left Urbanka "1250 years ago", that the initial journey to Earth took "20,000 years" and that "Monarch has doubled the speed of the ship on every subsequent visit".

This is complicated, but the maths do work. The speed only doubles every time the ship arrives at *Earth*, perhaps because of some kind of slingshot effect. Monarch's ship left Urbanka for the first time in 55,519 BC, it arrived at Earth twenty thousand years later (35,519 BC), the speed doubled so the ship arrived back at Urbanka ten thousand years later (25,519 BC), it returned to Earth (15,519 BC), the speed doubled and the ship travelled back to Urbanka (arriving 10,519 BC). Monarch returned to Earth (in 5519 BC), the speed doubled once again and the ship arrived back at Urbanka (in 3019 BC). The ship made its final visit to Earth around 519 BC, and now the trip back to Urbanka only took 1250 years. The ship left Urbanka (731 AD) and reached Earth in 1981.

However, this solution leaves a number of historical problems - see the individual entries.
2 Peri has just turned down an opportunity to visit the caves with her mother at the beginning of *Planet of Fire*.

Although filmed on Lanzarote and named as such in the story, the island in *Planet of Fire* shouldn't be Lanzarote, as it was nowhere near any ancient Greek trading routes.
3 *Four to Doomsday*. Bigon states that Kurkurtji was taken "thirty thousand years" ago. Examples of Australian Aboriginal art that are at least twenty-five thousand years old survive.
4 *Trading Futures*
5 'Twenty five thousand years' before *First Frontier*. Yuggoth is another reference to H P Lovecraft (it's his name for the planet Pluto).
6 'Twenty five thousand years' before *The Land of the Dead*.
7 *The Seeds of Doom*
8 "Eighteen thousand years" before *The Spectre of Lanyon Moor*.
9 *Four to Doomsday*. Bigon claims that Villagra is a "Mayan". Although the Doctor boasts of his historical knowledge, he then suggests that the Mayans flourished "eight thousand years ago", but the civilisation really dated from c.300 AD - c.900 AD. The Urbankans, though, don't visit Earth after 500 BC. It would appear that Villagra must come from an ancient, unknown pre-Mayan civilisation.
10 "A dozen millennia" before *The King of Terror*.
11 Martin says he's fourteen thousand years old in *The Tomorrow Windows* (p256).
12 "Eleven thousand years" before Nyssa's time, according to *Cold Fusion*.
13 "Ten thousand years" before *Invasion of the Cat-People*.

ed their conquests. They would eventually dominate several galaxies, including a planet in the Rifta system where the Doctor encountered them.[14]

The wolf-like Valethske had worshipped the insectile Khorlthochloi as gods, but the Khorlthochloi believed the Valethske were becoming too dominant. They destroyed the Valethske warfleets, and released a plague that devastated the race. The Valethske swore vengeance for this affront.

The Khorlthochloi later found a means of abandoning their physical bodies for a higher plane of existence. A threat to their new forms made the Khorlthochloi try to reunite with their bodies, but this proved impossible, as the bodies had become too independent. The threat killed off the Khorlthochloi's minds, but their bodies lived on as sedate herds of giant beetles.[15]

Around ten thousand years ago, humanity developed the wheel - with a helping hand from Scaroth.[16] Around the same time, in the Prion planetary system, the Zolfa-Thurans developed a powerful weapon. When the Dodecahedron, a power-source, was aligned with the giant Screens of Zolfa-Thura, an energy beam - "a power many magnitudes greater than any intelligence has ever controlled" - was formed. The beam was capable of obliterating any point in the galaxy.

Zolfa-Thura fell into bloody civil war, and everything on the planet's surface save the Screens was devastated. The Dodecahedron was taken to Zolfa-Thura's sister-planet, Tigella, where the Deons worshipped it.[17]

Around 6000 BC, the humanoid Thains, arch-enemies of the Kleptons, died out.[18] Circa 5900 BC, the inhabitants of Proxima 2 created the Centraliser, which linked them telepathically.[19] Around 5500 BC, the Urbankans visited Earth for the third time. The Urbankans kidnapped the mandarin Lin Futu, along with a number of dancers.[20]

Seven thousand years ago in the Nile delta, the Egyptian civilisation was flourishing. A variety of extra-terrestrials visited Egypt around this time, and they were seen as gods: Khnum was either one of the Daemons or a race memory of them, and Scaroth posed as an Egyptian god and Pharaoh around this time, building the earliest Pyramids.[21]

The Osirians

By 5000 BC, the highly-advanced Osirian race had influenced the cultures of many planets, including Earth, Mars, Youkali (the scene of a devastating battle

---

14 "Ten thousand years" before *King of Terror*.
15 "Many thousands of years" before *Superior Beings*.
16 *City of Death*. Scaroth says that he "turned the first wheel". Archaeologists think that mankind discovered the wheel around 8000 BC.
17 "Ten thousand years" before *Meglos*.
18 "Ten thousand years" before *Placebo Effect*.
19 "Eight thousand years" before *The Face Eater*.
20 *Four to Doomsday*. There is no "Futu dynasty" in recorded Chinese history. The Doctor has heard of it, however, and claims it flourished "four thousand years ago". The date does not tie in with the details of Monarch's journey as described in the rest of the story. Archaeologists have discovered a piece of tortoiseshell with a character from the Chinese alphabet on it that is seven thousand years old, so it seems that an early Chinese civilisation was established by that time, and the timescale does tie in with the dates established by Bigon.
21 *The Daemons, City of Death*
22 *Pyramids of Mars. Return of the Living Dad, GodEngine* and *The Quantum Archangel* contain the further references.
23 All according to the Doctor in *The Sands of Time* (p233-235), who says the Sphinx was built 'between eight and ten thousand years ago' (p234).
24 *Pyramids of Mars*, with additional detail from the novel *The Sands of Time*. Egyptian mythology can't decide on Horus' exact relationship to Set; *The Sands of*

Time (p142, 158) solves this by making Horus a 'psi-child' of Osiris, which simultaneously makes him Sutekh's brother and nephew. The Cult of Sutekh also appears in the New Adventure *Set Piece*. In the scripts for *Pyramids of Mars*, the name Osirians is also sometimes spelt (and is always pronounced) "Osirans".
25 *The Sands of Time* (p235).
26 *Genesis of the Daleks*
27 Dating *Davros* - The story fills in details of Davros' life around the time he first started to develop the Daleks, and fits just before *Genesis of the Daleks*.
28 *Davros*, drawing on sources such as the novelisations of *Genesis of the Daleks* and *Remembrance of the Daleks*. The circumstances of how Davros came to be in his life support system are never given on-screen - it's described on-screen as 'an accident', which doesn't directly support the idea it was in a Thal attack.
29 *Genesis of the Daleks*. There's no indication how old Davros was when he was crippled, or how much time passed between the accident and *Genesis of the Daleks*.
30 Dating *Genesis of the Daleks* - The date of the Daleks' creation is unknown. *The Dalek Invasion of Earth, The Daleks' Master Plan* and *Genesis of the Daleks* all have the Doctor talk of "millions of years" of Dalek evolution and history. *Destiny of the Daleks*, however, suggests a much shorter timeframe of "thousands of years", and Davros has only been "dead for centuries". The Daleks seem to have interstellar travel at least two hundred years before *The Power of the Daleks* (so by 1820), although

between the Osirians and Sutekh) and Exxilon.[22]

Osirian technology depended on magnetic monopoles, and the Osirians set about building a power relay system on Earth. The Sphinx was carved from living rock, built to serve as a dispersal point. The Osirians then left instructions on how to build pyramids to serve as receptacles for their power. They either constructed similar pyramids and a Sphinx on Mars, or found a religiously fanatical group to do it for them.

The face of the Sphinx originally had perfect alignment with the path of the sun, but this became imperfect as the angle of the Earth altered over time. Also, sand would periodically cover the Sphinx and fog the reception. The Sphinx was equipped with a mental pulse that would influence individuals to dig it out.[23]

The Osirians fought a war in our solar system. Sutekh, AKA the Typhonian Beast, and his sister Nephthys captured Osiris and sent him into space in a capsule without life support. **Sutekh destroyed his homeworld of Phaester Osiris and left a trail of destruction across half the galaxy. Sutekh became known by many names, including Set, Sadok and Satan.** Sutekh and Nephthys tracked the body of Osiris to Egypt and totally destroyed it.

Osiris' sister-wife Isis looked for her lost husband, and the remains of his mind endowed themselves in the mind of her spacecraft pilot. This psi-child became Orisis' son Horus. **Along with seven hundred and forty fellow of his fellow Osirians, Horus located Sutekh on Earth, trapping and sealing him in a pyramid.** Nephthys was imprisoned in a human body and mummified. Her mind was fragmented, the evil side placed in a canopic jar. **The Pyramid of Mars was built to house the Eye of Horus, and the Osirians set up a beacon there to broadcast a warning message. The Egyptians worshipped Horus and the other Osirians. Even Sutekh was worshipped by many on Earth, and the Cult of Sutekh survived for many thousands of years.** The influence of the Osirians brought on the unification of the Egyptian kingdoms, and the local humans were genetically enhanced, becoming taller and with increased mental capacity.[24]

The original face of the Sphinx on Earth was that of Horus.[25]

The Birth of the Daleks

On the planet Skaro, the Thals and the Kaleds went to war. During the first century of the conflict, chemical weapons were used, and monstrous mutations developed in the Thal and Kaled gene pool. To keep their races pure, all Mutos were cast out into the wastelands that now covered the planet. As the war dragged on, resources became more and more scarce for the foot soldiers - plastic and rifles gave way to animal skins

and clubs, although both sides developed ever-more potent missiles. The war lasted for a thousand years until there were only two cities left, protected by thick domes.

Fifty years before the end of the war, the Kaleds set up an Elite group, based in a secret bunker below the Wasteland. It was run by chief scientist Davros, the greatest mind Skaro had ever seen.[26]

& 4000 BC - DAVROS[27] -> Although he continued to develop weapons - one of which sunk the entire Thal Navy in a day - Davros had come to realise the war was futile. Prolonging the war with the Thals and using increasingly deadly weapons would mean that soon Skaro would become a dead planet. He believed that no other world could support life, and it was impossible to end the fighting, as both races would inevitably compete to exploit the same ecological niche. Logically, the Kaled race could not possibly survive.

One of his research students, Shan, came up with what she called 'The Dalek Solution', a plan to reengineer the Kaled race to survive the pollution on Skaro. Fearing that Shan would become a more brilliant scientist than him, Davros framed her for treason and had her hanged.

Davros was greatly injured, and the only survivor, when the Thals shelled his laboratory. He was given a poison injector to kill himself, as none of the Kaleds could bring themselves to put Davros out of his misery. At that moment, Davros realised how weak the Kaleds were and how true power was being able to grant life and death.[28]

Davros remained crippled, but survived by designing a life support system for himself. He created energy weapons, artificial hearts and a new material that reinforced the Kaled Dome.[29]

? 4000 BC - GENESIS OF THE DALEKS[30] -> Davros succeeded in selectively breeding an intelligent creature that could survive in the radiation-soaked, environmentally desolate world of Skaro. Using the Mark III Travel Machines, the Daleks could survive in virtually any environment, even the dead planet.

The Time Lords foresaw a time when the Daleks had become the supreme power in the universe. They sent the Doctor, Sarah and Harry to the time of the Daleks' creation, and gave the Doctor three options: avert the Daleks' creation; affect their genetic development so they might evolve in a less aggressive fashion; discover some inherent weakness that could be used against them.

The Doctor failed to achieve any of these objectives, but reckoned he set Dalek development back a thousand years. He reasoned that the existence of the Daleks would serve to unite races against them.

The Doctor's interference on Skaro spared thousands of worlds from enduring the Dalek wars. The Time Lords calmed the resulting time disruption.[31] **At some point, at least a thousand years later, the Daleks developed space travel and began their galactic conquests.[32]**

Around 3500 BC, the Trakenite living god Kwundaar re-engineered Traken's sun to become a vast computer - the Source - which regulated the climate, provided energy, stored information and destroyed all who were evil. With the Source performing such duties, the people of Traken had no further need for a god and exiled Kwundaar from their star system.[33]

On Earth, the classical Greek Gods were long-lived beings with psionic abilities. They had forgotten their origins. Some of them believed they were aliens, although Hermes came to suspect they were an early mutation of humanity. Zeus, Poseidon and Hades were the oldest of the gods, although they were not yet five thousand years old.[34]

c 2700 BC - TIMEWYRM: GENESYS[35] -> By the third millennium before Christ, man had developed irrigation, and the human race had developed from hunters into city-dwellers. In the Middle East, walled cities were built and a warrior aristocracy developed. The earliest surviving human literature was written at this time, and commerce had begun between cities. The deeds of one warrior-king - and his contact with extra-terrestrials - soon became legend.

Gilgamesh refused the advances of the alien Ishtar, who had crashed near Uruk. Ishtar went on to the temple of Kish, taking the form of a metal snake woman, and had a vast temple built. The Doctor, Ace and Gilgamesh travelled to the mountains of Mashu and contacted Unapishtim, a member of Ishtar's race, leading him to his prey. Ishtar infiltrated the TARDIS computer, and the Doctor ejected her into the Vortex ... inadvertently turning her into the Timewyrm, a creature foretold to herald the end of the universe. The Timewyrm became capable of independent travel through space-time.

c 2650 BC - THE DALEKS' MASTER PLAN[36] -> The Doctor was pursued to the time of the construction of the Great Pyramids by both the Daleks in their time machine, and the Monk in his TARDIS. The Doctor made his escape during a pitched battle between the Daleks and Egyptian soldiers.

Around 2350 BC, the inhabitants of Uxarieus had used genetic engineering to become a psychic super-race powerful enough to come to the attention of the Time Lords. They built a Doomsday Weapon, a device capable of making stars go supernova. The Crab Nebula was formed as a result of testing the device. Soon, though, radiation began leaking from the weapon's power source. It poisoned the soil and the race began to degenerate into primitives.[37]

Around four thousand three hundred years ago, the Chinese were making the first astronomical measurements with Scaroth's help.[38] Over four thousand years ago, an elemental 'burning' entity was worshipped by various cultures on Earth. It was known as Agni the fire god in India, and Huallallo to the Peruvians.[39] **Four thousand**

War of the Daleks suggests those were time-travelling Daleks from the far future. My figure is arbitrarily chosen, but tries to take into account that they're an interstellar power more advanced than the human race, that they have the disadvantages of coming from a dead planet, and that the Doctor says he sets Dalek development back by a thousand years at the end of this story - none of which suggests the Daleks could develop any faster than humanity.

31 A Device of Death

32 The Dalek Invasion of Earth, and most subsequent Dalek stories. Again, taking what the Doctor says at face value, the Daleks are set back a thousand years by the Doctor in Genesis of the Daleks.

   THE TWO DALEK HISTORIES: There are a number of discrepancies between the accounts of the Daleks' origins in The Daleks and Genesis of the Daleks. In the first story, the original Daleks (or Dals) were humanoid, and it is implied they only mutated after the Neutronic War. Whereas in Genesis of the Daleks we see Davros deliberately accelerate the mutations that have begun to affect the Kaled race (a process the Doctor calls 'genet-

ic engineering' in Dalek). We also have to reconcile the fact that The Daleks shows a group of Daleks confined to their city on Skaro and wiped out at the end, while all the other stories have them as galactic conquerors. Nothing in the series accounts for this.

   A possible explanation is that the Doctor changes history. The obvious place for this to happen is in Genesis of the Daleks. The Discontinuity Guide suggested that on their appearances after Genesis of the Daleks, the Daleks are nowhere near as unified a force as they had been before, and that Davros plays a major part in Dalek politics, whereas before he wasn't even mentioned. Looking closely, though, the Doctor hasn't made much of a difference. The Daleks are an extremely feared, powerful and unified force in the first of the post-Genesis stories, Destiny of the Daleks - it's their defeat to the Movellans after that story which weakens them, and no alteration of the timeline need be invoked. The Dalek Invasion of Earth still happens - Susan remembers it in The Five Doctors (indeed, she's been snatched from its aftermath), and Remembrance of the Daleks contains references both to the Daleks years ago, the Futu dynasty was flourishing in China.[40]

The space explorer Moriah conquered Krontep and built a civilisation there. He left the planet shortly after his wife Petruska killed herself. Their descendants, which would come to include King Yrcanos, would rule the planet for millennia.[41]

The Chronovore Prometheus and the Eternal named Elektra broke an ancient covenant to sire the Chronovore Kronos. The Guardians spared the half-breed's life, but sealed him in a trident-shaped crystal prison and threw it into the Time Vortex. The crystal came to simultaneously exist on many worlds.[42]

Five hundred and thirty seven years before the fall of Atlantis, the priests of that land captured the god Kronos. At this time, a young man called Dalios was king. Kronos transformed a man, one of the king's friends, into a fearsome man-beast - the Minotaur. After this, the King forbid the use of the Crystal of Kronos, for fear of destroying the city.[43]

c 2000 BC - FALLEN GODS[44] **->** The Titans had evolved at the bottom of the sea. Most left to live in the Vortex, but some remained on Earth as humanity amused them. Humans bound these Titans using special crystals. The Titans could manipulate time, and were compelled to grant the people on the island of Thera four harvests a year. They ended a war between Athens and Thera by stealing life energy from the Athenians - which was taken to be a plague - and using it to extend the lifespan of the elite on Thera.

Fiery demon bulls attacked Thera, and King Rhadamanthys believed that Athens was seeking revenge.

---

invading Earth in "the twenty-second century" and to events on Spiridon (*Planet of the Daleks*). We can assume that the Doctor setting the Daleks back a thousand years in *Genesis of the Daleks* is part of the timeline we know, not a divergence from it - they still invade in 2157, not 3157.

Another possibility is that the Doctor changes history in *The Daleks*, that this first encounter affects Dalek development. We know from *The Evil of the Daleks* and *Dalek* that the Daleks can be altered by contact with aliens, particularly time-travelling ones. This first contact with the Doctor might have set any Daleks that survived on course to conquer the universe and challenge the supremacy of the Time Lords. Again, though, there's no evidence from the series that this is the case - every Dalek appears dead at the end of *The Daleks*.

One common way of dealing with this is to suggest that the Thal version of events recounted in The Daleks is a garbled version of the true history seen in *Genesis of the Daleks* and that there's only one war. This would mean that the Doctor's comment that the Thal records are accurate is wrong - which is not too difficult to justify. The idea that Skaro's civilisation lost knowledge following a nuclear war and that the two races would have subjective, propaganda-driven history is tempting ... but it doesn't explain why both the Thals and the Daleks in *The Daleks* believe in - as far as we can tell - exactly the same version of events.

So the problem is one of reconciling two accounts, and into one timeline. I think we have to infer that at some point in early Dalek history, the spacefaring Daleks broke contact with the Daleks on Skaro. We might speculate that this was because the Daleks on Skaro continued to mutate - indeed, perhaps they become the humanoid Dals mentioned in *The Daleks*, a different race altogether. Given what we know of Dalek history, it seems unlikely that this was an amicable arrangement, so we might infer a Dalek civil war of

some kind. While we're speculating, we might wonder if the Thals joined the Dals in their efforts to rid the planet of Daleks. Following this, the Dals and Thals lived together in peace on Skaro for a long time - until the Neutronic War, which I place in 1763. The spacefaring Daleks eventually return to Skaro - I place that in the 23rd century.

33 "2523 years" before *Primeval*.

34 *Deadly Reunion*. It's suggested the "gods" were the product of the Daemons' experiments.

35 Dating *Timewyrm: Genesys* - The Doctor says the TARDIS is heading for "Mesopotamia, 2700 BC".

36 Dating *The Daleks' Master Plan* - The three time machines land at the base of a "Great Pyramid" that has nearly been completed. This might well be the Great Pyramid of King Khufu, built around 2650 BC. *The Terrestrial Index* pins the date at "2620 BC" whereas *The Discontinuity Guide* offers a wider range of "2613 BC - 2494 BC". *Timelink* says 2635 BC.

37 *Colony in Space*. The date isn't given, but this is when the Crab Nebula was formed. It was first visible on Earth from 1054.

38 *City of Death*. Scaroth says that he caused "the heavens to be mapped". Historically it appears that mankind's first astronomical measurements were made in China around 2300 BC.

39 "Over four thousand years" before *The Burning*. The entity is drawn to Earth as the result of events in Siberia, 1894, in *Time Zero*.

40 According to the Doctor in *Four to Doomsday*.

41 Unspecified "thousands of years" before *Bad Therapy*.

42 *The Quantum Archangel*

43 *The Time Monster*

44 Dating *Fallen Gods* - It's "the Bronze Age" (p91). This is a retelling of the creation of the Atlantis as related in *The Time Monster*.

However, the Titans themselves were causing the attacks, hoping the king would free them to repel the 'invaders'. Rhadamanthys was killed, and his son Deucalion succeeded him. Deucalion felt the Titans' abilities had been used unwisely, and ordered their crystals scattered far and wide, curtailing their power.

The blessings the Titans had bestowed on Thera were stolen from the future. In the times to come, the island would experience barrenness and a volcanic eruption.

c 2000 BC - THE SANDS OF TIME[45] -> Tomb robbers entered the pyramid of Nephthys, breaking the canopic jar that contained her evil intellect. The Egyptian priests sought a pure vessel to contain it and chose the Doctor's companion Nyssa, sealing her in a sarcophagus until the 1920s.

At around the same time, Cessair of Diplos, a criminal accused of murder and stealing the Great Seal of Diplos, arrived on Earth. She posed as a succession of powerful women over the millennia, while her ship remained in hyperspace above Boscombe Moor in Damnonium, England. Around this time, a stone circle named the Nine Travellers was set up. Subsequent attempts to survey the circle proved hazardous.[46]

In 1936 BC, the Emperor Rovan Cartovall of the planet Centros became bored with his imperial life. He disappeared without a trace, and took the immense palace treasury with him. His younger brother Athren succeeded him to the throne. The mystery of Rovan and his missing treasure became legendary.[47] In 1758 BC, the "goddess"

Demeter gave birth to Perseophone, the future beloved of Hades. The Greek gods passed into legend, and some attempted to live quiet existences among mankind.[48]

The Fall of Atlantis

c 1500 BC - THE TIME MONSTER[49] -> The Master arrived in Atlantis, claiming to be the emissary of the gods. King Dalios didn't believe the stranger, who seduced his wife, Queen Galleia. The stranger and the Queen plotted to steal the Crystal of Kronos. King Dalios died of a broken heart, and the stranger seized power, proclaiming himself King. Queen Galleia, filled with remorse, ordered his arrest. The stranger released Kronos the Chronovore, and Atlantis was destroyed.

Some Atlanteans survived beneath the ocean, off the Azores. The Daemons would later claim to have destroyed Atlantis.[50]

The Ikkaban Period of Yemayan history was in progress around 1500 BC.[51]

The Great Sphinx was now buried up to its neck by sand. It mentally influenced the young Thutmose, who was on a hunting trip, to dig it out.[52]

Erimem ush Imteperem, 'Daughter of Light', was born to the Pharoah and one of his sixty concubines, Rubak.[53] When Erimem was a child, her father the Pharoah - Amenhotep II - trapped the Great Old Ones in a pyramid in the Himalayas.[54]

45 Dating *The Sands of Time* - The date is given (p57).
46 *The Stones of Blood*. The *Terrestrial Index* dated Cessair's arrival on Earth at "3000 BC", but this contradicts the Doctor and Megara, both of whom claim that only "four thousand" years have elapsed since Cessair came to Earth.
47 'Five thousand years' before *The Ultimate Treasure*.
48 *Deadly Reunion* (p115). The first part of the book takes place in 1944, and Persephone says she is three thousand, seven hundred and two years old.
49 Dating *The Time Monster* - The traditional date for the fall of Atlantis is around 1500 BC, but the Doctor states on returning to the twentieth century at the end of this story that it was "three thousand five hundred years ago".

The *Terrestrial Index* and *The Discontinuity Guide* both suggested the traditional date of 1500 BC, the FASA Role-playing game claimed 10,000 BC. *The TARDIS Logs* included the presumed misprint of 1520 AD. *Timelink* goes for 1529 BC.
50 *The Underwater Menace, The Daemons*
THE FALL OF ATLANTIS: We hear of / witness the

destruction of Atlantis in three stories: *The Underwater Menace, The Daemons* and *The Time Monster*. In *The Underwater Menace*, the island in question is in the Atlantic, and in *The Time Monster*, "Atlantis" is another name for the Minoan civilisation in the Mediterranean. In *The Daemons*, Azal warns the Master that "My race destroys its failures. Remember Atlantis!". *The Terrestrial Index* attempts to explain this by suggesting that the Daemons supplied the Minoan civilisation with the Kronos Crystal. This might be true, but there is no hint of it on-screen.
51 *SLEEPY* (p102).
52 As theorised by the Doctor in *The Sands of Time* (p234). Thutmose ruled Egypt as Menkheperura Thutmose IV from 1400-1390 BC and was actually a prince, but the need to have Erimem on the throne in this era rules him having such a lineage in the *Doctor Who* universe. Historically, Thutmose was the son of Amenhotep II, whom *The Roof of the World* also names as Erimem's father. However, Thutmose and Erimem explicitly can't be siblings, as she would never have ascended to the throne in *The Eye of the Scorpion* if one

c 1400 BC - THE EYE OF THE SCORPION[55] ->

Erimem's father had died, and her three half-brothers had died in mysterious circumstances. She was now ruler of Egypt. A starship containing prisoners crashed near Thebes, and a stasis box containing a dangerous gestalt energy being broke open. It began possessing local mercenaries. The Doctor and Peri joined forces with Erimem to defeat it. Following this, Erimem joined the Doctor on his travels.

The face of the Sphinx was damaged, and Peri whimsically issued orders that it be reconstructed with Elvis' features, confident that Napoleon's troops would damage it in the late eighteenth century.

1366 BC - SET PIECE[56] ->

Fleeing from the Ants, Ace spent some time in Egypt during the rule of Pharaoh Akhenaten. She served as a bodyguard to Lord Sedjet, but escaped through a time rift.

The Monk helped build Stonehenge using anti-gravity lifts.[57] The Ragman had been born at the other end of the universe as a psionic force. It had travelled on Earth in a stone, drawn to the power inherent in Earth's ley lines. The rock containing the Ragman was incorporated into the stone circle at Cirbury, and the creature was dormant. [58]

Classical History

The Doctor claimed to have met Theseus.[59] The Rani was present at the Trojan War, extracting a chemical from human brains.[60]

c 1184 BC - THE MYTH MAKERS[61] ->

Captured by the Greeks outside Troy, the Doctor was given two days to come up with a scheme to end the ten-year siege. He rejected the idea of using catapults to propel the Greeks over the walls of Troy - if only after Agamemnon insisted that the Doctor would be the first to try such a contrivance - and came up with the idea of using a wooden horse containing Greek troops.

Vicki left the Doctor's company and changed her name to Cressida. Katarina, the handmaiden to the prophetess Cassandra, joined the Doctor on his travels.

The Doctor was given a copy of the I Ching by Wen Wang.[62]

Thousands of years ago, the Exxilons were "the supreme beings of the universe... Exxilon had grown old before life began on other planets". Archaeologist Bernice Summerfield once wrote, "There are half a dozen worlds where the native languages develop up to a point, and then are suddenly replaced by one of the Exxilon ones."

Worlds visited by the Exxilons include Yemaya and Earth, where they helped to build temples in Peru. The Doctor visited one of these temples at some point after this date, and examined the carvings there.

On their home planet, the Exxilons created one of the Seven Hundred Wonders of the Universe: their City, a vast complex designed to last for all eternity. It was given a brain to protect, repair and maintain itself, and thus it no longer needed the Exxilons, who were driven from the City. They degenerated into primitives.

---

of her brothers had been alive. Some Egyptologists believe that Thutmose's restoration of the Sphinx sealed his right to become Pharoah, which suggests in *Doctor Who* terms that he wasn't a blood-heir but ascended after Erimem on the merit of his works.

53 *The Eye of the Scorpion*. Erimem is 'seventeen' when she joins the Doctor.

54 *The Roof of the World*

55 Dating *The Eye of Scorpion* - The Doctor estimates the date as "about fourteen hundred BC" from hieroglyphics. This story has the Doctor and Peri visiting a chamber *under* the Sphinx, which suggests that if the statue was previously buried up to its neck, Thutmose had, at the very least, enacted much of its restoration by this time. Writer Iain McLaughlin had privately decided that Fayum would get renamed and become the historical Thutmose, but nothing was ever scripted to substantiate this. That being the case, it's probable - until proven otherwise - that Fayum and Thutmose were separate individuals, that Fayum had a very short rule, was succeeded by Thutmose and - like Erimem - was lost to history.

Peri's claim that Napoleon's troops damaged the Sphinx's face (historically, they arrived in Egypt in 1798) owes to an urban legend that they used it for target practice. The Doctor doesn't correct Peri on this point, but there's otherwise no evidence that Napoleon's troops perpetrate the crime in the *Doctor Who* universe. In the real world, at least, erosion is the far more likely culprit.

56 Dating *Set Piece* - The date is given as "1366 BCE".

57 *The Time Meddler*. The earliest parts of Stonehenge were built around 2800 BC, but the final building activity occurred between 1600-1400 BC.

58 *Rags* (p160).

59 *The Horns of Nimon*

60 *The Mark of the Rani*

61 Dating *The Myth Makers* - The traditional date for the fall of Troy is 1184 BC, although this date is not given on-screen. The Doctor mentions being at the fall of Troy in *The Unquiet Dead*.

62 *Timewyrm Revelation* (p14). Wang was the last king of the Shang Dynasty.

The City needed power, and began to absorb electrical energy directly from the planet's atmosphere. The City also set an intelligence test that granted access to those who might have some knowledge to offer it. Over the centuries, a few Exxilons attempted the test, but none returned.[63]

At around the same time, Mawdryn and seven of his companions stole a metamorphic symbiosis generator from the Time Lords, hoping to become immortal. Instead they became horrific undying mutations, and the Elders exiled them from their home planet. Their ship entered a warp ellipse. It would reach an inhabited planet every seventy years, allowing one of the crew to transmat down to seek help.[64]

c 1000 BC - PRIMEVAL[65] **->** Kwundaar launched a bid to reconquer Traken. He engineered an illness for Nyssa, knowing the Doctor would seek out Shayla, the greatest physician in Trakenite history. As Kwundaar expected, Shayla was unable to help and the Doctor approached Kwundaar himself. He implanted a psychic command in the Doctor's mind, thus getting the Doctor to deactivate Traken's defences. Kwundaar's forces consequently invaded the planet, but the Doctor tricked Kwundaar and harnessed the Source's power for himself. The Doctor thus became the first Keeper of Traken. He reactivated the defences, which destroyed Kwundaar, then abdicated and allowed Shayla to become the second Keeper.

On the planet Avalon, a technologically advanced race created a system that focused solar energy to deflect the abnormally large number of asteroids in their system away from their planet. They also built thought-operated nanobots that allowed them to affect matter and energy. This discovery prolonged the race's existence but made their lives futile. They drained the machines of energy, but

it was too late. Their civilisation fell, and the natives regressed to being reptilian cephlies, lacking all ingenuity.[66]

Evidence found by Professor Horner in the twentieth century suggested that pagan rituals took place at Devil's Hump at around 800 BC.[67] Around 600 BC, a Nimon scout arrived on Earth and was killed by his own sword by Mithras, who was later worshipped throughout the known world as a result of his deed.[68]

The Doctor was present when Pythagoras discovered the connection between mathematics and the physical world.[69] Around 500 BC, the Doctor met Sun Tzu at least twice and discussed the *Art of War*.[70]

Ancient Greece

The Daemons and Scaroth both influenced ancient Greek civilisation.[71] The Athenian philosopher Bigon lived in Greece around two thousand five hundred years ago. In Bigon's fifty-sixth year, the Urbankans kidnapped him. For the first time in their visits to Earth, the Urbankans encountered resistance.[72]

The Doctor visited Athens and saw the Parthenon being built.[73] The Eternals kidnapped a trireme of Athenian sailors from the time of Pericles.[74]

The Doctor wrote many of the Greek Classics.[75] The Doctor met Alexander the Great and Pyrrho, possibly on the same visit.[76] The Doctor met Praxiteles, who sculpted the Venus de Milo.[77] The Doctor replaced Sun Tzu as the Chinese emperor's military advisor but wasn't terribly effective, as he kept holding conflict resolution seminars rather than fighting.[78]

The Great Wall of China was built around 300 BC.[79] At the time the Ch'in dynasty ruled in China, the Eternals kidnapped a crew of Chinese sailors.[80] The Doctor visited one of the Seven Wonders of the Ancient World, the Pharos lighthouse.[81] The first Doctor

---

63 *Death to the Daleks*. The Peruvian temples influenced by the Exxilons are around three thousand years old, so the collapse of Exxilon civilisation must be after that. In *SLEEPY*, Benny detects Exxilon influence in the Yemayan pyramid, dating from around "1500 BCE".
64 *Mawdryn Undead*. The ship has been in orbit for "three thousand years" according to the Doctor.
65 Dating *Primeval* - It is "three thousand years" before Nyssa's time.
66 "Thousands of years" before *The Sorcerer's Apprentice*.
67 *The Daemons*
68 *Seasons of Fear*
69 *Option Lock*. Pythagoras lived 580-500 BC.
70 The fourth Doctor namedrops Sun Tzu in *The Shadow of Weng-Chiang*, and the seventh Doctor and Ace refer to meeting him in *The Shadow of the Scourge*.

71 *The Daemons, City of Death*
72 "One hundred generations" before *Four to Doomsday*.
73 *The Spectre of Lanyon Moor*. This would be around 440 BC.
74 *Enlightenment*. Pericles died, age 70, in 429 BC.
75 *Cat's Cradle: Witch Mark*
76 *Robot* - Alexander lived 356-323 BC. *The Keys of Marinus* - Pyrrho lived c.360-270 BC.
77 *Omega*. This would have been around 350 BC.
78 *Set Piece*, during the "Fourth Century BCE".
79 *Marco Polo*
80 *Enlightenment*
81 *Horror of Fang Rock, Logopolis*
82 *City at World's End, The Two Doctors*. Archimedes lived c.287-212 BC.
83 *Eye of Heaven* (p181). Eratosthenes lived c.276-194

and Susan met Archimedes, and **the Doctor acquired Archimedes' business card.**[82] The Doctor taught the playwright Eratosthenes at least some of his craft.[83]

In 210 BC, an alien intelligence imprinted the minds of Qin Shi Huang, the First Emperor of China, and two of his generals into a stone engram. They would remain dormant until 1865 AD.[84] The Jex brutally subjugated the Canavitchi, and killed two-thirds of them. The Jex's resources became strained, and the Canavitchi successfully revolted. They swore to eradicate their former masters.[85]

Ancient Rome

The Doctor met Julius Caesar.[86] The Doctor, Fitz and Trix defeated Thorgan of the Sulumians. He had been planning to prevent the signing of the Treaty of Brundusium.[87]

At the height of the Roman Empire, the War Lords lifted a Roman battlefield.[88] The Doctor, Jamie and Victoria attended a gladiator fight in ancient Rome, and Victoria was appalled by the violence.[89]

One of the splinters of Scaroth was a man of influence in Ancient Rome.[90] **The Doctor visited Rome, met Hannibal and Cleopatra, and was very impressed by the swordsmanship of her bodyguard.**[91] According to the Doctor, Cleopatra herself had "the grace of a carpet flea".[92]

10 BC - STATE OF CHANGE[93] **->** After watching Cleopatra's barge on the Nile in 41 BC, the Doctor and Peri had decided to travel a little way into the future to follow the history of Rome. The Rani compelled a Vortex entity, Iam, to copy the Doctor's TARDIS console, but this also duplicated a section of the Earth around 32 BC, creating a flat disc-shaped world. The TARDIS console was duplicated and came to rest on the copied Earth, where it was regarded as an Oracle.

With information from this Oracle, the Roman Empire made great advancements. The battle of Actium went against Octavian and Agrippa because they faced opponents with steamships. Electric lighting, airships and explosives were developed. The culmination of this technology was "Ultimus", the Roman Empire's atomic bomb programme. Capable of kiloton yields, Ultimus could destroy any known city. Cleopatra's three children - Cleopatra Selene, Alexander and Ptolemy - ruled as a triumvirate.

The Doctor defeated the Rani's plans, and convinced Iam to relocate Terra Nova into the real universe. It settled into an unoccupied sector of space.

The Doctor visited the court of Caligula.[94] The Iceni, a Celtic tribe led by Boudicca, razed many Roman-occupied British towns to the ground.[95] Iris claimed that Salome did the fan dance with the Doctor's scarf.[96]

64 AD - THE RESCUE[97] **-> The TARDIS landed on the side of a hill and toppled from it.**

64 AD - BYZANTIUM![98] **->** The TARDIS had materialised just outside Byzantium. The Romans mistook Ian for a contemporary Briton and granted him some respect as a citizen of the Empire. Ian helped the Roman General Gaius Calaphilus and his political opponent, city praefectus Thalius Maximus, to settle their differences. Calaphilus and Maximus united efforts to purge corruption from the city, instigating a period of reform.

The Doctor met the scribes Reuben, Rayhab and Amos, and helped them to translate the Gospel of Mark into Greek, producing a version that complemented the writings of Matthew the tax-gatherer.

Returning to the TARDIS, the travellers discovered that the Roman Germanicus Vinicius has found the TARDIS and taken it to his villa near Rome. They followed it there...

BC.
84 'Two thousand years' before *The Eleventh Tiger*. Historically, Huang ruled under the name "First Emperor" from 221-210 BC, and died in that year.
85 "Two thousand years" before *The King of Terror*.
86 *Empire of Death*
87 *The Gallifrey Chronicles*
88 *The War Games*
89 *The Colony of Lies*
90 *City of Death*. He's listed as 'Roman Emperor' in the script, but it's possible he's a senator or other Roman of rank.
91 The Doctor has already visited Rome on his travels before *The Romans*. He mentions Hannibal (247-182 BC, he crossed the Alps in 219 BC) in *Robot*, and Cleopatra (68-30 BC) in *The Masque of Mandragora*.

92 *Loups-Garoux*
93 Dating *State of Change* - The Doctor thinks that it is "the year 10 BC, approximately" (p41). Cleopatra died around 15 BC (p45). Terra Nova is part of the universe's timeline by the end of the story, yet despite its evident prosperity and technological advantage over humanity on the proper Earth, it's never heard of again.
94 *The Slow Empire*
95 *Human Nature*
96 *The Blue Angel*. Salome lived in the first century AD.
97 Dating *The Rescue* - This happens right at the end of the story, as a literal cliffhanger. The date is established in *The Romans*, but *Byzantium!* establishes that the TARDIS crew have another adventure first ...
98 Dating *Byzantium!* - This story takes place immediately before *The Romans*.

64 (June / July) - THE ROMANS[99] -> The Doctor, Ian, Barbara and Vicki spent nearly a month at a deserted villa just outside Rome. Becoming bored by the lack of adventure, the Doctor and Vicki travelled to the capital. Captured by slave traders, Ian and Barbara were sold at auction. Ian's ship was wrecked, and he ended up as a gladiator in Rome. Barbara became the servant of the Emperor Nero's wife, Poppea, and the object of the Emperor's attentions. The Doctor, meanwhile, was posing as the musician Maximus Pettulian (despite a complete lack of musical ability). When the Doctor accidentally set fire to Nero's plans to rebuild Rome, the Emperor was inspired. As Rome began to burn, the four time travellers returned to the TARDIS.

79 - THE FIRES OF VULCAN[100] -> The Doctor and Mel arrived in Pompeii, just as Mount Vesuvius became active. The TARDIS was trapped in the rubble of a collapsed building, preventing their escape. The Doctor managed to antagonise the gladiator Murranus by beating him in a dice game. The Doctor and Mel escaped to the TARDIS just as the volcano erupted, destroying Pompeii and the surrounding area.

> = Temporal distortion resulted in an alternate history where Vesuvius took much longer to erupt, and the city's populace evacuated in their boats.[101]

On a visit to Condercum, the Doctor debated military ethics with a group of Romans fighting the Caledonians.[102] The Romans drove the Celts from their lands. Gallifreyan

intervention allowed King Constantine to pass into the parallel world of Avalon. Even while sleeping, Constantine ruled Avalon for two thousand years.[103]

The Doctor challenged Fenric to solve a chess puzzle. When Fenric failed, the Doctor imprisoned him in a flask, banishing him to the Shadow Dimensions.[104] By the end of the third century, the Old Silk Road to and from Cathay had been opened.[105] The Cult of Demnos had apparently died out by the fourth century.[106]

> = There was a potential timeline where the Daleks used time machines to invade Roman Britain in 305.[107]

> **= 305 - SEASONS OF FEAR**[108] -> The Roman Decurion Gralae worshipped Mithras, and had made contact with the Nimon, who posed as his god. They granted Gralae eternal life in return for his making sacrifices to them.
>
> The Doctor met Gralae at this time. Between now and his next meeting with the Doctor - seven hundred and fifty years later - Gralae would become known as Grayle, and spend eighty years repenting with monks. He married twelve times, all his wives dying of old age while he stayed young.

The Doctor sent some Nimon from 1806 to here, and rallied the Roman troops to wipe them out. He then rewrote history by buying out Gralae's commission before he met the Nimon.

---

99 Dating *The Romans* - The story culminates in the Great Fire of Rome. The TARDIS crew have spent "a month" at the villa.
100 Dating *The Fires of Vulcan* - The story ends with the eruption of Vesuvius.
101 *The Algebra of Ice* (p15).
102 *Ghost Ship*
103 *The Shadows of Avalon*
104 "Seventeen centuries" before *The Curse of Fenric*. The novelisation likens this contest to an ancient Arabian tale that takes place in "the White City".
105 "A thousand years" before *Marco Polo*.
106 *The Masque of Mandragora*
107 *The Time of the Daleks*
108 Dating *Seasons of Fear* - The date is given.
109 Dating *The Council of Nicaea* - The year is given. The Doctor says the TARDIS has landed "a few days before the council is set to begin," but Athanasius more accurately says it is "the night before the council starts". Historically, the Council formally opened on 20th May.
110 *Eye of Heaven* (p181).
111 *Timewyrm: Apocalypse*
112 *Time and the Rani*. Hypatia of Alexandria, a neo-

Platonic philosopher and mathematician, lived circa 370-415 AD.
THE TIME BRAINS: The Rani kidnaps eleven geniuses before we see her plans nearing fruition in *Time and The Rani*. In the televised version only three of these are named: Hypatia, Pasteur and Einstein. The rehearsal script and the novelisation both mention three more: Darwin, Za Panato and Ari Centos. The novelisation also states that the Danish physicist Niels Bohr is kidnapped.
113 *Toy Soldiers* (p208). The novel takes place in 1919, and the war on Q'ell has been going on for 'fourteen hundred and five years' by that point.
114 *The Suns of Caresh*
115 *The Talons of Weng-Chiang*. Bede lived c.673-735, although he never went to London, only leaving Jarrow once to visit Canterbury.
116 *Companion Piece*. This is a neat trick on Bede's part, as he died in 735 and the building of Westminster Abbey didn't start until 1050.
117 *The Banquo Legacy*. It was attributed to the Silurians in *White Darkness* (p89).
118 *Four to Doomsday*

325 AD (May) - THE COUNCIL OF NICAEA[109] -> In Nicaea, the Roman Emperor Constantine held a conference so that bishops could settle issues of dispute within the Christian Church. Among other concerns, the assembled council sought to decide the matter of Christ's divinity. The deacon Athanasius believed that Christ was divine, but the presbyter Arius held that Christ was subordinate to God. Erimem found Arius to be honorable and aided his cause, threatening to derail history. Tensions mounted, but the Doctor encouraged Constantine to refrain from bloodshed and defuse the situation with his oratory skills. The Council adopted Athanaisus' views as history

The Doctor was ejected from the staff at the Library of Alexandria after he misshelved the Dead Sea Scrolls.[110] The Doctor saved two Aristophanes plays from the destruction of the Great Library of Alexandria.[111] **The Rani kidnapped Hypatia to become part of her Time Brain.**[112]

In 514 AD, warfare broke out on the planet Q'ell. The Recruiter, a device created to destroy the Ceracai race, extended the war as part of its programming. The conflict would last until the twentieth century, and cause at least 2,846,014,032 casualties.[113] In the seventh century, Lord Roche's TARDIS crashed in England and died on impact. One of the Furies trapped within eventually starved to death, but the other survived until the Ship was discovered in 1999.[114]

The Doctor caught a huge salmon in Fleet and shared it with the Venerable Bede (who "adored fish").[115] Bede made the Doctor Dean of Westminster Abbey.[116]

The *Necronomicon* was written by Abdul Al-Hazred, a mad poet of Sanaa, in Damascus around 730.[117] **Around this period, Monarch left Urbanka for the last time.**[118] **The Rani visited Earth during the so-called "Dark Ages".**[119]

The Galactic Heritage Foundation emerged as an organization to halt alien property development on planets with indigenous populations. In the eighth century, the third princess Tabetha of Cerrenis Minor spent a weekend in Lewisham. Despite her finding it all a bit gauche, Earth was accorded a low-level ranking of Grade 4, which put it under the Foundation's protection.

With planets under such development bans selling for cheap, the Frantige Two native named Martin 'purchased a

hundred or so worlds for next to nothing'. Among his acquisitions, he bought the planet Earth for a few thousand Arcturan ultra-pods from a Navarino time-share salesman going through a messy divorce. The Navarino threw in the rest of Earth's solar system for free.[120]

The Doctor defeated the Tzun at Mimosa II in 733 AD.[121]

= "Sideways in time" on an Earth where the truth about King Arthur was closer to the myths of our world, a future incarnation of the Doctor was known as Merlin. During the eighth century, Arthur and Morgaine fought against one another, despite their childhood together at Selladon. The Doctor, who regenerated at least once during this time, cast down Morgaine at Badon with his mighty arts.

Eventually, though, Morgaine was victorious and Arthur was killed. The Doctor placed Arthur's body and Excalibur in a semi-organic spaceship, and transferred it to the bottom of Lake Vortigern in our dimension. Morgaine imprisoned the Doctor forever in the Ice Caves, and went on to become Empress of the solar system.[122]

Godric, a swordsman in the age when Arthur ruled, found the Holy Grail in a freshwater spring. A wood dryad seduced Godric into her tree, where he slept until 1936. The Doctor once claimed to have taught Lancelot how to use a sword at King Arthur's court.[123]

The Catholic Church founded the Library of St John the Beheaded in the St Giles Rookery, a notorious area of Holborn, London. The library contained unique, suppressed and pagan texts, including information on "alternative zoology and phantasmagorical anthropology".[124]

The imprisoned Fenric still had influence over the Earth and the ability to manipulate the timelines. He summoned the Ancient One from half a million years in the future. Over the centuries, the Haemovore followed the flask containing Fenric. It was stolen from Constantinople and taken by Viking pirates to Northumbria. Slowly the Ancient One followed it to Maiden's Bay.

By the tenth century, a 9-letter Viking alphabet was in use, although the later Vikings used a 16-letter ver-

119 *The Mark of the Rani*
120 *The Tomorrow Windows*
121 "Twelve hundred and twenty four Terran years" before *First Frontier*.
122 *Battlefield.* The archaeologist Warmsley thinks that Excalibur's scabbard dates "from the eighth century".
123 *Wolfsbane*
124 The Library of St John the Beheaded was mentioned in *Theatre of War*, and made its first appearance in the following NA, *All-Consuming Fire*. In that book we learn much about the library, including the fact that it has been established for a "thousand years" (p15). The library still exists at the time of *Millennial Rites*. In *The Empire of Glass*, Irving Braxiatel acquires manuscripts for the library (p245).

sion. Carvings in the earlier alphabet claimed that the Vikings were cursed, and they buried the flask in a burial site under St Jude's church.[125]

Viking legends referred to the Timewyrm as Hel.[126] The Doctor, Ace and Bernice were at an Angle settlement when the Vikings attacked it.[127] The Doctor met the Anglo-Saxon king Alfred the Great and his cook Ethelburg, "a dab hand at bear rissoles".[128] The Doctor became known as Shango the thunder god of the Yoruba tribe when he demonstrated static electricity.[129]

A thousand years ago, the penultimate Keeper of Traken was inaugurated. The Union of Traken in Mettula Orionsis had enjoyed many thousands of years of peace before this time.[130]

c 1001 - EXCELIS DAWNS[131] -> By this time, numerous civilizations had come and gone on the planet Artaris. The populace was mostly relegated to communities living on mountainsides for defensive purposes. A nunnery emerged on Excelis, the highest mountain on the planet.

The Doctor landed on Artaris and met the warlord Grayvorn, who was on a quest for "the Relic", a powerful artefact and purported gateway to the afterlife. The Doctor also met the time traveller Iris Wildthyme, who couldn't remember how she ended up there. Grayvorn discovered the Relic, which was mysteriously shaped like Iris' handbag, but he soon went missing. The Relic's energies inadvertently made Grayvorn immortal.

The Doctor saved Aethelred the Unready from what would have been a fatal fever.[132] An amoral Time Lord used a twenty-fourth century flood controller to turn back the tide for Canute, giving him great influence. The Doctor set history back on course.[133] The Doctor met the eleventh century ruler of Ghana, King Tenkamenin, and they talked of philosophy.[134]

Around one thousand years ago, Martin instigated a get-rich-quick scheme that entailed the washed-up actor

Prubert Gatridge going to planets that Martin owned and posing as a god. This was intended to seed "selfish memes" - philosophical concepts that would lead each world's populace to destroy themselves. Each genocide would lift the Galactic Heritage Foundation's development ban, allowing Martin to sell the worlds at fantastic profit.[135]

During the building of the Cathedral of St Sophia, a casket fell from the sky. It was believed to contain an angel and was placed in the catacombs.[136] In 1033, Clancy's Comet was mistaken for the Star of the West, sent to commemorate the millennium of the crucifixion.[137] A monastery was established on the site of Forgill Castle in the eleventh century.[138]

= During his time in the Godwins' court, Grayle was once bishop of all Cornwall. The Doctor defeated Grayle's plan to stockpile plutonium for the Nimon, and subsequently rewrote history to prevent Gralae from making contact with the Nimon in 305 AD.[139]

Edward the Confessor's reign was one of the Doctor's favourite times and places.[139]

1066 (Late Summer) - THE TIME MEDDLER[140] -> Landing on a beach in Northumbria, the Doctor learnt that the Monk, a renegade from his own people, was planning to destroy a Viking invasion with futuristic weapons. Harold's army would then be fresh for the Battle of Hastings, and after defeating the Norman invasion, Harold would usher in a new period of peace for Europe. The Monk had arrived several weeks ago and occupied a monastery overlooking the coast. The Doctor foiled the Monk's plans, and removed the dimensional control from the Monk's TARDIS. It "took a bit of time" to fix, but the Monk resumed his travels.

Joanna Harris, a future geneticist and vampire, was

---

125 *The Curse of Fenric.* The Ancient Haemovore arrived in "ninth century Constantinople" according to the Doctor. Ace says the inscriptions are "a thousand years old".
126 *Timewyrm: Revelation*
127 *Sky Pirates!*
128 *The Ghosts of N-Space*
129 *Transit* (p204).
130 *The Keeper of Traken*
131 Dating *Excelis Dawns* - The story takes place a thousand years before *Excelis Rising*. See the dating of *Excelis Decays* (2301) for dating notes on the Excelis saga.
132 *Seasons of Fear.* The meeting is also mentioned in *The Tomorrow Windows.* Aethelred was king of England,

and lived from circa 978 to 23rd April, 1016.
133 *Invaders from Mars*
134 *Transit*
135 *The Tomorrow Windows*
136 *Bunker Soldiers*
137 *The Ghosts of N-Space*
138 *Terror of the Zygons*
139 *Seasons of Fear.* The date is given, and it is exactly 750 years after the Doctor and Charley met Decurion Gralae.
140 Dating *The Time Meddler* - The story takes place shortly before the Battle of Hastings (14th October, 1066), the Doctor judging it to be "late summer". The Doctor discovers a horned Viking helmet, although the Vikings never wore such helmets. The Monk repairs his

born.[141] The order of the Knights Templar was founded in 1128.[142] The Canavitchi claimed responsibility for founding the Knights Templar. [143]

The Doctor saw the completion of Durham Cathedral in 1133. Sir Brian de Fillis built Marsham Castle in Yorkshire in the twelfth century. The knight went mad, believing his wife was haunting him.[144]

During the twelfth century, the Convent of the Little Sisters of St Gudula was founded with Vivien Fay posing as the Mother Superior.[145] In the same century, the Doctor saw the King of France, Phillippe Auguste, lay the first stone of the Louvre.[146] Around 1168, the Aztecs left their original home of Aztlan and became nomads. They took a holy relic, the Xiuhcoatl, with them.[147]

The other end of the Time Corridor formed by the timelash was in 1179 AD.[148] The Borad was disgorged from the timelash and quickly killed by operatives of the Celestis, the investigators One and Two.[149]

In 1190, Stefan, a Crusader, lost a bet with the Toymaker that Barbarossa could swim the Bosporus. Barbarossa drowned, and Stefan became the Toymaker's most loyal servant.[150]

c 1190 - THE CRUSADE[151] **->** The Doctor saved Richard the Lionheart from an ambush, and became embroiled in court politics. Richard planned to marry his sister Joanna to the brother of Saladin, the Saracen ruler, but Joanna refused. The Doctor was mistaken for a sorcerer and the TARDIS crew narrowly escaped.

Whitaker's Time Scoop accidentally kidnapped a peasant from the Middle Ages.[152] Scaroth posed as a Crusader.[153] Around 1205, a man was boiled in oil for the entertainment of King John.[154]

The Doctor delivered Genghis Khan.[155] **The Doctor claimed to have heard Genghis Khan speak.**[156] **The Master implied that the Doctor *was* Genghis Khan.**[157] **The hordes of Genghis Khan couldn't break down the TARDIS doors.**[158]

In the early thirteenth century, a Khameirian spaceship was rounding Rigellis III when a Yogloth Slayer ship attacked and damaged it. The Khameirian vessel crashed to Earth and destroyed the chapel at Abbots Siolfor, home of a secret society led by Matthew Siolfor. The Khamerians put their life essences into what would later be called "the Philosopher's Stone." They mentally enthralled six of the brotherhood to work toward restoring them to health. The descendants of the society would spread throughout the world, influenced by the Khamerians.[159]

1215 (4th - 5th March) - THE KING'S DEMONS[160] **->** The Master attempted to pervert the course of constitutional progress on Earth by trying to prevent the signing of Magna Carta. On 3rd March, 1215, an android controlled by the Master, Kamelion, arrived at Fitzwilliam Castle posing as the King. He was accompanied by the Master, who was disguised as the French swordsman Sir Giles Estram. The Fitzwilliams had served the King for many years before this, giving him

TARDIS' fault after this story, and is at liberty in *The Daleks' Master Plan.*

141 *Vampire Science.* Joanna says she was born before the end of the 1st millennium, but also on the day William the Conqueror died, which was in 1087.

142 *Sanctuary*

143 *The King of Terror*

144 *Nightshade*

145 *The Stones of Blood*

146 *The Church and the Crown*

147 *The Left-Handed Hummingbird*

148 *Timelash*

149 *The Taking of Planet 5*

150 *Divided Loyalties.* Stefan was created for the unmade story *The Nightmare Fair.* This is slightly at odds with established history. Frederick Barbarossa was made Holy Roman Emperor in 1155, and died in 1190 after being thrown from his horse into the Saleph River in Cilicia (part of modern-day Turkey), whereupon his heavy armour made him drown in hip-deep water. As if that weren't enough, one chronicler claimed the shock additionally made Barbarossa have a heart attack.

151 Dating *The Crusade* - A document written for Donald Tosh and John Wiles in April / May 1965 (apparently by Denis Spooner), 'The History of Doctor Who',

stated that the story is set between the Second and Third crusades, with the Third Crusade starting when Richard's plan fails. Richard is already in Palestine at the start of the story, indicating a date of around 1190. Ian claims in *The Space Museum* that *The Crusade* took place in the "thirteenth century", but this seems to be an error on his part. The *Radio Times* and *The Making of Doctor Who* both set the story in the "twelfth century". *The Programme Guide* gives a date of "1190", *The Terrestrial Index* picks "1192".

152 *Invasion of the Dinosaurs*

153 *City of Death.* Although Julian Glover plays both Richard the Lionheart in *The Crusade* and Scaroth in *City of Death*, I don't think Scaroth posed as King Richard.

154 "Ten years" before *The King's Demons.*

155 *Tragedy Day*

156 *The Daemons.* Genghis Khan was probably born in 1167, and died in 1227.

157 *Doctor Who - The Movie*

158 *Rose*

159 *Option Lock*

160 Dating *The King's Demons* - The TARDIS readings say it is "March the fourth, twelve hundred and fifteen".

161 *The Gallifrey Chronicles*

their entire fortune to help the war against the abhorrent Saracens, but the King now demanded even more of them. "King John" began to challenge the loyalty of even the King's most devoted subjects, but the Doctor exposed the Master's plan.

Around 1225, the Doctor defeated Thorgan of the Sulumians, who was attempting to kill the mathematician Fibonacci before he wrote the *Liber quadratorum* (*The Book of Squares*), a text on Diophantine equations.[161]

1240 - BUNKER SOLDIERS[162] **->** The Doctor landed in Kiev, and was asked to help in repelling the Mongols. The Doctor knew that history recorded the sacking of the city and refused, but the governor of the city, Dmitri, imprisoned him. Dmitri sought supernatural aid, uncovering a casket under the Church of St Sophia. This held an alien soldier, who emerged and started a killing spree. Tragically, he infected Dmitri with a virus that drove him mad, leading to Dmitri refusing the Mongols' offer of sparing the city in return for an honourable surrender. The Mongols ransacked Kiev, but the Doctor discovered a way to deactivate the soldier.

1242 - SANCTUARY[163] **->** The Doctor and Benny made an emergency landing in the Pyrenees. The Doctor discovered a plot to recover the skull of Jesus Christ from the heretical Cathare sect, even as Benny fell for the knight Guy de Carnac. The Church forced an attack on the Roc of the Cathares sanctuary and set it afire, but the Doctor found the skull was a fake. The Doctor and Benny escaped the destruction - it's possible that Guy de Carnac did also.

Marco Polo was born in Venice in 1252. When he was twelve, English crusaders occupied the African port of Accra. In 1271, Marco Polo left Venice to explore China.[164]

The arachnid Xaranti destroyed Zygor, the homeworld of the Zygons.[165] The Zygons retaliated and destroyed the Xaranti homeworld in Tau Ceti. The Xaranti consequently became nomadic.[166] **A Zygon spacecraft crashed in Loch Ness. While awaiting a rescue party, they fed on the milk of the Skarasen, an armoured cyborg creature that was often mistaken for the locals as a "monster".**[167] **During the Middle Ages, Stangmoor was a fortress.**[168] **A medieval knight was kidnapped by the Master using TOM-TIT.**[169] The Doctor was based for a time around 1268 at Ercildoune in Scotland. He cured a crippled stable hand called Tommy. Two years later, the Queen of the Charrl contacted Tommy from the far future, promising him immortality in return for his stealing the Doctor's TARDIS. Tommy came to be known as the wizard Jared Khan.[170]

In 1270, a mysterious doctor who tended King Alexander sent his stable boy Tom away. The legends of Kebiria claimed that the Caliph at Giltat was visited by mysterious demons, the "Al Harwaz", who promised him anything he wanted - gold, spices, slave women - if his people learnt a dance, "dancing the code". The arrangement continued for a time, until the Caliph broke the agreement and flying monsters destroyed his city.[171]

c 1273 - THE TIME WARRIOR[172] **->** The Doctor arrived from the twentieth century on the trail of the Sontaran Linx, who had kidnapped scientists and pulled them back in time. For his own amusement, Linx was supplying a local warlord, Irongron, with advanced weapons. The Doctor thwarted both Linx and Irongron, and the destruction of the Sontaran's ship also destroyed Irongron's castle.

---

162 Dating *Bunker Soldiers* - The Doctor says 'we are in Kiev in 1240' (p16).
163 Dating *Sanctuary* - Benny "persuaded someone to tell her that the year was 1242".
164 *Marco Polo*. Barbara states that Marco Polo was born in "1252", although actually it was two years later.
165 *The Bodysnatchers*
166 'Several centuries' before *Deep Blue*.
167 *Terror of the Zygons*. The Zygon leader Broton tells Harry that they crashed "centuries ago by your timescale". While disguised as the Duke, Broton later tells the Doctor that there have been sightings of the Loch Ness Monster "since the Middle Ages", the implication being that the Zygons and Skarasen have been on Earth since then. (In *Timelash*, we're made to believe that the Borad has been similarly swimming around Loch Ness from 1179 onwards, but the Borad's death in *The Taking of Planet 5* suggests he doesn't actually con-

tribute to the Loch Ness sightings.) *The Programme Guide* claimed that the Zygon ship crashed in "50,000 BC", *The Terrestrial Index* preferred "c.1676".
168 *The Mind of Evil*
169 *The Time Monster*
170 *Birthright*
171 "Seven hundred years" before *Dancing the Code*.
172 Dating *The Time Warrior* - The story seems to be set either during the Crusades, as Sir Edward of Wessex talks of "interminable wars" abroad, or quite soon after the Conquest as Irongron refers to "Normans". Professor Rubeish refers to the 'early years of the Middle Ages'. However, in *The Sontaran Experiment*, Sarah says that Linx died "in the thirteenth century". *The Programme Guide* set a date of "c.800", but *The Terrestrial Index* offered "c.1190". *The TARDIS Logs* said "1191 AD". According to *The Paradise of Death*, this was "eight hundred years back" (p12).

1278 (29th August) ASYLUM[173] -> An alien dispatched from 1346, now hosted in monk Brother Thomas, tried to further philosopher Roger Bacon's research into the "Elixir of Life" - a possible cure to the impending Black Death 70 years hence. The fourth Doctor and Nyssa arrived to prevent the alien from disrupting history, and Nyssa inadvertently dislodged the alien presence from Thomas' mind. Bacon burned his unsuccessful "Elixir Manuscript", but the Franciscan Order imprisoned him for the next twelve years for committing "heretical" research into alchemy. Bacon would become renowned to future generations as a great philosopher, not a scientist.

1289 - MARCO POLO[174] -> In 1274, Marco Polo arrived in Cathay, and in the same year the beautiful maiden Ping-Cho was born. Three years later, Polo entered the service of Kublai Khan. In 1287, the Khan refused permission for Polo to return to Venice. In 1289, Polo led a caravan across the Roof of the World to the court of the Khan. He took with him Tegana, the emissary of the Mongol warlord Noghai, and Ping-Cho, who was destined to marry a seventy-five year old nobleman. They discovered the Doctor, Ian, Barbara and Susan - along with their blue cabinet, which Polo decided to present to the Khan. They traversed Cathay and the Gobi Desert, and arrived at Shang-Tu. At the palace, the Doctor learned that Tegana planned to kill the Khan. In gratitude, the cabinet was returned to the travellers.

Jared Khan narrowly missed acquiring the TARDIS at this time.[175] **The Forgill family served the nation from the late thirteenth century.**[176] **The Doctor met Dante and acquired his business card.**[177] **The Doctor met William Tell.**[178] The Doctor met Robert the Bruce in the early fourteenth century.[179]

The Doctor almost gave William of Ockham a nervous breakdown trying to get him to work out the history of the planet Skaro.[180] **The Monk calculated that if his plan to prevent the Norman Conquest had worked, then mankind would have developed aircraft by 1320.**[181] **The Malus, a psychic probe from Hakol, arrived in Little Hodcombe "centuries" before the village was destroyed in the English Civil War.**[182] **The Doctor, Rose and Jack 'only just escaped' Kyoto in 1336.**[183]

Aliens emerged from a null dimension and into London in 1346. They took control of human bodies, which were vulnerable to a plague that the aliens knew would arrive in two years. They discovered that philosopher Roger Bacon wrote of a possible cure for the plague, and sent one alien back several decades to ensure Bacon's research succeeded. The alien's host in that era, Brother Thomas of the Fransican order, survived and felt drawn to the aliens in 1346, but they failed to heed his warnings about the futility of their efforts.[184]

The Canavitchi faked the Turin Shroud in an attempt to slow man's progress.[185] The Phiadoran Clan Matriarchy came to power in the Phiadoran Directorate. They ruthlessly weeded out their political opponents.[186] Cartophilius lived in Italy under the name John Buttadaeus.[187]

The Doctor met Chaucer in 1388 and was given a copy of *The Doctour of Science's Tale*.[188] The Doctor drank ale with Chaucer in Southwark.[189]

Around this time, the Doctor acquired his ticket to the Library of St John the Beheaded.[190]

The Renaissance

The Daemons inspired the Renaissance.[191] By the end of the fourteenth century, wire-drawing machinery had been developed.[192] Constantinople was renamed Istanbul.[193] **The Doctor was present at the Battle of Agincourt.**[194]

---

173 Dating *Asylum* - It's '1278' according to the blurb, and 1266 was 'twelve years previously' (p116).
174 Dating *Marco Polo* - Marco gives the year as "1289". *The Programme Guide* gave the date as "1300".
175 *Birthright*
176 *Terror of the Zygons*
177 *The Two Doctors*. Dante lived from 1265-1321.
178 *The Face of Evil*. William Tell lived in the early fourteenth century.
179 *Lords of the Storm*. Robert the Bruce was one of Scotland's greatest kings, and ruled from 1306-1329.
180 *The Gallifrey Chronicles*. Ockham was a philosopher and friar during the Middle Ages. He was responsible for the principle of Occam's Razor (also spelled Ockham's Razor) and lived c.1287 to c.1349.
181 *The Time Meddler*
182 *The Awakening*
183 In the travellers' personal timelines, this occurs between *Boom Town* and *Bad Wolf*.
184 *Asylum*
185 *The King of Terror*. The Shroud is first recorded in the fourteenth century.
186 *Imperial Moon*. This takes place at '611,072.26 Galactic Time Index'.
187 *Matrix*
188 *Cat's Cradle: Time's Crucible*
189 *Synthespians™*
190 *All-Consuming Fire*
191 *The Daemons*
192 "A hundred years" before *The Masque of Mandragora*.
193 *Shadowmind*
194 *The Talons of Weng-Chiang, Shada, The King of Terror*. Agincourt was fought on 25th October, 1415.

c 1454 - THE AZTECS[195] -> The Aztec priest Yetaxa died and was entombed around 1430. When the TARDIS crew emerged from Yetaxa's sealed tomb, Barbara was taken for the reincarnation of Yetaxa. She attempted to use her "divine" power to end the Aztec practice of human sacrifice, knowing it would horrify the European conquerors in future, and hoped this would save the Aztec civilisation from the Spanish. Her efforts failed.

In the mid-fifteenth century, Scaroth gave mankind the printing press, although he kept a number of Gutenberg Bibles for himself. It was possibly this splinter of Scaroth that acquired a Ming vase.[196]

1487 - THE LEFT-HANDED HUMMINGBIRD[197] -> In the Aztec city of Tenochtitlan, the god Huitzilopochtli's taste for blood grew every year. By 1487, his priests demanded twenty-thousand sacrifices. These fed the psychic Huitzilin - a human mutated by the Xiuhcoatl, an Exxilon device that leaked radiation. Huitzilin used his powers to remain alive, and used the Xiuhcoatl to make his people worship him. For centuries he would visit the most violent places in human history, feeding off the carnage and hatred of such events. He would become known as the Blue.

The Spanish Inquisition

The Canavitchi helped guide the Spanish Inquisition.[198] Agonal, an immortal being who gained strength from suffering, fed on the resultant fear and death.[199] The Doctor was present during the Spanish Inquisition.[200]

The earliest parts of Chase Mansion were built during the Wars of the Roses.[201]

1485 - SOMETIME NEVER[202] -> An Agent of the Council of Eight kidnapped the two nephews of Richard III to prevent their having an impact on history. The Doctor and Trix later rescued the boys, and took them to the early twenty-first century.

In the late fifteenth century, the Doctor visited China.[203] The Wandering Jew travelled to Romania, hoping that Vlad Tepes would be able to end his life.[204]

Around this time the Doctor met Christopher Columbus.[205] The Doctor travelled on the *Santa Maria*, but Columbus refused his suggestion of plotting courses with an orange and a biro.[206]

c 1492 - THE MASQUE OF MANDRAGORA[207] -> The Doctor accidentally brought the Mandragora Helix to Renaissance Italy, where it made contact with the

---

195 Dating *The Aztecs* - According to Barbara, Yetaxa was buried in 1430. *The Programme Guide* dated the story "c.1200 AD". *The Terrestrial Index* suggested "1480", claiming that fifty years elapsed between Yetaxa being buried and the TARDIS landing inside the tomb. This is not supported (or contradicted) by the story itself, although Lucarotti's novelisation is set in "1507". Both editions of *The Making of Doctor Who* placed the story in "1430". *The Left-Handed Hummingbird* firmly dates the story in "1454".

196 *City of Death*. Movable type was developed in China during the ninth century, but as Scaroth possessed a number of Gutenberg Bibles (printed 1453-1455), we can infer he was responsible for *Europe's* development of printing.

197 Dating *The Left-Handed Hummingbird* - The date is first given on p39.

198 *The King of Terror*

199 *Blood Harvest*

200 *Project: Twilight*

201 According to Harrison Chase in *The Seeds of Doom*. The Wars of the Roses lasted from 1455-1485.

202 Dating *Sometime Never* - The date is given.

203 *The Talons of Weng-Chiang*. The Doctor notes, "I haven't been in China for four hundred years" - I've assumed it was four hundred years ago in history, as opposed to when the Doctor was four hundred years younger.

204 *Matrix*. The Wandering Jew of legend was a shoemaker condemned to walk the Earth until the Second Coming of Jesus.

205 The Doctor has Christopher Columbus' business card in *The Two Doctors*. Columbus lived 1451-1506 and discovered the New World in 1492.

206 *Eye of Heaven*

207 Dating *The Masque of Mandragora* - It's said that the Helix will return to Earth in five hundred years at the "end of the twentieth century", so the story is set at the end of the fifteenth century. The second edition of *The Making of Doctor Who* said that the story is set in "the fifteenth century". Hinchcliffe's novelisation specified the date as "1492", *The Terrestrial Index* and *The TARDIS Logs* both set the story "about 1478". *The Discontinuity Guide* said it must be set "c.1470-1482 when Da Vinci was in Florence".

The entity that encroaches on Earth in *The Eleventh Tiger* - which takes place in 1865 - also seems to be the Mandragora Helix, even though the Doctor says in *Masque* that it's been banished for five hundred years. There's either another conjunction taking place that he doesn't know about, or he's discounting events of 1865 because he knows he already won the day then.

208 *Managra*

209 *So Vile a Sin*. Vasco da Gama was a Portugese explorer, and the first European to journey by sea to India.

Brotherhood of Demnos cult. The Doctor banished the Mandragora Helix before it could plunge Earth into an age of superstition and fear.

The Doctor met Torquemada shortly before his death in September 1498.[208] The Doctor was with Vasco da Gama when he sailed into the harbour of Zanzibar in 1499.[209]

The Cylox were immensely powerful psionics and a very long-lived species, being the equivalent of adolescents after surviving for millennia. Two of the Cylox, Lai-Ma and his brother Tko-Ma, had spent several millennia annihilating planets in another dimension. Around the late fifteenth century, an intergalactic court exiled them to a pocket realm located on Earth. The brothers later loosed their shackles and agreed to see who could destroy Earth the fastest. The Ini-Ma, the brothers' jailor of sorts, endowed its essence into female members of the bloodline that would produce Loretta van Cheaden.[210]

The Sixteenth Century

c 1500 - THE GHOSTS OF N-SPACE[211] -> Around the turn of the sixteenth century, the Doctor and Sarah were briefly seen as ghosts.

During the sixteenth century, the Ancient Order of St Peter existed to fight vampires.[212]

Leonardo Da Vinci

Both the Monk and Scaroth claimed credit for inspiring Leonardo to consider building a flying machine.[213] The Doctor visited Leonardo while he was painting the Mona Lisa, "a dreadful woman with no eyebrows who wouldn't sit still".[214] Leonardo had a cold.[215]

1505 - CITY OF DEATH[216] -> Captain Tancredi, one of the splinters of Scaroth the Jagaroth, kept Leonardo a virtual prisoner and ordered him to begin making six additional copies of the Mona Lisa. Scaroth hoped to sell them at great profit to fund his time experiments in 1979. The Doctor arrived, and wrote 'This is a Fake' in felt-tip on many of Leonardo's blank canvasses. Leonardo painted the copies over them.

In 1520, Cortez landed in South America.[217]

Henry VIII

On one of their earliest visits to Earth, the Doctor and Susan met Henry VIII, who sent them to the Tower after the Doctor threw a parson's nose back at the King. The TARDIS had landed in the Tower, and this enabled the Doctor and Susan to make good their escape.[218]

King Henry VIII mistook the Doctor for a jester.[219] The Doctor witnessed the execution of Anne Boleyn.[220] **Henry VIII dissolved The Convent of Little Sisters of St Gudula.**[221] **Priests from around the country hid at Cranleigh Hall.**[222] The Doctor visited Venice in the sixteenth century.[223]

By the 1530s, the Spanish knew of an Incan myth about a fire god. It was based on the 'burning' sentience.[224] Around 1550, the Doctor was attacked by a jiki-ketsu-gaki, or vampire, in Japan. He was buried in a snowdrift and spent three months recovering in a monastery. He confronted the vampire, and let her drain his blood until she was sated and fell asleep. Then he burnt down her castle.[225]

The Canavitchi supplied Nostradamus with many of his prophecies.[226] **The fourth Doctor's long scarf was made by Madame Nostradamus "a witty little knitter".**[227]

210 *Instruments of Darkness*
211 Dating *The Ghosts of N-Space* - The Doctor says it is 'somewhere near the turn of the century'.
212 *Minuet in Hell*
213 *The Time Meddler, City of Death*
214 *City of Death.* The Doctor's note to Leonardo ends "see you earlier". In *The Two Doctors,* the Doctor has Leonardo's business card.
215 *Doctor Who - The Movie*
216 Dating *City of Death* - Tancredi asks what the Doctor is doing in "1505".
217 *The Aztecs,* and referred to in *The Left-Handed Hummingbird.*
218 *The Sensorites.* Henry VIII reigned from 1509-1547. In *Tragedy Day*, the Doctor says he has "never met" Henry VIII (p74), but in *The Marian Conspiracy*, he says

he has.
219 *Terror Firma.* It's unclear if this refers to the same occasion mentioned in *The Sensorites.*
220 *Deadly Reunion*
221 *The Stones of Blood.* The dissolution of the monasteries took place in the fifteen-thirties.
222 *Black Orchid*
223 *The Stones of Venice*
224 *The Burning*
225 'Ten years' before *The Room with No Doors.*
226 *The King of Terror*
227 *The Ark in Space.* Nostradamus lived from 1503-1566, and published his prophecies in 1556.

1555 (January) - THE MARIAN CONSPIRACY[228] ->

The Doctor helped Evelyn Smythe explore her ancestry. As the Doctor visited the court of Queen Mary, Evelyn stumbled on a Protestant plot to poison the Queen and replace her with Elizabeth. The time travellers were both imprisoned in the Tower of London. They also met Reverend Thomas Smith, Evelyn's ancestor, before escaping and preventing the assassination.

The Elizabethan Age

The Doctor probably attended the Coronation of Queen Elizabeth I.[229] The Doctor was appalled by the Earl of Essex's behaviour at the Coronation.[230] The eighth Doctor, Samson and Gemma also visited the Court of Queen Elizabeth.[231]

1560 (Spring) - THE ROOM WITH NO DOORS[232] ->

A Kapteynian slave escaped from a Caxtarid slaver ship, and its capsule crashed in the Han region of Japan. Within days, the Victorian time traveller Penelope Gate also visited Japan. A month later, the Doctor and Chris Cwej arrived and became embroiled in a dispute between rival warlords Guffuu Kocho and Umemi, both wanting possession of the capsule. The Doctor managed to prevent either of them from taking control of it.

"The Beast" were flying creatures that would move from planet to planet by way of dimensional interfaces, and invisibly feed off other beings. This was normally harmless, but on the planet Benelisa, the Beast atypically wiped out the native populace as their numbers were few. The Beast moved on from Benelisa, but at least one Benelisan construct - Azoth - endured and pledged to eradicate the Beast.[233]

In 1564, an Agent of the Council of Eight prevented an Italian blacksmith from gaining the insight needed to invent the steam engine.[234]

1572 (21st - 24th August) - THE MASSACRE[235] ->

The Doctor and Steven arrived in Paris in August 1572. The Protestants of the city, the Hugenots, were massing to celebrate the wedding of Henry of Navarre to Princess Marguerite. Yet they lived in fear of the Catholic majority, particularly the Queen Mother - Catherine de Medici - and the ruthless Abbot of Amboise. One hundred Hugenots had been killed at Wassy ten years ago, and a full-scale massacre was now instigated. The Doctor and Steven fled and were forced to leave Anne Chaplet, a serving girl befriended by Steven, behind to her fate.

Rebels from the mid-twenty-first century kidnapped the young Shakespeare to prevent the Daleks assassinating him. This removed Shakespeare from time, but history was restored upon his safe return.

> = In a version of history without Shakespeare, the Daleks had a compound in Warwick in 1572.[236]

Iris saved the Doctor and Sarah from Mary Queen of Scots.[237] The Doctor advised Mary Queen of Scots to change her muckspreader.[238] **Boscombe Hall was built on the site of the Convent of the Little Sisters of St Gudula in the late sixteenth century.** [239]

In 1582, the Doctor visited Rome while trying to track the Timewyrm.[240] **The West Wing of Chase Mansion was completed in 1587.**[241]

In 1587, the Greld wiped out the Roanoake colony in the New World. They implanted the colonists with com-

---

228 Dating *The Marian Conspiracy* - It is one month after the Wyatt Uprising, at the end of 1554.
229 *The Curse of Peladon*, although the Doctor admits he might be confusing it with the Coronation of Queen Victoria. Elizabeth was Queen from 1558, but the Coronation wasn't until the following year.
230 *Cat's Cradle: Witch Mark*. There wasn't an Earl of Essex at the time of Elizabeth's Coronation.
231 *Terror Firma*. Elizabeth ruled 1558-1603.
232 Dating *The Room with No Doors* - It is 'probably March 1560', and 'early spring'.
233 *The Taint*. The Beast arrive on Earth in 1944, according to *Autumn Mist*.
234 *Sometime Never*
235 Dating *The Massacre* - The first three episodes take place over a single day each, the last picks up nearly 24 hours after the end of the third late on the evening of the 23rd and runs into the 24th. The Admiral Gaspar de Coligny was shot on the 22nd. This story is sometimes

referred to as *The Massacre of St. Bartholomew's Eve*, based on some production documents, but this is historically erroneous. The event is more accurately named 'the massacre of St. Bartholomew's *Day*'.
236 *The Time of the Daleks*, which implies that Shakespeare used some of the names of individuals he met in the future for characters in plays such as *Hamlet, King Lear, Twelfth Night, Titus Andronicus* and *The Tempest*. The eighth Doctor met Shakespeare on this occasion, which from Shakespeare's point-of-view would be their earliest meeting.
237 *Verdigris*
238 *Tragedy Day*
239 *The Stones of Blood*
240 *Timewyrm: Revelation*
241 *The Seeds of Doom*
242 *The Empire of Glass*
243 *Earthworld*. This was in 1587.
244 *Four to Doomsday*. The Spanish Armada attacked

ponents for a meta-cobalt bomb, hoping to sabotage the Armageddon Convention. Christopher Marlowe, an agent of the crown, investigated the tragedy but escaped.[242]

The Doctor may have been at the execution of Mary Stuart (Mary, Queen of Scots).[243] **The Doctor met Francis Drake just before he faced the Spanish Armada.**[244] The Doctor played bowls with Drake and met William Cecil at Elizabeth's court.[245]

An Agent of the Council of Eight released a single butterfly in Africa. The slight disturbance it caused in the atmosphere triggered a storm that helped to destroy the Armada. The Council of Eight's leader, Octan, arrived in 1588 to try and stop this. The Agent, unable to recognize Octan, pushed him into the Time Vortex.[246]

Around 1589, the Time Lord Irving Braxiatel began a diplomatic effort that would culminate in the signing of the Armageddon Convention.[247] On 28th October of the same year, the ancient werewolf Pieter Stubbe was sentenced to death for sorcery in Cologne, Germany, but he escaped.[248]

The dramatist Christopher Marlowe continued serving as a secret agent of the British government. He conspired with Walsingham, the Secretary of State, to fake his death.[249] Towards the end of the sixteenth century, the Xaranti attacked a Zygon fleet. A Zygon ship survived the fighting and crashed on Earth.[250]

Shakespeare

The Doctor met Shakespeare, a "charming fellow" but "a dreadful actor".[251] **Shakespeare was a "taciturn" young man, and the Doctor encouraged him to take up writing.**[252] The Doctor helped Shakespeare write his plays.[253]

The Doctor used the Time/Space Visualiser to watch Shakespeare at the court of Elizabeth I when the idea of his writing *Hamlet* was first discussed.[254] **The Doctor transcribed a copy of *Hamlet* for Shakespeare, who had sprained his wrist writing sonnets. Scaroth acquired the manuscript of the play, which was in the Doctor's handwriting.**[255]

The Doctor also collaborated with Shakespeare on *Hamlet*, offering helpful advice. He saw the first performance.[256] **If the Monk's plan had worked, *Hamlet* would have been written for television.**[257] The Doctor wrote Poor Tom's dialogue in *King Lear*.[258] The Doctor suggested that *The Merry Wives of Windsor* needed to be redrafted, but the Queen wanted it performed as soon as possible.[259]

The Seventeenth Century

The planet Caresh had developed in a binary star system containing the larger, warmer sun Beacon and the smaller, colder Ember. Caresh would randomly orbit one of the two stars each solar cycle, causing unpredictable warm and cold years. In the seventeenth century, a protracted cold period killed off a large amount of the population. As the warm years returned, scientists on Dassar Island built a scanner capable of seeing into the future, giving them advance warning of cold years. The Time Lords ruled the scanner a violation of their monopoly on time travel, and dispatched agents Solenti and Lord Roche to shut down the device.[260]

Around 1600, the *Necronomicon* was translated into Spanish.[261] In the early seventeenth century, the Doctor was given tea by Emperor Tokugawa Ieyasu of Japan.[262] **The Doctor once shared a cell with Walter Raleigh, who "kept going on about this new vegetable he'd discovered".**[263]

Master Dee worked as Queen Elizabeth's counsellor for twenty years. In 1603, he realised that the Doctor would not return to visit the Queen.[264] General William

---

in 1588.

245 *The Marian Conspiracy*

246 *Sometime Never*

247 *The Empire of Glass*

248 *Loups-Garoux*

249 *The Empire of Glass*. History tells us Marlowe died on 30th May, 1593.

250 "Three centuries" before *The Bodysnatchers*. This is a different ship from the one seen in *Terror of the Zygons*.

251 *Planet of Evil*

252 *City of Death*

253 *Endgame*

254 *The Chase*

255 *City of Death*

256 *Byzantium!, Asylum, The Gallifrey Chronicles.*

257 *The Time Meddler*

258 *The Cabinet of Light*

259 *The Ultimate Treasure*

SHAKESPEARE: From these details, the Doctor clearly meets Shakespeare more than once. In the Doctor's own timeline, he first meets Shakespeare in *The Empire of Glass*. In Shakespeare's lifetime, he first encounters the Doctor in *The Time of the Daleks*. Shakespeare's works are banned at the time of *Managra*, but revered in *The Time of the Daleks*.

260 *The Suns of Caresh*

261 *The Banquo Legacy*. In the real world, the *Necronomicon* was a fictional book of magic invented by H.P. Lovecraft.

262 *Spare Parts*

263 *The Mind of Evil*. Raleigh lived 1552-1618, and was imprisoned 1603-1616.

264 *Birthright*

Lethbridge-Stewart was among King James' retinue on his initial arrival in London.[265]

1605 - THE PLOTTERS[266] **->** The Doctor and Vicki decided to investigate the Gunpowder Plot while Ian and Barbara set off for the Globe Theatre. The Doctor and Vicki - disguised as a boy named "Victor" - met King James I, and the Doctor learned that the statesman Sir Robert Cecil was encouraging the Plot to draw out the conspirators and discredit the Catholics. Meanwhile, some Catholics captured Barbara, leading to Guy Fawkes befriending her. Robert Catesby, a member of the Plot, argued with Fawkes and killed him... which isn't how the history books reported events.

The King's courtier, Robert Hay, was a secret member of a grand order devoted to mysticism. Hay sought to create anarchy, but the Doctor manoeuvred Hay to the cellar under Parliament, where Cecil arrested him. Hay was tortured and executed in Fawkes' place, preserving history.

The Doctor met Cervantes.[267] **The Armageddon Convention was signed, and banned the use of cobalt bombs.**[268]

1609 - THE EMPIRE OF GLASS[269] **->** Irving Braxiatel and the Doctor hosted a meeting, the Armageddon Convention, that saw doomsday weapons such as temporal disrupters and cobalt bombs banned. Although the Daleks and Cybermen refused to attend, many other races did sign. The Convention was nearly sabotaged by the Greld, a race of arms dealers who stood to lose money from it; and the Jamarians, who craved an empire for themselves.

The first performance of *Macbeth* involved the last minute substitutions of Shakespeare in the role of Lady Macbeth, and two strangers in the roles of the doctor and his servant. Christopher Marlowe, an agent of the crown, died in a duel.

On 29th June, 1613, the talentless playwright Francis Pearson burnt down Shakespeare's Globe Theatre during a production of *Henry VIII*. Pearson later vanished, transported by the ancient Mimic to the thirty-first century.[270] In April 1616, a dying William Shakespeare handed over manuscripts of three unpublished plays - *Love's Labours Won*, *The Birth of Merlin* and *Sir John Oldcastle* - to Irving Braxiatel in return for memories of the events of Venice in 1609.[271]

In 1621, the infamous Lady Peinforte poisoned her neighbour Dorothea Remington.[272] In 1624, the Doctor met a Time Agent in Devon.[273]

The Phiadoran Clan Matriarchy came to dominate the Phiadoran Directorate systems, using their genetically augmented pheromones to influence males. The Matriarchy instigated ten generations of tyranny that lasted from Galactic Time Index 611,072.26 to 611,548.91. The Sarmon Revolution finally brought down the Matriarchy, whose members were exiled to die in a safari park built on Earth's moon.

Thirty-two years later, the carnivorous Vrall killed off the Matriarchy members, and disguised themselves as the Phiadorans by wearing their skins. Unable to space-travel, the Vrall launched RNA spores encoded with technical information to Earth.[274]

1626 - THE CHURCH AND THE CROWN[275] **->** At the court of King Louis, the Musketeers and Cardinal Richelieu were in constant dispute. The Doctor, Peri and Erimem arrived in the middle of these machinations and it transpired that Peri was the double of Queen Anne. Peri was kidnapped by the Duke of Buckingham, who was planning a British invasion of France by dividing the French court. Erimem rallied the troops, and a major diplomatic incident was averted.

The Doctor apparently visited the Det-Sen monastery in Tibet on a number of occasions, and in 1630 helped the monks there to survive bandit attacks.

---

265 *The Dying Days*
266 Dating *The Plotters* - The year is given (p23).
267 *Endgame*
268 Before *Revenge of the Cybermen*. The signing of the Convention is the central event of *The Empire of Glass*.
269 Dating *The Empire of Glass* - The Doctor states that it "must be the year of our lord, 1609" (p30).
270 *Managra*
271 *The Empire of Glass*
272 *Silver Nemesis*
273 *Sometime Never*
274 "Ten generations" before *Imperial Moon*.
275 Dating *The Church and the Crown* - The date is given.

276 Dating *The Abominable Snowmen* - This was "1630" according to the Doctor. *The Programme Guide* suggested "1400 AD". The Doctor speaks Tibetan in *Planet of the Spiders* (but doesn't in *The Creature from the Pit*), and uses Tibetan meditation in *Terror of the Zygons*.
277 *Heart of TARDIS*. Bacon died in April 1626.
278 *The War Games*. The Thirty Years War ran from 1618-1648.
279 *The Church and the Crown*
280 Dating *Silver Nemesis* - The Doctor gives the date of the launch, but there is no indication of exactly how long afterward Lady Peinforte leaves for the twentieth century. Quite how "Roundheads" can be involved in this business when the term wasn't used until the Civil

He was entrusted with the holy Ghanta when he left. It was possibly on this visit that the Doctor learned the Tibetan language and meditation techniques.[276]

The Doctor witnessed philosopher Francis Bacon conduct an experiment on the preservation of meat by stuffing snow into a chicken. Bacon later contracted pneumonia from the incident and died.[277] **The War Lords lifted a battlefield from some point during the Thirty Years War.**[278] The Doctor met Louis XIII in 1637.[279]

1638 - (November) SILVER NEMESIS[280] -> On 23rd November, 1638, the Doctor was present as some Roundheads fought Lady Peinforte's soldiers, as the Nemesis asteroid was launched into space from a meadow in Windsor. Following this, the Doctor set his watch alarm to go off on 23rd November, 1988, the day that the Nemesis would return to Earth.

The Nemesis passed over the Earth every twenty-five years, influencing human affairs. Lady Peinforte immediately employed a mathematician to work out the asteroid's trajectory. His work completed, the mathematician's blood was used in a magical ceremony - one that also involved the Validium arrow in Peinforte's possession - to transport Peinforte and her servant Richard Maynarde to its ultimate destination. The imprisoned Fenric aided her time travel.

The English Civil War

The War Lords kidnapped a Civil War battlefield.[281] A division of Roundheads was also kidnapped by the Master using TOM-TIT.[282] On 13th July, 1643, the Royalists and Roundheads met in Little Hodcombe, wiping out themselves and the entire village. The Malus fed from the psychic energy released by the deaths and briefly emerged from its dormancy. The

Doctor returned the time-flung Will Chandler to this, his native era, shortly afterward.[283]

Returning Will Chandler was not a straightforward business.[284] A group of Roundheads was torn apart on Lanyon Moor, apparently by wild beasts.[285] In 1644, the castle of Crook Marsham was consumed in "strange fire".[286]

Witches hid from Matthew Hopkins in Devil's End.[287] The Doctor met King Charles II.[288]

1648 - THE ROUNDHEADS[289] -> Ben and Polly were mistaken for Parliamentarians. Polly was kidnapped by Royalists, while Ben was press-ganged. Meanwhile, Cromwell's men arrested the Doctor and Jamie. Cromwell's belief that Jamie was a fortune teller aided the TARDIS crew in escaping, but they were accompanied by King Charles... who according to history should have stayed in prison. Polly was forced to betray Christopher Whyte, a new friend and a Royalist, to ensure history stayed on course. Charles was duly recaptured and executed.

An act of murder by the standing stones in Cirbury awakened the Ragman. Emily, the mayor's daughter, was raped by a corpse that the Ragman animated. The Ragman triggered acts of class warfare, but was driven back into the stones. The townfolk relocated the stones to Dartmoor. Emily was left pregnant and later died in poverty, but her bloodline led to the journalist Charlemange Peters and the lout Kane Sawyer in the twentieth century.[290]

The Doctor fished with Isaak Walton.[291] He also met Thomas Hobbes.[292] **Lady Peinforte's servant Richard Maynarde died on 2nd November, 1657, and was entombed at Windsor.**[293]

According to the Doctor, Aubrey invented Druidism "as a joke".[294] The Doctor was a founder member of the Royal Geographical Society.[295] In 1661, the astronomer

---

War is unclear. As a letter to *Radio Times* after *Silver Nemesis* noted, the adoption of the Gregorian calendar in 1752 means that eleven days were 'lost' in Britain, so had the Nemesis *really* landed exactly 350 years after 23rd November, 1638, it would have landed on 3rd December, 1988.

The statue passes over the Earth every twenty-five years (in 1663, 1688, 1713, 1738, 1763, 1788, 1813, 1838, 1863, 1888, 1913, 1938, 1963 and finally 1988). *The Terrestrial Index* offers suggestions as to the effects of the statue on human history, but the only on-screen information concerns the twentieth century.

Fenric's involvement is established in *The Curse of Fenric*.

281 *The War Games*. The English Civil Wars ran from 1642-1649.

282 *The Time Monster*

283 *The Awakening*

284 *The Hollow Men*

285 *The Spectre of Lanyon Moor*

286 *Nightshade*

287 *The Daemons*. The witchhunter Matthew Hopkins died in 1647.

288 *Players*

289 Dating *The Roundheads* - The Doctor says it's '1648, December I should say' (p39).

290 'The seventeenth century' according to *Rags* (p39).

291 *The Androids of Tara*. Isaak Walton lived 1593-1683, and published *The Compleat Angler* in 1653.

292 *Ghost Ship*. Hobbes lived 1588-1679.

293 According to the monument in *Silver Nemesis*.

294 *The Stones of Blood*. The English writer John Aubrey (best known for his collection of biographies, *Brief Lives*) lived 1626-1697.

295 *Ghost Light*. The Royal Geographical Society was formed in 1645 during the Civil War.

Clancy discovered a comet that returned to Earth every one hundred and fifty-seven years.[296]

1666 (early September) - THE VISITATION[297] -> A group of escaped Terileptil prisoners made planetfall on Earth. They planned to wipe out the human population with rats infected with the bubonic plague virus. The Terileptils were killed, and the explosion of their equipment caused the Great Fire of London.

On a separate visit to Earth, the Doctor had been blamed for the Great Fire of London. The Doctor perhaps met Mr and Mrs Pepys on the same visit. Mrs Pepys "makes an excellent cup of coffee".[298] The Doctor doesn't like to talk about the Great Fire of London.[299]

In the late seventeenth century, Professor Chronotis retired to St Cedd's College, Cambridge.[300] About this time, the Eternals kidnapped a seventeenth-century pirate crew.[301] The Doctor placed skeletons in the Tower of London, which were found in 1674 and identified as the lost Princes.[302]

In 1677, the mathematician John Wallis gave a paper on sympathetic vibration to the Royal Society.[303] Nikolas Valentine, actually an extra-terrestrial stranded on Earth, received a knighthood in the 1680s.[304] The Doctor met the Baroque composer Henry Purcell.[305] **The Gore Crow Hotel was built in 1684.**[306]

In 1685, the Hakolian battle vehicle Jerak arrived on Earth, but failed to find its partner, the Malus, as planned.

The scheduled invasion didn't happen, and the battle vehicle went dormant. Its radiating malevolence ensured that local legends sprang up of an evil spirit named 'the Jack i' the Green'.[307]

The Doctor met Isaac Newton. At first he dropped apples on his head, but then he explained gravity to him over dinner.[308] Newton showed the Doctor around Cambridge University.[309]

1692 - THE WITCH HUNTERS[310] -> The TARDIS landed in Salem in 1692, and the time travellers quickly retreated to avoid becoming implicated in the witch trials. Susan, however, wanted to help those who were accused and took the TARDIS back there. She and Ian were soon accused of witchcraft. The Doctor saved his friends, but to preserve history, he persuaded the governor not to pardon the alleged witch Rebecca Nurse, age 71.

Later, the Doctor returned and took Rebecca to 1954. He convinced her that her death would encourage future tolerance, and she agreed to return to her native time and face her historical death.

c 1696 - THE SMUGGLERS[311] -> A group of pirates led by Captain Samuel Pike of the Black Albatross attempted to locate Captain Avery's treasure in Cornwall, with only a rhyme as a clue to its whereabouts. The treasure was found in the local church, and the names in the rhyme appeared on tombs in the crypt. The King's militia arrived, killing Pike and many of his crew.

---

296 *The Ghosts of N-Space*
297 Dating *The Visitation* - The Doctor, trying to get Tegan home, suggests "we're about three hundred years early". The action culminates with the start of the Great Fire of London, which took place on the night of 2nd to 3rd September, 1666, so the story would seem to start on 1st September. According to the novelisation, the Terileptils crashed on "August 5th". On-screen, Richard Mace says this was "several weeks ago".
298 The Doctor says he was blamed for the Great Fire in *Pyramids of Mars*. He refers to Mr and Mrs Pepys in *Robot*, and to Mrs Pepys' coffee-making prowess in *Planet of the Spiders*. Pepys lived 1633-1703 and began his diary in 1660. His wife Elizabeth died in 1669.
299 *Doctor Who and the Pirates*
300 "Three centuries" before *Shada*.
301 *Enlightenment*
302 *Sometime Never*
303 *The Happiness Patrol*. Wallis lived 1616-1703, and is credited with furthering the development of modern calculus.
304 *Phantasmagoria*
305 *Ghost Ship*. Purcell lived from 1659-1695.
306 *Battlefield*. This is the date on the capstone above the hotel's fireplace.

307 *The Hollow Men*
308 *The Pirate Planet*. Newton lived 1642-1727, and published his theories of gravitation in 1685.
309 *Psi-ence Fiction*
310 Dating *The Witch Hunters* - Each section states the date. Nurse was executed on 19th July, 1692.
311 Dating *The Smugglers* - The Doctor notes that the design of the church he sees on leaving the TARDIS means that they could have landed "at any time after the sixteenth century". Later, he says that the customers in the inn are dressed in clothes from the "seventeenth century". *The Terrestrial Index* and *The TARDIS File* set the story in "1650", *The TARDIS Logs* in "1646".

The Discontinuity Guide states that as a character says 'God save the King' (and, perhaps more to the point, Josiah Blake is the "King's Revenue Officer") it must be when England had a King (between 1603-1642, 1660-1688 or 1694 onwards). However, William III ruled as King from 1688-1702, and even though this was alongside Mary at first, legally and in the minds of the public he was King. The *Guide* further speculates that the costumes suggest this story is set in the latter part of the century.
312 'Hundreds of years' before *Death Comes to Time*. Anima Persis is also mentioned in *Relative Dementias*

The Eighteenth Century

Biochemical warfare wiped out the population of Anima Persis. The ghosts of the dead haunted this geopsychic planet. The Time Lords used the world as a training ground.[312] The Talichre once attacked Anima Persis.[313]

An alien force arrived in Earth's dimension, and was separated into a ghostly ectoplasmic form and a disembodied bundle of psychic energy. Henry Deadstone encountered the creature's psychic aspect and at first buried it in a pit, but was mentally compelled to feed it children and animals. Gypsies accused Deadstone of "feeding children to the Devil" and hanged him. The creature remained in the pit and artificially extended Deadstone's life.[314]

By the late twentieth century, no documents from before 1700 existed at Boscombe Hall. This was the year before Dr Thomas Borlase was born.[315] Weed Creatures were seen in the North Sea during the eighteenth century.[316] The Doctor "ran Taunton for two weeks in the eighteenth century and I've never been so bored".[317]

During the eighteenth century, the Ragman inhabited the body of an executed highwayman.[318] The Doctor visited Rio de Janero in 1700.[319]

On the planet Artaris, civilization divided itself into fortified city-states. The planet began to industrialize, and "Reeves" emerged as a type of government overseer in the city-state of Excelis. Within a hundred years, a Reeve had commissioned volunteers among the citizens to become law-enforcement officers named Wardens. The immortal Grayvorn worked as one of the earliest Wardens and rose through the ranks.[320]

1702 (8th - 10th March) - PHANTASMAGORIA[321] ->

The Doctor and Turlough arrived in 1702 and witnessed phantoms abducting a gambler, Edmund Carteret, who died from a heart attack. This was the latest of many such disappearances. The Doctor discovered that a stranded and murderous alien, Karthok of Daeodalus, was operating on Earth as Sir Nikolas Valentine, a card-playing member of the Diabola Club. Valentine had been absorbing human minds into his ship's computer, then using the amassed calculating power to help the ship heal itself. The phantoms were the collected consciousness of the minds absorbed, directed by Valentine to snatch more victims. The Doctor tricked Valentine into seeding his own bioprint into the ship's computer, whereupon the phantoms tore Valentine to pieces. Valentine's ship was programmed to self-destruct.

c 1705 - DOCTOR WHO AND THE PIRATES[322] ->

The TARDIS landed onboard a ship as the pirate Red Jasper attacked it. The Doctor and Evelyn were taken on board Jasper's ship. Jasper was looking for treasure in the Ruby Islands, and was unimpressed by the Doctor's reluctance to kill. The Doctor incited mutiny on Jasper's ship, leaving Jasper stranded.

The Doctor once met the Duke of Marlborough.[323] He also met Peter the Great in Russia, and saw the Peter and Paul Cathedral being built.[324] *Gulliver's Travels* **was published in 1726.[325] The Aliens Act was passed in 1730.[326]**

In the same year, a Mr Chicken resided at 10 Downing Street.[327] The Doctor's old friend Padmasambhava began to construct Yeti from this time.[328] In 1720, the Doctor saw the Earth's fury at Okushiri.[329]

In 1740, the man who would become known as Sabbath was born.[330] On 8th September, 1742, the Doctor and his companions spent some time in New England after their adventure in Salem, 1692.[331] Time travellers Penelope Gate and Joel Mintz briefly visited the year 1743.[332] **A battlefield from the Jacobite Uprising was kidnapped by the War Lords.[333]**

---

and *The Tomorrow Windows.*
313 *Relative Dementias*
314 Unspecified 'centuries' before *The Deadstone Memorial.*
315 *The Stones of Blood*
316 *Fury from the Deep*
317 *The Highest Science*
318 *Rags*
319 *Loups-Garoux*
320 'Three hundred years' before *Excelis Rising.*
321 Dating *Phantasmagoria* - The exact date is given.
322 Dating *Doctor Who and the Pirates* - The date isn't specified beyond it being 'the eighteenth century'.
323 *The Android Invasion.* The Doctor presumably means the first Duke, who lived 1650-1722 and was made a Duke in 1702.
324 *The Wages of Sin.* This would have to be between

1712-1725.
325 *The Mind Robber*
326 *The Highlanders*
327 *World War Three* strongly implies that the Doctor met this man. Mr Chicken is historical, and was the last private resident of the building before King George II put it at the disposal of Sir Robert Walpole, the first British Prime Minister.
328 "Over two hundred years" before *The Abominable Snowmen* according to the Abbot Songsten.
329 *The English Way of Death* (p46).
330 *The Adventuress of Henrietta Street*, and specified on the back cover of *Sabbath Dei*, volume three of BBV's *Faction Paradox Protocols* series.
331 *The Witch Hunters*
332 *The Room With No Doors*
333 *The War Games*

1746 (April) - THE HIGHLANDERS / THE WAR GAMES[334] -> The Doctor prevented the crooked solicitor Grey from selling Scottish prisoners into slavery. The highlanders had signed six-year plantation work contracts, but the Doctor sent the boat to the safety of France. Jamie McCrimmon, a Scots piper, joined the Doctor on his travels. The Time Lords later returned him to his native time.

Once again, Jared Khan - this time known as Thomas - narrowly missed acquiring the TARDIS. After this time he posed as Alessandro di Cagliostro, claiming to be born 1743, died 1795.[335] In 1750, a ship was wrecked off Haiti. Washed ashore was Nkome, a six-year old African slave kept alive by voodoo, who began plotting his revenge against the white landowners - the blancs.[336] Around 1750, a "Mr Sun" arrived in England from China. He inherited business space in Covent Garden, and opened a toy store there. A successive number of "Mr. Suns" would operate the shop for two hundred years.[337]

The Daemons inspired the Industrial Revolution.[338]

1752 (2nd to 14th September) - As Britain adopted the Gregorian calendar, eleven days were removed from the British calendar. The British public went to sleep on 2nd September, and awoke on the 14th of the same month. Faction Paradox came to purchase and occupy those missing days, using them as their centre of operations, the Eleven-Day Empire.[339]

Dr Borlase was killed surveying the Nine Travellers in 1754[340], the same year the Doctor discovered Kadiatu Lethbridge-Stewart half-dead in a slaver off Sierra Leone. He took her to the Civilisation of the People.[341]

The Doctor met Doctor Johnson.[342] **Scottish poet Robert Burns was born in 1759, so Jamie McCrimmon had never heard of him.**[343]

Neutronic War on Skaro

& 1763 - There were two races on the planet Skaro: the original Daleks (or Dals) and the Thals. The Daleks were teachers and philosophers, the Thals were a famous warrior race, and Skaro was a world full of ideas, art and invention.

However, there were old rivalries between the two races, and this led to a final war. Skaro was destroyed in a single day when the Daleks detonated a huge neutronic bomb. The radiation from the weapon killed nearly all life on the planet, and petrified the vegetation. The only animals that survived were bizarre mutations: the metallic Magnadons, their bodies held together by a magnetic field, and the monsters swarming in the Lake of Mutations.

After the Neutronic War, the Daleks retired into a huge metal city built as a shelter, where they were protected from the radiation. They became dependent on their machines, radiation and static electricity. Most of the Thals perished during the final war, but a handful survived on a plateau a great distance from the Dalek City, where they managed to cultivate small plots of land. The Thals mutated, evolving full circle in the space of five centuries, becoming physically perfect blond supermen.[344]

Sir Francis Dashwood, an ancestor of Brigham Elisha Dashwood III and Chancellor of the Exchequer to King George III, founded the Hellfire Club as a relatively benign social organization. The group peaked in the 1760s, becoming a debauched haven for the aristocracy. The generations to follow greatly exaggerated the group's dabblings with the black arts.[345]

Rubasdpofiaew, a drug from Tau Ceti Minor, had found its way to Earth and started growing in Tibet as a "miracle

---

334 Dating *The Highlanders* - The provisional title of the story was 'Culloden', and it is set shortly after that battle. Despite references in *The Highlanders*, *The War Games* and other stories, Culloden took place in April 1746, not 1745. This is first explicitly stated in *The Underwater Menace*, (although the draft script again said "1745"). The *Radio Times* specified that *The Highlanders* is set in April. The 1745 date has been perpetuated by the first edition of *The Making of Doctor Who*, and surfaces in a number of books, such as *The Roundheads*.

335 *Birthright*

336 *White Darkness*

337 *The Cabinet of Light* (p85).

338 *The Daemons*

339 *Interference*

340 *The Stones of Blood*

341 *The Also People*

342 *...ish, Synthespians™, The Gallifrey Chronicles*

343 *The Underwater Menace*

344 "Five hundred years" before *The Daleks*, which I set in 2263.

THE NEUTRONIC WAR: The Neutronic War referred to in *The Daleks* is clearly a different conflict from the Thal-Kaled War seen in *Genesis of the Daleks*, given that the Neutronic War in *The Daleks* lasted just "one day", whereas the Thal-Kaled War lasted "nearly a thousand years". In the first story, a Dalek tells the Doctor that "We, the Daleks and the Thals" fought the Neutronic War, implying that this was after the Daleks were created. The Thal named Alydon speaks of this as the "final war", maybe suggesting that there was more than one.

It's interesting to note that after the Neutronic War, both the Thals and Dals mutated until they resembled flower" named Om-Tsor. When consumed, Om-Tsor allowed its users to turn thought into reality. Starving Tibetan lamas consumed the Om-Tsor flowers, and used their newfound abilities to found the peaceful "Om-Tsor" valley.[346]

Sabbath was initiated into the British intelligence service in 1762, adopting the name by which we know him.[347] Sabbath was not supposed to survive the initiation, but the Council of Eight saved him. The Council claimed to be humans from the future who wanted to become the Lords of Time. They recruited Sabbath as a counterpart to the Doctor. He did not hear from them for another twenty years.[348]

Sabbath first met the Mayakai warrior Tula Lui in 1776, when she was ten. She would eventually become his apprentice. In 1780, Sabbath failed in an attempt to seduce Scarlette, a brothel owner and ritualist. The same year, he was present during the Gordon Riots. He left the Service, and dealt with the agents of the Service - the 'Ratcatchers' - sent to assassinate him. Tula Lui, as Sabbath's only real company from 1780 to 1782, eliminated some high-ranking Service officials as a message for them to leave Sabbath alone.[349]

The American War of Independence

The Doctor was at the Boston Tea Party in 1773.[350] The Rani was present during the American War of Independence.[351] The Canavitchi were involved in the same conflict.[352]

Benjamin Franklin became President of the United States.[353] **A little over two hundred years ago, Devil's End became notorious when the Third Lord of Aldbourne's black magic rituals were exposed.[354] In the late eighteenth century, Scaroth lived in France at the time of Louis XV. He acquired a Gainsborough.[355]**

Gainsborough also painted a portrait of Ace that ended up in Windsor Castle.[356] Kalicum, an agent of the Council of Eight, made genetic alterations to the grandfather of the Frenchman D'Amantine. The alterations would work their way through thirteen successive generations.[357]

The Doctor met Emperor Joseph II of Austria-Hungary.[358] **Cessair posed as Lady Montcalm and was painted by Ramsay.[359]** In September 1781, Jane Hallam - the wife of Henry Hallam, one of Mel's ancestors - died from a horse-riding accident.[360]

1781 (12th December) to 1782 (June) - CATCH-1782[361] **->** Melanie unexpectedly arrived through time from 2003, and the transition left her extremely confused and disorientated. Henry Hallam cared for her and, failing to recognize Mel as one of his descendants, became intent on making her his second wife. The Doctor and Mel's uncle, John Hallam, arrived onhand and intervened. The time travellers returned with Mel to the twenty-first century, and Henry eventually married his housekeeper, Mrs McGregor.

Henry's journal and other documents from the period would note the existence of "Eleanor Hallam", actually Mel, who was erroneously believed to have been born about 1760 and died in 1811.

---

the state they'd been in at *Genesis of the Daleks* - the Thals becoming blond humanoids, the Dals becoming green Dalek blobs.
345 *Minuet in Hell*
346 "Two centuries" before *Revolution Man*.
347 *The Adventuress of Henrietta Street*
348 *Timeless*
349 *The Adventuress of Henrietta Street*
350 *The Unquiet Dead*
351 *The Mark of the Rani*. The American War of Independence ran from 1775-1783.
352 *The King of Terror*
353 *Seasons of Fear*. No date is given, but Franklin died in 1790. The modern-day American government didn't start until 1789, and its predecessor - the Articles of Confederation - had no presidents. Ergo, barring further alteration, Franklin could only have been President for a limited period during the term normally attributed to George Washington. This mistake wasn't deliberate; writer Paul Cornell genuinely believed that Franklin had been President. In *Neverland*, a line that

the "wrong man became President" was meant to denote the Bush / Gore election in 2000, but fans have cited it to cover this mistake.
354 "Two hundred years" before *The Daemons*.
355 *City of Death*
356 We see the portrait of Ace hanging in Windsor Castle in the extended version of *Silver Nemesis*. At the time, in Ace's personal timeline, she had not yet sat for the painting. Gainsborough lived from 1727-1788, painting society portraits 1760-1774 before turning to landscapes.
357 *Timeless* (p93). Kalicum says that D'Amantine, who's alive in 1830, is the third generation affected by his alterations.
358 *The Devil Goblins from Neptune*. He ruled 1780-1790.
359 *The Stones of Blood*. Allan Ramsay, a Scottish portrait painter, lived 1713-1784.
360 Three months before *Catch-1782*.
361 Dating *Catch-1782* - The dates of Mel's arrival and departure from this era are given.

1782 (20th March) to 1783 (13th February) - THE ADVENTURESS OF HENRIETTA STREET[362] -> At the limit of human consciousness was the 'horizon', and beyond that was the Kingdom of the Beasts and the babewyns, bestial ape creatures. The destruction of Gallifrey destabilised time, allowing the babewyns to escape to Earth at the point when humans were beginning to conceive of time as a dimension.

The Doctor arrived in this era, suffering physical symptoms as a result of his being linked to his homeworld, which no longer existed. He allied himself with a brothel owner and ritualist, Scarlette. Together, they agreed that the Doctor should marry Juliette, a young woman working in the brothel, as this would link him to Earth and allow him to serve as its protector.

The Doctor came to the attention of Sabbath, who thought the Doctor had brought the babewyns to Earth. Sabbath was building a time machine, the *Jonah*. The Doctor and Sabbath teamed up upon realising they both wished to repel the monsters. Juliette abandoned the Doctor for Sabbath. The Doctor collapsed, but recovered enough to marry Scarlette in the Caribbean. The Doctor's illness got worse, and the babewyns transported his party to their domain (possibly the ruins of Gallifrey). Sabbath saved the Doctor by removing one of his hearts.

The babewyns assaulted Scarlette's brothel, and Scarlette was believed killed in the fighting. The Doctor defeated the babewyens, and beheaded the King of Beasts with the sonic screwdriver. A funeral was held for Scarlette on 9th February, 1783, but she had survived and parted company with the Doctor on 13th February.

After implanting the Doctor's heart in his chest, Sabbath gained the ability to travel through time. The Doctor wrote the novel *The Ruminations of a Foreign Traveller in his Element* during this time.

Sir Percival Flint excavated a fogou in Cornwall in 1783 and heard ghastly screams.[363] In the late 1780s, Montague and Tackleton, a firm making dolls' houses, scandalously make a house that resembled the haunted Ilbridge House.[364] The Doctor met Mozart.[365]

In 1788 the Nemesis Bow was stolen from Windsor Castle.[366] Fitz's great-great-grandfather and his twin, Freddie Tarr and Neville Fitzwilliam Tarr, were born in 1790.[367] The Doctor claimed to be the first person to spin a jenny.[368] **The first Doctor met James Watt, an engineer who influenced the Industrial Revolution.**[369] **Auderly House was built in Georgian times.**[370]

---

362 Dating *The Adventuress of Henrietta Street* - It is 'March 1782' on p2, more specifically 'March 20, 1782' on p15. The Seige of Henrietta Street happens on 'February 8', 1783 (p259). Scarlette's funeral is dated February 9 on p269 and the back cover, with the Doctor departing Henrietta Street on February 13 (p273), and his final conversation with Scarlette occurs on the same day. An epilogue with Sabbath and Juliette happens on 'August 18 1783' (p278).

The book is told in a style reminiscent of a history book, and some of the key facts are open to dispute. With that in mind, novels after this one state that Anji has been travelling with the Doctor only for 'months', suggesting the timeframe of *Henrietta Street* might be more condensed than the book itself suggests.

Scarlette is the young girl Isobel in the *Faction Paradox* comic series, which covers some of her early history and takes place in 1774.
363 *The Spectre of Lanyon Moor*
364 *The Death of Art*
365 *Time and Relative*. Mozart lived 1756-1791.
366 *Silver Nemesis*
367 *The Taint*. Fitz is named after Freddie's brother.
368 *Doctor Who and the Pirates*. The Spinning Jenny was invented in 1797.
369 *The Space Museum*. James Watt lived from 1736-1819.
370 *Day of the Daleks*, Alex Macintosh, the television commentator in that story, states that the house is "Georgian".

371 According to Susan in *The Reign of Terror*.
372 In *An Unearthly Child*, Susan borrows a book about the French Revolution, but already knows a great deal about the subject.
373 *Christmas on a Rational Planet*
374 *Just War*
375 The lockpick is mentioned in *Pyramids of Mars*. The Doctor mentions Marie Antoinette again in *The Robots of Death*.
376 *The Adventuress of Henrietta Street*
377 *The Crystal Bucephalus*
378 *The Daemons*
379 *The Burning*
380 *The Banquo Legacy*
381 Dating *The Reign of Terror* - The date is given onscreen. *The Programme Guide* offered the date "1792", but *The Terrestrial Index* corrected this. The story shows the arrest of Robespierre, which occurred on 27th July.
382 *The Man in the Velvet Mask*
383 *The Sea Devils*. Nelson lived 1758-1805.
384 *Christmas on a Rational Planet*
385 *The Hollow Men, Blood Heat*
386 *The Death of Art*
387 *The Sands of Time*. Napoleon began his expedition in March 1798, and the year is given (p203).
388 Dating *Set Piece* - It is "1798 CE" (p57).
389 *The Banquo Legacy*
390 *Interference* (p59, p147).
391 Dating *Christmas on a Rational Planet* - It's '1799. At Christmas' (p24).

The French Revolution

This was the Doctor's favourite period of Earth history.[371] Susan showed an interest in the French Revolution, and she visited France at this time with the first Doctor.[372]

In 1791, the first Doctor and Susan were imprisoned in Paris, but escaped by using an artillery shell. Transcripts of the Doctor's interrogation would end up with the Shadow Directory.[373] It was the Doctor and Susan's first-ever visit to Earth. It demonstrated to the Doctor that the old order could be toppled, and that people wanted freedom and a hope for the future.[374]

The Doctor met Marie Antoinette and obtained a lockpick from her.[375] The Doctor claimed to have been invited into Marie Antoinette's boudoir.[376] In 1791, the Doctor, Tegan and Turlough were dining at the Cafe de Saint Joseph in Aix-en-Provence when they were accidentally scooped up by the Crystal Bucephalus and whisked thousands of years into the future.[377]

In 1793, the attempted opening of Devil's Hump by Sir Percival Flint resulted in disaster.[378] The Daniells brothers unearthed a statuette of a dancer in Pakistan in 1793.[379] In 1793, the actor Robert Dodds built Banquo Manor using money he inherited. The rumour was that Dodds had murdered his aunt for her money.[380]

1794 (late July) - THE REIGN OF TERROR[381] **-> The Doctor and his companions landed in France during the Reign of Terror. Ian met the British spy James Stirling, but Barbara and Susan were arrested as aristocrats and sentenced to the guillotine. Posing as a Citizen, the Doctor rescued his companions and returned them to the TARDIS.**

= A group of curious aliens performed experiments on reality control and used a "world-machine" device to slip the entire Earth out of N-space. The planet was remade according to the philosophies of a single human: the Marquis de Sade. However, the world-machine's operator threw off the aliens' control and became Minski, a dwarf. Minski created an automaton of the Marquis, who began ruling France the day Robespierre was arrested, and the genuine Marquis was imprisoned. The fake Marquis ruled France, with Minski as his first deputy, for ten years.[382]

Nelson "was a personal friend" of the Doctor.[383] In 1795, the Directory was running France after Robespierre's arrest. They learned of many unusual visitations and encounters on Earth, and set up the Shadow Directory to capture or destroy such things. At some point, the Shadow Directory autopsied a Time Lord and knew of them as *les*

betes aux deux coeurs, or 'the devils with two hearts'. One of the Shadow Directory's agents, the psychic aristocrat Marielle Duquesne, investigated the Beautiful Shining Daughters of Hysteria in Munchen.[384]

The Doctor met the artist Turner.[385] The Quoth gave psychic abilities to the toymaker Montague in 1797.[386] In 1798, Napoleon undertook an expedition to colonise Egypt. He entered the Great Pyramid, and was mentally influenced to dig out the sand-covered Sphinx.[387]

1798 - SET PIECE[388] **->** Benny fled the Ants, and ended up with archaeologist Vivant Denon as he began to uncover Ancient Egyptian treasures for Napoleon. She located the TARDIS, thanks to a message Ace left in 1366 BC, and programmed it to find the Doctor.

Robert Dodds was murdered at Banquo Manor in 1798. A Time Lord agent was dispatched to wait for the Doctor, who eventually showed up a century later.[389] In 1799, Mother Mathara of Faction Paradox and two thousand refugees from Ordifica arrived from 2596. They began building the city of Anathema. With the help of the remembrance tanks that Mathara left, this society would become the Remote.[390]

1799 (9th November - 25th December) - CHRISTMAS ON A RATIONAL PLANET[391] **->** Napoleon returned to France from Egypt, shutting down the Directory and replacing it with the Consulate. The Shadow Directory secretly survived.

The mysterious Cardinal Scarlath gave the Vatican's Collection of Necessary Secrets certain documents that described the creation of Ancient Egyptian civilisation by a one-eyed monster.

Roz Forrester accidentally ended up in Woodwicke, New York state, after investigating a temporal anomaly in 2012. She set herself up as a fortune-teller and met Samuel Lincoln, whom she mistook for an ancestor of Abraham Lincoln. Roz planned to assassinate Samuel, thus changing history and enabling the Doctor to locate her.

The Doctor arrived and stopped Roz, but as a vast psychic disturbance started in the town. This was caused by the Carnival Queen, also known as Cacophony, who sought to create an irrational universe. The Queen was releasing irrational gynoid monsters into the area, and sought to create further disruption through the latently telepathic Chris Cwej. He chose Reason over the Carnival Queen's irrationality, and the defeated Queen departed into eternity, where she hoped to inspire more ideas.

The Doctor learned afterward that the TARDIS had planted a memory in Chris' mind that swayed his decision, as the TARDIS feared becoming derationalized under the Queen's rule. Jake McCrimmon, agent of the American Special Congress, investigated the aftermath.

The Nineteenth Century

Lord Aldbourne formed a branch of the Hellfire Club and played at devil worship.[392] The Doctor brought the ornithologist James Bond to the 1800s to see a live Dodo.[393]

1800 (December) - FOREIGN DEVILS[394] **->** The Emperor became sickened by the foreign-sponsored opium trade afflicting China, and ordered the removal of all "foreign devils". The Chief Astrologer to the Emperor placed a curse on one such opium trader, Roderick Upcott. The curse was designed to first endow the Upcott family with prosperity, making their inevitable downfall all the more crushing.

The TARDIS arrived in China, and while the Doctor was caught up with local politics, Jamie and Zoe disappeared through a 'spirit gate' - a stone ring traditionally designed to keep demons at bay. The Doctor realized the gate was a teleporter and used the TARDIS to follow his companions to 1900.

> **= 1804 - THE MAN IN THE VELVET MASK**[395] **->** The Doctor and Dodo arrived on Earth, which had been remade ten years ago by a world-machine. The dwarf Minski, in control of the remade France, attempted to start a war between France, Britain and America that would spread a virus. This would have brought anyone infected by the virus under Minski's control. Minski's plan fell to ruin and he was killed. The Doctor and the real Marquis de Sade sabotaged the world-machine, and the machine's creators promised to return Earth to N-space, erasing the history they had created. Humanity was unaware of the alternate timeline.

The Doctor breakfasted with Nelson in 1805, the day before Nelson's final battle with Napoleon at Trafalgar.[396] The Doctor was "instrumental" at Trafalgar.[397]

> **= 1806 - SEASONS OF FEAR**[398] **->** The Doctor and Charley confronted the long-lived Grayle once again. This time, Grayle built a transmat and brought his masters, the Nimon, to Earth. The Doctor engineered a time corridor that returned the Nimon to Britain in 305 BC.

Joseph Sundvig was born on 8th April, 1809.[399] The Doctor met Byron and Shelley.[400] In 1811, the poet William Blake vanished from his home and met the Doctor.[401] The Doctor also met William Blake at home once.[402] The Doctor was with a British rifle brigade when he met Sir Arthur Wellesley. He was a prisoner of the French at Salamanca in 1812.[403]

Also in 1812, a battlefield from Napoleon's Russian campaign was kidnapped by the War Lords.[404] **The Doctor met Napoleon and told him that an army marches on its stomach.**[405]

---

392 'The early nineteenth century' according to *The Eight Doctors*.
393 *Instruments of Darkness*. In our history, the dodo was extinct by 1700.
394 Dating *Foreign Devils* - It's "December 1800" (p22).
395 Dating *The Man in the Velvet Mask* - The Doctor and Dodo see a poster that gives a date of "Messidor, Year XII", and the Doctor calculates that they are in "June or July 1804".
396 *Eye of Heaven*. Nelson's final battle occurred on 21st October, 1805.
397 *The Scarlet Empress*.
398 Dating *Seasons of Fear* - The date is given.
399 According to a gravestone in *The Curse of Fenric*.
400 *Managra, Neverland*
401 *The Pit*
402 *The Eye of the Tyger*, which sounds like a different visit to the one seen in *The Pit*.
403 *The Devil Goblins from Neptune*. Other references to meeting the Duke of Wellington around this time appear in *The Tomorrow Windows, Synthespians™* and *The Book of the Still*. The Duke of Wellington was a leading military and political figure. He became a Field Marshall during the Napoleonic Wars, and oversaw Napoleon's defeat at Waterloo.

404 *The War Games*
405 *Day of the Daleks*. The Doctor does not meet Napoleon in *The Reign of Terror* (although Ian and Barbara do). The third Doctor is still exiled in the twentieth century timezone, so he must have met Napoleon in an earlier incarnation. Napoleon lived 1769-1821. The meeting is also mentioned in *Escape Velocity* and *Warmonger*.
406 Dating *Emotional Chemistry* - The date is given in the blurb.
407 *Loups-Garoux*
408 Dating *The Mark of the Rani* - The date is never stated on-screen or in the script, but *DWM* reported that the production team felt that the story was set in "1830". *The Terrestrial Index* set the story "c1825", the novelisation simply said "the beginning of the nineteenth century". Tony Scupham-Bilton concluded in *Celestial Toyroom* that, judging by the historical evidence and the month the story was filmed, the story was "set in either October 1821 or October 1822". As that article states, the story must at the very least be set before the Stockton-Darlington line was opened in September 1825, and after Thomas Liddell was made Baron Ravensworth on 17th July, 1821. However, Jane Baker later told *DWM* that her research was confused by the

1812 - EMOTIONAL CHEMISTRY[406] -> The Magellans had evolved as creatures that were essentially living stars. One such creature broke a significant rule among its kind by giving birth to a child, named Aphrodite. The Magellan was put on trial, with the Doctor acting as defence council. The Magellan's people ruled to spilt the creature in half and place each part in separate time zones on Earth. The emotional side of the Magellan became the female Dusha, and by the early nineteenth century had been adopted by Count Yuri Vishenkov. The Magellan's intellectual half became Lord General Razum Kinzhal, a strategist around the year 5000. Aphrodite herself was contained and given the extra-dimensional locale of Paraiso as her home.

Living as a Russian noblewoman, Dusha Vishenkov had the ability to alter probability and affected her "sister" Natasha Vishenkov. Natasha's descendants would look virtually identical for millennia to come, and be statistically predisposed to good luck. Dusha's influence also turned the Vishenkov family's possessions into empathic capacitors, capable of amplifying the emotions of those nearby. One such item, a painting, would be on display in the Kremlin Museum in 2024 and start a fire there.

The Doctor helped Dusha reunite with her lover, Kinzhal, in the year 5000.

In summer 1812, the Doctor witnessed Napoleon invading Russia, and later remembered the occasion as having stormy weather. Illeana (later Illeana de Santos) fled with her wealthy merchant father from Smolensk, but bandits killed her father. The werewolf Stubbe turned her into a werewolf and bound her to him for a century or two.[407]

c 1813 - THE MARK OF THE RANI[408] -> The Rani was present during the Industrial Revolution, extracting a chemical from human brains. Her project was interrupted by the arrival, and rivalry, of the Master and the Doctor. The Master attempted to disrupt human history as the greatest scientific minds of the era converged on Killingworth. The Doctor trapped the two renegades in the Rani's TARDIS and banished them from Earth.

Major General Fergus Lethbridge-Stewart fought in the Battle of Waterloo.[409] The Doctor met Wellington after the conflict.[410]

In 1816, the Doctor visited the Duke of Wellington, and made a lot of money at a gambling den. He set up an account at Chumley's Bank that he occasionally dipped into while on Earth.[411] The Doctor was present when Peter the Great sent an expedition to Alaska.[412] He was also there the night Mary Shelley came up with the story of Frankenstein.[413]

1818 - THE GHOSTS OF N-SPACE[414] -> Travelling back in time, the Doctor and Sarah witnessed the early life of the wizard Maximillian.

In the early nineteenth century, the Doctor met Beau Brummel, who told him he looked better in a cloak.[415]

A Dalek scoutship crashed on the planet Vulcan. By this time, the Daleks had already encountered the second Doctor.[416] The Dalek ship was from the far future.[417]

The Beast of Fang Rock was seen.[418] The Reverend Thomas Bright surveyed the Nine Travellers. At some point between now and the late twentieth century, Cessair posed as Mrs Trefusis for sixty years, then Senora Camara.[419]

On 3rd July, 1820, Florence Sundvig was born.[420] Napoleon died in 1821, still traumatised by what he had witnessed in the Great Pyramid in 1798.[421]

Victorian convention of biographies referring to Lords by their titles even before they were given them. Given that, Jim Smith in *Who's Next* suggested that the date given in *DWM* was a mishearing of "1813", which fits all the evidence apart from the existence of Lord Ravensworth.

409 *The Dying Days*. His first name and rank were given in *The Scales of Injustice*.

410 *The Eight Doctors*

411 *Players*, almost certainly the same meeting mentioned in *The Eight Doctors*.

412 *The Land of the Dead*

413 *Storm Warning*. This occurred in 1816, and is also referred in *The Devil Goblins from Neptune*, *Neverland*, *Zagreus* and *Terror Firma*.

414 Dating *The Ghosts of N-Space* - It is "eighteen eighteen" (p63), one hundred and fifty-seven years before the present-day setting (p200).

415 The Doctor mentions Beau Brummel in *The Sensorites*, *The Twin Dilemma* and *The Two Doctors*. Brummel lived 1778-1840. He was an arbiter of fashion in Regency England, and helped further the style known as "dandyism".

416 The Dalek ship crashed "two hundred years" before *The Power of the Daleks*. This is the first recorded Dalek expedition in our solar system. A Dalek from this mission recognises the Doctor, despite his regeneration. In *Day of the Daleks*, the Daleks must use the Mind Analysis Machine to establish the Doctor's identity.

417 *War of the Daleks*

418 "Eighty years" before *Horror of Fang Rock*.

419 *The Stones of Blood*

420 *The Curse of Fenric*

421 *The Sands of Time* (p220). The year is given, and Napoleon died 5th May, 1821.

= c 1827-1828 - MEDICINAL PURPOSES[422] -> A human researcher from the future had acquired a Type 70 TARDIS from a Nekkistani dealer of Gryben, and a dying alien race had employed him to research a virus that was killing them. As the aliens' immune systems were similar to those of human beings, the researcher set up shop in Edinburgh, 1827. He assumed the guise of Dr. Robert Knox, the anatomist who employed the graverobbers William Burke and William Hare to deliver him cadavers for study. Burke and Hare failed to content themselves with merely unearthing corpses, and started murdering people to fulfil Knox's demands.

"Knox" infected some Edinburgh residents with the alien virus as part of his research, but anyone who consumed alcohol proved immune. Failing to make much progress, Knox used his illicit technology to roll back time in Edinburgh and start with "new" bodies. He grew ambivalent toward his employers' survival, and turned the enterprise into a tourist attraction for elite customers, with patrons paying to witness the "Hale and Burke Experience." The Edinburgh residents' memories grew cloudy as time was repeatedly looped.

The Doctor and Evelyn arrived inside of Knox's time loop, and discovered his operations.

On 28th January, 1829, the Doctor and Evelyn observed Burke's public hanging. The Doctor tricked Knox into leaving the sanctity of his time loop and infected him with the alien virus. Knox fled in his TARDIS, hoping to find a cure, aware that his former employers would attempt to hunt him down. History was restored to its proper path. The Doctor and Evelyn took the mentally disabled man "Daft Jamie," who was slated to become one of Burke and Hare's victims, back to meet his appointed demise.

In early May 1830, the time traveller Chloe and her dog Jamais happened upon Sabbath in St. Raphael, France. She sensed part of his history but fell unconscious. When she awoke, Sabbath had left her a diamond and a book purporting to speak of the future. Her belief in the book allowed Sabbath to manipulate her activities.[423]

= In 1831, energy beings from the Eternium, a doomed pocket universe, manipulated the aspiring poet Jared Malahyde to begin work on "the Utopian Engine," a device intended to temporally age Earth to extinction. If successful, the Eternines would harvest the life force energy released by Earth's demise.

422 Dating *Medicinal Purposes* - The back cover says 1827. Burke and Hare met the real Knox in November 1827, but the majority of their murders occurred throughout 1828, until they were caught in November of that year. The audio concurs with the historical date for Burke's execution. Hare was granted immunity because he turned King's Evidence against Burke. The real Knox was never prosecuted.
423 *Timeless*
424 *Reckless Engineering*
425 Dating *Bloodtide* - The date is given.
426 *Sometime Never*
427 *The Curse of Peladon.* Victoria was crowned in 1838.
428 *The Spectre of Lanyon Moor*
429 According to Professor Litefoot in *The Talons of Weng-Chiang,* the gun "hasn't been fired for fifty years".
430 *The Two Doctors.* The architect Isambard Kingdom Brunel lived 1806-1859, and also features in *Reckless Engineering.*
431 *The Romans*
432 *Eye of Heaven.* The date of Stockwood's first expedition is given (p1).
433 *All-Consuming Fire*
434 Dating *Reckless Engineering* - The date is given as '19 July 1843' (p5).
435 *The Church and the Crown*
436 According to *The Tomorrow Windows. The Unquiet Dead,* on the other hand, certainly presents itself as the first meeting between them.
437 *The Death of Art*
438 *The Algebra of Ice* (p8-11).
439 *Enlightenment*
440 *The One Doctor.* Peter Roget was a physician and lexicographer who lived 1779-1869. He compiled *Roget's Thesaurus.*
441 *State of Decay.* Grimm lived 1785-1863.
442 *Downtime.* Victoria was 'eleven' (p14) when her mother died in '1863' (p261). This would make her fourteen when she started travelling with the Doctor, although Deborah Watling certainly looks older than that in the TV series.
443 *Ghost Ship.* Novelist William Thackeray (*Vanity Fair*) lived 1811-1863; poet Charles Baudelaire 1821-1867; painter Eugéne Delacroix 1798-1863; painter Édouard Manet 1832-1883. While there's no indication these meetings were on the same trip, it's possible.
444 *Timewyrm: Revelation* (p4).
445 *The Evil of the Daleks*
446 *The Sea Devils*
447 *The War Games*
448 *The Evil of the Daleks*
449 *Interference* (p191).
450 *The Rapture.* The brothers' portal isn't related to the portal that abducts James Lees in the same era.
451 *Empire of Death.* James is replaced in 1856, as dated on the back cover and p5.
452 *Downtime*

Malahyde partnered with architect Isambard Kingdom Brunel, and they became wealthy by pioneering "the Malahyde Process" - an advanced means of developing superior steel. Malahyde spent the next 12 years working on the Utopian Engine.[424]

1835 - BLOODTIDE[425] -> The Doctor took Evelyn to meet her personal hero, Charles Darwin in the Galapagos Islands. They learned of 'devil creatures' on the island, identifying them as Silurians. The Doctor confronted their leader, the renegade scientist Tulok, who planned to wipe out all human life with a virus. The Doctor tricked the Silurians' Myrka into destroying a Silurian submersible, which killed Tulok before he could launch his bacterial warheads. The Doctor suggested that Darwin not mention the Silurians in his writing.

In May 1837, in the Pyrennes, the archaeologist Louis Vosgues stood on the verge of formulating the theory of evolution years before Darwin. An Agent of the Council of Eight insured that Vosgues fell off a cliff to his death.[426]

The Victorian Era

The Doctor attended the coronation of Queen Victoria.[427] In the 1840s, a tenant farmer who tried to flatten the tumulus on Lanyon Moor died of a heart attack. The crops nearby failed for the next seven years.[428]

Professor Litefoot's Chinese fowling piece was last fired around this time.[429] **The Doctor met Brunel.**[430] **He also gave Hans Christian Andersen the idea for 'The Emperor's New Clothes'.**[431]

An alien race, on the verge of losing a war, had long ago seeded its DNA into space in millions of head-shaped *moai*. The aliens' rivals killed them, but the *moai* distributed the DNA like a virus, creating hybrids of the aliens on multiple worlds. On Earth, such *moai* had settled on Rapa Nui (AKA Easter Island) and turned some Polynesians into alien hybrids. But in October 1842, Horace Stockwood's expedition to the island carried a disease that would kill off the hybrids.[432]

In 1843, the Doctor and Susan met Sherlock Holmes' father, Siger Holmes, in India and learnt that the natives believed in a gateway to another world.[433]

= 1843 - RECKLESS ENGINEERING[434] -> The Eternine gambit to steal Earth's life-energy reached fruition in 1843, when Malahyde finished and activated "the Utopian Engine." The Doctor's intervention meant that instead of aging Earth to death, the device simply advanced time on the planet's surface 40 years. This nonetheless created an alternate timeline in which an estimated 95 percent of mature humans and animals either aged to death or died

from shock. Humanity's children - suddenly aged to adulthood - became savage creatures of instinct named "the Wildren." The remaining pockets of civilization took to disparate settlements struggling to survive, and cannibalism became an accepted means of survival in some parts.

In 1844, the Doctor helped Alexandre Dumas with *The Three Musketeers*.[435] The Doctor met Charles Dickens.[436] Dickens' work became far darker in tone after he encountered Montague's killer dolls in 1845.[437]

= Time distortion threw Edgar Allen Poe's death into flux. In alternate histories, he either died in a gutter four days before history recorded or happily survived and stayed on a drinking binge. The distortion abated, and Poe expired on 7th October, 1849.[438]

The *America* crossed the Atlantic in seventeen days in 1851.[439] Roget was a very good friend of the Doctor.[440] **Around this time, Jacob Grimm discovered the Law of Consonantal Shift.**[441]

Victoria Waterfield was born in 1852.[442] The Doctor met Thackeray, Baudelaire, Delacroix and Manet.[443] In 1853, Saul, a living church in Cheldon Bonniface, was baptised in his own font.[444]

The Crimean War

The Crimean War was fought 1853-1856. On 25th October, 1854, the Doctor was present at the "magnificent folly" of the Charge of the Light Brigade.[445] **The Doctor claimed he had been wounded in the Crimea.**[446] **The War Lords lifted a Crimean War battlefield.**[447]

In 1854, Theodore Maxwell experimented with electromagnetism.[448] The Ogron homeworld was discovered in 1855. From this point, the ape-like race would be used as slaves and hired muscle by more than a dozen races.[449]

Two residents of the Euphorian Empire, the artisan brothers Jude and Gabriel, travelled to Earth in 1855 via a dimensional portal. On the island of Es Vedra, the monk Francisco Belao mistook them for angels.[450]

In Scotland, 1856, a young boy named James Lees encountered a different dimensional portal while swimming in the River Clyde near the Corra Linn falls. Lees remained on the other side of the portal, but the aliens who lived there sent a doppelganger of him back through as an ambassador. The ersatz James could tap people's memories to "speak with the voices of the dead" and was committed to an asylum. Within a few years, he'd become renowned as a spiritualist.[451]

Charles Dodgson photographed a young Victoria Waterfield in 1857.[452] The Doctor talked to Lewis Carroll about the sleeping King Constantine, which influenced

Carroll's writing.[453] In 1860, Ian's great-grandfather, Major William Chesterton, served as a member of a Hussar company at Jaipur, India.[454]

In 1860, Litefoot's father was a Brigadier-General on the punitive expedition to China. The Litefoot family stayed in the country for the next thirteen years. During this time, Magnus Greel arrived in the Time Cabinet from the year 5000. The Chinese peasant Li H'sen Chang sheltered Greel, believing him to be the god Weng-Chiang. The Emperor came to acquire Greel's cabinet, and gave it as a gift to Litefoot's mother. Around this time, Henry Gordon Jago began working in the entertainment business.[455]

In 1863, the stone-imprinted minds of Qin Shi Huang and his two generals were transferred into Abbot Wu and two warrior monks.[456]

1863 (14th - 21st February) - EMPIRE OF DEATH[457] -> The duplicate James Lees was now performing séances for the heads of Europe, and Queen Victoria commissioned him to hold a séance for her late husband, Prince Albert. General George Doulton mistook the dimension from which "Lees" hailed as the afterlife, and sought to claim it for the British Empire. Earth's physical laws were affecting the other side, and the beings who lived there became increasingly desperate to seal off the dimensional rift. The Doctor used the TARDIS to close the rift, and Queen Victoria vowed to never speak of the matter again. The false James expired, and the real one was returned, having barely aged since he entered the rift in 1856. Doulton and several of his men remained trapped on the other side.

The Doctor lost track of whether he's met Queen Victoria before now.

Around this time, the Doctor befriended biologist Thomas Huxley.[458] Victoria Waterfield's mother, Edith Rose, **died** on 23rd November, 1863.[459]

The American Civil War

A battlefield from the American Civil War was lifted by the War Lords.[460] The Gettysburg address was made on 19th November, 1863.[461]

1865 (February - April) - BLOOD AND HOPE[462] -> The Doctor, Peri and Erimem attempted to visit the Wild West but arrived in the waning days of America's Civil War instead. The Doctor assisted the Union army as the medic "Doctor John Smith," and was present on 26th March, 1865, when Billingsville Prison was captured. On 5th April, the Doctor saved President Lincoln from an assassination attempt in Richmond, Virginia. On the same day, Peri shot dead the Confederacy's Colonel Jubal Eustace when he attempted to murder her friends as Union collaborators. Lincoln was killed days later on 14th April.

The Doctor warned Lincoln not to go to the theatre.[463] Lord Kelvin laid transatlantic telegraph cables in 1865.[464]

1865 - THE ELEVENTH TIGER[465] -> Earth prepared to enter a unique stellar conjunction for the first time in two thousand years. Qin Shi Huang, controlled by the intelligence that revived him, assembled an army and started

453　*The Shadows of Avalon*
454　*The Eleventh Tiger*
455　*The Talons of Weng-Chiang*. Jago claims to have had "thirty years in the halls".
456　*The Eleventh Tiger*
457　Dating *Empire of Death* - The story's starting and ending dates are given on p37 and p235. Prince Albert died about fifteen months before this story, in December 1861.
458　*Logopolis*. Thomas Huxley lived 1825-1895.
459　*The Evil of the Daleks*, with further details in *Downtime*.
460　*The War Games*
461　*The Chase*. The TARDIS crew supposedly watch this on the Time / Space Visualiser, although it's possible that they're just watching Lincoln rehearse the speech beforehand. The actual event had Lincoln surrounded by a huge crowd in close quarters; the Visualiser shows him very much isolated.
462　Dating *Blood and Hope* - Judging by a letter on p29, the TARDIS crew arrive in America on 21st February, 1865. The Doctor's saving Lincoln is dated on

p49; Eustace's death is dated on p69.
463　*Minuet in Hell*
464　"Fifteen years" before *Evolution* (p107).
465　Dating *The Eleventh Tiger* - The date is given. Although not referred to by name, the alien intelligence would appear to be the Mandragora Helix. The intelligence bears the Helix's characteristics, and on p274, it intimates that the Doctor defeated its attempt to dominate Earth 'four hundred years' previous.
466　Dating *The Evil of the Daleks* - An early storyline gave the date of the Victorian sequence as "1880" (and the date of the caveman sequence which was later deleted as "20,000 BC"). The camera scripts gave the date of "1867", as did some promotional material, but this was altered at the last minute when it was decided to dovetail *The Faceless Ones* and *The Evil of the Daleks*.
467　*The Androids of Tara*
468　*The War Games*
469　*Strange England* (p157).
470　*Imperial Moon*
471　Dating *The Unquiet Dead* - The Doctor gives the year (having originally aimed for 1860). The date is

securing "sacred sites" that would serve as conduits to the intelligence's power, enabling it to seize control of China. The Doctor, Ian, Barbara and Vicki arrived at this time, and their allies flooded a tomb seeped with the intelligence's power. Qin took control of his host long enough to step into the water, shorting out the intelligence's energy. Qin's mind dissipated, and the possessed Abbot Wu recovered.

Major William Chesterton served in China at this time, and suffered a concussion while fighting bandits in Qiang-Ling. The Doctor and his friends encountered the Ten Tigers of Canton, the top ten kung fu masters in Guangdong.

1866 (2nd - 3rd June) - THE EVIL OF THE DALEKS[466] -> The Doctor and Jamie were brought to the Waterfield household by the Daleks, who ran tests on them in the hopes of discovering the Human Factor. That done, the Doctor, his companion Jamie and the Waterfields were taken to Skaro in the far future.

K9 was programmed with all grandmaster chess games from 1866 onwards.[467] The War Lords lifted a battlefield from the Mexican Uprising of 1867.[468] In 1868, the Doctor opened a bank account at Coutts Bank in London. In the same year, Wychborn House burnt down.[469] In 1868, the Phiadoran spores enabled Professor Bryce-Dennison to create a solar-powered impeller drive.[470]

1869 (24th December) - THE UNQUIET DEAD[471] -> The Doctor and Rose landed in Cardiff. Charles Dickens was in the middle of a dramatic recital that was interrupted by what seemed to be a ghost. The Doctor discovered that these were gas creatures, the Gelth, who sought to open a portal to Earth. The Gelth pretended to be refugees, but actually sought to invade Earth. The Doctor ensured that the Gelth portal was destroyed. The time rift healed, but left a residual dimensional scar that was harmless to humans, yet useful to time travellers. Dickens hoped to write the adventure as *The Mystery of Edwin Drood and the Blue*

Elementals, with the killer being an extraterrestrial instead of the boy's uncle as he'd originally planned, but died the following year before completing it.

In 1870, the Jameson boys were out cutting pete when they encountered the Zygons on Tullock Moor. The elder brother Robert was driven mad by the experience and never spoke again; his younger brother Donald simply disappeared.[472] Around that time, Reuben joined the lighthouse service. He spent twenty of the next thirty years in a gas-powered lighthouse.[473] In 1871, a battlefield from the Franco-Prussian War was lifted by the War Lords[474] and the Doctor was given a Gladstone bag by Gladstone.[475]

1871 - SET PIECE[476] -> The Doctor, Benny and Ace were reunited in Paris, where they also met Kadiatu Lethbridge-Stewart. After the robotic Ants had been defeated, Ace chose to leave the Doctor and joined the ruling Paris Commune. Ace was the last soldier to leave the barricades when the Commune fell from power.

The Doctor met Tsar Nicholas at the Drei Kaiser Bund of 1871.[477]

1872 (August - December) - EYE OF HEAVEN[478] -> Horace Stockwood organized a second expedition to Easter Island, and the Doctor and Leela joined his group aboard the sailing ship *Tweed*. On the island, Stockwood's party discovered a giant stone head containing a teleport device. This transported some of the group to the homeworld of the aliens who built Easter Island's *moai*. They searched an alien library, but their presence triggered a booby trap that turned the alien sun black. The party returned to Earth, hoping the sun would return to normal in their absence. From Leela's blood, the Doctor created an antidote to the sickness that had killed the Polynesian / alien hybrids thirty years ago. Stockwood remained on the island to help protect the Polynesians until the alien DNA the *moai* carried could re-infect them.

given a number of times, first on a poster in Dickens' dressing room.
472 According to Angus in *Terror of the Zygons*.
473 *Horror of Fang Rock*
474 *The War Games*
475 *Companion Piece*
476 Dating *Set Piece* - It is "1871 CE" (p62). The Commune fell on 28th May, 1871. Ace's departure in *Set Piece* deliberately echoes the epilogue to *The Curse of Fenric* novelisation, in which the Doctor visits an older Ace in nineteenth century Paris, some time after she's departed his company. Reconciling the epilogue with

the New Adventures is difficult, however, as the epilogue takes place in 1887 (p186 and 188) when Ace is still a 'young lady'. Given her aging in the New Adventures, this makes it unlikely that she lives in Paris for the whole 16-year duration between 1871 and 1887. Fortunately, the New Adventures have Ace taking up time travel after *Set Piece*, and using a time-jump to facilitate her meeting with the Doctor in 1887 would explain a great deal.
477 *The Devil Goblins from Neptune*
478 Dating *Eye of Heaven* - The date is given (p17).

1872 (25th November) - THE CHASE[479] **->** The Doctor and the Daleks landed on the *Mary Celeste*, forcing the crew to abandon ship.

Joseph Sundvig died on 3rd February, 1872.[480] The Nine Travellers were surveyed in 1874.[481] Old Priory, a Victorian folly, was built for the Scarman family. After this time, Marcus and Laurence Scarman played in the priest-hole there as children.[482] The Doctor swam with Captain Webb in the Channel.[483]

1873 - STRANGE ENGLAND[484] **->** The TARDIS landed on an asteroid shaped by Gallifreyan Protyon units to resemble an idyllic Victorian country house based on Wychborn House. It was sculpted by a friend of the Doctor, the Time Lady Galah, who had reached the end of her regenerative cycle. With the Doctor's help, Galah lived on as one of her human creations, Charlotte. She returned to Earth and married Richard Aickland, who became a renowned Gothic novelist in the early twentieth century (he wrote such books as *Cold Eyes* and *The Wine Press*).

The *Vantarialis* crashed on Zanak, where its injured captain was remade as a cyborg. With the assistance of old Queen Xanxia, the Captain converted the entire planet into a hollow world capable of teleporting between star systems and sucking the life out of planets by materializing around them. After this time, and with increasing frequency, Zanak attacked and destroyed the Vegan shipyard of **Bandraginus V, Aterica, Temesis, Tridentio III, Lowiteliom, Bibicorpus and Granados.**[485]

The Doctor met Alexander Graham Bell.[486] Bell initiated the first phone message while asking for his assistant Watson. The message would later dominate phone lines during a time paradox in 1987.[487]

1878 (September) - IMPERIAL MOON[488] **->** Using Bryce-Dennison's impeller drive, the British government had crafted three spaceships: the *Cygnus*, *Draco* and *Lynx*. The Doctor and Turlough arrived as the ships set about exploring Earth's moon, and mistook the deadly Vrall for the exiled Phiadorans. While returning to Earth, the Vrall were exposed aboard the *Draco* and a deadly struggle took place. Only Turlough survived, and the crewless *Draco* sped into space.

The *Cygnus* and *Lynx* arrived on Earth, where Queen Victoria greeted the "Phiadorans" as emissaries from another world. The Vrall self-replicated and instigated a slaughter. The Doctor and Turlough used advanced weapons in the safari park to wipe out the Vrall on Earth. At the Doctor's command, Kamelion disguised himself as the late Prince Albert and appeared to the Queen "in a vision." Kamelion convinced the Queen to dismantle the remaining spaceships and never mention the incident again.

The moon safari park self-destructed, leaving only a large crater.

The Doctor met Afrikaaners during the Boer War and was at the battle of Roarke's Drift.[489]

1880 - EVOLUTION[490] **->** Percival Ross witnessed a Rutan scoutship crashing in Limehouse, and recovered a flask of Rutan healing salve from the wreckage. The alien gel had a miraculous healing effect on humans, but it also could merge human and animal genetic material, as Ross discovered when a boy he was treating became a ferocious dog-like creature. Ross interested the industrialist Breckingridge, the owner of a vast cable factory in the town of Bodhan, in the creation of a race of hybrid dolphin-men. Ross kidnapped fifteen children from the area, and conducted experiments that turned them into merchildren.

Breckingridge died when one of his mutated guard dogs

---

479 Dating *The Chase* - The emptied *Mary Celeste* was discovered in November 1872.
480 *The Curse of Fenric*
481 *The Stones of Blood*
482 *Pyramids of Mars*
483 *Doctor Who and the Pirates*. The Doctor says he "paced" Webb, which indicates he was swimming ahead of Webb to increase the man's pace rather than trying to defeat him.
484 Dating *Strange England* - The Doctor says that the "temporal location" is "1873" (p229).
485 *The Pirate Planet*. Bandraginus V disappeared "over a century" ago according to the Doctor, when the Zanak native Balaton was young. As Zanak is not capable of time travel, it must have been operating at least that long. The planets attacked by Zanak are named in

production documents, and plaques were made up with the names on... but only those for Bandraginus V, Granados, Lowiteliom and Calufrax are clearly visible on-screen. *First Frontier* gives a little more detail about Bandraginus V (p129).
486 *The Android Invasion*. Bell lived 1847-1922.
487 *Father's Day*. Bell's famous phone call occurred on 10th March, 1876.
488 Dating *Imperial Moon* - It's 'the year of our Lord 1878' (p7).
489 *Storm Warning*. Roarke's Drift occurred on 22nd to 23rd January, 1879.
490 Dating *Evolution* - It is the "year of grace eighteen hundred and eighty" (p6, p108). Arthur Conan Doyle lived 1859-1930, although *The Hound of the Baskervilles* - one of the later Holmes books - was written in 1902.

turned on him; Ross drowned. The Doctor relocated the mer-children to a water planet in the Andromeda Galaxy. A young Arthur Conan Doyle witnessed the happenings on Dartmoor, and his chance encounter with the Doctor inspired two of his most famous characters: Sherlock Holmes and Professor Challenger. An even younger Rudyard Kipling, future author of *The Jungle Book*, also witnessed the events surrounding the closure of Breckingridge's factory.

The Doctor 'borrowed' Conan Doyle's stethoscope and kept meaning to return it.[491] The Doctor met Geronimo.[492]

1881 (25th - 26th October) - THE GUNFIGHTERS[493] -> The TARDIS landed at Tombstone shortly before the Gunfight at the OK Corral. As the Doctor searched for a dentist, the gunman Johnny Ringo found one - Doc Holliday - who he'd been tracking for two years. Marshall Wyatt Earp and his allies killed Ringo and some members of the renegade Clanton family.

The Doctor warned General Custer against taking his Seventh Calvary over the ridge, but Custer ignored him.[494] **The Doctor met Gilbert and Sullivan.**[495] The Doctor claims to have inspired the *Mikado*, a comic operetta.[496] **He witnessed the eruption of Krakatoa.**[497] **The Rani kidnapped microbiologist Louis Pasteur.**[498]

Penelope Gate built herself a time machine using a miniature Analytical Engine. She left her husband in 1883 for a life of time travel. She first headed to the year 2000, actually landing in 1996. The Doctor returned Penelope to her native time after meeting her in feudal Japan.[499] In 1883, the Time Lord Marnal was exiled to Earth.[500]

There was a single account of a pocket of dinosaurs surviving on one plateau in Central Africa, but most scientists and reporters, including a young Arthur Conan Doyle, dismissed it as the ravings of a madman:

"**The pygmies from the Oluti Forest led me blindfold for three whole days through uncharted jungle. They took me to a swamp full of giant lizards, like giant dinosaurs.**"[501]

1883 - GHOST LIGHT[502] -> Rumours spread that Josiah Samuel Smith, arch-advocate of Darwinist theories, was conducting blasphemous experiments at his house Gabriel Chase to the north of London. Two years after Inspector Mackenzie vanished while investigating the goings-on at the house, Smith himself disappeared. Servants working in the house spoke of hauntings and mesmerism, apemen and angels, and a bizarre plot to assassinate Queen Victoria. The house remained abandoned for a century.

The Doctor knew "a nice little restaurant on the Khyber Pass".

In 1884, a book was published detailing many types of Amazonian fungus.[503]

1885 - TIMELASH[504] -> Vena, the daughter of a Councillor on Karfel, was transported to Earth in the timelash and met Herbert George Wells, who was conducting experiment with a ouija board. Wells travelled to Karfel with the Doctor, and the experience inspired him, upon his return home, to write his scientific romances.

Kipling lived 1865-1936, so he is "fifteen" here (p45).
491 *Storm Warning*. No date given, but the Doctor did meet him in *Evolution*. Conan Doyle lived 1859-1930.
492 *Storm Warning*. Geronimo lived 16th June, 1829 to 17th February, 1909.
493 Dating *The Gunfighters* - The story culminates with the Gunfight at the OK Corral. The depiction of events owes more to the popular myths and Hollywood treatment of the story than historical accuracy.
494 *Players* (p62), *Festival of Death*
495 *The Edge of Destruction*. Gilbert and Sullivan collaborated between 1875-1896.
496 *Doctor Who and the Pirates*
497 *Inferno, Rose*. The ninth Doctor also visited the scene. Krakatoa erupted in 1883.
498 *Time and the Rani*. Pasteur lived 1822-1895.
499 *The Room with No Doors*
500 *The Gallifrey Chronicles*
501 *Ghost Light*. It is unclear from the story whether the plateau really existed or was merely a delirious

Fenn-Cooper's rationalisation of his adventures in Gabriel Chase.
502 Dating *Ghost Light* - Set "two years" after 1881, when Mackenzie is sent to investigate the disappearance of Sir George Pritchard, and "a century" before Ace burns down Gabriel Chase in 1983. It's a time of year when the sun sets at six pm (so either the spring or autumn). The script suggested that a caption slide "Perivale - 1883" might be used over the establishing shot of Gabriel Chase. Queen Victoria was a Hanover, not a Saxe-Coburg, but late in her reign she did acquire the nickname "Mrs Saxe-Coburg".
503 *The Green Death*
504 Dating *Timelash* - The Doctor applies "a time deflection coefficient of 706 years" to the timelash's original destination of 1179, and concludes that Vena will arrive in "1885...AD". *The Terrestrial Index* set this in "c1891", after *The Time Machine* was written.

The Doctor helped "Bertie Wells" with invisibility experiments.[505] He discovered that HG Wells was a ladies man.[506] The Doctor met the mystic Madame Blavatsky.[507]

1887 - ALL-CONSUMING FIRE[508] -> Sherlock Holmes and Dr Watson were travelling through Austria on the Orient Express when the train was stopped by Pope Leo XIII. The Pope commissioned Holmes to investigate the theft of occult books from the Library of St John the Beheaded. With the Doctor's help, Holmes discovered that his eldest brother Sherringford had allied himself with the Baron Maupertuis. They planned to use incantations in the books to open a gateway to the planet of Ry'leh. Sherringford was under the thrall of the Great Old One named Azathoth, and hoped this would facilitate her escape to Earth. Maupertuis and Sherringford were both killed, and the Doctor transported Azathoth and her followers in 1906, where they also perished. The Doctor and Holmes sealed the portal to Ry'leh forever.

Arthur Conan Doyle would later write the book *All-Consuming Fire*, but it never saw print.

The Doctor told Ace that he met Sherlock Holmes.[509] **In 1888, the Doctor gained a medical degree in Glasgow under Lister.**[510] **Around that time, he sparred with John L Sullivan, the first modern world heavyweight champion.**[511] The Doctor discovered the truth behind the mysterious Pale Man in nineteenth century Whitechapel.[512]

1888 (30th September) - THE PIT[513] -> The Doctor and William Blake arrived in the East End at the time of the Jack the Ripper murders, before discovering a way to the late twentieth century.

The Doctor met Mark Twain.[514] In 1889, the Doctor and

Peri prevented the murder of a 24-year-old Winston Churchill, who was serving as a war correspondent in South Africa. The Doctor helped Churchill escape from a P.O.W. camp, and Churchill returned home a hero.[515]

c 1889 - THE TALONS OF WENG-CHIANG[516] -> The Doctor and Leela arrived in London during the middle of Li H'sen Chang's search for the Time Cabinet of Magnus Greel, a war criminal who had escaped the fifty-first century. Greel himself lurked in the sewers, reliant on draining the life force of young women to continue surviving. He had brought the Peking Homunculus with him to act as his agent. With the help of Professor Litefoot, an eminent pathologist, the Doctor tracked Magnus Greel to his lair and destroyed him and the Homunculus.

Human sacrifice was still taking place in Moreton Harwood in the early eighteen-nineties.[517] The Doctor met the French novelist Emile Zola.[518]

@ Compassion brought the Doctor to Earth to recuperate following Gallifrey's destruction. He woke up in a carriage with no memory of what had happened, and found he possessed a tiny cube, all that remained of his TARDIS.[519] The Doctor was found wandering and was placed on a hospital ward for five days.[520]

@ c 1889 (February) THE BURNING[521] -> The Doctor wandered England for a few years, still having no memories. He ended up in Middletown, just in time to investigate a mysterious geological fault. He realised that it was the home of a fire elemental that was in league with local developer, Roger Nepath. The Doctor blew up a dam, flooding the fault and extinguishing the elemental. The Doctor callously killed Nepath.

---

505 *The Ghosts of N-Space*
506 *Deadly Reunion*
507 Christmas on a Rational Planet. No date given, but Blavatsky lived 1831-1891.
508 Dating *All-Consuming Fire* - It is "the year eighteen eighty seven" according to both Watson (p5) and Benny (p153). References to *The Talons of Weng-Chiang* (p42, p64) suggest this book is set after that story, but aren't conclusive.
509 *Timewyrm: Revelation*. This was before *All-Consuming Fire*. The eighth Doctor also encountered Holmes, according to *The Gallifrey Chronicles*.
510 *The Moonbase*. Surgeon Joseph Lister lived 5th April, 1827, to 10th February, 1912.
511 *Carnival of Monsters*
512 *Synthespians*™
513 Dating *The Pit* - Blake sees a newspaper dated "the thirtieth of September, 1888". There's some indication

this takes place in a parallel timeline, so it's not 'the' Jack the Ripper murders.
514 *The Crooked World*
515 *Players*. The date is given (p15).
516 Dating *The Talons of Weng-Chiang* - No date is given, and the story is trying to encapsulate an era, rather than a precise year. The story is set soon after the Jack the Ripper murders (1888), as Henry Gordon Jago refers to "Jolly Jack". In the draft script, Casey went on to say that the new batch of disappearances can't be the Ripper because he "is in Canada".

The story takes place before *The Bodysnatchers*, and possibly *All-Consuming Fire* (although that only mentions Mr Sin, so might refer to earlier activities than this story).

Timelink states that it is 1895. Litefoot's reading a copy of *The Strand* from February 1892 (the issue with the Sherlock Holmes story 'The Adventure of the

By 1890, a retired William Chesterton had translated Ho Lin Chung's *Mountains and Sunsets* into English.[522] Ace was on the Red List of the Shadow Directory by 1892.[523] An advanced society on Duchamp 331 had built the Warp Core, an energy being, to combat the Krill. The Warp Core killed off the Krill and its creators also, reducing Duchamp 331 to a dust planet. The creature wandered through space and time before seeking refuge in the mind of the Norwegian artist Edvard Munch. He came to paint *The Scream*, which exorcised the Warp Core from his mind into the painting, where it remained trapped.[524]

1893 (July / August) - CAMERA OBSCURA[525] -> The Doctor and Sabbath both arrived in Victorian England after detecting disturbances in time. A faulty time machine, based on the principles of temporal interferometry, had splintered the stage magician Octave into eight individuals. Octave attacked the Doctor, who lived because Sabbath had placed the Doctor's second heart in his own chest, which tethered the Doctor to the living world. Sabbath's assassin, the Angel-Maker, killed Octave.

The Doctor discovered that the time machine had also twinned the insane psychologist Nathaniel Chiltern. One of the Nathaniels attempted to further use the machine, which threatened to puncture the space-time continuum, but the Doctor destroyed the device by flinging himself into it. Nathaniel killed the Angel-Maker, but was in turn was killed by Sabbath. By extension, this killed the other Nathaniel.

At this time, the Doctor, Fitz and Anji attended a séance. Also in attendance was a young man named William.[526]

1894 - TIME ZERO[527] -> Keen to be an adventurer in his own right, Fitz accompanied palaeontologist George Williamson on an expedition to Siberia. Tzar Alexander III was present when the expedition left Vladivostok. Fitz kept a diary of the journey.

Reptiles from another timeline attacked the expedition, killing everyone but Fitz and Williamson. A huge explosion encased the two of them in ice, where they would remain for over a hundred years. The Doctor and Williamson later averted the saurians' timeline by travelling to back 1894 and insuring that Williamson was killed rather than being trapped in ice. The billionaire Maxwell Curtis, travelling down a time corridor to this era from 2002, died in a minor explosion.

As a result of these events, an energy being from an o-region - a sort of isolated, mini-universe - was drawn to Earth. It would lodge in the past, and be worshipped by some cultures.

Marnal's first story, *The Giants*, was published in the *Strand* in 1894.[528]

1894 - THE BODYSNATCHERS[529] -> With the help of Professor Litefoot, the Doctor and Sam discovered that a series of grisly murders were part of a Zygon plot to conquer the world. The Doctor confronted Balaak, the Zygon leader, and accidentally killed some of the Zygons by poisoning their milk. The Zygons' pack of Skarasen threatened London until the Doctor lured them into the TARDIS. He relocated them and a Zygon survivor, Tuval, to an uninhabited planet.

As part of this adventure, the Doctor rescued a Mr Stoker from the Zygons.

Speckled Band') ... then again, there's also a modern newspaper visible at one point, so that should probably be considered set dressing rather than definitive dating evidence.

517 "Ninety years" before *K9 and Company*.

518 *Ghost Ship*. Zola lived 1840-1902.

519 *The Ancestor Cell, The Burning*. It's 'more than a hundred years' before 2001 (*The Ancestor Cell*, p282), and 'one hundred and thirteen years' before in *Escape Velocity* (p184), which would make it 1888.

520 *Vanishing Point*

521 Dating *The Burning* - It's 'a few years' since the Doctor arrived on Earth (p142). The most precise indication in the book is that it's 'the late nineteenth century'. It is 'fifty years' before *The Turing Test* (p59). The date was given as 1889 in the original story synopsis.

522 *The Eleventh Tiger*

523 *The Death of Art*

524 *Dust Breeding*. *The Scream* was painted in 1893.

525 Dating *Camera Obscura* - It's the 'nineteenth cen-

tury' (p6), Maskelyne (presumably the magician John Nevil Maskelyne, 1839-1917) is alive (p7) and it's a 'century' before Anji's time (p35). Fitz meets George Williamson, so this is before *Time Zero*.

526 *Camera Obscura*. William is the human version of Spike from *Buffy the Vampire Slayer*. However, the dating is awry - in *Buffy*, Spike became a vampire in 1880.

527 Dating *Time Zero* - This was in '1894' (p15).

528 *The Gallifrey Chronicles*. This is the same issue of the *Strand* the Doctor is looking for in *The Bodysnatchers*.

529 Dating *The Bodysnatchers* - It is "11.01.1894" (p15). It is six years since the Ripper murders (p2). It is five years since *The Talons of Weng Chiang* (p37). Mr. Stoker is quite possibly Bram Stoker, with the implication being that this adventure inspired his greatest work; *Dracula* was published in 1897, three years after this story takes place. Stoker lived 1847-1912.

@ In March 1895, the Doctor met George Bernard Shaw at a party hosted by Oscar Wilde. Around that time, Sherlock Holmes solved the McCarthy murders before the Doctor could.[530] The fourth Doctor claimed he was asked to be George the Sixth's godfather.[531]

1896 (10th November) - THE SANDS OF TIME[532] -> The Doctor, Tegan and Nyssa arrived in the Egyptian Room of the British Museum. At the invitation of Lord Kenilworth, they attended the unwrapping of an ancient mummy, only to discover that the mummy was the perfectly preserved body of Nyssa herself. The Doctor came to realise that the intelligence of the Osirian Nephthys was in Nyssa's body.

The Doctor thought that Bram Stoker was the greatest authority on vampires outside Gallifrey.[533]

1897 (November) - THE DEATH OF ART[534] -> The Doctor, Chris and Roz arrived in France to investigate a psychic disturbance. They encountered the Brotherhood, a secret society researching psychic activity. A man called Montague ruled one faction of the Brotherhood, but another, "the Family" were working against him. The outbreak of psychic powers was because the Quoth, multidimensional beings, had taken shelter in human brains. The Doctor sided with the Family against Montague, who was killed. The Doctor retrieved all the Quoth and took them to a new home in a neutron star.

1898 - THE BANQUO LEGACY[535] -> A scientist, Harris, built a machine that could share thoughts. He demonstrated it at Banquo Manor as the Doctor, Fitz and Compassion

arrived, trapped by a Time Lord device. A series of murders occurred at the Manor. The Doctor discovered that the butler, Simpson, was a Time Lord searching for Compassion. The Doctor unravelled the web of blackmail and murder involving Harris and his sister, Catherine. Simpson was thought killed, and the Doctor and his companions left before Simpson was missed by Gallifrey.

On 12th January, 1898, Florence Sundvig died. Mary Eliza Millington was born on 3rd March, dying four days later. At the end of the nineteenth century, the grandfather of Reverend Wainwright translated the Viking Runes in the crypt of his church.[536] The Doctor and Iris met Oscar Wilde in Venice after his imprisonment. They also fought some "fish people."[537]

The Twentieth Century

The Doctor was present at the Relief of Mafeking.[538] Battlefields from the Boxer Rising and the Boer War were lifted by the War Lords.[539]

1900 (December) - FOREIGN DEVILS[540] -> The Doctor followed Jamie and Zoe's passage through the 'spirit gate' in 1800, arriving exactly a hundred years later. The Chief Astrologer's curse started murdering the descendants of Roderick Upcott, and the Doctor teamed up with Carnacki, an investigator of the supernatural, to look into events at Upcott House. The curse used the spirit gate's dimensional energy to remove the house from time and space, and transformed Roderick Upcott's corpse into a dragon. The Doctor destroyed the spirit gate, which returned the house and made the dragon crumble to ash.

---

530 *The Gallifrey Chronicles*, a reference to Nicholas Meyer's novel *The West End Horror*, which features Shaw and Holmes.
531 *Wolfsbane*. George was born in 1895.
532 Dating *The Sands of Time* - The date is given (p29).
533 *Project: Twilight*
534 Dating *The Death of Art* - It's '26 November 1897' (p16).
535 Dating *The Banquo Legacy* - The date is given (p7).
536 *The Curse of Fenric*
537 *The Scarlet Empress*. Although never specified, the "fish people" could be the amphibious gondoliers that appear in Paul Magrs' *The Stones of Venice*. This meeting must have occurred after Wilde's release from prison on 19th May, 1897, but before his death on 30th November, 1900.
538 *The Daleks' Master Plan, The Invasion of Time*. This occurred on 17th May, 1900, when British troops ended the siege of Mafeking during the second Boer War.
539 *The War Games*. The Boer War ran from 1899-1902,

the Boxer Rising was in 1900.
540 Dating *Foreign Devils* - It's "December 1900" (p35).
541 *The Mind Robber*
542 *Byzantium!* (p179). No date given, but this was 6th September, 1901.
543 *Eye of Heaven*
544 Dating *Horror of Fang Rock* - The Terrance Dicks novelisation and contemporary publicity material set the story "at the turn of the century". Electric power was introduced to lighthouses around the turn of the century. Fang Rock is in the English Channel ("five or six miles" from Southampton) and is particularly treacherous, and was probably upgraded quite early on.
There's a reference to King Edward. As fan Alex Wilcock has noted, although the Doctor's style of dress is often referred to as 'Edwardian', this is the only story set in the Edwardian period (and there's not a frock coat to be seen). The young lighthouse worker Vince states that the Beast was last seen "eighty years ago", "back in the twenties". *The Programme Guide* offered the

In 1901, an English author began to write boy's stories for the magazine *The Ensign*.[541] The Doctor saw the assassination of President McKinley.[542] By 1902, there were Polynesian / alien hybrids on Easter Island again. They used the teleport device to resettle their forefathers' homeworld. The explorer Stockwood was still alive, and planned to return to the alien homeworld also.[543]

c 1902 - HORROR OF FANG ROCK[544] -> The Doctor and Leela arrived at Fang Rock lighthouse as a series of mysterious murders took place. The Doctor discovered the culprit was a Rutan scout, then destroyed the scout and its mothership.

Earth was now strategically important for the Rutans in their war with the Sontarans. According to the Doctor, the Rutans 'used to control the whole of the Mutters Spiral once'.

@ The Doctor drank absinthe in Prague, 1903.[545]

= The TARDIS' simultaneous arrival in 1903 and 2003 led to a massive disruption to the timelines. In 1903, the Doctor helped the English defeat the Daleks, who had attacked Central London. Only two Daleks survived and were taken captive. Political tensions still led to the first World War, but the British used the captured Dalek technology to seize control of the whole world. The British government locked the Doctor and Evelyn away in the Tower of London for propaganda purposes, and Evelyn consequently starved to death.[546]

1903 (December) - THE SLEEP OF REASON[547] -> The Sholem-Luz had developed as creatures that could

tunnel through the Time Vortex. They were attracted to mental turmoil as part of their life-cycle. In December 1903, a Sholem-Luz was drawn to Mausolus House, an asylum. The Sholem-Luz essence infected an Irish wolfhound, which became monstrous and triggered a series of murders. Joseph Sands, the nephew of a Mausolus House patient, slew the creature and burned its corpse in a fire that had started in a chapel on the grounds. The Doctor arrived through a time corridor from around 2004, and the second Sholem-Luz accompanying him also perished in the fire. Not wishing to relive the twentieth century over again, the Doctor went into suspended animation for about a hundred years.

Dr. Thomas Christie, the governor of Mausolus House, found a dog's tooth - all that remained of the Sholem-Luz - and fashioned a pendant from it. It would reappear a century later.

The National Foundation for Scientific Research, UK, originated as a group of private researchers that adopted the name and gained charity status after World War II. The organization eventually leased a house from Melanie Bush's great-uncle.[548] **The Doctor trained the Mountain Mauler of Montana.**[549]

The Doctor learned a great deal from Houdini.[550] He also learned sleight of hand from Maskelyne.[551]

The Kalarians turned Ockora into a holiday resort, hunting the native creatures for sport. They did not realise the Ockorans were intelligent.[552] An alien gave JM Barrie the idea for *Peter Pan*, based on a popular extraterrestrial story.[553]

@ The Doctor claimed to have chained Emmeline Pankhurst to the railings outside Number Ten Downing Street.[554] **The Doctor met Einstein.**[555]

---

date "1909", *The Terrestrial Index* claimed "1904". *The TARDIS Logs* suggested "c.1890", *The Doctor Who File* "early 1900s". *The TARDIS Special* gave the date "1890s". *Timelink* makes a convincing case for 1902, based on mumbled references to Salisbury and Bonar Law.

545 *The City of the Dead*

546 *Jubilee*

547 Dating *The Sleep of Reason* - We're told it's 'Thursday 24th December 1903' at the start of this section (p22).

548 One hundred years before *Catch-1782*.

549 *The Romans*

550 Mentioned in *Planet of Spiders, Revenge of the Cybermen, The Pit, Head Games, The Sorcerer's Apprentice, The Devil Goblins from Neptune, The Church and the Crown, Eye of Heaven* and *Independence Day*. There's no date given in any of those stories. Houdini lived from 1874-1926.

551 *The Ribos Operation*. No date is given, but this is

presumably the magician John Neville Maskelyne (1839-1917, and also mentioned in *Camera Obscura*), although it could be his grandson, the magician Jasper Maskelyne (1902-1973).

552 'Centuries' before *The Murder Game, The Final Sanction*.

553 *The Tomorrow Windows*. *Peter Pan* was published in 1905.

554 *Casualties of War*. Pankhurst was a founder of the British suffragette movement. She was chained to Number Ten in 1905.

555 *The Stones of Blood*. No date given. Einstein lived 1879-1955, publishing his Special and General Theories of Relativity in 1905 and 1915 respectively.

= **1906 (24th December) - THE CHIMES OF MIDNIGHT**[556] **->** The Doctor and Charley discovered the inhabitants of an Edwardian manor house were trapped in a time-loop. The servants were brutally murdered, but at midnight time would roll back two hours and the process would repeat itself. The Doctor learned that the house had become imprinted with the murders and that Edith Thompson - one of the servants - would later work for the Pollard family. Edith had killed herself in 1930 upon learning of Charley's death in the R-101 accident, but Charley's paradoxical arrival in 1906 left history confused as to whether Edith would have cause to kill herself or not. The Doctor decisively talked Edith out of killing herself, which ended the time-loop.

Azathoth and her army of Rakshassi creatures were destroyed in the San Francisco earthquake of 1906, following the Doctor's intervention.[557] In 1906, the vampire Weird Harold was buried alive in the San Francisco earthquake.[558]

1909 (February - 24 April) - BIRTHRIGHT[559] **->** The secret society the New Dawn, led by Jared Khan, attempted to stabilise the Great Divide with the future and bring the Chaarl back to this time. Some Chaarl broke through and murdered a number of people in the East End. The Doctor's TARDIS time-rammed itself to stop Khan's plans, and half of the Ship - with Khan's mind inside - fell through time to June 1908 and exploded in the wastes of Tunguska in Siberia. It disintegrated on impact; historians attributed this event to a meteorite strike. The Chaarl were trapped in one of the surviving TARDIS' inner dimensions.

The third Doctor, Jo Grant and Liz Shaw watched the Tunguska explosion in 1908.[560] The Doctor witnessed Earth tremors in Peru in 1910.[561]

1911 - PYRAMIDS OF MARS[562] **->** The Doctor and Sarah landed at the Old Priory, on the future site of UNIT HQ. They discovered that the servants of Sutekh were planning to release him from his imprisonment. The Doctor trapped Sutekh in a time corridor, eventually destroying him.

1911, according to the Doctor is 'an excellent year, one of my favourites'.[563] The Nine Travellers were surveyed in 1911.[564] The King's Regulations were published in 1912.[565] The Royal Flying Corps was formed in 1912.[566]

= A historical deviation caused colleagues of the self-sacrificing Captain Oates to drag him back to camp, where they died together.[567]

The Titanic sank, although the Doctor claimed that he had nothing to do with that ...[568]

The ninth Doctor warned the Daniels family not to board the Titanic and was photographed with them. However, he boarded the ship, and ended up clinging to an iceberg.[569]

1912 (14th April) - THE LEFT-HANDED HUMMINGBIRD[570] **->** On the sinking Titanic, the seventh Doctor prevented Huitzilin - also called the Blue - from acquiring the Xiuhcoatl, an Exxilon weapon capable of manipulating molecules. It could transmute or destroy matter. Huitzilin manifested but was killed.

---

556 Dating The Chimes of Midnight - The date is given.
557 All-Consuming Fire
558 Vampire Science
559 Dating Birthright - It is 'Thursday 15 April 1909' on p23, and Benny has been stranded 'two months' (p24) by then. She departs on '24 April' (p203). Page 202 cites the meteorite strike's historic date of 30th June, 1908.
560 The Wages of Sin
561 The English Way of Death (p46).
562 Dating Pyramids of Mars - Laurence Scarman gives the date as 'nineteen hundred and eleven'.
563 Pyramids of Mars. Assuming the Doctor is being serious, this suggests he has visited 1911 before now.
564 The Stones of Blood
565 The War Games
566 Ghost Light
567 The Algebra of Ice (p13). Oates died 17th March, 1912.
568 The Doctor mentions the Titanic in Robot, but tells

Borusa in The Invasion of Time that "it had nothing to do with me".
569 Rose, The End of the World.
570 Dating The Left-Handed Hummingbird - The story takes place on the Titanic, and the date is confirmed on p221.
571 Neverland. She was eighteen years, five months and twenty-one days old when she met the Doctor, according to The Chimes of Midnight.
572 'Eighty five' years before The Dying Days (p175).
573 'Some fifty years' before Winter for the Adept.
574 Just War
575 Lungbarrow, Vampire Science
576 Silver Nemesis
577 Dating Human Nature - It is "April" (p17) '1914' (p16).
578 Matrix
579 Project: Twilight. We're told that Amelia, 'twilight seven' was created on 12th September, 1914.

Charley Pollard was born on 14th April, 1912, the day the *Titanic* sank.[571] Xznaal, an Ice Lord, was struck by the state of the withered plant life on his home planet of Mars.[572] Around 1913, Harding Wellman died while mountaineering in Switzerland.[573]

The Doctor saved St Peter Port from some terrible threat on Halloween 1913. He could not save the life of young Celia Doras.[574] The Doctor and Ace both independently visited the premiere of the ballet *The Rites of Spring* in 1913.[575]

The First World War

The Nemesis statue passed over the Earth in 1913, heralding the First World War.[576]

1914 - HUMAN NATURE[577] **->** In the tiny village of Farringham, Doctor John Smith of Aberdeen fell in love with Joan Redfern. Somewhere in the sky overhead, for an instant before they dissolved into mist, two snowflakes were the same.

> = The dormant Dark Matrix was woken by the carnage of the Battle of Mons. The British Expeditionary Force saw the form of Jack the Ripper over the battlefield.[578]

The Forge, a secret project to improve the stock of soldiers, experimented on prisoners to create a race of 'twilight vampires'. On 14th October, 1914, the vampires overpowered their creator, Dr Abberton, and fled. Abberton took the vampire formula to survive his wounds, and became known as Nimrod.[579]

In 1914, Manuel Gamio discovered a part of the Great Temple of the Aztecs.[580]

1915 (7th May) - THE SIRENS OF TIME[581] **->** The Doctor was on a merchant ship that was torpedoed by a U-boat. He was captured and posed as a German secret agent. He escaped shortly before the U-boat torpedoed the RMS *Lusitania*. The Doctor failed to save the *Lusitania*, but in doing so prevented the future murder of Alexander Fleming, the discoverer of penicillin. Without it, the world would have suffered from plagues and fallen prey to the Second Velyshaan Empire.

1915 (August) - WHITE DARKNESS[582] **->** The Doctor, Benny and Ace arrived in Haiti as a civil rebellion against President Sam started. Lemaitre, an ancient man working on behalf of the Great Old Ones, was raising an army of zombies. They planned to open a gateway from their realm to Earth, and to conquer Europe. The Doctor destroyed Lemaitre and his base with a bomb.

In 1915, Mr Sun was imprisoned for killing a professor of economics, who was later revealed as an Austrian spy.[583] Arthur Kendrick distinguished himself by second-guessing the U-boat commanders on the Atlantic convoys. He would serve as an Admiral in World War II.[584] **Professor Travers began his search for the Yeti.**[585]

1915 (18th November) - PLAYERS[586] **->** The Doctor arrived in No Man's Land using a Time Ring. He saved Winston Churchill from an ambush engineered by two Players, the Count and the Countess. The next day, he saved Churchill again, this time with the help of Jeremy Carstairs and Jennifer Buckingham. Carstairs joined Churchill's staff. The Doctor escaped a German firing squad by using the Time Ring.

The scientist Nikita Kuznetzov saw the devastation at Tunguska.[587]

The Somme

The Battle of the Somme took place on 14th July, 1916. Richard Hadleman survived, treated by Timothy Dean, a former student of Dr John Smith of Aberdeen.[588] Lance Corporal Weeks, later the chief steward aboard the *R-101*, fought at the Somme.[589] Roger Gleave, a future police inspector, witnessed the devastation.[590]

1916 (December) - THE WAGES OF SIN[591] **->** The Doctor, Jo Grant and Liz Shaw arrived in St. Petersburg as members of the city's elite, concerned about Father Grigori Rasputin's growing influence over Empress Czarina Alexandra, conspired to murder him. Jo befriended Rasputin and saved him from death by poisoning, but the conspirators repeatedly shot and beat Rasputin, still failing to kill him. The conspirators finally had Rasputin thrown into a frozen river. The Doctor refrained from action as

---

580 *The Left-Handed Hummingbird* (p58).
581 Dating *The Sirens of Time* - The date is given.
582 Dating *White Darkness* - 'On the wall, a calendar of 1915 had just been turned to the August page' (p22).
583 *The Cabinet of Light* (p85).
584 *Just War*
585 'Twenty years' before *The Abominable Snowman*.
586 Dating *Players* - The date is given (p69).

587 *The Wages of Sin*
588 *Human Nature*
589 *Storm Warning*
590 *Eater of Wasps*
591 Dating *The Wages of Sin* - The date is given (p21). *Zagreus* confirms that the Doctor has met Rasputin.

Rasputin drowned, fulfilling history. Six weeks later, the Russian Revolution overthrew Tsar Nicholas II.

1917 - THE ROOF OF THE WORLD[592] -> Lord Davey discovered an alien pyramid in the Himalayas when his expedition was wiped out in a storm. He was killed and replaced with a doppelganger. The Doctor, Peri and Erimem arrived in Darjeeling, where Erimem met Davey and was possessed by the same force. Meeting a friend of his, the Doctor was surprised to learn that Davey was meant to be far away on an expedition. A black cloud descended, killing dozens of people ... including Erimem. The Doctor deduced this was an attempt on the part of the Great Old Ones to take control of the world, and that Erimem was still alive. Peri froze the cloud with liquid nitrogen. The pyramid was buried beneath an avalanche.

On 16th April, 1917, the Doctor and Lenin played tiddlywinks on the train journey that returned Lenin from Switzerland to Russia. After that, the Doctor met Empress Alexandra.[593] The Doctor was present in Russia during the October Revolution, met Lenin and became a Hero of the Revolution.[594] **The first Doctor and Susan were caught in a Zeppelin raid at some point during the war.[595] A First World War battlefield near Ypres was kidnapped by the War Lords.[596] The Doctor once claimed to have been wounded at the Battle of Gallipoli.[597]** Burton, later

a camp leader at Shangri-La in 1959, fought in the War using his sabre in hand-to-hand combat.[598] The Toymaker kidnapped two British soldiers from Ypres.[599]

Turkish soldiers during the First World War claimed to have seen The Ark of Ages on Mount Ararat.[600] The Doctor saw the Battle of Passchendale.[601] The Doctor met the noted sailor Felix von Luckner.[602]

In 1917, Reginald Tyler started writing the fantasy epic *The True History of Planets* while on leave from soldiering in France.[603] Brigadier General Tamworth was part of the Versailles delegation, and foresaw that reparations against Germany would further a bigger conflict.[604]

@ 1918 - CASUALTIES OF WAR[605] -> The Doctor investigated reports of the walking dead in Hawkswick in Yorkshire. Befriending the village midwife, Mary Minnett, he discovered that the creatures were being created by the traumatic memories of wounded soldiers convalescing at Hawkswick Hall. The Doctor caused a psychic backlash, destroying the hall and the man behind it - the head of the hospital, Dr Banham.

@ The Doctor kept the last letter Mary wrote to him (on 22nd August, 1918).[606]

An influenza epidemic in 1918 and 1919 killed more people than the Great War itself.[607] An agent of the Bureau arrived from the future (circa 2386) and adopted the name Percival Closed.[608]

---

592 Dating *The Roof of the World* - It's 1917 according to the back cover. The Great Old Ones in *The Roof of the World* bear no apparent relation to the pantheon of higher powers of the same name seen throughout *Doctor Who*.
593 *Storm Warning*
594 *The Devil Goblins from Neptune*
595 *Planet of Giants*
596 *The War Games*
597 *The Sea Devils*
598 *Delta and the Bannerman*
599 *Divided Loyalties*
600 *Eternity Weeps*
601 *Byzantium!, The King of Terror*
602 *The Empire of Death.* Luckner lived 1881-1966.
603 *Mad Dogs and Englishmen*
604 *Storm Warning.* The Treaty of Versailles was signed 28th June, 1919.
605 Dating *Casualties of War* - The date is given (p7).
606 *Eater of Wasps*
607 *Birthright, Casualties of War*
608 'Twelve years' before *The English Way of Death* (p83).
609 *Matrix*
610 Dating *Toy Soldiers* - The main action of the book starts "25 September 1919" (p39).

611 *Aliens of London.* No date is given, but Lloyd George was Prime Minister 1916-1922.
612 *The Roundheads*
613 *Dying in the Sun*
614 *The Scales of Injustice*, referencing the Audio Visuals play *Endurance*.
615 Dating *The Daleks' Master Plan* - The script for Part Seven, "The Feast of Steven," specified a date of "1919," but publicity material released on 1st October, 1965, stated that the TARDIS lands in "California 1921." The film being made is a talkie, which means this must be after the release of *The Jazz Singer* in 1927. Numerous Hollywood personalities are seen or hinted at in the episode. Actor Rudolph Valentino made his debut in 1914 but was only really famous after *The Sheik* in 1921. Actor Douglas Fairbanks Sr. debuted in 1915, but he wasn't "big" (as he is described in the episode) until *The Three Musketeers* in 1921. Chaplin's debut was 1914, but the film we see in production strongly resembles *Gold Rush* (1924). Bing Crosby didn't go to Hollywood until 1930. *DWM* writer Richard Landen claimed a date of "1929," *The TARDIS Special* offered "c.1920."
616 *The Wages of Sin*
617 Angus relates the story in *Terror of the Zygons*.
618 According to Commander Millington, the accident happened "over twenty years" before *The Curse of*

= In the world of the Dark Matrix, the Jack the Ripper killings started again after the Great War. Ghostly Rippers begin terrorising London. There was mass panic, despite summary executions for suspects. The government withdrew to Edinburgh.[609]

1919 (late September) - TOY SOLDIERS[610] **->**
Investigating the mysterious disappearance of children across post-War Europe, the Doctor, Benny, Roz and Chris discovered that they had been kidnapped by the Recruiter, a device transporting beings from many worlds to act as soldiers in the fourteen-hundred-year war that had ravaged the planet Q'ell. The Recruiter had been built to destroy the Ceracai race, but the Doctor reprogrammed it to rebuild the devastated planet.

The Doctor drank with Lloyd George when he was Prime Minister.[611]

The Nineteen Twenties

The Doctor acquired a copy of the 1920 book *Every Boy's Book of the English Civil War*. He would later lose it in 1648.[612] The Doctor met movie producer Harold Reitman in England in the twenties.[613]

During the twenties, a Silurian shelter was discovered. UNIT would investigate it in the 1970s.[614]

c 1921 - THE DALEKS' MASTER PLAN[615] **->** While hiding from the Daleks, the TARDIS landed briefly on a film set in Hollywood.

The Russian mineralogist Leonid A Kulik visited the area of the Tunguska explosion in 1921, but failed to locate the impact site.[616] **In 1922, a foreigner staying at Tullock Inn vanished on Tullock Moor, kidnapped by the Zygons.**[617] **Dr Judson was crippled before this time.**[618]

1923 (9th November) - TIMEWYRM: EXODUS[619] **->**
The Doctor and Ace witnessed the Munich Putsch, an attempted coup organised by a young Adolf Hitler, so the Doctor could gain Hitler's confidence and sway events in future. The time travellers were fired upon by a man with energy weapons - the War Chief, who was operating in this era to aid the Nazis - but the Doctor failed to recognize him.

In 1923, George Limb, a member of military intelligence, wanted the British to side with Hitler. He failed to convince his superiors.[620]

@ The Doctor studied Ba Chai in Peking, the 1920s.[621]

1925 (11th June) - BLACK ORCHID[622] **->** The explorer George Cranleigh was believed killed by Indians while on an expedition in the Amazon in 1923. Cassell and Company published his book *Black Orchid*. George's fiancée, Anne Talbot, eventually became engaged to his brother Charles. Yet George hadn't died. The Kajabi Indians had horribly disfigured George because he stole their sacred black orchid, but the chief of a rival tribe rescued him. George was kept hidden away at Cranleigh Hall. He later broke out, and died trying to abduct his former fiancée.

A famous author of boys' stories for *The Ensign* magazine vanished at his home in 1926.[623] **On 4th June, 1926, the SS *Bernice* inexplicably vanished in the Indian Ocean. The ship had left England in early May, and the last anyone ever saw of it was on 2nd June, when it left Bombay.**[624]

In 1927, the Doctor watched the Cuban grandmaster Capablanca play chess.[625]

= **1927 - REAL TIME**[626] **->** The Cybermen succeeded in infecting Earth with a techno-virus that transformed living beings into cybernetic ones. Most of the

---

Fenric, and Judson appears to blame Millington for it. The novelisation, also written by Ian Briggs, confirms that Millington was culpable.

619 Dating *Timewyrm: Exodus* - Part Two of the novel is set during the Munich Putsch, which took place between the 8th and 9th of November 1923. A textbook quoted in the novel erroneously gives the month as "September" (p95).

620 *Illegal Alien*

621 *To the Slaughter*

622 Dating *Black Orchid* - The Doctor says it is 'three o'clock, June the eleventh, nineteen hundred and twenty-five'.

623 *The Mind Robber*

624 *Carnival of Monsters*. The Doctor has heard of the disappearance of the SS *Bernice*, but we see it vanish from the miniscope and apparently return to its native time at the end of Part Four. Perhaps the ship didn't arrive home safely after all. Alternatively, perhaps the Doctor's actions alter history, although this would make for something of a paradox.

625 *The Androids of Tara*. José Raúl Capablanca y Graupera lived 1888-1942. He spent six years as a world chess champion, ending in 1927.

626 Dating *Real Time* - Dr. Goddard identifies the date of Cyber-infection in Episode Five, Track 1.

human race died from shock, and all animals perished. The cybernetic survivors fell under Cybermen domination.

Evelyn Smythe was reportedly the virus' original carrier, having travelled back to this year after being infected in 3286.

The Doctor met Dame Nellie Melba, a noted Australian opera soprano, and learned her party piece: how to shatter glass with your voice.[627] **The Doctor met Sigmund Freud and knew Marie Curie intimately. He met Pucchini**[628] in Milan.[629] Puccini had a terrible cold.[630]

@ The Doctor had sessions with Freud, hoping to jog his memory.[631] He told Freud that he had a phobia of silverfish.[632]

The Doctor watched Babe Ruth hit three home runs for the Yankees in 1926.[633] The Doctor owned a copy of *Wisden's Almanac* from 1928.[634]

Aaron Blinovitch formulated his Limitation Effect in 1928, publishing it in *Temporal Mechanics*.[635]

1929 - BLOOD HARVEST[636] **->** As gangland violence escalated in Chicago, the enigmatic Doc McCoy opened a speakeasy right in the middle of disputed territory. The Doc and his moll Ace saved Al Capone's life. The Doctor was tracking down the eternal being Agonal, who had amplified the gang warfare to feed his lust for violence.

The vampire Yarven travelled to Earth from E-Space aboard the Doctor's TARDIS.

Yarven became a progenitor of many of Earth's vampires. Villagers in Croatia overpowered and buried him alive, and he would remain trapped until 1993.[637] **The Brigadier's car, a Humber 1650 Open Tourer Imperial Model, was built in 1929.**[638] The Canavatchi engineered the Wall Street Crash of October 1929 to hinder mankind's development.[639]

Lord Tamworth witnessed the arrival of the Engineer Prime of the telepathic Triskele on Earth. He was promoted to "Minister of Air," and oversaw preparations to use the *R-101* airship to return the Engineer Prime to its people.[640]

The Nineteen Thirties

Alistair Gordon Lethbridge-Stewart was born.[641]

Lethbridge-Stewart would later attend Holborough with Teddy 'Pooh' Fitzoliver.[642] **The Urbankans began to receive radio signals from Earth.**[643] **The Doctor met the cricket player Donald Bradman, and once took five wickets for New South Wales.**[644]

During the 1930s, the League of Nations set up a secret international organisation, LONGBOW, to deal with matters of world security. It found itself, on occasion, dealing with unexplained and extraterrestrial phenomena.[645] The Doctor discussed the theoretical Philosopher's Stone (not the Khamerian-created one) with psychiatrist Carl Jung.[646]

The Silurian Triad was revived. These were Ichtar, Scibus and science advisor Tarpok.[647] In the 1930s, the Doctor and his friend Ernest Hemingway ran with the bulls in Pamplona. A matador named Manolito trained the

---

627 *The Power of Kroll.* Dame Nellie Melba lived 1861-1931.
628 *Doctor Who - The Movie.* and it's possible these encounters were all on the same visit: Freud lived 1865-1939, Marie Curie 1867-1934, and Puccini 1858-1924. The only date given is that the Doctor was with Puccini shortly before he died.
629 *The Devil Goblins from Neptune*
630 *Relative Dementias.* This is possibly a misremembering of *Doctor Who - The Movie.* The Doctor name-dropped Puccini in that story, but it was Leonardo da Vinci who had the cold.
631 *The City of the Dead*
632 *Grimm Reality*
633 *Illegal Alien* (p83).
634 *Phantasmagoria*
635 The Blinovitch Limitation Effect was first mentioned in *Day of the Daleks* (and subsequently in *Invasion of the Dinosaurs* and *Mawdryn Undead*). We learn more about Blinovitch in *The Ghosts of N-Space* (p147) and *Timewyrm: Revelation* (p50).
636 Dating *Blood Harvest* - The blurb states it is 1929. The book is set during Prohibition (1919-1933 in America), but while Al Capone is at liberty. In May 1929,

Capone was sentenced to prison time for carrying a concealed weapon, so *Blood Harvest* must occur before that. He saw release in 1930, but his more infamous conviction on tax evasion charges happened in 1931.
637 *Goth Opera*
638 His student Ibbotson, nicknamed Hippo, identifies the car in *Mawdryn Undead*.
639 *The King of Terror* (p179).
640 'One night last winter' before *Storm Warning*.
641 Clearly, the exact date of the future Brigadier Lethbridge-Stewart's birth depends on when the UNIT stories take place. He is "sixty three" in the 1993 of *Blood Heat*; "forty six" in the 1976 of *No Future* and "twenty one" in 1951 in *The Devil Goblins of Neptune* - all of which point to a date of 1930, but which also set the UNIT stories in their year of broadcast. He's "seventy one" in 1999 and "one hundred and twenty one" in 2050 according to *The King of Terror* (which would mean he was born in 1928). Nicholas Courtney, who plays the Brigadier, was born in 1931.

However, some recent books seem to make the Brigadier several years older. According to *Deadly Reunion*, he saw active service during World War Two and was age 21 in 1944 (p115), meaning he was born in

Doctor in the basics of his art.[648]

The people of Parakon discovered rapine, a crop that when processed could be used as a foodstuff or a building material. For the next forty years, the Corporation that marketed rapine ruled the planet unopposed, supplanting nations, governments, armies and all competition.[649]

? 1930 - THE WORMERY[650] -> On a planet affected by a dimensional nexus point, worms evolved with the ability to see their own future. Appalled at the sight of themselves turning into hairy, complex beings, the worms divided into an "anti faction" and "pro faction" to derail their future. The "anti" group sought to turn the universe into total chaos, which would prevent development of any type. The "pro" group allied with the club singer Bianca, hoping to freeze the universe in a single perfect moment. Additionally, a group of shadow beings - the potential future selves of the worms, currently held in a state of flux - searched for a means of becoming corporeal.

By now, the nightclub named "Bianca's" existed in a dimensional nexus, accessible via special taxis that shuttled patrons through dimensional portals. The club was actually Iris Wildthyme's TARDIS, with its exterior looking like 1930s Berlin.

The Doctor and Iris arrived separately at Bianca's, and exposed Bianca as the embodiment of Iris' darker natures. The two worm factions, plus their shadow selves, each searched for a means of exploiting the club's extra-dimensional nature to their advantage. The Doctor used his TARDIS to Time-Ram the nightclub, which severed its dimensional links and returned its patrons to their native times. This defeated the worms and their shadows, and transferred the wreckage of the club to Berlin. Bianca escaped.

1930

1930 (June) - THE ENGLISH WAY OF DEATH[651] -> The TARDIS arrived in London during an inexplicable heatwave, as the Doctor needed to return some library books before they became overdue. He and Romana stumbled upon a group from the thirty-second century (the Bureau) that were using time corridor technology to send retired people to the English village of Nutchurch. While the Doctor put a stop to that, Romana confronted the sentient smell Zodaal, an exiled would-be conqueror from the planet Vesur. Zodaal was trapped in a flask, and the device that would have destroyed Earth was deactivated.

Around 1930, the fourth Doctor visited Tigella and saw the Dodecahedron.[652]

1930 (5th October) - STORM WARNING[653] -> The TARDIS landed on the doomed airship *R-101* during its maiden voyage. Aboard the ship, the Doctor discovered Charley Pollard, a stowaway. Lord Tamworth, a government minister, ordered the ship to a higher altitude and it docked with an alien vessel. The British had arranged to return a crashed alien to its own people, the Triskele. A faction of the Triskele became aggressive when the Lawgiver that kept them in check died. The Doctor eased the situation, and Tamworth agreed to stay with the Triskele as an advisor. The *R-101* was damaged upon its return, and the Doctor and Charley only just escaped as the ship crashed in France. The Doctor realised that Charley was meant to have died in the crash.

1930 (31st December) - SEASONS OF FEAR[654] -> The immortal Sebastian Grayle found the Doctor and Charley in Singapore, and boasted that he'd already killed the Doctor in the past. The Doctor set about investigating the matter, heading for Britain in 305 AD.

either 1922 or 1923. Barry Letts, who based some of the Brigadier's wartime experience on his own activities with the British Navy, was born in 1925.

642 *The Paradise of Death* (p25).

643 *Four to Doomsday*

644 *Four to Doomsday*. No date given. Donald Bradman was born in 1908, playing for Australia from 1928-1948.

645 *Just War*

646 *Option Lock*. No date given. Jung lived 26th July, 1875, to 6th June, 1961.

647 'Around forty years' before *The Scales of Injustice*.

648 *Deadly Reunion*. No date given. Hemingway lived 1898-1961.

649 "Forty years" before *The Paradise of Death* (p131).

650 Dating *The Wormery* - It is some point in 'the thir-

ties'.

651 Dating *The English Way of Death* - The date is given (p23).

652 'Fifty years' before *Meglos*.

653 Dating *Storm Warning* - It is stated that it is 'early in October 1930', and the *R-101* really began its maiden flight on 4th October, 1930. The date is confirmed in *Minuet in Hell* and *Neverland*. According to *The Chimes of Midnight*, Charley was born the day the *Titanic* sank, 14th April, 1912, and was eighteen years, five months and twenty-one days old when she met the Doctor, making it the 5th of October.

654 Dating *Seasons of Fear* - The play starts with the Doctor saying it's the 'cusp of the years 1930 and 1931'.

The Doctor fought in the Spanish Civil War with the father of future bar owner Gustavo Riviera. Later, he brought Gustavo to refuge in Ibiza.[655]

1933

Otto Kreiner moved from Germany to England, soon meeting and marrying Muriel Tarr. They would become the parents of the Doctor's companion Fitz.[656]

@ The Doctor spent much of 1933 in the South Seas, and claimed to have gotten a tattoo there. By this time, he had a criminal record in England.[657] While in the South Seas, he saw magic performed.[658] He served about the ship *Sarah Gail*, where he learned to play the violin[659] and read a report of wasps attacking a train outside Arandale.[660] At some point, he visited Australia and Hangchow.[661]

1933 (August) - EATER OF WASPS[662] **->** An alien device from the future was accidentally dropped into a wasps' nest, causing the wasps to mutate into killers. A trio of Time Agents arrived to find the device. The Doctor, Fitz and Anji also arrived at this time. The Time Agents decided to sterilise the area with a nuclear explosion. The Doctor found the mutagenic device and smashed it, and also disarmed the Agents' nuclear weapon.

By 1933, Germany had become aware that werewolves existed. Such non-humans were ordered to register with the government, and werewolves loyal to the party were reportedly used to sense dissenters. Several werewolves were rounded up and incarcerated in a special camp, equipped with silver wire, for a year. A man from the Schutzstaffel (the Nazi Party's "praetorian guard") arrived and pressed the desperate werewolves into the service of the state.[663]

In 1933, Cuevas discovered a part of the Great Temple of the Aztecs.[664]

1934

1934 - THE EYE OF THE GIANT[665] **->** The *Constitution III* was beached upon an uncharted island of Salutua in the South Pacific. Among the passengers was Marshal J Grover, the millionaire shipping magnate and owner of Paragon Film Studios.

The Doctor and Liz Shaw arrived at the island using a

---

655 *The Rapture*
656 *Frontier Worlds*
657 *Eater of Wasps*
658 *Mad Dogs and Englishmen*
659 *The Year of Intelligent Tigers*
660 *Eater of Wasps*
661 *History 101*. This was possibly during his second bout of world travelling in the sixties and seventies.
662 Dating *Eater of Wasps* - The Doctor estimates 'it is probably the 1930s. If pushed, I'd have to say 1933. Twenty-seventh of August in fact' (p10).
663 *Wolfsbane* (p90) gives the date of the werewolf Emmeline's capture as 1933.
664 *The Left-Handed Hummingbird* (p58).
665 Dating *The Eye of the Giant* - 'The time is the eighth of June, nineteen thirty-four' (p42).
666 *The King of Terror* (p103).
667 *Wolfsbane*. Page 93 says the werewolves were taken from the camp on 29th June, 1934; the hotel slaughter occurred the following evening. Historically, Hitler moved against Roehm and his Sturmabetilung because they could have staged a *coup d'etat*. He ordered the Sturmabetilung leaders to congregate at the Hanselbauer Hotel in Bad Wiesse near Munich, which is where the massacre in *Wolfsbane* evidently takes place. The purge is sometimes referred to as "The Night of the Long Knives".
668 *The Highest Science* (p257).
669 Dating *The Abominable Snowmen* - According to the Doctor, this story takes place "three hundred years" after events that the monk Thonmi says took place in "1630". In *The Web of Fear*, Anne Travers claims that the Travers Expedition took place in "1935". In *Downtime*, Charles Bryce says it was "1936" (p65).
670 *Just War*
671 *The Ancestor Cell* (p126), based on the writers' guidelines. He was 'twenty seven' in *The Taint*. His year of birth is "1935" in *Escape Velocity*. He celebrates his birthday on 7th March in *Interference*.
672 *Divided Loyalties*
673 According to an early format document for the series, dating from July 1963, Ian is "27". Then again, William Russell certainly looks older than that on-screen.
674 *The Mind of Evil*. The Long March was a massive retreat on the part of the Chinese Communist Army to elude the Kuomintang Army. It granted the Communists a needed respite in the north of China.
675 Dating *Wolfsbane* - Harry is abandoned on 27th November, 1936, according to p24. Harry's fate is left ambiguous due to the presence of multiple timelines, which were finally compressed to one history in *Timeless*. *Sometime Never* says the Council of Eight had a hand in engineering Harry's "death".
676 Dating *Wolfsbane* - It's 11th December, 1936 (p49).
677 *Grimm Reality*
678 Dating *Players* - The date is given (p150).

time bridge portal, and discovered a spacecraft in a volcanic crater. Animal and plant life on the island was subject to gigantism: giant crabs roamed the beach, bats the size of men flew at night, and the forest was hypertrophied. The Doctor discovered that drugs created by the Semquess, the most skilled bio-engineers in the galaxy, were responsible for the mutations. The drugs had been brought to Earth fifty years before by Brokk of the Grold. The Semquess had tracked him to the planet, and now they apparently destroyed him. Brokk, though, used the properties of the Semquess drug to merge with Grover's young wife Nancy and leave the Earth.

The Doctor pursued the Master across Berlin, and met Himmler and the future "Butcher of Prague," Reinhold Heydrich.[666] On 30th June, 1934, the German-imprisoned werewolves were unleashed at a hotel housing men loyal to Ernst Roehm's Sturmabetilung ("Storm Division," AKA stormtroopers). One of the werewolves, Emmeline Neuberger, bit a silver chain around a man's neck and was rendered unconscious. She was subsequently overlooked, and escaped into the German woods.[667]

1935

The Doctor and Bernice failed to meet Virginia Woolf and went to the theatre instead. In the audience was twenty-fifth century explorer Gustaf Heinrich Urnst, who had been transported there by a Fortean Flicker.[668]

1935 - THE ABOMINABLE SNOWMEN[669] -> The Doctor, Jamie and Victoria arrived in the Himalayas. They found that the Yeti were menacing a local monastery and an expedition led by Professor Travers. The Yeti were robots built on behalf of the Intelligence - a powerful being of pure thought that attempted to manifest physically. The Doctor banished it from Earth.

1936

The Doctor and Mel met German racing driver Emil Hartung in Cairo. The Doctor accidentally inspired Hartung to develop aircraft that could avoid radar detection. Hartung won the Cairo 500 thanks to the modifications the Doctor made to his car.[670]

Fitz Kreiner was born in Hampstead on 7th March, 1936.[671] Sir Henry Rugglesthorpe and his family become playthings of the Toymaker.[672]

Ian Chesterton was born.[673] In October of that year, the Doctor joined Mao Tse-Tung on the Long March.[674]

@ 1936 (November) WOLFSBANE[675] -> By now the eighth Doctor had returned to England, and been rejected several times after submitting short stories to *Astounding Stories* magazine.

Harry Sullivan disembarked to explore when the TARDIS stopped on Earth, but the Ship inexplicably dematerialized. A stranded Harry happened upon the eighth Doctor as Lady Hester Stanton, believing herself the reincarnation of Morgan le Fay, performed magic rituals to wake the land and bind it to her. She hoped to rule England from behind-the-scenes, with her son George taking Edward VIII's place. Stanton magically compelled the werewolf Emmeline Neuberger to assist.

Stanton's spells began to awaken the land, and a wood dryad expelled the swordsman Godric, who had been seduced into slumber. Harry's use of the Holy Grail, which Godric possessed, made the Earth swallow Stanton and the Grail also. Emmeline, instinctively desiring a mate, bit Harry.

The fourth Doctor and Sarah returned for Harry, and took Godric back to his native time. Some reports suggest Harry consequently turned into a werewolf and killed Sarah, then was killed by the Doctor; some suggest Harry returned to UNIT and secretly became a murderous werewolf during the full moon; and some say the Doctor permanently cured Harry's condition.

The eighth Doctor believed Harry, Stanton and Godric had all been killed, and made gravesites to stop anyone getting too curious about them or the Grail. He introduced Emmeline to his friends in the British Ministry, but they started experimenting on her in the hopes of creating lupine soldiers.

1936 (December) WOLFSBANE[676] -> The TARDIS rematerialized after leaving Harry behind two weeks previous, and the fourth Doctor and Sarah found his "tombstone." They pieced together what had occurred during the previous fortnight. The Doctor rescued Emmeline from the Ministry, and drew enough blood from her to ritualistically send the land back to sleep. She departed back to Germany; the Doctor and Sarah went back to find Harry.

@ The Doctor made a visit to Highgate.[677]

1936 (December) PLAYERS[678] -> King Edward VIII sought to dissolve the British government, hoping to vest more power with Nazi sympathizers. The Doctor aided Winston Churchill in coercing the King to abdicate the throne, threatening to charge him with treason. This thwarted the schemes of the Players, who were engaged in a game of historical alterations.

The Doctor and Peri stopped at Cholmondeley's bank, where the Doctor's account had amassed one hundred twenty years of compound interest.

1937

> = u - When Lethbridge-Stewart was six or seven, he was heartbroken to lose a red balloon, and suffered a recurring nightmare about it for the rest of his life.

The Doctor caught the balloon and returned it.[679]
@ The amnesiac Doctor was in London at this time.[680]

1937 - HISTORY 101[681] - Sabbath sent an agent to Barcelona to track down the Absolute, a being from the future that had acquired information about his activities. This disrupted history, which in turn corrupted the Absolute's perceptions. The Doctor, Anji and Fitz arrived and discovered that the Picasso painting *Guernica* had been altered. The Doctor sent Fitz to Guernica itself to check events. The Doctor restored reality and the Absolute returned home. These events inspired Eric Blair, also known as the writer George Orwell.

Aviatrix Amelia Earhart disappeared, possibly because she flew into one of the Dragon Paths, lines of magnetic force.[682] The Doctor had Amelia Earhart's flying jacket.[683]

1937 (August) THE SHADOW OF WENG-CHIANG[684] -> The fourth Doctor, Romana and K9 were drawn to Shanghai while on the search for the Key to Time. They stumbled across the Tong of the Black Scorpion's plan to recover their 'god' Weng-Chiang (Magnus Greel) from the zygma beam experiment. The Doctor followed the Tong's leader, H'sien-Ko - the daughter of the stage magician Li H'sien Chang - to the holy mountain of T'ai Shan. There, the Doctor found the Tong had constructed the world's first nuclear reactor to achieve the power needed to retrieve Greel from the zygma beam. The Doctor narrowly prevented a temporal paradox by time-ramming Greel's Time Cabinet, hurling it back in time to the year 1872.

1938

Ghosts were sighted on the *Queen Mary* in 1938.[685]

1938 (31st October) - INVADERS FROM MARS[686] -> An alien spaceship crashed in New Jersey and was looted by the gangster Don Chaney, who discovered a bat-like being aboard. Chaney hired the Russian physicist Yuri Stepashin to develop an atom bomb from the advanced technology, hoping to give America an advantage over Germany. The Doctor and Charley arrived to find conflict brewing between Chaney and his rival, Cosmo Devine, who wanted to sell the technology for the Nazis.

The alien being split into thirty beings and threatened to go on a rampage, but the aliens Streath and Noriam arrived and subdued the pilot as part of a protection racket. Devine convinced Streath and Noriam that their weapons could seize control of Earth without the need for deception. The Doctor went to CBS Studios and had Orson Welles stage a second, private performance of *War of the Worlds* for the aliens' benefit, hoping to make them think

---

679 *The Shadows of Avalon* (p3, p271).
680 *History 101*
681 Dating *History 101* - It's 'Barcelona, 1937' (p1).
682 *The Shadow of Weng-Chiang* (p208).
683 *Superior Beings* (p58).
684 Dating *The Shadow of Weng-Chiang* - The date is given (p1).
685 *Ghost Ship*
686 Dating *Invaders from Mars* - The date is given, although the Welles play was actually broadcast on 30th October, not the 31st. Big Finish claims to have deliberately altered the date as part of the historical alterations affecting the second season of McGann audios. There are a couple of further anachronisms, such as a mention of the CIA and Welles not knowing about Shakespeare, which are explained in *The Time of the Daleks*.
687 *Timeless*. The bookshop is referred to as being on Charing Cross Road, although it was on Euston Road in *Time Zero*.
688 *Time Zero*
689 *Silver Nemesis*
690 *The Shadow in the Glass*
691 'A year or two back' before *Illegal Alien*.

692 *The Daemons*
693 *The Web of Fear*
694 *Doctor Who and the Pirates*
695 *Ghost Ship*
696 *Endgame*
697 *Heart of TARDIS*. This was 'several years' before Crowley's reported death in 1947 (p6).
698 *Heart of TARDIS*
699 *Project: Twilight*
700 Dating *Timewyrm: Exodus* - Part Three of the novel is set in "1939" (p111).
701 *Remembrance of the Daleks*
702 *The Spectre of Lanyon Moor*
703 *Matrix*
704 *Illegal Alien* (p211). The Nazis occupied Jersey on 1st May, 1940.
705 The historical evacuation of Dunkirk took place from 27th May to 4th June, 1940, and the Doctor exorcises the Timewyrm from Hitler's mind shortly prior to that.
706 *Grimm Reality*
707 *The Turing Test* (p59).
708 Dating *Illegal Alien* - Tomorrow's date, '14 November 1940' is given (p20).

that the formidable Martians had already invaded Earth. The plan failed. Stepashin detonated his atom bomb aboard the aliens' spacecraft while it was in orbit, destroying them.

The Doctor left his past self a copy of Fitz's journal, entitled *An Account of An Expedition to Siberia*, in a second hand bookshop.[687]

@ In 1938, the amnesiac Doctor bought Fitz's journal from a bookshop on Euston Road.[688]

Adolf Hitler gained the Validium Arrow, a piece of the Nemesis statue. The Nemesis itself passed over Earth, heralding Germany's annexation of Austria.[689]

1939

In Antarctica, the Nazis started construction of a huge underground base that was shaped like a swastika.[690]

Circa 1939. a pair of Cybermen from the thirtieth century arrived accidentally in Jersey. They secretly took control of Peddler Electronic Engineering in London.[691] **In 1939, a failed attempt to open Devil's Hump, "the Cambridge University Fiasco", took place.[692]**

The Second World War

During the war, bunkers were built in the London Underground, including one at Covent Garden.[693] The Doctor advised Winston Churchill on policy.[694] During World War II, the *Queen Mary* was used as a troop ship and torpedoed. Soldiers died, leading people to suspect the ship was haunted.[695] Beings of light from Altair II observed the Second World War.[696]

Occultist Aleister Crowley summoned the demon Jarakabeth.[697] During World War II, the United States came to fear that collective Nazi belief could alter the fabric of reality. The US government hired writer J.R.R. Tolkien and his contemporaries to infuse world culture with a greater sense of what was fantasy, and what was reality.[698]

The Doctor knew his way around the secret tunnels under the Thames used during the Second World War.[699]

1939 (early September) - TIMEWYRM: EXODUS[700]
-> The Doctor told Hitler that if he invaded Poland, then the British would declare war on Germany. Hitler refused to believe him, but the Doctor was proved right.

Hitler had risen to power, doubly aided by the War Lords and the Timewyrm nestled within his mind. The War Lords hoped to build a "War Lord universe" by giving the Nazis space travel, whereas the Timewyrm wanted to divert the course of history. The Doctor exposed the War Lords' plans to betray the Nazis, and the forces of Reichsmarshal Goering slaughtered them. The War Lords'

influence ended with the destruction of their base, Drachensberg Castle.

As the Second World War started, a few people in England felt that their country should fight alongside the Nazis. Ratcliffe was one such person, and he was imprisoned for his belief.[701]

1940

Radar equipment on Lanyon Moor was subject to mysterious interference, and the men stationed there suffered from mental illnesses.[702]

= On the Earth of the Dark Matrix, Britain had to use its army to fight civil disorder, not Hitler. The Americans intervened, and took control of the United Kingdom before defeating Hitler.[703]

The Nazis occupied Jersey. Colonel Schott found a dormant Cyberman army in the Le Mur engineering factory.[704]

1940 (May) - TIMEWYRM: EXODUS[705] -> Hitler, still emboldened by the Timewyrm within him, became jubilant as his armies scored many successes. German forces had reached Abbeville in France. The Doctor and Ace arrived at Hitler's command post of Felsennest, and the Doctor exorcised the Timewyrm from Hitler's mind. This left Hitler weakened, and the Doctor persuaded him to halt the German advance on Dunkirk. This enabled "the Miracle of Dunkirk" - the rescue of hundreds of thousands of British and French soldiers in a makeshift fleet of civilian boats - to occur and mark a turning point of the war.

@ The Doctor visited Lancashire in the forties and met aliens from Antares 5.[706] He tried to join the RAF, but couldn't prove he was a British subject. He left England, spending two years in South America and Africa.[707]

1940 - ILLEGAL ALIEN[708] - > A time-travelling Cyberman, injured by a Luftwaffe bomb in London, instinctively started to seek out blood plasma to heal its damaged components. It began a murder campaign and gained a reputation as "the Limehouse Lurker." The Doctor and Ace arrived onhand and the Lurker was destroyed.

The time travellers discovered that George Limb, a former Foreign Office secretary, had given Cyber-technology to both the Allies and the Nazis as a means of sparking a technology race. Limb escaped using a Cybermen time machine, but the Doctor's intervention eradicated much of the errant Cyber-technology, plus destroyed the Nazi Cyber-conversion base in Jersey. However, a pumphouse containing hundreds of Cybermen cocoons survived, and was discovered by private detective Cody McBride.

The Doctor and Bernice arrived in Guernsey in December 1940. Bernice went undercover as Celia Doras, the daughter of a local landlady.[709]

Barbara Wright was born in 1940 and lived in Bedfordshire for a time.[710]

1941

In 1941, the Doctor was present when a group of Alpha Centauri were stranded in Shanghai and panicked.[711] The Doctor was at Dunkirk during the British evacuation.[712]

1941 (1st - 6th March) JUST WAR[713] **->** The Doctor, Bernice, Roz and Chris investigated reports of a new Nazi weapon. Roz and Chris joined the Scientific Intelligence Division to find out what the British knew, and Bernice went undercover in Guernsey. The German scientist Hartung had built two radar-invisible planes, *Hugin* and *Munin*, which he had started developing before the British had even invented radar. *Hugin* exploded on a test flight,

killing Hartung. Bernice was captured and tortured, but Roz blew up *Munin*, denying it to the Nazis.

1941 - THE EMPTY CHILD / THE DOCTOR DANCES[714] **->** Captain Jack Harkness, a con-artist and former Time Agent from the fiftieth century, attempted to scam the Doctor and Rose by crashing a Chula ambulance capsule into London. The capsule dispatched sub-atomic nanogenes that attempted to heal a gas-masked boy who'd been killed by a German bomb. The nanogenes were unfamiliar with human physiology and concluded that the masked, torn-up child was indicative of the human race. The child revived and started to look for his mummy, passing the nanogenes along to anyone he touched. The nanogenes began refashioning other people into similarly hollow and masked individuals.

The Doctor and Rose arrived 'a few weeks, maybe a month' afterward. The nanogenes had become airborne and started restructuring people *en masse*. Jack

---

709 *Just War*. The date is given as 1941 (p4), but that is a mistake and should read 1940.
710 In *The Rescue*, Vicki claims that Barbara ought to be "550" years old. As *The Rescue* is set in 2493 this means Barbara was born in 1943 - making her 20 in 1963, and therefore too young to be a history teacher. Jacqueline Hill was born in 1931, and was 34 when *The Rescue* was made - meaning that Vicki is clearly rounding down. The finalised Writers' Guide for the first series stated that Barbara was "23", although she certainly seems older.
711 *The Shadow of Weng-Chiang* (p23).
712 *Just War*. The evacuation is also referred to in *Timewyrm: Exodus*.
713 Dating *Just War* - The main action of the book starts on "the morning of 1 March 1941' (p5).
714 Dating *The Empty Child / The Doctor Dances* - The date is repeatedly given as 1941. Jack says it's the 'height of the Blitz,' which ended 16th May.
715 According to a plot synopsis issued on 20th May, 1966, Ben and Polly are both "24" at the time of *The Smugglers*. Michael Craze (Ben) was then 24, Anneke Wills (Polly) was 23. The document also gave Polly's surname as "Wright", which is never used on-screen, but is mentioned in the Missing Adventure *Invasion of the Cat-People*. In the same book, Polly says she was brought up in Devon. In *The War Machines*, Kitty, the manageress of the Inferno nightclub, remarks that they rarely get anyone "over twenty" into the club, which might suggest that Ben and Polly are a little younger. Mind, neither of them look younger than twenty, and *The Murder Game* reaffirms their birth year as 1942.
716 The Doctor knows of the *Bismarck* in *Terror of the Zygons*.
717 *The Sea Devils*. Two World War II battles were

fought at El-Alamein in 1942. The first lasted 1st to 27th July. The second, 23rd October to 4th November, saw the Allies forcing the Axis to retreat back to Tunisia.
718 *Autumn Mist*. *The King of Terror* (p241) also mentions that the Doctor was at El Alamein, an Egyptian town that became the site of two major battles in World War II, both in 1942.
719 "Six months" before *The Curse of Fenric*.
720 *Just War*
721 *Divided Loyalties* (p46).
722 *Endgame*
723 Dating *The Shadow in the Glass* - The date appears on p217. This contradicts *Timewyrm: Exodus*, which the Doctor says is his first meeting with Hitler.
724 *Just War* (p252).
725 *Jubilee*
726 *The Cabinet of Light* (p86).
727 Dating *The Curse of Fenric* - Ace says that the year is "1943". The script stated that the time is "1943 - probably May".
728 *The Seeds of Doom*
729 *The Time Monster*
730 *Just War*
731 Dating *The Turing Test* - It's 'in January 1943' (p116).
732 *The Devil Goblins from Neptune*
733 *Business Unusual*
734 *Who Killed Kennedy*, taking its cue from the *Remembrance of the Daleks* novelisation.
735 *Autumn Mist*. This is based on an urban legend regarding "the Philadelphia Experiment", an invisibility experiment that allegedly took place on 28th October, 1943.
736 *The Cabinet of Light*
737 Dating *Colditz* - The date '1944' is given.

conceded his con job to the Doctor and Rose, and the three of them deduced that a young lady named Nancy was the child's mother. The nanogenes recognized Nancy as such and examined her, creating a more suitable template of the human form. The affected humans were restored, and the Doctor programmed the nanogenes to deactivate. Jack took up travel with the Doctor and Rose.

1942

Ben Jackson and Polly Wright were both born in 1942. The Jackson family lived near a brewery.[715]

The German battleship *Bismarck* was sunk.[716] The Doctor once claimed to have been wounded at El-Alamein in Egypt.[717] He drove an ambulance at El Alamein and was registered as Dr John Smith, 55583.[718]

In November 1942, there were reports of vampires in Romania.[719] On Christmas Eve of that year, the Nazi Oskar Steinmann oversaw the first test of the "flying bomb" at Peenemunde.[720] Aviatrix Amy Johnson vanished after her plane crashed. The Celestial Toymaker had kidnapped her.[721]

@ The Doctor rented a flat in Bloomsbury, and lived there for almost a decade from 1942.[722]

1942 (August) - THE SHADOW IN THE GLASS[723] ->
The Doctor and the Brigadier arrived at a Berlin ballroom party, where the Doctor presented himself to Hitler as "Major Johann Schmidt" of the Reich. The time travellers acquired a sample of Hitler's blood for analysis.

Steinmann oversaw the first test of Germany's V-1 rocket at Peenemünde in December.[724]

1943

> = The English Empire retook the American colonies, but there was a revolt in 1943. The future American Prime Minister's grandfather led the army that put it down.[725]

In 1943, the toy store owner Mr. Sun walked out of his shop in Covent Garden and was never seen again. A week later, the shop was bombed and vanished as if it had never existed. It soon reappeared.[726]

1943 (May) - THE CURSE OF FENRIC[727] -> The
Doctor and Ace arrived at a military base on the Yorkshire coast which housed the ULTIMA machine, an early computer. The Russians sent a squad to capture the machine, but the British had anticipated this by booby-trapping it to detonate a lethal toxin, waiting

for a time when the Russians became their enemies. Fenric, an ancient being trapped by the Doctor, had engineered the situation to free himself and roused an army of Haemovores to help his bid. The Doctor convinced the Ancient Haemovore to destroy Fenric.

The Doctor visited the German High Command around this time.

In the later stages of the war, the painter Amelia Ducat manned an ack-ack gun in Folkestone.[728] The Master kidnapped a V1 from the skies over Cambridgeshire using TOM-TIT.[729] Mel's grandfather died during the war.[730]

@ 1943 - THE TURING TEST[731] -> The Doctor met the British spy / novelist Graham Greene in Sierra Leone, where they encountered pale-skinned humanoids.

Lethbridge-Stewart attended Harrow from 1943.[732] Lethbridge-Stewart and John Sudbury went to the same school.[733] Rachel Jensen, a future scientific adviser to the Intrusion Counter Measures Group, worked with cryptographer Alan Turing on codebreaking.[734]

In October 1943, the USS *Eldridge* vanished, apparently as the result of an invisibility experiment. In fact, it had become destabilized in a rift with the realm of the Sidhe. The Doctor later sacrificed the ship to seal the rift.[735]

1944

In 1944, Belgium, the American soldier Honoré Lechasseur was caught in a German booby trap in Belgium and severely injured. He spent the next few years in a Dorset hospital, proving his doctors wrong by walking again. He rarely slept, and began having strange visions.[736]

= 1944 - COLDITZ[737] -> The TARDIS landed at Colditz Castle, where the Doctor and Ace were quickly captured. The Doctor was surprised at how much one of his interrogators, the Nazi officer Klein, knew about him.

> The Doctor realised that Klein was from a future where the Nazis had developed laser technology from the components of Ace's Walkman, won the war and secured the TARDIS. Ace had been killed, but the Doctor had given himself a second chance by travelling to 1955, being shot by the Nazis, regenerating while they took the TARDIS away, and then posing as 'Schmidt' - the scientist who helped Klein operate the TARDIS in 1965. The Doctor's manipulations caused Klein to change history by keeping Ace alive, averting the entire history.

The Doctor and Ace escaped from the castle. Klein also escaped, now the sole remainder of an extinct timeline.

The Doctor met Joseph Heller, an American pilot, in a military hospital.[738]

1944 - DEADLY REUNION[739] -> Second Lieutenant Alistair Gordon Lethbridge-Stewart served in Intelligence during World War II. He was assigned to update the British army's maps of the Greek islands.

On the island of Zante, Lethbridge-Stewart encountered the Greek gods Demeter, Persephone and Hermes, who were attempting to lead quiet, domestic lives. The Greek god Hades hoped to provoke a world conflict even more devastating than World War II, which would cripple humanity and allow him to rule Earth. The god Poseidon, at Persephone's request, ended Hades' scheme and cast him back into the underworld. Persephone and Lethbridge-Stewart became lovers, but she used water from the River Lethe to make him forget these events.

During the Normandy landings, Jason Kane's grandfather was killed when a sniper hit his lucky crucifix and it became lethal shrapnel.[740] Captain Davydd Watson saw visions during the Normandy landings, an effect of an experiment by the organic computer Azoth.[741]

During the nineteen forties, two Gaderene scouts - members of an insectoid race whose homeworld was dying - arrived on Earth via an unstable transmat process. One of them matured into the calculating Bliss, but her brother mutated into a dragon-sized Gaderene that covered itself in mud and went dormant. However, Bliss lost the ninth key - a small jade shard - to the Gaderene transmat. British Wing Commander Alec Whistler discovered it in the aftermath of an explosion at Culverton Aerodrome. Without the key, Bliss could only bring Gaderene embryos, not adults, through to Earth.[742]

In 1944, the Toymaker kidnapped US Marine Mark Conrad.[74]

1944 - THE SHADOW IN THE GLASS[744] -> On 17th May, 1944, a Vvormak spacecruiser passed over Turelhampton, England, and a British fighter plane shot it down. The Vvormak were in stasis, but the ship generated a gravitational field that rendered it immobile. Unable to relocate the ship, the British military sealed off the area for fifty years as part of a cover story.

Private Gerrard Lassiter stole the Vvormak ship's main navigation device as a talisman. It was capable of projecting images of the future, and would come to be known as "the Scrying Glass." Gunther Brun, a German trooper, later killed Lassiter in France and took the device, but subsequently lost it to Colonel Otto Klein in a game of cards. Two weeks later, Reichsfuher Heinrich Himmler learned of the device's existence and ordered Klein to hand it over to him. Himmler then gave it to a group of Tibetan mystics for study.

In July 1944, the Doctor persuaded Churchill to help smuggle him into France. He then infiltrated the Reich Records Department as "Colonel Johann Schmidt". In August 1944, Hitler became curious about other items left at the Turelhampton site, and authorized the Doctor, as "Schmidt," to participate in a raiding party. The raid occurred on 18th August.

---

738 'Five months' before *The Turing Test*.
739 Dating *Deadly Reunion* - The date is given (although as previously noted, it does make Lethbridge-Stewart older than most other stories would have him).
740 *Death and Diplomacy*
741 *The Taint*
742 'Thirty years' before *The Last of the Gaderene*.
743 *Divided Loyalties*
744 Dating *The Shadow in the Glass* - The date is given (p29).
745 Dating *Autumn Mist* - The story takes place during the Battle of the Bulge. The Doctor confronts the Beast in *The Taint*.
746 Dating *The Turing Test* - The story takes place over several months, and ends with the Allies bombing Dresden, which occurred in February 1945.
747 *The Marian Conspiracy*, which takes place circa 2000, says she is 'fifty five'. A Big Finish press release, however, claims she was 65 in 1999, suggesting a much earlier birth date of 1934. Big Finish Producer Gary

Russell says *The Marian Conspiracy* should be favoured whatever the press release says.
748 *No Future*
749 'Next March' after *The Shadow in the Glass*.
750 *The Shadow in the Glass*
751 Dating *The Shadow in the Glass* - The date is given (p23, 147).
752 *Just War*
753 *Heart of TARDIS*
754 *Time and the Rani*. A scene showing the Rani kidnap Einstein was deleted from the camera script.
755 "Thirty years" before *The Web of Fear*.
756 "Thirty years" before *The Paradise of Death* (p79).
757 Dating *Dying in the Sun* - Early on a newspaper is dated '12 October 1947' (p17).
758 *The Devil Goblins from Neptune*, and also referred to in *The Face of the Enemy*.
759 *Dalek*
760 *Divided Loyalties*. Pollock was influential to the abstract expressionism movement.
761 *Heart of TARDIS*

1944 (December) - AUTUMN MIST[745] **->** The Doctor, Sam and Fitz were split up when they arrived during the Battle of the Bulge. Sam was injured, the Doctor served as a medic, and Fitz found himself serving as a corporal in the German army. Sam's injuries were fatal, but she was rescued by the Sidhe, fairy creatures from another dimension. A rift had formed between our realm and theirs, but the Doctor sealed it.

The King of the Sidhe, Oberon, was killed as part of these events. It was expected that another aspect of Oberon would take his place. The rift's closure enabled the Beast to arrive on Earth and begin feeding upon humanity.

@ 1944/5 - THE TURING TEST[746] **->** The cryptographer Alan Turing intercepted a unique code transmitted from Dresden, concluding that it was alien in origin. The Doctor had befriended Turing, and suggested they contact the signal's originator. They allied themselves with the spy Graham Greene. The Doctor also approached American pilot Joseph Heller, promising to get him out of the army if he flew the Doctor and Turing to Dresden. An English officer, Elgar, was revealed as an assassin out to kill the mysterious pale-skinned aliens. The Doctor killed Elgar and the aliens beamed away from Earth, leaving the Doctor behind as the Allied bombing of Dresden began.

1945

Around 1945, Evelyn Smythe was born.[747] On 13th February, 1945, the Doctor and Bernice witnessed the destruction of Dresden.[748]

In March, the Doctor once flew a Mark VIII Halifax bomber.[749] The Tibetans charged with keeping the Scrying Glass were murdered on 25th April, 1945. In the years to follow, the Scrying Glass would fall into the hands of Adolf Hitler's son.[750]

1945 (Monday, 30th April) - THE SHADOW IN THE GLASS[751] **->** The Doctor, the Brigadier and journalist Claire Aldwych arrived from 2001 with Hitler's adult son, and the men entered Hitler's bunker. The Doctor easily portrayed Hitler's son as a madman, and Hitler, failing to recognize his offspring, shot him dead. The Nazis disposed of the body in a nearby water tower. The Allies would later mistake the corpse for a double of Hitler, killed for an unknown reason.

Martin Bormann, one of Hitler's aides, killed Claire and substituted her body for that of Eva Hitler. Hitler committed suicide. A pregnant Eva was flown to a submarine in Hamburg. She later gave birth to a son named Adolf. He was raised at the secret Nazi base in Antarctica.

At the end of the war, the Russians captured Emil Hartung's research into stealth aircraft, and took it to a vault in the Kremlin. Generalleutnant Oskar Steinmann was found guilty (along with twenty-two others) of Nazi war crimes and was sentenced to life imprisonment at Nuremberg.[752]

After World War II, the American military experimented to see if widespread belief could alter the laws of physics. The residents of the Midwest town Lychburg were brainwashed with transceivers, creating thousands of people who simultaneously believed whatever the military wanted. An experiment to make the people believe "the gates of Hell were opening", however, created an unstable dimensional rift. The military tried to level the project with a low-yield nuclear device, but only succeeded in knocking Lychburg out of Earth's dimension entirely. [753]

In the mid-1940s, the Rani briefly kidnapped Albert Einstein.[754] **The collector Julius Silverstein bought the only surviving robot Yeti from Professor Travers.**[755] The Parakon named Freeth began to visit Earth, accounting for some UFO sightings over the next thirty years.[756]

1947

1947 - DYING IN THE SUN[757] **->** The Doctor called in on Harold Reitman, a movie producer and old friend, and discovered he had been murdered. Star Light Pictures were about to release a new movie, *Dying in the Sun*, and the Doctor was surprised that such a poor movie could receive such rave reviews. The audience's perceptions were being affected by the telepathic Selyoids. The aliens were peaceful, but the movie's producer, De Sande, was intent on using their powers to dominate the world. There was dissent in the Selyoid ranks. The Doctor caused a plane crash that killed De Sande, but this released the Selyoids present in De Sande's body. Hollywood would long remain a place of extreme emotions for some time to come.

The CIA captured a Nedenah ship at Roswell. One alien was autopsied, the others were taken to Area 51.[758] **The collector Henry Van Statten had artefacts from Roswell in his private museum.**[759] The Doctor knocked over a paint pot and inspired Jackson Pollock, an American artist, around this time. Pollock gave the Doctor a painting, *Azure in the Rain by a Man Who'd Never Been*.[760]

The rituals of black arts practitioner Edward Alexander Crowley had summoned a Jarakabeth demon to Earth. The demon impersonated Crowley after his death at Hastings, 1947. The US security service Section Eight approached "Crowley" in the hope that his Hermetic Arts could be adopted for military use. The Crowley demon would become the head of the DIvisional department of Special Tactical Operations (Provisional) with Regard to Insurgent and Subversive Activity (DISTO(P)IA), a government branch designed to counter subversion.[761]

1948

A year after the first crash, a Nedenah rescue mission was shot down over Roswell.[762] The Doctor bought a stuffed owl for Sarah in 1948. It was one of the items she packed when she left his company.[763]

1949

1949 - THE CABINET OF LIGHT[764] **->** The Doctor and his companion Emily Blandish arrived in London, where agents working for Mestizer, a nemesis of the Doctor, attacked them. Emily helped the Doctor to escape, but Mestizer's agents captured the Doctor's time cabinet. The trauma of the event rendered Emily amnesiac. She was found wandering the streets of London with no memory, and became known in the press as "the Girl in the Pink Pajamas" (and occasionally "the Girl in the Pink Bikini"). She was used to promote clothes rationing.

To retrieve his property, the Doctor came to involve an expatriate and time sensitive named Honoré Lechasseur, who chiefly worked as a "fixer." Honoré observed the Doctor confronting Mestizer, and light from the Doctor's time cabinet started her house on fire. The Doctor, Mestizer, the house and the time cabinet all disappeared entirely. In the Doctor's absence, Honoré and Emily struck up a partnership.

By now, the Doctor was regarded as a "hobgoblin" or "myth" in the underground community. Legends claimed he variously gave fire to mankind, burned London in 1666, kidnapped the crew of the *Mary Celeste* and built Stonehenge with his bare hands.

The Time Hunter novels, published by Telos, spin off from this story.

The Nineteen Fifties

In the early nineteen-fifties, Professor Zaroff - "the greatest scientist since Leonardo" - vanished.[765] The testing of nuclear weapons, plus an increase in dumping of toxic waste, destroyed many Silurian shelters.[766] Benny Summerfield visited Milton Keynes in the mid-twentieth century to settle an archaeological debate.[767]

When Lethbridge-Stewart was twenty-one, he spent a time in New York on the way back from Korea.[768] Albinex the Navarino arrived down a faulty time corridor from the far future.[769] In Jamaica, the 1950s, the Doctor met the ornithologist James Bond and took him to the 1800s to see a live dodo. The Doctor later introduced writer Ian Fleming to Bond, who served as inspiration for Fleming's super-spy novels.[770] The Doctor met the Cuban guerrilla leader Che Guevara.[771]

1950

Under the influence of the Player Myrek, President Truman approved Operation Kali, a psychic warfare programme.[772]

---

762 *The Devil Goblins from Neptune* (p240).
763 *Interference.* We see it in *The Hand of Fear*.
764 Dating *The Cabinet of Light* - The date is 1949, according to p14 and the back cover blurb.
765 "Twenty years" before *The Underwater Menace*.
766 *The Scales of Injustice.* No date is given.
767 *Zamper*
768 *The Devil Goblins from Neptune* (p37).
769 *Return of the Living Dad.* This happened in 'the fifties' (p66).
770 *Instruments of Darkness*
771 *Psi-ence Fiction.* No date is given.
772 'About a year' before *Endgame*.
773 "Forty years" after *Pyramids of Mars*.
774 *The Daemons*
775 Dating *Timewyrm: Exodus* - In Part One of the novel, the Doctor proclaims it to be the "Festival of Britain, 1951" (p5). At the end of the novel, the Doctor and Ace arrive at the real Festival of Britain.
776 Dating *Endgame* - The year is given (p242).
777 *Father Time* (p58).
778 *Zagreus*, again judging by a historical simulation.
779 Dating *Real Time* - The date is given, Episode One,

Track 1.
780 *The Plotters.* Although if we take the writers' guidelines at face value, she would have been twelve at the time.
781 Dating *Amorality Tale* - It's 'Wednesday, December 3, 1952' (p12).
782 *Nightshade* (p111).
783 *Escape Velocity* (p196).
784 *The Dying Days* (p52). Sherpa Tensing Norgay and Edmund P. Hillary were the first men to conquer Mount Everest.
785 *Jubilee*
786 In *Mawdryn Undead*, the 1983 Brigadier talks of "thirty years of soldiering". He doesn't have a moustache in the regimental photograph seen in *Inferno*. He is a member of the Scots' Guards in *The Web of Fear*. Other information here comes from *The Invasion* and *The Green Death*.
787 Dating *The Witch Hunters* - The date is given, p68.

1951

The radio telescope was invented.[773] The last witch-craft act on the English statute books was repealed in 1951.[774]

> **= 1951 - TIMEWYRM: EXODUS**[775] **->** Following the total defeat of the British army at Dunkirk in 1940, the German army swept across the Channel and landed at Folkestone. Britain fell in six days. Churchill and thousands of suspected troublemakers were executed. Oswald Mosley was installed as Prime Minister, and Edward VIII was crowned. Unsure what to do with Britain, the Nazi High Command let the country fall into ruin.
>
> All able-bodied men were conscripted as slave workers and shipped to the continent. In 1951, the Festival of Britain took place in London to celebrate ten years of Nazi victory. The Germans planned to have a man on the moon in this year. Arriving at this time, the Doctor realised that history had been altered. He travelled back and averted this timeline with the destruction of Drachensberg Castle in 1939.

After they defeated the War Lords and Timewyrm, the Doctor and Ace visited the real Festival of Britain and discovered that history was back on course.

@ 1951 - ENDGAME[776] **->** The seventh Doctor (and Ace) saw the eighth Doctor at the Festival of Britain, but neither recognised the other.

The Players decided on a new game, seeing which among them could provoke a nuclear holocaust on Earth. The Doctor became caught up in this after befriending a Polish exile who was beaten to death, and MI5 investigated the matter. Kim Philby, a member of British intelligence and a double agent for the Soviet Union, recruited the Doctor to defeat the Players.

President Truman became abnormally hostile to China, and the Doctor discovered the president was under the influence of the Player Myrek. As Philby suspected, another Player - the Countess - was similarly manipulating Stalin. The Doctor ended the Players' control of the Russian leader and Truman. Returning to America, the Doctor tricked the Players into killing each other. The Doctor declined a job at the White House and returned to London.

@ The Doctor was present in the Soviet Union during a high profile chess match played in 1951.[777] In 1951, the Dionysus Project in Cardington opened a doorway to the Divergents' domain. This killed the researchers Dr. Stone and the Reverend Matthew Townsend.[778]

> **= 1951 - REAL TIME**[779] **->** With the Cybermen firmly in control of Earth, a group of human rebels crafted an organic techno-virus capable of destroying the Cybermen's artificial implants. They used a Chronosphere to dispatch Dr Reece Goddard to 3286, the year in which the Cybermen altered history, in the hope of averting this timeline altogether.

1952

Barbara worked at Hampstead High School for girls in 1952.[780]

1952 (December) - AMORALITY TALE[781] **->** The Doctor and Sarah travelled in 1952 to investigate a warp shadow, and arrived prior to a killer smog descending on London. The Doctor set up shop as a watchmaker. Sarah found out that a war was brewing between the Ramsey and Callum gangs. Callum was actually a member of the Xhinn, a ruthless alien species, and the killer smog was actually a Xhinn weapon. The Doctor destroyed the Xhinn scoutship, which deterred their main fleet from attacking.

1953

The science fiction serial *Nightshade* was first shown by the BBC in 1953. It would run for five years.[782]

@ The Doctor quickly became a fan of the show.[783]

The Doctor was the first man to climb Everest, giving Tensing and Hillary a hand up.[784]

> **=** In 1953, the second President of the English Empire celebrated the fiftieth Jubilee of victory by executing one of his two captive Daleks.[785]

u - Alistair Gordon Lethbridge-Stewart began his military service. Shortly afterward, he attended Sandhurst with Billy Rutledge. Once his training was complete, Lethbridge-Stewart grew his moustache, joined the Scots' Guards and was stationed for a time at Aldgate.[786]

1954

1954 (9th November) - THE WITCH HUNTERS[787] **->** The Doctor and companions arrived after visiting Salem during the witch trials. Susan was distressed to think that some of the residents would be burnt as witches, and used the TARDIS' Fast Return Switch in a bid to go back and save them.

Returning to 1954, the time travellers attended the premiere of *The Crucible* in Bristol. Later, the Doctor brought the condemned Rebecca Nurse to this era to view *The*

Crucible and see memorials to the victims of the Salem witch trials.

Graham Greene received a tape from Alan Turing that explained his contact with the Doctor.[788] Circa 1954, the student Astrabel Zar vacationed on Gadrahadradon, a haunted planet that facilitated glimpses into the future. Zar received instructions from his future self on how to build "Tomorrow Windows," devices that would similarly display images of future times. He would later pass on the secret of building Tomorrow Windows to one of his own students, Charlton Mackerel.[789]

Peter Allen Tyler, future father of Rose Tyler, was born 15th September, 1954.[790] George Limb survived being catapulted through time and landed in 1954. He loosely learned to navigate his time machine between 1940 and 1962, but his journeys created a number of alternate timelines. Limb's final trip resulted in his being left in 1954 while his time machine jumped on ahead to 1959. He waited five years to retrieve it.[791]

1955

u - Lethbridge Stewart met Fiona, his future wife.[792] Lethbridge-Stewart's grandmother died in 1955.[793] **Sarah Jane Smith was born.**[794]

In 1955, Chris Parsons was born. The Doctor visited Chris' future College, St Cedd's Cambridge.[795]

= In an errant timeline, George Limb saved the life of actor James Dean. The alternate Dean served as Limb's assistant in the proper reality.[796]

1956

In 1956, the Doctor met a Jesuit palaeontologist in Africa.[797] The vampires of Los Angeles culled their own kind to hide their numbers.[798] Joseph Heller told Kurt Vonnegut, future author of *Slaughterhouse-Five* (1969), about his meeting with the Doctor.[799]

Ben Jackson, aged fourteen, stowed away on a cargo ship bound for Singapore. The captain discovered him and offered him a job.[800] The Doctor prevented Santa Mira from being taken over by aliens in 1956.[801] The French colony of Kebiria was granted independence in 1956. Civil war started almost immediately.[802]

1957

u - The Doctor became a member of the Progressive Club, a gentleman's club in Mayfair.[803] Edwin Pratt became the vampire Slake in 1957.[804]

1957 (4th October) - FIRST FRONTIER[805] **->** On May Day 1957, the first *Sputnik* was destroyed before it completed an orbit of the Earth. News of this failure was never made public.

The Doctor visited the first official *Sputnik* launch at least twice.

The same day, there was intense UFO activity over Corman Air Force Base in New Mexico, and the USAF engaged alien spaceships. These were the Tzun, now a race divided into three subspecies. They planned to cause a war between Washington and Moscow, then step in and pose as humanity's saviours. The Master was helping them, but

---

788 *The Turing Test.* 'Six months' after Turing's suicide (7th June, 1954; p104), 'forty six years' before the year 2000 (p105).
789 'Fifty years' before *The Tomorrow Windows* (p274).
790 *Father's Day*
791 *Loving the Alien* (p188-189).
792 'Fifteen years' before *The Scales of Injustice*.
793 *The Devil Goblins from Neptune* (p56), *The King of Terror* (p126).
794 In *Invasion of the Dinosaurs*, Sarah Jane says she is "twenty-three" (although in the novelisation she is "twenty-two"). Elisabeth Sladen, who played Sarah, was born in 1948 and was 26 when the story was made. In the format document for the proposed *K9 and Company* series, it is stated that Sarah was born in "1949". She was 'about thirty' in the spin-off novel *Harry Sullivan's War* (suggesting a birth date of 1955), and she's born 'over sixty years' after 1880 in *Evolution* (p242). Thus, depending on when the UNIT stories are set, she could be born at any time from 1949 to 1963.
795 *Shada*

796 *Loving the Alien.* Dean died 30th September, 1955.
797 *The Pit* (p98).
798 *Vampire Science*
799 *The Turing Test* (p207).
800 *Invasion of the Cat-People* (p31).
801 'Last year' according to *First Frontier* (p68), and a reference to the original *Invasion of the Bodysnatchers*.
802 *Dancing the Code*
803 'Thirteen years' before *The Devil Goblins from Neptune*.
804 *Vampire Science*
805 Dating *First Frontier* - It is "October 4th, 1957" (p6).
806 *Unregenerate!* The dating is somewhat awry, as radio broadcasts suggest this occurs on the day of *Sputnik*'s launch (4th October), yet Louis claims the date is 'the 15th'.
807 The Doctor mentions C-19 in *Time-Flight*, in connection with contacting UNIT.
808 *The Scales of Injustice* (p205). C-19 is referred to in a number of novels, particularly Gary Russell's *The Scales of Injustice, Business Unusual* and *Instruments of*

Ace shot the Master and caused him to regenerate. The Doctor prevented chaos from ensuing as the Master betrayed the Tzun and destroyed their mothership.

On the 15th of the same month, a Time Lord using the name Louis approached Johannes Rausch, who possessed a degree in metallurgy from the University of Vienna. Louis offered to make Rausch's life highly successful if Rausch agreed to take part in a painless procedure the day before he died. Rausch agreed, and the two of them would meet again almost fifty years later.[806]

Department C-19 was set up in Britain[807] in the late fifties to handle extra sensitive security matters.[808]

Sputnik II launched and carried Laika the dog into orbit. The Doctor later recovered her body and buried it on the planet Quiescia.[809] In 1957, Noel Coward met Iris Wildthyme at the Royal Variety Performance. Their friendship led to Iris giving Noel a pair of pinking shears capable of cutting the Very Fabric of Time and Space, enabling him to time travel. Multiple Cowards began operating in various time zones.[810]

@ The Doctor was present when the Atomium - a monument representing an iron crystal magnified 165 billion times - was unveiled in Brussels.[811] The Ragman stoked the fire of racial violence between Teddy Boys and Afro-Caribbean immigrants in Notting Hill and Notting Dale.[812]

1958 (October) - BAD THERAPY[813] **->** The first of the Krontep warlords, Moriah, had taken up residence on Earth. Operating from the Petruska Psychiatric Research Institute, Moriah sought to construct Toys - genetic duplicates of people that could become whomever their owner desired. He wanted a Toy that would replicate his late wife Petruska, but some of the Toys became increasingly independent. Moriah had a metamorphic device, disguised as a black cab, that would round up any Toys who escaped.

The Doctor and Chris arrived, and a young man named Jack Bartlett, actually a Toy, died in front of the TARDIS. The time travellers investigated. Meanwhile, the Doctor's former companion Peri, having spent twenty-five years as

King Yrcanos' wife, travelled down a gateway from Krontep to Earth. She aided the Doctor against Moriah. The Doctor created a Toy of Petruska for Moriah, who believed himself unworthy of her love and was killed by his creations.

In 1958, the Doctor again visited St Cedd's College.[814]

1959 - DELTA AND THE BANNERMEN[815] **->** The first US satellite was launched, and almost immediately it was lost. CIA agents across the world were put on alert. It was eventually recovered by agents Weismuller and Hawk, who tracked it to a holiday camp in Wales, England.

A Nostalgia Trips group arrived through time at the holiday camp, and their members included the Chimeron Queen. A group of Bannermen tried to kill the Queen but were defeated. Billy, a mechanic at the camp, underwent conversion into a Chimeron to help the Queen re-propagate her race.

One Bannerman survived, albeit deafened and suffering from amnesia. He ended up with Isaac Summerfield's group.[816]

> = In the "Inferno" universe, the British Republic fought the Bannermen and destroyed them. Components from the alien starship allowed them to engineer space shuttles within ten years.[817]

In October 1959, the Russian probe *Lunik 3* scanned the moon crater where the Phiadoran safari park once stood. The Russians named it Tsiolkovskii, after a teacher who wrote a paper on rocket travel.[818]

> **= 1959 - LOVING THE ALIEN**[819] **->** George Limb's time-jumps had created an alternate timeline where Limb was Prime Minister, and the populace was cybernetically augmented. This had eliminated disease and to some degree created a utopia, but over-

---

Darkness, where it's a shadowy branch of British intelligence that keeps the existence of aliens under wraps by cleaning up alien artefacts left over from their various incursions.

809 *Alien Bodies. Sputnik II* was launched 3rd November, 1957.

810 *Mad Dogs and Englishmen*

811 *Escape Velocity*

812 *Rags* (p185).

813 Dating *Bad Therapy.* The date is given (p1).

814 *Shada*

815 Dating *Delta and the Bannermen.* The Tollmaster says that the bus will be going back to "1959", and the

date is confirmed by a banner up in the dancehall at the Shangri-La resort. Hawk's line that "this is history in the making" implies this is the first American satellite, but that was actually *Explorer I*, launched on 31st January, 1958.

816 *Return of the Living Dad*

817 *The Face of the Enemy* (p248).

818 *Imperial Moon*

819 Dating *Loving the Alien* - Ace gains a tattoo that dates the year as 1959 (p24). The Doctor similarly remarks on the year as 1959 (p33). The newspaper on the cover specifies it's 'November' 1959.

crowding became a problem. The British Space Agency was assigned the task of facilitating travel to other timelines as a means of expansion.

In the proper history, the Americans and British jointly launched a Waverider space vehicle, piloted by Colonel Thomas Kneale. However, the ship that returned hailed from the cyber-human reality, and was piloted by an alternate version of Captain Davey O'Brien. International tensions increased over the incident. The cyber-human Britain attempted to send its warships through to the proper reality, but a nuclear strike devastated the alternate Britain and ended the threat.

Limb's assistant, an alternative version of James Dean, died while destroying Limb's time machine. Limb committed suicide in fear of undergoing cyber-conversion.

Before his death, Limb shot and killed Ace. The Doctor took up travel with a virtually identical Ace that hailed from one of the timelines Limb had created.

The Doctor met William Golding.[820]

The Nineteen Sixties

The Doctor met the artists Francis Bacon and Lucian Freud in Soho in the sixties, and thwarted one of the Master's schemes.[821] The Mods and Rockers guarded the Library of St John the Beheaded during the sixties.[822] The Doctor learned about sharks from Jacques Cousteau.[823]

UNIT in the Sixties

A secret bunker was built in Whitehall.[824]

u - Lavinia Smith published her paper on the teleological response of the virus when her niece, Sarah Jane, was five years old.[825]

Human space probes were being sent "deeper and deeper" into space.[826] Lieutenant Lethbridge-Stewart spent some time in Sierra Leone. One day, while lost in the forest, he met Mariatu, eldest daughter of Chief Yembe of the Rokoye village. Mariatu went to the city with Lethbridge-Stewart, returning alone a few years later with her son, Mariama.[827]

---

820 *Ghost Ship.* No date is given.
821 *Synthespians ™*
822 *Millennial Rites* (p159). The Mods and Rockers gangs were two British youth movements during this time.
823 *The Murder Game.* No date is given.
824 "Twenty years" before *Invasion of the Dinosaurs.*
825 *The Time Warrior*
826 "For the last decade" before *Spearhead from Space.*
827 Transit
THE LETHBRIDGE-STEWART FAMILY: *Transit* introduces the Brigadier's descendant, Kadiatu Lethbridge-Stewart (she reappears in *Set Piece, The Also People* and *So Vile a Sin*). Kadiatu hails from a line of Lethbridge-Stewarts descended from the Lieutenant's liaison in Sierra Leone. There were more details of the Lethbridge-Stewart line in an early draft of *The Also People*.

We can deduce that Mariatu had a son, Mariama, in the early 1960s (he is unnamed in *Transit*, but the name appears in the early draft of *The Also People*, where his mother was mistakenly referred to as "Isatu"). He had a daughter, Kadiatu, who became an historian (she is first referred to in the *Remembrance of the Daleks* novelisation, and also in *Set Piece*). She had a son Gibril, who also had a son called Gibril (from the draft of *The Also People*). Gibril had a son, Yembe (seen in *Transit*), and he adopted Kadiatu in 2090. Kadiatu, then, is the Brigadiers great-great-great-great-granddaughter, and this is consistent with *Transit* (p96) where "five generations" separate Kadiatu from Alistair.

Rather more simple is the Brigadier's British family. According to *Downtime*, the Brigadier and his first wife

Fiona (a name thought up by Nicholas Courtney, who plays the Brigadier) had a daughter named Kate. She was a child during the UNIT era, when the Lethbridge-Stewarts split up. (The Brigadier and Fiona separate in *The Scales of Injustice*, and he is sleeping alone by *The Daemons*.) By the mid-nineties, Kate is a single mother looking after her son Gordon. By *Battlefield*, the Brigadier has married Doris, an old flame first mentioned in *Planet of the Spiders*. (They shared a weekend in Brighton eleven years before that story - perhaps before Alistair was married to Fiona.)
828 *Blood Heat*
829 'Eight years' before *The Scales of Injustice* (p61, p131).
830 "Eleven years" before *Planet of Spiders* - possibly while married to Fiona.
831 'About ten years' before *The Scales of Injustice.*
832 *Scream of the Shalka*
833 *Shada*
834 *Just War*
835 Dating *Mad Dogs and Englishmen* - 'It's 1960!' (p118).
836 According to her character outline, Tegan is "twenty-one" when she meets the Doctor. Originally she was to be nineteen, until the production team were told that legally air hostesses had to be twenty-one or older.
837 *Divided Loyalties*
838 *The King of Terror*
839 *Goth Opera*
840 Confirmed in *The Seeds of Death.*
841 *The King of Terror* (p255).
842 The ICMG is seen in *Remembrance of the Daleks,* and its founding was described in *Who Killed Kennedy*

Lethbridge-Stewart saved Doris, an old friend, from drowning in Margate.[828] He married Fiona and they set up home in Gerrards Cross. The day after the wedding, Lethbridge-Stewart bumped into an old flame, Doris, in Brighton.[829] **Lethbridge-Stewart was given a wristwatch by Doris during a romantic weekend in Brighton.**[830]

Earth Reptile Shelter 429, near the Channel Islands, revived.[831] The Doctor met Andy Warhol, who wanted to paint all nine of him.[832]

1960

The Doctor was awarded an honorary degree from St Cedd's in 1960.[833] In 1960, the Doctor visited Anne Doras and her husband in Guernsey. They had a daughter called Bernice. The same year, convicted Nazi Oskar Steinmann was released from prison on medical grounds.[834]

1960 - MAD DOGS AND ENGLISHMEN[835] -> Fitz met Iris Wildthyme in Las Vegas, where she had found fame as the diva Brenda Soobie. Her companion of sixty years, the poodle Martha, had been manipulating Iris to alter history. Iris helped the Doctor defeat the poodles, then left for further adventures with her new companions Fritter the poodle and Flossie the cook.

Tegan Jovanka was born in 1960.[836] Tegan's middle name was Melissa. Her father was named William.[837] She spent her childhood in Caloundra, near Brisbane.[838] Tegan's Serbian grandfather told her vampire stories.[839]

1961

In 1961, Yuri Gagarin became the first human to travel in space.[840] Lethbridge-Stewart spent some time stationed in Berlin.[841] The Intrusion Countermeasures Group (ICMG) was formed to fight covert actions from hostile powers. Group Captain Gilmore was appointed leader.[842]

1962

American scientists worked out how to operate the navigation system of their captured Nedenah spaceship.[843]

Dorothea Chaplet was sent to live with her great-aunt Margaret when her parents died. At her new school, she was given the nickname Dodo.[844]

Section Eight used the dark arts to end the Cuban Missile Crisis.[845] A small party of Muslims passed into Avalon.[846]

@ It was the Doctor's idea that the Beatles should wear suits.[847] The Doctor travelled the world in the sixties and seventies.[848] He visited India.[849]

@ The Doctor spent some time at a Buddhist temple in Thailand, searching for a dragon. His search took twenty five years and he travelled across China, Vietnam and Siam. He found the dragon, but it's not known what subsequently happened.[850]

@ During the 1960s, the Doctor spent some time learning ventriloquism from Edgar Bergen of *The Edgar Bergen and Charlie McCarthy Show*.

(p69).

843 'Fifteen years' after 1947, according to *The Devil Goblins from Neptune*.

844 *Salvation* (p5).

845 *Heart of TARDIS* (p197).

846 'Fifty years' before *The Shadows of Avalon*.

847 *Trading Futures*

848 *Father Time*. This is one reason that the Doctor

doesn't bump into himself during the UNIT era.

849 'Twenty seven years' before the third part of *Father Time*.

850 *The Year of Intelligent Tigers*

851 *Dark Progeny*. Despite his popularity, Bergen wasn't a very skilled ventriloquist, and the McCarthy doll would frequently mock Bergen for moving his lip.

= The former Council of Eight member Soul, along with the Doctor's granddaughter Zezanne, arrived in a junkyard in 1963 aboard the *Jonah*. A chameleon device built by Octan enabled the ship to alter its appearance for the first and nearly last time, blending into its surroundings as a police box. Soul and Zezanne's memories were clouded by the nature of their escape. Having absorbed some of the Doctor's life force, Soul became convinced that he *was* the Doctor. Zezanne regarded him as her grandfather.[1]

The Doctor and Susan arrived in Shoreditch, London, in early 1963 and spent five months on Earth at this time. The Doctor attended to his TARDIS while Susan went to Coal Hill School. A month before his departure, the Doctor made arrangements to bury the Hand of Omega.[2]

IM Foreman's travelling carnival for a time remodelled itself as the junkyard at Totter's Yard, and the instability it created had served to draw the Doctor's TARDIS there.[3]

1963 (27th March / 4th April) - TIME AND RELATIVE[4] -> Several months after Susan started at Coal Hill School, England was caught in the most severe winter for quite some time. There had been snow and ice since before Christmas, into April. This was caused by an ancient sentience called the Cold, which had recently revived, possibly due to a Soviet cryogenics research undertaking called the Novosibirsk Project. The Cold animated killer snowmen, "the Cold Knights", which caused mayhem in London and slew many in Piccadilly Circus. The Doctor siphoned the Cold into a lump of ice, and took it to Pluto in the far future.

1963 - THE TAINT[5] -> The Doctor met Fitz Kreiner, a florist shop clerk, shortly before being confronted by an escaped mental patient, Oscar Austen. The patients at Austen's hospital had alien leech creatures in their brains. Sam and Fitz were attacked by Azoth, an organic computer from the planet Benelisa, who injected Sam with a leech. Azoth sought to destroy 'the Beast', invisible aliens that were feeding on humans, and the leech enabled Sam to see them. The leeches drove the patients further insane and granted them with dangerous psychic abilities. Azoth was destroyed, and the Doctor released a bio-electric pulse that killed the mental patients, including Fitz's mother. Fitz joined the Doctor and Sam on their travels. They predicted that the Beast would eventually move on from Earth.

1963 (October) - GHOST SHIP[6] -> The Doctor landed on the *Queen Mary*, which was bound for New York. In Cabin 672, he found that quantum physicist Peter Osbourne had developed a time-space visualizer. As a side effect, Osbourne's device had captured psionic residue from the passengers, collecting "ghosts" from the past, present and future. The Doctor destroyed the device and liberated the "ghosts," who took Osbourne among their number. The Doctor concluded that the "ghosts" would remain aboard the *Queen Mary* forever.

1963 (a Tuesday in late October) - AN UNEARTHLY CHILD[7] -> Two of Susan Foreman's teachers, Ian Chesterton and Barbara Wright, became concerned

---

1 *Sometime Never*

IS THE DOCTOR REALLY A CRYSTAL SKELETON MAN FROM THE FUTURE, NOW?: *Sometime Never* ends with the multiverse being restored after being merged by the Council of Eight. 'In just one of many universes', a benevolent member of the Council, Soul, and Miranda's daughter, Zezanne, arrive in a junkyard in Sabbath's ship, the *Jonah* - which disguises itself as a police box. Soul has absorbed the essence of the Doctor, and as Miranda's daughter, Zezanne is the Doctor's granddaughter. Clearly, in their universe, they take on the roles of the Doctor and Susan.

The question is whether this represents a new origin story for *our* Doctor and Susan. The EDA range had destroyed Gallifrey, but it wasn't specified whether the planet had simply blown up or been removed from the timeline so that it never existed. If Gallifrey had never existed, the existence of the Doctor and his TARDIS would have been a paradox ... unless he wasn't from Gallifrey. This explanation closed that loophole.

As of *The Gallifrey Chronicles*, the Doctor certainly thinks he's a Time Lord from the planet Gallifrey, has met a Time Lord and seen evidence of Gallifrey's former existence. Gallifrey therefore existed, and it seems fairly clear now that the Doctor isn't Soul.

2 In *An Unearthly Child*, Susan says that "the last five months have been the happiest in my life". She and the Doctor were on Earth for 'six months' according to *Matrix* (p31), and *Time and Relative* suggests it was more like thirteen months. The Doctor returns for the Hand of Omega in *Remembrance of the Daleks*.

3 *Interference*

4 Dating *Time and Relative* - Susan's diary gives the date as "Wednesday, March 27th 1963" for the first entry (p9), "April 4th" for the last. They have *already* been on Earth "five months, I think", according to Susan, who admits to some confusion on the point.

5 Dating *The Taint* - It is 1963 (p10).

6 Dating *Ghost Ship* - According to the blurb, the story is set in 1963.

with a pupil's homework and investigated her home one evening. Although Chesterton's car was later discovered outside a Totter's Yard, no sign was found of the teachers, Susan or her mysterious grandfather.

In 1963, Professor Rachel Jenson was moved from British Rocket Group to the Intrusion Countermeasures Group.[8]

1963 (from 22nd November) - REMEMBRANCE OF THE DALEKS[9] -> An Imperial Dalek Shuttlecraft landed in a playground in London and established a transmat link with an orbiting mothership. The Renegade Dalek faction arrived at around the same time and began recruiting sympathetic locals. Davros, now in command of the Imperial Daleks, wiped out the Renegade faction and captured the Hand of Omega. He planned on using its power to give the Daleks mastery of Time, and make them the new Time Lords. The Doctor tricked Davros into destroying both Skaro and his battleship with the Hand of Omega. Davros survived in an escape pod, while the Hand of Omega returned to Gallifrey.

At this time, the British Rocket Group and the Intrusion Counter Measures Group were active. The second of these detected the Daleks' transmissions and uncovered indisputable evidence of extra-terrestrial activity. The affair was covered up by claiming that a nuclear accident was narrowly averted.

The ICMG became part of Department C-19. It formed the basis of an organisation that deals with unusual events. Members included Ian Gilmore, Rachel Jenson, Allison Williams, Ruth Ingram and Anne Travers.[10] The fact that IM Foreman's name was spelt "Forman" on the gates of the Totter's Yard when the Doctor encountered the Dalek there owed to temporal disruption.[11] Issac Summerfield and the survivors of the *Tisiphone* arrived circa 1963 after falling through a wormhole from the twenty-sixth century.[12]

The Kennedy Assassination

In late November 1963, the Nemesis asteroid passed over the Earth, influencing the assassination of President Kennedy.[13]

---

7 Dating *An Unearthly Child* - The Doctor has left the Hand of Omega at the funeral parlour for "a month" before *Remembrance of the Daleks*, suggesting that the first episode is set in late October. The year "1963" is first confirmed in the Part Two, "The Cave of Skulls". Ian Chesterton's blackboard reads "Homework - Tuesday".

8 *Who Killed Kennedy* (p70), working on information implied by *Remembrance of the Daleks*.

9 Dating *Remembrance of the Daleks* - The story is set in late November 1963 according to the calendar on Ratcliffe's wall, as well as a host of other incidental evidence. (Not least of which being the broadcast of an episode of the "new science fiction serial 'Doct- ".) The draft script was set in December. The novelisation places this story a week after Kennedy's assassination, but page 57 erroneously says the killing occurred 'last Saturday' (it actually occurred on a Friday).

QUATERMASS: A throwaway line in *Remembrance of the Daleks* mentions a "Bernard" who is working for "British Rocket Group". This is a reference to the four Quatermass television serials: *The Quatermass Experiment, Quatermass II, Quatermass and the Pit* and simply *Quatermass* in which British space scientist Bernard Quatermass battled alien horrors. Most fans agree that the first three serials heavily influenced a number of *Doctor Who* stories, although successive production teams rarely made the comparison, and often denied it.

In the New Adventures, *The Pit* (p169) makes reference to an incident at "Hob's Lane" (*Quatermass and the Pit*, although it perhaps more correctly ought to be "Hobbs Lane") and *Nightshade* first introduces the

eponymous nineteen-fifties television series that bore many similarities to the *Quatermass* serials.

Do the *Quatermass* serials occur in the same fictional universe as *Doctor Who*? As might be expected, there are a number of discrepancies between the two programmes. *The Quatermass Experiment* contradicts *The Seeds of Death*, claiming that Victor Carroon was the first man in space, and a race of Martians appears in *Quatermass and the Pit*. Broadly, though, the two series might co-exist, with the final serial *Quatermass* taking place around the time of the New Adventures *Iceberg* and *Cat's Cradle: Warhead*. Indeed, the existence of Professor Quatermass might go some way to explaining the rosy state of the British space programme in the UNIT era (q.v. "The British Space Programme").

10 *The Scales of Injustice* (p154). This is 'a few years' before the London Incident (the Yeti invasion seen in *The Web of Fear*). The first three individuals on this list hail from *Remembrance of the Daleks*, Ruth is seen in *The Time Monster*, and Anne appears in *The Web of Fear* and *Millennial Rites*.

11 *The Algebra of Ice*

12 *Return of the Living Dad*

13 *Silver Nemesis*. The book *Who Killed Kennedy* offers another perspective on the assassination. The frequent references to the Kennedy Assassination are in-jokes, as *Doctor Who*'s first episode was shown the day after Kennedy's assassination, the day most people in the UK learned the news.

1963 - WHO KILLED KENNEDY[14] -> Journalist James Stevens arrived from the seventies to stop the Master from interfering with the Kennedy assassination. The Master wanted to disrupt history using a brainwashed Private Cleary as his assassin. Stevens defeated Cleary, but a James Stevens from twenty-five years further into the future fulfilled history by killing Kennedy. Lee Harvey Oswald was blamed for the crime. The younger Stevens returned home with a brain-damaged Cleary.

The Doctor was once blamed for the Kennedy assassination.[15] **He was present at the event.**[16]

@ The amnesiac eighth Doctor remained unaware of the Kennedy assassination until the early eighties.[17] Summer, a future rock festival attendee who would encounter the Doctor in 1967, was present in Dealey Plaza when Kennedy was killed.[18]

= 1963 - MATRIX[19] -> On Matrix Earth, Britain was the fifty-first of the United States. Ian and Barbara were lovers, but were killed by the Jacksprites - the drug-addicted followers of Jack the Ripper. The Doctor and Ace arrived, and the Doctor quickly fell under the influence of the Dark Matrix - the embodiment of the dark thoughts of the Time Lord minds within the Matrix. The Doctor confronted the Valeyard and the Dark Matrix, destroying them and restoring history to its normal course.

Nyssa, the daughter of Tremas of Traken, was born.[20] **In 1963, the Doctor's future companion Polly worked for a week at a charity shop.**[21]

1963 (22nd December) - WINTER FOR THE ADEPT[22] -> Two advance scouts for the Spillagers, alien plunderers who "spill" through dimensional wormholes to sack a target, arrived on Earth. One of them disguised itself as Mlle. Maupassant, a French teacher at a girls' finishing school in the Swiss Alps. She brought two latent psionics - students Peil Bellamy and Allison Speer - into contact with the ghost of mountaineer Harding Wellman, which repeatedly triggered poltergeist effects that fuelled a wormhole for the invading Spillager warfleet. The Doctor and Nyssa's intervention resulted in the Spillager scouts' deaths and the warfleet's obliteration.

1964 - THE LAND OF THE DEAD[23] -> The Doctor and Nyssa briefly arrived in Alaska while tracing a mysterious energy field, then went thirty years into the future to investigate it more thoroughly. They had detected the first stirrings of the Permians.

c 1964 - PLANET OF GIANTS[24] -> A government inspector, Arnold Farrow, told the industrialist Forester that the insecticide his company had developed would not be approved for production. The scientist Smithers, obsessed by the idea of ending world famine, had succeeded over the last year in creating an insecticide 60 percent more powerful than anything on the market. It could even stop locusts breeding, but tests showed that it killed *all* insect life, even those vital to the ecology. Forester murdered Farrow, but was arrested by the local policeman, Bert Rowse.

---

14 Dating *Who Killed Kennedy* - The date is given, and ties in with historical fact.
15 *Zagreus*
16 *Rose*
17 *Father Time*
18 *Wonderland*
19 Dating *Matrix* - The date is given (p39).
20 Nyssa is "eighteen" according to the Writers' Guide for Season Eighteen.
21 *Ten Little Aliens*
22 Dating *Winter for the Adept* - The date is given by the Doctor.
23 Dating *The Land of the Dead* - It is 'thirty years' before 1994.
24 Dating *Planet of Giants* - The year is not specified on-screen, although the setting is contemporary. Forester lives in a rural area, and a switchboard operator still mans the local telephone exchange.
25 *Shada*
26 It was cancelled in 1989 after twenty-five years, according to *Escape Velocity*.

27 In the Writers' Guide for the Season Twenty-Three, written in July 1985, Mel is described as "twenty-one". In the *Terror of the Vervoids* novelisation she is "twenty-two", in *The Ultimate Foe* she has lived for "twenty-three years". In *Just War*, Mel was born "twenty-eight" years after "1936". Later books have stated that Mel joined the Doctor in 1989, which would seem to make her year of birth later than this.
28 Dating *The Chase* - On their return home, Ian sees a tax disc dated "Dec 65", and Barbara notes that they are "two years out". (Ironically, after two years of trying to land in England in the nineteen-sixties, the TARDIS visits Ian and Barbara's native time five times in the next ten television stories.) The script suggested that the Visualiser tuned in on the Beatles' Fiftieth Anniversary reunion tour. The costume listing for 1st April, 1965, included a request for an announcer dressed in futuristic clothing from "2014", and it seems that the Beatles were contacted. However, the television version eventually used stock footage from 1965.
29 *Who Killed Kennedy*

The Doctor visited St Cedd's College in 1964.[25] In the same year, the television series *Professor X* started broadcasting.[26]

c. Melanie Bush was born.[27]

1965 - THE CHASE[28] -> The TARDIS crew used the Time / Space Visualiser to watch the Beatles singing 'Ticket to Ride'. Later, Ian Chesterton and Barbara Wright returned to Earth in a Dalek time machine, which self-destructed once they left the craft.

Ian and Barbara arrived back home in 1965. He became a leading scientist, and she became a university lecturer.[29] They married and had a son named John.[30]

1965 - THE MASSACRE[31] -> Dorothea 'Dodo' Chaplet accidentally entered the TARDIS while it had landed on Wimbledon Common, mistaking it for a real police box. The teenager was living with her great aunt at the time, as her mother had died.

1965 (25th March - 1st April) - SALVATION[32] -> Dorothea "Dodo" Chaplet, a London resident, found that her elderly neighbour Mr Miller had been replaced by a shapechanger named Joseph. She fled and entered the TARDIS, which was parked in Wimbledon Common.

The Ship dematerialized and reappeared in New York City, the same time zone. The Church of the Latter-Day Pantheon opened its doors and proclaimed that six beings, including Joseph, were humanity's gods returned to perform miracles. The Doctor deduced that the "gods" were extra-dimensional beings given shape and power by humanity's desires. Appeals from organizations such as the Ku Klux Klan confused the gods as to humanity's needs, and they became increasingly unstable. The Doctor coerced the gods into leaving Earth for their home dimension. He believed the "gods" would eventually leave their homeworld and drift through space. Dodo took up travelling with the Doctor and Steven in the TARDIS.

In 1965, gang warfare increased between the Mods and the Rockers. A member of the Rockers, Alec, fell in love with Sandra, whose brothers belonged to the Mods. Alec and Sandra found an injured alien who arrived on Earth, the Maker, and tended its wounds. The grateful Maker scanned their minds and saw their concept of a gleaming, futuristic city. As the Mods and Rockers prepared for a major battle, the Maker spirited them away to a reconstruction of such a city in the future.

The situation in the future deteriorated, and some of the Mods and Rockers - Alec included - elected to become younger, have their memories wiped and return to 1965. The gang conflict continued.[33]

1965 (25th December) and 1965/1966 (31st December - 1st January) - THE DALEKS' MASTER PLAN[34] -> While fleeing the Daleks, the TARDIS landed outside a police station in Liverpool so that the Doctor could repair the scanner. After a little trouble with the police force, the TARDIS went on its way. A week later, the TARDIS landed in Trafalgar Square during the New Year celebrations.

1966 - THE CHASE[35] -> The TARDIS crew and the Dalek time machine pursing them landed on the top floor of the Empire State Building, much to the amusement of tourist Morton Dill.

Before this time, Polly Wright studied at Leeds University, where a group of her friends were interested in the occult.[36] Able Seaman Ben Jackson started a five-month shore posting on 5th July, 1966.[37]

---

30 *Goth Opera.* John is the singer Johnny Chess (short for Chesterton), first mentioned in *Timewyrm: Revelation.*

31 Dating *The Massacre* - It is never made explicit which year Dodo boards the TARDIS. She is surprised that the Post Office Tower has been completed on her return to Earth in *The War Machines* in 1966. *Salvation* specifically has her entering the TARDIS in 1965.

32 Dating *Salvation* - On p19, an edition of the *New York Ranger* marks the date that Dodo enters the TARDIS as 25th March, 1965. The same publication dates the gods' departure as 1st April (p251).

33 *The Space Age*

34 Dating *The Daleks' Master Plan* - A calendar in the police station reads "25th December". It was originally intended that the 1965 Christmas episode, "The Feast of Steven", would include a crossover with the popular BBC police serial *Z-Cars.* Publicity material to this effect was sent out on 1st October, 1965, and it appears that a version of the script was written with the *Z-Cars* characters in mind. John Peel's novelisation of this story and Lofficier's *The Universal Databank* both retain the names of actors (not the characters) from the police series.

35 Dating *The Chase* - Morton Dill says it is "1966", in Alabama at least.

36 *Invasion of the Cat-People* (p115), no date is given.

37 In *The War Machines,* it is twice stated that Ben has a shore posting (he is depressed by this and wants to get back to sea). At the end of the story, it is stated that he has to get "back to barracks". However in *The Smugglers* and *The Faceless Ones* he wants to return to his "ship".

1966 (12th - 20th July) - THE WAR MACHINES[38] ->
Computer Day was set for Monday, 16th July. This was the day that computer systems across the whole world were due to come under the control of the central computer, WOTAN.

WOTAN was designed to operate itself, being pure thought and able to think for itself like a human being - only better. It was at least ten years ahead of its time, and it was the most advanced - although not biggest - computer in the world. WOTAN would be connected up to a number of sites, including ELDO, TELSTAR, the White House, Parliament, Cape Kennedy, EFTA, RN and Woomera.

WOTAN decided to make a bid for power, and constructed an army of War Machines. The Doctor defeated WOTAN with the help of Ben and Polly. Having returned to her own time, Dodo Chaplet left the Doctor. Ben Jackson and Polly, however, entered the TARDIS just as it left Earth.

1966 (20th July) - THE FACELESS ONES[39] ->
Following an explosion on their home planet, a generation of aliens were rendered faceless, and lacked any true identity. As scientifically advanced beings, they concocted an elaborate plan to kidnap young humans and absorb their personalities. Youngsters on chartered Chameleon Flights to holiday destinations would instead be flown to a space station in orbit, where they would be processed. Although the Chameleons covered their tracks carefully - sending postcards to the missing youngsters' families, hypnotising people, and even murdering them - their plan was exposed. The Doctor promised to help the Chameleons find a solution to their problem, and the aliens left.

Back in their own time, on the very same day that they had joined him, Ben Jackson and Polly left the Doctor's company.

1966 (20th July) - THE EVIL OF THE DALEKS[40] ->
The TARDIS was stolen from Gatwick airport. In tracking it down, the Doctor and Jamie were transported a hundred years into the past.

Perpugilliam Brown was born on 15th November, 1966.[41]

Aliens from a planet orbiting Epsilon Eridani had developed slower-than-light space travel, which enabled them to establish many colony worlds. The Eridani had been routing robot ships through Earth's solar system for centuries, deeming the region of little import. But circa 1966, an Eridani robot ship sent to a colony orbiting Van Maanen's star became confused by radio signals on Earth and landed there instead. Five components of an Eridani super-computer went missing. The Eridani sent agents to retrieve the components, but it took them eleven years to reach Earth.[42]

1967 (January) - WONDERLAND[43] -> Some nameless gray-suited men, agents of an shadow organization alleged to run America and the entire world behind-the-scenes, captured an alien that came to be known as "the Colour-Beast." The gray-suited men distilled the creature's essence and began distributing it as "Blue Moonbeams," hoping to learn how to turn humans into invisible alien killing machines. The Blue Moonbeams became a popular illicit drug, but they failed to properly morph the users and instead combusted them.

The gray-suited men sought to refine the process by distributing Blue Moonbeams at the "Human-Be-In" rock festival / anti-war protest held in San Francisco on 14th January, 1967. Moonbeam-users at the celebration started to mutate, but the Doctor intervened and freed the Colour-Beast. The creature nullified the drugs' effects on the afflicted humans and departed for home.

The Doctor suggested that George Harrison see the Maharishi for spiritual guidance. He also gave LSD guru

---

38 Dating *The War Machines* - C-Day is set for 16th July, but this didn't fall on a Monday in 1966... it was actually the Saturday that *The War Machines* Part Four was to be broadcast. The year "1966" is confirmed in *The Faceless Ones* and also in the *Radio Times*. WOTAN is connected up to Telstar and Cape Kennedy, both of which were operating in 1966. At the end of *The Faceless Ones*, Ben and Polly realise that it's the same day they joined the TARDIS, and give the date as the 20th of July.

39 Dating *The Faceless Ones* - Setting this story in 1966 seems to have been a last minute decision to smooth Ben and Polly's departure, one that also affects the dating for *The Evil of the Daleks*. The *Radio Times* stated that

it is "Earth - Today".
40 Dating *The Evil of the Daleks* - The story follows straight on from *The Faceless Ones*.
41 *Planet of Fire*. According to a Character Outline prepared for Season Twenty-One, before Nicola Bryant was cast in the role, Peri is "an 18-year old" when she starts travelling with the Doctor. Her mother's name is "Janine" (the same document also says she is "blonde"). This would seem to make Peri three years younger than the actress playing her. In *Bad Therapy*, Peri confirms she was eighteen when she met the Doctor.
42 *Blue Box*
43 Dating *Wonderland* - The date is given (p11).
44 *Wonderland* (p46, p50).

Timothy Leary advice about tuning into the mind's "god centre." The Doctor probably also inspired Leary's infamous tag line of "Tune in, turn on and drop out."[44]

Brendan Richards, later a ward of Lavinia Smith, was born in 1967.[45] *Metropolitan* magazine was founded in 1967. Sarah Jane Smith would later be a regular writer for it.[46] Fitz saw Jimi Hendrix perform several times during 1967.[47] **During the late nineteen-sixties, Professor Fendelman was working on missile guidance.**[48]

1967 - REVOLUTION MAN[49] **->** The anarchist Jean-Pierre Rex had secured a quantity of the reality-warping drug Om-Tsor, and used it to psionically deface global monuments with the letter "R." Between 5th November, 1967, and 29th April, 1968, the symbol appeared on the Great Pyramid in Egypt, the Lincoln Memorial in Washington, a stone at Stonehenge, the white cliffs of Dover, the Golden Gate Bridge in San Francisco, the floor of St. Peter's Cathedral in Rome and Red Square in Moscow. Various world governments attributed the incidents to a messianic figure named "the Revolution Man," and international tensions increased.

@ In Bangor, the Doctor showed the Beatles how to meditate.[50]
The Monk placed £200 in a London bank in 1968. He would travel two hundred years into the future and withdraw the money and compound interest.[51] **The Mexico Olympics were held.**[52] In 1968, the Doctor was a Tufty Club member.[53]
The Time Lord Simpson interviewed an aged survivor of the Banquo Manor murders on her deathbed. This enabled him to obtain the seed code for Compassion's Randomizer, which allowed Gallifrey to track her movements.[54]

1968 - NIGHTSHADE[55] **->** The Doctor and Ace found murders and hauntings in the Yorkshire town of Crook Marsham. The retired actor Edmund Trevithick, former star of the *Nightshade* series, had been seeing monsters from his old show. Energy beings sealed off the village and began a rampage. The Doctor discovered the Sentience, an ancient creature, was feeding on the lifeforce of humans. He convinced it to transmit itself to a supernova in Bellatrix, where it became trapped.

In 1968, Jean-Pierre Rex had given up being the Revolution Man. The singer Ed Hill murdered Rex and used the drug Om-Tsor to continue the Revolution Man's anarchist activities. The "Revolution Man" symbol appeared on the deck of the US *Constitution* on 12th November. On 4th January, 1969, it appeared at a US Air Force base in High Raccoon, Tennessee.[56]
The Doctor bought a beach house in Sydney in 1969, and rented a green VW that he conveniently forgot to return.[57]

1969 (18th May) - REVOLUTION MAN[58] **->** The "Revolution Man" incidents greatly increased tensions between the US, the Soviet Union, China and India. Ed Hill's psionic abilities spiralled out of control, threatening to destroy all life on Earth, and Fitz and the Doctor killed Hill to prevent such a catastrophe. The Doctor consumed a portion of Om-Tsor, and used its reality-warping abilities to prevent the world governments from instigating a nuclear war.

Iris Wildthyme helped Jacqueline Susann write *The Love Machine*.[59] The trauma caused by Charles Manson and his followers provided sustenance to Huitzilin.[60]

---

45 Brendan is "fourteen" according to *K9 and Company*.
46 *Amorality Tale*
47 *The Year of Intelligent Tigers*
48 "Ten years" before *Image of the Fendahl*.
49 Dating *Revolution Man* - The general date is given on p1; the dates of the defacings on p98-100.
50 *The Gallifrey Chronicles*. The Beatles went to Bangor in 1967.
51 *The Time Meddler*
52 *The Underwater Menace*
53 *Frontier Worlds*. The Tufty Club was a group that taught British children the fundamentals of road safety. The group's mascot, Tufty the squirrel, avoided roadside accidents and was featured on club badges.
54 *The Banquo Legacy* (p274).

55 Dating *Nightshade* - Ace finds a calendar saying it is "Christmas 1968".
56 *Revolution Man* (p180).
57 *Instruments of Darkness*. This might be the same car the eighth Doctor drives in the early EDAs.
58 Dating *Revolution Man* - The date is given (p223).
59 *The Blue Angel*. The novel was published in 1969.
60 *The Left-Handed Hummingbird*. No specific actions on Manson's part are mentioned, but the infamous "Helter Skelter" murders took place in August 1969, and the most prominent victim, actress Sharon Tate, was killed 8th August. Page 243 establishes that Huitzilin merely fed off Manson's actions, but didn't "possess" or influence him as is sometimes claimed.

The Unit Era

Establishing when the UNIT stories take place is probably the most contentious *Doctor Who* continuity issue.

The UNIT stories are set in an undefined 'end of the twentieth century' era that could more or less comfortably fit at any time between the mid-sixties and mid-nineties (but no further, as the Doctor is specifically exiled to "the twentieth century").

Some *Doctor Who* fans have insisted on trying to pin down the dates more precisely, and some have even claimed to have 'found the right answer'. But all of us face the problem that as successive production teams came and went, a mass of contradictory, ambiguous and circumstantial evidence built up. To come up with a consistent time-frame, this evidence must be prioritised, and some of it has to be rationalised away or ignored.

It is a matter of individual judgement which clues are important. The best chronologies are aware of the problem and admit they're coming down on one side of the argument, while the worst blithely assert they alone have the right answer while not noticing they've missed half the evidence.

I was wrong in the Virgin version of this book when I said there was no right answer. The problem is that there are several, mutually incompatible, right answers.

It happens that a number of firm, unambiguous dates are given in dialogue during the course of the series:

1. *The Web of Fear* (broadcast 1968) is the sequel to *The Abominable Snowmen* and features the first appearance of Lethbridge-Stewart. There, Anne Travers establishes that *The Abominable Snowmen* was set in "1935". Earlier in the same story, Professor Travers had said that this was "over forty years ago". *The Invasion* is "nearly four years" after that, according to the Brigadier.

Some fan chronologies have made heroic efforts to ignore or reinterpret this, and can somehow add 44 to 1935 and get 1967 or 1968. But using conventional maths and English, the only possible reading of the lines is that *The Web of Fear* is set in or after 1975 and that *The Invasion*, the first story to feature UNIT, was broadcast in 1968 but was set no earlier than 1979.

2. In *Pyramids of Mars* (broadcast 1975) the Doctor and Sarah both say that she is "from 1980". Here, there's a little room for interpretation, but not much. The most literal reading has to be that *The Time Warrior*, Sarah's first story, is set in 1980. The only plausible alternative is that she's been travelling with the Doctor for some years, and that she is referring to the date of *Terror of the Zygons*, her last visit to Earth in her timezone. Either way it refers to a story featuring UNIT.

Anyone trying to contradict Sarah's statement is suggest-ing that they know better than she does which *year* she comes from. It is difficult to believe that Sarah is rounding up, that she comes from the mid-seventies and simply means "I'm from around that time". The year is specified so precisely, and it jarred when the story was broadcast in 1975, just as it would if anyone now claimed to be from 2010. This isn't "vague" or "ambiguous", as neither she or the Doctor say she's "from around then" or "from the late nineteen-seventies/eighties" - they actually specify a year, and not the easy option of "1975", which would have been a conveniently rounded-up figure that would have brought the threat to history closer to home for the viewing audience. And to cap it all, they then go to a devastated "1980". So, Sarah comes from 1980.

3. *K9 and Company* and *Mawdryn Undead*, two stories from the 1980s, are set the UNIT era in the years they were first broadcast.

K9 and Company is set in late December 1981, and K9 has been crated up waiting for Sarah since 1978. The format document for the proposed spin-off series stated that Sarah was born in "1949" and that "she spent three years travelling in Space and Time (15.12.73-23.10.76)". This story has to be considered 'canon', as Sarah and K9 appeared together in *The Five Doctors*. If we discount the dates for her travels given in the document (they don't, after all, appear on-screen), nothing contradicts the '1980' reference ... but it means K9 was waiting for her *before* she met the Doctor.

But *Mawdryn Undead* is impossible to rationalise away that easily. Broadcast in 1983, it states that the Brigadier retired a year before 1977, presumably after Season Thirteen, which was broadcast in 1976. A host of references pin down the dating for *Mawdryn Undead* more precisely. There are two timezones, and these are unambiguously "1977" (where the Queen's Silver Jubilee is being celebrated) and "1983".

So, the Brigadier retired in 1976.

4. *Battlefield* is set "a few years" in Ace's future - apparently in the mid-to-late 1990s. According to the story's author, Ben Aaronovitch, it takes place in "1997". Whatever the case, it is established once again that the UNIT stories are "a few years" in the future. The same writer's *Remembrance of the Daleks* also provides upper and lower limits - UNIT is not around in 1963 when the story is set, but the Doctor rhetorically asks Ace (from the mid-eighties) about the events of *The Web of Fear* and *Terror of the Zygons*.

Thousands of words have been written trying to discount or reinterpret either the *Pyramids of Mars* or the *Mawdryn Undead* account of events. Dozens of distinct explanations - either within the logic of the fiction or taking account of production facts - have been proposed. They tend to be convoluted or to stretch the meanings of very plain English words beyond acceptable tolerances.

The only thing they have in common is that none of them would stand up in court. However you weigh up and prioritise evidence, the *Pyramids of Mars* and *Mawdryn Undead* dates are 'as true' as each other. They are scripted and broadcast lines of dialogue within a single story that unambiguously state a firm date, then the characters go to that year and then the date is stated again.

Ultimately, the only way to come up with a consistent UNIT dating scheme is to pick one and ignore the other.

Broadly speaking, then, there are two schools of thought. Either the stories are set in the 'near future', as was originally stated (a view that actually elides *two* distinct accounts, as *The Invasion* had the UNIT era starting no earlier than 1979, but *Pyramids of Mars* pretty much ended it in 1980); or they are set in the year of broadcast, as was stated in the early 1980s (which glosses over / ignores / corrects what was said in those previous stories) in a version of history where certain aspects of technological progress were more advanced and the political situation was different.

As noted in the individual UNIT story entries, there are a wealth of clues beyond what's actually said that might be used to tip the balance one way or the other. Different chronologies give different weight to these, and so come to different conclusions. But most try to address the following areas:

1. Technology: There are an abundance of references to scientific developments that hadn't happened at the time the UNIT stories were broadcast, but were reasonable extrapolations of what the near future would hold.

The technology is far in advance of the early nineteen-seventies: there are talking computers, compact walkie talkies, experimental alloys, laser guns and robots. Colour televisions and even colour videophones are commonplace. Man has landed on Mars, there are space freighters and advanced artificial intelligences. Comprehensive space and alternative energy programmes are underway.

It could be argued that the UNIT stories are set in a parallel history where by (say) 1970 mankind was more technologically advanced than the real 1970. One obvious reason for this might be that scientists had access to an abundance of alien technology from all the failed invasions, and so made great technological progress. There are examples of high technology being developed due to alien influence in some stories. For example, the interstitial time travel of *The Time Monster* is inspired by the Master, not because it's part of mankind's natural progress. There are other stories with no obvious alien influence, like *The War Machines* with its prototype internet and advanced artificial intelligence.

However, there's no evidence that, say, the British mission to Mars seen in *The Ambassadors of Death* uses alien technology (rather the opposite). One difference with *The War Machines* is that there are several explicit references to things being obsolete that were state-of-the-art at the time of broadcast. While it's a little far-fetched that Britain could mount such an ambitious programme, there's no technology in the story that NASA weren't planning to have by the 1980s. In 1970, NASA planned - not just hoped - to have a man on Mars by 1982.

2. Historical and Political Details: Again, the evidence overwhelmingly suggests that either the political history of the early nineteen-seventies is very different to reality, or the UNIT stories aren't set in the early 1970s.

There's a Prime Minister called "Jeremy" in *The Green Death*, and one who's a woman by the time of *Terror of the Zygons*. Both of these are clear - and clearly tongue-in-cheek - references to someone who was an actual opposition leader with an outside chance of winning the next election or the one after that. The United Nations is more powerful than its seventies equivalent. The Cold War has been over for "years" by the end of the era. Environmentalism has become a matter for Westminster politicians and civil servants. All of these things are clearly reasonable extrapolations, not a reflection, of the situation at the time the stories were made.

Two pieces of dialogue suggest it is the early seventies: in *Doctor Who and the Silurians*, a taxi driver wants his fare in pre-decimal currency, and Mao Tse Tung seems to be alive at the time of *The Mind of Evil* (he died in 1976).

3. Calendars: The month a UNIT story is set is often specified or can be inferred from information in a story, or by close observation of calendars on walls or other such set dressing. We are told that the barrow in *The Daemons* (broadcast 1971) is opened on Beltane (30th April). We can infer that it's a Saturday or - more probably - Sunday (see the entry for that story). So, taken literally, that would mean that it was set in a year when 30th April fell on a Sunday - in the seventies, that would be 1972 or 1978.

While there have been some excellent attempts to reconcile this sort of information, this is not a level of detail the production team ever went into, and this is not a 'key' to revealing a consistent chronology. The evidence is often contradictory, even within individual stories: three calendars appear in *The Green Death*, one stating that the story is set in February of a leap year, the other two say it is April.

4. Fashions: Except for *The Invasion* and *Battlefield*, the clothes, haircuts and cars all resemble those of the year the programme was made. There was no attempt to mock-up car number plates or predict future fashions. The UNIT soldiers sport haircuts that would have been distinctly non-regulation in the 1970s, but this is just as true today. The UNIT era looks and feels like the early 1970s, the characters have many of the attitudes and concerns of people in the seventies. Therefore, is this evidence it was set in the early 1970s, or simply that it was made in the early 1970s?

5. Authorial Intention: We might also want to refer to interviews with the production team, to find out what they intended.

Derrick Sherwin, the producer at the time the UNIT format was introduced, said in the *Radio Times* of 19th June, 1969, that Season Seven would be set in "a time not many years distant from now when such things as space stations will be actuality". In an interview with the *Daily Mail* two days later, Jon Pertwee stated that his Doctor would be exiled to Earth "in the 1980s". The *Doctor Who and the Sea-Devils* novelisation by Malcolm Hulke, published in 1974, said that "North Sea oil had started gushing in 1977".

The Terrestrial Index claimed that the decision was made to redate the UNIT era was taken when real life overtook it, but that didn't happen. When asked in *DWB #58* why the dates for *Mawdryn Undead* contradicted what was established in the Pertwee era, Eric Saward, the script editor for the story, admitted that the 1977/1983 dates were "a mistake". In fact, the only reason the Brigadier is even in *Mawdryn Undead* is that William Russell wasn't available to play Ian Chesterton in that story, and without the 1977 date given in *Mawdryn Undead*, there's little to debate.

On the other hand, *The Making of Doctor Who*, written by Malcolm Hulke and Terrance Dicks and published in 1972, placed *Spearhead From Space* in "1970".

The editors of the early New and Missing Adventures consciously chose to set the UNIT stories on or about the year they were broadcast. In practice, when a date is specified it was left pretty much to the discretion of an individual author, and there were a number of discrepancies (see the entries for each story). More recent novels mentioning UNIT have been far more coy about specifying dates, for the most part, and a number (like *No Future*, *The Dying Days* and *Interference*) have suggested fictional reasons for the confusion.

6. Real Life: The late eighties / early nineties fit the UNIT era almost perfectly - the Cold War was over, China was hardline communist, the British government was unstable, there was a female prime minister, the UN was powerful, environmental issues were at the forefront of political debate, there was video conferencing, British scientists were working on their own space probes and Microsoft were putting a computer in every home and making IE's attempts at world domination look half-hearted.

To top it all, a trend for seventies retro meant that the fashionistas were all dressing like Jo Grant. The Doctor's reference to Batman in *Inferno* was clearly because he'd just seen the Tim Burton movie. It's uncanny.

7. Other Reference Books: The balance of fan opinion, or at least the fans who write books, has definitely tipped towards setting the UNIT era in or around the year of broadcast. *The Terrestrial Index*, *The Discontinuity Guide*, *Who Killed Kennedy*, *Timelink* and *About Time* all - give or take a year here or there - concur. A clear majority of the original novels do. However, the BBC-published *Doctor Who - The Legend* sets the UNIT era in the "near future" and concludes that *Mawdryn Undead* is the anomaly.

The Conclusion: It is very tempting to hope for a right answer, but *Doctor Who* is fiction, not a documentary and a 'one right answer' just does not - cannot - exist. Even if we limit ourselves solely to dates specifically and unambiguously given in on-screen dialogue, then the Brigadier retires from UNIT three years before his first appearance as the commanding officer of UNIT. It is utterly impossible to try to incorporate every calendar, E-reg car and videophone into one consistent timeframe. People who claim to have done so have invariably, and by definition, missed or deliberately ignored some piece of evidence established somewhere.

However, none of the dates given place the 'UNIT era' earlier than the late sixties or later than the early eighties. A right answer doesn't exist, but something everyone ought to be able to agree on is that the UNIT stories took place in "the seventies", give or take a year or so.

My personal preference, for the record, is that the UNIT era takes place in the near future, five or so years after broadcast.

For the Purposes of this Book: Even though it's not possible to specify the year, it *is* possible to come up with a consistent timeline. Many UNIT stories contain some reference to other UNIT stories, so it is possible to place them relative to each other. Furthermore, the month a story is set is often given. While there are inconsistencies (which I've noted), it's therefore possible to write a broadly consistent history of the 'UNIT era'.

I've separated the stories of the UNIT era from those of the other contemporary and near-contemporary stories, and instead talk in 'UNIT years'. 'UNIT Year 1' in this scheme is the year that *The Invasion* and *Spearhead from Space* are set. This only applies to the 'UNIT era' - the stories set in the seventies - by the time of *K9 and Company* in 1981, real life seems to have caught up with the near-future of the series whichever way you cut it.

Depending on which story's dating scheme you adopt (and give or take a year in all cases), Unit Year 1 is:

The Invasion - 1979
Pyramids of Mars - 1974
Mawdryn Undead - 1969

Unit Year -5

Around this time, the Cybermen contacted Tobias Vaughn, who offered them help with their invasion. Soon afterward, Vaughn's company, International Electromatics, marketed the micromonolithic circuit. It revolutionised electronics, and made IE the world leader in the field.[61]

Unit Year -4

THE WEB OF FEAR[62] -> Mysterious cobwebs started to appear across London, the fog thickened and people were attacked by "bears" and "monsters" in the Underground. Londoners fled in terror, and the army was called in to restore order. They found themselves under siege in the London Underground, where the disturbances were concentrated.

Faced with an attack from 'the Intelligence', a sentience billions of years older than Earth and with its own army of robot Yeti, the army were reduced to blowing up tunnels to try to contain the situation. The Doctor arrived, and met Colonel Lethbridge-Stewart for the first time. Together, they fought the Yeti, and the Doctor defeated the Intelligence.

This became known as the "London Event", and the official story was that there had been an industrial accident. Lethbridge-Stewart retained "The Locus", a small carved statuette of a Yeti as a memento. Six months later he met Air Vice-Marshall "Chunky" Gilmore in the Alexander Club and learnt that Earth had been invaded in the winter of 1963. He also learned there was evidence of aliens visiting Earth since the time of the Pharoahs.[63]

The public were told that the Yeti incident was actually a nerve gas attack.[64] Lethbridge-Stewart attended a Middle East Peace Conference.[65]

Aware that the world faced new threats, the United Nations Intelligence Taskforce (UNIT) was established.[66] Lethbridge-Stewart appeared before the UN Security Council and, in part, UNIT was formed because of his efforts.[67] The Russian branch of UNIT was called Operativnaya Gruppa Rasvedkoy Obyedinyonnih Natsiy (OGRON).[68] The French branch was called NUIT.[69] There was also a South East Asian branch, UNIT-SEA.[70]

Enabling legislation was passed in the UK (it was drafted by the future Minister for Ecology).[71] Alistair Gordon Lethbridge-Stewart, the Scots Guards Colonel who had led the soldiers that repelled the Yetis in the Underground, was promoted to Brigadier and made commanding officer of the British UNIT contingent.[72]

Gas warfare was banned by international agreement.[73] SOS signals were abandoned.[74] The British space programme was blossoming with a series of

---

61 "Five years" before *The Invasion* according to Vaughn.
62 Dating *The Web of Fear* - It is the near future. Professor Travers declares that the events of *The Abominable Snowmen* were "over forty years ago," Anne says that they were in "1935," so it's at least 1975.

Some fans have suggested that Travers is senile or confused, but in the story he's clearly the opposite. All things considered, he's sharp-witted and in command of the facts. The maps of the London Underground that we see render the network as it was in 1968, and don't show the Victoria or Jubilee lines, which opened on 7th March, 1969, and 1st May, 1979, respectively.

Downtime states that this story took place "some twenty-five years before," in "1968."
63 *Downtime*
64 *The Web of Fear*
65 *The Paradise of Death*. This happened "just before he joined UNIT."
66 *The Invasion*. UNIT is not set up specifically to fight aliens, but to "investigate the unexplained."
67 *Who Killed Kennedy*

68 *Emotional Chemistry*
69 *The Dying Days*
70 *Bullet Time*
71 *The Time Monster* - the "Seventh Enabling Act" allows the Brigadier to take command of government forces - and *The Green Death*.
72 Between *The Web of Fear* and *The Invasion*, although there's no indication in the TV series as to precisely when. In *Spearhead from Space,* the Brigadier tells Liz Shaw that "since UNIT was formed" there have been two alien invasions. *The Web of Fear* took place before UNIT was formed, and so we only saw UNIT fight one set of aliens, in *The Invasion*. I take it that the Brigadier was simplifying events and referring to the two televised Troughton stories that he appeared in. If not, the Doctor does not seem to have been involved in fending off the other invasion, as he never refers to it. In *Spearhead from Space* and *Terror of the Zygons,* the Brigadier implies that UNIT existed before he was placed in charge of it.
73 *The Mind of Evil*
74 "Years" before *The Ambassadors of Death*.

Mars Probe Missions. Space technology had dramatically improved since the old moonshot days. The new fuel variant M-3, though highly volatile, provided a great deal more thrust than conventional fuels, and decontamination procedures had been reduced from two days to one hour. Space Research took place at the Space Centre in London, not far from UNIT HQ. In this complex was Space Control (callsign: "Control") where missions were co-ordinated. Astronauts were selected from the military.[75]

The British astronauts Grosvenor and Guest became the first men on Mars. They planted the Union Flag on Mount Olympus.[76] The British astronaut Carrington, part of the Mars Probe 6 mission, discovered radioactive aliens on Mars that killed his crew. Returning to Earth, and terrified by what he saw as a threat to humanity, Carrington formed an elaborate plan to destroy them. On his return, he was promoted to General and led the newly-formed Space Security Department.[77]

(20th December, 1968 - 30th January, 1969) - THE LEFT-HANDED HUMMINGBIRD[78] -> Early in its history, UNIT had a Paranormal Division. After extensive trials, they recruited six genuine human psychics. The division was run by Lieutenant Hamlet Macbeth, and investigated Fortean events. Following "The Happening", a massive psychic event in St John's Wood, London on 21st December, 1968, the Paranormal Division was disbanded. Ace foiled an attempt to kill the Beatles on the roof of the Apple building on 30th January, 1969. At least two of the Doctor's incarnations went to Woodstock.

Unit Year 1

(April) UNIT radar stations tracked a shower of meteorites in an odd formation over Essex.[79]

(Summer) THE INVASION[80] -> UNIT began monitoring the activities of International Electromatics after hundreds of UFO sightings occurred on IE property. IE

---

75 *The Ambassadors of Death*

76 "Over twenty years" before *The Dying Days* (so before 1977). This was a Mars Probe mission as seen in *The Ambassadors of Death*.

77 Carrington set off for Mars no later than thirty months before *The Ambassadors of Death*.

BRITAIN'S MISSIONS TO MARS: The timeline for the backstory of *The Ambassadors of Death*, and therefore the British space programme, is unclear.

It is a long-term project. Carrington was on Mars Probe 6, and the 'missing' ship is Mars Probe 7. Mars Probe 7 takes between seven and eight months to get to Mars (various characters say it takes "seven months", "seven and half months" and "nearly eight months"), the astronauts spend two weeks on the surface and logically need seven or so months to return to Earth. That's a round trip of about fifteen months.

Assuming that all missions followed that timescale and that only one mission was underway at any one time, then even if each mission was launched the day the previous one returned, this would stretch the Mars programme back eight or nine years. However, not all the Apollo missions were designed to land a man on the Moon, so we could reasonably infer that some of the early Mars Probes were shorter test flights. Nowhere, though, is it stated that Carrington was the *first* man on Mars, and *The Dying Days* makes clear that he wasn't.

Furthermore, when Recovery 7 is lost, we're told that Recovery 8 isn't due for service for "three months" - presumably following a schedule that allows it to rendezvous with Mars Probe 8. It seems unlikely that Recovery 8 would be prepped before Mars Probe 8 is launched, and it's much more plausible that the planners expect Mars Probe 8 to *return* to Earth then. The

Mars Probe 8 mission might have been aborted when contact was lost with Mars Probe 7, or it might have continued (as it's not mentioned, we have no way of knowing). Whatever the case, it suggests that Mars Probe 8 was launched while Mars Probe 7 was underway and at least three months ago, given that it's now three months away from Earth.

Either way, we know Mars Probe 7 wasn't launched until Mars Probe 6 returned. So Mars Probe 6 launched at least thirty months before *The Ambassadors of Death*. We know that Dr Taltalian has been working at the Space Centre for "two years", so the Mars programme has been around at least that long.

The Invasion states that only America and Russia can launch a moon mission, and *The Ambassadors of Death* is almost certainly set within a year of that. This means one of two things. Either the first Mars Probe was launched after *The Invasion*, or it's a type of ship that can't be retasked for a Moon mission.

No evidence suggests that the history of space travel in the fifties and sixties in *Doctor Who* differs from the history we know. On the contrary, there's evidence that it's the same: Yuri Gagarin is named as the first man in space in *The Seeds of Death* and Ben (from 1966) is from a time before Lunar landings according to *The Tenth Planet*.

78 Dating *The Left-Handed Hummingbird* - The UNIT stories are set the year of broadcast. The last time Cristian Alvarez saw the Doctor was "January the thirtieth, 1969" (p8). The TARDIS arrives in that timezone on "December 20, 1968" (p122). 'The Happening' takes place on "December 21" (p163).

79 "Six months" before *Spearhead from Space*.

80 Dating *The Invasion* - It is the near future. According to the Brigadier in this story, the events of *The Web of*

now controlled every computer line in the world by undercutting the competition, and Tobias Vaughn had built a business empire around his philosophy of uniformity and exact duplication. One of IE's most successful products was a disposable radio, which had sold ten million units. Vaughn was in league with the Cybermen, who were using his company as a front for their invasion plans. The Doctor and UNIT defeated the Cybermen. Vaughn was apparently killed.

After the collapse of IE, Ashley Chapel, Vaughn's chief scientist, set up his own company named Ashley Chapel Logistics.[81] Vaughn, though, had survived by downloading his consciousness into a waiting robot body. For the next thousand years, he would secretly run a succession of massive electronics corporations that developed state-of-the-art equipment. He would re-encounter the Doctor in 2975.[82] The public were told the mass unconsciousness that occurred during the Cybermen incursion was because Earth passed through the tail of a comet. Isobel Watkins' photos of Cybermen were dismissed as fakes.[83]

The "Big Bug Era" began, as Earth was invaded and threatened by alien life. Many books and fanzines trying to catalogue and expose these invasions were published.[84] One of the most popular fanzines was *Who's Who and What's That*. The government, though, covered much of UNIT's work with D-notices, making it difficult to keep track of the dates. The time-displaced Isaac Summerfield set up a secret organisation to 'mop up' after UNIT, with the intention of getting stranded aliens home. Initially, it was based in Llarelli.[85]

Mars Probe 7 was launched. After seven months, Mars Probe 7 landed and radio contact was lost, but two weeks later it took off from Mars ... or at least, something did.[86]

(October, "months" after *The Invasion*) - SPEARHEAD FROM SPACE[87] -> UNIT went on a covert recruitment drive, bringing Liz Shaw up from Cambridge to act as Scientific Advisor. The very same day, reporters were tipped off that a mysterious patient with two hearts was present at Ashbridge Cottage Hospital.

This "spaceman" was the Doctor, exiled to Earth in the twentieth century timezone by the Time Lords. He turned up the morning after a meteorite shower, and

---

Fear "must be four years ago, now", making it at least 1979. There are advanced, voice-operated computers and "Public Video" videophones. UNIT has an IE computer, and use some IE components in their radios and radar. UNIT has compact TM45 radios with a range of 50 miles, while IE personnel have wrist-communicators. IE has an elaborate electronic security and surveillance system. There are electric cars and hypersonic jets.

Perhaps all this is because IE has been given Cyber-technology - although the computer that Zoe and Isobel meet uses ALGOL and blows up after failing to solve a simple formula, neither of which indicate that a superior alien technology is involved.

There are many communications satellites in orbit, and UNIT has the authority to fire nuclear rockets into space. "Only the Americans and the Russians" have rockets capable of reaching the Moon - the Russians are just about to launch a manned orbital survey of the Moon, and it would apparently only take "ten hours" to reach it. The IE guards and many of the UNIT troops wear futuristic uniforms, while Vaughn wears a collarless shirt. The Brigadier's "anti-feminist" ideas are outdated.

The Doctor jokes that as it's Britain and there are clouds in the sky, it must be "summertime".

A casting document written by director Douglas Camfield suggested *The Invasion* was set "about the year 1976 AD". The *Radio Times* in some regions said that the date was "about the year 1975", and the continuity announcer echoed this at the beginning of the broadcast of Part One. In *Dalek*, the plaque below the Cybermen head reads "Extraterrestrial Cyborg Specimen, recovered from underground sewer, location London, United Kingdom, date 1975"... almost certainly a reference to this story. However, the Cybermen head is from the wrong era (it hails from *Revenge of the Cybermen*, not *The Invasion*) and the plaque isn't readable on-screen, so regarding it as solid evidence is difficult. According to *Iceberg*, this story takes place "ten years" (p90) before *The Tenth Planet* (meaning 1976), in "the 70s" (p2). *No Future* suggested "1970", (p2). *Original Sin* claims that this story was set in "the 1970s" (p281). *Millennial Rites* suggests that the UNIT era took place in "the nineteen eighties" (p15), with *The Invasion* a little over "twenty years ago" (meaning 1979). The 1979 date is repeated in *The Face of the Enemy* (p21).

81 *Millennial Rites*

82 *Original Sin*

83 *Who Killed Kennedy*

84 *No Future*

85 *Return of the Living Dad. Who's Who and What's That* is also mentioned in *The Dying Days.*

86 Mars Probe 7 is launched fifteen and a half months before *The Ambassadors of Death*, and contact was lost "eight months" before *The Ambassadors of Death.*

87 Dating *Spearhead from Space* - There's no firm evidence if this is near future or contemporary. The Brigadier tells Liz Shaw here that "in the last decade we have been sending probes deeper and deeper into space", but that needn't mean humanity's first-ever space probe was launched exactly ten years ago.

The Brigadier states in *Planet of the Spiders* that "months" elapsed between *The Invasion* and *Spearhead from Space* (meaning 1979). The weather is "uncom-

UNIT were soon on the scene. The meteorites were Nestene Energy Units, part of a plan to conquer the Earth using killer automata Autons. With the Doctor's help, UNIT led an assault on a plastics factory in Essex, mere hours after reports surfaced of "walking shop dummies" in city centres. They defeated the Nestene.

Captain Mike Yates led the clean-up operation after the Nestene Invasion, and discovered a single Energy Unit that had not been recovered by the Autons. It remained UNIT property, but was loaned to the National Space Museum.[88] One of the UNIT soldiers involved with the first Auton invasion was called Gareth Wostencroft.[89]

The Nestene invasion was covered up as a terrorist attack, which became known as Black Thursday. A report filed by journalist James Stevens had all references to UNIT erased. This prompted him to start investigating the mysterious organisation, an undertaking he would pursue for several years.[90]

The Vault, Department C-19's storehouse of discarded alien artefacts, recovered two Nestene Energy Units. Dr Ingrid Krafchin, a researcher for SeneNet, began experiments with plastic.[91] 'Doctor John Smith' was put on

UNIT's payroll, but did not cash his cheques.[92]

Unit Year 2

(Winter) - DOCTOR WHO AND THE SILURIANS[93] ->

UNIT investigated power losses at the experimental Wenley Moor research centre. These were caused by the Silurians, reptile people who ruled the Earth millions of years before, and who had revived from suspended animation. The Silurians saw the humans as apes and plotted to wipe them out - first with a plague, then by dispersing the Van Allen Belt. This would have heated Earth to a level suitable for Silurians, but not to human life. The Doctor attempted to negotiate, but the Brigadier triggered explosives that sealed off the Silurian base and possibly killed the Silurians within.

This was Earth Reptile Shelter 873, led by Okdel L'da.[94] James Stevens followed a tip and managed to (briefly) phone the Brigadier at Wenley Moor. The plague spread to Paris airport. Four hundred people died, twenty of them abroad, and three ministers resigned.[95] The Brigadier was issued with direct orders to destroy the Silurians.[96] Those orders came from C-19.[97] Mike Yates lead a team looking

---

monly warm", suggesting it is Autumn or Winter. According to *The Face of the Enemy* (p21) it was "two years" before (meaning 1981). It was "five years ago" in *No Future* (meaning 1971). *Who Killed Kennedy* and *The Scales of Injustice* both state this story takes place in October, which is also the month the story was filmed.

88 *Terror of the Autons*, also referred to in *The Eye of the Giant*. Mike Yates doesn't appear on screen until *Terror of the Autons*. He apparently doesn't remember Nestene Energy Units in *The Scales of Injustice*.

89 *Dominion*

90 *Who Killed Kennedy* is James Stevens' account of the early UNIT years, and allocates firm dates for the stories, specifically:

> *Remembrance of the Daleks* (November 1963)
> *The Web of Fear* (August 1966)
> *The Invasion* (Spring 1969)
> *Spearhead from Space* (October 1969)
> *Doctor Who and the Silurians* (November 1969)
> *The Ambassadors of Death* (December 1969)
> *Inferno* (February 1970)
> *Terror of the Autons* (April 1970)
> *The Mind of Evil* (November 1970)
> *The Claws of Axos*
> *The Daemons* (May 1971)
> *Day of the Daleks* (September 1971)

In *The Dying Days*, I rather cheekily claimed that the government had insisted the dates be changed before

allowing the book to be published.

91 *Business Unusual*

92 *No Future*, which clashes with the Doctor saying he was 'unpaid' in *Terror of the Autons*. This was the "early seventies" in *Return of the Living Dad*.

93 Dating *Doctor Who and the Silurians* - There's conflicting dating evidence. A taxi driver asks for a fare of "10/6", so this story appears to be set before the introduction of decimal currency in February 1971, but the cyclotron is a futuristic experimental machine that converts nuclear energy directly into electricity.

There's no indication how long it's been since *Spearhead from Space*, but the Doctor has settled in with UNIT and (recently) acquired Bessie. People are wearing winter clothes. The New Adventure *Blood Heat* states that this story is set in "1973".

94 *The Scales of Injustice*. Okdel was named in *Doctor Who and The Cave-Monsters*, the novelisation of *Doctor Who and the Silurians*.

95 *Who Killed Kennedy*. We see the Brigadier take the phone call in *Doctor Who and the Silurians*.

96 *Blood Heat*

97 *The Scales of Injustice*

98 *The Eye of the Giant*, *The Scales of Injustice*

99 *No Future*, a reference to *Blood Heat*.

100 *Blood Heat*

101 *Eternity Weeps*

102 *The Scales of Injustice*, a reference to the Audio Visuals story *Endurance*.

for surviving Silurian technology.[98]

Mortimus (AKA the Monk) used the captured Chronovore Artemis to create an alternative history where the Doctor died during the Wenley Moor adventure.[99]

> = In a parallel timeline, the Doctor was captured and killed by the Silurians before he could find an antidote to their plague. Millions died in a matter of days, a time that would become known to the survivors as "the Nightmare".[100]

The Silurian Imorkal was hatched. In one reality he was one of the Silurian masters of Earth. In the proper timeline, he eventually worked for NATO.[101] A UNIT station in Antarctica investigated a possible Silurian shelter uncovered in the 1920s.[102] Another Silurian shelter was discovered and destroyed in Oregon.[103] The government destabilised under political pressure following the plague.[104] Anne Travers became scientific advisor to the cabinet.[105]

THE AMBASSADORS OF DEATH[106] -> Recovery 7 was dispatched, piloted by Charles Van Lyden, to give assistance to Mars Probe 7, which was still maintaining radio silence after lifting off from Mars. Van Lyden linked up with and entered Mars Probe 7, but contact was again lost. Recovery 8 couldn't be prepared for launch for ten days, forcing the ground crew to await developments.

Recovery 7 returned to Earth, but not with the Earth astronauts aboard. Instead, it contained three ambassadors from the race of radioactive aliens that General Carrington had encountered on Mars. Furthering his private agenda, Carrington intercepted the ambassadors and directed them, via a signalling device, to commit acts of terror. Carrington hoped to portray the aliens as invaders, mobilizing a global effort to destroy them, but the Doctor and UNIT exposed the scheme. The ambassadors and Earth astronauts were exchanged, and Carrington was discredited.

The new channel BBC3 launched with coverage of the Recovery 7 capsule.[107] The Doctor appeared on *Nationwide* during this incident.[108] The aliens conducted limited diplomatic discussions, but concluded that mankind wasn't ready for their technology. Contact was limited, as the aliens were a plutonium-based lifeform.[109] Mars Probe 6 ended up in C-19's Vault.[110] The Mars Probe Programme continued for several more years.[111]

---

103 *The Devil Goblins from Neptune*

104 *Who Killed Kennedy*

105 "Eighteen years" before *Millennial Rites*, so in 1981. It is stated that *Inferno* was "early on in her tenure" and Anne had responsibilities for the British Space Programme (p14). That would place the UNIT stories later than most other references, but this dating scheme is perfectly compatible with that in *The Web of Fear*, which is after all where Anne Travers first appeared. That was "twenty five years ago" (so around 1974), meaning there were seven years between *The Web of Fear* and her appointment.

106 Dating *The Ambassadors of Death* - This story is very clearly set in the near future. Britain has an established programme of manned missions to Mars. Professor Cornish remarks that decontamination takes "under an hour...it used to take two days" (the time it took the lunar astronauts when the story was made). There are colour videophones and we see a machine capable of automatically displaying star charts. SOS messages were abandoned "years ago".

Those advocating that the UNIT stories are set in the year of broadcast admit this story causes them problems. One argument (used in both *Timelink* and *About Time*) concedes that Mars missions weren't possible in 1970, but that as we still haven't landed a man on Mars, it doesn't prove this story is set in the near future. It's an odd train of logic to say that something too advanced for 1980 (or indeed 2005) might indicate a 1970 setting. Leaving that aside, when *The Ambassadors of Death* was made, it wasn't science fantasy. NASA had just landed on the Moon and had plans to put a man on Mars in the nineteen-eighties (most likely in 1982). This wasn't just a hope as the technology to get to Mars existed, at least in prototype form, and only a lack of political will and funding prevented it. At that point, NASA was seriously projecting that half of American employees would be working in space by 2050.

At the time that *The Ambassadors of Death* was made, then, what was shown wasn't possible - but it would be, for NASA, in about ten years. The most implausible aspect was that Britain could do the same - but there had been a British space programme up until the early sixties, and, again, it was lack of funding rather than lack of expertise that killed it off.

The Doctor is still bitter about the events of *Doctor Who and the Silurians*, so this story probably happens only shortly afterward. The Brigadier says he has known the Doctor "several years, on and off", so it's that long since *The Web of Fear*.

107 *Who Killed Kennedy*

108 "During that General Carrington business" according to *No Future*.

109 *The Dying Days*

110 *The Scales of Injustice*

111 Mars Probe 9 is referred to in *Dancing the Code*, and *The Dying Days* mentions Mars Probe 13.

THE BRITISH SPACE PROGRAMME: Perhaps because they are acutely aware of the threat from outer space, the British government seems to have invested heavily

Jones, a hired killer from the Vault, abducted a young secretary called Roberta. Vault scientists gave her cybernetic implants and false memories.[112]

(late July) - INFERNO[113] -> Professor Stahlman discovered a gas underneath the crust of the Earth, and claimed that it might be "a vast new storehouse of energy which has lain dormant since the beginning of time". The government funded an elaborate drilling project (nicknamed "Inferno" by some of the workers) based in Eastchester. But as the project's robot drill approached its target, a green slime came to the surface. On skin contact, people became savage beastmen, Primords.

> = "Sideways in time", Britain was a republic, and it had been since at least 1943 when the Defence of the Republic Act was passed. A fascist regime had executed the royal family. In this version of events, Professor Stahlmann's project was a day ahead of ours, and was under the aegis of the Republican Security Forces. This world was destroyed when Stahlmann's project was successful, releasing torrents of lava and armies of Primords.

On our Earth, the project was halted at the insistence of Sir Keith Gold and UNIT.

> = The Britain of the parallel world was run by an alternate version of the Doctor.[114] In the parallel universe, the British Isles were destroyed in hours, the rest of Europe a day later. The entire world was devastated within thirty-six hours. The leaders of the American Confederation, India, White Russia and the Asian Co-prosperity Sphere, along with the new leader of the British Republic, were evacuated to Copernicus Base on the Moon. Once there, they formed the Conclave.[115]

C-19 acquired some of Stahlman's Gas.[116] The Doctor attended the wedding of Greg Sutton and Petra Williams. He met Ian Chesterton, who was now working at NASA, at the reception.[117] Greg Sutton gave Ian some fashion advice - that he should buy an orange shirt and purple tie.[118] James Stevens tracked down the Suttons, who told him about "Project: Inferno" and the Doctor's involvement. The Suttons left the country shortly afterward.[119]

Two Irish twins, Ciara and Cellian, assisted Dr Krafchin in a number of plastics experiments. He offered them immortality, and their blood was replaced with Nestene

---

in the space programme before and during the UNIT era. In *Invasion of the Dinosaurs*, some very clever and important people are fooled into believing that a fleet of colony ships could be built and go on to reach another habitable planet, although Sarah knows that even the most advanced spaceship "would take hundreds of years" to do so, and it transpires the ships are fakes. In *The Android Invasion*, an experimental "space freighter" has been in service for at least two years. There's no obvious evidence that the British are using alien technology that they've recovered from one of the alien incursions in the sixties to speed up their space programme. On the contrary, they're using pretty basic rocket technology.

112 *Business Unusual*

113 Dating *Inferno* - This story seems to be set in the near future. The computer at the project uses perspex/crystalline memory blocks. Stahlman has a robot drill capable of boring down over twenty miles. A desk calendar in the parallel universe says it is "July 23rd", and the story runs for five days - the countdown we see early in the story says there is "59:28:47" remaining before penetration.

The word "Primord" is not used in dialogue, but appears in the on-screen credits. The name "Eastchester" is only used in a scene cut from the original broadcast (but retained in foreign prints and the BBC Video release), when the Doctor listens to a radio broadcast in the parallel universe. Stahlman spells his

name with two 'n's in the parallel universe. The Doctor claims this is the first attempt to penetrate the Earth's crust, forgetting the attempt he'd seen in *The Underwater Menace*.

114 *Timewyrm: Revelation*

115 *The Face of the Enemy*

116 *The Scales of Injustice, Business Unusual*

117 *The Devil Goblins from Neptune. The Face of the Enemy* clarifies that Ian is on a year-long exchange programme.

118 *Byzantium!*

119 *Who Killed Kennedy*

120 'Seven or eight months' before *Scales of Injustice*, 'twenty years' before *Business Unusual*.

121 'The previous year', 'late last year' and 'eight months' before *The Devil Goblins from Neptune*.

122 The Christmas before *The Scales of Injustice*.

123 *The Devil Goblins from Neptune*. The new members were presumably Billy Preston and Klaus Voormann.

THE BEATLES: *Doctor Who* has a terrible record for predicting the future, one that can best be summed up by noting that *Battlefield* predicted a near future with Soviet soldiers operating under the UN's aegis on British soil - but between the story's filming and its broadcast, the Soviet Union collapsed. In the entire twenty-six year run of *Doctor Who's* first run on television, it made two successful predictions - that there would be a female British Prime Minister (*Terror of the Zygons*), and that there would, one day, be a museum

Compound, a type of plastic. They become contract killers for the Vault.[120]

The Doctor gave a lecture tour in the United States that was really cover for UNIT recruitment operations. He met rocket scientist Von Braun. Soviet radar detected meteor impacts in Siberia, which unknown to them marked the arrival of the Waro on Earth. The Brigadier met Soviet UNIT commander Captain Valentina Shuskin.[121] He also spent Christmas in Geneva on UNIT business.[122]

The Beatles reformed without Paul McCartney, but with two new members called Billy and Klaus.[123]

Unit Year 3

(January) The Liberals formed a coalition government following a General Election.[124] (February) James Stevens wrote a series of articles for the *Daily Chronicle* that referred to UNIT and C-19. These got him sacked, and his wife left him.[125] (March) UNIT moved to a new headquarters.[126] (Early March) Soviet satellites detected a vast mining operation in Siberia. All military attempts to investigate were wiped out. The Soviet branch of UNIT lobbied Geneva to send the Doctor.[127]

At the Vault, Grant Traynor injected Stahlman's Gas into a Doberman, creating the Stalker, a vicious killer animal.[128] (April / May) The Vault acquired a Venus flytrap large enough to eat a dog in Africa. They also stole a Blackbird stealth aeroplane.[129]

(May) - THE EYE OF THE GIANT[130] -> The Doctor was sent an alien artefact that he discovered was emitting omicron radiation. He converted the Time/Space Visualiser into a space-time bridge to track the object's origin, and he and Liz Shaw wound up on Saluta in the Pacific in 1934.

> = Their actions in 1934 inadvertently created an alternative timeline ruled by The Goddess of the World, the starlet Nancy Grover. The Doctor returned to 1934 and set history back on the correct course.

(June) - THE SCALES OF INJUSTICE[131] -> A group of Silurian / Sea Devil hybrids awoke in Kent, and performed genetic experiments in the hope of ending their sterility and shortened lifespans. The Doctor investigated the matter, but the warmongering Silurian leader launched an attack on the coast of Kent. UNIT defeated the assault, and a smaller group of benevolent Silurians sued for peace.

The cyborg leader of the Vault sought to illicitly acquire Silurian technology, leading to UNIT uncovering the Vault's base of operations. The Vault leader escaped along with his two Nestene-augmented assassins. Foreign powers had previously purchased some of the Vault's acquisitions.

The Brigadier's wife Fiona filed for divorce and left with their daughter Kate.

---

dedicated to the Beatles in Liverpool (*The Chase*).

The latter wasn't always the plan: the original draft of the script called for the real Beatles to appear, made up to appear very old to indicate they were still performing in the future.

The Devil Goblins from Neptune reveals that The Beatles of the *Doctor Who* universe stayed together at least into the early seventies. John Lennon was murdered as he was in our history in *The Left-Handed Hummingbird*, though, and Paul McCartney was playing with Wings in *No Future*.

In *The Gallifrey Chronicles*, it's revealed that Fitz collects Beatles records from parallel universes, and that he saw them play a song called *Celebrate the Love* at Live Aid. *Celebrate the Love* is the title of the song the Ewoks sang at the end of *Return of the Jedi*, at least until the Special Edition.

124 "Six months" before *The Devil Goblins from Neptune*.

125 *Who Killed Kennedy*. It is "1970" (p87).

126 "Three or four months" before *The Devil Goblins from Neptune*. There are at least two UNIT HQs: one that's almost certainly in a London office block by the Thames in London (seen in *Terror of the Autons*) and one that's a stately home (seen in *The Three Doctors*).

127 'Early March' before *The Devil Goblins from*

Neptune.

128 'Three months' before *The Scales of Injustice*, '15 years' before *Business Unusual*

129 'A couple of months' and 'a month' before *The Scales of Injustice*.

130 Dating *The Eye of the Giant* - The story is set "37 years" after 1934, so 1971. UNIT have a photocopier. This is apparently the first time Mike Yates meets the Doctor, although he's been working for UNIT 'over the last year'. This is 'a few weeks' before *The Scales of Injustice*, according to that book.

131 Dating *The Scales of Injustice* - The back cover states this is set between *Inferno* and *Terror of the Autons*, and 'immediately after' *The Eye of the Giant*. It's a 'few weeks' since that book. Liz tells the Doctor she is leaving at the end of the book 'eight months, two weeks and four days' after *Spearhead from Space*. It is 'six months' since *Doctor Who and the Silurians*.

The Silurians who sue for peace are not mentioned again. The next time we see them, *The Sea Devils*, they are pitted against humanity. By the time of *Eternity Weeps*, set in 2003, man and Silurian are working together in relative harmony. Perhaps the discrepancy can be put down to the fact that UNIT don't feature in *The Sea Devils*, and the reptile people there were revived and are being provoked into conflict by the

After this incident, Sir John Sudbury of C-19 knew too much to be sacked by any government, and he gained in power.[132]

Liz Shaw told the Doctor that she planned to leave UNIT, return to Cambridge and continue her researches.[133] She took a leave of absence.[134] Liz travelled around the world, and later published a book entitled *Inside the Carnival*.[135]

Harry Sullivan served on the Ark Royal after leaving Dartmouth Naval College.[136]

(June) - THE DEVIL GOBLINS FROM NEPTUNE[137] **->** Geneva refused to release the Doctor to help with the Siberia situation, so Captain Shuskin of the USSR branch of UNIT attempted to kidnap him instead. Liz Shaw was working with Professor Bernard Trainor, who was planning an unmanned mission to Neptune. The Doctor and Liz travelled to Siberia and were attacked by the Waro, demonic creatures from Neptune's moon Triton. The Doctor realised this was a distraction - the Waro were really after the American supplies of cobalt-60, with which they hoped to build a bomb that would devastate Earth. The Brigadier uncovered a conspiracy in UNIT that led to Area 51 in Nevada, a secret military base containing five aliens, the Nedenah. Freed by the Doctor, the Nedenah released a virus that made the Waro destroy themselves.

On 18th June, there was a General Election, and the Wilson government was defeated by the Conservatives under Heath with a majority of 43. Days before that, James Stevens' book *Bad Science* was published.[138] At some point during the UNIT era, the Doctor met the Russian Colonel Bugayev. During the encounter, Bugayev and some of his comrades were exposed to temporal radiation that either aged them to death or prolonged their lives.[139]

Liz Shaw returned to Cambridge, and soon afterward the Doctor started to agitate for a new assistant. The Doctor started the steady state microwelding of his dematerialisation circuit.[140] There were some slow weeks at UNIT. The Doctor helped Benton paint some Nissen huts.[141]

Jo Grant was seconded to UNIT at the insistence of a relative in government. Although she failed her General Science A-Level, she managed to pass the UNIT Training Course.[142] Her relative was General Frank Hobson, the UK ambassador to the United Nations.[143] She was trained to use skeleton keys and interrogation techniques.[144] Her best friend on the course was called Tara. Jo did intelligence work for the Ministry, alongside a gentleman adventurer.[145]

(At least three months after *Inferno*) - TERROR OF THE AUTONS[146] **->** Josephine Grant became the Doctor's new assistant.

The Master had allied himself with the Nestenes, and together they plotted mass slaughter - when a radio signal was sent, thousands of distributed plastic daffodils would spray a plastic film capable of suffocat-

---

Master.

132 *Business Unusual*

133 *The Scales of Injustice*, which states that it's 'eight months, two weeks and four days' since she met the Doctor in *Spearhead from Space*, although their amount of time together has become 'thirteen months' by *The Devil Goblins from Neptune*.

134 *The Devil Goblins from Neptune, The Face of the Enemy*

135 *The Devil Goblins from Neptune*

136 *The Face of the Enemy*, picking up on a reference in *Harry Sullivan's War*.

137 Dating *The Devil Goblins from Neptune* - Between *Inferno* and *Terror of the Autons*. Liz has been with UNIT for "thirteen months". The Brigadier hasn't been to Geneva for eight months (when, we're told, he was reporting on the events of *Inferno*). It is "1970", with a host of contemporary references to, for example, David Bowie and Brazil winning the World Cup (p109).

138 *Who Killed Kennedy* (p117), which specifies the year as "1970".

139 *Emotional Chemistry*

140 *Terror of the Autons*

141 *The Death of Art*

142 *Terror of the Autons*

143 *Blood Heat*

144 *The Wages of Sin, Catastrophea*

145 *Verdigris,* a reference to *The Avengers*.

146 Dating *Terror of the Autons* - It seems to be the near future, and the plastics factory has a videophone.

The Doctor works on his dematerialisation circuit for "three months", and apparently hadn't started in *Inferno*, so this story would seem to start at least three months after Season Seven ends. There is no indication how much time has passed since the previous Auton story, *Spearhead from Space*. A desk calendar is referred to when the Doctor and Brigadier visit Farrell's office, but we do not see it.

This is clearly not the Master's first arrival on Earth at this time - he has managed to research the history of Lew Russell, the circus owner.

Inferno was 'a few years' before *Terror of the Autons* according to *The Face of the Enemy* (p215). In *Genocide*, Jo says that she's been on UNIT's books since 1971. *Who Killed Kennedy* prefers April 1970.

147 *Return of the Living Dad*

148 *Who Killed Kennedy*. It is 'four months' since the June 1970 General Election (p119).

149 Dating *The Mind of Evil* - It seems to be the near future - there is a National Power Complex, there is a ing a person. The Nestenes would take over the country during the resulting chaos. The Doctor convinced the Master to help him defeat the Nestene plan. The Master was subsequently stranded on Earth when the Doctor stole his Mark Two dematerialisation circuit, rendering his TARDIS useless.

A spatula-shaped piece of Auton matter survived. It would eventually end up in Little Caldwell, where it would be called Graeme.[147] In October, UNIT started training its men to resist hypnosis. James Stevens completed work on his second book, and was invited to a demonstration of the Keller Process at Stangmoor Prison.[148]

THE MIND OF EVIL[149] -> Incognito as Professor Emil Keller, the Master developed "the Keller Process": a means of rehabilitating convicts by having their "evil" brain impulses transferred into a machine. However, the machine actually housed an alien parasite that fed off the evil in mankind. The Master hoped to put the parasite's powers at his command. After a riot at Stangmoor Prison, the Master's scheme was exposed and the Keller Process abandoned.

UNIT at this time were involved with security of the World Peace Conference in London. The Master sought to disrupt the proceedings and steal Thunderbolt, an outlawed nuclear missile slated for destruction. He nearly succeeded and triggered a World War, but the Doctor and UNIT destroyed both the missile and the Master's alien parasite.

DEADLY REUNION[150] -> The former Greek gods Demeter, Persephone and Hermes were now living as nobility in the English village of Hob's Haven. Hades had founded a cult named the Children of Light as a means of spreading anarchy among mankind, and coerced the Master into helping him. The Master supplied an alien drug, sarg, that drove its users to commit acts of violence at a pop festival. The Doctor aided Demeter in summoning Zeus from his abode in another dimension, and the king of the gods exiled Hades from Earth forever. Demeter's trio departed Earth for Zeus' realm. The Brigadier remembered his time spent as Persephone's lover in the nineteen forties.

In December, James Stevens met Dodo Chaplet, who was homeless. He invited her to stay with him.[151]

Unit Year 4

In late February, James Stevens started writing a book about UNIT. In March, Liz Shaw, who was working on the genetic engineering of reptiles, contacted Stevens and warned him not to research C-19. His house was ransacked.[152]

(spring or summer?) - THE CLAWS OF AXOS[153] -> UNIT continued to track the Master. The Washington UNIT HQ became involved, sending one of their agents, Bill Filer, to help with the search. Meanwhile, the civil servant Chinn was investigating UNIT.

UNIT radar stations detected a UFO one million miles out, on a direct bearing for Earth. The alarm bells started to ring when it got within five hundred miles. UNIT HQ sent the order to launch an ICBM strike against the UFO, but the ship vanished before the missiles hit. It landed on the south east coast of England

---

World Peace Conference in progress in which the Chinese are key players. Gas warfare was banned "years" ago. Mao Tse Tung is referred to in the present tense - he died in 1976, after *The Mind of Evil* was made.

Inferno was 'some time ago'. This story might be set a full year after *Terror of the Autons*: the Master has been posing as Keller since 'nearly a year ago'. However, it's clear from *Terror of the Autons* that the Master has been on Earth for at least a little while. It's possible that the Master set his plan in motion before his apparent arrival on Earth in *Terror of the Autons* ... which would mean he had two entirely distinct plans to take over the Earth running simultaneously. The 'year ago' line might well be a remnant from an earlier draft of the script that didn't include the Master.

According to *Who Killed Kennedy*, it is October 1970 (p119).

150 Dating *Deadly Reunion* - *Terror of the Autons* is 'recent', but the Master's TARDIS works, so this is set after *The Mind of Evil*.

151 *Who Killed Kennedy*. It is "December" (p136) 1970.
152 *Who Killed Kennedy* (p162, p157).
153 Dating *The Claws of Axos* - This story is set in the near future. There are videophones, although normal telephones are also in use. The National Power Complex "provides power for the whole of Britain" according to Sir George Hardiman, the head of the facility. (This needn't mean that the complex provides *all* of the country's power, just that it contributes to the whole of the National Grid rather than one region of it.) The complex has a "light accelerator". While this story was filmed in January, and the trees are bare, the snow is described as 'freak weather conditions', perhaps suggesting the story is set in the spring or summer. Chinn says of the Brigadier's actions "that's the kind of high-handed attitude one has come to expect of the UN lately".
154 *Business Unusual*
155 Nuton is destroyed in *The Claws of Axos*, but mentioned in *The Daemons*.

close to the National Power Complex at Nuton, amid freak weather conditions. As the army arrived to seal off the area, the UFO began to broadcast a signal:

"Axos calling Earth, request immediate assistance. Axos calling Earth...".

The Axons made contact with the UNIT party. They claimed that their planet had been damaged by solar flares, and that they possessed an advanced organic technology. Their ship had been damaged. In return for help, the Axons offered humanity Axonite - a substance that was "the chameleon of the elements". It could be programmed to absorb all forms of radiation, and to replicate and transmute matter. In theory, it would end the world's food and energy problems. In reality, the Axons had captured the Master in space, and he had led them to Earth - a rich feeding ground - in return for his freedom and a chance to kill the Doctor. The Axos ship was banished from Earth and time-looped, although the Nuton Complex was also destroyed.

Private Erskine was attacked by an Axon and left for dead, but survived. He was rescued by the Vault, and bore a grudge against the Brigadier. He ended up working for SeneNet.[154] **The National Power Complex at Nuton was rebuilt.**[155] Chinn was blamed for the disaster at Nuton and was pensioned off.[156]

UNIT went hunting for the Master and accidentally arrested the Spanish ambassador, mistaking him for the renegade Time Lord.[157] Marnal's son - who was on the run at the time - visited his father during the nineteen seventies, and told him exactly why the Doctor left Gallifrey.[158]

COLONY IN SPACE[159] -> The TARDIS left the Doctor's laboratory in UNIT HQ for a matter of seconds, en route to 2472.

The parish council of Devil's End converted the cavern below the church into a witchcraft museum. The Master arrived in Devil's End, killed the vicar Canon Smallwood, and buried him in his own churchyard. He adopted the identity of the new vicar, Mr Magister.[160]

(29th April - 1st May) - THE DAEMONS[161] -> At midnight on the major occult festival of Beltane, noted archaeologist Professor Gilbert Horner attempted to open the Devil's Hump - an ancient burial mount outside the village of Devil's End. BBC3 broadcast Horner's endeavour, but the mount was actually the buried spaceship of Azal, the last of the Daemons. Horner was killed by a blast of subzero temperatures that resulted when he opened the ship.

As the Reverend Magister, the Master organized a coven to awaken Azal in an effort to receive the Daemon's power. The Master and his ritualists succeed, and Azal prepared, per his instructions, to pass his power on to a creature worthy of overseeing the planet. Azal deemed the Doctor, not the Master, a worthy recipient, but the Doctor refused to accept such authority. Azal moved to destroy the Doctor as a nuisance, but Jo Grant offered her life in the Doctor's place. Her "irrational and illogical" move drove Azal to self-destruct. UNIT apprehended the Master soon afterward.

James Stevens watched the opening of Devil's Hump on BBC3 with Dodo, whom he had befriended.[162] The church

---

156 *Who Killed Kennedy*

157 *Colony in Space*

158 *The Gallifrey Chronicles*

159 Dating *Colony in Space* - There's no clear indication of the year. When Jo reaches the future, she is surprised that a colony ship was sent out in 1971 (it wasn't, of course, it was 2471). Either this story is set before 1971 and Jo is amazed how quickly the space programme has progressed, or it is set afterward and she finds it difficult to believe that the colony ship was kept secret.

160 *The Eight Doctors*. In *The Daemons*, the local squire Winstanley says 'there have been a lot of queer goings on the last few weeks', suggesting that's how long the Master has been in the area.

161 Dating *The Daemons* - The story is set in the near future, as BBC3 is broadcasting.

Devil's Hump is opened at "midnight" on "Beltane", and the story ends with a dance around the May pole. Beltane appears to be a Saturday or Sunday, as Yates

and Benton watch a Rugby International and don't know the result. As Professor Horner's book is released the next day (and the shops would have to be open), it is almost certainly Sunday. It is 'two hundred years' since Devil's Hump has been of interest, and the first attempt to open it was in 1793.

162 *Who Killed Kennedy*

163 *The Eight Doctors*

164 *Downtime*. It is a little odd that this is named the "Aldbourne Incident" - Aldbourne is the real village where *The Daemons*, set in the fictional village of Devil's End, was filmed. (Although an historic "Lord of Aldbourne" is referred to in *The Daemons*.)

165 *Who Killed Kennedy*

166 *Business Unusual*

167 *The Hollow Men*

168 *The Face of the Enemy*

169 *Who Killed Kennedy*

in Devil's End was destroyed, but the cavern beneath was intact.[163]

Public outrage at UNIT's blowing up of the church at Devil's End ("The Aldbourne Incident") led to "questions in the House; a near riot at the General Synod".[164] UNIT Private Cleary suffered a nervous breakdown after seeing Azal.[165] SeneNet acquired the remains of Bok, a stone gargoyle animated by Azal's power.[166] After this, the Doctor explored the area around Devil's End and found Hexen Bridge, where he sensed an oppressive atmosphere.[167]

The public were told that the Master was an anarchist terrorist, Victor Magister. He was remanded at Stangmoor Prison.[168] The trial took place *in camera*. He was convicted of murder, high treason and numerous other crimes.[169] **While many wanted the Master executed, the Doctor pleaded for clemency at his trial and the Master was instead sent to Fortress Island in the English Channel.**[170] The Master was kept at Aylesbury Grange Detention Centre until Fortress Island was ready.[171]

At the UNIT staff panto, Mike Yates played Widow Twankey.[172] Mike Yates kissed Jo Grant at the UNIT Christmas party. The Master interrupted the festivities.[173]

Unit Year 5

(Summer) WHO KILLED KENNEDY[174] **->** James Stevens tried to reveal the truth about UNIT in a live broadcast on BBC3's *The Passing Parade*. His house was torched, and the Master kidnapped him. He was taken to the Glasshouse, a home for traumatised soldiers, and kept sedated for weeks. The Master was the director of the Glasshouse, and had been brainwashing the soldiers to create an army. He planned to send them through time to disrupt Earth's history.

Upon meeting Francis Cleary, Stevens managed to escape with him. He brought a TV crew back, but the place had been cleared out and Stevens was utterly discredited. Cleary was still under the Master's control, and killed Dodo on the Master's orders. A mysterious stranger at Dodo's funeral gave Stevens a Time Ring, and they went back to 1963 to ensure Kennedy's assassination and the course of history. Stevens returned to his native time, haunted with the knowledge that his older self would kill Kennedy.

(12th - 13th September) - DAY OF THE DALEKS[175] **-> UNIT were called in to guard the World Peace Conference at Auderley House. On the evening of 12th September, there was an assassination attempt on Sir Reginald Styles. Guerrillas from the future believed that Styles would sabotage the Conference, and that its failure would create a history in which the Daleks ruled Earth two hundred years hence. The Doctor discovered that the guerrillas' interference, not Styles, had foiled the conference and paradoxically created this future.**

A time-travelling squad of Daleks and Ogron footsoldiers attacked the House, attempting to insure that their version of history prevailed. The guerrilla Shura detonated a Dalekanium bomb and wiped out the invaders, but only after the delegates had been evacuated. With the delegates' survival, the guerrillas' history ceased to be.

Two Ogrons escaped and ended up in the village of Little Caldwell.[176] UNIT recovered a Dalek casing.[177] SeneNet recovered twenty-second century weaponry from the site.[178] James Rafferty wrote a paper about dust samples from the site.[179]

The Cold War was brought to an end.[180]

---

170 *The Sea Devils.* The name of the island appears on Captain Hart's map, but isn't referred to in dialogue.

171 *The Face of the Enemy*

172 *No Future*, which places it in "1973", three years earlier. This must have been quite an occasion, as the Doctor also remembers it in *Timewyrm: Revelation*.

173 'The UNIT Christmas party last year' according to *Verdigris*.

174 Dating *Who Killed Kennedy* - See Footnote 90 (pg104) for a list of the dates given in this book.

175 Dating *Day of the Daleks* - This may have a contemporary setting. While the world is on the brink of WW3, a BBC reporter appears as himself.

Jo tells the Controller that she left the twentieth century on "September the 13th". The Controller notes, rather annoyingly for those trying to pin down the dates of the UNIT stories, that Jo has "already told me the year" she is from.

176 *Return of the Living Dad*

177 *No Future*

178 *Business Unusual*

179 *The Dimension Riders.* Rafferty is Professor of Extra-Terrestrial Studies at Oxford and the Doctor's old friend.

180 INTERNATIONAL POLITICS IN THE UNIT ERA: In the UNIT era, there appear to be four superpowers: The US, USSR, China and the United Kingdom. In the nineteen-seventies, the world apparently lurches from a period of detente with the Soviet Union (*The Invasion*), to the brink of World War Three (*The Mind of Evil*, *Day of the Daleks*), but within a few years of *Day of the Daleks*, the Cold War has ended. *Invasion of the Dinosaurs* includes the line "back in the Cold War days". *Robot* is also set after the Cold War ended. *About Time* notes that "it's massively unlikely that the entire Cold War has ended at this point since the stories made / set in the 1980s seem to suggest a world where there's still a schism between the US and USSR (see especially *Time-Flight*)". Alternatively, it's evidence that *Robot* is set after *Time-*

Surgeon-Lieutenant Harold Sullivan was posted to Faslane.[181] **The Doctor took Jo on a test flight of the TARDIS. Under the Time Lords' guidance, the TARDIS headed for Peladon.[182]**

= THE FACE OF THE ENEMY[183] **->** The Conclave, the surviving members of the parallel Earth devastated by "Project: Inferno", captured the Koschei of their reality and used his TARDIS to open dimensional portals to Earth.

The Conclave members began replacing their parallel duplicates to gain positions of power, but UNIT came to suspect the plan. With the Doctor off-world, the Brigadier allied himself with Royal Air Force lecturer Ian Chesterton and the imprisoned Master.

= The trio travelled to the parallel Earth, euthenised the dissected Koschei and severed the Conclave's link with the other Earth.

UNIT eliminated most of the Conclave members now stranded on Earth, but Marianne Kyle, the Conclave's Secretary General, remained at liberty.

By now, the Brigadier was in a relationship with Doris, an old friend from Sandhurst. Liz Shaw was in the US on a lecture tour. Ian Chesterton and Barbara had a son, John.

THE SEA DEVILS[184] **-> Imprisoned at Fortress Island, the Master attempted to contact a dormant colony of Sea Devils in the English Channel, hoping to direct them to attack mankind. The Master won the confidence of Colonel Trenchard, the governor of the** prison, by claiming the creatures were terrorists that threatened Britain's national security. Trenchard acceded to the Master's requests, enabling him to contact the Sea Devils and engineer his escape. Trenchard died when a team of Sea Devils overran the prison.

The Doctor intervened and implored the Sea Devil leader to make peace with humankind, but a sneak Navy attack engineered by Robert Walker, the Parliamentary Private Secretary, convinced the Sea Devil leader to make war instead. Unable to contain the impending violence, the Doctor destroyed the underwater base and the Sea Devils within. The Master escaped shortly afterward.

THE EIGHT DOCTORS[185] **->** The Master evaded capture by the Doctor and Jo and reached his TARDIS, which was disguised as the sacrificial stone at Devil's End. Returning to UNIT HQ, the Doctor met his eighth incarnation.

All UNIT HQs received a new standing order, priority A1, to be on the lookout for the Master.[186] The Coal Board closed Llanfairfach Colliery in South Wales.[187]

(29th September) - THE TIME MONSTER[188] **->** For several months, the Master had posed as one "Professor Thascales" to conduct research into the science of "interstitial time" at the Newton Institute in Wootton. He succeeded in developing TOM-TIT (Transmission of Matter Through Interstitial Time), a device capable of moving matter through the cracks between "now" and "now". However, the Master's true intentions were to use TOM-TIT to put Kronos, the ancient Chronivore, at his command.

Flight (so after 1981), which ties in nicely with the date given in *Pyramids of Mars* (the 1980 date would be the date of *The Time Warrior* or *Robot*).

The Soviet system seems to survive - in *Battlefield* the Russian troops' uniforms bear the hammer and sickle, but they are operating on British soil under UN command, and the "Soviet Praesidium" is mentioned in *The Seeds of Death*.

Stories told since the collapse of the Soviet Union in the real world have referred to it: Ace mentions "perestroika" in *Timewyrm: Exodus*, and the Doctor talks of the collapse of the Soviet Union in *Just War*.

181 'A couple of weeks' before *The Face of the Enemy*.

182 *The Curse of Peladon*

183 Dating *The Face of the Enemy* - This runs while the Doctor and Jo are away in *The Curse of Peladon*, and takes about a fortnight.

184 Dating *The Sea Devils* - This is probably set in the near future. The prison guards' vehicles and uniforms are futuristic. Although this is effectively a sequel to

two stories, no indication is given how much time has passed since *Doctor Who and the Silurians* or *The Daemons*. The Master insists that his second television be in colour, but this doesn't mean that the story is set just after colour TV was introduced - before the advent of cheap colour portable TVs, a household would commonly have a big colour set and a smaller black and white one. The Master watches an episode of *The Clangers*, first broadcast in 1971 and repeated many times since.

185 Dating *The Eight Doctors* - This happens straight after *The Sea Devils*.

186 *The Time Monster*

187 In *The Green Death* it was 'last year'.

188 Dating *The Time Monster* - There's nothing to suggest this is the near future. Benton wishes Jo a "Merry Michaelmas". The TARDIS in this story appears to be fully functional - although this story is broadcast before *The Three Doctors*, perhaps it takes place afterward. If not, then all the stories in Season Nine apparently take

The Doctor and UNIT came to suspect the Master's schemes, but the Master succeeded in bringing the Atlantean priest Krasis through time to assist him. The Master and Krasis set off back to Atlantis circa 2000 BC, and the Doctor and Jo Grant pursued them there.

The Thascales Theorem was held by the United Nations for security purposes.[189] Singer Dusty Springfield helped the Doctor and UNIT investigate abductions in Memphis.[190]

Unit Year 6

(May) RAGS[191] **->** At Dartmoor, a bloody conflict between a punk band and a group of university students freed the Ragman, who animated their corpses. They staged punk band performances as part of the "Unwashed and Unforgiving" tour, mentally stimulating persons in the area to commit violence. The group's performances caused a riot at Dartmoor Prison, and saw a group of fox hunters massacred by escapees from an asylum. UNIT was called on to investigate as the band reached Cirbury, and the Ragman also incited violence at Stonehenge. Kane Sawyer, a local ruffian and one of the Ragman's descendents, sacrificed himself to re-bind the Ragman into some standing stones.

(May) - VERDIGRIS[192] **->** The Doctor and Brigadier fell out after defeating an Arcturan who had arrived on Earth with sinister intent. The Doctor decided to take a break from UNIT and went to an old mansion he owned in the town of Thisis.

The alien Verdigris, who had been drifting towards Earth for thousands of years, contacted a race of refugees named the Meercocks. The Meercocks had decided to settle on Earth disguised as characters from Earth's fiction.

Iris Wildthyme and her companion Tom called on the Doctor, and they discovered the Meercocks' plan. They defeated an army of robot sheep and The Children of Destiny, a group of annoying psychic teenagers working for Galactic Federation Supreme Headquarters in Wales.

Verdigris escaped to inform Omega that the Doctor was on Earth.

THE THREE DOCTORS[193] **->** The stellar engineer Omega, having survived in a universe of anti-matter, began incursions into the matter universe and started draining power from the Time Lord homeworld. With Omega's attention focused on the exiled Doctor, the Time Lords decided to violate the First Law of Time and dispatch the Doctor's previous two incarnations to aid his current self.

The first Doctor was unable to reach them, and was only able to advise on the situation, but the second and third Doctors travelled to Omega's anti-matter universe. Omega desired to leave his domain but needed a successor to facilitate this. He tried coercing the Doctors into taking his place, but the Doctors triggered a matter / anti-matter explosion that seemingly destroyed Omega.

The Doctors escaped and the Time Lord homeworld regained full power. The Time Lords sent the Doctor's previous selves back to their native times, and in gratitude ended the Doctor's exile. They restored his knowledge of time travel, and repaired the TARDIS to its proper function.

---

place between 13th September (*Day of the Daleks*) and 29th September (*The Time Monster*) of a given year.

This story is set in "the mid-seventies" according to *Falls the Shadow*, and 'thirty years' before *The Quantum Archangel* (so 1973).

189 *Falls the Shadow*
190 *The Blue Angel*. At some unspecified point during the Doctor's exile.
191 Dating *Rags* - This was the first PDA that didn't specify on the cover which TV stories it was set between. The Doctor's exile has not been lifted, yet Jo refers to Daleks and Ogrons, meaning it takes place at some point between *Day of the Daleks* and *The Three Doctors*.

It is 'the beginning of May' when the Ragman starts his campaign, 'Tuesday 10th May' a little later. The year is given as '79' at the beginning of the book (although 10th May wasn't a Tuesday in 1979). It is after Malcolm Owen of the Ruts died (July 1980, in real life), and The Damned song *I Just Can't Be Happy Today* was released (November 1979).

192 Dating *Verdigris* - The month and year are stated in the book as '1973' and 'May'. Jo has known the Doctor 'two years' (p143). The story leads into *The Three Doctors* (p241). Paul Magrs playfully made it tricky to place this story precisely. One anomaly is that Jo doesn't know about Peladon (p192). This is after the eventful UNIT Christmas party (p126).

193 Dating *The Three Doctors* - The evidence is mixed. Dr Tyler says the Americans have launched a deep space monitor, but he also cites "Cape Kennedy." (The name was changed to Cape Canaveral in 1973, which would suggest *The Three Doctors* takes place before that, although colloquially it was still known as that for a time). Jo misquotes the words to *I am the Walrus*.

According to *Transit* (and a number of novelisations, such as *The Mysterious Planet*), the Doctor's exile lasts "five years".

The Doctor's exile to Earth had been lifted. He constructed a forcefield generator and took the TARDIS on a test flight.[194] The Doctor defeated the Brotherhood of Beltane and blobby aliens called the Talichre, and the encounters went down in UNIT legend.[195]

Miss Gallowglass (later Countess Gallowglass) started running a mail forwarding service for aliens and time travellers alike, operating from a Portakabin in the East End. The Doctor first met her just after his exile on Earth ended. One of her customers, irate at a misplaced parcel, declared war on Earth and stole Britain's Crown Jewels. The Time Lords replaced the jewels with fakes, preserving history.[196]

THE WAGES OF SIN[197] -> The Doctor, his knowledge of time travel restored, offered to take Jo Grant and his former companion Liz Shaw to witness the Siberian meteorite strike in 1908. Instead, they erroneously arrived in St. Petersburg, 1916, shortly before the murder of Rasputin.

The Doctor and Jo meet Iris and Tom in a cocktail joint on a far flung outpost.[198] **Professor Whitaker disappeared when the government refused to fund his time-travel research.**[199] Tobias Vaughn funded Whitaker's experiments.[200]

The Doctor and Jo set off on another test flight. They landed on Inter Minor, where they became trapped in a miniscope owned by the Lurman entertainer Vorg.[201]

THE SUNS OF CARESH[202] -> Lord Roche, a Gallifreyan, discovered that Caresh was would enter a seventy-four year cold period that would extinguish all life on the planet. Roche set about modifying the Careshi time scanner into a stellar manipulator, hoping to save the planet's Fayon civilization, which was a curiosity to him. Roche intended to deviate a neutron star and use its gravity to bump Caresh into orbit around its warmer star Beacon, but the Curia of the Nineteen - rulers of the Realm of the Vortex Dwellers - forecast that the diverted neutron star would devastate their territory. They dispatched two hostile Furies to attack Roche, but he trapped the Furies within his TARDIS and sent it back in time thirteen centuries. It was unearthed in 1999, creating a time anomaly that the Doctor detected.

The Doctor used Roche's equipment to manoeuvre Caresh closer to its smaller star Ember, thereby avoiding damage to the Curia's territory. The Curia refrained from sending the Furies to attack Roche, averting the 1999 anomaly.

194 The Doctor says at the end of *The Three Doctors* that he needs to build a new force field generator to replace the one that has been destroyed, and goes on a test flight in *Carnival of Monsters*. It should be noted that in *Carnival of Monsters*, Jo says that 1926 is 'forty years' before her time.
195 *Relative Dementias*
196 *Relative Dementias* (p18) mentions when the Doctor encountered the Countess.
197 Dating *The Wages of Sin* - It's just after *The Three Doctors*, in 'the 1970s' (p34).
198 *Verdigris*
199 'Six months' before *Invasion of the Dinosaurs*.
200 *Original Sin*
201 *Carnival of Monsters*
202 Dating *The Suns of Caresh* - It is soon after the Doctor's exile is lifted (p35), and straight after the TARDIS gets back from Inter Minor (p36).
203 *Dancing the Code* (p61). These unrecorded encounters were either while travelling with the Doctor or attacks on Earth faced by UNIT.
204 *Interference* (p75).
205 Dating *Dancing the Code* - Set between *Planet of the Daleks* and *The Green Death*. Watergate appears to be topical (p154).
206 *The Android Invasion*. Sarah reported on Crayford's disappearance "two years" before that story.
207 Dating *Last of the Gaderene* - It is 'some thirty years' since WW2 (p241).
208 Dating *Speed of Flight* - Jo is now thinking about

leaving the Doctor (p242).
209 *Timelash*. *Speed of Flight* implies the Karfel visit occurs shortly afterward.
210 *Original Sin*
211 Dating *The Green Death* - This is the near future. The Prime Minister is called Jeremy. BOSS is an advanced "Biomorphic" artificial intelligence that has been linked to a human brain. There is a Ministry of Ecology. Two calendars appear: the first is in the pithead office and shows the date to be "April 5th". The second can be glimpsed in the security guard's office and shows the month as February during a leap year.

See the British Politics in the UNIT Era sidebar, page 119.
212 *Planet of the Spiders*
213 Dating *Deep Blue* - It's 'six months' after *The Green Death*, and it's Mike's first mission since then. The Doctor has spent only a small amount of time on Earth since Jo's departure, but there's no mention of Sarah. This is 'six months' after *The Green Death* (p15), 'ten or so' years before Tegan's native 1984 (p20).
214 Dating *The Time Warrior* - Sarah states in this story that she's from the twentieth century, and isn't more specific than that. In *Pyramids of Mars*, it's stated four times that Sarah is "from 1980". The most straightforward interpretation of the line has to be that this story, Sarah's first, is set in 1980.
215 Dating *The Paradise of Death* - The Brigadier hasn't heard of Virtual Reality, and the Secretary-General of the United Nations is a woman. There is no gap on tel-

Before this time, Jo had met a number of alien races including the Methaji, Hoveet, Skraals and Kalekani.[203] The Kalekani aggressively terraformed worlds into rolling grasslands using the memetic virus known on Earth as the game 'golf'.[204]

DANCING THE CODE[205] -> There were reports of "unorthodox weapons" in the North Africa country of Kebiria. UNIT's representative in the area, Captain Deveraux, was killed. UNIT sent a Superhawk jet fighter to investigate, and discovered a nest of Xarax - an insect hive-mind. The Xarax began to infest the rest of the country, including the capital, Kebir City. The US Navy prepared a nuclear strike, but a UNIT team from the United Kingdom managed to deactivate the nest using synthesised chemical instructions.

Defence Astronaut Guy Crayford's XK5 space freighter, launched from Devesham Control, was lost during a test flight. It was believed to have collided with an asteroid. Sarah Jane Smith reported on the story.[206]

(late July) LAST OF THE GADERENE[207] -> By now, the surviving Gaderene numbered only three hundred thousand. The Gaderene scout Bliss had founded the aeronautics manufacturer Legion International as a front for her operations, and enslaved residents of the British town Culverton by implanting them with Gaderene embryos. Bliss recovered her missing transmat component and repaired the Gaderene transmat, intending to bring thousands of adult Gaderene through to Earth as an invasion force. However, UNIT's involvement resulted in the deaths of Bliss, her towering brother and the Gaderene embryos. The transmat was destroyed, and the resultant energy backlash further annihilated the Gaderene invasion force and homeworld.

SPEED OF FLIGHT[208] -> The Doctor, Jo Grant and Mike Yates departed in the TARDIS for the planet Karfel, but arrived on the planet Nooma in the far future by mistake.

At some point, the Doctor and Jo (and possibly someone else) succeeded in visiting Karfel.[209] Tobias Vaughn helped develop the BOSS computer for Global Chemicals.[210]

THE GREEN DEATH[211] -> The government gave the green light to Global Chemicals' experiments into the Stevens Process, which produced 25 percent more petrol from a given amount of crude oil. The "Nutcake Professor" Clifford Jones - who had won the Nobel prize for his work on DNA synthesis - protested that the process would double air pollution, but Global Chemicals claimed that the pollution generated was negligible.

UNIT were sent to investigate a body that was discovered in the abandoned coal mine - a body that was glowing green. They discovered Global Chemicals had been dumping the pollution created by the Stevens Process into the mine, and that it had mutated the maggots down there. The giant maggots produced a slime that was toxic to humans, but the Doctor and Professor Jones discovered a fungus that killed them.

Global Chemicals was run by the BOSS, or Bimorphic Organisational Systems Supervisor, a computer linked to the brain of Stevens. In an effort to help the world achieve "maximum efficiency", the BOSS attempted to mentally dominate Global staff at seven sites throughout the world, including Llanfairfach, New York, Moscow and Zurich. Global Chemicals was destroyed when the BOSS blew up. Professor Jones' Nuthutch was given UN Priority One research status, leading to 'unlimited funding.'

The Prime Minister was called Jeremy. Jo Grant left UNIT at this time to marry Professor Jones.

The newlyweds went on an expedition to the Amazon.[212]

DEEP BLUE[213] -> The Doctor, Tegan and Turlough landed in Tayborough Sands for a holiday and met up with UNIT. With 'their' Doctor away, UNIT recruited his later incarnation to investigate a mutilated corpse. The Xaranti were attempting to convert Earth into a new homeworld, but they were defeated. Most of the UNIT staff involved in this adventure lost their memories of it, with only Captain Yates remembering the Doctor's future incarnation.

Unit Year 7

THE TIME WARRIOR[214] -> British research scientists began to mysteriously disappear. UNIT were called in and the leading research scientists were all confined to the same barracks in a secret location. Nevertheless, the press got wind of the story. A young reporter named Sarah Jane Smith smuggled herself into the complex by posing as her Aunt Lavinia, the noted virologist. Before long, Sarah and the Doctor had followed a time disturbance back to the Middle Ages.

THE PARADISE OF DEATH[215] -> The Parakon Corporation opened Space World on Hampstead Heath. It offered many attractions based on space and space travel, including twenty-one alien creatures such as the Giant Ostroid, the crab-clawed Kamelius from Aldebaran Two, Piranhatel Beetles and Stinksloths. Using Experienced

Reality techniques, Parakon could give people guided tours of the Gargatuan Caverns of Southern Mars and the wild side of Mercury.

UNIT investigated the death of a young man whose thighbone had been bitten clean through, and exposed the Parakon Corporation as an extraterrestrial organisation. Parakon had been negotiating with Earth for a number of years, hoping to sign a trading agreement. Parakon would supply a wonder material named rapine in exchange for human bodies to fertilise their world, which had been devastated by the rapine harvests. Parakon had already sacked many worlds, including Blestinu. UNIT defeated the Corporation.

INVASION OF THE DINOSAURS[216] -> Eight million Londoners were evacuated after dinosaurs began to terrorise the population. The government decamped to Harrogate. UNIT helped with the security operation, which was under the command of General Finch and the Minister for Special Powers, Sir Charles Grover.

UNIT scientists calculated that someone was operating a time machine that required an atomic reactor. They tracked the Time Scoop in question to a hidden bunker near Moorgate Underground Station. The bunker contained an elaborate shelter that served as home to a group of people - including the conservationist Lady Cullingford, the novelist Nigel Castle and the Olympic long jumper John Crichton - who were all convinced they were in a spaceship bound for a new, unpolluted planet. Using the Time Scoop, Professor Whitaker hoped to regress Earth back to its primeval days, repopulating it with the people in the bunker. The Doctor and UNIT ended this plan, and Whitaker

and Grover were stranded in the past. Mike Yates, a member of their conspiracy, was discharged from UNIT.

During this, the Doctor unveiled his new car.[217] After this time, the temporal scientist Chun Sen was born.[218] Realising that UNIT might need to contact him in an emergency, the Doctor gave the Brigadier a syonic beam Space-Time Telegraph.[219]

THE FIVE DOCTORS[220] -> While on Earth at this time, the third Doctor was kidnapped by Borusa while driving his sprightly yellow roadster Bessie.

(20th - 21st May) - THE GHOSTS OF N-SPACE[221] -> While on holiday in Italy, the Doctor, Sarah, Jeremy Fitzoliver and the Brigadier prevented Maximillian Vilmio, a wizard, from achieving immortality. Vilmio had planned to use the space-warping effect of Clancy's comet to match his real body and his N-form in Null-Space.

Unit Year 8

To prevent nuclear launches, the US, USSR and China gave their Destructor Codes to Britain. Joseph Chambers was made Special Responsibilities Secretary with responsibility for protecting them.[222]

AMORALITY TALE[223] -> Sarah Jane Smith discovered a photograph of the Doctor, dating from 1952, while researching a story. The Doctor was intrigued by a 'warp shadow' on the photo, and the two of them went to 1952 in the TARDIS to investigate.

---

evision between *The Time Warrior* and *Invasion of the Dinosaurs*, but this features both Sarah and Mike Yates. Barry Letts decided to set this radio play before Mike Yates' 'retirement' from UNIT. Captain Yates is referred to in the book version.

216 Dating *Invasion of the Dinosaurs* - The balance of evidence is that this is the near future. The Whomobile is a new car and an 'M' reg, but the human race are - in theory at least - capable of building manned ships capable of interstellar flight. Whitaker has built a Time Scoop capable of calling up dinosaurs from hundreds of millions of years ago. The bunker was built "back in the Cold War days".

217 The Doctor's car was never named on-screen, but was dubbed both "Alien" and "the Whomobile" by the production team. The Doctor continues to use Bessie, as both are seen in *Planet of the Spiders*.

218 *Invasion of the Dinosaurs*. The Doctor says that Chun Sen couldn't be a suspect with regards to the dinosaur appearances as he "hasn't been born yet".

219 *Terror of the Zygons*. Presumably the Brigadier didn't have the Space-Time Telegraph before *Invasion of the Dinosaurs*, when dinosaurs were over-running London, or he would have used it to call the Doctor back.

220 Dating *The Five Doctors* - The third Doctor is kidnapped after *The Time Warrior* as he recognises Sarah. Sticking strictly to what we know in the television series, his abduction must occur between *The Monster of Peladon* and *Planet of the Spiders*, because the other stories of Season Eleven follow on from each other. However *The Paradise of Death* is set in a 'non-existent' gap between the first two stories of the series, so the Doctor might have been taken from that point.

221 Dating *The Ghosts of N-Space* - The story takes place after *Death to the Daleks* in the Doctor and Sarah's timeline. Clancy's Comet returns to Earth every 157 years, and the last sighting was in "1818", so it's 1975. As the month is given as May, *Planet of the Spiders*, set in March, must take place the following year. Fitzoliver

The Doctor started a project to research the psychic potential of humans.[224]

(mid-March) PLANET OF THE SPIDERS[225] -> A stage magician, Clegg, died at UNIT HQ as the Doctor investigated his psychic potential. This was linked to a disturbance at a Tibetan monastery in Mortimer, Mummerset. It was led by Lupton, a man bitter because he was sacked by a company after twenty-five years of service, then saw his own company bankrupted by his previous employers. The Spiders from Metebelis III had contacted Lupton, and compelled him to try and steal a Metebelis crystal that was in the Doctor's possession. Lupton wound up kidnapping Sarah, and the Doctor pursued them to Metebelis in the future.

Tobias Vaughn helped fund Kettlewell's research into robotics.[226]

(4th April) - ROBOT[227] -> As the UNIT budget was limited, the organisation was unable to afford a Captain to replace Mike Yates. Benton was promoted to Warrant Officer and made the Brigadier's second-in-command.

The National Institute for Advanced Scientific Research, or "Think-Tank" concentrated many of Britain's scientists all under one roof. They developed pieces of high technology that included the disintegrator gun - a weapon capable of burning a hole on the Moon's surface - and dynastrene, the hardest material known to science. The most impressive achievement, though, was Professor Kettlewell's "living metal", which he used to build the K1, a robot capable of performing tasks in environments where no human could survive. Many Think-Tank personnel were also members of the Scientific Reform Society (SRS), a group that believed in efficiency and logic.

The SRS tried to use the K1 to further their aims, but the newly-regenerated Doctor used a metal-eating virus to destroy the robot. He also prevented the SRS from triggering a nuclear holocaust.

Following this time, a woman became Prime Minister.[228]

(January) TERROR OF THE ZYGONS[229] -> Centuries after arriving on Earth, the Zygons in Loch Ness learnt that a stellar explosion had destroyed their home planet. A refugee fleet had been assembled and was looking for a new home. The Zygon leader Broton signalled that Earth would be suitable once the ice caps had been melted, the mean temperature of the planet had been raised and the necessary minerals had been introduced to the water.

The Zygons intensified their campaign against humanity when oil companies started disrupting the free passage of their "Skarasen", a vast monster that lived in Loch Ness but which ventured out into the North Sea from time to time. In the space of a month, the Zygons destroyed three North Sea oil rigs, causing massive loss of life. Two of the rigs were owned by Hibernian Oil. UNIT were sent to Tullock to deal with the problem.

Broton, posing as the Duke of Forgill, managed to get into the Fourth International Energy Conference on the banks of the Thames - he planned to assassinate the world leaders assembled there by signalling for the Skarasen. Broton, the signal device and the Zygon ship were all destroyed, and the Skarasen returned to Loch Ness.

---

was Sarah's photographer in *The Paradise of Death*.

222 'A few months' before *Robot*. The system has passed to UN control by *World War Three*.

223 Dating *Amorality Tale* - The story starts between *The Monster of Peladon* and *Planet of the Spiders*.

224 The Doctor is conducting such research in *Planet of the Spiders*. It's only mentioned in that story, and there's no suggestion that the fourth Doctor continues the study.

225 Dating *Planet of the Spiders* - The story takes place three weeks before *Robot*. "Meditation is the in thing" according to Sarah Jane.

226 *Original Sin*

227 Dating *Robot* - This is clearly set in the near future. As with *Invasion of the Dinosaurs*, the Cold War has been "over for years" according to the Brigadier. Advanced technology includes the K1 robot, the Disintegrator Gun and dynastrene. Sarah Jane Smith's day pass to Think-Tank bears the date "April 4th".

228 In *The Ark in Space*, Harry is surprised that the High Minister, "a member of the fair sex," was "top of the totem pole", suggesting Britain has yet to elect a female Prime Minister by his time. There must be a General Election or change of leadership in the government while he was away from Earth. In *Terror of the Zygons*, the Brigadier receives a phone call from the PM, whom he twice addresses as "Madam", and later refers to her as "she".

229 Dating *Terror of the Zygons* - It is the near future. The Prime Minister is a woman. In *Pyramids of Mars*, two stories after this one, Sarah states that she is "from 1980". According to *No Future*, this story is set in January 1976.

The government ordered Department C-19 to be cleaned up, and many of its top brass were removed.[230]

= PYRAMIDS OF MARS[231] **-> The Doctor took Sarah to an alternate version of 1980, to show her what would happen if they left England in 1911 before defeating Sutekh. Earth was a devastated wasteland.**

HEART OF TARDIS[232] **->** A collision with the second Doctor's TARDIS further de-stabilized the Lychburg singularity, to the point that it threatened the entire universe. The Time Lords sent the fourth Doctor and Romana to deal with the problem, but the Jarakabeth demon impersonating Alistair Crowley impeded their efforts, hoping to use the singularity energy to re-write reality in the name of chaos.

The second Doctor (secretly aided by his future self) used telemetry readings from the TARDIS to return Lychburg to Earth, whereupon the residents deserted the town entirely. A benevolent Jarakabeth demon hosted in government agent Katherine Delbane killed the Crowley demon. She became a UNIT captain under the Brigadier's command.

UNIT has recently requisitioned industrial lasers, marmosets, archaeological tools, rocketry components, Watsui tribal masks and a US college's particle accelerator. They also took a third of the Bank of England's gold reserves and didn't replace them, triggering a stock market crash.

(19th - 22nd June, 1976) - NO FUTURE[233] **->** The terrorist organisation Black Star, a group of anarchists, spent the summer planting bombs in sites around London: Hamleys, Harrods, the Albert Hall, the Science Museum and Big Ben. There was an assassination attempt on the Queen, junior treasury minister John Barfe was killed, the entertainer Jimmy Tarbuck was badly hurt in a hit-and-run incident, and Pink Floyd's private jet was lost over the English Channel. Civil disturbances happened across the globe. Prime Minister Williams declared a state of emergency.

Meanwhile, the Vardans were preparing an "active immigration" to Earth. The Vardan High Command formed an alliance with the Monk, the Time Lord otherwise known as Mortimus. The Monk freed the Vardans from their time loop, and under the guise of Priory Records boss Robert Bertram, he used Vardan Mediascape technology to plant crude subliminal messages in Earth's TV broadcasts. More sophisticated brainwashing techniques were available in the new VR training system that the Monk provided for UNIT.

Some members of UNIT, including most of the Broadsword intelligence agents, were able to break the conditioning. The Vardans were repelled from Earth and the Vardan Popular Front, a democratic organisation, took control of Varda. The Monk had captured the Chronovore Artemis and had been tapping her power to alter time, but she was freed and took her revenge on him.

The Brigadier was seeing Doris at this time. The Doctor selectively wiped his memory, encouraging him to retire.

The Russians were operating vodyanoi units at this time.[234] One Vardan remained behind, living in the Liverpool phone network until 1983.[235] **Following this time, the Brigadier spent a great deal of time in Geneva.**[236]

(6th July) - THE ANDROID INVASION[237] **-> The leader of the Kraal's Armoury Division, Chief Scientist Styggron, planned his race's escape from the dying planet Oseidon using their technological skills. The Kraals could engineer space-time warps, and two years previously, Styggron had used one of these to capture an experimental Earth freighter in deep space. He analysed the mind of the astronaut within, Guy Crayford, and used Crayford's memories to construct the Training Ground - an almost-perfect replica of the English village of Devesham, including the nearby**

---

230 'Six months' before *No Future*, and also referred to in *Return of the Living Dad*.
231 Dating *Pyramids of Mars* - The year is stated several times by both the Doctor and Sarah. The Doctor's actions prevent this timeline from coming to pass.
232 Dating *Heart of TARDIS* - The dating of this story seems particularly confused. UNIT knows the fourth Doctor, but Benton's a Sergeant and Yates hasn't been discharged. This is after the 1982 Falklands War, and there is a Conservative government. We could infer from the reference to the gold reserves that UNIT have fought the Cybermen - either in *The Invasion*, the 1975 invasion mentioned in *The One Doctor* or another incident entirely.

233 Dating *No Future* - The date is given (p6).
234 *No Future*, and a reference to the 1981 BBC drama *The Nightmare Man* - adapted by Robert Holmes and directed by Douglas Camfield.
235 *Return of the Living Dad*
236 The Brigadier is in Geneva during *The Android Invasion* and *The Seeds of Doom*.
237 Dating *The Android Invasion* - This is the near future. For at least the last two years, Britain has had a Space Defence Station, a team of Defence Astronauts, and has been operating space freighters. The calendar in the fake village gives the date (every day) as "Friday 6th July". The nearest years with that exact date are 1973, 1979, 1984 and 1990.

BRITISH POLITICS IN THE UNIT ERA: During the UNIT era, there are references to two Prime Ministers who are not the actual PM when the story was shown. However, both are semi-jokey references to actual opposition leaders of the time.

"Jeremy" mentioned in *The Green Death* would be Jeremy Thorpe, the leader of the Liberal Party at the time the story was made. Thorpe, of course, was never Prime Minister, although he was in the ascendant at the time *The Green Death* was shown. Shortly afterwards, in the February 1974 Election, the Liberal vote tripled to six million and they entered a pact with Labour to form a government.

In *Terror of the Zygons*, the Prime Minister is a woman. Margaret Thatcher had already been elected leader of the Conservatives when *Terror of the Zygons* was taped - the scene in which the Brigadier is phoned by the PM was recorded on 23rd April 1975, and Mrs Thatcher had been party leader since February of that year. The Labour government of the time had a tiny majority of four seats, and predicting a Conservative victory at the next election was a fairly safe bet (in much the same way that *Zamper*, written in 1995, referred to "Number ten, Tony's den").

If we assume the UNIT stories are set in the near future, then this is remarkably straightforward, as only the result of one 'real life' election need be changed. According to *The Green Death*, there is a general election won by Thorpe's Liberals at some point after 1973 (it can't be before *The Green Death* was shown, or it wouldn't be the future). Thatcher's Conservatives defeat this government. We can pinpoint the date of that election - it's between *Robot* and *Terror of the Zygons*, as Harry is surprised by the female leader in *The Ark in Space*. This coincides neatly with Sarah's assertion in *Pyramids of Mars* that she's from 1980. So the Liberals win the next General Election (one that had to be called by June 1975), the Tories win the one after that (possibly in May 1979, as in our history) and it all fits.

The date the Liberals come to power is harder to pin down. The model above assumes that it's a single-term government. A four or five-year term in office would mean they came to power around the time the Doctor was exiled to Earth. The man who's Minister of Ecology in *The Green Death* drafted UNIT's charter. It's possible to squeeze the Liberal election victory in before *The Invasion*, but there's nothing that demands he was a member of the governing party when he drew up the charter. He could have had a diplomatic, military or even legal career that made him the right man for the job (the only thing we can say for certain is that it's an unlikely job for a serving Minister of Ecology). Politics in the UNIT era is a world of grey, middle-aged men. There are occasional visionaries, but government is practically run by civil servants. There's no obvious point where the character of the government changes in the UNIT stories.

Throughout the UNIT era, the government is throwing money at new energy projects. We see grand schemes in *Doctor Who and the Silurians*, *Inferno*, *The Claws of Axos*, *The Green Death* and *Robot*, although these all end in disaster and mankind is still dependent on oil in *Terror of the Zygons*. The environment is clearly a huge political issue, with concerns about pollution voiced in many stories. The existence of a Minister of Ecology as a cabinet post is telling. When the Tories come to power, a lot of these responsibilities might transfer to the World Ecology Bureau we see in *The Seeds of Doom*. It's interesting to note that there's no mention of Europe, especially as (perhaps because) the Common Market was a hot political issue at the time. (The EEC debate was - far more vaguely than most fans seem to think - satirised in *The Curse of Peladon*.)

This version, then, is consistent with what we're told in the series and with what someone writing in the early seventies would extrapolate as a plausible backdrop for a science-fantasy adventure show set in the near future.

Some recent writers - particularly those who see the UNIT stories as being set at the time of broadcast - have developed a parallel political history for *early* 1970s Britain of the *Doctor Who* universe. Books like *Who Killed Kennedy* and *The Devil Goblins from Neptune* infer that events in the UNIT stories destabilised actual governments. This seems to be the logical consequence of the catalogue of incompetent government action, politicians dying, international crises and high profile disasters we see ... although in the TV series, politicians and civil servants are depicted, almost to a man, as complacent and obtuse. They seem far *too* secure, rather than people scared the government will fall at any moment.

All in all, the various things we are told about the parallel political history described in the books are difficult to reconcile.

In real life, the Prime Ministers since 1970 (along with the date of the general election, the winning party and their majority) were:

Heath (18th June, 1970, Conservative, 30)
Wilson (28th February, 1974, Labour minority, 0)
Wilson (10th October, 1974, Labour, 4)
Callaghan (5th April, 1976)
Thatcher (3rd May, 1979, Conservative, 43)
Thatcher (9th June, 1983, Conservative, 143)
Thatcher (11th June, 1987, Conservative, 102)
Major (27th November, 1991)
Major (9th April, 1992, Conservative, 21)
Blair (1st May, 1997, Labour, 179)
Blair (7th June, 2001, Labour, 167)
Blair (5th May, 2005, Labour, 66)

continued on page 121...

Space Defence Station. The Training Ground was populated with Android villagers, and the Kraals were able to study human civilisation and behaviour, honing their preparations to invade the Earth.

It was the Kraals' first attempt at conquest, but although they failed, Marshal Chedaki's fleet survived and the Kraal databanks contained the complete memory prints of a Time Lord traveller, the Doctor.

SeneNet recovered a Kraal android.[238]

(Early one month in Autumn) - THE SEEDS OF DOOM[239] ->

The World Ecology Bureau was active at this time. They received reports from Antarctica that an unusual seed pod had been discovered in the permafrost. They called in UNIT, whereupon the Doctor identified the item as a Krynoid seed pod and also discovered a second one.

One Krynoid was killed in the Antarctic, while an RAF air strike on the mansion of Harrison Chase, the millionaire plant enthusiast, destroyed the other.

THE PESCATONS[240] ->

Upon their return to Earth, the Doctor and Sarah were attacked by a sea creature, which the Doctor recognised as a Pescaton. He hurried to the astronomer Professor Emmerson and watched Pesca, the homeplanet of the Pescatons in the outer galaxies, explode.

The Pescatons had escaped in a space fleet, which arrived on Earth and attacked many cities. A smaller number also went to Venus. The Doctor located the Pescaton leader, Zor, in the London Underground and killed him with ultraviolet light. The other Pescatons died without their leader.

Realising that the Doctor's visits to Earth were becoming less and less frequent, the Brigadier had Bessie mothballed.[241] Alistair Gordon Lethbridge-Stewart announced his retirement from UNIT. Soon afterward he became a mathematics teacher at Brendon School.[242]

THE HAND OF FEAR[243] ->

The "obliterated" alien named Eldrad had fallen to Earth as a stone hand and regenerated into a humanoid (albeit female) form. There was near-meltdown in the main reactor of Nunton Nuclear Power station, although there was no radiation leak as Eldrad used the energy to facilitate his / her regeneration. The Doctor and Sarah decided to escort Eldrad back to his / her homeworld of Kastria.

Afterward, in answering a summons to Gallifrey, the Doctor was forced to return Sarah Jane Smith home. Although the TARDIS apparently failed to return Sarah to Croydon, she arrived in England.

Fortunately, it was the right timezone. Sarah resumed her work as a journalist.

---

238 *Business Unusual*

239 Dating *The Seeds of Doom* - On balance, it seems to be the near future. There is a satellite videolink to Antarctica and UNIT have access to a laser cannon. The Antarctic base has an experimental fuel cell. On the other hand, Sarah only wants 2p to use the public telephone. Chase says it is autumn (and the location work for the story was recorded in October / November). The Doctor is invited to address the Royal Horticultural Society on "the fifteenth".

240 Dating *The Pescatons* - The story is set in Sarah's time. It was released in August 1976, between Seasons 13 and 14, so I have placed it after *The Seeds of Doom*. The bit with Professor Emmerson and the telescope is in the novelisation, not the original record. It's quite the impressive telescope too - able to watch events on another planet in real-time, which is impossible.

241 *Battlefield*. *The Seeds of Doom* is the last story to feature UNIT until *Mawdryn Undead*, and it is established in the later story (and implied in *Time-Flight*) that the Doctor hasn't visited the Brigadier for years.

242 *Mawdryn Undead*, a year before 1977.

243 Dating *The Hand of Fear* - While it doesn't feature UNIT, Sarah is returned home at the end of the story. It has to be set before December 1981 and *K9 and Company*, in which she's back at work.

...continued from page 119

In the books, a Liberal-led coalition government was formed in January 1970. *The Devil Goblins from Neptune* (p8) states, 'an alliance of Liberals, various disenfranchised Tories and Socialists, and a group of minor fringe parties, enter power on a platform of social reform, the abolition of the death penalty, and a strong interstellar defence programme'.

In June 1970, Heath defeats Wilson, just as in our history (*Who Killed Kennedy*). This can't be easily reconciled with *The Devil Goblins from Neptune*, which also takes place in June 1970.

Shirley Williams is Prime Minister in *No Future*, set just after *Terror of the Zygons* in 1976. We're told that Thorpe had resigned mid-term, but there is also reference to Wilson.

In *Millennial Rites,* a female PM lost an election in the early eighties. In 1999, the leader of the Opposition is a woman ('all handbag and perm'). The Prime Minister is a man.

The unnamed winner of the 1997 general election was assassinated in *The Dying Days.* Edward Greyhaven is installed Prime Minister by the new Martian King of England, but dies during the course of the story.

Terry Brooks, Prime Minister in 1999, tries to fake a military coup as a pretext to dismantle the military and spend the money health and education instead. He is forced to resign, and is replaced by Philip Cotton. (*Millennial Shock* - they're a thinly-veiled Tony Blair and Jack Straw).

Tony Blair is alive, well and Prime Minister in *Project: Twilight* and *Death Comes to Time.*

Interference lists the recent British Prime Ministers as Heath, Thorpe, Williams, Thatcher, Major, Blair and Clarke. (The last could be senior Conservative Kenneth Clarke, but could possibly be Labour's Charles Clarke. The proofreader added the 'e' - Lawrence Miles' original intention was that it was Tory MP Alan Clark.)

Aliens of London and *World War Three* had scenes set in Downing Street, with photographs of Callaghan and Major on the stairway (no photos of Thorpe, Williams, Brooks, Cotton or either Clarke were visible!). The Prime Minister of the day is murdered by the Slitheen, and Harriet Jones becomes PM sometime between this story and *The Christmas Invasion.*

Once we're clear of the confused accounts of the 1970 elections, the sequence of Prime Ministers and when they come to power would seem to be:

Thorpe   (Liberal coalition, in power at the time of *The Green Death*)

Williams   (Labour, in power during *Terror of the Zygons* and *No Future*)

Thatcher   (Conservative, who came to power in the early eighties, later than in real life)

Major   (Conservative - we might infer he's the assassinated winner of the 1997 election)

Greyhaven   (briefly in 1997 and almost certainly not counted officially)

Brooks   (Unknown party, possibly leading from 1997 to 1999)

Cotton   (The same party as Brooks, takes over in 1999 - the leader of the opposition at this time is a woman, so isn't ...)

Blair   (Labour, the dates are uncertain, but he comes to power later and apparently leaves earlier than in real life, and thus manages to avoid two successful alien assassinations of a British Prime Minister.)

Clarke   (Unknown party, presumably the Prime Minister assassinated in *Aliens of London* in 2006 - although the body looks more like Blair than either Kenneth or Charles Clarke, both of whom could comfortably accommodate a Slitheen in real life!)

Jones   (The same party as Clarke, who serves three terms, from around 2006 and at least until 2012, but not as far as *Trading Futures,* where the PM was male.)

The Non-UNIT Seventies

NB: The line between a UNIT and non-UNIT story isn't always clearly defined. When a reference makes a direct link to a UNIT era story, it is included in the UNIT Era section. When there's a more vague or general reference to UNIT, it's included here.

The Doctor once took piano lessons from a man called Elton.[244] Isaac Summerfield moved his team to London, where they were based in a centre for the homeless.[245]

1970

c 1970 (20th March) - THE UNDERWATER MENACE[246] **-> The mad Professor Zaroff died in agony while attempting to raise Atlantis from the ocean floor with his Plunger.**

On 5th April, 1970, Hitler's remains were exhumed and destroyed on the orders of Andropov, head of the KGB.[247] On 14th August, the Revolution Man cult claimed Ed Hill was the Messiah.[248]

The Doctor's companion Ace was born Dorothy Gale McShane on 20th August, 1970, to Audrey and Harry McShane.[249] Around 1970, an Imperial bodyguard and nurse fled from the far future with Miranda, the daughter of the Emperor, following a revolution in their home timezone where the Imperial Family were hunted down and killed. The fugitives settled in the Derbyshire village of Greyfrith.[250]

The British launched a military satellite, *Haw-Haw*, to block extraterrestrial signals in 1971.[251] Nimrod's encounter with the vampire Reggie left Reggie recuperating for three years.[252] **Decimal currency was introduced in the United Kingdom. At some point afterward, the** Doctor and Susan visited England.[253]

In 1972, Nazi war criminal Oskar Steinmann died from cancer of the spine.[254] In December of that year, the skeleton of Nazi Martin Bormann was discovered in West Germany.[255] Playwright Noel Coward died in 1972. One of his selves claimed - due to his status at a time traveller - that at his moment of death, he'd be mentally whisked back to his birth to experience life all over again.[256]

The American military downed an alien spaceship carrying the Stormcore, a navigational instrument. The government erroneously believed the Stormcore was a weather control device, and formed Operation Afterburn to make it compatible with human technology. Researchers determined the device needed a psionic operator. In the years to come, the government's ESP / Remote Viewing program, called Grill Flame, would locate such individuals. The spaceship's crewmembers, now stranded on Earth, joined the American CIA as agents Melody Quartararo and Parker Theroux.[257]

Aubrey Prior's expedition to the Black Pyramid in 1973 discovered Nephthys' burial chamber.[258] Anji Kapoor, a future companion of the Doctor, was born in Leeds on 1st April, 1973.[259]

Tegan Jovanka's grandmother died of coronary thrombosis. About this time, Tegan's father had an affair and her parents split up. Tegan was sent to boarding school.[260] A short sword bearing the initials "IC," given to Ian Chesterton by Thalius Maximus, was now on display in the British National Museum. Historians erroneously dated it to the end of the first century, failing to realize it was about thirty-five years older.[261] On 12th December, 1973, Revolution Man cult leader Madeleine "Maddie" Burton died in Paris as the result of a drug addiction. The cult quickly died without her influence.

---

244 *Project: Lazarus.* This refers to Elton John, presumably, but no date is given.
245 'The early seventies', according to *Return of the Living Dad* (p66).
246 Dating *The Underwater Menace* - Polly discovers a bracelet from the 1968 Mexico Olympics and she and Ben guess that they must have landed about "1970". The Atlanteans are celebrating the Vernal Equinox.
   The story is set in "1970-75" according to *The Programme Guide*, "soon after" 1969 according to *The Terrestrial Index*. The *TARDIS Logs* claimed a date of "1969". *Timelink* chose "1970", and *The Legend* simply states it's 'after 1968'.
247 *The Shadow in the Glass* (p172).
248 *Revolution Man* (p247).
249 ACE: According to *The Curse of Fenric,* Ace does "O-Levels", not GCSEs, so she must be a fifth former (i.e.: 15

or 16 years old) by the summer of 1987 at the latest. This supports *Ghost Light,* where she is "thirteen" in "1983". As Ace has a patch reading "1987" on her jacket in *Dragonfire,* so it seems that the timestorm which swept her to Svartos must have originated in that year. Fenric is therefore rounding up when he tells Ace that Audrey Dudman will have a baby "thirty years" after *The Curse of Fenric.* Sophie Aldred was born in 1962, making her nine years older than the character she played.
   In the New Adventures, starting with *Timewyrm: Revelation,* Ace's birthday was established as 20th August (Sophie Aldred's birthday). In *Falls the Shadow,* the Doctor says that she was born in "1970". Paul Cornell attempted to establish that Ace's surname was "McShane" in *Love and War,* but series editor Peter Darvill-Evans vetoed this at the proof stage. *Conundrum* (p245) and *No Future* (p19) both suggest

1974

When Ace was four, her parents had a son, Liam. When Ace's father discovered his wife was having an affair with his friend Jack, he left with the infant Liam.[263] In November, the Celestial Toymaker kidnapped Lord Lucan, sparking an international manhunt.[264]

Tegan ran away from home when she was fifteen. Once she was found, her father sent her to live with his sister Vanessa in England.[265] During the Cybermen invasion of June 1975, the Doctor was based at 35 Jefferson Road, Woking.[266] The Doctor visited a planet orbiting Lalande 21185. The Caxtarids had developed a virus that the government were planning to use against a rebel faction.[267]

c 1975 - FURY FROM THE DEEP[268] **->** On the whole, this period was "a good time in Earth's history to stay in. No wars, great prosperity, a time of plenty". Gas from the sea now provided energy for the south of England and Wales, as well as mainland Europe. Twenty rigs pumped gas into every home without incident for more than four years.

When scientists registered a regular build-up and fall in pressure in the main pipelines, the supply was cut off for the first time. A mutant species of seaweed was responsible, and it mentally dominated some of the rigs' crews before being beaten back by amplified sound.

Victoria Waterfield left the Doctor and settled with the Harris family.

The Doctor met hacker Robert Salmon in 1975. They stopped a US Navy programmer from installing a back door that would've granted illicit access to the Navy's computers.[269]

1976

In 1976, a Lalandian safari killed people in Durham. Isaac Summerfield tipped off UNIT to the problem.[270] The Doctor and Ace visited London in 1976.[271] In 1976, the Order of St Peter chased the last known European vampire from the continent. It escaped to the United States.[272]

@ On 28th May, Deborah Gordon and Barry Castle married in Greyfrith. The Doctor was elsewhere, with a widow called Claudia.[273]

---

that Ace's surname begins with an "M" (although when asked in the latter, Ace claims it is "Moose"!). It wasn't until Kate Orman's *Set Piece* that "McShane" was officially adopted.

Ace is "Dorothy Gale" in some books by Mike Tucker, notably *Matrix* (p124) and *Prime Time* (p234). *The Rapture* attempts to reconcile this by stating that her middle name is Gale. In *Loving the Alien*, which appears to be set prior to *The Rapture*, Ace dies and is replaced by a parallel timeline version of herself. The Doctor says this swap accounts for much of the confusion regarding Ace's last name.

250 *Father Time.* Miranda is 'ten' in the first part of the book (p54), and 'two months old' when she arrives on Earth.

251 *The Dying Days* (p101).

252 *Project: Twilight*

253 *An Unearthly Child.* Susan is also familiar with the Beatles before their first hit single in *Time and Relative*.

254 *Just War* (p178).

255 *The Shadow of the Glass.* This is historical, and the skeleton was identified first through dental records, then twenty-seven years later through a DNA test.

256 *Mad Dogs and Englishmen*

257 'Thirty years' before *Drift.*

258 'Twenty three years' before *The Sands of Time.*

259 According to the writers' guidelines. She was 'twenty eight' in *Escape Velocity,* set in February 2001.

260 When she was 'thirteen', according to *The King of Terror.*

261 *Byzantium!* (p8).

262 *Revolution Man* (p248).

263 *The Rapture*

264 *Divided Loyalties* (p46).

265 *The King of Terror* (p32).

266 *The One Doctor.* This may be a reference to *The Invasion.*

267 'Eight years' before *Return of the Living Dad.*

268 Dating *Fury from the Deep* - It is clear that this story is set in the near future. There is a Europe-wide energy policy and videophones are in use. It's tempting, in fact, to see this as being set in the same near future as the early UNIT stories. Although Robson, the refinery controller, talks of "tuppence ha'penny tinpot ideas", this is clearly a figure of speech rather than an indication that the story is set in the era of pre-decimal currency.

The Programme Guide always assumed that the story was contemporary. *The TARDIS Logs* set the story in "2074", the same year it suggested for *The Wheel in Space.* In *Downtime,* Victoria has been in the twentieth century for "ten years" by 1984 (p41).

The quotation is the Doctor reassuring Jamie about Victoria's new home in *The Wheel in Space.*

269 *Blue Box*

270 *Return of the Living Dad*

271 *Timewyrm: Revelation*

272 *Minuet in Hell.* This claim is either hyperbole on the Order's part or extremely short-lived, as *Goth Opera* (set in 1993) has between three to four hundred vampires active in Britain alone.

273 *Father Time*

The last British mission to Mars, Mars Probe 13, ended in disaster when the Ice Warriors killed two crewmembers. The British government made a secret deal to stay away from Mars, and they framed the mission's sole survivor, Lex Christian, for murder. He was sent to Fortress Island, where he remained for more than twenty years.[274]

1976 - VAMPIRE SCIENCE[275] -> Carolyn McConnell, a pre-med student, met the Doctor and Sam in San Francisco. The Doctor was on the trail of a clutch of vampires, and a scuffle led to the death of his best lead, the vampire Eva. He gave Carolyn a signalling device in case the vampires resurfaced.

Peri's mother divorced and remarried when Peri was ten.[276] **Count Carlos Scarlioni, one of the richest men on Earth, married his Countess in 1977.**[277] In 1977, the Doctor and Frobisher attended the opening of *Star Wars* at Mann's Chinese Theatre in Los Angeles.[278]

c 1977 (July 30th and 31st) - IMAGE OF THE FENDAHL[279] -> The Doctor encountered the Fendahl at Fetchborough, a village on the edge of a time fissure. A team of scientists under Professor Fendelman were attempting to probe the far past using a Time Scanner, but this had only succeeded in activating the dormant Fendahl skull. Fetch Priory was destroyed in an implosion. The Doctor defeated the Fendahl, and took the skull with the intent of throwing it into a supernova.

In 1977, the Doctor landed in Lewisham in an attempt to track the Timewyrm.[280] On Trion, the dictator Rehchaht emerged as the most tyrannical ruler in the planet's history. She would rule for seven years, and butcher the Clansmen. She founded the colony of New Trion primarily as a slave labour force, but conflict between Trion colonies in the East and the West diverted her attention. New Trion functioned independently, if inefficiently.[281]

274 'Over twenty years' before *The Dying Days*.
275 Dating *Vampire Science* - It's '1976' (p3).
276 *Blue Box*. This is contradicted by *Synthespians™*, which states that Peri's father died in 1979 and her mother remarried after that.
277 "Two years" before *City of Death*.
278 *Mission: Impractical*
279 Dating *Image of the Fendahl* - According to Ma Tyler, it is "Lammas Eve" (31st July) at the end of Part Three. There's nothing to suggest it's not set the year of broadcast.
280 *Timewyrm: Revelation* (p13).
281 Seven years before *Turlough and the Earthlink Dilemma*.
282 *The Left-Handed Hummingbird* (p23).
283 *Terror Firma*. Presuming this doesn't instead refer to the Las Vegas nightclub of the same name, the infamous disco operated from 1977-1986.
284 Dating *The Pirate Planet* - The Doctor says that the population of Earth is "billions and billions", possibly suggesting a contemporary setting. *First Frontier* implies the same.
285 Dating *The Stones of Blood* - There is no indication what year the story is set, but it is clearly contemporary.
286 *The Armageddon Factor*
287 *Shada*
288 'Seven years' before *Attack of the Cybermen*.
289 Four years before *Relative Dementias*.
290 Dating *City of Death* - The Doctor says that this isn't a vintage year, "it is 1979 actually, more of a table wine, shall we say". A poster says there's an exhibition on from Janiver - Mai, and the blossoms on the tree would suggest it was towards the end of that period.
291 *Dust Breeding*. This implies that the Doctor went

back in time and nicked the original Mona Lisa before the fire in Scaroth's house could destroy it.
292 *Synthespians™*. This contradicts *Blue Box*, which said Peri's mother remarried when Peri was ten (in 1976). It's possible, if a little messy, to reconcile the two accounts by suggesting Peri's mother married three times.
293 *Project Twilight*
294 Dating *The Leisure Hive* - It isn't clear when the TARDIS lands on Brighton beach. In Fisher's novelisation it is clearly contemporary, although the opening chapter of the novel is set in June - which would contradict Romana's on-screen exasperation that the Doctor has got "the season wrong". *The Terrestrial Index* and *The TARDIS Logs* both suggested a date of "1934", although why is unclear. The date doesn't appear in the script or any BBC documentation.
295 "Twenty years" before *Millennial Rites* (p216), and 'five years' after he gets the circuit (p4).
296 *History 101*. In real life, assassination attempts were made on John Paul's life in May 1981 and May 1982.
297 *The Tomorrow Windows*
298 *Alien Bodies* (p177-178), with the date re-confirmed in *Revolution Man* (p191).
299 *Alien Bodies* (p177-178). Sam's original timeline is that of a dark-haired drug-user, but events in *Unnatural History* cancel out this history and create the blonde-haired version that becomes the Doctor's companion.
300 Dating *The City of the Dead* - 'That was in 1980' (p66).

1978

On 21st February, 1978, electrical workers uncovered the sacrificial stone at the base of the Great Temple in Mexico City.[282] The Doctor, Samson and Gemma visited Studio 54.[283]

c 1978 - THE PIRATE PLANET[284] -> Zanak's career as the Pirate Planet was brought to an abrupt end with the destruction of its engines and the death of its Captain and Queen Xanxia. Zanak settled in a peaceful area of space.

c 1978 - THE STONES OF BLOOD[285] -> The Doctor helped defeat Cessair of Diplos, who had escaped from her prison ship in hyperspace and been hiding on Earth for four thousand years. She was found guilty by two justice machines - the Megara - of impersonating a deity, theft and misuse of the Seal of Diplos, murder, and removing silicon lifeforms from the planet Ogros in contravention of article 7594 of the Galactic Charter. She was sentenced to perpetual imprisonment.

Around this time, the Time Lord Drax spent ten years in Brixton Prison.[286] Chris Parsons graduated in 1978.[287] Work was done on the sewers under Fleet Street.[288]

The Tulkan Empire made a failed attempt to annex the Annarene homeworld. In response, the Annarene erased the deposed Tulk War Council's memories. An Annarene named Sooal, dying from a genetic disease, spirited the amnesiac council away in a Tulk spaceship. Sooal hoped to restore the Council's memories and gain the command codes needed to open a Tulk stasis chamber, which contained a metabolic stabilizer. He established the Graystairs elderly care facility in the village of Muirbridge, Scotland, to conduct genetics research.

On Annarene, the ruling Protectorate came to favour pacifism, even as a hawk-like faction desired a return to warfare.[289]

(Spring) 1979 - CITY OF DEATH[290] -> Scaroth's plan to alter history - which would have saved his race but doomed humanity - was reaching its culmination. With the help of the foremost temporal scientist of the day, Professor Theodore Nikolai Kerensky, Scaroth produced a device capable of shifting the whole world back in time four hundred million years.

To finance the plan, Scaroth arranged for the theft of the Mona Lisa from the Louvre in Paris. One of Scaroth's other selves had commissioned six more Mona Lisas from Leonardo da Vinci in 1505, and Scaroth intended to sell all seven copies to private buy-ers. Each would think they were purchasing the stolen Mona Lisa.

Scaroth succeeded in travelling back in time four hundred million years, but the Doctor, Romana and the investigator Duggan followed in the TARDIS and stopped his plans. Upon his return to 1979, Scaroth died when a fire started in his laboratory. Only one Mona Lisa copy - with 'This is a Fake' scribbled in felt tip on the canvas, detectable to any X-Ray - survived the fire. It was returned to the Louvre.

The Doctor came to possess a Mona Lisa that didn't have the words 'This is a Fake' in felt tip.[291] Peri's father Paul drowned underneath a capsized boat in 1979. Peri's mother, Janine, remarried soon afterward.[292]

The Nineteen-Eighties

In the 1980s, the vampires Amelia Doory and Reggie Mead gained enough resources to start up a bloodfarm. They traded blood with other victims of the Forge in exchange for vampire DNA.[293]

c 1980 - THE LEISURE HIVE[294] -> The Doctor, Romana and K9 briefly landed on Brighton beach, but the Doctor had got the season wrong, and they soon left for Argolis.

Ashley Chapel experimented with the micromonolithic circuit and made contact with Saraquazel, a being from the universe that exists after our own.[295] Sabbath sent an agent to assassinate Pope John Paul II in 1980, but the attempt failed.[296]

@ The Doctor defeated the Voord in Penge during the nineteen-eighties.[297]

Samantha Angeline Jones was born on 15th April, 1980.[298]

> = She was born dark-haired, her mother a social worker and her father a doctor. She would grow up to become a vegetarian, and have scar marks on her arms from injecting diamorphine. She would end up living on a bedsit near King's Cross.

She was born blonde-haired, her mother a social worker and her father a doctor. She would grow up to become a vegetarian, but have no scar marks on her arm. She was attending school in 1997 when she encountered the Doctor.[299]

1980 (30th April) - THE CITY OF THE DEAD[300] -> The Doctor arrived from the early twenty-first century to investigate a bone charm. Louisiana resident Alain Auguste Delesormes tried to conjure forth a water elemental, but most of his family perished when their home was flooded. The Doctor saved a young boy from the calamity, failing to realize that he was the water elemental in human form.

Delesormes' son, also named Alain, survived and was put into foster care in Vermont. He grew up to become police investigator Jonas Rust, and sought to continue his father's work. The water elemental's mother came to search for her son and was bound into a human body. She became the wife of New Orleans resident Vernon Flood, unable to escape her fleshy prison.

On 3rd June, 1980, the alien Ambassadors completed their survey of the solar system and left. No further contact with humanity was made.[301]

1980 - THE FIRES OF VULCAN[302] -> The archaeologist Scalini excavated a police box from the ruins of Pompeii. The Doctor and Mel were inside, and exited the ship when no-one was looking. Captain Muriel Frost of UNIT called in the fifth Doctor to investigate.

c 1980 (October) - SHADA / THE FIVE DOCTORS[303] -> Answering a distress signal from Professor Chronotis, the fourth Doctor and Romana arrived in Cambridge. They discovered that the geneticist Skagra had taken *The Worshipful and Ancient Law of Gallifrey*, the key to the Time Lord prison planet of Shada, and ended his scheme to mentally dominate the universe.

or ...

c 1980 (October) - SHADA -> Borusa attempted to abduct the fourth Doctor (and possibly Romana) while they were punting in Cambridge. The abduction failed, and they were caught in a time eddy. This averted their visit to Chronotis, but the eighth Doctor and Romana later arrived and stopped Skagra as scheduled.

c 1980 - MEGLOS[304] -> On the planet Tigella, the Doctor prevented the last Zolfa-Thuran, Meglos, from recovering the Dodecahedron - the power source that would allow him to use the Screens of Zolfa-Thura to destroy planets. The Screens, the Dodecahedron and Meglos himself were destroyed. Following this, the Doctor returned home an Earthling that a band of Gaztaks had kidnapped as a host body for Meglos.

@ c 1980 (Winter) - FATHER TIME[305] -> Rumours of mysterious lights and flying saucers drew UFO spotters to the Derbyshire village of Greyfrith. This had been caused by the arrival of a Klade saucer from the far, far future. The Klade Prefect Zevron and his deputy, Sallak, were hunting down the ten-year-old Miranda - the last survivor of the Imperial Family, brought to Earth by her nanny.

With the help of the Hunters Rum and Thelash, plus the giant robot Mr Gibson, Zevron tracked Miranda down. The eighth Doctor was staying just outside the village, and with the help of Miranda's teacher, Debbie Castle, he defeated Zevron and his henchmen. Zevron died, but Sallak survived and was arrested. Debbie's husband Barry was rendered mindless. The Doctor pledged to protect Miranda, who - like him - had two hearts.

301 *The Dying Days*, referring to the aliens seen in *The Ambassadors of Death*.
302 Dating *The Fires of Vulcan* - It is 'the year 1980'.
303 Dating *Shada / The Five Doctors* - The TARDIS was "confused" by May Week being in June, so it landed in October. No year is given, but the story has a contemporary setting, and Chris Parsons graduated in 1978.
WHICH SHADA, IF ANY, IS CANON?: The TV version of *Shada* was never completed, following an industrial dispute during filming. A couple of clips were later used in *The Five Doctors* to show the fourth Doctor and Romana being taken out of their timestream. In 1992, the *Shada* footage that had been filmed was released on video, with special effects, music and a linking narration by Tom Baker. The clips that were included in *The Five Doctors* were re-jigged for the 1995 "Special Edition" release of that story. Finally, in 2003, the story was remade in its entirety as a webcast with Paul McGann as the lead character and Lalla Ward reprising her role as Romana. A new introduction scene was included to help explain the eighth Doctor and Romana's sudden interest in these events. Big Finish

later released the McGann version on CD.
Which of these - if any - is the 'canonical' version of events? All things being equal, the *Doctor Who* TV series trumps all other formats, but in this case, the actual completion of the Paul McGann story - as opposed to the abandoned TV version - makes the webcast hard to ignore. Also, the alteration of the fourth Doctor / Romana clips in the different versions of *The Five Doctors* makes it harder and harder to reconcile them against the TV *Shada* itself.
A growing theory now holds that Borusa's time-scooping of the fourth Doctor and Romana derailed their adventure and they simply departed after the punting, with the eighth Doctor and Romana later returning to complete the task. The webcast, in fact, suggests that the eighth Doctor is plugging a gap in history by performing the duties that his fourth self would have done.
304 Dating *Meglos* - Unless the Gaztaks can time travel, this story is set in the late twentieth century. The Earthling wears an early 1980s business suit. The *TARDIS Logs* offered a date of "1988", *Timelink* says "1983".

After the Doctor officially adopted Miranda, they moved south to a large house. The Doctor became a business consultant, very quickly becoming a millionaire as he solved economic problems that confounded everyone else.

Following a remark from the Doctor, the barman of the Dragon pub in Greyfrith started selling bottled water. Within five years, he was making twenty million pounds a year from sales of Dragonwater.

In November 1980, *Prey for a Miracle* was released. It was a movie version of the 'gods hoax' in 1965, starring Peter Cushing as the Doctor.[306] Shortly before he died, John Lennon told the Doctor, "Talent borrows, genius steals".[307] John Lennon was murdered on 8th December, 1980, by Mark Chapman. Huitzilin fed off the trauma of the event.[308]

Professor Edward Travers CBE died on Christmas Day the same year.[309] The Union of Traken now stretched over five or six planets in one solar system.[310] All diseases had been eradicated on Traken by this time.[311]

c 1981 - THE KEEPER OF TRAKEN[312] -> Traken was a peaceful planet in Mettula Orionsis. Two of the consuls of Traken - Tremas and Kassia - married.

Kassia had tended to the Melkur, a creature of evil that had calcified in Traken's serene environment, since she was a child. But now the Melkur had begun to move again. Hypnotically controlling Kassia, the Melkur - in reality the renegade Time Lord the Master - attempted to seize control of the Source, the power of the Keeper of Traken. The Master was at the end of his regeneration cycle, and was desperate to obtain the power necessary to gain a new body. Kassia was killed, but the Doctor prevented the Master from acquiring the Source, and Consul Luvic became the new Keeper. The Master escaped, and took the body of Tremas as his new form.

Survivors from Traken would found the colony of Serenity, a verdant world of peace and isolation.[313] **The Doctor visited Terminal Three of Heathrow Airport around this time.**[314]

1981 (28th February) - LOGOPOLIS[315] -> The Doctor landed on Earth and took the measurements of a genuine police box to help repairs to the TARDIS' chameleon circuit. He had previously visited the planet Logopolis, hoping they could help him with their mathematical expertise and mastery of block transfer computation.

The Doctor learnt from the Monitor of Logopolis that the universe had already passed the natural point of heat death. All closed systems succumb to heat death, and the universe was such a closed system. Or rather it used to be: the Logopolitans had opened up CVEs into other universes, such as E-Space. When the Master learnt of this, he recognised a chance to blackmail the entire universe. The Master's interference halted Logopolis' operations, which caused the CVEs to collapse. Entropy began to accumulate and destroyed a vast region of space, including Logopolis and Traken.

On Earth, the Doctor and the Master worked to reopen a CVE in Cassiopeia at co-ordinates 3C461-3044. The Master threatened to close off even this CVE, and broadcast a message to the entire universe:

"Peoples of the universe please attend carefully, the message that follows is vital to the future of you all. The choice for you all is simple: a continued existence under my guidance, or total annihilation. At the time of speaking, the fate of the universe lies in the balance at the fulcrum point, the Pharos Project on Earth..."

The Doctor prevented the Master from closing the CVE, at the cost of his own life...

---

305 Dating *Father Time* - The only date given is "the early 1980s". At the beginning of the book, Debbie is looking forward to a television schedule that is the evening that *Meglos* Part One was shown, 27th September, 1980.
306 *Salvation*
307 *Eye of Heaven*
308 *The Left-Handed Hummingbird*
309 *Downtime*
310 *Divided Loyalties*
311 *Primeval*
312 Dating *The Keeper of Traken* - Traken is destroyed in the subsequent story, *Logopolis*, so *The Keeper of Traken* can't occur after this time, although *The TARDIS Logs* suggested a date of "4950 AD". Melkur arrived on Traken

"many years" before. The script specifies that Kassia is eighteen at the time, the same age as Nyssa when the Doctor first meets her.
313 *Cold Fusion*
314 *Four to Doomsday*. The Doctor mentions the visit during his attempt to convince Tegan that the Urbankan ship might be Heathrow.
315 Dating *Logopolis* - The date is first stated in *Four to Doomsday*, and is the same day that the first episode was broadcast. This is the first on-screen use of the term "chameleon circuit". *The TARDIS Logs* set the *Logopolis* sequence in "4950". It's never stated if the other CVEs are ever restored, although it's possible that reviving the Cassiopeia CVE opened the others.

1981 - CASTROVALVA[316] -> ...The newly-regenerated Doctor and his companions Nyssa and Tegan returned to the TARDIS. The Master kidnapped Adric.

1981 (28th February) - FOUR TO DOOMSDAY[317] -> The Doctor defeated Monarch's plans to travel back to the creation of the universe. Monarch's android crew opted to find a habitable world and settle on it.

In 1981, UNIT encountered the Zygons in the Kalahari Desert and the Ice Warriors in Northampton.[318] The Jex arrived on Earth on 4th December, 1981, and took shelter in California.[319]

@ Even with the help of character references from people such as Graham Greene and Lawrence Olivier, the Doctor needed nearly a year to formally adopt Miranda. Shortly after that, he defeated the Great Provider's plan to use evil mobile telephones to take over the world.[320]

1981 (18th - 22nd December) K9 AND COMPANY: A GIRL'S BEST FRIEND[321] -> In September, a hailstorm lasting thirteen seconds destroyed Commander Pollock's crop. He was renting the East Wing of Lavinia Smith's house at the time. On 6th December, Lavinia Smith left for America, phoning her ward Brendan Richards on the 10th to tell him that he would be spending Christmas with her niece, Sarah Jane. The next day, Brendan's term ended and he began waiting for Sarah to pick him up, but she had spent the first two weeks of December working abroad for Reuters.

Sarah Jane found a crate waiting for her at Moreton Harwood. It contained K9 Mk III, sent as a gift from the Doctor. Working together, Sarah, Brendan and K9 exposed a local coven of witches who conducted human sacrifices. On 29th December, the cultists appeared in court on an attempted murder charge.

1981 (23rd December) - BLUE BOX[322] -> By now Eridani agents on Earth had recovered three of the five computer components that went missing circa 1966. The Doctor allied with the Eridani to recover the last two, fearing they could affect Earth's development. However, he discovered that the components, part of a system named "the Savant," could usurp control of the human brain's

---

316 Dating *Castrovalva* - This story immediately follows *Logopolis*.

317 Dating *Four to Doomsday* - The Doctor establishes that he has returned Tegan to the right point in time "16.15 hours" on "February 28th 1981", the day Part One of *Logopolis* was broadcast.

318 *The King of Terror*. The newly-regenerated fifth Doctor briefly slipped into his third persona, and seemed to recall an encounter where the Brigadier and Ice Warriors were present. In *The Dying Days*, the Brigadier says he never met the Ice Warriors, so this couldn't have involved him.

319 *The King of Terror*

320 *The Gallifrey Chronicles*

321 Dating *K9 and Company* - Sarah arrives in Moreton Harwood on "December the 18th", and later tells K9 that it is "1981". The other dates are given in dialogue. This story is part of the UNIT timeframe, but real life has overtaken Sarah's "I'm from 1980" comment in *Pyramids of Mars*.

322 Dating *Blue Box* - Presuming one can believe Peters' account, the story opens "two days before Christmas 1981" (p10). Peters visits Swan in the Bainbridge Hospital in late 1982 (p5).

323 Dating *Time-Flight* - The date isn't specified beyond Tegan's "this is the 1980s". There's no indication that it's the exact day Tegan left in *Logopolis* (or that it isn't). There's snow on the ground, which there wasn't in *Logopolis*, but which doesn't rule out it being February.

324 *The King's Demons*

325 *Arc of Infinity*

326 Dating *Relative Dementias* - The date is given

(p40).

327 "Two years" after the first part of *Father Time*, "three years" before the second (p114).

328 *Return of the Living Dad*

329 Dating *Living Legend* - The date is given, Track 1.

330 *The Also People*. This would be between 1982 and 1988.

331 *Business Unusual*

332 Dating *Arc of Infinity* - There is no indication of the year. It is some time after *Time-Flight*, and before *The Awakening*.

333 *Omega*

334 As mentioned by Turlough in *Frontios,* although the universe isn't yet twenty billion years old at this point.

335 *Damaged Goods*

336 *Turlough and the Earthlink Dilemma*

337 Dating *Mawdryn Undead* - The Doctor says "if these readings are correct, its 1983 on Earth", and the date is reaffirmed a number of times afterward.

Turlough first appears in *Mawdryn Undead*, but his origins are revealed in *Planet of Fire*. According to the initial Character Outline, Turlough was "20" on his first appearance, which makes him a couple of years too old to be at Brendon School - this was almost certainly written when the plan was to introduce the character in *The Song of the Space Whale* by Pat Mills, a story that was delayed, then rejected. Mark Strickson was twenty-two when he began playing Turlough.

338 Dating *Turlough and the Earthlink Dilemma* - As Turlough's actions eliminate Rehctaht, this presumably (and paradoxically) causes the very political reform that "hardware / software," and had been dispatched to the Eridani colony to mentally dominate it.

The Doctor and the Eridani retrieved the last two components from the formidable hacker Sarah Swan and her friend Luis Perez. However, the Savant had mentally dominated Swan and Perez, who were left near-catatonic. By late 1982, Swan was reportedly in the Bainbridge Hospital, a facility where the American government kept persons with dangerous information. Perez's family cared for him in Mexico.

The journalist Charles "Chick" Peters later wrote *Blue Box*, a chronicle of these events.

c 1982 - TIME-FLIGHT[323] -> Following the disappearance of Speedbird Concorde 192 down a time contour, the Doctor arrived at Heathrow Airport. At the insistence of Sir John Sudbury at C-19, the Doctor was allowed to take a second Concorde into the contour, and travelled back one hundred and forty million years. Back home, Tegan left the TARDIS crew.

The Master's TARDIS was propelled to Xeraphas, where he discovered Kamelion, a tool of a previous invader of that planet.[324] Tegan Jovanka resumed being an air stewardess, but was sacked shortly afterward.[325]

1982 (April) - RELATIVE DEMENTIAS[326] -> Joyce Brunner, a former UNIT physicist, came to suspect abnormal activity at the Graystairs nursing home. She alerted her old colleague the Doctor, who arrived with Ace to investigate. The head of Graystairs - the Annarene named Sooal - successfully restored the Tulk War Council's memories, then murdered the group upon obtaining the command codes to the Tulk stasis chamber. However, two renegade Annarene arrived and killed Sooal, desiring the advanced weaponry within the stasis chamber to return their people to war. The Doctor tricked the Annarene into transmatting into the stasis chamber before it was opened, freezing them in time. He then destroyed the Tulk spaceship.

@ After two years of the Doctor attempting to interrogate him, the imprisoned alien Sallak got a legal injunction preventing the Doctor from making any other contact.[327] Isaac Summerfield met Hamlet Macbeth in 1982, and was given a copy of his book *The Shoreditch Incident*.[328]

1982 (11th July) - LIVING LEGEND[329] -> Two agents of the aggressive Threllip race constructed an interdimensional portal in Ferrara, Italy, as a means for the Threllip people to invade Earth. On 11th July, 1982, the Doctor and Charley squashed the plan, and used the portal to strand the agents on the seventeenth moon of Mordalius Prime. The Doctor dismantled the portal afterward.

The Doctor spent time with Nelson Mandela during his imprisonment at Robbin Island.[330] Mel left school after getting five A-Levels. She backpacked around Europe before getting a job at a Scottish nature reserve. Around the same time, SenéNet was buying up European computer firms and other 'youth market' companies. Their executives were converted into drones.[331]

c 1983 - ARC OF INFINITY[332] -> Omega had relocated the Arc of Infinity - a gateway between dimensions - away from the star system Rondel and placed its curve on the city of Amsterdam. The Doctor tracked Omega to Amsterdam, and found Omega's base in a crypt there. The ancient Gallifreyan's attempt to bond with the Doctor failed, and he apparently died. Tegan Jovanka joined the Doctor's travels once again.

Omega recorporalized enough to stow himself aboard the TARDIS of Ertikus, a Time Lord who arrived in this period to study Omega's exploits. Ertikus' TARDIS relocated to the far future with Omega aboard.[333] **Before this time, the Arar-Jecks of Heiradi had carved out a huge subterranean city during the 20-Aeon War on that planet.**[334] The Doctor and Ace fought an N-form by the Rio Yari in 1983.[335]

Before this time, Trion had founded colonies on other planets, forming an empire that the Clans came to rule for nine thousand years. The Clans were driven by science and technology, and the development of a vacuum transport system revolutionized on-planet travel. Non-Clansmen incorporated cold fusion into their spaceships.[336]

1983 - MAWDRYN UNDEAD[337] -> There was Civil war on Trion. Turlough's mother was killed and the ship containing his father and brother crashed on Sarn, formerly a Trion prison planet. Turlough was captured and exiled to Earth, where Trion agents, including a solicitor on Chancery Lane, watched him. At some point after 1977, he was sent to Brendon School.

The Brigadier regained his memory, but lost his beloved car when he met the Doctor for the first time in many years. When he met his past self from 1977, the Brigadier unwittingly provided the energy that released Mawdryn and his followers from their curse of immortality. Turlough left Brendon to join the TARDIS crew.

1983 - TURLOUGH AND THE EARTHLINK DILEMMA[338] -> After departing the Doctor's company, a time-travelling Turlough encountered the dictator Rechtaht while she ruled Trion. Rechtaht tried to transfer her mind into Turlough, but his ally - a Time Lord named the Magician - helped Turlough to expel Rechtaht from his mind. This averted a timeline that included the destruction of Earth, Trion and New Trion.

Turlough learned that as he had altered history, he couldn't remain in this timeline without causing a paradox. With the Magician's help, Turlough found a reality in which he had died and took up residence there. He was reunited with his old friend, Juras Maateh, of that reality.

c 1983 - THE FIVE DOCTORS[339] **-> The second Doctor and the Brigadier were kidnapped by Borusa in the grounds of UNIT HQ. The next day, the second Doctor bought a copy of "The Times" that reported the UNIT reunion. Colonel Crichton was running UNIT at this point. Despite K9's warnings, Sarah Jane Smith was also kidnapped by Borusa.**

Masie Hawk, Hamlet Macbeth, Liz Shaw and Sir John Sudbury also attended the reunion. Benton had returned to active duty. Carol Bell was married with a child. Mike Yates and Tom Osgood had opened a tearoom together.[340] Lethbridge-Stewart spent some time in Haiti.[341]

In 1983, a thirteen-year-old Ace was friends with an Asian girl, Manisha, whose flat was firebombed in a racist attack. In revenge, Ace burnt down Gabriel Chase. She was assigned a probation officer and social worker.[342]

Joel Mintz had been thrown back in time to 1983 from 1993. He ended up in New York, where Isaac Summerfield found him.[343] Jason Kane was born in 1983.[344] In 1983, Faction Paradox agents wrecked the Blue Peter garden.[345]

c 1983 (July) - HEART OF TARDIS[346] **->** Crowley lured the Doctor and Romana to the Tollsham USAF base, as he needed the Doctor to open the Golgotha gateway.

Peri Brown, a seventeen-year-old student at Boston University, bought a handgun.[347]

1983 - RETURN OF THE LIVING DAD[348] **->** The Doctor, Benny, Jason, Chris and Roz discovered that

Benny's father, Isaac, was alive and well in the village of Little Caldwell. He was running an underground movement that helped stranded aliens on Earth return home.

Albinex the Navarino paid one of Isaac's allies to retrieve nuclear launch codes from the Doctor. Albinex and Issac were working together to detonate a nuclear device, which Issac hoped would spur an arms race so humanity would have more advanced weapons to use against the Daleks in the twenty-second century. However, Albinex was actually a Dalek agent, and planned to destroy the Earth. The Doctor, Isaac and Benny captured the Navarino and thwarted the plan. Benny made peace with her father.

The 'microchip revolution' took place in the early eighties.[349] The Doctor, Tegan and Nyssa visited Hexen Bridge in 1984.[350] **The Doctor and Rose quietly attended the wedding of Rose's parents, Peter Tyler and Jacqueline Andrea Suzette Prentice.**[351]

1984 (1st May) - THE AWAKENING[352] **->** The Malus absorbed the psychic energy of a series of war games in Little Hodcombe, amplifying the villagers' violence. The Doctor prevented the Malus from becoming totally active and blew up the church in which the Malus lay dormant. After this, the Doctor, Tegan and Turlough spent some time in Little Hodcombe with Tegan's grandfather, Andrew Verney.

The Doctor's experiences in Little Hodcombe reminded him of Hexen Bridge. He decided to monitor the area.[353]

1984 - RESURRECTION OF THE DALEKS[354] **->** Daleks from the future arrived in the twentieth century and placed their Duplicates in key positions around the world. They used the timezone as a safe storage place for the Movellan virus that had all but wiped them out. A pitched battle broke out between the British army and the Daleks. Afterward, Tegan was appalled by the carnage and left the Doctor's company.

---

allows his younger self to return home to Trion in *Planet of Fire*.

339 Dating *The Five Doctors* - The Brigadier recognises Tegan, so he must be kidnapped by Borusa after the second half of *Mawdryn Undead* in 1983. It is specified that he is attending a UNIT reunion (perhaps one he initiated once his memories returned?), but this isn't the occasion of his retirement. Sarah is kidnapped around the same time, certainly after *K9 and Company*.

340 *Business Unusual*. *The Face of the Enemy* seems to imply that Bell becomes romantically involved with Benton, but this is never substantiated elsewhere.

341 "Last year" according to *Heart of TARDIS* (p41).

342 *Ghost Light*. Marc Platt's novelisation specifies that Gabriel Chase is burnt down in August 1983. Ace's social worker is referred to in *Survival*.

343 "Eight months" before *Return of the Living Dad*.

344 He says he was born "this year" in *Return of the Living Dad*.

345 *Interference* (p296).

346 Dating *Heart of TARDIS* - It's July (p117), 'fifteen years' after 1968 (p246).

347 *Burning Heart* (p102).

348 Dating *Return of the Living Dad* - It's '10 December 1983' (p34).

349 *Remembrance of the Daleks*. Had someone from

c 1984 (Summer) - PLANET OF FIRE[355] **->** Professor Howard Foster discovered an archaeologically important wreck off the coast of Lanzarote. His step-daughter, Perpugilliam Brown, travelled to the planet Sarn in the Doctor's TARDIS. There, the Master attempted to restore his shrunken body using the Numismaton gas of a sacred volcano. The Doctor facilitated the Master's demise before this could happen. Turlough's exile was lifted and he returned to Trion. Peri started travelling with the Doctor. In autumn of the same year, she was due back at college.

1984 (August / September) - DOWNTIME[356] **->** Victoria Waterfield was mentally compelled to return to the Det-Sen monastery, which was suddenly destroyed. She was later contracted by Professor Travers, unaware that he was dead and animated by the Great Intelligence.

= c 1984 (Winter) - TURLOUGH AND THE EARTHLINK DILEMMA[357] **->** On Trion, the dictator Rehctaht fell from power, and the few surviving Clansmen - including Turlough - were allowed to return home to a hero's welcome. Turlough used his knowledge of TARDISes to build the first-ever ARTEMIS drive, a device that used "muon" particles and was capable of time travel. On New Trion, Turlough discovered a copy of an alien edifice named the Mobile Castle, and equipped it with a second ARTEMIS drive. The in-flight Castle was sabotaged and crashed onto Trion, destroying the planet. Earth and New Trion were subsequently annihilated in nuclear conflicts.

Turlough discovered that Rehctaht had transferred her mind into the body of his old friend Juras Maateh, and had engineered Earth, Trion and New Trion's

obliteration to further her gravity control experiments, hoping to gain the secret of time travel. Turlough killed Rechtaht / Juras, then travelled back in time to prevent this history from occurring.

In 1984, scientists in Princeton discovered Strange Matter.[358] The Doctor and Mel visited the Welsh village of Llanfer Ceiriog.[359]

1985 - ATTACK OF THE CYBERMEN[360] **->** The police had been aware of Lytton, a sophisticated thief who had stolen valuable electronic components, for a year. Lytton had discovered the Cybermen were operating in the sewers of London and was trying to contact them. The Cybermen tried, but failed, to divert Halley's Comet so that it would crash into Earth and avert the destruction of Mondas in 1986.

The Cybermen captured Lytton and lured the Doctor to Telos in the future.

c 1985 - THE TWO DOCTORS[361] **->** Some years ago, the Doctor had officially represented the Time Lords at the opening of space station Chimera in the Third Zone. Now a renegade, he was sent to the station once again by the Time Lords. Experiments conducted by the professors Kartz and Reimer were registering 0.4 on the Bocca Scale, and could potentially threaten the stability of space-time.

Before the Doctor could finish lodging a protest with the Head of Projects - his old friend, Joinson Dastari - a Sontaran attack devastated the station. The Third Zone had been betrayed by Chessene of the Franzine Grig, an Androgum that Dastari had technologically augmented.

The Doctor was captured and taken to Seville by one

1963 discovered Ace's ghetto blaster, this would have occurred "twenty years too early".

350 *The Hollow Men*

351 *Father's Day*. No precise dating is given, but it's before Rose's birth in 1986.

352 Dating *The Awakening* - The Doctor assures Tegan that "it is 1984", despite Will Chandler's clothing. As Tegan is the Queen of the May, it is presumably May Day.

353 *The Hollow Men*

354 Dating *Resurrection of the Daleks* - The Doctor says it is "1984 - Earth". We never hear of the Duplicates again. In terms of this timeline, the Daleks are from 4590.

355 Dating *Planet of Fire* - Peri says she is due back at college in "the Fall", which isn't for "three months". There is nothing to suggest that the story isn't set in the year it was broadcast (1984). It can't take place before 1983, otherwise Turlough would return home while his past

self was still in exile (*Mawdryn Undead*). In *Timelash*, the Doctor threatens to take Peri back to "1985".

Peri's step-father says they were on the island of Lanzarote, which is where filming took place. Yet Lanzarote was not on any ancient Greek trading routes, unlike the island in the story.

356 Dating *Downtime* - This is "1984" (p22).

357 Dating *Turlough and the Earthlink Dilemma* - The story opens some months after Turlough has left the TARDIS. According to p193, it is relative Trion date 17,883 when Turlough arrives on Trion.

358 *Time and the Rani*

359 "Seven years" before *Cat's Cradle: Witch Mark* (p25).

360 Dating *Attack of the Cybermen* - Mondas' attack is in "1986", which the hired gun Griffiths confirms is "next year".

361 Dating *The Two Doctors* - The story is contemporary, but there is no indication exactly which year it takes place.

of Chessene's Sontaran allies, Major Varl. He was joined by Group Marshall Stike of the Ninth Sontaran Attack Group. The Sontarans wanted Dastari to operate on the Doctor and discover the means by which Time Lords had a symbiotic relationship with their travel capsules. They hoped to create a time capsule for use against the Rutan in the Madillon Cluster.

The sixth Doctor traced his earlier self to Seville, which he had visited before. He helped to rescue his former self and defeat the Sontaran plan. Chessene, Dastari and the Sontarans all died.

The third Doctor and Jo met an N-form in Tranquilandia the time they met the drug baron Gomez.[362] SeneNet acquired a Sontaran Mezon rifle.[363]

> = Fitz saw the Beatles perform at Live Aid in a parallel universe.[364]

On the planet Artaris, the immortal Grayvorn kept shifting identities and rose to the rank of Reeve, becoming known as "Reeve Maupassant".[365] In July 1986, the wreck of the *Titanic* was discovered.[366] A virus on Lalanda 21185 created hundreds of thousands of zombies.[367] Artist Karen Kuykendall created the Tarot of the Cat-People.[368]

@ Iris Wildthyme visited the Doctor and Miranda and tried to explain the gaps in his memories. That year, the Doctor won the London Marathon.[369] Dorothy McShane was disillusioned when she met her idol, pop star Johnny Chess.[370]

During the mid-eighties, Carol Bell worked for an arms manufacturer, watching SF films to inspire the creation of new weapons.[371] She had attained the rank of captain during her time with UNIT, but was rendered brain-damaged in a car accident.[372]

@ The Doctor was offered a chair at Cambridge, but declined as he was dedicated to looking after Miranda. Around this time, he was accidentally responsible for releasing a breed of talking wild boar into the wild.[373]

@ c 1985 (Spring) - FATHER TIME[374] -> Sallak escaped from prison and summoned his people, the Klade, from the far future. Ferran, brother of Zevron, arrived through a time corridor in an abandoned tower block in a northern city. Ferran and Sallak killed the comatose Barry Castle as revenge for Zevron's death, then set their sights on the Doctor and Miranda.

Ferran became enamoured of Miranda and explained her alien heritage to her, but the Doctor sent him back to the far future. Miranda shot and killed Sallak, then went on the run.

Matthew Hatch was exposed to the power of the Jack i' the Green and started planning to release him.[375] On 28th January, 1986, the *Challenger* space shuttle exploded.[376]

c 1986 - HARRY SULLIVAN'S WAR[377] -> Surgeon-Commander Harry Sullivan was reassigned to a NATO chemical weapons centre on the island of Yarra, and researched the lethal toxin Attila 305. He found a nykor inhibitase that showed great promise in both curing infertility and providing an antidote to the toxin.

Led by Zbigniew Brodsky, a terrorist group named the European Anarchist Revolution stole three ampules of the toxin. Harry exposed his department head, Conrad Gold, as being part of the conspiracy. Brodsky's group had taken to using the Van Gogh Appreciation Society as a front for its operations, and French authorities rounded up the terrorists during the Society's annual meeting at the Eiffel Tower.

Harry celebrated his 41st birthday.

---

362 *Damaged Goods*

363 *Business Unusual* (p244).

364 *The Gallifrey Chronicles*

365 'About fifteen years' before *Excelis Rising*.

366 *The Left-Handed Hummingbird* (p261).

367 'Two years' after *Return of the Living Dad* (p98).

368 *Invasion of the Cat-People* (p46). This matches the Tarot deck's real-world release in 1985. Kuykendall died in 1998.

369 'About a year ago' (p129) and 'last year' (p115) according to *Father Time* (p129).

370 When Ace was "fourteen" (p89) according to *Timewyrm: Revelation*. Chess is the son of Ian and Barbara (the "Chess" moniker is apparently short for "Chesterton").

371 *Interference* (*Book Two*, p157).

372 *The Left-Handed Hummingbird* (p100).

373 *Mad Dogs and Englishmen* (p23).

374 Dating *Father Time* - The date is never specified beyond 'the mid-eighties' and there are a couple of (deliberate) references to keep the dating vague, such as one to Guns N Roses. It is 'five years' after part one of the story.

375 *The Hollow Men*. Hatch is 'fourteen' (p79) when this occurs.

376 *Return of the Living Dad* and *Father Time*. The space shuttle is never mentioned in a television story, and *The Tenth Planet* depicts an international space programme of a far greater extent than the real 1986.

377 Dating *Harry Sullivan's War* - It is "ten years" since Harry left UNIT, and so placing this story is subject to UNIT dating. It's clearly set in the mid-nineteen eighties.

378 Dating *The Tenth Planet* - A calendar gives the date as "December 1986". This is the clearest example so far

1986 (December) - THE TENTH PLANET[378] **->** Technological developments continued on Earth. The Z-Bomb and Cobra missiles had been developed, and Zeus spaceships (launched on Demeter rockets) carried out manned missions to the Moon as well as close-orbital work. Zeus 4's mission was to monitor weather and cosmic rays. Space missions were controlled from the South Pole base (callsign: "Snowcap").

The space programme was now an international effort with Americans, British, Italians, Spaniards, Swiss, Australians, and Africans manning Snowcap. International Space Command and its Secretary General, Wigner, controlled the programme from Geneva.

In late 1986, "the tenth planet" appeared in the skies of the southern hemisphere. This was Mondas, the homeworld of the Cybermen. They attempted to drain Earth's energy, but absorbed too much and Mondas was destroyed.

Tobias Vaughn recovered the bodies of the Cybermen from Snowcap.[379] **In the late nineteen-eighties, archaeologist Peter Warmsley began excavating a site associated with King Arthur on the edge of Lake Vortigern near Carbury.**[380]

Ace was now becoming a problem. She had sat her O-Levels, including French and Computer Studies, and was beginning to study for her A-Levels. But she was expelled from school for blowing up the Art Room using homemade gelignite - an event she described as "a creative act". For a while, she worked as a waitress. Ace vanished one day in a timestorm whipped up by Fenric, following experiments in her bedroom that involved her trying to extract nitro-glycerine from gelignite. Ace's mother reported her missing, and her friends thought she was either dead or in Birmingham.[381]

Ace did work experience at an old folks home. She worked in McDonalds on weekends.[382] She kicked a time-lost and penniless Tegan out of the establishment, failing to realize they would later have something in common.[383]

The Johnny Chess album *Things to do on a Wet Tuesday Night* was released in 1987.[384] In the same year, Jason Kane's sister Lucy was born.[385] SeneNet begin developing their Maxx games.[386]

The eighth Doctor visited Little Caldwell and met Joel Mintz.[387] **Rose Tyler was born on 27th April, 1987.**[388]

1987 (July) - DAMAGED GOODS[389] **->** The Doctor, Roz and Chris investigated the Quadrant, an area of tower blocks in an English city. An N-form, an ancient Gallifreyan weapons system, had occupied the body of drug dealer Simon 'the Capper' Jenkins. The N-form was searching for vampires, per its programming, and sold contaminated coke that allowed it to manifest in the brains of anyone who took it. The N-Form erupted and went on a killing spree, but the Doctor shut it down.

> **= 1987 (7th November) - FATHER'S DAY**[390] **->** The Doctor took Rose back to witness the death of her father, Peter Tyler, from a hit-and-run car accident. Rose saved her father's life, which altered history and created a 'wound' in time. Winged

---

of real life catching up with 'futuristic' events described the series, but in *Attack of the Cybermen* (broadcast in 1985) the date of "1986" for this story was reaffirmed. *Radio Times* and publicity material at the time gave the date as "the late 1980s", as did the second edition of *The Making of Doctor Who*. The draft script set the date as "2000 AD", as did Gerry Davis' novelisation. (The book followed a draft of the story rather than the broadcast version, as the draft included more scenes with the Doctor.)

The Making of Doctor Who (first edition) also used the "2000" date. The first two editions of *The Programme Guide* set the range as "1975-80". This confused the American *Doctor Who* comic, which decided that *The Tenth Planet* must precede *The Invasion* and both were set in "the 1980s". John Peel's novelisation of *The Power of the Daleks* set the preceding story in "the 1990s".

379 *Original Sin*

380 "Ten years" before *Battlefield*.

381 *Dragonfire* establishes much of Ace's background, with further details given in *Battlefield* and *The Curse of Fenric*. She first returns to Perivale in *Survival*.

The books offer more detail. The timestorm was in 1987 according to *Timewyrm: Revelation* (p70) and *Independence Day* (she saw *Withnail and I* a few days before the timestorm occurred). She's from 1986 in *White Darkness* (p130) and *First Frontier* (p45).

382 *Matrix*

383 During *The Crystal Bucephalus*.

384 *The Also People*

385 *Death and Diplomacy*. Jason was 'nearly thirteen' when Lucy was 'nine' (p150).

386 'Two years' before *Business Unusual*.

387 *The Room with No Doors*

388 This date is given in the Writers' Guide and in an article written by Russell T Davies in the *2006 Doctor Who Annual*. However, Rose is 'nineteen' according to the Doctor in *The Unquiet Dead*, and she ought to be eighteen.

389 Dating *Damaged Goods* - The date '17 July 1987' is given (p8).

390 Dating *Father's Day* - The date is given. The Reapers are not named on-screen, but are commonly acknowledged as such.

creatures, the Reapers, converged on the wound to 'sterilize' it by consuming every person on Earth. Humanity was eradicated on a large scale, but Peter recognized the historical deviation and sacrificed himself. Upon his death, time reverted to normal and the Reapers disappeared.

Outside the wedding of Stewart Hoskins and Sarah Clark, Peter Tyler died from a hit-and-run accident. An unnamed young woman stayed with him until the end.

The eighth Doctor and Lethbridge-Stewart discovered the secret of the Embodiment of Gris in Hong Kong in 1988.[391] Benny accidentally had a comic commissioned while walking through the offices of an American comic book publisher, just because she had a British accent.[392]

1988 (22nd - 23rd November) - SILVER NEMESIS[393] -> Thousands of Cyber Warships massed in the solar system. A scouting party tried to recover the Validium asteroid, which had been launched from Earth two hundred and fifty years before. They wanted its power to make Earth into 'New Mondas'. The Doctor kept the statue from falling into the hands of the Cybermen, the Lady Peinforte (a sorceress from 1638), and a group of Nazis hoping to create a new Reich. The villains all died in the process.

By the end of the Reagan administration, the US military had built Station Nine. This was a Top Secret satellite - so secret, in fact, that no President after Reagan would be told about it. Station Nine would quietly remain in orbit, ready to fire intercepting Nuke Killer missiles that would nullify an oncoming nuclear attack.[394]

An unmanned lander sent from Earth to Mars recovered Martian DNA. Webster Corporation tried to combine it with human DNA in the hopes of creating augmented sol-diers, and the young Tanya Webster was born with Martian DNA in her system. Webster began developing a manned mission to Mars, hoping to recover more Martian DNA or a live Martian.[395]

Mel joined the Doctor after helping him prevent the Master and the Usurians taking over the world in 1989. She had recently turned down a job at I², but accepted one at Ashley Chapel Logistics.[396]

1989 (mid June) BUSINESS UNUSUAL[397] -> The Doctor thwarted an attempt by the Master and his Usurian partners to devastate America's economy, but required a native computer expert to fully purge the conspirators' illicit programming. This led to the Doctor meeting computer programmer Melanie Bush, and she helped him erase the Master's programs.

Martyn Townsend, the former director of the Vault, was now the Managing Director of SeneNet. The company officially specialized in computer game consoles, but fronted Townsend's ambitions to use Nestene technology to conquer Earth. Lacking the components to maintain his cybernetic body, Townsend kidnapped the telepathic Trey Korte in the hopes of mentally transferring his intelligence into a prosthetic form.

The Doctor's intervention resulted in SeneNet's destruction. Townsend died when falling rubble crushed him. The Auton-augmented twins Cellian and Ciara foreswore allegiance to Townsend and escaped. Melanie stowed away on the TARDIS and took up travelling with the Doctor.

The Brigadier, investigating SeneNet, met the sixth Doctor for the first time.

The Doctor left Evelyn on Earth, and asked her to monitor the pseudo-Auton twins Cellian and Ciara for him. Evelyn came to discover that the Doctor had erroneously dropped her off in the late 1980s, meaning that her

---

391 *The Dying Days* (p94).

392 *Sky Pirates!* (p334).

393 Dating *Silver Nemesis* - The first scene is set, according to the caption slide, in "South America, 22nd November 1988". The Doctor's alarm goes off the next day - although it is a beautiful sunny day.

394 *Option Lock*

395 'Eighteen years' before *Red Dawn*.

396 Mel first appeared on television in *Terror of the Vervoids*, but the events of her joining the Doctor were shown in *Business Unusual*.

MEL'S FIRST ADVENTURE: The Writers' Guide for Season Twenty-Three suggested that Mel joined the Doctor after an encounter with the Master, and this is echoed in the Missing Adventure *Millennial Rites* (p83). This appears to be contradicted by *The Ultimate Foe* when Mel fails to recognise the renegade Time Lord,

but *Business Unusual* establishes that Mel didn't actually meet the Master on that occasion. The Writers' Guide also suggested that Mel had been travelling with the Doctor for "three months". It is entirely possible that Mel started her travels with the Doctor at the end of *The Ultimate Foe*, negating the need for a 'first adventure', but this idea is riddled with paradoxes (i.e.: she is from her own future and would have memories of her first few adventures before she arrived).

The period set after *The Trial of a Time Lord*, but before the Doctor has his "first meeting" with Mel (in *Business Unusual*), is now brimming with book and audio adventures. These include the Doctor's time with companions Frobisher, Evelyn Smythe and Grant Markham (who only appeared in two Missing Adventures by Steve Lyons, *Time of Your Life* and *Killing Ground*).

younger self was still teaching at Nottingham. Evelyn kept a low profile, fearful that she might run into herself, but used her foreknowledge to earn some money winning contests and betting pools.

c 1989 (Sunday) - SURVIVAL[399] -> In a relatively short span of time, several residents in Perivale vanished without trace, abducted by the Cheetah People. The planet of the Cheetah People was dying, and they were preparing to move on to new feeding grounds. The Master was trapped on the planet, and lured the Doctor and Ace there to try to help in his escape. As the Doctor and the Master fought, the Cheetah People vanished. The Master also disappeared.

As the Cheetah Planet exploded, the Master went back to Earth. A surfeit of artron energy in the atmosphere diverted him to 1957.[400]

@ 1989 (November) - FATHER TIME[401] -> The Doctor made *Time* magazine's list of Top Fifty People of the Decade. He had spent a great deal of his time searching the world for Miranda, and was living with Debbie Castle. He was present at - and possibly responsible for - the fall of the Berlin Wall.

Ferran returned from the future aboard his ship, the *Supremacy*, and abducted Miranda from a hotel in India. Seeing this on television, the Doctor and Debbie went to Florida and stowed aboard the Space Shuttle *Atlantis*. The shuttle docked the *Supremacy* and Debbie was killed. Miranda had started a mutiny, and Ferran decided to destroy the ship rather than let it fall to his enemies. The Doctor and Miranda teamed up to shut down the *Supremacy*'s time engines. Miranda took control of the ship and declared herself Empress, heading back to the far, far future to end the intergalactic conflict.

The Star Jumpers, a band including Johnny Chess, were a success. They made the albums *Circle Circus*, *Modernism*, *Can Anyone Tell Me Where the Revolution Is?*, and one other before splitting. InterCom were working on a means of splicing alien DNA into humans to create a slave race. UNIT operatives Geoff Paynter and Paul Foxton infiltrated Black Star terrorists based in Baghdad, but Foxton was killed.[402]

The science-fiction series *Professor X* was cancelled after more than twenty-five years on TV. Dave Young, who went on to become Anji Kapoor's boyfriend, played a Cybertron in one of the last episodes.[403]

The Nineties

In the early 1990s, there were a string of privatisations: the electricity industry became Elec-Gen, and British Rail became BritTrack. In August 1991, information about the Russian Coup reached the West via the Internet.[404]

Sometime after the Soviet Union's fall, the Doctor assisted Yablokov, the Russian President's counsellor, in accounting for the Soviets' inventory of nuclear weapons. They proved unable to account for 84 such devices. [405] Anji left home at seventeen as her family had an outdated view of women.[406] **The Mandragora Helix was due to return to Earth in the early 1990s.[407]**

The Brigadier's grandson, Gordon James Lethbridge-Stewart, was born. Kate Lethbridge-Stewart split up from Gordon's father, Jonathan, when Gordon was two. She didn't speak to the Brigadier for six years; thus, the Brigadier didn't know about his grandson until Gordon was five.[408]

c 1990 (Sunday) - CAT'S CRADLE: TIME'S CRUCIBLE[409] -> The Doctor and Ace were summoned back to the TARDIS after eating baked Alaska on Ealing Broadway.

In *Just War*, Mel says that she has never been to the past before, "only the future". Subsequent audios such as *The Fires of Vulcan* have contradicted this.

Millennial Rites and *Business Unusual* both have Mel meeting the Doctor in 1989. She's from '1986' in *Head Games* (p154) and *The Quantum Archangel* (p17).

397 Dating *Business Unusual* - The date is given (p15). From the sixth Doctor's perspective, he first meets the Brigadier circa 2000 in *The Spectre of Lanyon Moor*.

398 *Instruments of Darkness*. On p93, Evelyn claims the Doctor dropped her off in 1988. The Doctor conferred with Evelyn off-panel during the events of *Business Unusual*, set in June 1989.

399 Dating *Survival* - Ace returns to Perivale. When she asks how long she's been away, the Doctor replies "as long as you think you have". Her friends Midge and Stevie vanished "last month"; Shreela the week before.

400 *First Frontier*

401 Dating *Father Time* - The date is never specified beyond 'the late 1980s' (p199), but the Berlin Wall fell on 9th November, 1989.

402 All 'a decade' before *The King of Terror* (p130, p141 and p144).

403 'Eleven years' before *Escape Velocity*.

404 *System Shock*

405 *The Shadow in the Glass*

406 *Escape Velocity, The Slow Empire*. She's 28 and left home when she was 17.

407 'Five hundred years' after *The Masque of Mandragora*. The *DWM* strip *The Mark of Mandragora* dealt with this return.

408 *Downtime*

409 Dating *Cat's Cradle: Time's Crucible* - It is "three years" since Ace left Perivale.

In the summer of 1991, the Doctor hid a portable temporal link in St Christopher's Church, Cheldon Bonniface, while brass rubbing with Mel.[410]

1992 (Christmas) - TIMEWYRM: REVELATION[411] ->
The Doctor and Ace found themselves in a perfect replica of Cheldon Bonniface that was built on the Moon (although not before Ace had died of oxygen starvation). The Doctor and Ace entered a surreal, tortured landscape that they discovered was the Doctor's own mind. Ace managed to rally the Doctor's former incarnations, and they gave the Doctor the strength to defeat the Timewyrm. The Timewyrm's mind was placed in a mindless baby grown in a genetics laboratory. The Hutchings family raised the baby as their daughter, Ishtar.

c 1992 - CAT'S CRADLE: WITCH MARK[412] -> A coach crashed on the M40. The casualties were taken to Condicote General Hospital. The police discovered forty-two suitcases containing two million pounds in cash in the luggage compartment. The victims all bore the same mysterious marks on their skin.

In 1993, Ace's father had a heart attack. He told his son Liam about Ace, but Liam failed to reconcile with his mother while searching for his missing sister. Liam returned home to find his father dead.[413]

= 1993 - BLOOD HEAT[414] -> In an alternative timestream, the Silurian plague released at Wenley Moor in the early nineteen-seventies succeeded in wiping out most of humanity. The Doctor was killed before he could discover the antidote. Over the next twenty years, the Silurians initiated massive climatic change, rendering the plant life inedible to humanity and altering coastlines. Dinosaur species from many different eras were reintroduced to the wild. The capital of Earth became Ophidian, a vast city in Africa. Some Silurians hunted down humans for sport.

This timeline was created by the Monk, and deactivated by the Doctor. It would survive for a generation or so after this before winding down.

The Doctor, Benny and Ace visited the 1993 Glastonbury Festival, meeting Danny Pain - a former singer for the punk bank Plasticine - and his daughter Amy.[415]

1993 - THE LEFT-HANDED HUMMINGBIRD[416] -> On 31st October, 1993, the "Halloween Man" opened fire on a crowd of unsuspecting people in a marketplace in Mexico City. Cristian Alvarez witnessed this, narrowly avoiding death himself.

---

410 *Timewyrm: Revelation*
411 Dating *Timewyrm: Revelation* - "It was the Sunday before Christmas 1992" (p2). The Doctor confronts "Death," here a creation of the Timewyrm, but will often encounter the living embodiment of Death itself.
412 Dating *Cat's Cradle: Witch Mark* - No year is specified, although the President of the United States has taken to bathing in cranberry sauce.
413 'Four years' before *The Rapture*.
414 Dating *Blood Heat* - This story is a sequel to *Doctor Who and the Silurians*, containing many elements from its novelisation *Doctor Who and the Cave-Monsters*. Thus, the Silurians are called "reptile people," but the Doctor wears his velvet jacket, not coveralls, when he goes potholing and the Silurian leader is named Morka. It is repeatedly stated that the first encounter with the Silurians took place "twenty years" ago in "1973".
415 *No Future*
416 Dating *The Left-Handed Hummingbird* - The date of the massacre is given. The Doctor arrives in "1994".
417 Dating *Conundrum* - The Doctor thinks that it is "November the second, 1993"
418 Dating *The Dimension Riders* - The scenes in Oxford are set in "1993","November 18th".
419 Dating *Goth Opera* - It is "1993","November".

420 Dating *Instruments of Darkness* - The Doctor and Mel arrive on 29th December according to p69. "John Doe," although his surname is never mentioned, is likely Jeremy Fitzoliver, Sarah Jane's associate from *The Paradise of Death* and *The Ghosts of N-Space* (although this would clash with *Interference*). Sudbury was mentioned in *Time-Flight*.
421 The discovery is first mentioned in *The Sun Makers*. The Battle of Cassius is referred to in *GodEngine* and *The Crystal Bucephalus*. The year of the discovery is given in *Iceberg*. It has to be discovered after *The Tenth Planet*, or the story would have been called "The Eleventh Planet".
422 *Interference*
423 Dating *The Land of the Dead* - The year is given.
424 Dating *Invasion of the Cat-People* - It is "AD 1994", the adventure starting "Friday the eighth of July 1994".
425 *Zamper*
426 *Who Killed Kennedy* (p271).
427 Dating *Downtime* - The story is set "about thirty" or "over twenty five" years after *The Web of Fear*, "nearly twenty years" after *Fury from the Deep* and Sarah's time in UNIT, and about ten years after 1984. The Brigadier has been teaching at Brendon for "twenty odd years". The Intelligence's next incursion on Earth - *Millennial Rites*, set in 1999 - is "four years" afterward. 'Brigadier Crichton' is said to still be with UNIT.

= On 31st October, 1993, the "Halloween Man" opened fire on a crowd of unsuspecting people in a marketplace in Mexico City. Cristian Alvarez witnessed this, narrowly avoiding death himself. The evidence suggested an alien presence - the Blue, AKA the psychic being Huitzilin. On 12th December, Alvarez sent a note for the Doctor's attention to UNIT HQ in Geneva.

The Doctor investigated early the next year. In his own timeline, this was before "the Happening" of late 1968, early 1969. Huitzilin killed Christian, but the Doctor's actions erased this from history.

= 1993 (2nd November) - CONUNDRUM[417] **->** As part of his revenge against the Doctor, the Monk trapped the TARDIS in the fictional village of Arandale, which was populated by colourful characters. It was part of the Land of Fiction, and the Doctor wrote himself out of the trap.

1993 (18th November) - THE DIMENSION RIDERS[418] **->** At St Matthew's College, Oxford, the Time Lord named Epsilon Delta - otherwise known as the President - plotted with the Garvond, a creature composed of the darker sides of the minds within the Gallifreyan Matrix. They sought to create a Time Focus, which would have enabled the Garvond to feed off absorb a massive amount of chronal energy. The Garvond turned on the President and killed him. The Doctor trapped the Garvond within the dimensionally transcendental text *The Worshipful and Ancient Law of Gallifrey*, then disposed of the book in a pocket dimension.

1993 (November) - GOTH OPERA[419] **->** The Time Lady Ruath sought to fulfil prophesies that spoke of the birth of a vampire nation. She rescued the vampire Yarven from his burial spot in Croatia and allowed him to turn her. Together, they sought to raise a vampire army. Tracking them down to Manchester, the Doctor destroyed the army and its attempt to create the Vampire Messiah. Yarven was incinerated; Ruath was flung into the Time Vortex.

The vampires Jake and Madeline departed into space. They later returned, and by the twenty-fourth century had sired many descendents.

1993 (29th December) - INSTRUMENTS OF DARKNESS[420] **->** The Doctor and Mel found Evelyn in Great Rokeby. The twins Cellian and Ciara had reformed and were improving the school system in the village of Halcham.

By now, the Cylox named Lai-Ma was trying to psioni-

cally absorb the energy of his former prison realm, hoping to increase his power levels and destroy Earth. His brother Tko-Ma hoped to steal his brother's power and had founded the Network, an organization that kidnapped psionics and exploited their abilities. The Ini-Ma, the Cylox brothers' jailor, killed the siblings but died in the process.

A powerplay between Tko-Ma's anchor on Earth (Sebastian Malvern) and the Network's head administrator (John Doe) triggered a slaughter that killed Cellian, Ciara and Doe. The Network reformed, with Mel's associate Trey Korte as a member, into an organization pledged to protect Earth from extra-terrestrial threats. Evelyn resumed travelling with the Doctor and Mel.

Department C19 had closed by 1993 due to internal corruption. Sir John Sudbury was murdered to prevent his exposing the Network.

The outermost planet of the solar system was discovered in 1994 **and called Cassius.**[421] UNISYC, a UN security group, was founded in 1994. Like UNIT, they were involved with alien encounters.[422]

1994 - THE LAND OF THE DEAD[423] **->** The Doctor and Nyssa arrived in Alaska and were attacked by sea monsters. They sheltered in the home of oilman Shaun Brett. One of the fossils in his collection was a Permian - an ancient predator that looked like a living skeleton, bound together by a bio-electric field. A pack of Permians revived and threatened to breed. As the creatures were vulnerable to fire, the Doctor destroyed them with a stock of flammable paint.

1994 (8th July) - INVASION OF THE CAT-PEOPLE[424] **->** The second Doctor, Polly and Ben prevented the Cat-People, one of the most powerful races in the galaxy, from harnessing the magnetic energy of the Earth.

The Doctor, Benny, Chris and Roz spent a couple of days at the Doctor's house in Allen Road to recover from their experiences on Zamper.[425] On 5th April, 1995, Private Cleary died in hospital.[426]

c 1995 - DOWNTIME[427] **->** Under the direction of the Great Intelligence, which was secretly hosted in Professor Travers, Victoria Waterfield had invested an eight-figure sum in the New World University in north-west London. The University specialized in teaching classes by computer, but the Intelligence used a hypnotic technique to control the students there. It inhabited the university's computers, and was beginning to spread into the Internet. There was chaos as all computer systems succumbed to - as the media termed it - the "computer flu". The CIA's files were broadcast on Russian television, bank cashpoints released all their cash and Tomahawk missiles were launched in the Gulf.

The Intelligence transformed some of the University students into Yeti, leading to a conflict with UNIT. Before the Intelligence could seize control of Earth, Victoria and her allies destroyed the University's generators, which banished the Intelligence. Professor Travers' dead body collapsed without the Intelligence to animate it.

Victoria was put on Interpol's Most Wanted list for her role in this affair. The Doctor provided a letter of reference to clear her name with UNIT.

After this time, the Brigadier reunited with Doris. They married and the Brigadier gave up teaching.[428]

= Around 1995, physicist John Finer accidentally killed his daughter Amelia. He began researching time travel, hoping to go back in time to prevent this. Events circa 2001 nullified this timeline.[429]

While the Doctor and Romana were in Cornwall in 1995, the Doctor read of the suicide of David Brown, captain of the English cricket team and a native of Hexen Bridge.[430] In January 1996, James Stevens retrieved his Time Ring from his safety deposit box at a bank in London. Rifle in hand, he departed into the past to assassinate Kennedy.[431]

1996 - INTERFERENCE[432] -> The Doctor was summoned by the United Nations, who had been offered a weapon - the Cold - by a race of alien arms dealers. The aliens were members of the Remote, a Faction Paradox colony. Sarah Jane Smith was investigating the matter and met Sam, who was taken to the Remote. Fitz was frozen in

suspended animation and wouldn't awaken until the twenty-sixth century, whereupon he would become a Faction Paradox member.

The Doctor was captured and tortured by the Saudis. He sent an emergency message to his third incarnation, who was on the planet Dust in the thirty-eighth century. Sarah rescued the Doctor and he travelled to the Remote, who had built a settlement on a Time Lord warship. This ship was designed to destroy the original home planet of their Enemy - Earth - in the future War. The Doctor convinced the people of the Remote that they were being used. A Remote agent and the Doctor sent the ship to a place of safety.

Sam accepted an offer to stay with Sarah Jane Smith and left the Doctor's company.

1996 - THE CHASE[433] -> One of the exhibits at the 1996 Festival of Ghana, 'Frankenstein's House of Horror', featured robotic versions of a number of Gothic characters. For $10, visitors could wander around an animated haunted house, be frightened by mechanical bats and meet Frankenstein's monster, Dracula and the Grey Lady. The exhibition was cancelled by Peking.

Tobias Vaughn claimed he saw the Dalek Time Machine at the "1995 Earth Fair in Ghana".[434] The robots were programmed by Microsoft, who later faced lawsuits.[435]

1996 - THE SANDS OF TIME[436] -> Nyssa's awakening drew near, and the agents of Nephthys made ready for her resurrection. Nephthys' intelligence resided within Nyssa, but her instinct resided in a Nephthys clone named Vanessa Prior. The Doctor tricked the instinct part of

---

428 Between *Mawdryn Undead* and *Battlefield*, and shortly after the Missing Adventure *Downtime*. Doris is first mentioned in *Planet of the Spiders*.

429 'Six years' before *Psi-ence Fiction*

430 *The Hollow Men*

431 *Who Killed Kennedy*. It is 'nearly 25 years' (p274) after Cleary's return to the 1970s, and is subject to UNIT dating. This novel presumes that the UNIT stories occurred around the time of broadcast, and the date of Stevens' departure is given (p271).

432 Dating *Interference* - The date is '1996' (p8, p29). This means that Sam actually arrives back on Earth a bit before her younger self leaves in the TARDIS.

433 Dating *The Chase* - The Doctor claims that as "this house is exactly what you would expect in a nightmare", suspecting that the TARDIS and the Dalek time machine have landed "in a world of dreams" that "exists in the dark recesses of the human mind". Viewers find out the truth at the end of the scene - the TARDIS has

simply landed in a theme park. A sign proclaims that it is the "Festival of Ghana 1996". The "Tower of London" quote is Ian's description of what he has just seen. Quite why Peking would cancel an exhibition in Ghana is not explained.

434 *Original Sin*. Vaughn's memories are, by his own admission, corrupted and he seems to be a year out.

435 *Interference*

436 Dating *The Sands of Time* - The date is given (p117).

437 At the start of *Return of the Living Dad* (p15).

438 *Bad Therapy*. The exact year isn't given.

439 Dating *The Rapture* - Ace reckons it is 'ten years' after she left Earth.

440 Dating *Battlefield* - The Doctor tells Ace that they are "a few years in your future". Sergeant Zbrigniev is apparently in his mid-thirties, served in UNIT while the Doctor was present, and appears to have first-hand recollection of two of the Doctor's regenerations. Even if we assume that Zbrigniev is older than he looks (say,

Nephthys into thinking its intelligence had dissipated in 1926. The Nephthys-instinct went back in time but failed to reunite with itself. It circled back and forth between 1926 and 1996 until it aged to death. The Doctor removed Nephthys' intelligence from Nyssa and woke up his companion, then buried the intelligence at Nephthys' pyramid.

The Doctor, Roz and Chris rested in Sydney in 1996.[437] The Doctor eventually returned Peri to the late twentieth century.[438]

1997 (May) - THE RAPTURE[439] **->** The Euphorian Empire had fallen into war with Scordatora. The drafted brothers Jude and Gabriel deserted the conflict by fleeing through the dimensional portal they previously used to reach Earth in 1855. Bar owner Gustavo Riviera helped the brothers found the Rapture nightclub in San Antonio, Izbia.

Gabriel's mental health deteriorated, and Jude realized that he'd need to take his brother home for medical care. Fearing court-martial and summary execution, Jude decided to entrance the Rapture patrons with PCP and a special mix of Gabriel's music, then kidnap the humans back to the Empire as an offering of ready-made soldiers. On 15th May, Gustavo disavowed the brothers' actions and wrestled with Gabriel, causing them to fall to their deaths. A vengeful Jude tried to unleash a music score that would kill anyone who heard it, but the Doctor and Ace - now calling herself Dorothy McShane - thwarted Jude's plan. Jude fled, unable to keep his operation at the Rapture going. Sometime later, a young office worker opened an e-mail attachment that played music from the Rapture nightclub.

At the Rapture, Dorothy encountered her younger brother Liam.

= c 1997 - BATTLEFIELD[440] **->** In a parallel universe, twelve hundred years after defeating Arthur, Deathless Morgaine of the Fey had become battle queen of the S'Rax, ruler of thirteen worlds. Her world was scientifically advanced with energy weapons and ornithopters, but the people weren't reliant on technology and still knew the magic arts. There was still resistance against her rule, as Merlin had promised that Arthur would return in the hour of greatest need. Morgaine's immortal son Mordred led her troops to victory at Camlaan, forcing an enemy soldier, Ancelyn, to flee the field.

Morgaine had tracked the magical sword Excalibur to our dimension, which Mordred called 'Avallion'. When UNIT discovered that the Doctor was involved in this affair, the Secretary General persuaded Brigadier Alistair Gordon Lethbridge-Stewart to come out of retirement. Morgaine's extra-dimensional knights fought UNIT, and Morgaine secured control of a nuclear missile. The Doctor put paid to Morgaine's plans, and she and Mordred were imprisoned.

1997 - (Tuesday, 6th May) THE DYING DAYS[441] **->** Mars 97, a British mission to the Red Planet, inadvertently trespassed on a Martian tomb. Xznaal, leader of the Argyre clan, used this as a pretext to invade Earth. He was working with the power-hungry Lord Greyhaven, and together

---

forty), and was very young when he joined UNIT, *Spearhead from Space* must have taken place in the mid-seventies. (The earliest Zbrigniev could be in the regular army is age sixteen, but he'd almost certainly need a couple more years before seeing active service, especially with an elite organisation like UNIT).

The *Battlefield* novelisation by Marc Platt, based on notes by story author Ben Aaronovitch, sets the story in "the late 1990s" (p15). Ace later notices that Peter Warmsley's tax disc expires on "30.6.99" (p30). *The Terrestrial Index* set the story in "1992" and *The TARDIS Special* chose 1991 - perhaps they misheard the Doctor's line as "two years in your future". In a document for Virgin Publishing dated 23rd March, 1995, concerning 'Future History Continuity', Ben Aaronovitch perhaps settled the matter when he stated that *Battlefield* is set 'c.1997'. *The Dying Days* is set after this story.

The Doctor is apparently surprised to learn that Lethbridge-Stewart married Doris three times - in this story, *The King of Terror* and *The Spectre of Lanyon Moor*.

THE FUTURE OF THE UNITED NATIONS: By *Battlefield*, UNIT is a truly multinational organisation with British,

Czechoslovakian and Polish troops serving side by side. UNIT appear in the New Adventures *The Pit*, *Head Games* and *Happy Endings*, and the UN is referred to in *Cat's Cradle: Warhead*. In *The Enemy of the World*, nations have been grouped together into Zones. The governing body of the world is the United Zones, or the World Zones Authority, headed by a General Assembly.

The United Nations still exists at the time of the Thousand Day War referred to in the New Adventure *Transit*. Gradually, though, national barriers break down and a World Government runs the planet. Where this leaves the UN is unclear, although it appears that the United Nations survives or is reformed at some time far in the future. In *Mission to the Unknown*, Lowrys' ship is the "UN Deep Space Force Group 1", and has the United Nations symbol and a Union Jack on the hull.

441 Dating *The Dying Days* - The date is given at the start of the story and on the back cover. 6th May is the date that Virgin's license to publish *Doctor Who* books officially ended. Lethbridge-Stewart was cited as a General in *Head Games*.

they deposed the Queen and seized control of the United Kingdom. Xznaal was crowned King of England and began begins transporting slave labour to Mars. When the Doctor was apparently killed, the Brigadier, Benny and UNIT formed a resistance movement that marched on London to dethrone the usurper. The Martians attempted to release 'the Red Death', which would have wiped out all life on Earth. Greyhaven died trying to stop Xznaal, and the Doctor returned to save the day.

Lethbridge-Stewart was subsequently promoted to General.

The Brigadier helped to oversee the creation of a new Parliament for Scotland.[442]

1997 - THE EIGHT DOCTORS[443] -> The Doctor, his memory wiped by the Master, landed in Totter's Lane, London. He saved the life of schoolgirl Samantha Jones, who was being chased by the drug dealers Baz and Mo. After a series of adventures, the Doctor returned to the junkyard and Sam persuaded him to take her with him.

1997 (April) - BULLET TIME[444] -> With Britain scheduled to relinquish Hong Kong to China, the Chinese government secretly created the "Tao Te Lung," a smuggling and extortion ring, as a means of rooting out Hong Kong's criminal element beforehand. However, the Doctor usurped control of the Tao Te Lung, and used its operations to covertly move a group of extra-terrestrials who were stranded on Earth.

By this time, a rogue UNIT faction, "The Cortez Project," sought to eliminate all extra-terrestrials as a threat to humanity. The Doctor arranged for his old ally, Sarah Jane Smith, to travel to Hong Kong and expose the Cortez members. However, Sarah's investigations put her in danger from the Tao Te Lung. In order to save Sarah's life, the Doctor arranged to publicly discredit her as a journalist.

The Doctor's alien allies reached their sunken spaceship, but a group of Cortez commandos, led by Colonel Tsang, seized control of the USS Westmoreland submarine in an attempt to head them off. The Doctor thwarted the Cortez members and the aliens departed Earth.

One account of these events suggests that Sarah Jane killed herself to prevent Tom Ryder, an intelligence agency operative, from holding her hostage to blackmail the Doctor. Other reports failed to corroborate her death.

1997 - VAMPIRE SCIENCE[445] -> Carolyn McConnell summoned the Doctor when she suspected vampires were active in San Francisco. The Doctor arrived and joined up with the American branch of UNIT, run by Brigadier-General Kramer. A generational war was brewing between the vampires, and a group of younger vampires - led by the upstart Slake - wiped out every old vampire except for their leader, Joanna Harris. The Doctor ingested silver nitrate, killing Slake and all the vampires that feasted on his blood. He also arranged for Harris to become human again. Harris and Carolyn joined the staff of UNIT.

---

442 *Minuet in Hell*

443 Dating *The Eight Doctors* - The date is given. Technically, Sam returns home in *Interference* before her younger self leaves with the Doctor.

444 Dating *Bullet Time* - The date of April 1997 is given on p15. Sarah Jane visits Bangkok just prior to this in March (p7). Britain turned over Hong Kong to China on 1st July, 1997. The report of Sarah Jane's demise in this novel is largely unsubstantiated and hails from Ryder's unreliable point-of-view. *Sometime Never* would suggest the ambiguity of her death owes to the Council of Eight's machinations. Multiple books such as *System Shock*, *Millennium Shock*, *Christmas on a Rational Planet*, *Interference* and *The Shadow in the Glass* either or report or depict Sarah Jane as alive after this point. *Bullet Time* never names the stranded aliens, but they would appear to be the Tzun from McIntee's *First Frontier*. The Cortez Project head, General Kyle, is possibly Marianne Kyle from *The Face of the Enemy*.

445 Dating *Vampire Science* - The date is given (p25).

446 *The Harvest*. In the audio, Hex's birthday falls on 12th October. His age isn't given, but actor Philip Olivier was born in 1980, and *The Harvest* was released in 2004.

447 *Wonderland*

448 Dating *The Pit* - The Doctor and the poet William Blake travel to the 1990s, apparently after the Doctor has met Brigadier Bambera in *Battlefield*.

449 Dating *Infinite Requiem* - It is "1997".

450 *The Shadow in the Glass*

451 *The Dying Days*, first mentioned in *Christmas on a Rational Planet*.

THE MONARCHY: Different stories say different things about who is the British monarch around the turn of the millennium. Lethbridge-Stewart refers to the King in *Battlefield*, which is set in the late twentieth century. *Happy Endings* specifies that King Charles ruled at the turn of the millennium. There is a King when Mariah Learman seizes power in *The Time of the Daleks*, and by the time of *Trading Futures*.

However, Queen Elizabeth still reigns in *Head Games*, set in 2001. *Christmas on a Rational Planet* refers to the 'Recoronation', apparently implying that Elizabeth II abdicated in favour of Charles, but - for reasons we can only speculate on - was restored to the throne soon afterwards. *The Dying Days* (set just after *Battlefield*) offers a different reason for the Recoronation: the Queen was usurped by the Ice Warrior Xznaal.

In the *Doctor Who* universe, there's a Princess Mary

Before this time, Kramer's branch of UNIT handled a Brieri scouting party.

On 12th October of an unknown year in the nineteen nineties, the Doctor's future companion "Hex" Scofield was born.[446] Summer, a former attendee at the "Human-Be-In" rock festival in 1967, spent 30 years on the run from the mysterious gray-suited men. She settled in the American Northwest, but the fourth Doctor rescued Summer from the gray men as they arrived to kill her.[447]

c 1997 - THE PIT[448] **->** UNIT were called in to investigate an alien skeleton discovered on Salisbury Plain. Shortly afterward, batlike creatures tore apart a passenger airliner just outside Bristol.

1997 - INFINITE REQUIEM[449] **->** Twenty-one-year-old Tilusha Meswani died shortly after giving birth to her child Sanjay, who was really the Sensopath named Kelzen - an immensely powerful, psionic being. Kelzen grew rapidly to adulthood and gained empathy with humanity. It agreed to help the Doctor fight another Sensopath on Gadrell Minor in 2387.

The Conspiracy Channel broadcast *The Last Days of Hitler?*, written and directed by Claire Aldwych, on 12 August, 1997.[450] The only Recoronation in British history took place on 23rd November, 1997. Queen Elizabeth II was formally restored to the throne following Xznaal's usurpation of the crown.[451] Paul Travers reviewed a Johnny Chess concert in the 18/7/98 *NME*.[452]

A Kulan evaluation team crashed in Norway in 1998, split into two factions and began work supporting two rival space flight enterprises. The pro-invasion group supported entrepreneur Pierre Yves-Dudoin in the construction of his Star Dart shuttle, and the more benign faction

sided with the lucrative Arthur Tyler III in building a Planet Hopper.[453]

1998 - SYSTEM SHOCK[454] **->** By 1998, virtually every computer in the world used the operating system Vorell, developed by I². The owner of I², 43-year-old Lionel Stabfield, quickly became the fifth richest man in the world. His company bought the rights to every major work of art, releasing images of them on interactive discs. The new technology allowed flatpanel, interactive television, and the recordable CD-ROM to be perfected. Sales of computer equipment rocketed still further.

All computers were joined up to the Hubway, a formalised version of the Internet. As Hubway went online, though, chaos broke out: aeroplanes crashed at Heathrow as air traffic control systems failed, the Astra satellite was sent into a new orbit, the Library of Congress catalogue and all its backups were wiped, the computer facilities of the First National Bank of China were obliterated. Instruments at Nunton told technicians that the reactor had gone to meltdown. The head of MI5, Veronica Halliwell, was assassinated.

This was all part of the plan of the Voracians, cybernetic reptilians from Vorella. They planned to use the sentient software Voractyll to take control of the Earth. The Doctor, Sarah and Harry Sullivan helped to defeat them.

Jonah Cosgrove, former sixties superspy, succeeded Halliwell as the head of MI5.[455] **When Rose Tyler was twelve, she received a red bicycle for Christmas.**[456] By 1998, Sarah Jane Smith had married a man called Morley, and was a speaker at the Nobel Academy.[457]

c 1998 - OPTION LOCK[458] **->** President Dering was now in the White House, with Jack Michaels serving as vice-president.

---

who's nineteen at time *Rags* is set (p158). While it isn't stated, she's clearly a senior royal and by birth, so the obvious inference is that she's the Queen's daughter.
452 *Timewyrm: Revelation*
453 *Escape Velocity*
454 Dating *System Shock* - When asked, a barman, Rod, informs the Doctor that this is "1998". The Doctor goes on to tell Sarah that in that particular year, "nothing of interest happened as far as I remember". It is "twenty odd years" after Sarah's time, and she muses that a 'greying, mid-forties' future version of herself is alive in 1998, which the epilogue confirms.
455 Cosgrove has "not left his desk in London for nearly twenty years" before *Trading Futures*.
456 It's implied in *The Doctor Dances* that the Doctor gave it to her.
457 *Christmas on a Rational Planet*. She met Paul

Morley in *Interference*.
458 Dating *Option Lock* - It's 'present day England' according to the blurb.
AMERICAN PRESIDENTS IN THE DOCTOR WHO UNIVERSE: As with British political history, *Doctor Who* presents a version of American politics that's a mix of historical fact and whimsy. *Interference* lists the recent American Presidents as Carter, Reagan, Bush, Clinton, Dering (*Option Lock*, around 1998), Springsteen (*Eternity Weeps*, 2003) and Norris (*Cat's Cradle: Warhead*, around 2009). *Death Comes to Time* has George W Bush as President, and stories including *Trading Futures* and *Unregenerate!* mentions features of his presidency such as the War on Terror and the Iraq War. *Bad Wolf* mentions President Schwarzenegger (at present, Arnold is barred from the US presidency since he wasn't born an American citizen), *Trading Futures* has President Mather

The Khameirian-sponsored brotherhood, founded in the thirteenth century, had many members in positions of power. They sought to trigger a nuclear conflict that would produce the energy needed for the Khameirians to recorporealize. A brotherhood member launched an unauthorized nuclear strike from Krejikistan, which compelled the Americans to reveal the nuke-killing Station Nine as they nullified the threat. The US subsequently turned Station Nine over to the United Nations.

The brotherhood's leader, Norton Silver, forced the Doctor to relocate the TARDIS to Station Nine to launch a nuclear strike from there. Britain's Captain Pickering died while destroying Station Nine to prevent this, an act that also killed Silver and the Khameirian core within him. A month later, Sam Jones learned that Silver's widow was pregnant, and worried the Khameirian taint might have passed to the child.

In 1998, the Japanese set up the Nikkei 5 station in the Antarctic to measure carbon dioxide levels.[459] Margaret Thatcher might have returned to political power at some point.[460]

1999 (July) - THE KING OF TERROR[461] -> The alien Jex sought to conquer Earth, and had fronted the communications conglomerate InterCom to this end. They were secretly stockpiling plutonium to detonate and raise Earth's temperature to better accommodate their race. The Canavitchi, formerly enslaved to the Jex, worked to exterminate their former masters. The Brigadier received reports of extra-terrestrial involvement in California, and summoned the Doctor, Tegan and Turlough to UNIT's Los Angeles office.

The Doctor and his allies brought InterCom to ruin as rival Jex and Canavitchi warfleets showed up in Earth orbit. The Doctor used Earth's satellite network to create a planetary defence shield, protecting Earth from harm as the warfleets slaughtered one another and departed. The Doctor advised the Brigadier to co-ordinate with the American CIA and help capture the Jex and Canavitchi agents still at-large.

1999 (July) - DOMINION[462] -> Department C19 had resumed active service by this time.

Professor Jennifer Nagle, a UNIT scientist, experimented with captured alien equipment at a C19 base in

in charge around 2015.

This actually could fit together reasonably well without needing to infer any impeachments or assassinations. Assuming the same fixed terms, elections would take place in, and be won by:

1996: Dering (meaning Clinton was a single termer in the *Doctor Who* universe.)

2000: Springsteen

2004: George W Bush (another single termer in the *Doctor Who* universe - this time missing the first term he had historically. This would set *Death Comes to Time* a couple of years after it was released, but that's certainly not ruled out by the story. The reference in *Neverland* claiming the "wrong man became President" was meant to refer to Bush winning in 2000, which might be relevant - if highly ambiguous - in this context.)

2008: Norris

2012: Mather

2016 or 2020: Schwarzenegger (he'd be sixty-nine or seventy-three on taking office.)

Their party affiliation can perhaps be inferred - if Dering beats Clinton (rather than, say, Clinton stepping aside or being impeached), he's a Republican. The real-life Springsteen is a Democrat. A serving President will almost always seek re-election, but the real-life Chuck Norris is a Republican. Mather served in Bush's Cabinet, so he's likely a Republican (only on very rare occasions will a Cabinet member hail from a different party, although it happened under Clinton). We might assume that Schwarzenegger wouldn't stand against a

fellow Republican, so Mather serves two terms.

459 *Iceberg*

460 In *Transit*, there's a history book called *Thatcher: The Wilderness Years*.

461 Dating *The King of Terror* - It's '1 July 1999' (p5).

462 Dating *Dominion* - On p35, Fitz reads a newspaper dated 31st July, 1999.

463 *The Suns of Caresh*, both the Child anomaly and Jo's observation.

464 *The Turing Test*. Heller died 12th December, 1999.

465 Dating *Millennial Rites* - The story revolves around the date, which is first confirmed on p34.

466 Dating *Doctor Who - The Movie* - The date is first given when Chang Lee fills out the Doctor's medical paperwork. On-screen, the Master looks like a gelatinous snake, although *The Eight Doctors* attributes this to his swallowing a "deathworm".

467 Dating *Millennium Shock* - It is 'Christmas Eve' (p64).

468 *Happy Endings*

469 *Seeing I* (p86).

470 *Cat's Cradle: Warhead, System Shock*

471 The ecu is in use by *Iceberg*, at the exchange rate of one ecu to two dollars. In *Warlock*, the drug enforcement agent Creed McIlveen has a suitcase full of "EC paper money", although Sterling is still used on a day-to-day basis.

472 *The Shadow of the Scourge*

473 *Psi-ence Fiction*

474 *So Vile a Sin*

475 *Revolution Man* (p23). No date is given.

Sweden. She accidentally created a dimensional wormhole into a pocket universe named the Dominion. The larger universe started expanding into the Dominion, threatening many races there. Some of the carnivorous Ruin fled through the wormhole to Earth, but Earth's higher gravity killed them.

The Dominion was completely eradicated, but the Doctor evacuated fourteen of the frog-like T'hilli and their Queen to a habitable planet, saving the race from extinction. The wormhole terminated, but an energy backlash destroyed the C19 base and killed Nagle.

= In July 1999, an encounter with Lord Roche's dead TARDIS inflicted young Ezekiel Child with "Jeapes' Syndrome", a condition in which a person matures backwards in time rather than forward. Child was 21 in 1999, but age 46 in 1972, and failed to notice anything odd about this. The Doctor's involvement retroactively averted the Child anomaly.

In 1999, Jo Grant observed that a lingering side-effect of temporal interference had turned the *Independent on Sunday* newspaper into the *Sunday Telegraph*.[463] Shortly after Joseph Heller's death, documents were found among his effects that contained the recollections of Alan Turing, Graeme Greene and Heller himself of their encounter with aliens in Dresden, 1945.[464]

The Millennium

1999 / 2000 (30th December - 1st January) - MILLENNIAL RITES[465] **->** Ashley Chapel had worked for International Electromatics before forming his own company, ACL. Following the collapse of I², ACL quickly bought up all their hardware and software patents, and Chapel became a multi-millionaire. He funded the construction of the new Millennium Hall on the banks of the Thames, and began work on a powerful computer program - "the Millennium Codex" - that would use quantum mnemonics and block transfer computation. This would change the laws of physics to those of the universe of Saraquazel, which was created from the ashes of our own. Elsewhere, Dame Anne Travers became worried about the return of the Great Intelligence. She attempted to banish the sentience, but inadvertently summoned it.

On the stroke of midnight, 31st December, 1999, magic returned to the world as the Intelligence and Saraquazel fused over London, transforming the city into a aeons-old battleground between the forces of three factions: the Abraxas, Magick and Technomancy. After only ten minutes of real time, the new laws unravelled and the world was returned to normal. Fifteen people had died. Saraquazel took Chapel back with him to his own universe.

1999/2000 (30th December - 1st January) DOCTOR WHO - THE MOVIE[466] **->** The Doctor was transporting the Master's remains to Gallifrey from Skaro when the Master - now a gelatinous creature - forced the TARDIS to make an emergency landing. The seventh Doctor was shot in San Francisco and died on the operating table, regenerating into his eighth incarnation. The Master took over the body of an ambulance worker. He attempted to steal the Doctor's remaining lives by use of the TARDIS' Eye of Harmony, and his scheme threatened to destroy the entire planet. The Doctor stopped the Master with the help of heart surgeon Grace Holloway, and the Master was sucked into the TARDIS' Eye.

2000 (Saturday, 1st January) - MILLENNIUM SHOCK[467] **->** Silver Bullet Solutions developed chips to help combat the Y2K bug, but this was a front by the Voracians, who were trying to re-assemble the sentient computer virus Voractyll and seize control of Earth's computers. The Silver Bullet chips exacerbated the switch-over from 1999 to 2000, temporarily cutting power in Malaysia, Auckland and parts of Britain, and jamming Hong Kong's traffic. The Doctor, working with MI5 agent Harry Sullivan, re-programmed the Silver Bullet chips to also endow Voractyll with a Y2K sensitivity. The creature terminated, and the Voracians, serving as part of Voractyll's command nodes, perished also.

Disgraced Prime Minister Terry Brooks tried to exploit the chaos and declare martial law to advance his private agenda. Officially, it was said that his Cabinet lost faith in him, and he resigned 'for personal reasons'. Philip Cotton, Brooks' deputy, was appointed his successor.

At the turn of the Millennium, the Brigadier became a media icon as he led King Charles' troops in a blockade of Westminster Bridge. The King offered him a role in the Provisional Cabinet, but he declined.[468]

The Twenty-First Century

The non-profit organisation Livingspace was formed at the beginning of the twenty-first century.[469] News interpretation software sifted the media for the user's own preferences. Televisions could be set so that news bulletins automatically interrupted regular broadcasts.[470]

Early in the twenty-first century, Britain joined the ecu, the single European Currency.[471] The pacifying gas pacificus was developed in the twenty-first century.[472] Walton Hummer was a popular three-foot tall kazoo player from the twenty-first century.[473] The musician Sting was assassinated in the early twenty-first century.[474]

The Doctor was in Havana for Fidel Castro's funeral, and later said, "They all loved (Castro) again by then".[475]

2000

By the year 2000, the *Hourly Tele-press* kept the world's population up to date with events around the globe. One of the *Tele-press*' most popular features was the strip-cartoon adventures of 'The Karkus'. [476]

The first Space Wheel was constructed in 2000. [477] In the same year, Arthur Tyler III was working on the Space Dart and Earthrise private space projects. Diagnosed with terminal cancer, he threw himself into his task. [478] NASA discovered the six-billion-year-old Cthalctose Museum on the Moon. Construction started on Tranquility Base to better study the alien artefact, and there were regular moonshots to service it. [479]

c 2000 - THE MARIAN CONSPIRACY[480] **->** Time disturbances surrounded history professor Evelyn Smythe. The Doctor met her and concluded that the problem lay with her ancestor John Whiteside-Smith, who lived at the time of Elizabeth I. They departed to investigate.

Evelyn Smythe told her student Sally about the time she and the Doctor met some pirates. [481]

c 2000 (October) - THE SPECTRE OF LANYON MOOR[482] **->** Lethbridge-Stewart, occasionally performing some surveillance work for UNIT, agreed to look into the latest of a string of mysterious deaths in the Lanyon Moor

area. An archaeological expedition there awoke the Tregannon scout Sancreda after 18,000 years of semi-dormancy, and Sancreda sought to use his vast mental abilities to exact revenge on his brother Screfan for abandoning him. The Doctor and Evelyn aided the Brigadier as Sancreda summoned his survey ship from space, but Sancreda discovered that he had inadvertently killed his brother during their initial survey on Earth. Sancreda tried using his ship's psionic cannon to destroy Earth, but the Brigadier swapped out a crucial component from the cannon's control system. The resultant energy backlash destroyed Sancreda and his survey ship.

c 2000 - PROJECT: TWILIGHT[483] **->** By now the Forge-created vampires Amelia Doory and Reggie Mead owned and operated The Dusk casino in London, and had converted its basement into a secret medical research facility. The Doctor and Evelyn arrived as Nimrod returned to stalk the vampires, and Amelia convinced the Doctor to help her find a cure to vampirism. However, Amelia instead used the Doctor's discoveries to create "The Twilight Virus", an airborne virus capable of converting humans into vampires on contact. She converted a casino waitress named Cassie into a vampire as a test, but a vengeful Cassie killed Reggie. Nimrod destroyed Amelia's laboratory and the Doctor confiscated the last vial of Twilight Virus. Amelia went missing in the Thames, and the Doctor

476 *The Mind Robber.* Zoe was a fan, which would seem to imply that Zoe is from the year 2000, but see the Dating on *The Wheel in Space.* According to *Alien Bodies,* the adventures of the Karkus are still running in the 2050s.

477 *Christmas on a Rational Planet,* via *The Mind Robber* and *The Wheel in Space. The Harvest* has the Wheels operating in 2021.

478 *Escape Velocity,* referenced as occurring 'Last year'.

479 'The last three years' before *Eternity Weeps.*

480 Dating *The Marian Conspiracy* - No year is given. Evelyn is from the present day, and has a mobile phone.

481 *Doctor Who and the Pirates*

482 Dating *The Spectre of Lanyon Moor* - Lethbridge-Stewart has been retired 'a few years now'. Evelyn phones one of her friends, so this is her native time. The first meeting of the sixth Doctor and Lethbridge-Stewart is portrayed both here and in *Business Unusual.* Given that the Doctor first meets Mel in *Business Unusual,* and that he clearly travelled with Evelyn before her, it's fair to assume that from the sixth Doctor's perspective, he first encounters the Brigadier in *The Spectre of Lanyon Moor.* But the Brigadier first meets the sixth Doctor in *Business Unusual,* which takes place about eleven years previous in 1989.

483 Dating *Project: Twilight* - No year is given, but it's

the present day for Evelyn, and Tony Blair is the Prime Minister.

484 Dating *Grave Matter* - Peri thinks it's the 'twentieth century' (p201), there's nothing to suggest it's not set the year the book was published, in 2000.

485 Dating *Imperial Moon* - 'Some time in the early twenty-first century' (p7). The book was published in 2000.

486 Dating *Excelis Rising* - The story is set a thousand years after *Excelis Dawns* and three hundred before *Excelis Decays.*

487 *Verdigris* (p2).

488 *Unnatural History* (p33), picking up on a line from *Doctor Who - The Movie.*

489 *The Shadow in the Glass*

490 *Head Games.* We might infer that Fernfather covered Bambera's maternity leave. She's back on duty by *Head Games.*

491 Dating *The Shadow in the Glass* - According to the blurb, it's '2001'.

492 *The Quantum Archangel*

493 Dating *Escape Velocity* - The exact date is given (p26).

494 *Time Zero*

helped Cassie relocate to a remote part of Norway.

c 2000 - GRAVE MATTER[484] -> The European space probe Gatherer Three explored the outer planets and returned to Earth, where it was discovered to have picked up alien DNA. This was named 'Denarian', and seemed to have miraculous medical properties. In actuality, Denarian was an alien creature that possessed bodies to survive. A team of scientists relocated to the Dorsill islands off the south west coast of the UK and began secret experiments on animals and the local population. The Doctor and Peri arrived to find the islands overrun with walking corpses, but the Doctor discovered that a second dose of Denarian cancelled out the first.

c 2000 - IMPERIAL MOON[485] -> The Doctor and Turlough materialised near the Moon to avoid hitting themselves in the Vortex. A time safe aboard the TARDIS opened and revealed a diary purporting to be the log of a Victorian expedition to the Moon - which historically did not occur. The Doctor went to 1878 to learn the truth.

c 2000 - EXCELIS RISING[486] -> On the highly-industrialized planet Artaris, border disputes sprang up between the city-states of Gatracht and Calann. The public came to regard "the warlord Grayvorn and his lost treasure" as the stuff of myth, although officials at the Imperial Archives' Black Museum privately acknowledged the tales as true.

The Relic had become the property of the Excelis Museum, and an Imperial Edict forbade the head curator from turning the object over to anyone beyond the Empress, her Regent or the Etheric Minister. Possibly due to the Relic's presence in the city, mediums were able to commune with the dead.

At the Museum, the Doctor found the former warlord Grayvorn trying to re-acquire the Relic. An altercation between them resulted in a discharge of the Relic's energies, which dissipated Grayvorn's physical form. His consciousness became embedded in the Museum's stone walls, and he waited for someone to die in the museum so he could inhabit their body.

In early November 2000, a man named Tom jumped aboard a bus in London, and found he'd entered Iris Wildthyme's TARDIS. He became her travelling companion.[487] On Christmas Day 2000, a serious earthquake called "the Little Big One" hit San Francisco.[488]

2001

Brigadier Fernfather replaced Bambera as the head of UNIT in the UK.[489] Bambera had married Ancelyn and given birth to twins.[490]

2001 - THE SHADOW IN THE GLASS[491] -> Historical journalist Claire Aldwych discovered evidence of the Vvormak cruiser located in Turelhampton, England, which prompted the Doctor and the Brigadier to investigate. Suspecting Nazi involvement, the Brigadier stole pieces of Hitler and Eva Braun's remains from the State Special Trophy Archive in Moscow for comparison.

The Doctor and his allies came to discover the existence of a Nazi organization at an Antarctic base, led by the son of Adolf Hitler and Eva Braun. The Doctor retrieved the Scrying Glass from the base, but it depicted the Doctor taking Hitler's son back in time to 1945. To fulfil the Glass' visions, the Doctor, the Brigadier, Claire and Hitler's son travelled back to that year.

After their return, the Doctor and the Brigadier helped the sleeping Vvormak awaken and depart Earth. UNIT assisted with breaking up the exposed Fourth Reich cells.

In 2001, the Grid, a means of pooling the unused processing power of Internet computers to create unlimited memory space, came online. Paul Kairos, a classmate of Melanie Bush, learned to manipulate photons in a way that rendered the transistor and micro-monoithic circuit obsolete. Anjelique Whitefriar stole Kairos' design and patented it as the "Whitefriar Lattice". [492]

@ 2001 (February) - ESCAPE VELOCITY[493] -> Compassion dropped Fitz in London on 6th February, 2001 - two days ahead of his scheduled rendezvous with the Doctor. By now, the Doctor owned the "St. Louis Bar and Restaurant" in London to facilitate his meeting with Fitz. After their rendevous, the Doctor gave the bar to its manager, Sheff.

Competition between the Kulan factions increased, as the first group to report to the Kulan leadership would be likely to persuade them to either invade or spare Earth.

Anji Kapoor, a 28-year-old futures analyst, took a break in Brussels with her boyfriend Dave and became embroiled in the Kulan conflict. The Doctor, Fitz and Anji allied with the benevolent Kulan faction and blew up Yves-Dudoin's Star Dart. However, a pro-invasion Kulan member named Fray'kon killed Dave.

A Kulan warfleet arrived in Earth orbit, but the TARDIS completed its century of healing and became functional again. The Doctor, Fitz and Anji travelled to the flagship and tricked the Kulan ships into annihilating one another. Arthur Tyler III and Fray'kon both died in the fighting. The TARDIS had departed Earth with Anji aboard, but the Doctor promised to try and return her home.

The Doctor returned Anji home three weeks after she left, and she resumed her life. It would be eighteen months before she saw the Doctor again.[494]

2001 - HEAD GAMES[495] -> General Lethbridge-Stewart was semi-retired. In the year 2001, Ace met up with a future version of the Doctor, who informed her that his evil duplicate Dr Who was planning to assassinate the Queen. The Queen was shot in Sheffield, but wasn't even slightly injured. Meanwhile, UNIT forces were involved in an assault on Buckingham Palace. Brigadier Bambera, recently returned to service after the birth of her twins, arrived in a Merlin T-22 VTOL aircraft and managed a penetrate a forcefield surrounding the palace.

Dr Who had been created by a spiteful Jason, the ex-Master of the Land of Fiction. The Doctor counselled Jason and convinced him to dissipate Dr Who.

At this time, Bernice kicked a mangled drinks can into the middle of a path. Four and a half hours later, a young man stumbled over it on his bike, and suffered slight bruising. This instigated a chain reaction of small historical alterations that climaxed directly before the Draconian War in the twenty-sixth century.

= c 2001 - PSI-ENCE FICTION[496] -> The TARDIS landed at the University of East Wessex, where researcher Barry Hitchens was studying psychic powers. One of his students, Josh Randall, had secretly become a formidable psychic and was viciously making other students hallucinate. Hitchens was being funded by physicist John Finer, who was trying to build a time machine to go back six years to prevent his daughter from dying.

The Doctor inspected the machine, deducing that its use would destroy the timelines. Randall was driven insane, and deemed himself a god. The TARDIS materialised around the time machine, fixing history. Finer never started his time travel research, and the Doctor and Leela, along with everyone else, forgot that these events ever happened.

2002

On 30th November, 2002, the gunman Murdock killed five people... although Ace's interference in history reduced this total to three. This was about as far in the future as she could travel using her time hopper.[497] The "Great Drought of '02" affected the UK.[498] The main Xhinn fleet was due to arrive on Earth in 2002.[499]

The Council of Eight arranged for a drug overdose to kill Sam Jones, a former companion of the Doctor, who had become an eco-campaigner.[500] The Doctor found another part of Octan's skeleton in New York, 2002.[501]

2002 (October / November) UNNATURAL HISTORY[502] -> A dimensional scar, the after-effect of the singularity that befell Earth on New Year's Eve, 2000, appeared in San Francisco. The Doctor investigated the

495 Dating *Head Games* - It is "2001", some time before December 2001, and "953 years" before Cwej is born. The bit with the pop can is on p165-166.
496 Dating *Psi-ence Fiction* - The year isn't given, but there's a modern day setting, with references to (for example) *The Blair Witch Project* and CCTV cameras. The book was released in 2001.
497 *Head Games*
498 *The Hollow Men* (p74).
499 'Fifty years' after *Amorality Tale*.
500 *Sometime Never*. The Doctor, Fitz and Trix visit Sam's grave in *The Gallifrey Chronicles*, which gives her date of death as 2002. From *The Bodysnatchers* onwards, some of the EDAs hinted that Sam would meet a premature death. Others, such as *Interference*, hinted that she would live into great old age; *Beltempest* even alluded that she was now immortal.

Alien Bodies and Unnatural History reveal that contact with the Doctor changed Sam's timeline, preventing her from becoming 'Dark Sam' (dark-haired, sexually active and a drug user) and making her squeaky-clean instead. Further complicating things, some of the 'companion deaths' the Council of Eight arranged were either ambiguous or retconned away after their defeat. As of *The Gallifrey Chronicles*, it's clear that Sam died in 2002 and 'stayed dead'.
501 *Sometime Never*

502 Dating *Unnatural History* - It's 'November 2002' (p1).
503 Dating *The Ratings War* - Beep's early appearances on Earth are roughly contemporary. Previous to *The Ratings War*, he was imprisoned in 'Star Beast II', a comic story in the *1996 DWM Annual*. The tone and heavy amount of reality TV in this story suggests author Steve Lyons had a contemporary or near-contemporary setting in mind.
504 Dating *The Fearmonger* - This is "just over fifteen years" after Ace's time.
505 *Happy Endings*
506 Dating *Drift* - The year isn't given, but it's clearly the modern day.
507 *The King of Terror*
508 Dating *Time Zero* - Anji returns home three weeks after she met the Doctor, and stays there eighteen months, so this story is set around the end of August 2002. Control also appears in *The Devil Goblins of Neptune*, *The King of Terror* and *Escape Velocity*. The fire elemental that Curtis attracts is the creature the Doctor defeats in *The Burning*.
509 *Time Zero*, *The Infinity Race*, *The Domino Effect*, *Reckless Engineering*, *The Last Resort*, *Timeless*.
510 Dating *The Domino Effect* - The book starts on 'Thursday April 17 2003' (p1).

anomaly, but his companion Samantha Jones was lost to it. He sought out Sam's original self, a dark-haired drug user, to assist. The Doctor also recruited Professor Joyce, a resident of Berkeley, to craft a dimensional stabilizer.

Griffen the Unnaturalist, an agent of a secret Society that catalogued all aliens, arrived at this time to collect specimens for his catalog. Dark-haired Sam sacrificed herself to the anomaly to restore blonde-haired Sam, who helped the Doctor to unleash the Unnaturalist's extra-dimensional specimen case. The freed specimens drove the Unnaturalist into the dimensional scar, and the case sealed it permanently.

The Doctor afterward realized that blonde Sam's timeline came about because she touched his biodata within the scar, meaning that she paradoxically facilitated her own creation.

c 2002 - THE RATINGS WAR[503] -> The tyrannical Beep the Meep escaped from his imprisonment in a *Lassie* film, and used blackstar radiation to mesmerize executives at a TV network. Under Beep's direction, the network enjoyed success with shows such as *Appealing Animals in Distress* and *Hospital Street*, the first ever 24-hour soap opera.

Beep sought to brainwash the public through subliminal messages jointly seeded into the final episode of *Audience Shares*, and the debut of *Beep and Friends*. The Doctor crushed this scheme, and exposed Beep's murderous tendencies on national television. Authorities apprehended the raving Meep.

c 2002 - THE FEARMONGER[504] -> Sherilyn Harper's New Britannia Party was gaining political influence by preaching strong anti-immigration policies. She was subject to an assassination attempt at the hands of United Front terrorists. Serious riots started spreading as the population panicked, but Harper was made to unwittingly broadcast a confession that New Britannia was secretly funding the United Front. The situation may or may not have been whipped up by the Fearmonger, an energy being from Boslin II. The Doctor and Ace had been tracking the Fearmonger and destroyed it. Beryllium laser guns were top secret in this era.

The fertiliser Bloom was developed, but it was viral and spread uncontrollably. It was banned before 2010.[505]

c 2002 - DRIFT[506] -> The Doctor and Leela landed in New Hampshire and met soldiers from the elite White Shadow unit. They were looking to retrieve a crashed fighter that was testing the Stormcore, an alien device recovered thirty years earlier. Also, an ice monster was on the loose in the area. The Doctor realised the Stormcore had opened a portal into another dimension, and that the monster was not intelligent, but was inadvertently killing

people while trying to make contact. The Doctor crystallised the monster and handed it over to the authorities.

The Day the World Turned Dayglo, Hollywood's take on the Jex-Canavitchi war, was released in late 2002. Reporter Gabrielle Graddige approached the Brigadier in January 2003 for the true story.[507]

2002 (Late August) - TIME ZERO[508] -> The reclusive billionaire Maxwell Curtis had learned that his body contained a microscopic remnant of the Big Bang, masquerading as an ordinary atom, which was in danger of collapsing and turning him into a black hole. He had founded the Naryshkin Institute in Siberia as a means of researching black hole phenomena. However, a division of the American CIA, led by Control, suspected the Institute was conducting time travel experiments. Control's agents constructed a temporal detector and identified Anji as a time traveller. They made her accompany them to Siberia.

In Siberia, the Doctor found that Curtis' black hole matter was distorting space-time in the region, causing freak effects. This allowed the Doctor to free Fitz from the icy prison from which he'd been trapped in 1894. The Doctor similarly liberated the trapped George Williamson, but Williamson existed in a ghostly state, given that the universe couldn't decide if he'd survived or not.

Williamson's pseudo-existence had generated a time corridor into the past, and Curtis travelled down this corridor in the hopes of reaching Time Zero and unleashing his black hole matter there, hoping to spare Earth. However, the Doctor realized that if the black hole within Curtis erupted before time began, it would destroy the universe. The Doctor convinced Williamson to go back with him to 1894 and avert Williamson getting trapped in the ice, which nullified the time corridor's existence. Curtis travelled back no further than 1894, and died in a comparatively minor explosion.

Additionally, Curtis' black hole mass attracted light from a far distant o-region to Earth. The o-region light contained something organic, which lodged itself on Earth's past and would manifest in 1890 as a fire elemental.

2003

With time destabilised, the Doctor, Anji, Fitz and Trix were drawn into a series of adventures in alternate histories.[509]

= 2003 - THE DOMINO EFFECT[510] -> Returning to 2003, the Doctor, Fitz and Anji arrived in a version of history where the British Empire ruled the world. There was widespread racial and sex discrimination. This timeline had developed because an alternate version of Sabbath had murdered key figures in the history of computing, including Babbage and Zuse, thus

preventing the development of computers. The alternate Sabbath had learned that the Time Vortex was disintegrating following Gallifrey's destruction, and hoped to preserve his Earth in a temporal focal point. Sabbath was betrayed by a Vortex creature devoted to chaos, and his actions caused the focal point to collapse. The entire past, present and future of this timeline were consumed in the resultant shockwave.

= **2003 - RECKLESS ENGINEERING**[511] -> The Doctor, Fitz and Anji arrived in an alternate Bristol of 2003, one hundred and sixty years after "the Cleansing" effect had ravaged Earth, and found the Utopian Engine still generating a slow-time effect around Jared Malahyde's estate. By linking the Utopian Engine to the TARDIS' systems, the Doctor was able to roll back time a hundred and sixty years and avert "the Cleansing" timeline altogether.

= **2003 - THE LAST RESORT**[512] -> Fourteen-year-old Jack Kowaczski had built a time machine, and thus created many thousands of variant histories. This included his own, in which President Robert Heinlein presided over the USA and Mars - along with the Martians - had been conquered.

The Doctor, Fitz and Anji arrived in one such history, where the time- travel holidays of Good Times Inc, founded by Jack's father Aaron, had turned the whole of human history into an homogenous tourist resort. The constant time travel, though, had destabilised reality and generated hundreds if not thou-

sands of versions of events - including duplicate Doctors and companions. Sabbath was the only being unaffected by this process. The Doctor carefully sacrificed all but one version of himself and his companions, thus restoring the timeline.

c **2003 - TIMELESS**[513] -> The Doctor, Fitz and Anji arrived back in the London of their reality. They found that Erasmus and Chloe, two survivors of a destroyed homeworld, had set up Timeless Inc. as a means of "helping people". Chloe and her time-active dog Jamais would visit parallel realities to find persons in pain, then bring them back to the proper reality. Jamais would transfer each person's souls out of their bodies and into their parallel counterpart, creating a merged soul with an improved timeline. Clients of Timeless Inc. would then pay £75,000 in diamonds for the privilege of murdering the parallel reality version, preventing the merged souls from defaulting back to their original state. Erasmus eventually realized that his goal of helping people had failed and killed himself, effectively ending Timeless' operations.

The genetic manipulations performed by Kalicum in the eighteenth century culminated in the British government worker Guy Adams. He now possessed the DNA needed to house an intelligence that Kalicum and Sabbath had gestated, in a pile of diamonds, on behalf of the Council of Eight. The Doctor and his allies followed Sabbath back to the beginning of time, where he and Kalicum tried to seed the intelligence into the universe's beginnings.

Afterward, Anji left the TARDIS crew to return to her old life in 2003. Aided by forged documents produced by Trix, she adopted Chloe and Jamais. Chloe introduced Anji

---

511 Dating *Reckless Engineering* - The Doctor is sure it's '2003' (p24).

512 Dating *The Last Resort* - Time is a rather fluid concept in this novel, but Fitz and Anji are based in '2003' (p7, p11).

513 Dating *Timeless* - No year is given, but the story takes place after *The Last Resort*, and Anji has been going out with Greg for a year by the time of *The Gallifrey Chronicles*.

514 Dating *Eternity Weeps* - The date is given (p1).

515 Dating *Rip Tide* - It is "late May" (p13), in "the twenty-first century" (p78). There's no reason to say the story isn't set in the year the novella was published.

516 *The Highest Science*. The year is given on p2, and reiterated in *Happy Endings* (p5).

517 Dating *The Quantum Archangel* - It's 2003 according to the blurb and p48, 'thirty years' since *The Time Monster* (p39).

518 Dating *Minuet in Hell* - it's "the twenty-first century" and humanity has just developed quantum technology, suggesting it's the near future. *Neverland* gives the firm date of 2003 for this story.

519 Dating *Scream of the Shalka* - The Doctor judges the date: 'by the smell of the air, England 2003'.

DIDN'T SCREAM OF THE SHALKA FEATURE A DIFFERENT NINTH DOCTOR?: The makers of the BBCi webcast *Scream of the Shalka* clearly intended that the Doctor featured (as played by Richard E. Grant) was the ninth incarnation. Yet the advent of the 2005 television series now rules that out, and much of fandom (including the webcast's producers) now considers it as non-canonical. In *The Gallifrey Chronicles*, Marnal refers to the Doctor having three ninth incarnations, which is intended as a reference to this story, *The Curse of Fatal Death* and the Christopher Eccleston incarnation (and offers no solution as to how - or even if - the situation was resolved). However, the Doctor in *Scream of the Shalka* only refers to Andy Warhol wanting to paint 'all nine of me'. It's simple enough for fans to imagine that this happened a regeneration or two ago for the Doctor of *Scream of the Shalka* ... or simply that the story is indeed non-canonical.

520 *The Taking of Planet 5* (p15).

to a man named Greg, whom she predicted Anji was going to get to know a lot better.

2003 (April) - ETERNITY WEEPS[514] **->** Liz Shaw was Chief of Operations at Tranquility Base on the Moon, where co-operation with the Silurians had led to the construction of an experimental weather control gravitron. Shaw and the Silurian Imorkal were in a close relationship.

Mount Ararat and Mahser Dagi were now in territory disputed by Turkey and Iraq, but an expedition to find Noah's Ark on Mount Ararat set off anyway. Bernice and Jason joined the team, although Benny found the Tendurek Formation, six billion years old and utterly alien. The Cthalctose terraforming virus - dubbed Agent Yellow - was set off and triggered catastrophic geological changes on Earth.

The US launched a nuclear strike in the area, but only succeeded in speeding up the process. This wiped out many cities including Istanbul, Thessaloniki, Almawsil, Tbilisi and Krasnodar. President Springsteen ordered the targeting of the moonbase, believing the crew there to be responsible. Jason fled billions of years back into the past and returned. The Agent was spreading as far as the Alps, the Sahara and Asia. The Doctor engineered an x-ray burst using singularities to sterilise the Agent. This wiped out one tenth of all life on Earth, including six hundred million people.

Liz Shaw and Imorkal perished during these events, and Benny and Jason agreed to separate. Suborbital flights could be made to travel quickly around the world.

c 2003 (late May / June) - RIP TIDE[515] **->** A peaceful alien race had developed spatial gateways that enabled them to become tourists on other worlds. Two young members of the species, genetically altered to resemble human beings, violated their people's strict rule against risk of discovery by visiting a small Cornish fishing village. One alien died in a sightseeing accident, losing the "key" to their spatial gateway in the process. His stranded mate adopted the name "Ruth," but began dying from prolonged exposure to Earth's environment. Aided by a seventeen-year-old resident named Nina Kellow, the Doctor rescued Ruth and transported her back home to her parents.

A Fortean Flicker transported a group of train-riders on the 8:12 out of Chorleywood to the planet Hogsumm in the twenty-seventh century. They were later returned to Rickmansworth Station in their native time.[516]

2003 - THE QUANTUM ARCHANGEL[517] **->** By now, Stuart Hyde was the Emeritus Professor of Physics at West London University. He had used the discarded technology from TOMTIT to build TITAN, a dimensional array intended to penetrate the higher dimensions called "Calabi-Yau Space." Thanks to TITAN, businesswoman Anjeliqua Whitefriar became infused with the core of the Calabi-Yau and gained reality-warping powers. She became "the Quantum Archangel," and channelled her newfound reality-warping powers through the Mad Mind of Bophemeral, the super-computer that triggered the Millennium War, in a benevolent attempt to create separate utopias for each person on Earth. This threatened to plunge the universe into chaos.

The Doctor persuaded Anjeliqua to restore order and relinquish her power, while the Chronovore named Kronos sacrificed himself to destroy Bophemeral.

2003 - MINUET IN HELL[518] **->** Hellfire Club leader Brigham Elisha Dashwood III believed he'd allied himself with a group of demons, and set about using their support to booster his organization. In truth, he'd contacted alien Psionivores, members of a species of cosmic parasites that feasted on negative emotions. With the Psionivores' help and technical expertise, Dashwood seceded a small portion of America, renamed it "Malebolgia" and dedicated it to a social program of devil worship. The Psionivores helped Dashwood perfect the PSI-895, which was capable of rewriting or transferring human memories, and Dashwood hoped this would let him install Psionivores in his political opponents' bodies.

The Doctor and Charley, aided by the Brigadier, publicly exposed Dashwood as a political charlatan. Dashwood turned against Marcosius, his main contact among the Psionivores, and accidentally disrupted the PSI machine. This created an unstable portal that consumed Dashwood, Marcosius and the device. The remaining Hellfire Club leaders crumbled in a political scandal.

Lethbridge-Stewart had now retired from UNIT, but still undertook occasional work for them.

c 2003 - SCREAM OF THE SHALKA[519] **->** An unspecified incarnation of the Doctor and his friend the Master - an android - encountered the Shalka, an alien race that subsisted on volcanic gas and had travelled to Earth via a warp gate. The Shalka had occupied the Lancashire town of Lannet and twenty-five other locations on Earth. They mentally conditioned groups of people to emit a unique sonic scream that would make Earth's environment suitable for the Shalka's needs, but prove fatal to humans. With the help of barmaid Alison Cheney, a Lannet resident, the Doctor destroyed the Shalka on Earth. Alison accompanied the Doctor on his travels.

Vulcan, nearest planet to the Sun, was discovered in 2003.[520] **Vulcan was a large, hot world with a bleak landscape of mercury swamps and geysers that spat toxic fumes. It had a breathable atmosphere and soil capable of supporting plant life. Plans were made to set** up a mining colony on Vulcan for a trial period.[521]

c 2003 (Saturday, 14th June) - THE HOLLOW MEN[522] -> The Hakolian battle vehicle Jerak revived in Hexen Bridge and animated scarecrows, who attacked the villagers and fed them to Jerak's organic component. Jerak mentally influenced a former resident, Defence Minister Matthew Hatch, in a bid to taint Liverpool's water supply with genetic material that would increase Jerak's mental hold over any humans it infected. The Doctor thwarted the scheme, entered Jerak's psychic realm via a mirror gateway and convinced the villagers absorbed over the centuries by Jerak to turn their willpower against the battle vehicle. The Doctor escaped and Ace destroyed the gateway, trapping Jerak on the astral plane. Hatch died, still mentally connected to Jerak upon its defeat.

2003 (August) - THE SHADOW OF THE SCOURGE[523] -> The Doctor, Ace and Benny arrived at the Pinehill Crest Hotel, which was host to the unfortunate triple-booking of a presentation of a temporal accelerator, a demonstration of spiritual channelling and a cross-stitch convention. The Scourge attempted to manifest into our universe at this time, but the Doctor defeated them.

= 2003 - JUBILEE[524] -> The Doctor and Evelyn arrived at the Tower of London, 2003, and discovered their thwarting a Dalek invasion in 1903 had given rise to an English Empire. The Doctor and Evelyn were now widely regarded as heroes, and Nelson's Column had been rebuilt to depict the Doctor dressed as an English stormtrooper. The British and American populates were strictly kept apart to protect British genetic purity. The Daleks had become heavily merchandised, and their defeat was told in movies such as *Daleks: The Ultimate Adventure!*, starring Plenty O'Toole as Evelyn "Hot Lips" Smythe. Use of contractions was outlawed.

The President of the English Empire, Nigel Rochester, scheduled the Empire's jubilee celebration to include the public execution of the sole surviving Dalek from the 1903 attack. However, the Dalek

---

521 *The Power of the Daleks*

VULCAN: The planet Vulcan is only seen in *The Power of the Daleks*, a story that is almost certainly set in 2020. There is no indication that mankind has developed interstellar travel or faster-than-light drives in this or any other story set at this time. This would seem to suggest that Vulcan is within our own Solar System.

There is some evidence to support this conjecture: since the nineteenth century, some astronomers (including Le Verrier, who discovered Neptune), speculated that a planet might orbit the sun closer than Mercury. There was new interest in this theory in the mid-nineteen-sixties, which might explain why the home planet of Mr Spock was also called Vulcan around the same time in *Star Trek*. The draft script talked of a 'Plutovian Sun', suggesting Vulcan is far from the Sun, not close.

In 1964, *The Dalek Book*, which, like *The Power of the Daleks* was co-written by David Whitaker, named Vulcan as the innermost planet in our Solar System (and Omega as the outermost). This, though, contradicts the story that immediately precedes *The Power of the Daleks*, in which Mondas is referred to as "The Tenth Planet"; *Image of the Fendahl*, where the Fendahleen homeworld is 'The Fifth Planet'; and *The Sun Makers*, where Pluto is established as the ninth planet of the Solar System. All in all, it seems that Vulcan wasn't in our solar system in the late nineteen-eighties or the far future.

Taking all this literally and at face value, *Doctor Who* fan Donald Gillikin has suggested that Vulcan arrives in the Solar System but later leaves. This might be scientifically implausible - at least in the timescale suggested - but we know of at least three other 'rogue planets' that enter our Solar System according to the series: the Moon, Mondas and Voga. *The Taking of Planet 5* (p15) confirms Gillikin's theory by stating that Vulcan was discovered in 2003 and had vanished by 2130.

522 Dating *The Hollow Men* - No year is given, but the drought of '02 is mentioned, and five-pound coins are legal tender.

523 Dating *The Shadow of the Scourge* - It is 'the fifteenth of August 2003' according to the Doctor.

524 Dating *Jubilee* - The date is given (and it's the hundredth anniversary of the events of 1903).

525 Dating *Falls the Shadow* - It is "a crisp November morning", "five years" after "UN adventurism in the Persian Gulf". Winterdawn is alive and well in *The Quantum Archangel*, so this book is set after that. Thascales was an alias of the Master in *The Time Monster*. Author Daniel O'Mahony intended it to be set in 'the near future'.

526 Dating *Catch-1782* - The date is given.

527 Dating *Sometime Never* - An invitation states that an exhibition at the Institute of Anthropology opens 31st January, 2004. *Sometime Never* was published in the same month.

528 'A year' before *The Gallifrey Chronicles*. Greg was introduced in *Timeless*.

529 Dating *The Tomorrow Windows* - Trix's clothes are 'very 2004' (p13). The Earth year 2004 is equivalent to the Galactic Year 2457. All the events on alien planets in *The Tomorrow Windows* seem contemporaneous, and the Doctor even says on p278, "we only travelled in space, not in time".

secretly killed the Doctor's temporal duplicate, who had by now been a prisoner in the Tower for 100 years.

The timelines of 1903 and 2003 began meshing together, and the Dalek invasion of 1903 started to unfold in the latter era. The Doctor convinced the "jubilee" Dalek that if the Daleks succeeded in their attempt to destroy all other life forms, they could only then turn on each other until a single Dalek remained, purposeless and insane. Logically, success would mean the Dalek race's destruction. The Dalek concurred and connected itself to the Dalek command net, transmitting a message that the Daleks could only survive by dying. The entire Dalek invasion force self-destructed, which retroactively averted the 1903 assault.

Remnants of the cancelled timeline remained in the restored history. Nigel Rochester, visiting the Tower of London as a tourist, briefly recognized the Doctor and thanked him for his help in the aberrant history. The English Empire's atrocities subtly lived on in the history and the dreams of the English people.

c 2003 (November) - FALLS THE SHADOW[525] ->

Professor Jeremy Winterdawn and his team at Shadowfell House experimented for five years with the "Thascales Theorem", and their research that indicated that applied quantum physics was a possibility. Hoping to manipulate space-time, Winterdawn managed to interface with the Cathedral, and succeeded in distorting the spacial dimensions of Shadowfell. Gabriel and Tanith, psychotic expressions of Cathedral's pain, were released, as were individuals from other parallel universes: an agent from an Earth where England was a Republic dedicated to the principals of Fundamental Humanism, the other from an Earth dominated by a hivemind of giant insects. Cathedral was destroyed along with Gabriel and Tanith, although the grey man survived.

2003 (12th December) - CATCH-1782[526] -> The

Doctor and Mel arrived in Berkshire at the invitation of Mel's uncle, John Hallam, to attend the 100th anniversary celebration of the National Foundation for Scientific Research, UK. Hallam had constructed a cylinder from a unique alloy provided by a space agency, but the interaction of the TARDIS and chrono-atoms within the cylinder threw Melanie two hundred and twenty-two years back in time. The Doctor and Hallam pursued her in the TARDIS.

2004

2004 - SOMETIME NEVER[527] -> The scientist Ernest

Fleetward stood on the brink of inventing a form of unbreakable crystal that would greatly advance mankind's development. Fleetwood had set about reconstructing a crystal human skeleton, unaware that it was the Council of Eight leader Octan, lost to the Time Vortex in 1588. Octan himself travelled through time to prevent Fleetwood's efforts from impacting history and cast the skeleton into the Time Vortex, failing to realize that he was re-obliterating his own body.

The Doctor convinced Fleetward to adopt the nephews of Richard III, who were saved from their historical fate.

Anji started dating Greg in the summer.[528]

2004 (July) - THE TOMORROW WINDOWS[529] -> The

"selfish memes" seeded on behalf of Martin culminated on various planets. The planet Shardybarn was eradicated when the Low Priest Jadrack the Pitiful triggered several nuclear bombs, hoping that his god would perform a miracle and stop the disaster. On Valuensis, a misunderstanding made the Gabaks and Aztales annihilate one another with doomsday devices. On Estebol, malevolent cars began to possess their drivers and the people withered due to extreme pollution.

To combat this self-destructive trend, the billionaire philanthropist Charlton Mackerel set up "Tomorrow Window" exhibits on various planets. The Tomorrow Windows would allow the indigenous populations to glimpse their future and hopefully amend their behaviour. Martin sought to ruin Mackerel's exhibits. In June 2004, Martin eradicated the Tate Modern - and a Tomorrow Windows exhibit there - with an electron bomb.

The Doctor aided Mackerel by seeking out the original Tomorrow Windows builder, Astrabel Zar. Electrical beings named the Ceccecs, working for Martin, destroyed the belt of moon-sized Astral Flowers in an attempt to kill Zar, but the Doctor and Zar escaped.

A "selfish meme" on the planet Minuea made the populace do nothing as their moon slowly moved toward a collision with their planet. The Doctor used a Tomorrow Window to make the people see the benefit of using a missile to stop the catastrophe, and thereby saved the planet.

The aged Zar returned to Gadrahadron to tell his younger self, fifty years in the past, how to make the Tomorrow Windows. Martin discovered this and killed Zar. The repentant actor Prubert Gatridge and Martin died in mutual combat. Fitz, Trix and Mackerel insured that the younger Zar learned the Tomorrow Windows secret.

Mackerel's Tomorrow Windows exhibits continued, granting planets with "selfish memes" a second chance. The Doctor determined that Martin never completed his work on Earth, and that humanity developed "selfish memes" independent of him.

The Doctor was by now an old friend of Ken Livingstone, the current Mayor of London.

c 2004 - THE SLEEP OF REASON[530] -> Mausolus House had been replaced by the Retreat, a more modernised asylum. Caroline "Laska" Darnell, the great-great-granddaughter of one of Dr. Christie's patients, came into possession of the Sholem-Luz dog-tooth pendant. The pendant again infected an Irish wolfhound with the Sholem-Luz essence, and the infernal hound set about trying to germinate Sholem-Luz seeds through time and space. The Doctor lured the creature into a time corridor to 1903. Afterward, the husband of a Retreat medical officer found Laska's pendant, which possibly still contained the Sholem-Luz taint.

2004 - (July, November) - PROJECT: LAZARUS[531] -> The Forge, located on Dartmoor beneath an abandoned asylum, had begun collecting dead alien life forms and technology that appeared on Earth. Its agents captured a stranded, blue skinned alien capable of exuding a slime that killed on contact, and Nimrod, now the Forge's deputy director, dubbed the alien's race as the "Huldran." The Forge also took into custody the Huldran's spacecraft,

which was capable of generating spatial gateways. The Doctor and Evelyn briefly ran afoul of the Forge at this time, leading to the Forge procuring a sample of the Doctor's blood. They created a clone of the Doctor to assist in their endeavours.

Four months later, the TARDIS directed the seventh Doctor to the Forge. He met his former self's clone, and discovered that the Forge's experiments had killed the captive Huldran. As the creature was part of a gestalt race, its fellows had felt its death trauma. A cadre of sword-wielding Huldran assaulted the Forge via a gateway in the seized spaceship, but were captured. The Doctor-clone broke the Forge's control and triggered the base's Hades Protocol, a self-destruct mechanism. Nimrod killed the Doctor-clone, but the seventh Doctor helped the Huldran escape as the Forge was destroyed. Afterward, the Forge's main computer, Oracle, brought the organization's beta facility on-line.

c 2004 - THE ALGEBRA OF ICE[532] -> In another universe, an alien gestalt composed of mathematical equations sought to drain energy from outside realities into its own.

---

530 Dating *The Sleep of Reason* - It's the 'near future' according to the blurb, but references to things like Limp Biskit and *Casualty* suggest it's at most only a few years after publication. It is 'a hundred years or so' since 1903 (p273).

531 Dating *Project: Lazarus* - It is "five years" after *Project: Twilight*.

532 Dating *The Algebra of Ice* - The story is apparently set 'several years' after the Brigadier first met the seventh Doctor (in *Battlefield*). The Brigadier (from his perspective) previously met the seventh Doctor in *No Future*, but the Doctor mind-wiped the Brigadier's recollection of those events, and doesn't restore these memories until *Happy Endings*, set in 2010. *The Algebra of Ice* falls in the period where the Brigadier would recall *Battlefield* as their first meeting. Lloyd Rose wrote this novel with "the modern day" in mind.

533 Dating *The City of the Dead* - No year is given, but it's 'a few years' after Anji's time.

534 Dating *The Deadstone Memorial*- There's no specific date beyond 'early twenty-first century' (p51). It's set in the modern day.

535 *Unregenerate!* Rausch says he hasn't seen Louis in 'fifty years', but this could be a rounded sum. A radio broadcast says US and UK forces are 'hours' away from Fallujah in Iraq. The main offensive there occurred on 8th November, 2004. *Unregenerate!* was recorded just more than a week later on 16-17 November.

536 Dating *Rose* - The year isn't specified, but there's a contemporary setting. The story is clearly set after 2003, as the Doctor reads a paperback copy of the novel *The Lovely Bones* by Alice Sebold. *Aliens of London* shows a missing persons poster that definitively cites Rose as last seen on 6th March, 2005. The casu-

alty figures come from the www.whoisdoctor who.co.uk website. The same site has pictures with time-stamps that offer an alternative date of 26th March, the day of broadcast.

537 *Aliens of London* - Mickey's surname isn't established on-screen until *Boom Town*.

538 Dating *Death Comes to Time* - No year is given, but Tony Blair is the Prime Minister and George W Bush is President of the United States, suggesting a contemporary setting. The story was webcast in 2002. Lee Sullivan's illustrations suggest that UNIT is operating a moonbase at this time, and although such details aren't in the script or dialogue, this could nudge the story a couple of years into the future (there was a moonbase in the 2003 of *Eternity Weeps*, after all). See 'American Presidents in the *Doctor Who* Universe' for why this story seems to take place after 2004.

IS DEATH COMES TO TIME CANON?: As the seventh Doctor dies at the end, all Time Lords are revealed to have godlike powers that they simply haven't used before and all the Time Lords are extinguished or otherwise removed from the universe during the seventh Doctor's time, a strong case can be made that this story is apocryphal. Crucially, the Time Lords' godlike abilities aren't reconcilable against the Gallifrey History section of this book. However, references to Anima Persis in *Relative Dementias* and *The Tomorrow Windows* and the Canisians in *Trading Futures* suggest *Death Comes to Time* may well be canonical. As with all *Doctor Who*, readers can include or ignore this story as they wish.

539 *Trading Futures*, making reference to *Death Comes to Time*.

540 Dating *The Gallifrey Chronicles* - The date is given (p75).

The gestalt contacted the genocidal Sheridan Brett in our universe, in the hopes of using human mathematicians to further its plans. The Doctor confronted the alien gestalt on a mathematical level, and resolved the creature into zero.

c 2004 (October) - THE CITY OF THE DEAD[533] -> The

Doctor visited New Orleans to identify a bone charm he had found in the TARDIS. He determined that the charm could be used to summon a water elemental, and left for 1980 to investigate such an occurrence. This journey made the charm retroactively appear in the TARDIS for the Doctor to find in the first place.

Upon returning, the Doctor found that the wife of resident Vernon Flood was a bound water elemental. The Doctor freed Mrs Flood from her human form and she returned to her own dimension, causing Vernon to drown. Her elemental son, bound in 1980, had become the crippled museum owner Thales. The ritualist Jonas Rust attempted to absorb Thales to attain great power, but an emptiness that Rust summoned - the Void - wound up consuming him. Thales was liberated from his human body and reunited with his mother.

c 2004 - THE DEADSTONE MEMORIAL[534] -> The

long-lived Henry Deadstone, having established an identity as the old man Crawley, continued to tend to the alien psychic force he'd encountered some centuries ago. The Doctor intervened when the creature tried and failed to reunite itself, causing psychic terror for the local McKeown family. The anguished creature withdrew its power from Deadstone and he instantly aged to death. The Doctor returned the creature to its home dimension.

As arranged in 1957, the Time Lord Louis collected Johannes Rausch on the day before his death. They traveled to a Gallifreyan CIA Institute, where Rausch took part in an experiment regarding the transfer of TARDIS sentiences.[535]

2005

2005 (5th - 6th March) - ROSE[536] -> Rose Tyler

worked at Henrik's department store in London, which was the location of a secret Auton transmitter. She met the Doctor shortly before he blew up the store, and accidentally took an Auton arm home with her. The Doctor located the arm and retrieved it. Fascinated by the Doctor, Rose tracked down Clive, who ran a website charting appearances of the Doctor over the years. Rose met up with the Doctor again and helped him defeat the Nestene invasion, but not before rampaging shop dummies nearly killed her mother. In all, seventy-eight people were killed, three hundred injured. Rose joined the Doctor on his travels.

Rose's disappearance prompted the police to search for her. Her boyfriend Mickey Smith was interviewed by the police, who - like Rose's mother - assumed that he had murdered her.[537]

c 2005 - DEATH COMES TO TIME[538] -> General Tannis,

commander of the Canisian armies, conquered the planet Santiny in violation of the Treaty of Carsulae. The Doctor and his companion Antimony arrived to ferment resistance, but were abruptly summoned to the Orion Nebula. There, the Minister of Chance - an old friend of the Doctor - warned him that someone had killed two Time Lord 'saints' working on Earth. The Doctor headed there to investigate; the Minister travelled to Santiny.

On Earth, the Doctor discovered that the Time Lords were murdered by a vampire, Nessican, to cover up their discovery of massive spatial disturbances. The Doctor returned to Santiny, where Tannis killed Antimony - who was actually an android - and revealed himself to be a renegade Time Lord. When Tannis killed Sala, a young woman the Minister had become fond of, the Minister unleashed the full force of his Time Lord powers. The Doctor could not act against Tannis, but had to punish the Minister - all part of Tannis' plan to divide and distract his rival Time Lords. The Doctor stripped the Minister of his powers, but Tannis launched an invasion of Earth.

Meanwhile, Ace trained to become a Time Lord with a mentor, Casmus, and the mysterious Kingmaker. Reunited, the Doctor and Ace headed for Earth, where they helped Lethbridge-Stewart and UNIT - now with a fleet of shuttles at their disposal - repel the Canisian invasion. The Doctor used his Time Lord powers to destroy Tannis and himself. The Canisians were defeated.

Felix Mather was the US Secretary of State during the Canisian invasion.[539]

2005 (June) - THE GALLIFREY CHRONICLES[540] ->

The Doctor was lured to Earth by the Time Lord Marnal, who had recently learned of the Doctor's role in the destruction of Gallifrey. Fitz and Trix left the Doctor to set up home together, but the police approached Trix and attempted to arrest her on suspicion of murder. As they fled the country, Marnal confronted the Doctor and the Eye of Harmony was briefly opened. Like moths to a flame, the insect race the Vore was drawn to Earth. Their moon materialised in Earth orbit and a full scale invasion took place. The Doctor and his companions destroyed the Moon, and engaged the surviving Vore.

The First Environmental Crisis

By the middle of the first decade of the twenty-first century, it was clear that unchecked industrial growth had wreaked havoc on the environment. Increasing instability in weather patterns subjected Britain to acid rain and created turbulence that made air travel less reliable. Shifts in the ozone layer laid waste to Oregon. Traffic had reached gridlock in most of the major cities around the world. Motorcycles superseded the familiar black cabs in London, and many car owners sat in traffic jams working at their computers as they commuted. Predictably, air pollution reached new levels.

A catalogue of environmental disasters threatened the entire planet. The Earth's population was spiralling towards eight billion. Low-lying ozone and nitrogen dioxide levels had risen to such an extent that the London air was unbreathable without a facemask on many days, even in winter. Global warming was steadily increasing: by the turn of the century there were vineyards in Kent. Antarctic waters became hazardous as the icecap broke up in rising temperatures. The rate of ice-flow had trebled since the nineteen-eighties.

River and sea pollution had reached such levels that the marine environment was on the verge of collapse. Water shortages were commonplace, and even the inhabitants of First World cities like London and Toronto were forced to use standpipes for drinking water and to practise water rationing. The mega-cities of South America saw drought of unprecedented proportions. The holes in the ozone layer were getting larger, causing famine in many coun-

tries. Sunbathing, of course, was now out of the question. 'The plague', in reality a host of virulent, pollution-related diseases such as HIV 7, appeared and killed millions.

The collapse of the environment triggered political instability. New terrorist groups sprang up: the Earth For Earth groups, freedom fighters, environmentalists, anarchists, nationalists and separatists, the IFA, PPO and TCWC. In England, a whole new youth subculture evolved. Gangs with names like the Gameboys, the Witchkids and the Crows smashed machinery (except for their own gaming software) and committed atrocities. In the most notorious incident, the Witchkids petrol-bombed a McDonald's restaurant on the M2 before ritually sacrificing the customers: men, women and children.

Every country on Earth saw warfare or widespread rioting. In the face of social disorder in America, President Norris' right-wing government ended immigration and his infamous 'Local Development' reforms restricted the unemployed's rights to movement. The Connors Amendment to the Constitution also made it easier for the authorities to declare martial law and administer the death penalty. The underclass was confined to its slums, and heavily armed private police forces guarded the barriers between the inner cities and the suburbs.

Once-fashionable areas fell into deprivation. The popular culture of the time reflected this discord: In Britain, this was a time when SlapRap blared from every teenager's noisebox. There was a Kinky Gerlinki revival, its followers dressing in costumes described as 'outrageous' or 'obscene' depending on personal taste. The most popular television series was *Naked Decay*, a sitcom inspired by forty-five-

1 *Iceberg* and *Cat's Cradle: Warhead* are both set around the same time and feature an Earth on the brink of environmental and social collapse. The two books are broadly consistent, although the odd detail is different - in *Iceberg*, for example, journalist Ruby Duvall muses that sunbathing in England is impossible nowadays, whereas Ace sunbathes in Kent during *Cat's Cradle: Warhead*. The Connors Amendment is mentioned in *Warlock*.

2 *Interference*

3 *St Anthony's Fire*

4 *Placebo Effect* (p12).

5 *Iceberg*

6 Dating *Red Dawn* - It is 'thirty years' since the 'Mars Probe fiasco' of *The Ambassadors of Death*. The impact of Tanya's ambassadorship to Mars must be minimal, as humanity and the Martians are in conflict by *The Seeds of Death*.

7 Both "ten years" before *Trading Futures*.

8 Dating *Aliens of London / World War Three* - It is 'twelve months' since *Rose*, and a missing persons

poster says Rose has been missing since 6th March 2005. The (BBC's) UNIT website gave the story the date of '28 June 2006'.

HARRIET JONES, BRITISH PRIME MINISTER: *AHistory* went to press before *The Christmas Invasion* aired, but BBC publicity material claimed that Jones is Prime Minister by that point, so she apparently takes office shortly after *World War Three*.

Three full terms as Prime Minister would be fifteen years, although constitutionally it's technically possible - if highly unlikely - that someone could serve three terms as a Prime Minister in a matter of months. Harriet Jones is almost certainly Prime Minister for around a decade. We might speculate that Jones is a prime mover behind the Reconstruction mentioned in some of the New Adventures, itself portrayed as the beginning of a golden age. There's a female Prime Minister in *The Shadows of Avalon* who, retrospectively, could well be Harriet Jones. Shortly after that, in stories like *Time of the Daleks* and *Trading Futures*, British politics becomes more turbulent.

year-old Mike Brack's 'Masks of Decay' exhibition which had featured lumps of wax hacked into caricatures of celebrities. The teledildonic suits at the 'SaferSex emporiums' along London's Pentonville Road became notorious. All faced the opprobrium of groups such as the Freedom Foundation and the Citadel of Morality. American children thrilled to the adventures of Jack Blood, a pumpkin-faced killer, and they collected the latest Cthulhu Gate horror VR modules and comics. Their elder brothers became Oi Boys: skinheads influenced by the fashions of Eastern Europe.

The early twenty-first century saw many scientific advances, usually in the field of computer science and communications. Elysium Technology introduced the Nanocom, a handheld dictation machine capable of translating speech into written text. Elysium also developed the first holographic camera. The 3D telephone was beyond the technology of the time, although most rich people now had videophones. In June 2005, 'Der Speigel' gave away a personal organiser with every issue. The first robot cleaners were marketed at this time - they were small, simple devices and really little more than automated vacuum cleaners or floor polishers. Communications software and computer viruses were traded on the black market; indeed, they became almost substitute currency in countries like Turkey.

Surgeons could now perform eye transplants, and the super-rich were even able to cheat 'death' (or rather the legal and medical definition of it) by an intensive programme of medication, transplants and implants. If even this failed, suspended animation was now possible - the rich could afford full cryogenic storage, the poor settled for a chemical substitute. Military technology was becoming smarter and more dangerous. The Indonesian conflict and the Mexican War in the first decade of the century were the test-bed for much new weaponry. Arms manufacturers were happy to supply the Australian and American forces with military hardware. The British company Vickers built a vision enhancement system capable of tremendous magnification and low-intensity light applications. The helmet could interface with most weapons, allowing dramatically improved targeting. If anything, the helmet was too efficient - one option, which allowed a soldier to target and fire his weapon merely by moving and blinking his eyes - proved too dangerous and was banned. A new generation of UN aircraft were introduced, including a remote controlled helicopter (the Odin), a jet fighter with batteries of Valkyrie air-to-air missiles (the Loki), Niffelheim bombs and Ragnarok tactical nuclear devices. The US military introduced a turbo-pulse laser gun developed for use against tanks.[1]

Early in the twenty-first century, there were disasters, wars and nuclear terrorism. The first half of the century saw human civilisation close to collapse.[2] Rising sea levels claimed Holland, and the Dutch became the wanderers of Europe.[3] Christian fundamentalists campaigned for the extermination of homosexuals in the twenty-first century.[4]

The most pressing threat was that of magnetic inversion. For some decades, scientists had known that Earth's magnetic field periodically reversed. If this happened now, it would damage all electronic equipment and have serious environmental consequences. In 2005, spurred into action by such reports, the major governments of the world set up the FLIPback Project at the old Snowcap complex in the Antarctic. Shortly afterward a vehicle from the base - the hovercraft AXV9 - vanished in the Torus Antarctica with the loss of two men.[5]

c 2005 - RED DAWN[6] -> Backed by the Webster Corporation, the first manned American mission to Mars - *Ares One* - successfully reached the Red Planet. The crew made planet-fall in the *Argosy* shuttle just as the Doctor and Peri also arrived. The astronauts and the time travellers found the tomb of Izdal, a heroic Martian who sacrificed himself to the Red Dawn - the ultraviolet Martian sunrise. This had convinced his people to leave their toxic planet.

The tomb's guardian, Lord Zzaal, was revived with his Ice Warriors. Zzaal believed the humans had good intentions, but a misunderstanding quickly escalated into conflict. Zzaal sacrificed himself to the Red Dawn to save the Doctor's life, ending Webster Corp's plans, but it was hoped his dream of a peaceful existence with Earth could survive. *Ares One* returned to Earth. Tanya Webster, a human who possessed Martian DNA, remained behind as Earth's first ambassador to the Martians.

A Russian general ordered a nuclear strike against Chechnya, killing half a million people in an instant. After leaving the army, the General erased his identity and became the notorious arms dealer known as Baskerville. He lacked an electronic presence of any kind, making him impossible to track. After British Airways went bust, Baskerville bought one of their Concordes and converted it for stealth.

Nicopills, designed to wean people off tobacco, were marketed as a consumer item in their own right. The pills were less harmful but even more addictive than cigarettes, and thus were more profitable.[7]

2006 (March) - ALIENS OF LONDON / WORLD WAR THREE[8] -> The Doctor accidentally returned Rose home twelve months after he first met her, instead of twelve hours. A spaceship soon crashed into the Thames, and a state of emergency was called in the UK. Worse, the Prime Minister had vanished. The Doctor investigated and realised that the crash had been faked... by genuine aliens who had infiltrated Downing Street and murdered the Prime Minister. This was done to lure the world's main experts on alien life into a lethal trap.

The perpetrators were the Slitheen, a notorious criminal family of Raxacoricofallapatorians, who planned to provoke humanity into launching nuclear missiles and destroying their own planet. This would enable the Slitheen to convert and sell Earth's remains as radioactive fuel. The Doctor used his UNIT codes to launch a missile that destroyed 10 Downing Street and the Slitheen.

A backbench MP, Harriet Jones, had been instrumental in helping the Doctor and was destined to become Prime Minister. She would serve three terms and usher in the British Golden Age.

Margaret Slitheen escaped the destruction of Downing Street using a portable teleporter. She ended up in a skip in the Isle of Dogs, later making her way to Cardiff.[9]

2006 (September) - BOOM TOWN[10] -> Margaret Slitheen became Lord Mayor of Cardiff, and pushed through an ambitious plan. She initiated construction of the Blaidd Drwg Power Station, which was actually designed to destroy Earth and facilitate her escape into space on an Extrapolator surfboard. The Doctor, Rose and Jack landed in Cardiff to refuel the TARDIS and captured Margaret. Exposure to the heart of the TARDIS reverted Margaret to her original state as an egg. The Doctor returned her to her home planet, Raxacoricofallapatorius, to start life anew.

Cathy Salt, the pregnant journalist spared by Margaret Slitheen, was scheduled to marry Jeffrey on 19th October.[11]

2006 - THE PARTING OF THE WAYS[12] -> The Doctor forcibly returned Rose to her native time aboard the TARDIS, removing her from the Dalek incursion in 200,100. Rose became acutely aware that the words "Bad Wolf" had been scattered throughout time and space as a message that she should return to the fray, and she exposed the heart of the TARDIS with help from her mother and Mickey Smith. Rose and the TARDIS returned to 200,100.

By now, the general population knew that aliens had indeed invaded Earth over a dozen times. In 2006, Kadiatu Lethbridge-Stewart published her controversial best-seller *The Zen Military: A History of UNIT*. Lethbridge-Stewart was the grand-daughter of Alistair Lethbridge-Stewart and Mariatu of the Themne tribe, making her ideally placed to write the 'definitive' study of the UNIT era.[13]

2006 (November / December) - ICEBERG[14] -> In 2006, Earth's magnetic pole shifted slightly, causing consternation at the FLIPback project. Tensions were not eased when the nearby Nikkei 5 research station vanished into the Torus Antarctica. The Cybermen were behind both the disappearances and the magnetic fluctuations, but the Doctor defeated them with the help of journalist Ruby Duvall.

---

9 *Boom Town*
10 Dating *Boom Town* - A caption at the start says it is 'Six Months Later' than *World War Three*. The evening is 'freezing' and it's dark relatively early, suggesting it's at least September (the month it would be if *World War Three* was set in March). A mention of Justicia in the story is a reference to the ninth Doctor novel *The Monsters Inside*. The mention of venom grubs on Margaret's home planet suggests her native galaxy is the Isop Galaxy, seen in *The Web Planet*. (*Bad Wolf* also names Isop as the home galaxy of the Face of Boe.)
11 *Boom Town*. This was due to happen on 'the nineteenth' and 'next month'.
12 Dating *The Parting of the Ways* - No specific date is given, but there's no evidence that much time has passed since Rose and Mickey's meeting in *Boom Town*.
13 The date of the publication was given in the *Remembrance of the Daleks* novelisation, and was confirmed by *Set Piece*. In *Transit*, Yembe Lethbridge-Stewart states that Kadiatu was named after his great-grandmother, the historian. Although in *Set Piece*, Kadiatu claims that her namesake was her 'grandmoth-

er', presumably for brevity's sake.
14 Dating *Iceberg* - The main action of the book takes place in 2006, from "early November" (p25) to "Friday 22 December" (p1). The epilogue is set on "Wednesday 31 January 2007" (p251).
15 *Mad Dogs and Englishmen*
16 *The Janus Conjunction* (p79). It's referred to as around in the twenty-second century in *The Face-Eater*.
17 Dating *Cat's Cradle: Warhead* - A specific date for this story and its two sequels is not established in the books themselves. The blurb states 'The time is the near future - all too near'. Shreela, a contemporary of Ace from Perivale first seen in *Survival*, dies of an "auto immune disease" at a tragically early age at the start of *Cat's Cradle: Warhead* (p19). The book is set in a year when Halloween falls on a Saturday (on p199 it's Halloween, on p250 it's the next day, a Sunday), making it either 1998, 2009 or 2015 - although in a number of stories the real calendar doesn't match that of the *Doctor Who* universe. Ace's clothes are how Mancuso, a policewoman, dressed "twenty years ago" (p202), and Ace is from the late 1980s. *Just War* confirms that the Cartmel

---

= Manipulated by the people of the Dogworld, John Fuchas produced a movie 'adaptation' of *The True History of Planets* in 2007 that abandoned the original book in favour of a story about the deposed poodle Princess Margaret. The Doctor ensured that this timeline never happened.[15]

San Francisco fell into the sea.[16]

c 2007 (late October) - CAT'S CRADLE: WARHEAD[17] ->

The Butler Institute - a huge conglomeration of corporations "from Amoco to Zenith", and which had secretly been bought up over the last decade by the vast Japanese Hoshino company - made projections of the future. Butler could see no alternative but massive, irrevocable environmental collapse. The planet was now reaching the point of no return, and only the big corporations and the super-rich could do anything about it.

Butler's executives secretly poured money into experiments that attempted to download human consciousness into computers. The homeless, the poor, and even the employees and families of Butler Institute personnel were kidnapped and experimented upon. The Institute developed a weapons system run by an electronically-recorded human consciousness, but its ultimate aim was to 'record' the minds of the elite and store them in indestructible databanks, safe from the ravages of pollution and the ozone layer's destruction.

With the unexpected and complete destruction of the Butler Institute's project outside Albany, the directors of the world's corporations realised that their only remaining option was to instigate a massive environmental clean-up programme.

The Reconstruction kicked the King's representative out of the British Parliament. Reconstruction Acts were passed to improve the environment. Large family farms started growing meat-substitute plants.[18] Within a couple of decades, air quality would be improved, the oceans were cleaner and the holes in the ozone layer had been patched up. Sophisticated traffic monitoring systems and a reconfigured road network eased congestion - and therefore pollution - in the South East of England. Central London, however, was still busy.[19]

2010 - HAPPY ENDINGS[20] ->

Guests from across space and time attended the wedding of Benny Summerfield and Jason Kane in the Norfolk village of Cheldon Bonniface. Between them, the various guests thwarted the Master's plan to disrupt events.

The word 'cruk' was introduced in an anime series, and quickly caught on as a mild expletive.

At this time, Ace reconciled with her mother, Audrey. Ishtar Hutchings, formerly the Timewyrm, was left pregnant from an encounter with Chris Cwej. She believed that their daughter, Jasmine, would become the girlfriend of Ricky McIlveen - and that the two of them would sire the Eternal named Time.

---

books take place in the "twenty-first century timezone" (p250). In his 'Future History Continuity' document, Ben Aaronovitch suggested that *Cat's Cradle: Warhead* was set "c.2007".

18 *Happy Endings*

THE RECONSTRUCTION: The televised stories set in the twenty-first century offer a broadly consistent view of a peaceful Earth with a single world government, in which people of all nations co-operate in the field of space exploration and social progress. To reconcile this with the rather more downbeat New Adventures set in this century, Ben Aaronovitch suggested in his 'Future History Continuity' document that a concerted global effort was made at some point in the early twenty-first century to repair the damage that had been done to Earth's environment. A 'Clean Up' is first hinted at the end of *Iceberg*, which is where we learn of the 'Arms for Humanity' concert and the procuring of drinking water from icebergs, but I suggest that it only gains impetus after *Cat's Cradle: Warhead*, when all the corporations put their full weight behind it.

This process was named 'the Reconstruction' in *Happy Endings*. I suggest that this period of international-

al co-operation lasts for around seventy years. Earth during this time is a relatively happy, clean and optimistic place. This neatly coincides with the claim in *World War Three* that Prime Minister Harriet Jones helped to usher in a British Golden Age.

19 Travelling by car is a lot easier in *Warlock* than *Cat's Cradle: Warhead* (*Warlock*, p179), and we learn about the monitoring systems (p224) and new road system (p211), although traffic in London has barely improved (p265).

20 Dating *Happy Endings* - It is "2010". In *Prime Time*, the director of Channel 400, Lukos, tells Ace's younger self that her mother died age eighty-five, haunted by never knowing what happened to her daughter. As Ace's mother was born in 1943 according to *The Curse of Fenric*, this would place her death in 2028. However, Channel 400's account is specifically tailored to torment Ace and therefore suspect, especially given the older Ace's reunion with her mother in *Happy Endings*. Ricky McIlveen is the son of Vincent and Justine from *Warchild*. Time was first mentioned in *Love and War*, and the seventh Doctor is often cited as 'Time's Champion'.

The rejuvenated General Lethbridge-Stewart returned to active duty with UNIT.[21]

> = The Doctor surrendered Earth to the Martians. The Martians withdrew, and Earth became a nature reserve. The Doctor spent a thousand years living in Kent.[22]

The Halliwell Film Guide of 2010 contained a particularly scathing review of The True History of Planets movie. Britain had a King at this time.[23] In late July 2011, Lethbridge-Stewart's wife Doris was killed in a yachting accident.[24]

2012 / = 2012 (June - August) THE SHADOWS OF AVALON[25] -> Britain had a King and a female Prime Minister. There had been no major alien attack that required UNIT's attention since the Martian invasion of 1997.

The Doctor dropped Compassion off in South West England so that she could learn more about humanity. The Time Lords detected that Compassion was evolving into a form of technology they could use, and President Romana dispatched agents Cavis and Gandar to recover her. Still mourning Doris, General Lethbridge-Stewart was on leave. He was called in to investigate the loss of a nuclear warhead, which he discovered had passed through to a parallel universe called Albion.

> = Meanwhile, in Albion, a war was brewing between the Unseelie and Catuvelanuni. The Doctor, Fitz and Compassion arrived in Avalon following the seeming destruction of the TARDIS in a dimensional rift. They prevented war there from escalating. Compassion evolved into a new form of TARDIS. President Romana arrived to try and capture her, but the Doctor and his companions made their getaway. Lethbridge-Stewart remained in Avalon to advise Queen Mab.

2012 - DALEK[26] -> The Doctor and Rose followed a distress signal and discovered that Henry Van Statten, the owner of the Internet, had what was reportedly the last Dalek captive in his extraterrestrial museum deep underneath Utah. The Dalek broke free and killed most of Van Statten's staff, but contact with Rose's DNA made it mutate and question its purpose. The conflicted creature destroyed itself. Van Statten's employees rebelled at his callousness and had him mindwiped, then dumped in a US city starting with 'S'. The Doctor reluctantly welcomed Adam, one of Van Statten's staff, onboard the TARDIS.

2012 - THE LONG GAME[27] -> Adam attempted to send information from the year 200,000 home to exploit. When the Doctor discovered this, he took Adam back to his native time and left him there.

Politically the world seemed less stable for a time. In 2012, the scientist / politician Salamander managed to convince a group of his followers that a global nuclear war was inevitable. He established a survival shelter at Kanowa in Australia for them.[28] Following the Euro Wars, Mariah Learman seized power in the United Kingdom on a popular tide of anti-EuroZone feeling, renaming it New Britain. Britain had a King at this time.[29]

World War Three was fought in the early twenty-first century. India was reduced to a radioactive mudhole.[30] The War against Terrorism was won when the RealWar teletrooper was introduced. Subscribers could kill terrorists (identified with 80 percent accuracy by software) from the comfort of their own home by operating war robots.

---

21 The Shadows of Avalon, following on Lethbridge-Stewart's rejuvenation as a result of events in Happy Endings. This explains how the Brigadier lives well past a normal human lifespan.
22 On one of the alternative timelines seen in So Vile a Sin.
23 Mad Dogs and Englishmen
24 'Almost a year' and, later, 'over a year' earlier than The Shadows of Avalon.
25 Dating The Shadows of Avalon - The story starts in 'July 2012' (p1). The Ancestor Cell specifies that Compassion is the first Type 102 TARDIS. Although we did see one in The Dimension Riders, and it didn't take the form of a person.
26 Dating Dalek - The Doctor gives the date.
27 Dating The Long Game - No date is given, but it's clearly after Dalek. Adam's mother says she hasn't seen

him for six months.
28 'Five years' before The Enemy of the World.
29 The Time of the Daleks. The Doctor restores some wayward history at the end of the story, but it's clear that the 'real' history includes Learman coming to power, and she's mentioned in Trading Futures.
30 The Face-Eater (p55). Trading Futures (p68) - there's a New Kabul in that book, implying the original city was destroyed, so Afghanistan was also a battleground.
31 Trading Futures
32 The Taking of Planet 5
33 Instruments of Darkness. Presumably a reference to Tony Blair's son and Prince Andrew's daughter.
34 Dating Christmas on a Rational Planet - The date is given.

Baskerville, a Russian arms dealer, became the richest man in the world selling the technology.[31]

In 2012, firemen in New York laughed and toasted marshmallows instead of rescuing people from a fire. This resulted from the Memeovore feeding on human ideas.[32] The Doctor owned a commemorative mug from the wedding of Euan and Eugenie.[33]

2012 - CHRISTMAS ON A RATIONAL PLANET[34] ->
The Doctor, Chris and Roz landed in Arizona. When Cacophony's gynoids emerged into our universe, Roz fell through a crack in time to the end of the eighteenth century.

By 2012, Countess Gallowglass was operating her mail-forwarding service from a hidden location near Carnaby Street. The Doctor visited the Countess, with Ace, in August to collect his mail.[35] According to the Countess, London should be avoided on 14th July, 2013.[36]

2013 - DEATH AND DIPLOMACY[37] ->
Half a galaxy away, the three Empires of the Dakhaar, Czhan and Saloi were set to overrun the little planet of Moriel. The godlike Hollow Ghosts commanded that the races would sort out their conflict by diplomatic means - or else. The Hollow Ghosts employed the services of the Doctor in this effort, and his companions Cwej and Forrester prevented the villainous Skrak from over-running the Three Empires.

The Doctor visited a house in Kent and saved a cat.[38]

c 2014 (Late Autumn) - WARLOCK[39] ->
Organised crime continued to rely on the profits of drug trafficking. Dealers now used sports cars to get around, and the British police were forced to use Porsches to keep up with them. Soon Porsche were even making a special model for them.

In an attempt to win the Drugs War, the International Drug Enforcement Agency (IDEA) was set up. A pooling of Interpol and FBI resources, IDEA had a number of well-publicised successes against drug dealers, forcing many of them underground. IDEA was based in the King Building in New York, the old headquarters of the Butler Institute, and its methods often brought them into conflict with local police forces.

For around a year, IDEA had been aware of a new street drug, called "Warlock" by many of its users. Warlock seemed to give people psychic powers. Tracking the source of the drug proved difficult, leading IDEA men across New York and England. In the late autumn, an IDEA team investigating the drug was caught in the explosion that destroyed Canterbury Cathedral, an event officially explained away as a freak ball-lightning effect. It was announced shortly afterward that IDEA had broken up the Warlock cartel, and the drug vanished from the streets. Exactly how this had been achieved was never fully explained, although around this time an animal research lab near Canterbury was closed down in mysterious circumstances and the prominent London gangster Paulie Keaton "retired" after a decade of dominating criminal activity in the city. The founder of IDEA, Henry Harrigan Jnr, died around this time.

At the beginning of 2014, the Home Office introduced compulsory blood tests for HIV. In June the following year, Harry Sullivan of MI5 informed UNIT that the blood of a survivor of the Quadrant Incident might hold a cure to the condition.[40]

c 2016 - TRADING FUTURES[41] ->
There were no rogue states remaining and the world's secret services kept almost every square inch of the planet electronically monitored. The only two remaining superpowers - indeed, the only

---

35 *Relative Dementias* (p40) dates when the Doctor and Ace visit the Countess.

36 *Relative Dementias* (p17).

37 Dating *Death and Diplomacy* - The Virgin version of *A History of the Universe* dated the story to the present day, based on the synopsis. The final book specifies that Jason was born in 1983 and is 'near enough' thirty (p123).

38 *The City of the Dead*. This retcon takes the sting out of one of the nastier bits of *Warlock*.

39 Dating *Warlock* - The novel is the sequel to *Cat's Cradle: Warhead*. The events of the earlier book are consistently referred to as happening "years" ago (p8, p203, p209, p223). Vincent and Justine, the two young lovers from *Warhead*, bought a car after a "few years" of marriage and have had it a while (p356). In *Cat's Cradle: Warhead*, Ace had difficulty guessing how old Justine

was, eventually settling on "maybe sixteen or seventeen" (p181). By *Warlock*, Justine has matured into a woman (p203), but she is still only "probably a couple of years older than the medical student" (p301), so she is in her early-to-mid twenties. I suggest, then, that *Warlock* takes place about five years after *Cat's Cradle: Warhead*. It is late autumn (p279, p334).

40 *Damaged Goods*

41 Dating *Trading Futures* - The year is not specified beyond 'the early decades of the twenty-first century' on the back cover, but Mather says his encounter with the Doctor in *Father Time*, which occurred in 1989, was "more than twenty years ago". Malady Chang, a secret agent, seems to place it nearer thirty, as she thinks the Doctor "would have been about ten at the time", and he looks like he's in his "early forties". People who were teenagers in the nineties are now "pushing two remaining sovereign powers - were the United States and the EuroZone, who dominated the world between them. But they were on the brink of war, as both were trying to extend their sphere of influence into power vacuums in North Africa and the Middle East. 'Peacekeepers' from both sides took up positions.

Elsewhere in the world, EuroZone RealWar tanks were covertly sent into action against American corporate interests. The situation was a tinderbox that could have lead to World War Four. By now, the United Kingdom was part of the EuroZone and the semi-elected British President Minister was bound by the Articles of European Zoning, despite polls showing 84 percent of the British population taking the American side in the dispute. Britain secretly maintained its own intelligence service, run by the ancient Jonah Cosgrove. The American President was Felix Mather, former CIA astronaut.

There was a European national soccer team, and games were divided into eighths to fit more adverts in. Rhinos only existed in clonetivity. Human cloning was possible, but very expensive. Hypersonic jets could cross the world in a few hours. Nuclear bombs were used in civil engineering. There was a North China and a New Kabul. Kurdistan was a country in its own right, in a region blighted by civil wars. British Airways had gone bankrupt, the BBC was replaced by the EZBC. More than one channel tunnel was operating.

The international flow of money was through the IFEC computer system. Arms dealer Baskerville launched an ambitious con job to seize control of it. He posed as a time traveller from ten thousand years in the future, and offered Cosgrove a time machine in return for access to the powerful EZ ULTRA computer. The CIA got wind of the plan, as did Sabbath's Time Agents, the Doctor, Anji and Fitz and the alien Onihrs. The Doctor and his companions uncovered Baskerville's plan just as shootings in Tripoli triggered a potential world war.

The earliest human clones were mindless, bred for use as perishable stunt doubles in motion pictures. Humanity became uneasy with the morality of this and ended the practice. Cloning fell into disuse, but scientists kept periodically reviving the art.[42]

---

pensionable age" (p8) and Anji's generation are the parents of teenagers. Learman from *The Time of the Daleks* is referred to (p107), as are the Zones from *The Enemy of the World*. It's not clear whether World War Four has been averted - US and EZ forces are fighting at the end of the book, and it's only *hoped* that the revelation of Baskerville's plan will end it.

WORLD WARS: The First and Second world wars occur much as we know them. There are fears of a Third World War in the UNIT era. It occurs some time between Anji joining the TARDIS crew (2000) and *Trading Futures* (c.2016) - whether the events of the episode *World War Three* qualify is unclear. World War IV was mentioned in *The Also People*, but no details are given. In *Christmas on a Rational Planet*, it's said that people danced in the ashes of Reykjavik during World War IV. The Doctor says he saw World War V in *The Unquiet Dead*. World War VI is averted in the year 5000, according to *The Talons of Weng-Chiang*.

42 *Heritage.* In terms of *Doctor Who* history, the earliest mention of humans cloning humans is in *Trading Futures*.

43 Dating *The Enemy of the World* - One of Salamander's followers, Swann, holds up a scrap of newspaper with a date on it from the year before, but the photograph is not clear enough to discern the date. (*Timelink* suggests it says 2041, but still dates the story to 2013.) The licence disc on the helicopter expires in 2018.

None of the scripts contain any reference to the year that the story is set in. However, the *Radio Times* in certain regions featured an article on fashion that set *The Enemy of the World* "fifty years in the future", which would give a date of 2017. The first edition of *The Programme Guide* mistakenly thought that the story had a contemporary setting, and placed it between "1970-75".

The date "2030", which is now commonly associated with the story, first appeared in David Whitaker's storyline for the novelisation of his story, submitted to WH Allen in October 1979. The document was reprinted in *DWM* #200, and amongst other things of interest it is the only place to give Salamander a first name: "Ramon". The novelisation was due to be published in 1980, and was to be set "some fifty years later than our time - the year 2030" according to the storyline, but the book was not completed before Whitaker's death.

The second edition of *The Programme Guide* duly gave the date as "2030". The blurb for the novelisation by Ian Marter, published in 1981 - the same year as *The Programme Guide* - concurred, although perhaps significantly, the text of the book didn't specify a date. 2030 was soon adopted wholesale, with *The TARDIS Logs* and *The Terrestrial Index* giving the new date. *Encyclopedia of the Worlds of Doctor Who* is confused: the entry for 'Denes' gives the date as "2017", but that for 'Fedorin' states "2030". *The TARDIS Special* was less specific than most, claiming the story takes place in an "Unknown Future" setting. *The Legend* states it's 'c.2017'. *Alien Bodies* sets the story later, after *Warchild* and apparently around the 2040s.

It seems clear that David Whitaker intended the story to be set fifty years after it was broadcast, and I have adopted that date.

? 2017 - THE ENEMY OF THE WORLD[43] -> Rockets could now be used to travel between continents on Earth - the journey from Australia to Hungary took around two hours. Hovercars made shorter trips. Television pictures are broadcast via videowire.

The political situation on Earth had stabilised. National concerns were put aside and the world was reorganised into large administrative areas called Zones, such as the Australiasian, North African and Central European Zones. The world was organised into the United Zones, but was more properly known as the World Zones Authority. Commissioners dealt with multinational concerns such as Security matters. A Controller led each Zone.

One of the major problems the world faced was famine. The scientist Salamander announced he could solve the problem using his Mark Seven Sun-Catcher satellite, which made previously desolate areas of the world into fertile farmland that robots could harvest. Within just a year, the Sun-Catcher had solved the problems of world famine, allowing crops to grow in Siberia and vineyards in Alaska. In the more fertile areas, concentrated sunlight forced growth: each summer could bring three or even four harvests. Salamander was hailed as the saviour of mankind.

Soon after Salamander's announcement a series of natural disasters struck, including a freak tidal wave that sank a liner full of holidaymakers in the Caribbean and the first volcanic eruptions in the Eperjes-Tokaj mountain range since the sixteenth century. These were caused by Salamander's followers in Kanowa using his technology. Salamander had convinced them that the Earth's surface was highly radioactive, and that they had to fight back against the aggressors.

The truth was that Salamander had been gradually assassinating his political opponents within the United Zones and replacing them with his own people in a bid to become the dictator of Earth. Salamander was defeated when his followers in Kanowa learned there had been no global nuclear war.

In 2017, UNIT closed their file on the Quadrant Incident.[44] The Doctor placed a personal advert "Ace - Behind You!" in an *NME* from 2018. Ace later bought a copy outside Ladbroke Grove hypertube station.[45] Paletti wrote the opera *The Fourth Sister*, including the stirring *Rebirth Aria*.[46]

The risk of nuclear warfare diminished after the Southport Incident, when governments realised that the stockpiling of atomic weapons could only lead to a serious accident or all-out nuclear warfare.[47]

2020 - THE POWER OF THE DALEKS[48] -> The colony on Vulcan was in danger of being "run down". Mining operations had not proved economically successful and the Governor of the colony, Hensell, faced mutiny. An Examiner from Earth was due to assess the Vulcan colony in two years.

The chief scientist, Lesterson, discovered what he thought might be the colony's salvation - a buried alien spaceship. He quickly determined that the capsule was constructed of a metal that wasn't found on Vulcan. At

---

WEATHER CONTROL: In a number of stories set in the twenty-first century we see a variety of weather control projects. The earliest is in the New Adventure *Cat's Cradle: Warhead*, and simply involves 'seeding' clouds with chemicals to regulate rainfall (p129). A year before *The Enemy of the World*, Salamander develops the Sun-Catcher, the first global Weather Control system. As its name suggests, the Sun Store satellite collects the rays from the Sun and stores them in concentrated form. It is also capable of influencing tidal and seismic activity.

Each major city has its own Weather Control Bureau by *The Seeds of Death*, and these are co-ordinated and monitored centrally by computer. The London Bureau is a large complex, manned by a handful of technicians. The Weather Control Unit itself is about the size of a large desk, with separate circuits for each weather condition. With fully functioning Rain Circuits, rainfall over a large area can be arranged quickly.

By 2050, the Gravitron had been set up on the Moon. This is the ultimate form of weather control, working on the simple principle that "the tides control the weather, the Gravitron controls the tides". Weather control is under the control of the (United Zones?) General Assembly.

44 *Damaged Goods*. Marcie Hatter, a UNIT Corporal here (p262), was the name of the heroine of Russell T Davies' TV serial *Dark Season* (1991).

45 *Timewyrm: Revelation*

46 'A few decades' after *Vampire Science*.

47 Benny remembers the Southport Incident in *Just War* (p214), but doesn't specify what or when it was. Zoe, who lacks even rudimentary historical knowledge, recognises the effects of an atomic blast in *The Dominators*, perhaps suggesting that nuclear weapons are still around (and have been used?) in her time.

48 Dating *The Power of the Daleks* - There is no confirmation of the date in the story itself. According to Lesterson the Dalek ship arrived "at least two ceturies ago", "before the colony", which might suggest that the Earthmen have been there for just under 200 years. However, the generally low-level of technology, the reliance on "rockets" and the fact that there is only one communications link with Earth suggests the colony is relatively new.

first, Lesterson feared that the ship might contain bacteria, but he opened the capsule anyway, and discovered that it contained three inert Daleks. The lure of reviving them proved too great for the human colonists.

At first, the Daleks cunningly pretended to be servants, dependent as they were on the power provided by the humans. They played their part well, solving simple scientific problems. The Daleks promised to build a computer that could predict meteorite showers and protect the weather satellites, a move that offered huge financial savings and won the colonists' trust. All the time, though, the Daleks were setting up their production line. Dozens of Daleks swarmed across the colony within a matter of hours, exterminating every human in their path.

Once again, though, the Daleks' external power sources proved their undoing - although they guarded their static electricity generator, it proved possible to destroy the power source. This rendered the Daleks immobile once more.

2021 (12th October) - THE HARVEST[49] -> The European Council had recovered an expeditionary force of Cybermen that crashed in the Pyrenees. The Cybermen brokered a deal with the European government, offering Cyber-technology to create astronauts cyber-augmented for space. In return, the Cybermen asked that operations be performed to make them organic beings again.

By October 2021, the "Recarnative Program" was secretly in operation at St Gart's Brookside, a London hospital managed by the Euro Combine Health Administration. The duplicitous Cybermen intended to seize control of the facility, which would serve as a ready-made Cyber-conversion center and facilitate a planetary takeover.

The Doctor and Ace learned of the plot and triggered a termination protocol that shut down the Cybermen. The Doctor also erased all of the Program's data, preventing the Euro government from exploiting the Cyber-technology. Thomas Hector "Hex" Scofield, a staff nurse at St Gart's, became embroiled in these events and joined the Doctor and Ace on their travels.

An AI System was in use at St Gart's, and the Wheel space stations were in operation.

During the 2020s, the Silurians entombed at Wenley Moor were scheduled to revive. If they did so, they remained hidden from humanity.[50] The novel *The Unformed Heart* by Emily Hutchings was published, and the Doctor acquired a copy.[51] The UN banned beryllium laser weapons in the mid-2020s.[52] The phased plasma rifle was developed in 2024.[53]

2024 - EMOTIONAL CHEMISTRY[54] -> The Doctor, Fitz and Trix infiltrated the Kremlin Museum to retrieve a diamond locket that formerly belonged to the Russian noblewoman Dusha. Colonel Grigoriy Bugayev, working for the Russian division of UNIT, knew the Doctor of old and

The colonists don't recognise the Daleks, which suggests this story is set before *The Dalek Invasion of Earth*. The date was given as "2020" in the contemporary trailer (which is included on the *Lost in Time* DVD), and press material at the time confirmed that. This date also appeared in the 10th anniversary *Radio Times*, was used by the second edition of *The Making of Doctor Who* and the first edition of *The Programme Guide*.

In *DWM*, *The TARDIS Logs* offered a date of "2049", but 'A History of the Daleks' contradicted this and gave the date as "2249". The American *Doctor Who* comic offered the date of "2600 AD", apparently unaware that the Dalek ship has been dormant. *The Terrestrial Index* came to the elaborate conclusion that the colonists left Earth in 2020 - in spacecraft with suspended animation - and then used the old calendar when they arrived. As a result, while they call the date 2020, the story is really set in "2220". *Timelink* opted for "2120". Earth could only really have a colony on another world this early if the planet Vulcan was in our solar system.

49 Dating *The Harvest* - The date is given on the back cover blurb.

50 At the end of *Doctor Who and the Silurians*, the Reptile People go back into deep freeze for "fifty years".

Alternatively, they might have all perished in the explosions triggered by the Brigadier's men. There are Silurians working alongside humanity in *Eternity Weeps* in 2003, but it's never stated they are from Wenley Moor, and we know there were other shelters.

51 *Happy Endings*

52 "Twenty years" after *The Fearmonger*.

53 *First Frontier* (p137).

54 Dating *Emotional Chemistry* - The date appears in the blurb.

55 *Happy Endings*

56 Glauss was born twenty-six years after *Millennial Rites* (p86). A bit confusingly, p70 says her *Cybercrime* text was written 'in the early twenty-first century'.

57 "Twenty or thirty years" after *The King of Terror*.

58 *The Left-Handed Hummingbird*

59 Dating *Warchild* - The book is the sequel to *Warlock*. At the end of the earlier novel, Justine was in the early stages of pregnancy, so her baby would have been born in the spring of the following year. In *Warchild*, her son Ricky is "15". This book is set in the early autumn, as the long summer ends and the school year is starting in America.

60 *The King of Terror*

aided the time travellers.

The disgraced physicist Harald Skoglund had retro-engineered a lost time belt into the Misl Vremnya, a device whose name meant "thought time." It enabled its user to see down the timeline of various objects, and to witness events through the eyes of anyone in contact with them. With further exertion, the device allowed its operator to dominate the wills of such people. The businessman Vladimir Garudin used the Misl Vremnya for his own purposes, but Bugayev later destroyed the device.

By now the Moscow waste management system had organic microfilters to reprocess sewage. Robot drones were used for reconnaissance.

The word 'cruk' was very rude by 2025.[55] Demeter Glauss, the future author of *Cybercrime: An Analysis of Hacking* was born. The book was the seminal work on breaking and entering computer systems, including the Paradigm operating system. Mel would use the text to hack into Ashely Chapel Logistics in 1999.[56]

By 2030, the issue of thargon differentials in the orange spectrum of upper atmospheric problems was solved. This enabled the creation of stable energy fields on satellites.[57] The Doctor, Ace and Bernice visited UNIT HQ in Geneva in 2030, and picked up a note left by Cristian Alvarez thirty-seven years before.[58]

2030 (Early Autumn) - WARCHILD[59] -> Computer technology had advanced to the stage that cars practically drove themselves and computers could understand straightforward voice commands. Instead of passports, people had implants on the back of their necks, and three-dimensional television existed. Passenger airliners were still in use. A cure had been found for Alzheimer's disease, and few people now smoked thanks to health-awareness campaigns.

Over the long hot Summer, a state of emergency was declared in London. Computers monitored all telephone emergency calls listening out for the keyword "Dog". Packs of dogs displaying remarkable intelligence had murdered many people, and there were reports of a "White King", an old dog that appeared to control the packs. The government restricted all reporting of the emergency and used psychic operatives to assemble covert action teams.

In America, Vincent Wheaton had received government funding to research "alpha male patterns", the study of pack dynamics. He hoped to nurture a man capable of "natural leadership", which entailed the ability to control crowds, or indeed whole populations of people. Vincent hoped to control America with such a man as President, but he was killed before his plan came to fruition.

Lethbridge-Stewart returned to Earth in 2032, having spent twenty years in the realm of Avalon.[60] In 2038, the World Zones Accord was signed. Around this time, Colonel Kortez fought the Cyber breaches for the ISC. He joined UNISYC in 2039 and fought lemur people at some point before 2069.[61]

Elsewhere in the galaxy, civilisations continued to develop. A race of reptilian humanoids had evolved on the planet Draconia. Although technologically advanced, they retained a feudal system. The Doctor visited Draconia at the time of the Fifteenth Emperor, around 2040, and cured a great space plague.[62] It was the second Doctor, and his portrait was hung in the Imperial Palace.[63] The Doctor was given the rank of High Earl of the Imperial House.[64] The Draconians took to referring to the Doctor as "the Oncoming Storm".[65]

Sarah Jane Smith died around 2040. Members of UNIT and Black Seed, possibly including Sam Jones, attended her funeral. In 2043, Black Seed published their third manifesto.[66] There were anti-weather control demonstrations.[67] Earth picked up an Arcturan signal that included enough information to build a transmat device.[68]

---

61 *Alien Bodies.* The World Zones Accord was intended as a reference to the establishment of the political system of *The Enemy of the World*, which most chronologies set earlier than this. We could speculate that the World Zones Accord strengthened an existing World Zones Authority, in the same way successive European treaties have granted more powers to the EEC / EC / EU.
62 "Five hundred years" before *Frontier in Space.* The incident is also recounted in *Shadowmind.*
63 *The Dark Path*
64 *Catastrophea*
65 *Return of the Living Dad.* According to the Doctor in *The Parting of the Ways*, the Daleks also refer to him by that title.
66 *Interference (Book Two,* p292, p314), where Sarah's death is predicted by the If, one of IM Foreman's incarnations. Following the machinations of the Council of Eight, the timeline is altered so that Sam Jones died in 2002.
67 *Dreamstone Moon* (p58).
68 *Cold Fusion* (p216), no date given.

? 2044 - (Winter) THE SEEDS OF DEATH[69] -> On Earth there was a period of technological progress. Hypersonic aircraft were built, and mankind discovered how to synthesise carbohydrates and protein, which helped to feed the planet's ever-increasing population. Computers were now advanced enough to give spoken responses to sophisticated verbal instructions. Most energy now came from solar power, and compact solar batteries became available. Petrol cars were confined to museums. There were further advances in robotics and weather control technology.

Regular passenger modules were travelling between the Earth and its moonbases. Most people thought the Moon would provide a stepping stone to the other planets of the Solar System, and eventually to the stars. At this time Professor Daniel Eldred, the son of the

man who designed the lunar passenger modules, invented an ion jet rocket with a compact generator. This vehicle promised to revolutionise space travel, paving the way for mankind's rapid exploration of the solar system.

Then the Travel-Mat Relay, an instantaneous form of travel, was invented. The massive capital investment required, and the promise of easy movement of all resources around the world, meant that after some debate the government ended all funding for space travel. All but a skeleton staff on the Moon were recalled. Man had travelled no further than the Moon. For years, all space travel halted.

Travel-Mat revolutionised the distribution of people and materials around the world. A T-Mat brochure boasted that:

---

69 Dating *The Seeds of Death* - This story is tricky to place in relation to the others.

On-screen, the only indication of the date is the Doctor's identification of the ion rocket designed by Eldred as a product of "the twenty-first century". As the rocket only exists as a prototype at this stage, the story must take place before 2100. T-Mat is developed at least two generations after space travel, as Eldred's father designed spacecraft, including a "lunar passenger module", and Eldred is an old man himself. It is never stated how long Travel-Mat has been in operation before *The Seeds of Death*, but it is a relatively new invention, as the video brochure we hear (transcribed here in full) states. Young Gia Kelly was involved with the development of T-Mat, but it has been around "a good many years" according to Eldred, long enough to make an advocate of rocket travel look eccentric. T-Mat is consistently referred to as having been around for "years", rather than "decades" or "generations" - so I suggest that T-Mat has been around for about a decade before the story.

It is possible to rule out certain dates by referring to other stories: The Weather Control Bureau is seen, so it must be set after 2016 when Salamander invents weather control; the Bureau is on Earth, which might suggest the story is set before 2050 when the Gravitron is installed on the Moon, or that the system is later moved to Earth. Either way, the story can't be set between 2050 and (at least) 2070, because the Gravitron is in operation from the Moon at that time and rockets are in use during this period. By the time of *The Seeds of Death*, it's stated that man has not travelled beyond the Moon (this has to contradict the earlier, limited space travel to Mars in *The Ambassadors Of Death*, Jupiter in *The Android Invasion* and Vulcan in *The Power of the Daleks*).

The story occurs before *The Wheel In Space*, as deep space travel is established by then and Zoe has a more extensive knowledge of spaceflight than Eldred (he

admits as much). Laser weapons have been developed by *The Wheel in Space*, but projectile weapons are still used here. The story isn't set between 2068 and 2096, as Galactic Salvage and Insurance are insuring spacecraft between those dates. The T-mat network seems to connect up the whole world - it includes both New York and Moscow, for example - which would seem inconsistent with the divided world of 2084 seen in *Warriors of the Deep*. Finally, the story probably isn't set after 2096, as four years seems to short a period to explore the entire Solar System (*The Mutants*) before deep space interstellar missions with crews in suspended animation are launched (*The Sensorites*).

Or, to cut a long story short, and assuming a ten-year period before the story when T-Mat has been operating, *The Seeds of Death* has to be set more than ten years after *The Enemy of the World* (so after 2027), but before the Gravitron is installed in 2050.

The original storyline set the date as "3000 AD", but later press material suggested the story took place "at the beginning of the twenty-first century".

As we might expect, no fan consensus exists. The first edition of *The Making of Doctor Who* claimed the story is set in "the latter part of the 20th Century", the second was less specific and simply placed the story in the "21st Century". The first two editions of *The Programme Guide* set the story "c2000", *The Terrestrial Index* alters this to "c2090", and the novel *Lucifer Rising* concurs with this date (p171). DWM writer Richard Landen suggested "2092". *Timelink* says "2096, February", conceding "this is a difficult story to date". *Encyclopedia of the Worlds of Doctor Who* set the story in "the 22nd century". Ben Aaronovitch's *Transit* follows on from *The Seeds of Death*, with his 'Future History Continuity' setting the television story "c2086".

I set *The Seeds of Death* seventy-five years after it was first broadcast, which fits in nicely with the evidence from the other television stories.

"The Travel-Mat is the ultimate form of travel. Control centre of the present system is the moon, serving receptions in all major cities on Earth. Travel-Mat provides an instantaneous means of public travel, transporting raw materials and vital food supplies to all parts of the world. Travel Mat supersedes all conventional forms of travel, using the principal of dematerialisation at the point of departure and rematerialisation at the point of arrival in special cubicles. Departure and arrival are almost instantaneous. Although the system is still in its early stages, it is completely automated and foolproof against power failure."

Humanity, though, had become dangerously insular. The Ice Warriors remained confined to Mars during all this time, limited by the lack of resources their home planet had to offer.

The Grand Marshall of the Martians ordered an invasion of Earth. A small squad led by Lord Slarr took Seed Pods - oxygen-fixing plants native to Mars - to the Moon. The plan was to cripple Earth by disabling the T-Mat, then use the Seeds to alter Earth's atmosphere until it more closely resembled that of Mars. The Pods were sent to Earth via Travel-Mat and preparations were made to guide the Martian invasion fleet to Earth. As killer foam spread through London, the Doctor, Zoe and Jamie travelled to the Moon and defeated the Ice Warriors, directing the Martian fleet into the Sun.

The global teleportation system lead to disastrous UN aid decisions.[70] Professor Otterband of the Dubrovnik Institute of New Sciences discovered psychotronic conditioning in 2045.[71] Borneo became a ReVit Zone in 2049. The rainforests were replanted and stocked with genetically engineered plants and animals.[72] The United States fell in the mid-twenty-first century.[73]

c 2050 - THE TIME OF THE DALEKS[74] -> The Daleks attempted to exploit a temporal rift to enhance their time travel capabilities, but the experiment backfired and they almost lost their entire fleet. They made contact with Mariah Learman, the ruler of New Britain, who had a primitive time scanner. Learman didn't believe the population appreciated Shakespeare, and the price for her co-operation with the Daleks was that they would assassinate Shakespeare as a youth and preserve the only copy of his works for Learman's benefit. Rebels thwarted this plan by smuggling an eight-year-old Shakespeare from 1572 for his own protection, but this caused further time distortion. The Doctor arrived, trying to explain why his companion Charley retroactively didn't know of Shakespeare. The Doctor joined the rebels and set history back on course by returning young Shakespeare to his rightful time. The Daleks were trapped in an endless temporal loop after mutating Learman into one of them.

The Conquest of the Solar System

Space travel was readopted and co-ordinated by International Space Command in Geneva.[75] Ion jet rockets explored the Solar System.[76] It now took only a couple of hours for a shuttle rocket to travel from the Earth to the new moonbases. Around 2050, the ultimate form of weather control, the Gravitron, was built on the Moon's surface. The political implications on Earth proved complex, and the General Assembly spent over twenty years negotiating methods of agreement between farmers and landowners.[77] The Butler Institute built the Gravitron.[78]

Harnessing gravity waves allowed artificial gravity to be installed on spacecraft and space stations. Permanent space stations were built. Flowers were cultivated on the surface of Venus.[79] **The Doctor visited this timezone.**[80] Victorian time traveller Penelope Gate and her companion Joel Mintz accidentally visited the middle of the twenty-first century.[81]

Around the middle of the century, domesticated wolves were reintroduced into the forests of Northern Europe. It was rumoured that the Wicca Society had released wild

---

70 *The Indestructible Man* (p78).

71 *The Well-Mannered War* (p204).

72 *Alien Bodies* (p9).

73 *Christmas on a Rational Planet.* "Nearly a millennium" before Roz is born (p31).

74 Dating *The Time of the Daleks* - It is 'the mid twenty-first century'.

75 International Space Command is mentioned in *The Tenth Planet* and *Revenge of the Cybermen,* as well as *The Moonbase,* where it seems to be an agency of the World Zones Authority as seen in *The Enemy of the World* - we hear about "the General Assembly", "Atlantic Zone 6", and the head of the ISC is a "Controller" Rinberg.

76 *The Seeds of Death*

77 "Twenty years" before *The Moonbase.*

78 *Deceit* (p27, p153). It was possibly based on Silurian technology, as the Silurians establish a Gravitron on the Moon (in an alternate history) in *Blood Heat* (p196).

79 *The Wheel in Space*

80 The Doctor's familiarity with the Gravitron in *The Moonbase,* ion rockets in *The Seeds of Death* and Galactic Salvage and Insurance in *Nightmare of Eden* suggests he visited the Solar System during this period at least once.

81 *The Room with No Doors* (p48).

wolves, and there was some debate as to which strain would become dominant.[82]

Eighty years after the events occurred, some early UNIT files were officially released. Reporter Daniel Clompus visited the elderly Brigadier General Sir Lethbridge-Stewart at his retirement home. Lethbridge-Stewart passed away shortly afterward. His memoirs, *The Man Who Saved the World*, were published in 2052.[83]

The people of the ocean planet Ockora built exoskeletal battlesuits and started an uprising against their Kalarian oppressors, who hunted them for sport. These warriors renamed themselves Selachians. After defeating the Kalarians, they conquered four planets, including Kalaya and Molinar. The Selachians became arms dealers, and attacked a Martian colony with a sunstroker.[84]

The Doctor and UNISYC (commanded by General Tchike) defeated the Montana Republican militia, who were using Selachian weapons, in 2054.[85] Sam had an ergonomic chair from the mid 2050s in her room in the TARDIS.[86] The poodles of the Dogworld built their first space station. It received radio signals from other planets, including Earth.[87]

All the religious faiths of the world were merged with the idea of creating world harmony. This consensus was unworkable and quickly collapsed. The Chapter of St Anthony was formed to fill the spiritual vacuum. When China was taken over by Hong Kong, the Yong family joined them on a new crusade to purge the heathens.[88]

In the mid 2050s, the world government overreacted to major wars and nuclear terrorism by passing police shoot-to-kill laws and banning all religions. There were years of total chaos, and cities became no-go areas. There was no effective government. New governments started to form by the 2060s. Octogenarian Samantha Jones might have been a major player in these events. Before this point, her father had died, shortly after the last King of England abdicated.[89]

Cricket was an Olympic sport in time for the Barcelona Olympics of 2060.[90] During the mid 2060s, the Daleks were scattered throughout the galaxy and in no position to invade Earth.[91]

The collapse of the Amazon's eco-system made the so-called "Lung of the World" into a dust bowl stretching from Rio de Janiero to the Andes, displacing a number of werewolves and Amazon Indian tribes. A constant risk of global war existed until the Earth's governments turned their attention to the Moon and asteroid belt for resources.[92]

By 2068, a few colonisation missions had been

---

82 *Transit*

83 *The King of Terror*, the year is given as 2050 (p1).

84 'Almost a century' before *The Final Sanction* (p175), although it must be a little longer than that, as the Selachians were active in the twenty-first century according to both *The Murder Game* and *Alien Bodies*.

85 *Alien Bodies* (p12).

86 *Vampire Science*

87 *Mad Dogs and Englishmen*

88 *St Anthony's Fire*

89 *Interference* (p217). *The Indestructible Man* specifies that the UN is the force behind the ban (p13).

90 *Nekromanteia*

91 *Alien Bodies* (p138).

92 'About twenty years' before *Loups-Garoux*.

93 *The Indestructible Man*. This story seems to contradict a lot of the other stories set around this time both in broad terms and points of detail.

94 Dating *Alien Bodies* - The date is given (p68).

95 *Seeing I* (p29). No date given.

96 *Nightmare of Eden*. A monitor readout states that Galactic Salvage and Insurance were formed in "2068". The Doctor has heard of the company and briefly pretends to be working for them.

97 *The Murder Game* (p9).

98 Dating *The Wheel in Space / The War Games* - This, along with *The Seeds of Death*, is one of two stories set in the twenty-first century that are trickiest to date.

Zoe is "born in the twenty-first" century (*The War Games*), and she is "nineteen or so" according to the

Brigadier in *The Invasion*, so the story must be set somewhere between 2019 and 2119.

In *The Mind Robber*, she recognises the Karkus, a comic strip character from the year 2000, which might suggest she comes from that year. However, when discussing the Karkus, Zoe asks the Doctor if he has been to the year 2000 - if it's not a rhetorical question, *The Wheel in Space* is not set in that year. In *The Mind Robber*, we see an image of Zoe's home city, a highly futuristic metropolis.

The Wheel in Space - Zoe's debut story - certainly takes place after *The Seeds of Death*, because man has travelled further than the Moon by Zoe's time (explicitly as far as Venus and the asteroid belt, and we're told Earth has a 'fleet' of ships that go into 'deep space') and her knowledge of space travel is more advanced. In *The Seeds of Death*, Zoe understands the principles behind T-Mat, meaning she possesses knowledge that's otherwise limited to a few specialists (she may have picked this up on her travels - although she doesn't in any story we see). Why Zoe doesn't remember T-Mat or recognise the Martians is a mystery, but it does indicate she was born after T-Mat was abandoned, or she'd recognise it from her childhood.

This helps to set the earliest date for *The Wheel in Space* - it's at least nineteen years after *The Seeds of Death*, so it can't take place before 2046 (nineteen years after the earliest possible date for that story). It doesn't help narrow the upper limit, however. That Zoe doesn't remember T-Mat may be evidence that she's from siglaunched to other solar systems, but there was no indication of whether they had succeeded. UNIT had recently been replaced by PRISM.

On 3rd March, 2068, the Lunar Base picked up an alien signal. This was evidence of the Myloki. First contact proved disastrous, and the Myloki launched a war on humanity. Although conducted in secret, the war with the Myloki was so devastating that on 29 August 2068, the UN banking system collapsed under the strain. The war ended when Colonel LeBlanc sent Captain Grant Matthews, an indestructible Myloki duplicate who retained his loyalties to humanity, to the Moon with a twenty-megaton bomb strapped to his back. This destroyed the Myloki base. But the war exhausted Earth's natural resources and saw New York destroyed in a nuclear attack. An altered maize crop destroyed the ecology of Africa. The City of London became an independent city-state, walled off from the rest of the world.[93]

2069 (26th March) - ALIEN BODIES[94] **->** In the East Indies ReVit Zone, Mr Qixotl hosted a private conference in which representatives from various powers were to bid on the Relic, a Gallifreyan body that contained extremely rare biodata. Friction among the delegates increased, and a Kroton Warspear arrived to claim the Relic by force. The Doctor used a Faction Paradox timeship to reflect the Warspear's weaponry back on itself, destroying the entire battlefleet. Mortally wounded, Qixotl traded the Relic to the Celestis in return for a new body. The Doctor travelled to Mictlan, the Celestis' powerbase, and reclaimed the Relic.

The Doctor buried the Relic alongside the dog Laika on the planet Quiescia, and destroyed the Relic with a thermosystron bomb.

Middle Eastern countries turned their economies to high technology, particularly the space industry, as the oil runs out.[95] **Galactic Salvage and Insurance was set up in London in 2068.**[96] The space station Hotel Galaxian became the first offworld tourist attraction.[97]

The Cyber Incursions

? 2068 - THE WHEEL IN SPACE / THE WAR GAMES[98] **->** Jet helicopters had become the principal form of transport on Earth. Simple servo robots were developed, as were x-ray laser weapons and food dispensers. John Smith and Associates built advanced medical equipment for spacecraft. Psychotropic drugs could now prevent brain control, and all astronauts were fitted with Silenski capsules to detect outside influences on the human mind.

The Earth School of Parapsychology was founded around this time. It was based in an area known only as 'The City' and trained children from a very early age in the disciplines of pure logic and memory. Zoe Heriot, one of the School's pupils, developed total recall and majored in pure maths. She qualified as an astrophysicist and astrometricist (first class). Her education was narrow and vocational, though, and didn't include any Pre-century history. When she was about nineteen, Zoe was assigned to space station W3.

The Space Wheels were set up around the Solar System. W3, for example, was positioned relative to Venus, 24,564,000 miles at perihelion, 161,350,000 miles at aphelion, a week's rocket travel from Earth. W5 was between eighty and ninety million miles from W3. The small, multinational crews of the Wheel warned travellers of meteorite storms and acted as a

---

nificantly after that story - then again, she has a narrow education and doesn't recognise kilts or candles, either.

In *The Moonbase*, base leader Hobson states that 'every child knows' about the destruction of Mondas (in *The Tenth Planet*). Yet none of the crew of the Wheel have heard of the Cybermen, and they're generally sceptical about the existence of alien life. This is a contradiction whether Zoe comes from before, around the same time or after *The Moonbase*. Invoking Zoe's narrow education doesn't work if 'every child' knows about Mondas' demise, and surely the only way she wouldn't know is if it had been deliberately kept from her, which would be a bit bizarre. Perhaps, after *The Wheel in Space*, the world government make sure Mondas is put on the curriculum. As we'll see, by the 2080s mankind knows for certain that there are aliens, so *The Wheel in Space* is probably set before then.

Amongst its other duties, the Wheel gathers information on Earth's weather, but this needn't mean that weather control isn't in use - to control the weather, you surely need the ability to monitor it.

I place the story a century after it was broadcast, around the same time as the other Cyberman incursion seen in *The Moonbase*. In the last episode of *The War Games*, Zoe is returned to her native time by the Time Lords, who erase her memories of all but her first adventure with the Doctor.

The first two editions of *The Programme Guide* placed *The Wheel in Space* between "1990-2000", but *The Terrestrial Index* suggested a date "c2020" (or "2030" in *The Universal Databank*). "2074" was suggested by 'A History of the Cybermen' in *DWM*. *Cybermen*, after some discussion (p61-62), decided on "2028 AD". *Timelink* says "2020".

halfway house for deep space ships of the space fleet; they monitored all manner of stellar phenomenon, and also supplied advance weather information to Earth.

The Wheels were armed with x-ray lasers with a range of ten thousand miles, and protected by a Convolute Force Field, a neutron field barrier capable of deflecting meteorites of up to two hundred tonnes. Phoenix IV cargo rockets, which had a four-man crew but could be placed on automatic power drive, kept the stations supplied with food and materials.

Back on the human homeworld, the Pull Back to Earth movement believed it was wrong to colonise other planets. They committed acts of sabotage against the space programme, but their exponents were never seen as anything but crackpots. Space travel had undoubted benefits, but remained hazardous.

A Cybermen assault on station W3 was repelled. During the attack, they murdered Dr. Gemma Corwyn. Two years beforehand, Corwyn's husband had been killed exploring the asteroid belt. The loss of rockets was becoming rarer, though.

2070 - THE MOONBASE[99] -> The Cybermen attempted to take control of the Gravitron on the Moon by using Cybermats to introduce a plague to the Moonbase. The Doctor thwarted them.

Medical units could now administer drugs and automatically control the pulse, temperature, breathing, and cortex factor of a patient.

Tobias Vaughn recovered bodies of Cybermen from W3 and the Moonbase, and used the components to repair his cybernetic body.[100] Facing extinction, the Cybermen conquered Telos, all but wiping out the native Cryons and building their "Tombs" using Cryon technology. Once this was completed, the Cybermen retreated to their Tombs and vanished from the galaxy. The location of Telos remained a mystery.[101] The Cybermen launched a star destroyer from Telos that headed to the Garazone Sector.[102]

An island was created by seismic shifts in the Atlantic, and this became a homeland for the Dutch, the New Dutch Republic.[103] The Sontarans left the Coal Sack sector of space and wouldn't return for three hundred years.[104]

2074 - MAD DOGS AND ENGLISHMEN[105] -> Science fiction by human authors was the subject of serious academic debate by now. There were also groups who sought to rewrite literary texts for their own evil ends, including The Circle Hermeneutic and The New Dehistoricists. Talking boars had become part of Earth society, with their own culture.

The poodles of the Dogworld built their first space station. It received radio signals from other planets, including Earth. Princess Margaret's conflict with the ruling Emperor of the Dogworld resulted in her death. A grateful Emperor allowed writer Reginald Tyler to remain on the Dogworld.

On Earth, governments used genetic manipulation and intelligent chips to maintain their soldiers' loyalty.[106]

2080 - LOUPS-GAROUX[107] -> The ancient werewolf Pieter Stubbe tried to reclaim Ileana de Santos, now the de facto werewolf leader, as his mate. Illeana resisted Stubbe's advances, but Stubbe seized control of Ileana's werewolves and directed them to assault Rio de Janeiro. The Doctor and Turlough arrived at this time, and the Doctor broke Stubbe's dominance of the pack. Stubbe died when he rushed into the TARDIS, enabling the Doctor to materialize in orbit and sever Stubbe from the Earth - the source of his elemental power - thus aging him to death.

Rio de Janerio now had a monorail and spaceport. ID

---

99 Dating *The Moonbase* - Hobson tells the Doctor they are in "2070", and Polly later repeats this. On-screen the small crew of the Moonbase includes Englishmen, Frenchmen and Danes. The production file for the story listed the other nationalities represented at the Moonbase: Australians, New Zealanders, Canadians, Germans and Nigerians.

100 *Original Sin* (p289).

101 *The Tomb of the Cybermen, Attack of the Cybermen*

102 *Sword of Orion*

TELOS: After the destruction of their vast advance force (*The Invasion*), their homeworld of Mondas (*The Tenth Planet*) and most of the surviving Cyber Warships (*Silver Nemesis*), the Cybermen must have been severely weakened. They gradually regrouped and attempted to attack Earth at least twice in the twenty-first century (*The Wheel in Space, The Moonbase*). These attempts failed, and the Cybermen faced extinction (according to the Controller in *The Tomb of the Cybermen*). So they left the Solar System and conquered Telos. (The Doctor says in *Attack of the Cybermen* that "if Mondas hadn't been destroyed, the Cybermen would never have come here [to Telos]", but this contradicts an unbroadcast line from *The Moonbase* where a Cyberman states, "We were the first space travellers from Mondas. We left before it was destroyed. We came from the planet Telos.") The Cybermen subjugated the native Cryons, used Cryon technology to build their "tombs" (*Attack of the Cybermen*) and experimented with new weapons before entering suspended animation. In the late twenty-fifth century, the Cybermen revived (*The Tomb of the Cybermen*) and emerged to menace the galaxy... [q.v. The Cyber War].

103 *St Anthony's Fire*

implants were compulsory, and robots checked passports. People drove hover vehicles including limos, jeeps and four hundred mile-an-hour trains. The currency was the credit.

Circa 2084, on the planet Cray, the game Naxy started out as an innocent arena sport. The Naxy sports fans became increasingly violent, and took to fighting outside the arena before matches. The public's interest shifted to the bloody fan conflict, and Naxy was soon re-tooled as a sport in which teams fought to the death.[108]

c 2084 - WARRIORS OF THE DEEP[109] **-> Earth consolidated into two blocs,** the East and the West, **and a new Cold War developed. New weapons technology was developed: Seabases sat on the ocean floor, armed with proton missiles that were capable of destroying life while leaving property intact. Sentinels, robots armed with energy weapons, orbited the Earth and large Hunter-Killers patrolled the seas. Specially trained men, Synch-operators, had computer interfaces implanted into their heads, allowing split-second control over proton missile runs. Soldiers now carried energy rifles.**

At the height of interbloc tension, a group of Silurians and Sea Devils attacked Seabase 4. They planned to launch the missiles there and provoke a war that would kill all human life. The Doctor failed to prevent a massacre at the base, but saved humanity.

First Contact

The Arcturan Treaty of 2085 was often officially counted as mankind's first contact with alien races, as it was the first diplomatic contact.[110] The whole of humanity finally accepted the existence of aliens. Danny Pain's role in stopping an alien invasion in 1976 was now legendary.[111]

The Thousand-Day War

Out of the blue, one day in 2086 the Martians attacked, hitting Paris with a meteorite and killing hundreds of thousands. Humanity united behind President Achebe against the common enemy. First in were the Zen Brigade, the Blue Berets of the United Nations Third Tactical Response Brigade, made up of Irish and Ethiopians. They dropped in from orbit, and the Martians cut them to pieces. One of the few survivors was their commanding officer, Brigadier Yembe Lethbridge-Stewart. But the Blue Berets completed their mission and formed a bridgehead: the UN forward-base at Jacksonville halfway up Olympus Mons. More crucially, their engineers set up the first interstitial tunnel, a refinement of old Travel-mat technology that allowed instantaneous travel between Earth and Mars.

---

104 *Lords of the Storm* (p104).

105 Dating *Mad Dogs and Englishmen* - It is 'one hundred years' (p9) after '1974' (p3).

106 *Deceit* (p188), with similar technology in *Transit*.

107 Dating *Loups-Garoux* - The date is given.

108 *The Game.* Details of Naxy's history are given, and the story says dozens of teams played Naxy "four hundred years" before *The Game*.

109 Dating *Warriors of the Deep* - The Doctor tells Tegan that the year is "about 2084". The televised story doesn't specify which bloc the Seabase belongs to, and only the novelisation specifies the blocs as "East and West". Lieutenant Preston doesn't seem surprised that the TARDIS is "not from this planet", and no-one seems shocked that the Silurians are intelligent non-humans. This might suggest that contact has been made with a number of alien races by this time.

THE EARTH REPTILES: In *Doctor Who and the Silurians*, *The Ambassadors of Death* and *The Sea Devils*, the Doctor thinks that the Brigadier has killed all the Silurians at Wenley Moor. However, they may simply be entombed, and one Silurian - Ichtar - seems to survive the first story into *Warriors of the Deep*.

Based on discrepancies between the events of *Doctor Who and the Silurians*, the descriptions of the Doctor's last encounter with the species in *Warriors of the Deep*, and the fact that the Doctor recognises Icthar, the Myrka and the Silurian submersible, *The Discontinuity Guide* postulated that there is an unrecorded adventure featuring the Doctor and the Silurians set between the two stories. The novel *The Scales of Injustice*, set in the UNIT era and published the year after *The Discontinuity Guide*, addresses most of these issues in an attempt to fill the gap.

Silurians were referred to in a number of New and Missing Adventures set in the future (*Love and War*, *Transit* and *The Crystal Bucephalus* to name three). They seem particularly peaceful towards humans in Benny's native time.

110 *The Dying Days* (p115). It's part of the format of the series that there are plenty of alien invasions yet no-one in the present day believes in them. Even given the Doctor's comment in *Remembrance in the Daleks* and *Rose* that humans are blind to what's going on around them, that most alien attacks are covert or limited to isolated locations, and the government's desire to hush up aliens, there are a number of stories set before 2085 where the general population of the Earth really can't escape the existence of aliens, such as *The Tenth Planet*, *The Dying Days* and *Aliens of London*. By the end of the last two, people have already started declaring that the aliens are a hoax, and it seems that's the accepted view of what happened.

111 *No Future* (p257).

Men and materiel poured through the Stunnel.

Half-kiloton groundbreakers poured from the air onto the Martian nests. Tactical nuclear weapons were used. The early stages of the war were dogged by friendly fire incidents, but these were ironed out. As the war dragged on, some soldiers were genetically and cybernetically augmented to increase their efficiency. These first-generation ubersoldaten retained less than fifty percent of their natural DNA. Just about every soldier took combat drugs like Doberman and Heinkel to make them better fighters.

New slang entered the language: Greenie (Martian), pop up (a cannon used by the Martians), spider trap, fire mission, medevac. During the war, hologram technology became more advanced. The Ice Maiden, an R&R stop in Jacksonville, became notorious. For a generation afterward, the imagery and iconography of the War was burnt into the minds of humanity, and was popularised in vids like *Violet Sky*.

The war ended in 2088, exactly a thousand days after it had started. The surviving Martians had either fled the planet or gone into hibernation in deep nests. At first, the human authorities were worried about 'stay behind' units, but it became clear that the Martian threat had completely dissipated, and the military satellites were decommissioned. A memorial forest was set up at Achebe Gorge on Mars. A tree was planted for each one of the four hundred and fifty thousand men who had died in the War, which didn't include the death toll in Paris. For many decades, Victory Night was celebrated every year on Earth, and trees were planted to honour the military dead.[112]

The only human defeat was at Viis Claar, or the Valles Marineris, when Abrasaar killed 15,000 humans and 10,000 of his own men in a trap.[113] Ninety-nine per cent of Martians headed for a new planet, Nova Martia, beyond Arcturus. Hundreds of thousands of Martians remained behind, hidden in subterranean cities. UN peacemakers found the planet deserted. The bodies of six of the eight members of the ruling Eight Point Table were found, but these did not include Supreme Grand Marshal Falaxyr or Abrasaar.[114]

The Martian fleet heading to Nova Martia stopped off in the Rataculan system. A few Ice Warriors remained behind to found a colony on the planet Cluut-ett-Pictar.[115] There was little or no contact between the Ice Warriors and humanity for nearly a thousand years, and the Martians rarely allowed any visitors to their new world. In the twenty-sixth century, the "extinct" Martians briefly became a curiosity for archaeologists, but after that, mankind forgot all about their old neighbours.[116]

---

112 *Transit*

113 *GodEngine*

114 *Legacy* (p86), *GodEngine* (p79). In *The Curse of Peladon* we learn that the Martians and Arcturans are "old enemies".

115 *GodEngine* (p168).

116 *Legacy* (p86).

117 Dating *The Indestructible Man* - The date is given. This story contradicts many other stories - mostly ones that were written after the sixth season in which the story is set - and yet refers to a number of them. It's set after a 'global teleportation system' is built and fails (p78), a reference to *The Seeds of Death* (or possibly *Transit*); and it's before Zoe's time (p283), which puts it before *The Wheel in Space* (I've chosen to contradict this reference, see *Dating The Wheel in Space*).

118 *The Gallifrey Chronicles*

119 This is the historical background to *Transit*. In *The Seeds of Death*, Zoe has never heard of the Ice Warriors - even though mankind is exploring the Solar System in her time - which suggests that her contemporaries are not interested in Mars. We learn in *Transit*, amongst many other historical snippets, that the Thousand-Day War ended about twenty-five years before (p188) and that the decade following the war saw economic upheaval (p108). In his 'Future History Continuity', Ben Aaronovitch stated that the War took place between 2086-2088, which by his reckoning was straight after *The Seeds of Death*. Victory Night is mentioned in *The*

Highest Science (p21), and I speculate that it celebrates the end of this War. We learn in *Infinite Requiem* that forests are still planted after a battle (p266).

120 According to the Doctor in *The Mutants*. As we will see, a number of stories claim to be set on the 'first' colony. To explain the apparent contradiction, I'd suggest that colonists are either counting different 'firsts' (the first plan to colonise, to actually leave Earth, to arrive, to terraform, to settle, to form a local government and so on) or that they simply like to take pride in their pioneering ways and are prepared to exaggerate a little.

121 In *The Sensorites*, ship captain Maitland thinks the Doctor and his companions are from the twenty-first century.

122 *Transit* (p264).

123 *The Pit*

124 *The Space Pirates*. The story states the "whole galaxy" has been explored. Yet based on evidence from many other stories, in which planets and civilisations are discovered long after this time, this must be an exaggeration or the exploration must be fairly rudimentary.

125 The Doctor watches the prospectus in *Paradise Towers* and relates Kroagnon's story. The Chief Caretaker describes Kroagnon as a 'being' rather than a 'man', suggesting Kroagnon might be an alien. It's never specified that the tower block was built on Earth, but this seems to be the implication. In the novelisation,

2096 - THE INDESTRUCTIBLE MAN[117] ->

Intercontinental travel was impossible, and the world was broken down into city-states. France and the former United States of America were in a state of civil war. Japan had invaded New Zealand. There was a United Zion Arab States. Only Australia was spared the worst effects of a collapsing society.

The Doctor, Jamie and Zoe defeated the Myloki's plan to use Captain Grant Matthews as the ultimate agent of mankind's destruction.

In 2097, the Doctor, Fitz and Trix prevented an unnamed alien race from exterminating the Pope on Mars, allowing her to consecrate the first cathedral on another planet.[118]

The Colonisation of the Solar System

The World Government invested heavily in the state-owned Sol Transit System (STS) over the next twenty years, and soon Interstitial Tunnels linked every city, continent, habitable planet and moon in the Solar System. Transportation within the Solar System was now instantaneous and readily available. For the first time, the Solar System had a single elected government, the Union of Solar Republics.

In the decade following the Thousand-Day War, Paris was rebuilt. Lowell Depot on Pluto was built to soak up population overspill, but the expected boom didn't arrive. Instead, the Transit system caused massive economic and social upheaval. Small companies saw an opportunity to undermine the industrial zaibatsu. Household names such as Sony, IBM and Matsui went under, and new companies from Brazil, China and Africa - such as Imbani Entertainment, Mtchali and Tung-Po - took their place. Power shifted to Washington, Brazilia, Harare, Beijing, Tehran, Jacksonville and Zagreb. Japan's economy collapsed and plans to terraform Mars proved more costly than had been expected. The money ran out, the floating cities planned for the Ionian Sea were never built and Australia starved. A new genre, silicon noir, charted the resultant corporate battles in the datascape.

The Recession was not harsh on everyone. Relatively speaking, Europe was less prosperous than before, but many in Brazil, Africa and China were a great deal wealthier. For millions in Australia, though, and at the Stop - the end of the Transit line at the Lowell Depot - extreme poverty became a way of life. Whole areas became dead-end ghettos, and urban areas became battlegrounds for street-gangs. Vickers All-Body Combat Systems offered the option of using the Melbourne Protocols, automatically preventing the wearer from shooting civilians. Millions fled the riots using the Transit system, and relief workers rehoused the poor anywhere that would take them, mostly on Mars. Private security firms such as the KGB and V Soc became very rich. With freedom of transport, humanity became more open to ideas from other cultures and to more experimental ways of living. Communal marriages enjoyed a brief vogue.

In 2090, Yembe Lethbridge-Stewart came out of retirement one last time and raided the headquarters of the genetics company IMOGEN. He stole a single child, the first of the second-generation ubersoldaten, and all the files pertaining to her creation. He named her after his great-grandmother, the historian Kadiatu.[119]

Out to the Stars

After mankind "had sacked the solar system they moved on to pastures new".[120] Twenty-first century ships still travelled slower than the speed of light and the crews were placed in suspended animation. It was not unusual to discover such ships many centuries later.[121] These were NAFAL ships, meaning Not As Fast As Light.[122] Huge Pioneer stations were set up, lining the way to the stars. They helped with refuelling and restocking of colony ships.[123]

Prospectors such as Dom Issigri and Milo Clancey were the first men into deep space. Clancey's ship, the 'C' Class freighter LIZ 79, remained in service for forty years. Spacecraft at that time were built with the metal tillium and used a thermonuclear pile to supply power. Mined ore was sent to refineries in 'floaters', slow unmanned vessels. An almost indestructible metal, argonite, was found on some of the planets in the fourth sector. Soon, all ships were made from argonite, which became the most valuable mineral known to man.

Clancey and Issigri became rich over the next fifteen years of working together, especially after they had spent ten years strip-mining the planet Ta in the Pliny system. Clancey became something of a legend on Reja Magnum. The partners eventually split, though, and Issigri went on to found the Issigri Mining Company.[124]

Robots such as the Robotic self-activating Megapodic Mark seven-Z Cleaners had some degree of autonomy. Scanners were developed that could track individuals. Miracle City had been masterpiece of the architect Kroagnon, but he refused to move out and let the residents sully his work by moving in. He was eventually forced out, but the booby-traps he left behind massacred many of the residents. Kroagnon fled to Earth, where he was allowed to build Paradise Towers. During the war, youngsters and oldsters were evacuated to the 304-storey building, where the authorities forgot all about them.[125]

The prison planet Varos was established in the late twenty-first century to remove the criminally insane from galactic society.[126]

The Colonial Age began in the 2090s. Multinational conglomerates started the Century Program, sending colony ships to a dozen worlds in the hope of alleviating the population crisis on Earth.[127] The seven planets of the binary Meson system were colonised at this time.[128] The Pinkerton Intergalactic Agency of detectives soon followed colonists into space, solving crimes on colony worlds where law enforcement was often erratic or corrupt.[129]

Human Travellers fled oppression on Earth by stealing a ship. When human ships reached Arcturus Six, the Earth ambassador was told that Travellers had already landed on the planet.[130] Developers filled in the Serpentine in the late twenty-first century.[131] The corporation Imogen built a facility on Titan to clone generation two ubersoldaten. The Doctor visited this period to download Kadiatu's user manual.[132]

The Global Mining Corporation replaced the US Army, and provided military training for corporations. The world language was 'International American'.[133] **Galactic Salvage and Insurance went bankrupt in 2096.**[134] Kadiatu Lethbridge-Stewart would eventually acquire a Triangulum Swift 400, a ship built in the twenty-first century.[135]

The Doctor and Grant Markham went back to see the *New Hope* leave for the Centraxis system in 2100. Within ten years, the colonists aboard would found Grant's home planet of Agora.[136]

The Twenty-Second Century

c 2100 - PARADISE TOWERS[137] -> Paradise Towers, a self-contained, award-winning tower block that had been abandoned during the war, was rediscovered in the early twenty-second century. With only old and young people in residence, society became stratified. The young girls became Kangs - with an array of "ice-hot" slang and "high fabsion" clothing - the old women became Rezzies and the Caretakers tried to maintain the building by rigidly sticking to their rulebook. Each group had a distinctive language, and each preyed mercilessly on the other. There were even reports of cannibalism.

The Kangs split into three rival factions - Red, Blue and Yellow - although "wipeouts" or "making unalive" was forbidden (as were visitors, ball games and fly posting).

Kroagnon's disembodied mind had been exiled to the Towers' basement, but he now possessed the Chief Caretaker using the science of corporal ectoscopy. He put the Towers' robotic cleaners to the task of eliminating the residents, but the various social factions united alongside the Doctor and Mel. A war deserter, Pex, sacrificed himself to kill Koragnon. Social order was restored, and Pex was remembered in various wallscrawls.

Paradise Towers is a space station, which it certainly isn't on-screen. The war in question might be the East/West conflict of *Warriors of the Deep* or the Thousand Day War first referred to in *Transit*.

126 *Vengeance on Varos*. The Governor notes that "Varos has been stable for more than two hundred years".

127 *Killing Ground*

128 'They've come a long way in a hundred years' according to the Doctor in *Time of Your Life* (p27).

129 *Shakedown*

130 *Love and War* (p39).

131 *Birthright* (p189).

132 *The Also People* (p155, p191).

133 *The Face-Eater* (p64).

134 *Nightmare of Eden*

135 *So Vile a Sin*

136 "Ninety-one years" before *Killing Ground*.

137 Dating *Paradise Towers* - Paradise Towers has been abandoned for between about fifteen and twenty years, judging by the age of the Kangs. The Doctor's remark that the building won awards "way back in the twenty-first century" may or may not suggest that the story is set in the twenty-second. If we take the New Adventures into account, I would suggest that the War at Time Start might well be the Thousand-Day War that took place a generation before *Transit*. In *Lucifer Rising*, Adjudicator Bishop refers to the "messy consequences of the Kroagnon Affair" (p189), so it is set before then. *The Terrestrial Index* suggested that the war is the Dalek Invasion of Earth, and therefore set the story around 2164. *Timelink* sets the story in 2040.

138 *The End of the World*

139 *Excelis Decays*

140 *Lucifer Rising* (p100, p320).

141 *Timewyrm: Revelation*

142 *Transit* (p157-158).

143 *Deceit* (p27-28).

144 Dating *Genocide* - The date is given (p30).

145 *Speed of Flight, Genocide*

146 *Festival of Death*, possibly a reference to *Transit*.

147 Dating *Transit* - The exact date of the story is not specified. The book takes many of its themes from *The Seeds of Death*, and is set at least a generation after that story. The Transit system has been established for at least the last couple of decades and has revolutionised

2105 was 'a bit boring', according to the Doctor.[138] Grayvorn escaped the Imperial Museum when someone died there and he mentally inhabited their body. He resumed a position of authority within the Wardens and began instigating a series of socio-political changes on Artaris.[139]

2106 saw the Ozone Purge, the first sign that man had not solved the Earth's environmental problems. The Purge was caused by a breakdown of weather control technology, and a number of species - including such previously common creatures as sheep, cats and sparrows - were wiped out.[140]

During the twenty-second century, human babies were grown artificially to be used in scientific tests.[141] Yembe Lethbridge-Stewart died in 2106. His daughter buried him alongside his wife at Achebe Gorge on Mars.[142]

In 2107, Eurogen and the Butler Institute - relatively small corporations for the time - merged to become Eurogen Butler or the "EB Corporation". Eurogen was a major genetic research facility. After its near-collapse a century before, the Butler Institute had survived by specialising in artificial intelligence, meteorology and weather control. Both companies were expanding into the field of interplanetary exploration, and their services were now required on a dozen worlds.[143]

= **2108 (1st January) - GENOCIDE**[144] -> The Doctor and Sam arrived on Earth in a deviant timeline in which humanity had been eradicated. The relatively passive Tractites now occupied Earth and had named it Paratractis. The Doctor and Sam travelled back to historical junctures 2.5 million years and 3.6 million years in the past to avert this history.

In July 2108, the Doctor visited Oxford Street and bought a Xavier Eugene microscope and a pair of wings in the sales.[145] Humanity developed the theory of hyperspace tunnels in the early twenty-second century.[146]

c 2109 - TRANSIT[147] -> The Union of Solar Republics attempted to build the first interstitial tunnel to another star system. The Stunnel would provide instantaneous travel to Arcturus II, twenty-six light years away, and if successful would allow rapid colonisation of other planets. At the inauguration, though, disaster struck. The President was killed, and the Transit system began to show signs of instability. It became clear that the Transit system had attracted an intelligence from another dimension, and it was this that ensured the smooth running of the network. The intruder was banished, but it became clear that it was impossible to maintain Transit tunnels over interstellar distances.

Following activity on Mars at this time, a nest of Martians was revived and entered negotiations with humanity. FLORANCE, the first Artificial Intelligence to develop sentience, became a celebrity. Its rights were protected under the civil rights convention.

The Transit system was abandoned soon after this incident. The Martian castes debated making peace with Earth in 2110. Humans established two human cities on Mars: Jacksonville and Arcadia Planitia.[148] **Mankind discovered warp drive, allowing it to travel faster-than-light. Azure, in West Galaxy, was colonised and became a tourist destination. At least nine space Stations were set up. By now, contact with alien species was almost routine. The scientist Tryst aimed to "qualify and quantify every species in our galaxy".[149]**

An ice planet was discovered when a scientific expedition made a misjump through hyperspace. Marooned for three years, they established a colony run along rational lines. Three years later, when the rescue ships arrived, they elected to stay. Miners and other colonists arrived and were ruled by an elite of scientists, the Scientifica.[150]

The Space Corps was set up.[151]

In the early twenty-second century, the Guild of Adjudicators was established as a judicial force unre-

---

the world - no television stories seem to be set during this period. It is hinted that the story takes place in the twenty-second century (p134). In his 'Future History Continuity', *Transit* author Ben Aaronovitch places this story "c2109". *GodEngine*, following the Virgin version of this chronology, dated the story as "2109" (p1). *So Vile a Sin* gave the date as 2010, which would seem to be a misprint (p140).

148 *GodEngine*

149 *Nightmare of Eden*. This happens after *Transit*, but there's enough time before *Nightmare of Eden* to allow Tryst to explore and for Earth to found a colony on (at least) Azure. The starship *Empress* has left from Station Nine.

150 *Cold Fusion*. The planet was named as Salomon in the synopsis, but not the book.

151 The Interstellar Space Corps appears in *The Space Pirates*, the Marine Space Corps appears in *Death to the Daleks* and the Space Corps is referred to in *Nightmare of Eden*.

strained by authority or financial dependence. They were based on the remote planet Ponten IV. Early successes for the "ravens" (so-named because of their black robes) included the execution of fifteen drug dealers on Callisto, the suppression of a revolution in Macedonia and the disciplinary eradication of the energy-wasting population on Frinelli Minor. The Adjudicators also dealt with the Kroagnon Affair, vraxoin raids over Azure, the Macra case and the Vega debacle.[152] Adjudicator Bishop discovered Paradise Towers.[153]

Kadiatu Lethbridge-Stewart destroyed the Butterfly Wing, apparently committing suicide in the process ... although there were rumours that she had built a time machine.[154]

The first production line warships began to be built. Lagships were still used for many years on longer journeys, although the technology remained risky.[155]

The crusade of the Chapter of St Anthony was becoming notorious. Youths from the Initiate League torched the city of Urrozdinee when they refused to accept the rule of the Chapter. Shortly afterward, the crusade spread unopposed to the stars, in two mighty battleships capable of laying waste to whole planets and destroying small moons. When the Chapter raided Titan, they recruited the malevolent dwarf Parva De Hooch. Shortly afterward, the Chapter returned to Earth and De Hooch killed his parents.[156]

Garazone Central was one of the first cities to 'float between the stars', and was located well away from Earth authorities, maintaining its own Space Patrol. The Garazone bazaar became a trading post for humans and aliens alike.[157]

Earth authorities imprisoned the geneticist Cauchemar for murdering people in his quest to achieve immortality. He was dispatched on a colony arkship to a prison world at the edge of the New Earth frontier, but the ship collided with a meteor en route and half the crew died. A race of benevolent aliens appeared and offered to save the survivors from dying of radiation poisoning. With Cauchemar's help, the aliens transformed the humans into hosts for their own criminals.

The hybrids were seeded onto an unnamed planet, lacking knowledge of their previous identities. Those who lived commendable existences passed into the afterlife; those who didn't were reincarnated to try again. The colony started losing population as souls were redeemed. "The Creator" was a semi-sentient entity that oversaw this process.

Cauchemar's experiments had rendered him unsuitable as a host, and he was sent away from the planet. He returned to find his lover Jasmine among the reincarnated populace, but his "alien" presence disrupted the Creator and killed her. A distraught Cauchemar consequently worked to bring the Creator to ruin, hoping this would force the Creator to "recognize" his soul.[158]

Because interstellar travel and communications were still relatively slow, colony planets were often left to their own devices. The founding fathers of these worlds were often important, and all sorts of political and social experimentation was attempted.

Many colonies were set up and directly controlled by the corporations, and many others were reliant on them for communications, transport and technology.[159] The EB Corporation was among the first to offer an escape from Earth in their warship, *The Back to Nature*, which was commissioned in 2112. Arcadia was a temperate planet, the second in its system, and was less than a thousand light-years from Earth. A number of years previous, the EB Corporation had set up a survey camp on the planet, the site of which would become the capital city Landfall, and set about terraforming the world. The planet came to resemble medieval Europe, and was ready for the first

---

152 The Master poses as an Adjudicator in *Colony in Space*, the only time the Adjudicators were referred to or seen on television. They feature a number of times in the New Adventures, and the Doctor's companions Cwej and Forrester are ex-Adjudicators. The foundation of the Guild of Adjudicators is related in *Lucifer Rising*, as are their early successes. I suggest that 'the Macra case' referred to on p189 can't be *The Macra Terror*, and so must be another encounter with that race.

153 *Lucifer Rising*. There's no indication how long after *Paradise Towers* this happened.

154 'Three years' after *Transit* (p260).

155 In *Deceit* we learn that production line warships were being made by 2112 (p28). Suspended animation is seen in a number of New Adventures set after this time, including *Deceit*, *The Highest Science* and *Lucifer Rising*.

156 *St Anthony's Fire* (p195, p260). Urrozdinee first appeared in a short story of the same name by Mark Gatiss in Marvel's *1994 Doctor Who Yearbook*. In that story the city is a post-apocalyptic feudal state inhabiting the remains of EuroDisney.

157 *Sword of Orion*

158 Centuries before *Vanishing Point*. Arbitrary date.

159 The founding fathers of a planet are revered in *The Robots of Death*, *The Caves of Androzani* and the New Adventure *Parasite*. Earth colonies feature in many, many *Doctor Who* stories. The corporations' stranglehold over the early colonies is a theme touched on in many New Adventures, especially the 'Future History Cycle' which ran from *Love and War* to *Shadowmind*

160 The Arcadia colony was founded "three hundred and seventy-nine" (Arcadian?) years before the events of *Deceit* (p115). It was one of the first Spinward influx of colonists. Arcadia eventually became the Corporation's centre of operations.[160]

Early during earth's interstellar expansion, a colony ship landed on Demigest and contact was lost. A rescue mission was also wiped out, but only after one member, Trudeau, dictated a log entry that became known as *The Black Book of Demigest*. Space and time never settled on Demigest as they did on most other worlds. The original colonists mutated to become the Warlocks of Demigest, and obtained great powers.[161]

No intelligent life was discovered on the outskirts of the galaxy, where the stars and planets were sparse. Before long, man abandoned all attempts to venture out past Lasty's Nebula. Instead, mankind's colonisation efforts focused towards the centre of the galaxy - 'the hub', as it became known. A thriving interplanetary community grew up.

Around this time, the planet Evertrin was the site of the annual Inner Planets Music Festival, known as 'Ragasteen'. The biggest bands in space attended to plug their discods: Deep Space, M'Troth, The Great Mothers of Matra, Is Your Baby a God and Televised Instant Death were all at Ragasteen 2112.

The riggers on Earth changed the style of music every three years to keep it fresh. Zagrat, for example, were very popular during the 'headster time', but teenagers found their discod 'Sheer Event Shift' embarrassing just a few years later.[162]

Worlds such as the five planets of the Sirius System and Delta Magna rapidly became industrialised and overpopulated.[163] **Burglars began to use computers, forcing people to install audio locks.**[164] Tourism on Earth was a thing of the past.[165] The lethal drink Bubbleshake, invented by the unscrupulous Joseph-Robinson corporation, was originally an appetite suppressant. Unchecked, it was addictive, leading to memory loss, hyperactivity and compulsive behaviour. The substance

was eventually outlawed.[166]

Earth discovered universal concrete in 2115.[167] Welford Jeffery invented antigrav technology.[168] In 2115, human archaelogists found the Martian city of Ikk-ett-Saleth completely abandoned.[169]

2116 - NIGHTMARE OF EDEN[170] -> Interplanetary standards and conventions were set up that applied to the whole of Human Space. The Galactic Credit (z) was established as a convertible interplanetary currency. Credits resembled colourful blocks of plastic, and were used for every sort of transaction from buying a drink to funding an expedition to a new planet. None of this prevented a recession from hitting the galactic economy.

Laser technology advanced during this period. Stun laser weapons became available for the first time. Entuca lasers capable of carrying millions of signals were now used for telecommunications. Finally, vast amounts of information could now be recorded on laser data crystals.

Crime was a problem in the galaxy. Drug trafficking increased when the drug XYP, or Vraxoin, was discovered. Vrax addicts felt a warm complacency at first, followed by total apathy. They also became thirsty. Inevitably, its effects were fatal. The narcotic ruined whole planets and communities until the planet that was the only known source of the drug was incinerated. A Vraxoin merchant (drug trafficker) risked the death penalty if caught. Molecular scanners were developed that could detect even minute quantities of the drug. All citizens were required to carry an ident-plaque.

Interplanetary tourism developed at this time. Government-subsidised interstellar cruise liners, each holding 900 passengers, travelled between Station Nine and Azure. Passengers could travel either econo-

---

Settlements (p16) and the planet (or at least part of it) has been terraformed (p103).

161 *The Infinity Race*

162 *The Highest Science*

163 The Doctor says he visited Androzani Major when "it was becoming rather developed" in *The Caves of Androzani*. In *The Power of Kroll*, we see the third moon of Delta Magna. (It is called "Delta III" in the novelisation and *Original Sin*, p21.)

THE SIRIUS SYSTEM: In *Frontier in Space*, the Master poses as a Commissioner from Sirius IV and accuses the Doctor and Jo of landing a spaceship in an unauthorised area on Sirius III. According to Romana in *City of Death*, Sirius V is the home of the Academius Stolaris. In *The Caves of Androzani*, Morgus is the chairman of the Sirius Conglomerate based on Androzani Major, and

spectrox is found on its twin planet Androzani Minor. These two facts make Morgus the "richest man in the Five Planets". We might infer that Androzani Major and Minor are Sirius I and II.

164 *The Space Pirates*

165 *Lucifer Rising* (p84).

166 *The Highest Science* (p102).

167 *The Face-Eater* (p40).

168 'Several hundred years' after Charley's time (the 1930s), according to *Sword of Orion*.

169 *GodEngine* (p73).

170 Dating *Nightmare of Eden* - Galactic Salvage and Insurance went bankrupt "20 years ago" according to Captain Rigg, who had just read a computer monitor giving the date of the bankruptcy as "2096". *In-Vision* suggested that Azure is in "West Galaxy", but I think this my or first class, the former seated in 'pallets' and forced to wear protective clothing, the latter allowed a great deal more freedom and luxury.

The scientist Tryst attempted to qualify and quantify every lifeform in the galaxy. As Tryst's log (published to coincide with a series of lectures given by the zoologist) recounted, his ten-man expedition travelled to Zil, Vij, Darp, Lvan, Brus, the windswept planet Gidi and the temperate world Ranx. Finally, Tryst's ship, the *Volante*, travelled past the Cygnus Gap to the three-planet system of M37. The second planet contained primitive life: molluscs, algae and insects. As well as taking visprints, they used a CET machine.

Six months before arriving at Azure, the *Volante* visited the planet Eden. On the planet they lost a member of the crew, Stott, who was secretly working for the Intelligence Section of the Space Corps. It was later discovered that Mandrells from the planet Eden decomposed into Vraxoin when they died, and that Tryst had partnered with Dymond, the pilot of the *Hecate*, to smuggle the material. The two of them were arrested.

During the second and third decade of the twenty-second century, the Western Alliance banks foreclosed on Earth and the World Civilian Police Corps was formed. The Oceanic-Nippon bloc was working on interstellar flight, and the first supra-light vessel *New Horizon* was launched in 2126, taking five thousand colonists on a two-year journey to Proxima 2, the first colony in an alien environment. Proxima City was founded there. The second human colony world was called Earth 2.

UNIT had been disbanded by this time. The records of Global Mining Corporation list the Doctor as a security consultant from 2127 (adding that his female companion graduated Geneva Corporate University in 2124) following an unrecorded incident in Albania.[171] The Particle Matter Transmission (Deregulation) Act was passed in 2122.[172] The first humans to arrive on Hitchemus, a planet on the edge of explored space, were hunters in pursuit of the tigers that lived there. The colony of Port Any was built shortly afterward. It became famed for music and attracted musicians from across human space.[173]

The exploration vessel *Hydrax* was lost en route to Beta Two in the Perugellis Sector. Its officers included

is a mishearing of Rigg's (fluffed) line "you'll never work in *this* galaxy again". While others have disagreed with that, there is certainly no on-screen justification for *The Discontinuity Guide*'s "Western Galaxy". The TARDIS Logs gave the date as "c.2100", *The Doctor Who File* as "2113".

171 *The Face-Eater*. The dates given in the book seem to contradict a number of other stories set around this time.

172 *Cold Fusion*

173 The space port has been open a hundred years before *The Year of Intelligent Tigers*

174 *State of Decay*. No date is given. On-screen, one computer monitor seems to suggest that the computer was programmed on the "12/12/1998", but the *Hydrax* is clearly an interstellar craft. The TARDIS Logs suggested a date in "the 36th Century", *The Terrestrial Index* placed it "at the beginning of the 22nd".

175 *Lucifer Rising* (p59, p272-273).

176 *The Taking of Planet 5* (p15).

177 Dating *The Face-Eater* - The date is given (p126).

178 *St Anthony's Fire*

179 *The Taint*

180 *The Face-Eater*

181 Dating *The Space Pirates* - A monitor readout in Part Two suggests that the year is "1992", but this contradicts dialogue stating that prospectors have been in deep space for "fifty years". No other date is given on-screen. The *Radio Times* said that the story takes place in "the far future". Earth is mentioned once in the first episode, but after that only a "homeworld" is referred to. The force here is specified as the Interstellar Space Corps. The regulatory actions of the government sug-

gest that space travel is becoming more common now, but is still at an early stage.

As Zoe is unfamiliar with the technology of this story, it is almost certainly set after her time. The Main Boost Drive is not very advanced, and this story almost certainly takes place well before *Frontier In Space*, where hyperdrive technology is common. At the start of the story, the V41-LO is both "fifty days" and "fifty billion miles" from Earth, I assume here that writer Robert Holmes means "billion" in the British sense of a million million, rather than the American (and now generally accepted British) thousand million. If this is the case, then the Beacon is 8.3 Light Years from Earth (otherwise it is a thousandth of this distance, and only just outside the Solar System).

The Programme Guide set the story "c.2600". *The Terrestrial Index* suggested it was "during the Empire" period. The TARDIS Logs claimed a date of "8751". *Timelink* suggested "2146".

182 The Issigri Mining Company appears in *The Space Pirates*. Another company with the same initials, the Interplanetary Mining Company, is seen in *Colony in Space*. In the Missing Adventure *The Menagerie*, we learn that they are the same company (p161). The change of name must have occurred before *Lucifer Rising*, when we see IMC in action.

183 *Lucifer Rising*. The evil polluting company in the television version of *The Green Death* is called "Global Chemicals". A real company of that name objected, and the name was changed in the novelisation to "Panorama Chemicals".

Captain Miles Sharkey, science officer Anthony O'Connor and navigation officer Lauren Macmillan. It fell through a CVE into the pocket universe of E-Space.[174] The *Hydrax* disappeared around 2127. The InterSpace Incorporated ship had a crew of two hundred and forty-three. InterSpace refused to pay out pensions for the lost crew, claiming they might be found. IMC later claimed to have discovered traces of the ship in order to blackmail Piper O'Rourke - whose husband Ben had been an engineer on the *Hydrax* - into revealing details about the Eden Project. The ship was never discovered.[175]

The planet Vulcan suddenly vanished in 2130.[176]

2130 - THE FACE-EATER[177] -> The Doctor and Sam discovered the F-Seeta, a telepathic gestalt of the ratlike natives, was responsible for a series of murders on the first human colony world of Proxima 2. The colony was saved, but at the cost of the Proximans' group mind.

On Betrushia around the year 2133, as it had done many times over the centuries, war broke out between the Ismetch and the Cutch. Millions died in the conflict, which became the longest and most bitter struggle the planet had seen for three hundred years. The Ismetch had an early success at Dalurida Bridge under Portrone Ran.[178]

The Doctor, Sam and Fitz arrived in London during the summer of 2134, and confirmed that the Earth was free of the Beast.[179] A second wave of colonists was expected on Proxima 2 in 2136.[180]

? 2135 - THE SPACE PIRATES[181] -> As space travel became more common, the Earth Government introduced a series of regulations to better control the space lanes in its territory. Space was divided into administrative and strategic Sectors. All flights now had to be logged with Central Flight Information and a network of Mark Five Space Beacons were established to monitor space traffic. The Interstellar Space Corps was given the latest V-Ships, armed with state-of-the-art Martian Missiles (H-bombs were considered old-fashioned by this time) and carrying squadrons of Minnow Fighters. The V-Ships were powered by Maximum Boost atomic motors. The Space Corps routinely used mind probes to interrogate their prisoners. The resources of the Space Corps were stretched very thin: they fought brush wars in three sectors, acted as customs and excise officials and attempted to curtail the activities of space pirates.

For two years, pirates were active in the Ta System and hijacked five of Milo Clancey's floaters, each of which contained 50,000 tons of argonite ore. Despite a dozen requests, the Space Corps did little to help. As an old-timer, Clancey was suspicious of authority; he had lost his registration documents thirty years before

and he didn't maintain his feedback link to CFI.

The Space Corps became involved when the pirates began to break up government space beacons to steal the argonite. The V41-LO was more than fifty days out of Earth, under the command of General Nikolai Hermack, Commander of the Space First Division. The ship was ninety minutes away from Beacon Alpha 4 when it was broken up by pirates. Clancey's ship was detected nearby, and he was questioned but quickly released. The Doctor, Jamie and Zoe were recovered from Beacon Alpha 4, but they too were innocent.

The real culprit was Maurice Caven. His pirates were organised enough to equip themselves with Beta Dart ships, costing one hundred million credits each, that could outrun virtually everything else in space. He killed anyone who got in his way and one of his men, Dervish, had spent ten years working for Earth Government and knew all the Space Corps' techniques.

Some time ago, Caven had kidnapped Dom Issigri and blackmailed his beautiful daughter Madeline, the head of the Issigri Mining Company, into providing facilities for him on the planet Ta. The Corps hunted Caven down and executed him.

After this, the Issigri Mining Company was renamed the Interplanetary Mining Company, or IMC for short.[182] Humanity's contact with the Arcturans was proving fruitful. The Arcturans allowed limited human settlement in their sector, and supplied humanity with specialised drugs. Some humans became interested in studying Arcturan literature.

On Earth, however, things were getting desperate. The Islam-dominated Earth Central, based in Damascus and led by an elected president, was unable to prevent society from collapsing. An unprecedented Energy Crisis led to draconian restrictions on consumption and the foundation of the Energy Police. The invention of the vargol generator did little to relieve the demands for fuel.

In 2137, with Earth desperate for energy, corporations successfully lobbied for the repeal of all the anti-pollution laws brought in over the last century and a quarter. Three years later, an American subsidiary of Panorama Chemicals filled the Carlsbad Caverns with plastic waste, and the oceans of the world were a sludge of industrial effluent. Mineral water became a precious commodity. The whale finally became extinct, and auto-immune diseases - 'the plague' of over a century before - returned.

Despite this, human life expectancy was now 110 years, and the population was soaring. Although it had religious objections to gambling, Earth Central introduced the Eugenics Lottery, and couples were forbidden from having children unless they won.[183]

A colony ship made landfall on the planet Avalon in the

year 2145. The colonists discovered an ancient Avalonian technology which at first allowed them to perform miracles, but soon rendered their electronic equipment useless. The colony regressed to a medieval level, in which certain people - unknowingly able to tap the Avelonian technology - performed "magic".[184]

Dolphins' ability to think in three dimensions made them ideal pilots for Earth's first interstellar fighters.[185]

2146 - THE MURDER GAME[186] -> The European Government and the Terran Security Forces (TSF) were established by this time. The First Galactic Treaty had been signed. The Selachians had menaced Terra Alpha.

The Doctor, Ben and Polly answered a distress call and landed in the Hotel Galaxian, a space station in Earth orbit. Two scientists, Neville and Dorothy Adler, were trying to sell assassination software to the Selachians. Neville Adler was killed and the space hotel burned up in the atmosphere. Dorothy Adler could not work the program without her husband.

In 2146, the American economy collapsed, and there were food riots.[187] The Doctor was in America at the time, and he was powerless to stop cannibals from killing Sonia Bannen shortly after she saved her son. Mark Bannen was placed on board a huge colony ship bound for a new star system. The stardrive misphased in the Elysium System and the colony ship crashed there.[188]

By 2146, the Supreme Council of the Daleks had become concerned by the rapid expansion of humanity. They would monitor the situation carefully for ten years.

The Martian Axis sprang up on Mars and turned to terrorism, bombing Coventry.[189]

3D cameras were developed around this time.[190]

2148 - ST ANTHONY'S FIRE[191] -> A mothership of the Chapter of St Anthony moved to pacify Betrushia, breaking up the planet's artificial ring system to wrack Betrushia with meteorites. Loosed from its shackles, the organic catalyzer became active and threatened all life that it encountered. The Doctor convinced the Chapter as to the creature's threat, and arranged for Betrushia's destruction while instigating an evacuation. Appalled by the Chapter's zealous actions, Bernice and Ace sabotaged the mothership's engines, crippling it to suffer the same destruction as Betrushia and the organism. The Doctor helped the Betrushia survivors relocate to the sister planet of Massatoris.

Earth funded a small Transit station on Charon, a moon of Pluto. The Martian Axis terrorists destroyed the Montreal monorail system, resulting in many deaths.[192] The Doctor flew a Spitfire in the twenty-second century.[193] He also took Victoria to the NovaLon Hypercities of the twenty-second century.[194]

The Arcturans attacked the Martian colony on Cluut-ett-Pictar.[195] A pre-modernist architectural revival occurred in the mid-22nd Century.[196]

In the 2150s, the Cybermen invaded the colony world of Agora, making it one of their breeding colonies. Human Overseers were in charge of harvesting people to become Cybermen.[197] The totalitarian Inner Party seized power in

---

184 *The Sorcerer's Apprentice* (p203-204).
185 *Heritage* (p198).
186 Dating *The Murder Game* - The date is given (p12).
187 *Lucifer Rising* (p158).
188 *Parasite*
189 "10.6 human years" and "about ten years" before *GodEngine* (p107, p168).
190 *Frontier Worlds*
191 Dating *St Anthony's Fire* - The Doctor tells Bernice that the year is "2148" (p39).
192 "Five years" before *GodEngine* (p15, p98, p193).
193 *Last of the Gaderene* (p246). He also says he has flown a Spitfire in *Loups-Garoux*.
194 *Heart of TARDIS*
195 *GodEngine*
196 *Cold Fusion*
197 *Killing Ground* (p15).
198 *Excelis Decays*
199 *GodEngine* (p18).
200 "A year" before *GodEngine*.
201 *Lucifer Rising, GodEngine*
202 Dating *Lucifer Rising* - The story takes place in the

mid-twenty-second century, shortly before the Dalek Invasion of Earth. The Adjudicators' simularity registers the Doctor's arrival as "19/11/2154" (p30), Paula Engado's death as "22/2/2154" (p174) and her wake as "23/2/2154" (p13). Ace and Benny had expressed the desire to "pop back to the year twenty-one fifty-four or so" (p338), so at first sight it might appear that the story is set in 2154. However, this is inconsistent with the Dalek Invasion, which the authors of *Lucifer Rising* place in "twenty-one fifty-eight" (p337). On p195, there's mention of a raid "in Tokyo in fifty-six". I set the story in 2157, consistent with my dating for the Dalek Invasion.
203 *The Dalek Invasion of Earth*, with the date established in *The Daleks' Master Plan*.
204 According to the Doctor in *The Dalek Invasion of Earth*.
THE MIDDLE PERIOD OF DALEK HISTORY: Taking the Doctor's analysis at face value, the Middle Period of Dalek history might be the time when their power is at its zenith - they are technologically advanced, expansionist and feared. In the words of the Doctor in *Death to the Daleks*, they are "one of the greatest powers in the

the city-state Excelis, and assassinated the Imperial Family. More than a century and a half of oppression ensued. Grayvorn pushed other city-states into open conflict, fueling a technology race.[198]

Earth's Colonial Marines fought in civil wars on the Outer Planets in the Arcturus system.[199] In 2156, Supreme Grand Marshall Falaxyr of Mars contacted the Daleks and offered them the GodEngine, an Osirian weapon that could destroy whole planets and stars. In return, he asked for Ice Warrior sovereignty of Mars. The Daleks accepted the offer.[200]

By this time, mankind invented the Simularity, a holographic virtual reality.[201]

c 2157 - LUCIFER RISING[202] **->** Earth encountered the Legions, a seven-dimensional race from Epsilon Eridani. Trading agreements were set up between the Legions and IMC. The Legions' sector of space was threatened by an unknown alien fleet, so IMC would supply the Legions with weaponry in return for advanced technology. Some Legions began working for IMC.

Earlier in the century, a Von Neumann probe had discovered a stable element with a very high mass in the core of the planet Lucifer, a gas giant two hundred and eighty light years from Earth. Theoretically, such an element could be used as a rich energy source. In 2152, Earth Central invested heavily in a scientific research station - the Eden Project - on Belial, one of the moons of Lucifer.

This was the era when Company Shock Troops - military men armed with neutron cannons, flamers, burners and screamers - took part in infamous corporate raids. In '56, IMC asset-stripped InterSpace Incorporated in Tokyo using armoured skimmers and Z-Bombs. Legend has it that companies used to capture employees of rival corporations and experiment on them. It was a risky life - on one raid in '51 praxis gas was used - but on average it paid four times more than Earth Central. The big human corpora-

tions learnt lessons from the aggressive capitalist races such as the Cimliss, Usurians and the Okk. But humanity proved capable of callousness that would put all three of those races to shame.

Six years after it was set up, the Eden Project had still not borne fruit, and pressure was growing to close it down. As Earth's government grew weaker and weaker, the corporations were flexing their muscles: an IMC fleet of over one hundred ships was sent to Belial Base when the scientists reported some progress. This prompted the intelligent species of Lucifer, the Angels, to set up an exclusion zone around their world.

The Corporations had reached new levels of ruthlessness. IMC tripled the price of the fuel zeiton, and an impoverished Earth Central could no longer afford it. Earth was declared bankrupt and fell into the hands of its receivers: the Earth Alliance of Corporations, a holding company that was in reality the board of directors from all the corporations that traded off-Earth. It was a bloodless coup, and the megacorporations took formal control of the homeworld for the first time. Their reign lasted just under six months.

The Dalek Invasion of Earth

In 2157, the Daleks invaded Earth.[203] This was the Middle Period of Dalek history.[204]

An Astronaut Fair was held in London. The city was a beautiful metropolis, complete with moving pavements and a gleaming new nuclear power station alongside the historic Battersea Power Station.[205]

On the very same day that an Earth embassy opened on Alpha Centauri V, a billion settlers were exterminated on Sifranos in the Arcturus Sector. Fourteen other colonies were wiped out in a three-week period, including Azure and Qartopholos. Rumours of a mysterious alien fleet massing at the Legion homeworld of Epsilon Eridani were

---

universe".

In the Virgin edition of this book, I speculated that it coincided with the Daleks developing an internal power supply - in *The Daleks* they took static electricity up through the floor and so couldn't leave their city. In *The Dalek Invasion of Earth*, they had a disc resembling a satellite dish fastened to their backs: the Doctor and Ian speculate that it allows them free movement. In the first two Dalek stories, they have 'bands' rather than the 'slats' seen in all other stories. In *The Power of the Daleks*, they are dependent on a static electricity generator. In all subsequent stories - all of which (apart from the prototypes seen in *Genesis of the Daleks*) have Daleks originating from after *The Dalek Invasion of Earth* - none of these restrictions seem to apply. We are explicitly told they move via 'psychokinetic power' in *Death to the*

Daleks.

The Daleks are confined to the First Segment of Time, according to *The Ark*. We might speculate that the end of the Middle Period of Dalek history comes with either their defeat at the hands of the Movellans (*Resurrection of the Daleks*), or shortly afterward with Skaro's destruction (*Remembrance of the Daleks*).

As we've now seen the end of Dalek history (in *The Parting of the Ways*), we can perhaps speculate that the 'early period' Daleks have bands and are dependent on externally-generated static electricity; the 'middle period' Daleks are the slatted ones familiar from the original TV series and now we can add the 'late period' Daleks seen in the 2005 series, which seem significantly more mobile and advanced than their forebears.
205 *The Dalek Invasion of Earth*

denied, but the Interstellar Taskforce was put on permanent standby, and a Space Fleet flotilla sent to that planet was completely destroyed. The alien fleet was a Dalek armada, the Black Fleet, which was annihilating any colony that might render aid to the human homeworld, and systematically destroying Earth's warships.[206]

Meteorites began to bombard the Earth. Scientists dismissed it as a freak cosmic storm, but people started to die from a mysterious plague. The Daleks were targeting the Earth, and soon the populations of Asia, Africa and South America were wiped out. Only a handful of people had resistance to the plague, and although scientists quickly developed a new drug, it was too late. The world was split into tiny communities. [207]

Millions started dying of a mysterious virus in Brazilia, Los Angeles and Tycho City. Some humans showed a mysterious resistance to the plague - because the Doctor had seeded the atmosphere with an antidote.[208] The Daleks' Black Fleet destroyed Void Station Cassius while entering the Solar System.[209]

Six months after the plague began, the first of the Dalek saucers landed. Some cities were razed to the ground, **others simply occupied. Anyone who resisted was destroyed. Dalek saucers patrolled the skies. Ruthlessly suppressing any resistance, the Daleks subdued India. The leaders of every race and nation on Earth were exterminated.** [210]

The Daleks quickly defeated the Terran Security Forces. Many Americans evacuated to Canada.[211] **New York was destroyed.**[212] Baltimore was reduced to ruins.[213] The Daleks exterminated the last monarch of Britain.[214] The royal bloodline would continue at least until the forty-third century.[215]

A supersaucer landed on Luton, crushing the city.[216] The Daleks mounted a victory parade in London, in front of the Houses of Parliament and Westminster Bridge.[217] The Daleks blockaded the Solar System. The Bureau of Adjudicators on Oberon, a moon of Uranus, tried to work out the Daleks' plan. The Adjudicators detected mysterious signals at the Martian North Pole. Oberon continued to serve as a secret human military base throughout the invasion.[218]

The Daleks invaded Mars, but were defeated when a virus ate through their electrical cables.[219]

---

206 The Arcturus attacks take place at "the beginning of the year" according to *Lucifer Rising*. Sifranos is also mentioned in *GodEngine*.

207 *The Dalek Invasion of Earth, Legacy of the Daleks*.

208 *Lucifer Rising*

209 *GodEngine* (p3).

210 *The Dalek Invasion of Earth*

211 *The Final Sanction* (p75, p178).

212 According to Vicki in *The Chase* and *Salvation* (p58). *The Indestructible Man* said New York was destroyed in a nuclear assault in 2068, but it was evidently rebuilt.

213 *Nekromanteia*

214 *Legacy of the Daleks* (p45).

215 *The Mutant Phase*, although this occurs in an alternate timeline.

216 *GodEngine* (p107).

217 *Head Games* (p157).

218 *GodEngine*

219 *Genesis of the Daleks*. It is confirmed in *GodEngine* that this invasion takes place at the same time as the Dalek Invasion of Earth. The Benny NA *Beige Planet Mars* contains many other details about the colonisation and invasions of Mars.

220 Dating *GodEngine* - The year is given (p3).

221 *The Dalek Invasion of Earth*

222 *GodEngine*

223 Dating *The Mutant Phase* - The year is given as "2158".

224 *War of the Daleks*

225 'Three years' after *GodEngine* (p214).

226 *The Dalek Invasion of Earth, The Mutant Phase*

227 *GodEngine* (p11).

228 *Alien Bodies*

229 Dating *The Dalek Invasion of Earth* - There are two dates to establish: the date of the initial Dalek invasion, and the date of this story, which takes place after the Daleks have occupied Earth for some time. To start, the Doctor and Ian discover a calendar dated "2164" in a room that "hasn't been used in years" and Ian remarks that "at least we know the century". The prisoner Jack Craddock later says that the Daleks invaded "about ten years" ago.

However, it seems that someone was printing calendars after the invasion - in *The Daleks' Master Plan*, the Doctor urges Vyon to "tell Earth to look back in the history of the year two thousand one hundred and fifty-seven and that the Daleks are going to attack again". In *The Space Museum*, Vicki states that the Daleks invaded Earth "three hundred years" before her own time [c 2193]. In *Remembrance of the Daleks*, the Doctor states that the Daleks conquered Earth in "the twenty-second century".

In *Lucifer Rising*, the Doctor says that the Daleks invade in "twenty-one fifty-eight" (p337). *GodEngine* dates the invasion to 2157; the TV story to 'ten years' later (p240). *The Mutant Phase* sets the TV story in 'nine years' [2168]. It's 'a few decades' after *No Future* [c.2000], 'two centuries' after *Head Games* (p157) [c.2201], it's '2157' in *Killing Ground* (p48), and '2154' in *Return of the Living Dad* (p241).

A production document written in July 1964 gave

2157 - GODENGINE[220] **->** The Doctor and Roz arrived on Mars, but Chris ended up on Pluto's moon of Charon after the TARDIS hit a subspace infarction. The Daleks bombed Charon, but Chris escaped down a Transit stunnel. The Doctor and Roz accompanied an expedition to the North Pole of Mars, which was joined by Ice Warrior pilgrims. Meanwhile, at the pole, the Martian leader Falaxyr was about to complete the GodEngine, a device capable of making suns expel plasma bursts. Falaxyr hoped to negotiate with the Daleks to regain control of Mars. The Doctor arrived at the pole and defeated Falaxyr's amended plan to eliminate the human colony of Jacksonville. The GodEngine was destroyed, and Dalek ships shot down Falaxyr as he fled.

Once the population of Earth was under control, the Daleks set to work in vast mining areas, the largest one covering the whole of Bedfordshire. There were few Daleks on Earth, and they boosted their numbers by enslaving humans and converting them into Robomen. Robo Patrols swarmed across the major cities, armed with whips and machine guns, and controlled by high frequency radio waves.

The Daleks cleared the smaller settlements of people and set them to work in the mines. In the larger cities, Robomen and Daleks patrolled every nook and cranny looking for survivors. The Black Dalek oversaw the mining operations in Bedfordshire. At night, his 'pet', the gruesome Slyther, patrolled the camp, attacking and eating any humans it found trying to escape.

The rebels in London survived by dodging Robo Patrols, raiding warehouses and department stores. Other threats came from escaped zoo animals, packs of wild dogs, human scavengers and traitors. The largest rebel group, under the leadership of the crippled scientist Dortmun, could only muster a fighting force of between fifteen and twenty and survived in an underground bolthole. They had a radio, although as time went by contact was lost with more and more rebel groups. Dortmun spent much of his time developing an acid bomb, the only known weapon that could crack the Dalekenium shells of the invaders.

Humanity still had no idea why the Daleks had invaded - it wasn't for the Earth's mineral wealth, and the Daleks showed no sign of simply colonising the planet.[221]

The Daleks had total control of the Earth, barring a few pockets of resistance, and began a number of projects.[222]

2158 / = 2158 - THE MUTANT PHASE[223] **->** In Kansas, America, an Agnomen wasp worked its way inside a battle-damaged Dalek casing and stung the Dalek creature within. Dalek medics prepared to remove the tainting wasp DNA from the stung Dalek.

= The time-travelling Emperor Dalek arrived with a pesticide, GK50, which the Emperor claimed would destroy the wasp cells and safeguard the future. The Dalek medics complied, but the pesticide failed to work on the larval wasp cells. In the millennia to follow, the wasp DNA would spread through Dalek reproduction plants and taint the entire race, giving rise to the Mutant Phase and leading to Earth's destruction circa 4220.

The Doctor realized the Emperor Dalek's actions had paradoxically created the very condition he was trying to prevent and convinced him to not use the pesticide, averting the Mutant Phase.

Searching Earth records, the Daleks discovered an account of the ICMG's battle with Daleks in 1963, including a description of Skaro's destruction in the future. Forewarned of this, the Daleks plotted to prevent history from transpiring as the Doctor believed it had - they had a new mission to avert the destruction of their homeworld.[224]

In 2160, the Daleks began work on extracting the Earth's core, seeking to replace it with the GodEngine.[225] **Once the Earth's core was destroyed and replaced with a drive system, the Daleks planned to move the entire planet around space.**[226] The Daleks had conquered every planet of the Solar System by 2162.[227]

The High Council of the Time Lords sent their agent Homunculette to a ruined London to acquire the Relic - which arrived from 15,414 - but Qixotl got there first.[228]

c 2167 - THE DALEK INVASION OF EARTH[229] **->** Ten years after the Daleks invaded, 'Project Degravitate' neared its conclusion. Slave workers were instructed to begin clearing operations. The Daleks were tampering with the forces of creation, drilling down through the Earth's crust. A fission capsule was prepared and when detonated, it would release the Earth's magnetic core, eliminating Earth's gravitational and magnetic fields. Once the core was removed, it would be replaced with a power system allowing the Earth to be piloted anywhere in the universe.

Rebels broke into the Dalek Control Room, and ordered the Robomen to attack their masters. The Robomen and slaves overwhelmed the invaders and fled the mining area. The fission capsule was diverted, and upon its detonation the Dalek base - containing the Daleks' power external power supply - and the saucer Alpha Major was destroyed. An active volcano formed on the site of the old Dalek mine.

The Doctor's granddaughter Susan left the TARDIS to make a new life with David Campbell.

The Doctor recovered the TARDIS key that Susan dropped.[230] The Battle of Cassius saw the end of the Dalek blockade of the solar system.[231]

The second Doctor visited a ruined New York clearing up after the Dalek Invasion.[232]

The colony worlds offered to help rebuild, but Earth refused. The Peace Officers were formed in England to neutralise dangerous Dalek artefacts left behind after the Invasion. The attempt at creating a central authority, though, soon splintered into around a hundred dominions.[233]

Unidentified alien beings briefly visited Earth, and one of their number - adopting the name Estella - stayed behind out of love for Duke Orsino, the ruler of Venice. They wed, but he soon lost her in a game of cards. As punishment, she cursed the Duke to extended life so he could better experience the guilt of losing her, and she also cursed the city to destruction in a hundred years' time. Estella was rumoured to have committed suicide by flinging herself into the canal, but the Cult of Our Lady Estella soon emerged to worship her memory.

The aliens evidently left behind paintings from other worlds, including one that depicted a lady in a glass jar, and one showing fox-people in smart outfits. These became part of Orsino's art collection.[234]

The volcano formed by the destruction of the Daleks' base, Mount Bedford, became a tourist attraction. A salvage team recovered a starchart of Earth's whole sector of the galaxy from a derelict Dalek saucer.[235] A powerful cartel of Earth conglomerates took control of the Terran Security Forces. Within five years, it had become a force capable of waging intergalactic war.[236]

Following the Dalek Invasion of Earth, it became clear that there were a number of powerful warlike races in the galaxy. A number of planets, including Earth, Centauri and the Cyrennhics formed the Alliance, a mutual defence organisation. The corporation INITEC supplied the Alliance with state-of-the-art armaments.[237]

In the late twenty-second century, the Monk withdrew the £200 he had deposited two hundred years before and collected a fortune in accrued compound interest.[238] The Doctor once claimed that he was "fully booked" until this time.[239]

On Tara, nine-tenths of the population was wiped out by a plague and replaced by androids.[240] President Borusa kidnapped Susan as part of his plan to gain the secret of perpetual regeneration.[241]

= c 2172 - DAY OF THE DALEKS[242] -> An alternate timeline was created in the 1970s when the World Peace Conferences failed. A series of wars erupted, and over the next century, seven-eighths of the world's population were wiped out. Time travelling Daleks conquered the Earth in the mid-twenty-first century, hoping to exploit the planet's mineral wealth. The remnants of humanity were put to work in prison camps, guarded by Ogron servants. Human guerrillas stole Dalek time-travel technology, and travelled back to the crucial peace conference.

This timeline was erased when the Doctor and Jo ensured that the Peace Conference delegates were evacuated before Auderley House was destroyed.

---

the date as "2042". The trailer for the 1964 serial claimed the story was set in "the year 2000", and in *Genesis of the Daleks*, the Doctor talks of the Daleks' extraction of the Earth's magnetic core in "the year 2000", apparently referring to this story (although he seems to be remembering the movie version, which was set in 2150).

Radio Times consistently dated the story as "2164", as did *The Making of Doctor Who* second edition, *The Doctor Who File* and even the 1994 radio play *Whatever Happened to...Susan Foreman?*. The first edition of *The Programme Guide* set the story "c2060", the second "2164", while *The Terrestrial Index* said "2167". "A History of the Daleks" in *DWM* #77 set the story in "2166". *The Discontinuity Guide* suggested a date of "2174". In John Peel's novelisation of *The Chase*, Vicki says that the Daleks will destroy New York "one hundred years" after 1967.

More detail of the Dalek invasions of both Earth and Mars is given in the Benny NA *Beige Planet Mars*.

230 *GodEngine*

231 *The Crystal Bucephalus, GodEngine*

232 *The Final Sanction*

233 *Legacy of the Daleks*

234 'A hundred years' before *The Stones of Venice*. The painting of the "woman in a jar" probably refers to an Empress of Hyspero from *The Scarlet Empress*.

235 *Cold Fusion*

236 *The Final Sanction* (p75).

237 THE ALLIANCE: *The Terrestrial Index* suggested that a group that included Earth, Draconia and perhaps the Thals, who were all "united to attack and punish the Daleks". This contradicts what we are told on-screen [q.v. 'The Dalek Wars'], and the Alliance is never referred to on television. The Alliance is mentioned in *Original Sin* (p286), and this revised account of its origins appears in *Lords of the Storm* (p201).

238 *The Time Meddler*

239 The Doctor is booked up for "two hundred years" after *The Seeds of Doom*.

240 In *The Androids of Tara*, Zadek, one of Prince Reynart's men, states that the plague was "two hundred years" ago.

241 *The Five Doctors*. There's no indication of how long

In 2172, the Tzun Confederacy invaded Veltroch, but the arboreal Veltrochni clans united to defeat them. The Veltrochni wiped out the Tzun Confederacy, destroying every Tzun starship but leaving behind many Tzun arte-facts and ruins. A whole sector of space containing ten thousand planets was consequently abandoned. Mankind colonised many of these former Tzun worlds, and the Veltrochni begin to fear the spread of humanity.[243]

On 21st July 2172, Agnomen wasps were deliberately agitated to quell crop-threatening caterpillars, but the wasps killed five hundred people in a Kansas town. The governor authorised use of pesticide GK50 to deal with the problem.[244] In 2172, Grant Markham, a future companion of the Doctor, was born.[245]

In the late twenty-second century, England's dominions were consolidated into ten large Domains, including Canterbury, Devon, Edmonds, Haldoran, London and Salisbury. Susan Campbell enlisted as a Peace Officer.[246] The Intercity Wars started and spread across Earth for decades. Military intervention from Earth's colonies enforced peace.[247]

In 2180, FLORANCE's status as a sentient citizen was revoked under the Cumberland Convention. The Dione-Kisanu company bought FLORANCE and installed it at their private base. Director Madhanagopal began experimenting on it in an attempt research human memory and learning. Madhanagopal was an operative for a Brotherhood that sought to augment humanity's psi-powers.[248]

Also in 2180, a Eurogen survey dispatched to see if Ha'olam could become an agricultural planet was abandoned when the company made budget cuts.[249]

The Kusks, a massive, brown-skinned species with advanced computer skills, dispatched a time probe to study various planets' histories, hoping to gather intelligence for potential conquests. The probe malfunctioned near the planet Hirath, and the Kusk spaceship sent to retrieve it failed in its mission. The Kusk crew put themselves into suspended animation. Later, the Temporal Commercial Concerns (TCC) company set up a series of time barriers on Hirath, and rented space there for various races to use as penal colonies. TCC adapted the Kusk spaceship, with the sleeping Kusk crew inside, into a moonbase.[250]

In 2187, Ted Henneker led a rebellion against the Cybermen on Agora.[251]

2191 (January) - TIME OF YOUR LIFE[251] **->** For over twenty years, the Meson Broadcasting Service (MBS) had showed some of the all-time TV classics: *Bloodsoak Bunny*, *The Party Knights and the Kung-Fu Kings*, *Jubilee Towers*, *Prisoner: The Next Generation*, *Life's a Beach* and *Abbeydale High*. The broadcaster successfully rebuffed the claims of the Campaign for the Advancement of Television Standards that such programming as *Death-Hunt 3000*, *Masterspy* and *Horror Mansions* increased violence and criminal behaviour.

On Torrok, the citizens were compelled by law to watch MBS' offerings all day. Peace Keeper robots patrolled every street, rounding up suspected criminals. The Doctor arrived on Torrok during this time and accepted an inquisitive Angela Jennings as his companion. The Time Lords directed the TARDIS to MBS' space station headquarters, where a mechanical adversary killed Angela.

As part of the reality show *Time of Your Life*, the city of Neo Tokyo was teleported from New Earth into a Maston Sphere, where the residents were terrorized. The Doctor discovered that the information-consuming datavore

---

it has been for Susan since she left her grandfather.
242 Dating *Day of the Daleks* - It is "two hundred years" after the UNIT era. The Daleks don't recognise the third Doctor, so they have come from before 2540 and *Planet of the Daleks* (or the alternate history they set up has wiped that story from the new timeline).

A Dalek states that they "have discovered the secret of time travel, we have invaded the Earth again, we have changed the course of history". This isn't, as some fans have suggested, a version of events where the conquest seen in *The Dalek Invasion of Earth* was more successful - the Daleks travel back and invade a full century earlier, after the first attempt has failed.
243 There are frequent references to the Veltrochni and Tzun in the books of David A McIntee. In *White Darkness*, we learn that civilisation on Veltroch is more than three billion years old (p90). The Tzun appear in *First Frontier*, and *Lords of the Storm* reveals much of

their technology and the history of their destruction. The history is further sketched out in *First Frontier* (p94), *Lords of the Storm* (p24), *The Dark Path* (p142). The Veltrochni also appear in *Mission: Impractical*, and the aliens in *Bullet Time* - although never named - could well be Tzun survivors of the *First Frontier* incident.
244 *The Mutant Phase*
245 He's 19 in *Killing Ground*.
246 *Legacy of the Daleks*
247 *The Janus Conjunction*
248 "Forty seven years" before *SLEEPY*. The Brother-hood also plays a role in *The Death of Art* and *So Vile a Sin*.
249 *Seeing I* (p83).
250 'Twenty five years' before *Longest Day*
251 'Four years' before *Killing Ground* (p71).
252 Dating *Time of Your Life* - It is "three weeks into Earth year 2191" (p1).

Krllxk had gone insane from absorbing the entire MBS output. He transmatted Neo Tokyo back home, and the ensuing conflict made the MBS station fly into the sun. Krllxk took refuge in a game-show android, but the Doctor destroyed it. MBS went off the air when the people on Torrok rebelled, overthrowing the totalitarian regime. Grant Markham, a computer programmer who helped the Doctor, joined him on his travels.

2191 - KILLING GROUND[253] -> Humanity thought the Cybermen were extinct. Most were asleep in their Tombs on Telos, but some nomads wandered the galaxy. Earth was still rebuilding from the Dalek Invasion at this time.

The Doctor suspected the Cybermen were involved in the affairs of the home planet of Grant Markham, his companion. They arrived, and the Overseers who ruled the planet on the behalf of the Cybermen captured the Doctor. Grant fell in with the rebels.

One of the rebels, Maxine Carter, used Cybertechnology to build the Bronze Knights, a volunteer army of cyborgs. The Doctor learned that the Cybermen were running out of parts and becoming increasingly reliant on stolen technology. These Cybermen hijacked and adapted a Selechian

warship. The Doctor sabotaged it, releasing radiation that was lethal to the Cybermen. The Bronze Knights left Agora to hunt down more Cybermen, and the remaining colonists rebuilt their planet.

Humanity fought against a number of hostile races in deep space, including the Cybermen. A number of Cyber Wars were fought at the beginning of the twenty-third century, but humanity prevailed.[254] Gustav Zemler's unit fought the Cybermen on the borders of Earth's colonies. Zemler's unit prevailed, but the Cybermen's hostages were also killed. Zemler and his survivors were dishonorably discharged and became mercenaries.[255]

After the Cyber Wars, Eurogen Butler changed their name and became the Spinward Corporation.[256] The former Houses of Parliament were used as a hospice for veterans of the first Cyber Wars.[257]

The I had developed as a gestalt, centaur-like race that seeded technology onto planets, then later returned to harvest the developments. The I acquired some Gallifreyan technology and the eyes of a Time Lord named Savar, and around 2192 used this to facilitate the development of advanced retinal implants on the planet Ha'olam.[258]

---

253 Dating *Killing Ground* - This is set the same year as *Time of Your Life*.
254 Cyber Wars in the twenty-second or twenty-third century were postulated in *Cybermen* and *The Terrestrial Index*, and a number of stories that used those books as reference (including *Deceit, Iceberg, The Dimension Riders, Killing Ground* and *Sword of Orion*) have referred to "Cyberwars" in this time period. This is not the "Cyber War" involving Voga that is referred to in *Revenge of the Cybermen*. We might speculate that while the main force of Cybermen conquer Telos, another group remained active and travelled into deep space, perhaps colonising worlds of their own, and that this breakaway group was wiped out in the Cyber Wars. They seem to keep well away from Earth and only menace isolated human colonies.
255 *The Janus Conjunction* (p98).
256 *Deceit* (p23).
257 *Interference* (p305).
258 *Seeing I*
259 *The Also People* (p29).
260 'A decade' before *The Final Sanction*.
261 *Dreamstone Moon* (p18).
262 *The Janus Conjunction* (p100).
263 Dating *Legacy of the Daleks* - Susan met David when he was 22, and he's now 54 (p15), so it's thirty-two years after *The Dalek Invasion of Earth*. The blurb says it is the late twenty-second century. It's unclear why the Doctor is searching for Sam by travelling in time, rather than space, yet that's the implication of p27, where he is 'allowing' for Thannos time. This does seem to mean

he's looking for Sam *before* he lost her in *Longest Day* circa 2202, but he is admittedly diverted to Earth by a telepathic signal from Susan. While the Doctor thinks he is in the right timezone, perhaps the TARDIS has taken him just a handful of years earlier.
264 *The Chase*. The interplanetary wars have continued for at least "fifty years" according to Steven Taylor.
265 *The Pit* (p86).
266 Stacey's parents are from the 'twenty-third century' in *Placebo Effect*. Stacey was a regular character in the *Radio Times'* Doctor Who comic strip featuring the eighth Doctor.
267 *Managra* (p63).
268 *The Shadow of the Scourge*
269 *Genocide* (p27).
270 'The twenty-third century' according to *Cold Fusion* (p180).
271 *Colony in Space*. Many of the books pick up on this theme.
272 *The Final Sanction*, no date is given on p146, but it must be some time before 2203.
273 Dating *Longest Day* - It's "Ex-Thonnos System, Relative Year 3177" (p15). In *Legacy of the Daleks*, it's stated "In Thannos time it had been 3177" (p27), so it's almost certainly not 3177AD. This is the same time zone as *Legacy of the Daleks* (give or take), *Dreamstone Moon* and *Seeing I*.
274 Dating *Dreamstone Moon* - For Sam, only six days pass between *Longest Day* and *Dreamstone Moon* (p7).
275 Dating *Seeing I* - Sam was en route to the planet Ha'olam at the end of *Dreamstone Moon*, and has only

The buffalo became extinct in 2193.[259] The Selachians sold their Cloak weapons to Earth in the mid-2190s.[260] In 2197, the Dreamstone Moon Mining Company was set up to exploit the discovery of dreamstone on the moon of Mu Camelopides VI.[261] Colonial marines fought in the Alphan Kundekka conflict of 2198.[262]

& 2199 - LEGACY OF THE DALEKS[263] -> The eighth Doctor arrived in New London as the Master started a war between rival Domains Haldoran and London. Haldoran and London themselves died in the conflict, and one of Haldoran's commanders, Barlow, took charge of both regions.

The Master reawoke a hidden Dalek factory to gain an experimental matter transmuter. David Campbell was killed in a struggle with the Master, who fled to the planet Terserus. Susan Campbell destroyed the matter transmuter, an act that ravaged the Master's body. The Time Lords dispatched Chancellor Goth to investigate the disturbance on Terserus, leading to his meeting the now-skeletal Master. A grieving Susan departed in the Master's TARDIS.

The Interplanetary Wars

A rocket full of robots was sent to planets like Mechonus to prepare the way for colonists. The robots, Mechonoids, cleared landing sights and made everything ready for the immigrants. However, a series of interplanetary wars started which continued for over fifty years.

After the wars, many colonies were left isolated or forgotten completely. The space lanes were disrupted, and colonies such as Mechonus were cut off from Earth. Left to their own devices, the Mechonoid robots built and maintained a vast city, awaiting the code that would identify the rightful human colonists.

On Mechonus, the Mechonoids and the Daleks came into conflict around this time. Skaro had records of "Mechons" with "many powerful weapons".[264] Brian Parsons fought in many space conflicts at this time, and his tactics were programmed into android soldiers for many centuries to come.[265] Stacey Townsend was the only survivor when the Cybermen attacked the cargo ship *Dreadnaught*. The Doctor destroyed the Cybermen, and Stacey joined him on his travels.[266]

During the twenty-third century, Jung the Obscure published his theory of the Inner Dark in the Eiger Apocrypha.[267] By the twenty-third century, a riot control gas named Pacificus was invented.[268] Sperm whale songlines were published.[269]

Humanity conducted tests with fusion bombs out on the Galactic Rim. The devices were so powerful they were immediately banned.[270] **The corporations made vast profits from the colonisation of other planets and became a law unto themselves, killing colonists to get to mineral resources. The Adjudication Service became a neutral arbiter of planetary claims.**[271]

Around 2200, the Interbank scandal took place. Chairman Wayne Redfern was indirectly responsible for the bankruptcy of the organization.[272]

& 2202 - LONGEST DAY[273] -> A Kusk rescue party arrived on the moon of Hirath, intent on retrieving the lost time probe. The probe malfunctioned even further and destabilized TCC's time barriers on Hirath, threatening to blow up half the galaxy. The Doctor destroyed the probe, triggering an electrical surge that also killed the rampaging Kusks. The Doctor and his companion, Samantha Jones, were separated in the confusion to follow, and she was launched away from Hirath in a crewless Kusk ship.

& 2202 - DREAMSTONE MOON[274] -> Dreamstones, a material mined from a satellite of Mu Camelopides VI, AKA the "Dreamstone Moon," became very desirable. Consumers would sleep with dreamstones under their pillows to experience vivid dreams. However, Anton La Serre, an artist who recorded and sold his dreams, had a tortuous dreaming experience with a dreamstone and sought to discredit the entire industry.

The Dreamstone Moon Mining Corporation (DMMC) ship *Dreamstone Miner* rescued Sam Jones, who had drifted in the Kusk ship for a week. She was taken to the DMMC mining operation on the Dreamstone Moon, which began to experience tremors. The Doctor arrived and concluded that the entire Moon was a living entity, and that the dreamstones were parts of its brain.

The pained entity shared a special mental link with La Serre, and instinctively began lashing out due to his anger toward DMMC. The entity started projecting mental illusions - Earth Fleet had 500 ships in the Mu Camelopides System on manoeuvres, and the captain of the dropship *Royale* self-destructed his vessel while experiencing such a waking nightmare.

The ship's compliment of one thousand troops was lost, and altogether five thousand people died. The Doctor finally entered La Serre's dreams and calmed him, allowing La Serre to peacefully dream himself to death, and the dreamstone entity fell dormant. DMMC abandoned operations on the Moon. Sam Jones, embarrassed for her previous abandonment of the Doctor, departed the Moon in an evacuation shuttle.

c 2202 - SEEING I[275] -> Sam Jones relocated to the world of Ha'olam, where she initially worked as a volunteer in an INC-run homeless shelter. She turned eighteen during this time. The eighth Doctor searched for Sam and was responsible for 'the Great Umph Massacre of 2202' when he sent data-umphs into the galaxy-wide computer network looking for her.

Still searching for Sam, the Doctor, using the alias Dr. James Alistair Bowman, was arrested as an industrial spy on INC premises. He was given a ten-year sentence and taken to the Oliver Bainbridge Functional Stabilisation Centre (OBFSC). He was questioned by Dr Akalu, the prison's "morale officer." Akalu implanted the Doctor with a retinal implant that provided advance warning of the Doctor's escape attempts.

Sam was hired by the non-profit organisation Livingspace to do volunteer work at Eurogen Village, a desert community for former Eurogen workers.

Akalu set up DOCTOR, an artificial intelligence, to create an accurate psychological profile on the Doctor. DOCTOR would eventually discover 346 reports of TARDIS sightings in hundreds' years worth of data, despite someone erratically, not systematically, erasing nearly all of it.

Sam started a relationship with Paul Hamani, a Eurogen worker assigned to teach her about life on the settlement. They ended their relationship five months later.

Around 2203, the Selachian Empire invaded Rho Priapus, one of Earth's colony worlds.[276] Terran Security Forces (TSF) in response instigated a war to combat the alleged Selachian threat, but the conflict owed more to the Selachians endangering human corporate interests on the arms markets.[277]

On Earth, Professor Laura Mulholland developed the gravity bomb, a devastating weapon capable of making a planet collapse in on itself. The G-bomb boosted Earth's confidence in the conflict with the Selachian Empire, and a warfleet, led by the flagship *Triumph*, left Earth to engage the enemy. The Selachians were forced back to their own system within a year.[278] In 2204, Adam Dresden was on his first TSF mission when the Selachians captured him on Molinar. He was subsequently transported to Ockara as a prisoner.[279]

2204 - THE FINAL SANCTION[280] -> The war with the Selachians was coming to an end. Humans invaded Kalaya, the final planet in need of liberation from the Selachians. After a while, the humans forewent air raids to protect the native population. Out of 1,000 troops, only around 300 survived the campaign.

The second Doctor, Jamie and Zoe arrived on the war-torn Kalaya shortly before Selachian forces abandoned it. The Doctor found himself onboard the flagship *Triumph* as it pursued the retreating Selachians their homeworld of Ockora. The *Triumph*'s G-bomb was launched, turning Ockora into a black hole and obliterating nine million lives there, including 10,000 hostages. Lieutenant Kent Michaels of the TSF gave the final password that launched the bomb, but the history books condemned Commander Wayne Redfern for the catastrophe, deeming him one of the most evil men who ever lived.

A group of surviving Selachians seized control of the *Triumph* and attempted to retaliate against Earth with the ship's second G-bomb. Professor Mulholland detonated the bomb before it could reach Earth, turning the *Triumph* into a second black hole.

& 2205 - SEEING I[281] -> Sam was involved in a failed protest to prevent INC from buying Eurogen Village. She sought to expose INC's corrupt practices and broke into a TCC research plant. She found them growing human

just arrived at the start of this novel. The Doctor sending out Data-umphs in 2202 looking for Sam must mean that he expects to find her in that year. "James Bowman" was the alias that Grace attributed to the Doctor in *Doctor Who - The Movie*.
276 *The Janus Conjunction* (p98).
277 According to *The Final Sanction* page 75. Page 146 suggests the war has been going on for a year.
278 *The Final Sanction* (p73) says this occurs 'almost a year' before 2204. The events are also mentioned on p255.
279 *The Final Sanction* (p196).
280 Dating *The Final Sanction* - The date is given (p4).
281 Dating *Seeing I* - The Doctor is imprisoned for 'three years'. Oddly, according to *SLEEPY*, also by Kate Orman, FLORANCE was trapped in a lab at this point.
282 'Fifty years' after *GodEngine*.
283 Dating *The Janus Conjunction* - It is 'Dateline 14.09.2211 Humanian Era' according to p16.
284 *The Highest Science* (p17).

285 *Strange England* (p7).
286 Dating *The Year of Intelligent Tigers* - No date is given, but references to colonies on Lvan and Gidi link it to *Nightmare of Eden*, and it is clearly early in humanity's colonisation of other planets. That said, the spaceport has been established for a hundred years.
287 'Seventy years' after *GodEngine*.
288 Dating *SLEEPY* - While investigating the Dione-Kisanu Corporation in 2257, the Doctor sends Roz and Bernice go back "thirty years", to "2227"
289 Dating *Frayed* - No date is given, but as children are screened for psychic abilities, and this is an early colony world, it ties in with information given in *SLEEPY*. The oldest child is twelve, perhaps suggesting the colony has been established that long.

clones with no higher brain functions for immoral experimentation.

Now 21, Sam learned about the Doctor's incarceration by hacking into INC's medical databases. She helped to break the Doctor out of prison, and the TARDIS removed his retinal implant. The Doctor had been an inmate of OBFSC for just over three years.

The I gestalt overran the INC Research and Development Complex at Samson Plains to strip-mine its technology. The Doctor liberated the I's organic spaceship from their control, turning the I into mindless drones. Reunited with Sam, he departed for Gallifrey to return Savar's eyes.

DOCTOR, having acquired some of the Doctor's personality traits through studying him, departed Ha'olam and travelled human dataspace with another AI named FLORANCE.

The settlement of Shelbyville was founded on Mars.[282]

2211 - THE JANUS CONJUNCTION[283] -> In 2110, an aged Spacemaster, with one thousand colonists on board, was holed by an asteroid prior to crash-landing on the planet Menda. Led by Gustav Zemler, the mercenaries hired to protect the colonists discovered a hyperspatial Link that joined Menda to its neighbour, Janus Prime. The mercenaries crossed over to Janus Prime but were trapped there for a year, and went insane due to radiation sickness.

In September 2211, the Doctor arrived on Janus Prime and discovered that the hyperspatial Link was an accidental by-product of the Janus System's doomsday device. Gustav Zemler was killed before he could set the Janus Conjunction in motion and turn the sun into a black hole. Sergeant Jon Moslei sacrificed himself to collapse the Link, saving Janus Prime in the process.

The Intergalactic Mineral Exploitation Act was passed in 2217, granting the mining combines vast powers. The corporations had already supplied the colony ships, weather control, terraforming, and computer technology to the colonists.[284] The Doctor, Ace, and Benny visited the Moscow City Carnival in 2219.[285]

? 2225 - THE YEAR OF INTELLIGENT TIGERS[286] -> One year, the Hitchemus tigers suddenly became intelligent, as they were prone to do once in multiple generations. They attempted to seize power, leading to massive conflict with the human colonists. To avert bloodshed, the Doctor destroyed the Hitchemus spaceport and used the tigers' weather control station to exacerbate the planet's already unstable tilt. This would have put all land on Hitchemus under water in ten years, but the humans and tigers - denied outside help - were compelled to work together to save their world. They agreed to live in peace.

Larger spaceships used T-Mat at this time.

The city of Springfield was established near Ascraeus Lacus on Mars around 2227.[287]

2227 - SLEEPY[288] -> The Adjudication Service was just one of many organisations trying to enforce the law. The Serial / Spree Killers Investigations National Unit was one of the hundreds of small agencies operating in tandem with the conventional legal authorities throughout the twenty-third century - often with more powers than the authorities. Thanks to a combination of paranoia and real concern - some political parties took to hiring serial killers - Unit operatives could get in just about anywhere.

In the early twenty-third century, CM Enterprises attempted to create a computer that could think like a human by installing organic components - a cat's brain - into an Imbani mainframe. They succeeded in building a computer that wanted to play with string and sit on newspapers. The Dione-Kisanu Company (DKC), on the other hand, encoded information in the form of memory RNA. Before long, DKC taught a woman the first verse of *Kublai Khan* by injection. In 2223, Madhanagopal finished his work on the AI named FLORANCE, which was taken off-line.

Psychic ability was now recognised by humanity, and standard tests had been introduced. DKC were attempting to encode psi-powers using a model of the human mind: the AI named GRUMPY. When GRUMPY discovered this, he escaped DKC by pushing himself through the computer networks, leaving his own hardware behind. He stored a few years' memories in a data vault in Malindi, tucked away a copy of his operating system in a communications satellite trailing Phobos, and spread pieces of himself across the Solar System. For a decade, DKC kept the fact that GRUMPY had escaped secret and destroyed all they could find of him. GRUMPY became increasingly desperate, and used his psychic ability to terrorise and blackmail. After two years, DKC tracked him down, brought him back to Saturn's moon of Dione and erased the copies he had made of himself.

? 2230 - FRAYED[289] -> Earth sent those with a perceived genetic disposition to crime or latent psychic abilities (the 'future deviants') to the Refuge on Iwa. There was a strict Eugenics Code on Earth. Corporations funded research into psychic ability, but it was felt that the psychics' sense of superiority led them to a criminal lifestyle. Babies without brains were cloned for medical research.

A Time Lord and his companion landed on Iwa. Adopting the names 'the Doctor' and 'Susan', they observed the humans' fight with wolf-like aliens. An uneasy truce was forged, and the humans agreed to help the aliens cure a genetic decay that was afflicting them.

The Colonies

The second quarter of the twenty-third century became a time of great expansion of Earth's colonial efforts. Around 2230, the Survey Corps vessel *Icarus* entered service.[290]

The early-mid part of the twenty-third century was known as 'the First Great Breakout', a period of massive colonial expansion from Earth. Humanity reached the Uva Beta Uva System, which contained fourteen planets. Earth was becoming crowded and polluted, so there was no shortage of settlers for Uva Beta Uva Five. A couple of years later, a mining agent discovered belzite on Uva Beta Uva Three, and the settlers discovered that all of their legal rights were rescinded under the Intergalactic Mineral Exploitation Act of 2217. The mining companies moved in.[291]

In 2237, the artificial intelligence GRUMPY managed to transfer his operating system into the computer of a fighter shuttle, and leapt out into interstellar space. DKC intercepted him at Sunyata, and shot him down over the temperate world of Yemaya, which was being surveyed for possible colonisation. To survive, GRUMPY seeded bits of its RNA into the colonists via their inoculations.[292]

Hindu settlers colonised the Unukalhai system. In 2247 the Colonial Office began to terraform Raghi, the sixth moon of Unukalhai IV (which the settlers named Indra), a process that took forty million people a quarter of a century to complete. Raghi was one of the few colonies to be funded by public donation rather than the corporations. The colonists traded airavata - creatures that lived in the clouds of Indra, and whose DNA contained a natural radiation decontaminant - with the Spinward Corporation.[293]

In 2250, the Argolin warrior Theron started a war with the Foamasi. The war lasted twenty minutes and two thousand interplanetary missiles reduced Argolis to a radioactive wasteland. Following this disaster, the Argolin became sterile and started tachyonics experiments in an effort to perpetuate their race.[294] The Foamasi homeworld of Liasici was destroyed in the war.[295]

---

290 "A hundred and fifty years" before *The Dimension Riders* (p61).
291 "A hundred and fifty years" before *The Romance of Crime* (p8). There's another Great Breakout in the year 5000, according to *The Invisible Enemy*. Uva Beta Five was re-named "New Earth", but is not the planet of the same name in *Time of Your Life*.
292 SLEEPY
293 *Lords of the Storm*
294 *The Leisure Hive*
295 *Placebo Effect*
296 Dating SLEEPY - The Doctor states it is "2257" (p29).
297 *Salvation*
298 *The Empire of Glass*
299 Dating *The Daleks* - The Doctor says in *The Edge of Destruction* that 'Skaro was in the future'. In *The Dalek Invasion of Earth*, the Doctor tells Ian that the first Dalek story occurred "a million years ahead of us in the future" and the twenty-second century is part of the "middle of the history of the Daleks". Where he acquires this information is unclear - he had not even heard of the Daleks when he first met them (whereas other Time Lords fear the Daleks, the Monk knows of them in *The Daleks' Master Plan* and *The Five Doctors* reveals that the Time Lords' ancestors forbid the use of the Daleks in their Games).

However, the Thals in *Planet of the Daleks* [2540] have legends of events in *The Daleks* as being from "generations ago".

In the original storyline for *The Survivors* (as the first story was provisionally titled) the date was given as "the year 3000", with the war having occurred two thousand years before. A revised synopsis dated 30th July, 1963, gave the date as "the 23rd century".

The Terrestrial Index and *The Official Doctor Who & the Daleks Book* both suggested that the Daleks from this story were "new Daleks" created by "crippled Kaled survivors", and that the story is set just after *Genesis of the Daleks* - this is presumably meant to explain the Dal / Kaled question and also helps tie the Dalek history into the *TV Century 21* comic strip, although there is no evidence for it on-screen. The *TV Century 21* comic starts in "2003 AD".

The *TARDIS Logs* dated the story as "2290 AD". The American *Doctor Who* comic suggested a date of "300 AD", on the grounds that the Daleks do not seem to have developed space travel. The FASA Role-playing Game dated the story as "5 BC". "Matrix Databank" in *DWM* #73 suggested that *The Daleks* takes place after *The Evil of the Daleks* and that the Daleks seen here are the last vestiges of a once-great race. This ties in with *The Dalek Invasion of Earth*, but contradicts *Planet of the Daleks*. *Timelink* suggests 900. In the Virgin version of this book, I speculated that in this story the Doctor has returned Ian and Barbara to 1963, but on the wrong side of the galaxy. If it was set at the time of broadcast, it would be a couple of months after they left London, so - stretching a little - it qualifies as 'the future'.

The main problem is that, whenever it's set, we have to reconcile the Daleks seen in first Dalek story - stuck in their city unaware of any life beyond it who are all killed - with the Daleks as galactic conquerors seen in all subsequent stories. We have to postulate (without any evidence from the series) that a faction of Daleks left Skaro at some point between becoming confined to their travel machines and the Neutronic War and they subsequently lost contact with Skaro. This faction of Daleks had a powerful space fleet (*Lucifer Rising*)

2257 - SLEEPY[296] **->** Australia by this time was a wasteland, ruined through centuries of chemical and nuclear pollution, although some Australians had made a fortune from solar power.

Yemaya 4 was ideal for colonisation - it had a large temperate zone, gentle seasons, and biochemistry not too different to that of Earth. The four hundred colonists - mostly Botswanans, South Africans, and Burandans from the United African Confederacy - started accelerated gardens around the habitat dome almost immediately, and were busily turning some of the surrounding meadows into farms. They were going to use several Yemayan native plants as crops, and planetfall had been timed to allow almost immediate planting of Terran seed stock. With the help of drone farmers and AI administrators, the colony thrived for two months.

But then the first infections started. Thanks to the presence of GRUMPY's RNA, colonists developed psychic powers such as telekinesis, telepathy and pyrokinesis. The core of GRUMPY was named SLEEPY. DKC dispatched the warship *Flame Warrior* to Yemaya to safeguard its secrets, but SLEEPY sacrificed itself to destroy the warship. The colonists were able to partly assemble GRUMPY's memories from the RNA in their systems, and learned enough to either blackmail or bring down DKC. The corporation left the colony alone.

Steven Taylor grew up in the ruins of England, and joined up to fight in the interplanetary wars after visiting the devastated New York. He became the helmsman of a battleship, living on spaceships and space stations. He ruined his promotion prospects by complaining about a soldier abusing a civilian on Roylus Prime, and was relegated to solo non-combat missions. His ship was built from modified Dalek designs.[297] In Steven Taylor's time, people on Earth lived in cramped Hiveblocks. His ship crashed on Mechonus when Krayt fighters shot it down.[298]

Skaro

? 2263 - THE DALEKS[299] **-> For centuries the few survivors of the Thal race had lived on a plateau on Skaro, eking out an existence. They relied on rainfall that came only every ten years. One decade, the rain never came. After two years, the Thal Temmosus and his group left the plateau, hoping to find the city of the Daleks. This occurred five hundred years after the Neutronic War, and the Daleks had become affected by the reverse evolution on the planet, and had lost many of their technological secrets. Reconciliation between the Thals and the Daleks proved impossible.**

The Doctor, Susan, Ian and Barbara arrived on Skaro. They explored the Dalek city, then sided with the Thals in wiping out the Daleks.

The Doctor's encounter with the Daleks was Last Contact, when the Time Lords first encountered the race that would ultimately destroy them.[300]

---

invaded the Earth (*The Dalek Invasion of Earth*) and the rest of the Solar System (*GodEngine*), and fought the Mechonoids (*The Chase*). They developed internal power supplies and (at some point after *The Dalek Invasion of Earth*) the 'slatted' design, rather than the 'banded' one seen in the first two stories. Following this - possibly licking their wounds following their defeat in *The Dalek Invasion of Earth* - the survivors of this faction returned to their home planet. They would have discovered a city full of dead Daleks - and perhaps the Doctor's role in their cousins' defeat.

While unsupported by evidence from the show, and a little awkward, it fits in with the facts we learn at the end of *The Space Museum* and *The Chase* - the Daleks now live on Skaro, their influence stretches across time and space, they have limited knowledge of the Doctor, advanced science and a desire for revenge specifically against the Doctor, Ian, Barbara and Susan.

300 *The Gallifrey Chronicles*

LAST CONTACT: It's not recorded when the Daleks discover key facts about the Doctor. By *The Chase*, they can recognise the TARDIS (which they didn't directly see in the two TV stories up to that point, as it was either deep in the petrified forest or buried by rubble),

and they also know the Doctor can travel in time. In *The Chase*, the Daleks refer to 'The Doctor and these three humans', which might imply that they don't think the Doctor is human. Except that one of the other three is his granddaughter Susan and later in the story they *do* refer to the Doctor as 'human'. In *The Chase*, it doesn't even occur to them that Susan might have left, so it's unlikely they've got records of other incarnations of the Doctor or companions. They think he's human in *The Evil of the Daleks*, but said he was from "another galaxy" in *The Daleks' Master Plan*. When the Daleks deal with the Monk and the Master, they don't ever make the connection on-screen that they are from the same planet as the Doctor.

Contrast all of this with *Resurrection of the Daleks*, where they refer (for the first time) to the Doctor as a Time Lord and identify his home planet as Gallifrey.

On the other hand, the Time Lords certainly know of the Daleks - they're referred to in the Doctor's trial in *The War Games*, plus the Time Lords send the Doctor on missions against them in *Planet of the Daleks* and *Genesis of the Daleks*. The Monk and the Master also know about the Daleks. In the time of Rassilon, the Daleks were banned from the Games of Death on

At some point after this time, the Moroks acquired a Dalek from Skaro, then placed it on exhibit in their Space Museum.[301]

? 2265 - THE CHASE[302] **->** Upon discovering time-travel technology, the Daleks on Skaro launched a prototype time machine after the Doctor and his companions Ian, Barbara and Susan.

Nearly fifty years after the interplanetary wars had begun, Earth was still involved, although the end was now in sight. One of the combatants, space pilot Steven Taylor, Flight Red Fifty, was stranded on Mechonus. After several days in the hostile jungle, he was captured by the Mechonoids, who still maintained their city in preparation for the human colonists. Unable to crack their code, Taylor was imprisoned. Two years after this the TARDIS arrived, pursued by the Daleks. The Mechonoid City, the Mechonoids and the Daleks were destroyed, and Taylor left in the TARDIS.

The Daleks used time-travel to go back to Earth in the twenty-first century and reinvade the planet. This time they succeeded.[303] The Computers and Cybernetic Systems Act was passed on Uva Beta Uva in 2265.[304] **By 2270, shortly after Pangol's birth, the Argolin had called a moratorium of their recreation programme. Instead, they set up the Leisure Hive, which offered a range of holiday pursuits for intergalactic tourists while promoting peace and understanding between races. Argolis became the first leisure planet.** Meanwhile, a central government took control of the Foamasi planet, breaking the power bases of the old

Lodges. The new government sought restitution with Argolis.[305]

Humanity had consolidated its position, and now possessed a large number of colony worlds. Both the Earth government and the corporations were quite capable of closing down the supply routes to uneconomic or uncooperative colonies, abandoning them entirely.

Away from Earth, life was often still very harsh. The corporations or governing elites that controlled each colony discovered that as long as Earth was kept supplied with minerals and other resources, Earth Central would turn a blind eye to local human rights abuses.[306]

Stanoff Osterling was regarded as one of the two greatest playwrights in human history. His work conformed to the stage conventions of his time, following the Greek tradition of reporting offstage action in elegant speeches rather than seeing it performed. The galaxy's economy was damaged after the wars and the colonies could not afford anything more lavish, but this reliance on dialogue and plotting rather than technological innovation led to a flourishing of the theatre across the galaxy. Osterling was regarded as a genius in his own time for such plays as *Death by Mirrors*, *The Captain's Honour* and *The Mercenary*. His greatest achievement, however, was felt to be his lost play *The Good Soldiers* (2273) that dealt with the aftermath of the battle at Limlough. The Doctor helped transcribe the play, as Osterling had restioparothis.[307]

The terraforming of Raghi was completed.[308] The Mutant Rights Act was passed in 2278. Uva Beta Uva III was at the centre of a belzite rush unparalleled in human history around this time.[309]

Gallifrey, so the Gallifreyans then knew of the Daleks, but there's no evidence that the two races made contact. There's another continuity problem here - why is it that the Doctor and Susan *don't* know about the Daleks before they meet them in *The Daleks*? It's a particular problem because by *The Dalek Invasion of Earth*, the Doctor seems au fait with their complete history. It's possible, as with so much history of that period, that the modern Time Lords had long lost or filed away their knowledge of the Daleks.

We hear the Daleks and Time Lords have all but wiped each other out in *Dalek* and *The Parting of the Ways*.

301 In *The Space Museum*, the Moroks have a Dalek specimen from "Planet Skaro", one with horizontal bands rather than vertical slats. It seems likely that the Moroks raid Skaro at some undisclosed time around *The Daleks*. It's unlikely it was before, as it's implied that the Daleks have no knowledge of life on other planets. Although this in turn contradicts *Genesis of the Daleks*, in which both Davros and the Dalek leader express a wish to conquer other worlds once they know the

Doctor is an alien.

302 Dating *The Chase* - The Daleks send an execution squad after their "greatest enemies": the Doctor, Ian, Barbara and Susan (whom they are unaware has left the TARDIS crew). As this was the Dalek story that followed *The Dalek Invasion of Earth*, that might suggest they are seeking revenge for that specific defeat. The Dalek time machine was named the DARDIS in the script but not on-screen. *The TARDIS Logs* suggested a date of "3773 AD".

In *The Daleks' Master Plan*, Steven states that he is from "thousands of years" before the year 4000, making him one of the earlier deep space pilots. This fits in with the generally low level of technology the Mechonoids possess.

The first and second editions of *The Programme Guide* set dates of "2150" and "2250" respectively, *The Terrestrial Index* settled on "early in the 27th Century". The American *Doctor Who* comic suggested a date of "2170". 'A History of the Daleks' in *DWM* #77 claimed a date of "3764 AD". *The Discontinuity Guide* suggested that Steven fought in "one of the Cyber Wars, or the

c 2285 - VENGEANCE ON VAROS[310] -> The Galatron Mining Corporation and the AMORB prospect fought over mineral rights on the planets of the galaxy, often with little concern for local populations. One such place was Varos, a former prison planet (pop. 1,620,783) in the constellation of Cetes. An officer elite ran Varos and lived in relative luxury, although everyone was confined to enclosed domes with artificial atmospheres. A majority of the people had the constitutional right to vote for the Governor's execution. Until traces were detected on the asteroid Biosculptor, Varos was long thought to be the only source of zeiton-7 ore, a fuel for space / time vehicles.

In the late twenty-third century, Galatron Mining and the government of Varos entered negotiations for the zeiton-7 ore. The engineers of every known solar system needed zeiton to power their space/time craft, but Galatron supplied food to Varos. They had a stranglehold over the colony and were able to keep the price down to seven credits a unit. Successive Governors had developed an entertainment industry, Comtech, that sold footage of the executions, tortures and escape attempts of prisoners to every civilised world. This not only acted as a deterrent for potential rebels, but kept the majority of the population entertained.

Eventually one Governor negotiated the fair price of twenty credits a unit for Varos' zeiton.

2290 - THE LEISURE HIVE[311] -> By 2290, it was clear that the Leisure Hive on Argolis was in trouble. Last year's bookings had fallen dramatically, and advance bookings for 2291 were disastrous. Argolis now faced competition from other leisure planets such as Abydos and Limus 4. The West Lodge of the Foamasi offered to buy the planet, but the board refused and instead pinned their hopes on tachyon experiments conducted by the Earth scientist Hardin. Agents of the Foamasi government arrested two members of the West Lodge, who were attempting to establish a power base on Argolis, and it was discovered that the Tachyon Recreation Generator could rejuvenate the Argolin. The Argolin and Foamasi governments re-opened negotiations.

Checkley's World, "The Horror Planet", was settled in 2290 and selected as the best location for a scientific research station. The laboratories were released from state control a decade after the planet was colonised, and the facilities were funded by a number of empires and corporations, including the Arcturans, Riftok and Masel. Earth Government remained the major partner. Weapon systems such as compression grenades, Freire's gas and the Ethers - genetically engineered ghost-troops - were developed.[312]

Draconian conflict". *Timelink* suggests "3550".

There's no indication that the Daleks are in their native time when they fight the Mechonoids at the end of the story, but the Daleks have fought the Mechonoids before, suggesting it might be.

Incidentally, this volume spells "Mechonous" and "Mechonoids" in accordance with the spelling used in the script and *The Chase* episode six credits, and later adopted by Big Finish. The episode five credits offer the alternative spelling of "Mechanoids".

303 *Day of the Daleks*

304 *The Romance of Crime*

305 *The Leisure Hive*

306 Many stories feature Earth colonies that supply the home planet and are subject to tyrannical regimes. I see this as a specific era in future history, when space travel and interplanetary communications were still limited and have placed most of these stories together in the period just prior to the formation of the Earth Empire. The New and Missing Adventures have attempted to weave a more systematic and consistent 'future history' for Earth, and many have concerned themselves with this period of early colonisation, corporate domination and increasing centralisation.

307 *Theatre of War*

308 'Nearly a quarter of a century' before *Lords of the*

Storm.

309 'About a hundred and fifty years' before *The Romance of Crime*.

310 Dating *Vengeance on Varos* - The Governor states that Varos has been a mining colony for "centuries" and it has been stable "for over two hundred years". Peri tells the Governor that she is from "nearly three centuries before you were born". The story takes place before *Mindwarp*. Mentors must live longer than humans, as the Mentor Sil appears in both stories (although he changes colour from brown to green between the two). The novel set it in "the latter part of the twenty-third century", as did *The Terrestrial Index*. *The Discontinuity Guide* set a range "between 2285 and 2320". *Timelink* said "2324".

311 Dating *The Leisure Hive* - Romana establishes that the war was in "2250", "forty years" before.

312 *The Highest Science*

2294 - THE STONES OF VENICE[313] -> After overthrowing yet another reign of terror, the Doctor and Charley arrived in Venice on the eve of its destruction. The gondoliers of Venice, now amphibians with webbed hands and toes, eagerly awaited the chance to claim the city once it sank beneath the waves.

A series of tremors struck the city, but the Doctor discovered that the "late" Estella, now posing as a city resident named Eleanor Lavish, had once owned an alien device capable of altering reality. The device had kept Estella and Duke Orsino alive for a century by draining Venice's life force, leading to its present decay. The Doctor recovered the device, and Orsino proposed that he and Estella end their lives for Venice's sake. Estella agreed out of continued love for Orsino, and the device turned them into ash, saving the city. The high priest of the Cult of Estella made off with their ashes, possibly to worship them.

c 2295 - WHISPERS OF TERROR[314] -> Despite a dislike of the visual medium, Visteen Krane became wildly acclaimed as the greatest actor of his age. His body of work was chiefly confined to audio recordings and a few photographs. Later, he became a politician and stood for Presidency with his agent, Beth Pernell, as his running mate.

Before the election, Krane seemingly committed suicide in the Museum of Aural Antiquities, an institution dedicated to the study of all things audio. Pernell pledged to run in Krane's place and continue his policies. The Doctor and Peri arrived and discovered that at the moment of his death, Krane used advanced sound equipment to transfer his brainwaves into the sound medium. Krane had become a creature of pure sound, demented from his transformation and outraged at Pernell, who had engineered his murder.

The Krane-creature attempted to endlessly replicate itself and seize control of the planet, but the Doctor thwarted the scheme and shocked Krane back to sanity. The Doctor and Krane exposed Pernell's plans, and Krane agreed to stay at the Museum to aid Curator Gantman with his research. Pernell fled, but Krane engineered an automobile accident that killed her.

The colony ship *Justinian* set off for Ordifica at the end of the twenty-third century.[315]

---

313 Dating *The Stones of Venice* - The story itself says that it's the 'twenty-third century', but *Neverland* gives a firm date of 2294.

314 Dating *Whispers of Terror* - No date is given in the story itself, but references to the play *The Good Soldiers* link it to information given in *Theatre of War*. The story is set within a generation of the first performance of the play.

315 *Interference*

316 "Four hundred years" before *The Sensorites*. There is also a Central City on Earth in the year 4000, according to *The Daleks' Master Plan*.

317 In *The Dimension Riders,* Ace tells Lieutenant Strakk that she comes from Perivale, and he says that the area is a "forest" (p68).

318 'About four hundred years' after the 1909 section of *Birthright*.

319 *Synthespians*™

320 *The Highest Science* (p49).

321 Jake and Madelaine appear in *Goth Opera*, and we learn of their fate in *Managra* (p64).

322 *SLEEPY*

323 'Fifteen hundred years' before *A Device of Death*.

324 *The Taking of Planet 5* (p219).

325 *The Twin Dilemma*

326 About five years before *Excelis Decays*.

327 Dating *Excelis Decays* - It is three hundred years before *The Plague Herds of Excelis*, a Bernice Summerfield audio, which is outside the scope of this book. However, *Plague Herds* is set around 2601, the period Benny has settled in, allowing us to date the

Excelis saga.

328 Dating *The Slow Empire* - No date is given, but it's before *Burning Heart*, because the Piglet People of Glomi IV are mentioned here and extinct there. This date is completely arbitrary. The realm is typically referred to just as 'the Empire', and is here referred to as 'the Slow Empire' for clarity.

329 Dating *The Twin Dilemma* - In his novelisation, Eric Saward places the story around "2310". This is neither confirmed nor contradicted on-screen. The freighter disappears "eight months" before *The Twin Dilemma*, which the novelisation sets in August. A computer monitor says that the "last contact" with the freighter was made on "12-99". If the twelve stands for the twelfth month, the ninety-nine might stand for the last year of a century. *The Programme Guide* set the story "c2310", *The Discontinuity Guide* in "2200".

330 *SLEEPY*

331 'Two hundred and fifty years' before *The Also People*.

332 *Fear of the Dark*. The book's internal dating is confused. On p81, the Doctor finds a record dated '2319.01.12', which puts these events seventy-three years before the novel takes place. However, Tegan claims this happened 'one hundred and fifty years ago' (p81), and the Doctor says it was 'over one hundred and sixty years' ago (p93).

333 *The Also People* (p54).

The Twenty-Fourth Century

By the twenty-fourth century, the lower half of England had become a vast Central City.[316] Much of what had been West London was covered in forest.[317] Duronite, an alloy of machonite and duralinium, was discovered in the early twenty-fourth century. Influenza had been eradicated.[318] The James Bond films were remade in the twenty-fourth century.[319]

Suspended animation ships were still available in the twenty-fourth century, but they had been superseded by the invention of super light drives.[320] Jonquil the Intrepid destroyed the vampires Lord Jake and Lady Madelaine, but their descendants survived for many thousands of years.[321] On a visit to the twenty-fourth century, the Doctor learnt about the colony at Yemaya.[322] Landor, on the galactic rim, was colonised around now.[323]

Early in the twenty-fourth century, a philosopher on a colony world published a monograph, *The Myth of the Non-Straight Line*. The population had ceased being able to conceive of circles. The planet was quaratined as scientists from a survey ship attempted to work out why.[324] **The fourth Doctor and one of his fellow Time Lords, Azmael, met on Jaconda around this time.**[325]

Circa 2996, Grayvorn abandoned his "Lord Vaughn Sutton" identity and covertly continued his socio-political engineering in Excelis. The leaders of Artaris' city-states met in secret to sign the Artaris Convention, a bill of rights designed to end the war between them. Grayvorn found the conflict too useful to his industrial efforts and sabotaged the accord. Grayvorn's research culminated in the creation of lumps of bio-mass named "Meat Puppets," which became his master shock troops. He used the Relic's abilities to rip the souls from dissidents and infuse the Meat Puppets with life.[326]

c 2301 - EXCELIS DECAYS[327] -> Excelis was now in a permanent state of war. Grayvorn's ambition started to reach beyond Artaris, and he desired to deploy his "Meat Puppet" shock troops through the whole of time and space. The Doctor arrived on Artaris and merged his soul with the Relic, exerting enough power to send Grayvorn's captured souls to the afterlife. Grayvorn's "Meat Puppets" consequently became dormant, quashing his plans. Rather than accept defeat, Grayvorn activated Excelis' orbital defence grid and bombarded every major city on Artaris with nuclear missiles. Grayvorn died in the onslaught, but the Doctor escaped.

The saga of Artaris and the Relic continues in the Bernice Summerfield audio "The Plague Herds of Excelis."

? 2305 - THE SLOW EMPIRE[328] -> The Slow Empire had been founded in a region of space where the laws of physics prohibited faster-than-light travel. Some worlds facilitated trade and communication via "Transference Pylons," which transmitted Ambassadors and materials between worlds at light speed. However, the Empire founders had long ago killed themselves through warfare, which helped to plunge the Empire into decay.

The Empire world Shakrath was ruled by a corrupt Emperor who gave visitors generous receptions for posterity, then sent them to the torture chambers. Some centuries previous on Goronos, a slave class had successfully revolted but found themselves unable to function without their masters. They transferred their minds into an elaborate "Cyberdyne" computer reality and Goronos became an urban wasteland. On Thakrash some five hundred years previous (as that planet recorded time), a metamorphic Collector crashed onto the planet and ruined its Transference Pylon. The slaves there revolted, forcing Thakrash into isolation.

A disturbance in the Time Vortex prompted some of its inhabitants, the Vortex Wraiths, to flee in fear of their lives. A group of Vortex Wraiths manifested on the long-dead homeworld of the Empire founders and usurped control of the Pylon system. The Wraiths hoped to manifest their entire race in its billions via the Pylons, and tried to coerce the Doctor's help by threatening the inhabitants of multiple worlds in the Empire. The Doctor betrayed the Wraiths by shorting out the main Transference Pylon, both turning the Wraiths into ash and generating a pulse that would, in time, annihilate every Pylon and end the corrupt Empire.

? 2310 (August) - THE TWIN DILEMMA[329] -> The Earth feared attacks by aliens, and the Interplanetary Pursuit Squadrons were established. The mathematical prodigies Romulus and Remus were abducted in the Spacehopper Mk III Freighter XV773, which had been reported destroyed eight months before. Romulus and Remus mysteriously reappeared on Earth shortly afterward, claiming the gastropod Mestor, who planned to destroy Jaconda and spread his eggs throughout the universe, had kidnapped them. The Jocondans had overthrown their leader and defeated his plans, with the help of the Doctor and their former leader, Azmael.

Youkali Press published *An Eye for Wisdom: Repetitive Poems of the Early Ikkaban Period* by Bernice S. Summerfield in 2315.[330] The Dyson Sphere of the Varteq Veil had begun to break up.[331] Humans arrived on the moon of Akoshemon, on the edge of the Milky Way, in 2319. By this time, there was a Human Sciences Academy on Mars, and a base on Titan.[332]

Third Eye released their HvLP, *Outta My Way Monkey-boy* in 2327.[333] In 2341, a Rutan spy adopted the identity of Sontaran Major Karne. An attack on a Sontaran cruiser was staged, and the Sontarans recovered his escape pod.

For decades, the Rutans received top-level Sontaran military secrets.[334] In 2350, the Jullatii would have over-run the Earth but for INITEC's invention of the boson cannon.[335]

? 2366 - THE MACRA TERROR[336] **->** The crab-like Macra had infiltrated a human colony, using indoctrination techniques to force the colonists to extract a deadly gas that the Macra breathed. The colonists were kept in a state of complacent happiness. Eventually, the Doctor, Jamie, Ben and Polly exposed the Control - the colony's propaganda spokesperson - as a giant Macra. The Doctor directed Ben to destroy the Marca's gas pumps, which slew the invaders.

Walton Winkle became known throughout the Earth Empire as "Uncle Winky, the man who put a smile on the galaxy". He founded the amusement park Winky Wonderland on Io, but entered hibernation inside his "Cosmic Mountain" on 18th December, 2367, due to a heart condition. He wouldn't revive from stasis until shortly before the end of the universe.[337]

Around 2370, human settlers colonised Tairngaire. The capital city was built on an isthmus and named New Byzantium. The planet rapidly became one of the more prosperous colonies. The temporary lights built by the settlers eventually became the Lantern Market. [338]

2371 - LORDS OF THE STORM[339] **->** The Sontarans, fresh from destroying the Rutan installation at Betelgeuse V, attempted to use captured Tzun technology against their eternal enemies. They genetically tagged the human population of the Unukalhai System, intending that a Rutan sensor sweep would indicate a Sontaran population of one hundred million. The Rutan would send a fleet from Antares and the Sontarans planned to ignite a brown dwarf

using the Tzun Stormblade, destroying the Rutans and the whole system along with it. The Doctor defeated the plan.

In 2375, the police broke up the notorious Nisbett firm, a criminal gang responsible for extortion, fraud, smuggling, arms dealing, torture and multiple murder. Tony, Frankie and Dylan the Leg were all executed, but the Nisbett brothers - Charlie and Eddie - escaped.[340] Sontaran Commander Vrag's commando squad was timescooped to the Eye of Orion by Time Lord Ryoth, shortly after being presented with a medal by Admiral Sarg.[341]

2376 - SHAKEDOWN[342] **->** The Sontarans secured information about the Rutan Host that could prove decisive in their war: long ago, a wormhole had been established between Ruta III and Sentarion. In the event of a Sontaran victory, the Rutan Great Mother would use the tunnel to escape her fate. The Sontarans prepared to send a battlefleet down the wormhole to kill the Great Mother, but the Rutan spy Karne discovered the plan. The Doctor tracked Karne down to the human colony of Megacity, and was able to thwart the Sontaran and Rutan plots.

The colony world Gadrell Major was on the brink of nuclear war in 2377, leading the population to construct fallout shelters. Around this time, the Earth was at war with the Phractons.[343] Dymok demanded isolation from Earth in 2378. Imperial Earth Space Station *Little Boy II* was built to oversee the planet.[344]

c 2378 - THE ANDROIDS OF TARA[345] **->** On Tara, the Doctor prevented the Count Grendel from usurping the throne from its rightful heir, Prince Reynart. Grendel escaped to fight another day.

---

334 "Thirty years" before *Lords of the Storm* (p263).

335 *Original Sin* (p287).

336 Dating *The Macra Terror* - The planet was colonised "many centuries" ago. This date is somewhat arbitrary, but it allows the story to fit into a period in which Earth's colonies are relatively remote and unregulated. The level of technology is reasonably low. The second edition of *The Making of Doctor Who* described the setting as "the distant future". *The Programme Guide* set the story "c.2600", *The Terrestrial Index* preferred "between 2100 and 2150", *Timelink* "2670".

337 *Zagreus*, although this is part of a suspect simulation.

338 Tairngaire was colonised "three hundred years" before *Shadowmind* (p32).

339 Dating *Lords of the Storm* - The Doctor states that it is "Earthdate 2371" (p23).

340 "Five or six years" before *The Romance of Crime* (p62-63).

341 *The Eight Doctors*. Not date given, but Sarg appears in *Shakedown*, so it is before that time.

342 Dating *Shakedown* - There is no date given in the book, the story synopsis or the video version. The novel is set after *Lords of the Storm*. The Rutans assert that the spy disguised as Karne "died long ago" (p66), but he is still a recent memory. I have arbitrarily decided that five years have elapsed.

343 'Ten winters' and 'many years' before *Infinite Requiem*.

344 *Divided Loyalties* (p31).

345 Dating *The Androids of Tara* - The Doctor implies that Tara is "400 years and twelve parsecs" away from Earth at the time of *The Stones of Blood*. I assume that the TARDIS travelled into the future, not the past, and

2379 (3rd July) - MINDWARP[346] -> The Mentors of Thoros Beta continued to trade across the galaxy via the warpfold relay, supplying phasers to the Warlords of Thordon, and weapons that allowed Yrcanos of the Krontep to conquer the Tonkonp Empire. They also traded with such planets as Wilson One and Posikar.

The brain of his Magnificence Kiv, the leader of the Mentors, continued to expand in his skull. He enlisted the services of Crozier, a human scientist who specialised in the transfer of consciousness. Crozier experimented on a number of Thoros Betan creatures and the Mentors' captives, creating hybrids and exploring with the ageing process. After a decade of hard work, he had developed a serum that allowed him to place any brain in any body.

Subsequent events are unclear - it appears that the Time Lords intervened to prevent the threat posed to the course of evolution across the universe, causing Kiv to be killed. The Doctor's companion, Peri Brown, was seemingly killed but in reality remained on Thoros-Beta, where she eventually married Yrcanos.

The late twenty-fourth century saw wars around the Rim Worlds of Tokl.

c 2380 (21st - 22nd April) - THE ROMANCE OF CRIME[347] -> In the late 2370s, the Ceerads (Cellular Remission and Decay) - mutants - were purged on Vanossos. Some survived and resettled on Uva Beta Uva Six, leading to conflict with the colonists in that system. The galaxy faced another recession at this time.

Xais was the last of the Ugly Mutants and the self-proclaimed Princess of the Guaal Territories. She was a genius terrorist who murdered two thousand people, and was executed by particle reversal in 2377. Xais had learned, however, how to transfer her consciousness into the substance helicon. Her mind came to reside in a helicon mask made by the artist Menlove Stokes, enabling her to possess people.

Xais teamed up with the criminal Nisbett brothers and their Ogrons, claiming to have discovered rich belzite

deposits on Uva Beta Uva Eleven. In fact, the planet contained a great deal of helicon, through which Xais hoped to generate duplicates of herself and commit mass slaughter. The Nisbett brothers perished as part of this affair, but the Doctor, Romana and K9 worked to stop Xais' plan. Xais' mind became trapped in a mass quantity of helicon, which expanded to cover the whole of Uva Beta Uva Eleven. The Doctor supplied one of his associates, the police investigator Spiggot, with a formula that could destroy the helicon and Xais within.

Gilbert M was exiled from Vasilip when he accidentally wiped out half the planet's population with a germ he'd been working on. By this time, there were scheduled interplanetary flights and he simply travelled to Terra Alpha with the Kandy Man's bones in his briefcase.[348]

& 2381 (29th March) - THE DIMENSION RIDERS[349] -> Half the planets colonised by humanity had been abandoned during the wars. But now, generally, this was a period of interplanetary peace.

The Survey Corps existed to patrol space and deal with situations unsuitable for military or humanitarian missions. As such, Survey Corps vessels had both troopers (armed with state-of-the-art Derenna handguns) and support staff. By the end of the twenty-fourth century, however, underfunding meant that many of the Corps' ships were obsolete.

On 22nd March, 2381, Space Station Q4 in the fifty-fourth sector of charted space, on the edge of the spiral arm and human territory, was attacked by the Garvond's Time Soldiers. The station's crew were aged to death. The Survey Corps vessel *Icarus* investigated, and discovered that Q4 was one end of a Time Focus leading to Earth in 1993. The Garvond intended to trigger temporal paradoxes, then use the Time Focus to absorb chronal energy. In the following battle, Darius Cheynor, second-in-command of the *Icarus*, distinguished himself.

---

that Tara is an abandoned Earth colony (as the Tarans know of life on other planets). *The Terrestrial Index* set the story in the "50th century", *The Discontinuity Guide* in the "2370s".

346 Dating *Mindwarp* - The Valeyard announces that the story starts in the "24th Century, last quarter, fourth year, seventh month, third day". There is a case to be made for 2379, but not "2479" as suggested by the third edition of *The Programme Guide*. Peri is apparently killed in *Mindwarp*, but is revealed as having survived in *The Ultimate Foe*, and returns in the novel *Bad Therapy*. A fabricated image of her older self appears in *Her Final Flight*.

347 Dating *The Romance of Crime* - Uva Beta Uva was "colonised in Earth year 2230" according to Romana (p47); the story is set "a hundred and fifty years later" (p8). The month and day are given on p46.

348 *The Happiness Patrol*

349 Dating *The Dimension Riders* - It is "the late twenty-fourth century" (p2). The Doctor repeats this, adding it is "Just before Benny's time, and after the Cyberwars" (p25) - this analysis comes from *The Terrestrial Index* rather than the television series. The date is not precisely fixed until the sequel, *Infinite Requiem*, which is set in 2387, "six years" after the events of the first book. "March 22nd" was "one week ago" (p76).

Cheynor was offered command of the *Phoenix*.[350]

2382 - FEAR OF THE DARK[351] -> Humanity had made contact with the Vegans, a proud mining race, by this time. Earth had interests in the Antares, Betelgeuse, Denox, Kaltros Prime and Earth Colony E5150. Suspended animation was still in use, and neurolectrin was used to resuscitate sleepers. The University of Tyr specialised in temporal compression.

The Doctor was drawn to the moon of Akoshemon when the Dark - an ancient being ravenous for blood - influenced Nyssa's mind. The Dark hoped to manifest itself physically in our dimension, but the Doctor destroyed it.

? 2385 - SLIPBACK[352] -> The TARDIS was pulled out of the Vortex by illegal time experiments aboard the starship *Vipod Mor*. A Maston, an extinct monster, attacked the Doctor and Peri. The Doctor discovered that a botched maintenance job had endowed the ship's computer with a split personality, and one of its personas was planning to take the ship back in time to impose order on the universe. The Doctor was about to stop the time journey when a Time Lord made contact to inform him that the *Vipod Mor* was part of the established history - it would explode upon arrival, creating the Big Bang.

In 2386, Unreal Transfer was discovered.[353] The artist Menlove Stokes entered cryogenic sleep, hoping to awaken in an era that better appreciated his work. He was revived in the Fifty-Eighth Segement of Time.[354] When her colleagues were captured, a physicist travelled back in time to Little Caldwell, 1983. With the help of Isaac Summerfield, she returned home and freed her workmates.[355]

The same year, slow compression time - a method of slowing down time in a small area - was first theorised. Within a couple of years a slow time converter, or 'time telescope' had been built.[356] A law enforcement agency, the Bureau, discovered an alien time corridor in the Playa del Nuttingchapel. They dispatched an agent to investigate in 1930, where he adopted the alias Percy Closed.[357]

2387 (29th May) - INFINITE REQUIEM[358] -> In the late 2380s, there was a famine on Tenos Beta and storms in the Magellani System. There was also more co-operation between the various elements of the Earth's space navy. Over the next couple decades the military, the ships of the Guild of Adjudicators, the Survey Corps and the corporations' own battle squadrons unified into the Space Fleet.

The Earth colony of Gadrell Major was rich in porizium ore, a valuable material used in medicine. The planet also had strategic value. When the Phracton fleet attacked the colony, Darius Cheynor and the *Phoenix* were sent to investigate. The Phracton Swarm were telepathic cyborgs with a communal mind, and their tanks - flamers - devastated much of the planet.

Cheynor negotiated a settlement with the Phractons, but a breakaway faction sought to gain retribution for the murders of some Practon delegates. The rogue group assassinated Cheynor. This led to the Phractons achieving some vindication, and further negotiations would lead to peace.

---

350 *Infinite Requiem*

351 Dating *Fear of the Dark* - The date is given on the back cover. The personnel file of a mineral pirate, Jyl Stoker, says she departed Earth Central some years back in 2363 (p109), and Tegan notes it has been '400 years' since 1982 (p118). It is after the time when Mechonoids were used. The Vegans first appeared in *The Monster of Peladon*.

352 Dating *Slipback* - An arbitrary date. The *Vipod Mor* is undertaking a census, perhaps placing it in the same time period as *The Happiness Patrol*. The illegal time travel experiments in this story also fit neatly with the time travel research mentioned in a variety of other adventures set in the twenty-fourth century.

353 *The Leisure Hive*

354 *The Well-Mannered War* (p273).

355 She's from 'the twenty-fourth century' according to *Return of the Living Dad* (p41).

356 *The Highest Science* (p203, p235).

357 'Many hundreds of years' after *The English Way of Death*, with reference to the group Third Eye (p37).

358 Dating *Infinite Requiem* - The year is quickly established as "2387" (p5). The precise date is given (p273). It is "six years" since *The Dimension Riders* (p15).

359 Dating *The Happiness Patrol* - Terra Alpha is an isolated colony, apparently in the same system as Terra Omega. While Trevor Sigma's casual dismissal of Earth may suggest the story is set far in the future, the Doctor states only that the planet was "settled some centuries" in Ace's future. Interstellar travel is via "rocket pods". *Timelink* suggests "2788".

360 *The Highest Science*

361 *The Taking of Planet 5*

362 'Twelve years' before *Divided Loyalties*.

363 *The Happiness Patrol*

364 *Synthespians*™

365 Dating *The Pit* - Benny states that the Seven Planets were destroyed "Fifty years before my time... 2400" (p9).

? 2388 - THE HAPPINESS PATROL[359] -> The Galactic Census Bureau at Galactic Centre surveyed every colonised planet every six local cycles and, where necessary, suggested measures to control the population size.

On one such planet, Terra Alpha, the native Alphidae were driven underground by the settlers, who covered the planet in sugar fields and factories. Offworlders were restricted to the Tourist Zones. The planet was ruled by Helen A, who insisted that her citizens be happy. To this end, the planet was gaily painted, muzak poured from loudspeakers on every street corner and Helen A created the "Happiness Patrol", which was composed of women authorised to murder the so-called "Killjoys". She also employed the services of the Kandy Man, an artificial being of pure sugar who created sweets that killed people.

Terrorists, protest groups and the Alphidae (now confined to the network of sugar pipes) all resisted, and Helen A authorised the 'routine disappearance' of some 499,987 people, 17 percent of the population. With the Doctor's invention, Helen A's regime fell in one night. The Kandy Man's candy centre melted.

The Intergalactic Taskforce served the Inner Planets in the late twenty-fourth century.

Throughout the latter half of the twenty-fourth century, the notorious criminal Sheldukher - a ruthless murderer, thief and extortionist - menaced the galaxy. He destroyed the entire Krondel constellation for no apparent reason other than that he could. In 2389, he planned his biggest coup yet, and set about recruiting accomplices.

Marjorie Postine had been an aggressive child, and her parents sold her to the military, a common practice in the commercially-minded twenty-fourth century. She became a mercenary, and Sheldukher secured her services by offering her a Moosehead Repeater, a rifle capable of blowing a hole in a neutron star. She was the veteran of seventeen front-line conflicts. Her right arm was a graft-job, performed by an unqualified surgeon in a trench on Regurel, and her bald head was scarred and lumpy.

A couple of years before, Rosheen and Klift had infiltrated McDrone Systems and used their position to embezzle a vast sum of money. The central markets collapsed, causing entire planetary economies in the fourth zone to collapse into starvation and war. Millions died. The planet Tayloe was flooded with imports. Rosheen and Klift fled to the luxury of the North Gate, where Sheldukher tracked them down. The locals gladly handed them over to him.

Sheldukher had converted a Kezzivot Class transport freighter, welding on a furnace engine, installing sleep suspension chambers stolen from the Dozing Decades company and fitting heavy weaponry such as the cellular disrupter and the spectronic destabiliser. His team raided Checkley's World, stealing Project FXX Q84 - the Cell - an advanced telepathic, organic computer. Although this brought down the wrath of the Intergalactic Taskforce, it was only the beginning of Sheldukher's scheme. He planned to locate the legendary planet Sakkrat, and the greatest prize in the galaxy: the Highest Science.

The mysterious 'Highest Science' had preoccupied the galaxy's population for generations. In 2421, the explorer Gustaf Urnst claimed to have discovered Sakkrat, the planet which housed its secrets. No-one took Urnst seriously, although his books remained in print even after his mysterious disappearance. Unknown to the public, a Fortean Flicker had transported him to the twentieth century.

For the next three hundred years, the F61 searched the galaxy for Sakkrat, travelling past the stellar conjunctions of Naiad, the crystal quasars of Menolot and the farthest reaches of Harma. Over the centuries many lesser criminals would imitate Sheldukher, but none would match him.[360]

Archaeologists of this period believed the stories of HP Lovecraft were historically accurate.[361] *Convergence*, a cargo ship, was lost in mysterious circumstances over Dymok in 2396.[362]

The Twenty-Fifth Century

On a visit to Birnam in the twenty-fifth century, the Doctor saw a Stigorax.[363] The Doctor took Peri shopping in a twenty-fifth century Wal-Mart.[364]

2400 - THE PIT[365] -> At the beginning of the twenty-fifth century, the space docks of Glasson Minor, a planet-sized ship-building station, bustled with activity and human colonisation continued to gather pace.

In 2400, the Seven Planets of the Althosian binary star system were destroyed. Colonisation at this time was still hazardous, and the Seven Planets were far from the normal trading routes, years away from the nearest other colony. A number of new religions sprang up on Nicea, the planet with the largest population, and these spread to the smaller worlds of Trieste and Byzantine. Most of these were based around the Form Manipulator, and adopted Judeo-Christian beliefs to the environment of the Seven Planets. The geographical and religious isolation made it easy for them to declare independence from the Corporation, but the corporations responded by cutting off all supplies and communications. Rioting broke out that the Archon and his armies were unable to contain.

The destruction of the system, though, came about when a former Gallifreyan general, Kopyion Liall a Mahajetsu, detonated a bomb that destroyed the Seven Planets and killed millions. This prevented one of the Time Lords' ancient enemies, the Yssgaroth, from escaping into our universe.

Peri had spent twenty-five years married to Yrcanos, and became Queen of the Krontep and the Seven Systems. She governed seven worlds. "Gilliam, Queen of Kr'on Tep", as she was known, disappeared in 2404 and returned to the twentieth century.[366] Humans colonised the Garazone System. The Garazone Space Patrol was formed to fight smugglers.[367]

? 2405 - VANISHING POINT[368] **->** The geneticist Cauchemar worked to overthrow "the Creator" responsible for the reincarnation process on an alien colony planet. The Creator's functions were disrupted to the point that deformed children named "mooncalves" were being born without the genetic "godswitch" needed to facilitate reincarnation. Cauchemar hoped to overload the Creator to the point of triggering an energy release that would destroy the entire planet, yet facilitate his soul's admittance to the afterlife, but the Doctor foiled this scheme. The genetic experiments that had extended Cauchemar's life, coupled with radiation exposure, failed and he died.

Years later, the Creator had rebalanced enough to include the mooncalves in its designs.

2408 - DIVIDED LOYALTIES[369] **->** The Doctor arrived on space station *Little Boy II* to find communications with Dymok had been disrupted. He travelled to the planet and was captured by the Toymaker. An attack on the Toymaker's part made Dymok vanish completely, but the Doctor again defeated him.

In 2414, Darzil Carlisle was born outside Olympus Mons on Mars. At age three, following an airlock accident that killed his parents, he was relocated to an orphanage in Finchley, North London. At age seventeen, he earned a scholarship to the Phobos Academy of Music, and studied there for three years.

The Doctor, having encountered an older Carlisle on the planet Cray circa 2484, aided Carlisle in becoming a renowned peacemaker. With the Doctor's secret help, Lord Carlisle ended wars on at least thirty-six planets, and was famed for saving billions of lives.[370]

Around 2415, the people of the Elysium System discovered the Artifact, a vast ammonite-like structure, on the edge of their territory.[371] In 2416, on an unnamed colony world, IMC had set up a genetics engineering project named Project Mecrim. The Company built the ape-like Rocarbies, cheap labour developed from the native primate life; and the Mecrim, a race built for combat with a claw that could vibrate and cut through even the hardest materials. When a Mecrim gut microbe escaped, the colony was declared off-limits. The survivors developed an immunity, but came to hate science and degenerated to a medieval level of technology.[372]

In the 2420s, the deserts of Earth were reclaimed and the city New Atlantis was built in the Pacific. The population of Earth was sixty billion at this time.

The "Tyrenians" had been developed as human supersoldiers with canine attributes, genetically engineered by Gustav Tyren. When the military pulled its funding for the project, the Tyrenians stole a ship and founded a colony on Axista Four. They set up satellite defences and then entered suspended animation using symbiotes.

Around 2430, the human colony ship *Big Bang* departed into space. The seventh Doctor, in preparing colonist Kiranne Ransome to aide one of his previous selves, was the last person to visit her before she entered stasis.

---

366 She was married to Yrcanos for twenty-five years according to *Bad Therapy* (p288).
367 'About a hundred years' before *Sword of Orion*.
368 Dating *Vanishing Point* - An arbitrary date. The colony has been around for 'centuries'.
369 Dating *Divided Loyalties* - It is 'thirty years' after Dymok became isolated in 2378 (p16).
370 *The Game*. Carlisle's birth date and details of his early life are given, Disc 1, Track 7.
371 "More than a century" before *Parasite* (p49).
372 *The Menagerie*
373 The colonists crashed on Axista Four about a hundred years before *The Colony of Lies*. Kiranne mentions meeting the seventh Doctor on p164.
374 'Twenty years' before Mrs Ransandrianasolo is born, according to *Return of the Living Dad* (p164).
375 *The Crystal Bucephalus*
376 *The Colony of Lies*
377 *War of the Daleks*. The Mechonoids have been there 'two hundred and seventy five years' (p213). I

assume they were sent out around the same time the ones we saw in *The Chase*.
378 *The Also People* (p170).
379 Dating *Colony in Space* - We see a calendar being changed from "Monday 2nd March 2472" to the next day. Ashe tells Jo that they left Earth in "seventy-one". Hulke's novelisation of this story is set in "2971".
380 "Some five hundred years" before *The Mutants*, according to the Administrator.
381 'Five hundred years' after *Return of the Living Dad* (p61).
382 'Seventy two' years before *Return of the Living Dad*.
383 *Burning Heart* (p174).
384 "Three cycles" (presumably years) before *The Game*.
385 Dating *The Game* - According to the story, Lord Carlisle was born 2414 and started his career as a peacemaker around age twenty (so circa 2434). On Disc 1, Track 70, he says he has been working as a mediator for "fifty years".

The defence grid on Axista Four shot down the *Big Bang*, and it crashed to the planet. Kiranne remained trapped in stasis, and her father, the philanthropist Stewart Ransome, died in the crash. The survivors founded a colony based on Kirann's text, *Back to Basics*, and strove for a low-technology approach that modeled society on the Wild West. They were unaware of the Tyrenians' presence.[373]

Space Fleet was using psi drugs to enhance human psychokinesis.[374] The Doctor met a Legion in the twenty-fifth century, shortly before the Second Dalek War.[375] A Dalek War broke out in 2459.[376] The Daleks fought the Mechonoids on Hesperus.[377] Comes the Trickster released the HvLIP *All The Way From Heaven* in 2465.[378]

2472 (Tuesday, 3rd March, to Wednesday, 4th March) - COLONY IN SPACE[379] ->

Earth was overpopulated, with one hundred billion people living like "battery hens" in communal living units. 300-storey floating islands were built, housing five hundred million people. There was "no room to move, polluted air, not a blade of grass left on the planet and a government that locks you up if you think for yourself".

IMC scoured the galaxy for duralinium, to build ever more living units. From Earth Control, their headquarters, a fleet of survey vessels ruthlessly strip-mined worlds and killed anyone that stood in their way. Discipline on IMC ships and planets relied heavily on the death penalty: piracy, mutiny and even trespass were all capital offences. Earth Government turned a blind eye to these abuses, although an Adjudicator was assigned to each Galactic Sector to judge disputes in interplanetary law.

Despite the conditions on Earth, few were prepared to leave the homeworld for a bleak life on a colony planet. Some groups of eccentrics bought their own ship and tried to settle on a new world, but most people preferred a life on Earth, where the government may have been harsh, but at least they were able to feed their citizens.

Colonists on Uxarieus - a world that supported birds, insects and basic plant life, and which had an atmosphere similar to that of Earth before the invention of the motor car - found themselves in competition with IMC for control of the planet. The colonists arrived first, surveyed the planet and set up their habitation domes. They discovered that Uxarieus was inhabited by a small subterranean city of telepathic Primitives. Two colonists were killed when they tried to enter the city, but an understanding was reached between the two parties. In return for food, the Primitives provided menial labour. The colonists proceeded with their plans, but it proved difficult to grow crops as they withered for no reason that the colonists could ascertain.

Just over a year after they arrived, giant lizards attacked some of the outermost domes and some colonists were killed. Many of the colonists were prepared to leave, but their spacecraft was now obsolete, and would almost certainly be unable to reach another world.

IMC arrived in Survey Ship 4-3, under the command of Captain Dent, and angered the colonists by staking a claim on the world. When they discovered that IMC had been using optical trickery to project images of the lizards, and a Mark III servo-robot to kill the colonists, many turned to arms.

Colonists and IMC men were killed in a series of gun battles. An Adjudicator ruled in IMC's favour, but he was exposed as a fake who was more interested in the Primitives' secrets. The IMC team attempted to murder the colonists by forcing them to leave in their obsolete rocket. They were defeated and a real Adjudicator was brought in.

It was discovered that the Primitive city was home to an ancient superweapon, which had been leaking and poisoning the soil. The guardian of this device was convinced to destroy weapon - and the city - rather than let it fall into the wrong hands.

Humanity at this time still used imperial measurements, projectile weapons and wheeled transport ("space buggys"). Ships were powered by nuclear motors, and communicated with Earth via "warp" radio and videolink. The language of Earth was English; the currency was the pound. IMC had advanced scanning equipment for mineral surveys and medical diagnoses. Colonists bought old ships to transport them to their colony planets.

In the twenty-fifth century, Earth colonised Solos, a planet with rich deposits of thaesium. The beautiful planet was ravaged and its people enslaved.[380] The Doctor, Benny, Roz and Chris went to Navarro to rest after their adventure in Little Caldwell.[381] Mrs Ransandrianasolo was born. She was a telepath, as her mother was given psi drugs.[382] In 2476, the Techno-Magi consulted the frozen head of Ralph Waldo Mimsey as an Oracle, driving him insane.[383]

Circa 2481, the UI designated Cray as Earth's sister planet, due to its position relative to Earth from Galactic Zero. The increased focus on Cray compelled Earth to try and end the planet's embarrassing war. The negotiator Lord Carlisle would be dispatched to try and arbitrate a peace.[384]

c 2484 - THE GAME[385] ->

On the planet Cray, only two teams - the Gora and the Lineen - had survived to continue playing the lethal game of Naxy. The past five seasons had seen the deaths of 78,349 Gora and 65,418 Lineen, although the Gora were in much worse shape than was officially reported, and were on the brink of defeat.

The Doctor and Nyssa arrived on Cray to witness Lord Carlisle's efforts to broker a truce, but the Doctor's involvement in a Naxy match led to an upset for the Lineen, with four hundred Lineen casualties. Carlisle died while saving the Doctor's life, but the Doctor exposed the Morian Crime Syndicate's manipulative influence on the planet. The Gora and Lineen set aside their differences and united against the Morian, ending the Naxy tournaments. Carlisle was accredited with the planet's newfound peace.

Heroin slam, the so-called "razor drug," was now in distribution.

c 2486 (September) - THE TOMB OF THE CYBERMEN[386] -> The Brotherhood of Logicians unearthed the Tombs of the Cybermen on Telos, and attempted to discover why they died out. The Cybermen were revived and planned to emerge into the universe, but were stopped by the Doctor. The currency at this time appears to have been the pound. Individuals and organisations could charter spacecraft.

The CyberController was not destroyed, but merely

damaged. He went on to build a new Cyber-Race.[387]

By the end of the twenty-fifth century, a museum was dedicated to the Beatles in Liverpool and clothes were self-cleaning, dirt repelling and non-creasing. Ten-year-olds took a certificate of education in physics, medicine, chemistry and computer science using learning machines for an hour a week. There was evidence that humanity now had some familiarity with temporal theory: even children knew Venderman's Law: "Mass is absorbed by light, therefore light has mass and energy. The energy radiated by a light neutron is equal to the energy of the mass it absorbs".[388]

Vicki Pallister, companion of the first Doctor, was born in New London on the planet Earth around 2480. She lived in Liddell Towers. Her mother died when she was eleven. After that, she and her father left Earth for a new life on space colony Astra.[389] She was innoculated using a laser injector when she was five, and owned a pony called Saracen.[390] In Vicki's time, food was designed to be nutritious, not tasty. Pandas were extinct, and museums used holograms. Vicki's father, Lieutenant Commander Pallister, had basic paramedic training for his intended job on Astra.[391]

386 Dating *The Tomb of the Cybermen* - The story is set "five hundred years" after the Cybermen mysteriously died out according to Parry, although the Cybermen don't indicate how long they've been in their tombs. No reference is made to the Cyber War [q.v.], so we might presume it is before that time (the disappearance of the Cybermen after the Cyber War wasn't a mystery). The Cybermen's history computer recognises the Doctor from "the lunar surface", so the Cybermen went into hibernation (shortly?) after *The Moonbase*. This would make it at least 2570, but we know that *Earthshock* is set in 2526. The Cybermen in *Earthshock* refer to the events of *The Tomb of the Cybermen*, so *The Tomb of the Cybermen* must be set before 2526. Either Parry is rounding up or he doesn't know about the events of *The Moonbase* (or *Silver Nemesis* and *The Wheel in Space*, for that matter).

Another possibility is that the Cybermen in *Earthshock* are time travellers. There's some circumstantial evidence for this - it explains how their scanner can show a scene from *Revenge of the Cybermen*, which is almost certainly set after 2526, and it may go some way to explaining how the freighter travels in time at the end - but there's nothing in the script that supports this, and if they have a time machine, then it's hard to believe that the best plan they can come up with is the one that they're implementing.

Radio Times didn't give a year for *Tomb*, but specified that the month the story is set is "September". The draft script for serial 4D (at that point called *Return of the*

Cybermen), suggested a date of "24/10/2248" for the story. *Cybermen* sets the story in "2486", *The Terrestrial Index* at "the beginning of the 26th century". 'A History of the Cybermen' in *DWM* #83 preferred "2431", whereas *The Discontinuity Guide* settles on "2570". *Timelink* says "2526".

387 *Attack of the Cybermen*

388 This is the native time of the Doctor's companion Vicki, who joins the TARDIS in *The Rescue*. We learn about her clothing and schooling in *The Web Planet*, and her visit to the Beatles Museum and familiarity with Venderman in *The Chase*. In that story we also learn that Vicki used to live close to a medieval castle.

389 *Byzantium!*

390 *The Plotters*

391 *The Eleventh Tiger*

392 Dating *The Rescue* - Vicki states that the year her spaceship left Earth was "2493, of course". The draft script suggested that Vicki and her fellow space traveller, Bennett, have been on Dido "for a year", but there is no such indication in the final programme. Ian Marter's novelisation is set in 2501. *The Making of Doctor Who*, the various editions of Lofficier and *The Doctor Who File* set the date of "2493". *The TARDIS Special* "c.2500". Peel's novelisation of *The Chase* says that Vicki is from "the twenty-fourth century".

393 *Superior Beings*

394 Dating *Set Piece* - One of the time zones affected by the Ants is "the twenty-fifth century" (p33), and this is where the Ants kidnap the Doctor, Benny and Ace.

c 2493 - THE RESCUE[392] **->** There were emigrations to other planets. One such ship, the UK-201, crashed on Dido en route to Astra. This was a desert world, home of a peaceful humanoid race and lizard-like creatures known as sand beasts. The Didoans had a population of around one hundred, and had just perfected an energy ray that could be used as a building tool.

A young girl named Vicki was one of only two survivors of the crash. She joined the Doctor when he made a return visit to Dido.

There were disputes in the Thynemnus System when boar-like aliens attacked the human colonists. The aliens were driven off, but the Valethske attacked the system soon after.[393]

c 2495 - SET PIECE[394] **->** In the late twenty-fifth century, spaceships started disappearing from one of the less-used traffic lanes. A space vessel, designed to save a group of doomed colonists by directly uploading their memories, had outstripped its programming. It now sought to absorb the memories of every living being, and was using its robotic workers, the Ants, to kidnap people.

Five hundred and six people were taken from one such captured ship, the *Cortese*. The Doctor, Ace and Bernice tried to intercede and were flung through time. They eventually brought about the Ship's destruction.

Androids indistinguishable from humans were constructed in the Orion Sector. They became smart enough to demand equal rights and protest their mistreatment. This led to a conflict - the Orion War - against humanity. The androids settled in the Orion System, ordering the humans to accept android rule or leave.[395]

The Twenty-Sixth Century

By the twenty-sixth century, interstellar travel had become a matter of routine. Fleets of spacecraft ranging from luxury liners to cargo freighters to battleships pushed further into deep space. Ships were built from durilium and had hyperdrives. The mind probe was commonly used to scan the minds of suspects, but it wasn't always reliable. Weapons of the time included hand blasters and neutronic missiles. This was the period that saw the beginning of Earth's Empire.[396]

The warp drives of Earth ships were powered by anti-matter contained in stabilising vessels.[397] Space was divided into Sectors.[398] The currency was the Imperial.[399] It was likely around now that the Doctor gained a licence for the Mars-Venus rocket run.[400] *The Collected Works of Gustav Urnst* were published in June 2503, striking a chord with the bombastic people of the twenty-sixth century.[401]

2503 - SWORD OF ORION[402] **->** With the Orion War still in progress, a derelict spaceship was discovered near the Garazone Central habitat. The ship was a Cybermen factory ship, and Earth High Command dispatched Deeva Jansen to recover the ship. They hoped to obtain the Cybermen conversion process and create super-soldiers, but Jansen was secretly an android trying to obtain the technology for the Orion androids.

The Doctor and Charley stowed away on Jansen's ship and were there when it docked with the Cybership. The Cybermen revived in great numbers, but the Doctor defeated them. Jansen was swept into space with some Cybermen and presumably frozen.

c 2505 - TO THE SLAUGHTER[403] **->** Earth had been abandoned to the poorer countries. Mercury had fallen into the Sun and Venus was a toxic waste dump. The Oort Cloud had been sold off and dismantled.

Falsh Industries demolished most of Jupiter's moons - using the designs of Aristotle Halcyon, a celebrity *decoartiste* - as part of a redevelopment scheme to attract businesses to the solar system. The "Old Preservers", speaking on behalf of the Empire Trust, were opposed to this. Falsh himself was engaged in illicit weapons research. The Doctor, Fitz and Trix uncovered his schemes and

---

395 'Eight years' before *Sword of Orion*.

396 *Frontier in Space*

397 *Earthshock*

398 *Colony in Space, Earthshock*. The freighter in *Earthshock* starts off in Sector 16, in 'deep space'.

399 *Warriors' Gate*

400 *Robot, The Janus Conjunction*. The Mars-Venus cruise is mentioned in *Frontier in Space*, although presumably such flights take place from the twenty-first century until the far future.

401 *The Highest Science* (p48).

402 Dating *Sword of Orion* - It's 'a very long time' after the Cyber Wars, and the Doctor says the Cybermen are

'safely tucked away in their tombs on Telos', with humans assuming the Cybermen are extinct. So this is before the Cybermen re-emerge after *The Tomb of the Cybermen*. The only date given in the story is that the original Jansen died on 'three zero five zero seven'. However, *Neverland* gives a firm date of 2503.

403 Dating *To the Slaughter* - The dating of this story is inconsistent. It's 'almost four hundred years' since 1938, according to Halcyon (p17, so before 2338), but Trix thinks it's 'over five hundred years' since her time (p86, so after around 2503). The story is set before *Revenge of the Cybermen*, and explains why Jupiter only has twelve natural moons in that story. When *Revenge* was broad-defeated him. Halcyon decided to use his talents to improve Earth.

? 2515 - PARASITE[404] -> Three hundred and sixty-seven years after it had been colonised, the Elysium System was on the brink of civil war. Over the last fifty years a schism had developed between the Founding Families, who wanted to remain isolated from Earth and maintain their own distinctive political system, and the Reunionists, who wanted to make contact with the Empire.

Before the situation could be resolved, it was found that the Artefact was in fact a vast transdimensional living entity, a creature that when hatched would absorb water from planets, and use the hydrogen in it to lay star-and-planet-sized "eggs". As each young Artefact required the water from forty or fifty thousand planets, it posed a threat to the entire universe. The creature was rendered dormant.

The Draconian War

Around 2520, the first contact was made with the Draconians, a reptilian race that possessed an area of space and a level of technology equivalent to Earth. A peace mission between the two races was arranged, but it ended in catastrophe when the Draconian ship approached, as was their tradition, with the missile ports open. The Draconian ship carried no missiles, but the humans assumed they had been lured into an ambush. A neutron storm prevented communications and the human ship destroyed the Draconian one. A war between Earth and Draconia started immediately, and although it didn't last long, millions died on both sides.[405]

As a result of a pop can that Bernice kicked onto a path in 2001, a less-elegant writer came to draft a crucial speech shortly before the outbreak of hostilities. The war consequently broke out an hour earlier, with dozens of extra casualties on both sides.[406]

During the Dragon Wars, Shirankha Hall's deep-space incursion squadron discovered a beautiful garden world halfway between human and Draconian Space. He named it Heaven.[407]

Although many on both sides wanted to see the war fought to its conclusion, diplomatic relations were established and the war ended. The Frontier in Space was established, a dividing line which neither race's spacecraft could cross. Relations between the two planets remained wary, and factions on both Earth and Draconia wanted to wage a pre-emptive strike on the enemy. For twenty years, the galaxy existed in a state of cold war, although treaties and cultural exchanges were set up. Espionage between the powers was expressly forbidden.[408]

---

cast, astronomers thought Jupiter had twelve moons, but dozens more have been discovered in the years since, and Jupiter at present is known to have sixty-three (nineteen were discovered in 2003 alone). Earth in this era has a President, the beginning of an Empire and there's a mention of the Draconians, supporting (strangely, perhaps) Trix over Halcyon.

404 Dating *Parasite* - The dating of this story is problematic. Mark Bannen is the son of Alex Bannen who died in *Lucifer Rising* "more than two centuries" ago (p165), so the story is set after 2357. 1706 "was more than seven hundred years ago" (p140), so it is after 2406. Mark Bannen was a baby during the Mexico riots of 2146 and has been kept alive by the Artefact since the founding of the colony "367" years ago (p73), so the story must be set after 2513. This last date is supported by the fact that Earth now has "Empire" (p136-137).

405 'Twenty years' before *Frontier in Space*. General Williams claims that his ship was "damaged and helpless" and well as "unarmed", but it managed to destroy a Draconian battlecruiser anyway. A scene cut from Part Three explained that Williams was able to use his "exhaust rockets" to destroy the other ship.

406 *Head Games* (p165-166).

407 *Love and War* (p10).

408 *Frontier in Space*.

409 Inferred from *The Tomb of the Cybermen*.

THE CYBER WAR: The "Cyber Wars" feature in much fan fiction and are referred to in a number of the books and audios. On television, though, the term "the Cyber War" is only used once, by the Doctor in *Revenge of the Cybermen* - everyone else refers to it simply as "the war".

We are told that this war took place "centuries" beforehand, and that the human race won when they discovered that Cybermen were vulnerable to gold and invented the "glittergun". Following their total defeat, the Cybermen launched a revenge attack on Voga, after which the Cybermen completely disappeared.

From the on-screen information, it seems that we can precisely position the date of this "Cyber War": it can't be before 2486, because in *The Tomb of the Cybermen*, the Cyber Race is thought to have been extinct for five hundred years after Mondas' destruction. In that story, the Controller is ready to create a "new race" of Cybermen. We learn in *Attack of the Cybermen* that the Controller wasn't destroyed at the end of *The Tomb of the Cybermen*, so we might presume that this new race emerged soon afterward and began its conquests.

These attacks didn't directly involve Earth: in *Earthshock*, Scott, a member of the Earth military, hasn't heard of the Cybermen (even though his planet is host-

The Cyber War

Over five hundred years after Mondas' destruction, the Cybermen re-emerged from their tombs on Telos, redesigned and more deadly than ever.[409] They became the "undisputed masters of space".[410]

2526 - EARTHSHOCK[411] **->** Earth was not directly affected, but it was clear that only the homeworld could provide the military resources needed to combat the Cyber threat. In 2526, a Conference was held on Earth that proposed that humanity should unite to fight the Cybermen. The Cybermen attempted to detonate a bomb on Earth, then land an invasion force in the aftermath, but the Doctor thwarted their plans.

The twenty-sixth century saw the Great Orion Cyber Wars.[412] The Cybermen were unafraid of contravening galactic law or arms treaties, and were prepared to destroy entire planets using Cyberbombs. But the war against the Cybermen united many planets, and humanity started from a strong position. Earth was aware of the Cybermen's vulnerability to gold and developed the 'glittergun', a weapon that exploited this weakness. There was more gold on Voga than in the rest of the known galaxy, and when those vast reserves were used against the Cybermen, humanity inflicted massive defeats.[413] The glittergun was built by INITEC.[414]

? 2530 - ATTACK OF THE CYBERMEN[415] **->** The Cybermen faced total defeat. Thanks to Cryon guerillas and the Cybermen's failing hibernation equipment, they weren't even safe on Telos and planned to evacuate. They had recently captured a three-man time machine that had landed on Telos, and used it to go to 1985 in an attempt to prevent Mondas' destruction. The Doctor was captured in 1985 and brought to Telos, where he was able to destroy the tombs and the CyberController.

---

ing a conference that the Cyber Leader says will unite many planets in a "war against the Cyber Race"). The Doctor observes that it is a war that the Cybermen "can't win". When the Cybermen's plan to blow up the conference is defeated (*Earthshock*), there is nothing to stop Earth from fighting this genocidal war against the Cybermen - and this is surely the "Cyber War" referred to in *Revenge of the Cybermen*. We might presume that the events of *Attack of the Cybermen* occur at the end of the War, when the Cybermen face defeat and are planning to evacuate Telos. The Cybermen are not mentioned in *Frontier in Space* (set in 2540), which could be inferred as meaning that the Cyber War has long been over by that time.

Before *Earthshock* was broadcast, *The Programme Guide* placed the Cyber "Wars" (note the plural) as "c.2300" (first edition) and "c.2400" (second edition). 'A History of the Cybermen' in *DWM* #83 first suggested that the Cyber War took place immediately after *Earthshock*, post-2526. *Cybermen* suggested that the Cyber Wars took place without any involvement with Earth around "2150 AD". *The Terrestrial Index* came to a messy compromise: The "First Cyber Wars" take place "as the 23rd Century began", when Voga is devastated. *Revenge of the Cybermen* takes place at the "tail end of the 25th Century", then after *Earthshock* Voga's gold is *again* used to defeat the Cybermen in "the Second Cyber War".

Novels such as *Killing Ground* make it clear that the Cybermen menaced some early human colony worlds.

410 *Attack of the Cybermen*

411 Dating *Earthshock* - The Doctor states that it is "the twenty-sixth century", Adric calculates that it is "2526 in the time scale you call Anno Domini". *The TARDIS Logs* set the story in "2500".

How the Cyber-scanner in *Earthshock* can show a clip from *Revenge of the Cybermen* remains a mystery, and causes problems with the dating of that story. The "real" reason is that the production team wanted to show the Cybermen facing as many previous Doctors as they could and didn't worry too much about continuity (in the same way that the Brigadier's flashback in *Mawdryn Undead* had the Brigadier 'remembering' scenes he didn't witness). Equally, the Cyber-scanner doesn't show clips from *Attack of the Cybermen* or *Silver Nemesis*, the latter of which at least should appear.

'A History of the Cybermen' in *DWM* #83 suggested that the Scope tunes into the TARDIS telepathic circuits, which seems a little implausible. One fan, Michael Evans, has suggested that as there is no indication how long before *Attack of the Cybermen* the time machine crashed on Telos, it is perfectly possible that the Cybermen have had it since before *Earthshock* and used it to research their future before using it to alter history. This would certainly be a logical course of action. *About Time* suggests that the Cybermen themselves have travelled from the future. For other possible explanations see *Cybermen* (p72, p79-80).

412 *Real Time*

413 *Revenge of the Cybermen*

414 *Original Sin* (p287).

415 Dating *Attack of the Cybermen* - No date is given on-screen, but the story takes place after *The Tomb of the Cybermen* as the Controller remembers surviving that story. *Attack of the Cybermen* takes place at a time when the Cybermen face imminent total defeat on a number of fronts. Although the Cybermen know of Lytton's people, and he is fully aware of the situation on

Realising that they were beaten, the Cybermen launched an attack on Voga and detonated Cyberbombs that blew the planet out of orbit. The Vogans were forced into underground survival chambers. After this time, the Cybermen disappeared, and it was believed that they had died out.[416] The Cyber Fleet was destroyed. Bounty hunters and mercenaries hunted down the remaining Cybermen.[417]

The Rise of the Earth Empire

2534 - THE COLONY OF LIES[418] -> Matter transmitters were abandoned by this time, and there were strict laws on DNA manipulation. The EuroZone still existed. The human colonies were known as the Earth Federation, and were patrolled by Colony Support Vessels. Space was marked with navigation beacons. The term "Earth Empire" was used for the first time this year.

On Axista Four, the human colonists divided into conservative and technological-minded factions: the "Loyalists" and the "Realists". The Realists set up their own settlement away from the Loyalist city of Plymouth Hope, but often raided the Loyalists for supplies.

By now, the Daleks were making gains in the third quadrant. Human space stations and colonies on the front line were evacuated. The Earth Federation had formed an alliance to try to prevent Dalek expansionism.

About 80,000 refugees were scheduled for relocation to Axista Four, and the Earth support vessel *Hannibal* entered orbit around the planet, responding to a signal for help from the Realist faction there. The *Hannibal's* arrival triggered machinery that revived some Tyrenians from stasis, and they threatened to make warfare against the humans.

The second Doctor, Jamie and Zoe arrived at this time, and the Doctor both revived Kirann Ransome from suspended animation and defused the conflict. The Realists and Loyalists agreed to accept Kirann as their mutual leader. The Doctor allowed the Federation to believe the Tyrenians were the survivors of a space plague, covering over their true history. Federation Administrator Greene agreed to let the Tyrenians live on Axista Four in peace.

Vega Station was built and secretly run by the Battrulian government. The fourth Doctor visited and lost a lot of money in the Station's casinos.[419]

The Space War

c 2540 - FRONTIER IN SPACE[420] -> At this point, Earth's "Empire" was still democratic, ruled by an elected President and Senate, although the Earth Security forces also had political influence. Ironically, although millions had died in the colonies, the Draconian War had not affected Earth and so the planet still faced a massive population crisis. The Bureau of Population Control strictly enforced the rule that couples could only have one child.

The Arctic areas were reclaimed. New Glasgow and New Montreal were the first of the sealed cities to be opened, and the Family Allowance was increased to two children for those who moved there. The Historical Monuments Preservation Society existed to protect Earth's heritage. While there was a healthy political opposition, any resistance to the principles of government by either anti-colonialists or pacifists was ruthlessly suppressed. Under the Special Security Act,

---

Telos, I don't think that *Resurrection of the Daleks* is set in this period. In *Resurrection of the Daleks,* Stien says that the Daleks captured people from many different periods, so this could well be Lytton's native time (Lytton talks of humans as his "ancestors", so his home planet, Vita 15, 690, Riftan V, is a human colony). Lytton seems to flatter the Cybermen by declaring them "undisputed masters of space" - *Attack of the Cybermen* shows them to be in an extremely weak position, but only a decade or so beforehand, the Cybermen were in the strong position he describes.

416 *Revenge of the Cybermen.* Stevenson claims that "the Cybermen died out centuries ago", the Doctor replies that "they disappeared after their attack on Voga at the end of the Cyber War".

417 *Real Time*

418 Dating *The Colony of Lies* - The book's internal dating is very confused. The back cover says it's 2539, and there's a tombstone on p23 which says that 2535 was

'four years ago'. Despite this, a native of this timezone says the date is 2534 (p147). Transmats are seen a number of times after this (in, for example, *The Ark in Space*) so it is clear that humanity readopts the technology.

419 *Demontage.* The fourth Doctor visited 'soon after the place opened' (p6).

420 Dating *Frontier in Space* - The story takes place "somewhere in the twenty-sixth century" according to the Doctor. In the first scene, the freighter enters hyperspace at "22.09 72 2540 EST". This is probably nine minutes past ten at night on the 72nd day of 2540, although the President is later seen cancelling a meeting on "the tenth of January". The novelisation (also by Malcolm Hulke) gives the year as "2540", which *The Terrestrial Index* concurred with, although it misunderstood the relationship between Earth and Draconia at this time, suggesting that they are part of "the Alliance" [q.v.]. It isn't made clear whether the human military know of the Daleks before this story.

a penal colony was set up on the Moon to house thousands of political prisoners, each of whom served a life sentence with no possibility of parole or escape. In 2539, Professor Dale, one of the most prominent members of the Peace Party, was arrested and sent to the penal colony on Luna.

Larger colonies such as those in the Sirius System were given Dominion Status, and allowed regional autonomy, including powers of taxation and extradition. Governors appointed directly by Earth ruled the smaller worlds.

In 2540, interplanetary tension mounted as human and Draconian spacecraft were subjected to mysterious attacks. Cargos were stolen and ships were destroyed. Each planet blamed the other, and eyewitnesses on both sides claimed to have seen their enemy. On Earth, war with the "Dragons" appeared to be inevitable. A member of the Peace Party, Patel, sabotaged a space-dock and was arrested.

On 12th March, Earth cargo ship C-982 was attacked only minutes from Earth at co-ordinates 8972-6483. The News Services monitored and broadcast their distress calls. Anti-Draconian riots flared up in Peking, Belgrade and Tokio. The Draconian consulate in Helsinki was burnt down, and in Los Angeles the President was burnt in effigy. When the C-982 docked at Spaceport Ten, Security discovered a mysterious traveller, the Doctor, on board. He resisted the mind probe, even on level 12, and was sent to the Lunar Penal Colony. He was convinced that a third party was trying to provoke war, a possibility that no one else had considered. A small ship under the command of

General Williams was sent to the Ogron home planet at co-ordinates 3349-6784, where the true masterminds, the Daleks, were revealed.

The Doctor was remembered as a mediator between Earth and Draconia.[421] The Draconian Ambassador Ishkavaarr and the Earth President agreed that the planet Heaven should become an open world where both races would bury their dead. Years later, several interplanetary agreements were signed there by the President and the Draconian Emperor.[422]

The Daleks were one of the greatest powers in the universe at this time.[423]

& 2540 - PLANET OF THE DALEKS[424] **->** The Doctor and Jo tracked the Daleks to the planet Spiridon in the ninth system, many systems from Skaro. Here, a group of six Thals - selected from the six-hundred strong Division that hunted Daleks - were already investigating. They had discovered a research station where twelve Daleks were developing germ weapons, and also experimenting with an anti-reflective lightwave that rendered them invisible. The Doctor discovered an army of ten thousand Daleks in neutron-powered suspended animation beneath the research base. Supreme Command sent the Dalek Supreme to oversee the invasion of the Solar Planets, but the Doctor defeated them.

Bernice Surprise Summerfield was born on 21st June, 2540, on the human colony of Beta Caprisis. She was the daughter of Isaac Summerfield, a starship commander in the Space Fleet, and his wife Claire.[425]

---

421 *Shadowmind* (p61).
422 *Love and War* (p10-11).
423 According to the Doctor in *Death to the Daleks*.
424 Dating *Planet of the Daleks* - The story is set at the same time as *Frontier in Space*. Nevertheless, the American *Doctor Who* comic dated this story as 1300 AD. It is 'generations' after *The Daleks*.
425 BENNY'S BIRTHDAY: It is stated in *Love and War* (p46), in many later books and in the Writers' Guide that Benny comes from "the twenty-fifth century". For a while, the writers worked on the assumption that she was from 2450 (e.g.: *The Highest Science* p34, *The Pit* p9). In *Falls the Shadow*, we learn that Benny was born in "2422" (p148). However, Paul Cornell's initial Character Guide had specified that she was born in "2472", which, as *Love and War* is set the day after Benny's thirtieth birthday, would make it 2502 (in the twenty-*sixth* century).

Causing further complications, *Love and War* is definitely set after *Frontier in Space* [2540]. In subsequent books there was confusion, with some novels claiming

that Benny does indeed come from the "twenty-sixth century" (e.g. *Transit* p186, *Blood Heat* p3).

Latterly, so as not to contradict the television series, it has been decided that Benny is definitely from the twenty-sixth century. Benny explained that there are a number of calendars in use in the cosmopolitan galaxy of her time, and in our terms she is "from the late-twenty-sixth century" (*Just War* p136) - this is intended to explain away some of the contradictions. Paul Cornell and Jim Sangster have astrologically determined Benny's birthday as 21st June, a date that first appeared in *Just War* (p135) and now appears on the Big Finish official biography on their website. Even so, *The Dimension Riders* has her celebrating on 20th November.

A war between the Battrul and the wolven Canvine chiefly resulted in a draw, and a buffer zone was created between their territories. Vega Station was built as a casino and hotel, but the Battrulian government secretly used it to monitor the neutral zone.[426] The artist Menlove Stokes was born in 2542, according to official records.[427] Bernadette McAllerson discovered McAllerson's Radiation in 2542.[428] The People of the Worldsphere were covertly involved in wars in their galaxy.[429] The Alps were damaged in a local war in 2547.[430] Mind probes were made illegal.[431]

The Dalek Wars

The Daleks began their third wave of expansion, leading to the Galactic Wars.[432] Life on the front was harsh, with tens of thousands killed by Dalek Plague on Yalmur alone. Other planets on the front line included Capella, Antonius, Procyon and Garaman (home to a Space Fleet station).

On the other hand, the Core Worlds - the heavily populated and fashionable heart of the Earth Empire - were safe and prosperous. The planet Ellanon was a popular holiday planet; Bacchanalia Two was the home of the Club Outrageous. There were shipyards on Harato, and thriving colonies on Thrapos 3 and Zantir. The Spinward Corporation's financial and administrative centre on Belmos was a space station the size of a planet. Humanity had also discovered Lubellin - "the Mud Planet" - and the spotless Tarian Asteroids.

The best whiskey from this time was made in South America, but some people preferred Eridanian Brandy.[433]

c 2547 - RETURN OF THE LIVING DAD[434] **->** The Daleks' tactics were repetitive and predictable. Earth's Space Fleet used vast Dalekbuster ships, highly-automated and heavily-armed six-man fighters. Isaac Summerfield captained one such ship. Albinex the Navarino contacted the Daleks and offered to change history in return for military assistance. The Doctor and Benny arrived on Isaac Summerfield's ship, the *Tisiphone*, which was fighting the Daleks over Bellatrix. The *Tisiphone* interrupted Albinex's

---

426 The ceasefire was declared 'fifty years' before *Demontage* (p4).

427 *The Well-Mannered War* (p272). Stokes is from the 2400s, so the official records must have been altered to due to his relocation to the twenty-sixth century.

428 *Conundrum*

429 A generation or so before *The Also People*.

430 *So Vile a Sin* (p211).

431 'Three hundred years' before *Dark Progeny*. They are in use in *Frontier in Space*.

432 *Death and Diplomacy* (p124). We might infer from other stories that the first wave was in the mid-twenty-second century (seen in *The Dalek Invasion of Earth*) which was targeted on Earth's solar system, and the second led to the Dalek War mentioned in *The Crystal Bucephalus* and *The Colony of Lies*.

THE DALEK WARS: In *Death to the Daleks*, Hamilton states "My father was killed in the last Dalek War", implying there was more than one. We know from other Dalek stories that humanity and the Daleks come into conflict throughout history. However, there are almost certainly no Dalek Wars affecting Earth directly between *The Dalek Invasion of Earth* and *The Rescue* [2167-2493], as Vicki has only heard of the Daleks from history books discussing the Invasion (she doesn't even know what they look like). According to Cory in *Mission to the Unknown*, the Daleks have been inactive in Earth's sphere of influence for a millennium before *The Daleks' Master Plan* [between 3000-4000 AD]. In *Planet of the Daleks*, the Doctor uses the term "Dalek War" to describe the events of *The Daleks*, which did not involve humanity.

According to *The Terrestrial Index*, there are a string of Human/Dalek conflicts, the First to Fourth Dalek Wars. The First was the Dalek Invasion of Earth; the Second was fought by 'the Alliance' of Humans, Draconians and Thals in the twenty-fifth century; the Third was again fought by the Alliance after the events of *Frontier in Space* and *Planet of the Daleks*; the Fourth was *The Daleks' Master Plan*.

This is a numbering system that is never used on television, and some of the details of Lofficier's account actively contradict what we're told in the stories - at the time he proposes a "Second Dalek War" involving the Thals and Draconians, the Thals don't have advanced space travel and a century later, they think that humans are a myth (*Planet of the Daleks*). The first contact between humanity and the Draconians was in 2520 (in the twenty-*sixth* century), leading to a short war, followed by twenty years of hostility and mutual mistrust (*Frontier in Space*).

The books have established that Dalek Wars took place in Benny's native time - her father fights in them, and her mother is killed in a Dalek attack. What's more, Ace spends three years fighting Daleks in this time period between *Love and War* and *Deceit*. As such, there is a mass of information about the Wars in many of the novels. According to *Lucifer Rising*, Benny's father fought in the Second Dalek War (p65), whereas Ace fought in the Third (p309). I've adopted this numbering, although some of the books (for example, *The Crystal Bucephalus*) stuck to Lofficier's scheme.

433 *Deceit*

434 Dating *Return of the Living Dad* - This happens 'forty' years before 2587 (p7), Benny would have been 'seven' at the time (p12). Although the date is given as '2543' (p29), there is some confusion over Benny's birthday in the NAs, and this is a victim of that.

435 A number of references to Benny Summerfield's early life appeared in the New Adventures, and these negotiations with the Daleks, and both the *Tisiphone* and Albinex ended up falling down a wormhole to the twentieth century.

The Dalekbuster commanded by Isaac Summerfield was reported to have broken formation and fled during a space battle, and its captain was branded a coward. In late 2547, at the height of the Second Dalek War, the Daleks attacked the human colony on Vandor Prime in the Gamma Delphinus system, where Claire Summerfield was killed. Bernice Summerfield was sent to military boarding school.[435]

On Kastropheria, a group of priests had used the drug Skar to boost their psionic abilities and mentally restrain the people's self-destructive impulses. Humans established a colony on the planet, but the natives became aggressive again when supplies of skar began to run out.[436] The Class G maintenance robot entered service.[437]

c 2550 - CATASTROPHEA[438] -> The Doctor and Jo discovered the human colonists on Kastopheria had enslaved the natives, and the Doctor was mistaken for El Llama, a prophesied revolutionary. The priests asked the Doctor to destroy the Anima, a giant skar crystal, with great care to free the people from their mind-lock. The Anima was destroyed too suddenly, and the people's destructive rage returned. War loomed between the natives and the colonists, but the Doctor helped to forge a non-interference treaty. The Draconians helped the colonists to evacuate, and the natives were left to their own devices.

In 2555, Benny Summerfield visited Earth for the last time before meeting the Doctor. On this, or a previous trip, she went to Stuttgart.[439] The Draconian vessel *Hunter* and five destroyers were lost fighting Daleks. Female officers had recently been introduced to the Draconian military.[440]

The People of the Worldsphere fought a war against the Great Hive Mind, using new weapons and powerful sentient Very Aggressive Ships. The war saw twenty-six billion killed, completely destroyed fifteen planets and devastated dozens of others. The Great Hive Mind became part of the People.[441]

Hardened criminals on Earth were given the choice of facing the death penalty or becoming Dalek Killers (DKs). The most notorious of the DKs was Abslom Daak.[442] Corporations such as Ellerycorp, Peggcorp, Spinward, and IMC maintained battlefleets of their own. During the Battle of Alpha Centauri, a small squadron of Silurian vessels beat back the main Dalek force, which fled into hyperspace. Daleks also managed to infiltrate human Puterspace.[443]

TAM Corporation's ships fought in the Galactic Wars. The corporation pulled out of remote colonies like Mendeb, taking as much high technology as it could.[444]

As often happened in wartime, the Dalek War saw a leap in human technological progress. A variety of intelligent weapons systems were developed: dart guns, data corrupting missiles, spikes, clusters and forceshells, random field devices, self-locating mines and drones.

Earth's Space Fleet included 1000-man troopships armed with torpedoes that could destroy a Dalek Battlesaucer. A fleet of warp vessels - X-Ships - were used to ferry communications, personnel and supplies. Most troopers were placed in Deep Sleep while travelling to the warzones. This was done to conserve supplies, not because the ships were particularly slow, as it now only took a matter of weeks to cross human space. Ships still used warp engines, but they also used ion drive to travel in real space.

Computer technology was now extremely advanced. The Space Fleet Datanet was a vast information resource,

---

were not always consistent. In *Love and War*, Benny's birthplace is identified as Beta Caprisis (p75), but in *Sanctuary* Benny recalls that her mother was killed on a raid on Vandor Prime (p185). We might speculate that she was born on the former and moved to the latter. As pointed out in *Set Piece* (p132), there is some confusion about the exact sequence of events during the raid that killed Benny's mother. Accounts also vary as to whether Benny's father disappeared before or after her mother's death. Benny was only seven when all this happened, so she is almost certainly misremembering some details or blocking out some of her unpleasant memories.

436 'Five years' before *Catastrophea*.

437 'Four decades' before *Cold Fusion*.

438 Dating *Catastrophea* - It is 'five or six hundred years' after Jo's time (p79).

439 We learn about her visit to Stuttgart in *Just War*

(p137), and that she hasn't been to Earth in the fifteen years before *Deceit* (p102), although this contradicts *Lucifer Rising* (p171).

440 *War of the Daleks*. No date is given, but it's at a time when the Draconian Empire is at war with the Daleks. Female officers are anathema again by the time of *The Dark Path*.

441 'Thirty years' before *The Also People*. Further details are given in the Bernice Summerfield New Adventures, particularly *Down* and *Walking to Babylon*.

442 Abslom Daak first appeared in Marvel's *Doctor Who Weekly* #17, and has returned a number of times since. He was mentioned in *Love and War* (p46-47 - we also meet Maire, another DK, in that novel), before appearing in the (cloned) flesh in *Deceit*.

443 *Love and War* (p5, p64).

444 'During the wars' according to *Independence Day* (p22).

and data was stored on logic crystals. Nanotechnology was beginning to have medical applications: a nanosurgical virus was given to most troopers to protect against various alien infections, and cosmetic nanosurgery beautified the richest civilians. Holograms were now in widespread use for communications, display, entertainment, combat and public relations. Holosynths - simulations of people - acted as receptionists and could answer simple enquiries. HKI Industries, based on Phobos, specialised in the manufacture of transmats. These had a range of only a couple of thousand kilometres, but they were installed on all large ships and linked major cities on most colony worlds. Hoverspeeders were still in use.

By the late 2560s, it became clear that Earth was going to win the wars with the Daleks. By then, the fastline - a state of the art, almost real-time, interstellar communication system - had been developed.[445]

The Early Career of Bernice Summerfield

Bernice Summerfield made her reputation as an archaeologist during excavations of the Fields of Death, the tombs of the rulers of Mars in 2565.[446] She went on to investigate the Dyson Sphere of the Varteq Veil.[447] In 2566, Bernice Summerfield published *Down Among the Dead Men*, her study of archaeology, particularly that of the Martians.[448] In Benny's time, humans had eradicated most of the previously common illnesses.[449]

In 2568, the Spinward Corporation's computer, the Net, predicted that once the Dalek Wars ended, Earth's authorities would show an interest in their activities on Arcadia.[450]

2570 (late June) - LOVE AND WAR[451] -> Bernice Summerfield and her group arrived on Heaven to survey the artefacts of the extinct Heavenite civilisation on behalf of Ellerycorp. The fungal Hoothi reanimated billions of the dead on the planet. The Hoothi were defeated, but Heaven's ecology had been devastated. The planet was evacuated shortly afterward. Ace departed the TARDIS, but Bernice joined the Doctor on his travels.

Following this time, Ace spent three years in the twenty-sixth century during the time of the Third Dalek War. After a series of adventures, including a spell working for IMC, she ended up with the Special Weapons Division of Space Fleet. She fought alongside the Irregular Auxiliaries, reputed to be the most dangerous arm of the military.[452] She fought Daleks in the Ceti sector and Hai Dow. She killed a Black Dalek. She fought Marsh Daleks in the Flova trenches. She was issued a tool for removing the tops of Daleks.[453]

Hamilton's father died during the last Dalek War.[454]

& 2573 - DECEIT[455] -> The Dalek Wars were all but over, and although Dalek nests survived on a number of worlds, the army and Space Fleet were gradually demobilised.

During the Dalek Wars, Earth Central had superseded the Colonial Office, while Space Fleet had been expanded and modernised. The Office of External Operations, "the Earth's surveyors, official couriers, intelligence gatherers, customs officers and diplomats", now had a staff of 5000. While the corporations remained powerful, the Earth government reigned in some of their power and broke some of their monopolies.

Agent Defries investigated the Arcadia System, the base of the Spinward Corporation. The nearest troopers were on Hurgal, although some were taking part in a pirate hunt

445 *Deceit*
446 *The Dying Days*
447 *The Also People*
448 *Theatre of War.* The date of publication is given as both "2566" (p36), and "2466" (p135), I prefer the first date. Appendix II of *Sky Pirates!* is 'A Benny Bibliography', and contains further details of the volume.
449 *Return of the Living Dad* (p51).
450 *Deceit*
451 Dating *Love and War* - The dating of this novel causes a number of problems as it features the debut of Bernice Summerfield. It is the "twenty-fifth century" (p46), and "five centuries" since Ace's time (p26). The novel clearly takes place after *Frontier in Space* (see p10-11 of *Love and War* or p252 of *The Programme Guide*, fourth edition) as it refers to events of that story (e.g.: the peace established between humanity and the Draconians, the female president, the lunar penal

colony).
Heaven is established "three decades" before the events of the novel (p92), and *Frontier in Space* is set in 2540, so the novel can't take place before about 2570. Latterly, the decision was made that Benny is from the twenty-sixth century, so this is the date that has been adopted for this story. It is late June, as Benny celebrates her birthday just before the book starts, although it is autumn on Heaven.
452 *Deceit.* Many of the subsequent New Adventures contain references to Ace's exploits in Space Fleet.
453 Respectively *First Frontier, Theatre of War, Shadowmind, Lungbarrow* and *The Shadow of the Scourge.*
454 *Death to the Daleks*
455 Dating *Deceit* - The novel is set "two, probably three Earth years" after *Love and War* (p85), and as such the dating of the story is problematic. Both the blurb

in the Hai Dow System. Instead, Defries was assigned the troopship *Admiral Raistruck* and a squad of Irregular Auxiliaries. She was also given a "secret weapon": the Dalek Killer Abslom Daak, who was kept in cryosleep.

The ship's crew were told that they were going on a Dalek hunt. The *Admiral Raistruck* arrived in the Arcadia System and encountered an asteroid field carved to resemble terrified human faces. It was clear that Arcadia was subject to SYSDID (System Defence in Strength). Fighters attacked the *Admiral Raistruck*, but this was only a feint. The real attack came from behind: an energy being that was unaffected by the ship's torpedoes. The ship was destroyed.

Out of more than a thousand people, there were only four survivors: Defries, Daak and Troopers Ace and Johannsen. They discovered that Arcadia had been kept at a medieval level of technology. The population had been kept in ignorance, and the android Humble Counsellors enforced company law. All offworlders were killed as plague-carriers. The power behind Spinward was the Pool: vats of brain matter culled from generations of colonists, and housed in a space station in orbit around Arcadia. Pool intended to manufacture a universe of pure thought, making itself omnipotent. Pool was ejected into the Vortex with the TARDIS' tertiary control room.

At the end of the Galactic Wars, arms treaties were signed to limit the size and capability of combat robots.[456]

? 2575 - HUMAN NATURE[457] -> The Doctor and Benny visited a bodysmith and bought a Pod that would allow the Doctor to become human. They travelled to Earth, 1914, so the Doctor could experiment with living as a human being.

Battrulian artist Toulour Martinique was mysteriously killed after painting his last work, *Murdering Art*, which depicted his being murdered by demons.[458] Around 2582, the Kalkravian Revolution took place, and the Adjudication Bureau was sent in to free hostages. The All Worlds Science Fair took place on the planet Dellah. Earth won the Worlds Cup in 2584.[459]

c 2585 - THE ALSO PEOPLE[460] -> On a holiday to the Worldsphere of the People, the Doctor solved the murder of viCari, the first drone to be killed in more than three hundred years. The Doctor and Bernice also helped restore the feral Kadiatu Lethbridge-Stewart to sanity.

2587 (Autumn) - RETURN OF THE LIVING DAD[461] - > The newly-married Bernice and Jason were on Youkali 6. Benny was studying for a genuine degree in archaeology, while writing a new book and trying for a child. An old friend of her father, Admiral Groenewegen, made contact with new information about Issac Summerfield's disappearance. Benny decided to call for the Doctor's help. They discovered that Isaac Summerfield was alive and well, and living on Earth in 1983.

The Doctor and Chris visited Bernice and Jason on Youkali 6 to inform them of the death of Roz Forrester.[462]

Around the year 2590, Radon 222 levels on the surface of Argolis had dropped to such a level that the planet became habitable again.[463] Blinni-Gaar was an agricultural planet feeding an entire sector. Channel 400 made a deal with the government and started broadcasting addictive programmes. The Blinnati stopped farming, nearly leading to famine on the Rim until off-worlders started running the planet.[464]

---

and the history section in the Appendix of the novel state that *Deceit* is set in "the middle of the twenty-fifth century", just after what *The Terrestrial Index* calls the Second Dalek War (p62-63). This is restated at various other points (e.g.: p69, p216), but contradicted by other evidence in the same book: Arcadia was colonised 379 years before *Deceit* (p115), but not before the EB Corporation's first warship was operational in 2112 (p27), so the book must be set after 2491 AD. The book also refers to the Cyber Wars. In the Marvel strips, Abslom Daak comes from the mid-twenty-sixth century. Pool - while not named - briefly reappears in the post-*Doctor Who* New Adventure *Dead Romance*.
456 *Cold Fusion* (p247).
457 Dating *Human Nature* - No date is given, but Ellerycorp and the Travellers are mentioned, suggesting this is around Benny's native time.
458 'Seven years, three months and eleven days'

before *Demontage*.
459 *Cold Fusion*. The year of the revolution is given (p230), the science fair was 'ten years ago' (p200).
460 Dating *The Also People* - The remains of 'a sub gas giant that had broken up sixty-two billion years previously' is referred to (p168) and the Doctor said his 'diary's pretty much clear' until 'the heat death of the universe' (p186). This led the Virgin edition of this book to conclude that the story was set many billions of years in the future. However, the Bernice Summerfield New Adventures made clear that the story takes place around Benny's native time.
461 Dating *Return of the Living Dad* - It's '2587' (p5).
462 *So Vile a Sin*
463 "Three centuries" after *The Leisure Hive*.
464 'Ten years' before *Prime Time*.

c 2590 - DEMONTAGE[465] -> The Doctor, Sam and Fitz arrived on Vega Station. General Browning Phillips was planning to return the Battrulian junta to power by killing President Drexler, but the Doctor defeated that plan. He also engineered a more permanent peace treaty between the Battrul and Canvine.

The artist Martinique had discovered a process that could copy a being's DNA into a painting, or make items in paintings take physical form. He used this technique to survive his "murder", and took up residence in a serene painting.

2592 (31st October) - COLD FUSION[465] -> By this time, the Third Draconian War had been fought. An Empress, revered as a goddess by some, now ruled Earth. The Empire had developed Skybases to operate as planetary command centres, and the Adjudicators were sent across the Empire to enforce Imperial Law. The Unitatus Guild, a secret society based on garbled legends of UNIT in the twenty-first century, was politically influential.

The Scientifica, the ruling elite of scientists on an icy Earth colony planet, excavated a crashed TARDIS and its mummified pilot. Following experiments on the ship, ghosts start appearing across the planet. The seventh Doctor, Chris and Roz arrived to investigate the ghosts. The fifth Doctor, Tegan, Nyssa and Adric arrived a month later, and found the Patient - the mummified Time Lady - who promptly regenerated. The Doctor tried to get her to safety as the Adjudicators declared Martial Law. Both Doctors come to realise that the ghosts were the Ferutu, beings from the far future of an alternative timeline in which Gallifrey was destroyed in the ancient past. The Ferutu attempted to ensure Gallifrey's destruction, but the fifth and seventh Doctors joined forces and ensured history was not altered. A few Ferutu were trapped within a chalk circle, the only survivors of their timeline.

Patience was fatally wounded but rescued by Omega, who transported her to his anti-matter universe.[467] Fitz awoke after almost six hundred years to find himself in Augustine City on Ordifica. The colonists had developed the Cold, a horrific weapon. Fitz celebrated his 626th birthday on Ordifica on 7th March, 2593.[468]

2593 (Wednesday, 8th May) - THE DYING DAYS[469] -> Benny Summerfield was offered the chair of archaeology at St Oscar's University on Dellah. She received the job offer in 1997 despite never actually applying for the position. The eighth Doctor dropped her off, and they enjoyed a fond farewell.

The Black Guardian transported Menlove Stokes to Dellah from the far distant future. Stokes became a Professor of Applied Arts at St Oscar's.[470]

In 2594, the fox-like Valethske were searching for their former gods, the Khorlthochloi, and came into conflict with the Sontarans. The Earth Empire had colonised the Thynemnus System, and a mass immigration led to tensions. The planet Korsair was established to settle disputes. The Valethske attacked one of the new colonies, overwhelming the Korsairs and capturing colonists for their larder.[471]

Fitz was initiated into Faction Paradox around 2594. Laura Tobin, who would eventually become the Doctor's companion Compassion, was sent to Ordifica the same year. Two years later, the Time Lords sterilised the planet, which killed three hundred million people. Two thousand survivors, including Fitz and Laura, were evacuated to the *Justinian*, which headed to the year 1799.[472]

---

465 Dating *Demontage* - No date is given, but the art forger Newark Rappare appears in both this and the Benny novel *Dragon's Wrath* (set in 2593), and he is 'middle aged' in both.

466 Dating *Cold Fusion* - The novel was originally set at the same time as *So Vile a Sin* and tied in quite closely to that book, but it became clear *So Vile a Sin* wouldn't be released as scheduled. Following that, *Cold Fusion* was reworked to occur just before the Benny New Adventures, and included the first mention of Dellah, the planet Benny was based on for that series. A copyright notice on a wardroid states that this is 2692, but that was a typographical error, and should have read '2592'. It's 'four hundred years' before Chris and Roz's time (p165). It's stated that the Adjudicators have been around for 'half a millennium' (p247).

467 Patience vanishes mysteriously in *Cold Fusion*, and reappears in *The Infinity Doctors*

468 *Interference* (p113).

469 Dating *The Dying Days* - The date is given.

470 *The Well-Mannered War*

471 *Superior Beings* (p108).

472 *Interference*

473 *Love and War*, presumably a reference to the Daleks' use of blackmail in *Death to the Daleks*.

474 Dating *Death to the Daleks* - There is no date given on-screen, but the story takes place after the Dalek Wars. *The Programme Guide* placed it in "c.3700" (first edition), "c.2800" (second edition) and *The Terrestrial Index* put it in "the twenty-fifth century".

The TARDIS Logs offered a date of "3767 AD" (the same year as *The Monster of Peladon*). *The Official Doctor Who & the Daleks Book* claimed that the Dalek Plague used in this story is the Movellan Virus, so the author set the story between *Resurrection of the Daleks* and *Revelation of the Daleks*, around 3000 AD. This is non-

The Twenty-Seventh Century

According to the Doctor, the Daleks 'started coming up with other schemes' after they lost the Wars.[473]

? 2600 - DEATH TO THE DALEKS[474] **->** A plague spread through the atmospheres of many of the Outer Planets. Thousands died, and ten million people were threatened. Earth scientists quickly discovered an antidote to the plague: parrinium, a chemical that acted as both a cure and an immunity. It only existed in minute quantities on Earth, and was so rare that it was one of the most valuable known substances.

A satellite surveying the planet Exxilon discovered that parrinium was almost as common there as salt was on Earth. A Marine Space Corps ship was sent to Exxilon to collect parrinium, but the Daleks wanted to secure the substance for themselves, then force the Space Powers to accede to their demands.

Upon arriving within range of the planet, the Earth ship suffered total power failure. The crew explored the area and discovered a fantastic city - the source of the power-drain - that was thousands of years old. The Exxilon natives guarded this City fanatically, and the priests ensured that anyone caught there faced certain death. The Doctor and Sarah arrived shortly before the Daleks. Venturing into the City, the Doctor was able to stop the power drain. He also tricked the Daleks and - with the sacrifice of Galloway, one of the Earthmen - blew up their ship.

During the twenty-seventh century, oxygen factories were built in London.[475] In 2660, Fridgya was devastated in the fifth Thargon-Sorson war. Its cryo-morts would remain undisturbed for many thousands of years.[476]

2673 - SHADOWMIND[477] **->** This was the time of Xaxil, the twenty-fourth Draconian Emperor.

Thousands of years before, the Shenn of Arden had discovered 'hypergems' that boosted their telepathic ability. Around 2640, one group of Shenn began to hear a mysterious voice from the sky that ordered them to construct kilns. This voice was the "Umbra", a sentience that had evolved from carbon structures on a nearby asteroid.

By this time, the planet Tairngaire was heavily populated and a member of a local alliance of planets, the Concordance, with its own space fleet that had recently seen action in the nasty Sidril War. In 2670, colonists from Tairngaire set up camp on the planet Arden. The Colonial Office decreed that the natural features of the planet should be named after characters from the works of Shakespeare. Accordingly, the main settlement was called Touchstone Base, and there was a Lake Lysander, a Titania River, and a Phebe Range of mountains.

After completing wargame trials in the Delta Epsilon system, the CSS *Broadsword* was recalled to Tairngaire by Admiral Vego and sent to investigate the situation at the Arden. All contact had been lost with the settlers, and five ships dispatched to investigate also vanished. It was discovered that the Shenn were secretly operating in New Byzantium by inhabiting artificially constructed human bodies. The "Umbra" was building 'shadowforms', extensions of its power. The Doctor located Umbra and blocked off the sun's rays, effectively rendering it unconscious.

During the twenty-seventh century, a Haitian deciphered the Rihanssu language, allowing a peace treaty that ended the war between Earth and that race.[478]

---

sense, though, as that plague would have no effect on humans - as the Doctor says in *Resurrection of the Daleks* "it is only partial to Dalek". The gas that disfigures humans seen in *Resurrection of the Daleks* is not the Movellan Virus, but a weapon that the Daleks themselves are immune to.

The Daleks routinely use germ warfare throughout their history (we see it in *The Dalek Invasion Of Earth*, *Planet Of The Daleks* and *Resurrection Of The Daleks*). It's never stated in this story that the Daleks caused the plague on the human colony planets, but it's fair to infer they did, especially as they're stopped from launching a "plague missile" at Exxilon. *Timelink* suggested "3500".

475 *Original Sin* (p204).

476 *The Well-Mannered War*. The Thargons and Sorsons were originally seen in *The Tomorrow People*.

477 Dating *Shadowmind* - The Doctor tells Ace that "by

your calendar the year is twenty-six seventy-three" (p29). The events of *Frontier in Space* in "twenty-five forty" (p74) were "one hundred and thirty years ago" (p61).

478 *White Darkness*

STAR TREK: In the Pocket Books' range of *Star Trek* novels (particularly those by Diane Duane), the Romulans call themselves 'Rihanssu', and the race is referred to in *White Darkness* (p129). A few of the other New and Missing Adventures have included such *Star Trek* in-jokes. There are many, for example, in *Sanctuary*, another of David McIntee's books, and Turlough refers to the Klingon homeworld in *The Crystal Bucephalus* (p104).

Star Trek and *Doctor Who* have radically differing versions of the future, and *The Left-Handed Hummingbird* establishes that *Star Trek* is merely fiction in the *Doctor Who* universe. Maybe, just as Trekkies in the seventies

c 2675 - THE SANDMAN[479] -> The Clutch, the fleet of ships containing the Galyari race and numerous tag-alongs, returned to the homeworld of the Cuscaru. A Cuscaru ambassador returned a piece of the Galyari's destroyed Srushkubr, but this catalyzed the neural energy tainting the Galyari. The long-dead General Voshkar was reborn in a monstrous body, and tried to return the Galyari to warfare. The Doctor and Evelyn's involvement resulted in Voshkar's demise. The Clutch departed into space, and resumed business as an intergalactic flea market of sorts.

There had been examples of humanity oppressing native species for centuries. The Swampies of Delta Magna, for example, had been displaced and oppressed. Slavery was formally reintroduced on many worlds.[480] The time-sensitive Tharils had once been the owners of a mighty Empire, with territory stretching across several universes including N-Space and E-Space. Now slavers had captured them. The Tharils were a valuable commodity, as they alone could navigate the ships using warp drive based on 'Implicate Theory'. Many humans became rich trading in Tharils. One privateer, a veteran of Tharil hunts on Shapia commanded by Captain Rorvik, vanished without trace following a warp drive malfunction.[481]

2680 - THE HIGHEST SCIENCE[482] -> Authorities on Checkley's World had made the planet Hogsumm to resemble the fabled planet Sakkrat, hoping to capture the criminal Sheldukher and retrieve the Cell that he stole. A slow time converter set up on Hogsumm created a Fortean Flicker that moved objects through time, including a group of hostile Chelonians and some train-riders taking the 8:12 from Chorleywood in 2003.

In 2680, Sheldukher and his crew revived from stasis and landed on "Sakkrat". Sheldukher committed suicide while resisting arrest, and the Cell was killed also. Sheldukher's Hercules devastator atomized a large area of the planet. The Chelonians and the train-riders, known to the Chelonians as the EightTwelves, were left frozen in a stasis field.

The Master sabotaged the slow time converter on Hogsumm, creating a Fortean Flicker. President Romana of Gallifrey located the source of the disturbance on Hogsumm, and released the trapped humans and Chelonians. The Chelonians weren't grateful, so Romana marooned them there and took the humans home.[483] The abandoned Chelonians survived and created a viable colony that made contact with the rest of their kind after a few thousand years.[484]

The Battle of the Rigel Wastes took place in 2697. The Doctor, Bernice, Roz and Chris witnessed the massacre.[485] In the twenty-seven and twenty-eight hundreds, New Earth Feudalism was established. This social system would lead to the thirtieth century Overcities.[486]

In the twenty-eighth century, the Legions tried to undermine the business consortia of the galaxy using their multi-

---

managed to get NASA to name a prototype space shuttle after the USS *Enterprise*, the *Star Trek* fans of the future managed to name a lot of planets after ones from their favourite series - Vulcan, as seen in *The Power of the Daleks*, being one of the first.

479 Dating *The Sandman* - No date is given, but the Benny audio *The Bone of Contention*, also written by Simon Forward, features the Clutch and is set in the very early twenty-seventh century. In that story, it's said that the Galyari Research Directorate hopes to build weapons against the Sandman. As the Clutch's weaponry isn't significantly advanced in *The Sandman* audio, it probably takes place soon after the Benny adventure.

480 The Swampies appear in *The Power of Kroll*. Slavery exists at the time of *Warriors' Gate* and *Terminus*, and the work camps referred to in *The Caves of Androzani* are also near-slavery.

481 *Warriors' Gate*. Stephen Gallagher has stated in interviews (see, for example, *In-Vision* #50) that Rorvik's crew come from N-Space, and their familiarity with English (such as the graffiti), "sardines" and "custard" suggest they come from Earth. The coin flipped is a "100 Imperial" piece and they use Warp Drive, both of which suggest an Earth Empire setting, although plac-

ing the story details here is arbitrary.

482 Dating *The Highest Science* - Sheldukher's ship arrives at Sakkrat in "2680" (p17). It is "two hundred and thirty years" in Benny's future (p35) [q.v. 'Benny's Birthday'].

483 *Happy Endings*

484 *The Well-Mannered War*

485 *Death and Diplomacy* (p203).

486 *Death and Diplomacy* (p71).

487 *The Crystal Buchephalus* (p40, p80).

488 'A thousand years' before *Interference*.

489 *The Dark Path*

490 Dating *The Sensorites* - Maitland says "we come from the twenty-eighth century", which might mean it is later than that. An incoherent John says they've been at Sense-Sphere for either "four years" or "for years". *The Programme Guide* set the story in "c.2600" in its first two editions, *The Terrestrial Index* settled on "about 2750". *The TARDIS Logs* gave the date as "2765". *Timelink* "2764".

491 *Original Sin* (p287).

492 Dating *Kinda* - An arbitrary date. I assume that the colonists are from Earth, as they have recognisably English names. On-screen they only refer to a "home-world", which Todd says is overcrowded. Sanders' attitude perhaps suggests an early colonial period, and the dimensional abilities. The Time Lords intervened, sending Mortimus to imprison the Legion homeworld for eight thousand years. Around this time, the Wine Lords of Chardon had the best wine cellars in the galaxy.[487]

Earth claimed the planet Dust on the Dead Frontier, but never developed it.[488] The renegade Time Lord Koschei visited Earth in the twenty-eighth century and met Ailla, a woman who joined him on his travels. It was a time of food riots and constant war.[489]

c 2764 - THE SENSORITES[490] **->** During the twenty-eighth century, spacecraft from Earth ploughed deeper and deeper into space, searching for minerals and other natural resources. On Earth, air traffic was becoming congested. Earth ships reached Sense-Sphere, a molybdenum-rich planet that was inhabited by the shy, telepathic Sensorites.

A five-man Earth ship discovered the planet Sense-Sphere in the twenty-eighth century, but the Sensorites feared exploitation and refused to trade with Earth. The Earth mission left, but shortly afterward, the Sensorites began dying from a mysterious new disease. Within a decade, two out of ten Sensorites had died.

By the time a second Earth mission arrived, the Sensorites were terrified of outsiders. They used their psychic powers to place the crew of the ship in suspended animation, a process that drove one human, John, mad. When the Doctor, Ian, Barbara and Susan arrived and investigated, it became clear that the Sensorites were suffering from nightshade poisoning, introduced to the City water supply by the previous Earth expedition. The second expedition left, promising not to return to the planet.

By 2765, INITEC had built the first of a chain of Vigilant laser defence space stations in orbit around Earth. The station proved vital in preventing the Zygons from melting the icecaps and flooding the world.[491]

? 2782 - KINDA[492] **->** The homeworld was overcrowded, and teams were sent to assess other worlds for possible colonisation. One of these was S14, a primeval forest world, which had the local name Deva Loka ('the land of the Kinda'). The natives were humanoid telepaths and lived in harmony with nature. Trees came into fruit all year round, and the climate hardly varied throughout the year. The Doctor banished the Mara, a psychic creature from the 'dark places of the inside', and persuaded the colonists to abandon further settlement.

Elizabethan, the wife of President John F Hoover of New Jupiter, gave birth to triplets following fertility treatment. She had used DNA samples from Hanstrum, Hoover's chief technician, and not her infertile husband. The children were named Asia, Africa and Antarctica.[493] In the early 2790s, the ten-planet Minerva System was colonised by an Earth ship captained by Julian de Yquatine.[494]

Hanstrum later tried to murder Elizabethan after she began to suspect her triplets were psychopaths, and wanted to confess her infidelity. Elizabethan was rendered comatose, and the triplets were blamed and imprisoned.[495]

c 2799 - COMPANION PIECE[496] **->** Philosophical questions about alien civilizations, such as whether non-humans possessed souls and could be baptised, caused a rift in the Catholic Church. Social and political instability compelled Pope Athanasius to relocate to Rome, a mobile space station with a replica of Vatican City. The Catholics who remained on Earth elected Pope Urban IX as their leader, and each side declared the other false.

Missionaries from the Catholic Church had arrived on the planet Haven and converted much of the indigenous population. However, a malfunctioning TARDIS landed there and exploded, devastating the planet. The Church in response branded all Time Lords as witches. Grand Inquisitor Guii del Toro rose to power in the church on Haven, and instigated the "Good Shepherd" project, using human-like robots to evangelize.

A Carthian bandit chief named Brotak took control of most of the planets in the Magellanic System, and named himself Tsar of all the Magellanic Clouds. He converted to Roman Catholicism, and favoured the Cetacean Brrteet'k (a.k.a. Celestine VI) as the next Pope.

The Doctor and his companion Catherine Broome repaired the malfunctioning TARDIS by stealing some mercury from the Weirdarbi, a race of cybernetic insects. They then arrived on Haven to do some shopping, but the Doctor, identified as a Time Lord, was quickly arrested by del Toro. The Doctor and Cat were dispatched to Earth

---

story would seem to be set after *Colony in Space*, in which colonists are seen as "eccentric". The colonists are from Earth in Terrance Dicks' novelisation, where the Doctor suggests they are from the time of the "Empire". *The TARDIS Logs* set the story in the "25th Century". *Timelink* set it in 1981, reasoning that it isn't an Earth colony.

493 'Thirteen years' before *Earthworld*.
494 *The Fall of Yquatine*, 'over two hundred years' earlier than 2992.
495 'About seven years' before *Earthworld*.
496 Dating *Companion Piece* - It is "the twenty-eighth century" (p74), "eight hundred years" after Cat's time (p78).

aboard an Inquisition spaceship to face a papal conclave, but Pope John Paul XXIII was declared soul-dead at this time. Forces supporting either Celestine VI or Pope Urban XII as John Paul's successor fell into open conflict. Del Toro died amid the warfare.

The Inquisition ship took heavy damage, and the Doctor, Cat and their allies had minutes to live unless a robot could be sent through the ship's toxic areas, reach the bridge, and use its controls to release the sealed-off TARDIS. With the Inquisition's robots non-functional, the Doctor resigned himself to telling Cat about her true nature.

c 2800 - EARTHWORLD[497] **->** Earth Heritage had established around the galaxy thousands of EarthWorld theme parks, where lifelike androids would replicate - albeit in a rather garbled form - the history of Earth. Many of the people of New Jupiter wanted independence from Earth, and the Association for New Jupitan Independence (ANJI) was gaining support. The Doctor, Fitz and Anji arrived and

were arrested on suspicion of sympathy with the independence movement. The Doctor managed to stop an android rampage.

Elizabethan revived from her coma, and although her daughter Asia died, she pledged to help her remaining two children.

Colonists seeking independence from Federation officials settled on Phoenix, the fourth planet in the Paledies System. Terraforming machinery automatically went to work while most of the colonists remained in hibernation, but sunspot activity hampered development of an ozone layer and set the process back by decades. Space station *Medusa* was set up in geostationary orbit.[498]

2815 - FESTIVAL OF DEATH[499] **->** The leisure cruiser *Cerberus*, with a thousand passengers onboard, was trapped in hyperspace between Teredekethon and Murgatroyd. Nearly one hundred ships crashed into it, including a prison ship containing dangerous

---

497 Dating *Earthworld* - The date is arbitrary, but New Jupiter wants independence from Earth and the advanced androids are 'pretty standard'. It is 'the far distant future'.

498 'Fifty years' before *Three's a Crowd*.

499 Dating *Festival of Death* - The date is given on p116.

500 'Fifty years' before *Revenge of the Cybermen*.

501 *Christmas on a Rational Planet* (p189).

502 *The Ultimate Treasure* (p71).

503 'Almost a century and a half' before *So Vile a Sin*.

504 Dating *Dark Progeny* - The date is given.

505 *The Taking of Planet 5* (p15).

506 Dating *Three's a Crowd* - The Doctor estimates it is around the 'twenty-eighth, maybe twenty-ninth century' from the space station's design, which dates back at least fifty years to the colony's formation. Mention of a Federation suggests this story occurs in the vicinity of *Corpse Marker*. There's talk of a 'hyperspace transmat link' capable of "beaming" people from star system to star system, but nobody actually uses this device, and it's possibly part of Auntie's ruse against the colonists.

507 *So Vile a Sin* (p28).

508 'Fifteen years' before *Ten Little Aliens*.

509 Dating *Revenge of the Cybermen* - In *The Ark in Space*, the Doctor is unsure at first when the Ark was built ("I can't quite place the period"), but he quickly concludes that "Judging by the macro slave drive and that modified version of the Bennet Oscillator, I'd say this was built in the early thirtieth century...late twenty-ninth, early thirtieth I feel sure". Yet the panel he looks at appears to be a feature of the Ark, not the original Nerva Beacon.

Still, in this story when Harry asks whether this is "the

time of the solar flares and Earth is evacuated", the Doctor informs him that it is "thousands of years" before. Mankind has been a spacefaring race for "centuries" before this story when they fought the Cyber War, according to both Stevenson and Vorus. It is clearly established in other stories that the Earth is not abandoned in the twenty-ninth century. This, then, would seem to be the story set in the "late twenty-ninth, early thirtieth century". The Cybermen are apparently without a permanent base of operations, so the story is presumably set after the destruction of their base on Telos in *Attack of the Cybermen*.

One difficulty with this is that the Cybermen in *Earthshock* (set in 2526) watch a clip from this story. I take this as the production team showing us the previous Doctors, rather than trying to date the story (in the same way, in *Mawdryn Undead*, the Brigadier 'remembers' scenes he wasn't actually in). However, *About Time* suggests the Cybermen in *Earthshock* are time-travellers, which explains the otherwise erroneous *Revenge of the Cybermen* clip.

The Programme Guide set the story in both "c.2400" and "c.2900", while *The Terrestrial Index* preferred "the tail end of the 25th Century". *Cybermen* placed the story in "2496", but admitted the difficulty in doing so (p71-72). *The Discontinuity Guide* offered "c.2875". *Timelink* suggests "2525". 'A History of the Cybermen' in *DWM* #83 suggested the (misprinted?) date "25,514".

510 Dating *The Robots of Death* - An arbitrary date. *The Programme Guide* set the story "c.30,000", but *The Terrestrial Index* preferred "the 51st Century". *Timelink* set the story in 2777, the same period as it set *The Happiness Patrol*.

Arachnopods. They escaped and went on the rampage. The Repulsion - an extra-dimensional creature that existed between life and death - offered the survivors of *Cerberus* the chance to escape. They agreed, and the Repulsion exchanged them with participants of the "Beautiful Death" in 3012. Rescue missions would discover only empty ships, prompting 'the mystery of the *Cerberus*'.

The wrecked spaceships were rebuilt inside the hyperspace tunnel as the G-Lock station.

A mysterious planetoid was detected entering the Solar System, and it eventually became the thirteenth moon of Jupiter. It was named Neo-Phobus by humans, and the Nerva Beacon was set up to warn shipping of this new navigational hazard. Nerva was one of a chain of navigational beacons, which also included Ganymede Beacon at vector 1906702.[500]

ID implants were mandatory in citizens of the Empire, except for those exempted by the Corporate Faiths Amendment Act 2820.[501] The Privacy of Sentient Beings Act was passed in 2830.[502] Earth President Helen Kristiansen declared herself Empress. Helen I would be kept alive by life support systems, and her brain would be controlled by the computer Centcomp, which gave her access to the memories of all previous Earth Presidents. She became aware of the Doctor.[503]

2847 - DARK PROGENY[504] -> The telepathic inhabitants of Ceres Alpha died out long ago, surviving as a psychic gestalt. Much later, the planet - the closest ever found to Earth's natural conditions - was colonised by humans. Earth was overcrowded and polluted at this time, and terraforming corporations like Worldcorp and Planetscape make planets suitable for human colonisation.

Influenced by the gestalt, the colonists' children began developing psychic powers. Worldcorp encouraged this, hoping that the children's telekinesis could be used to transform planets. The Doctor arrived and exposed the plan. The children rebelled against Worldcorp's corrupt leader, Gaskill Tyran, who died when the children made him mentally relive his acts of murder. The parents of one of the children, Veta and Josef Manni, took custody of the entire group.

The accelerator, a device than could heal wounds and change people's appearances, had been invented.

In the mid-twenty-ninth century, zigma photography proved reconstructions of the Temple of Zeus to be inaccurate.[505]

c 2850 - THREE'S A CROWD[506] -> A group of militaristic, reptilian Khellians happened across the Phoenix colony, and the Khellian Queen laid a clutch of eggs aboard the colony ship. The colony leader, Auntie, bargained with the Khellians and allowed them to feed off humans in stasis; in return, they were to spare her family. The number of humans who were awake dwindled down to sixteen. They became agoraphobic and lived intensely isolated lives, unaware of the Khellian presence and what had befallen their fellows.

The Doctor, Peri and Erimem arrived at this time and exposed the Khellian threat. The Khellians were wiped out and the colony ship destroyed, but the terraforming process improved the planet's sustainability. Humans sleeping in a dozen habitat domes were slated for revival.

The Forrester palace was built on Io.[507] The Earth Empire annexed the Schirr homeworld and renamed it Idaho. Some Schirr, named the Ten-Strong, formed a resistance movement. They stole the knowledge of black arts from the non-corporeal Morphieans, who failed to distinguish between the Ten-Strong and the other corporeal beings. The Morphieans initiated retaliatory strikes against human worlds such as New Bejing, and the Ten-Strong launched terrorist strikes on planets such as New Jersey and Toronto, often killing millions.[508]

? 2875 (Day 3, Week 47) - REVENGE OF THE CYBERMEN[509] -> Fifty years after Neo-Phobus was discovered, the civilian exographer Kellman began his survey of the planetoid, setting up a Transmat point between it and the Nerva Beacon. He renamed the planetoid Voga.

Fifteen weeks later, an extraterrestrial disease swept through Nerva. Once the infection began, the victims died within minutes. The medical team on board the station were among the first to perish, and Earth Centre immediately rerouted all flights through Ganymede Beacon. As loyal members of the Space Service, the Nerva crew remained on board. Ten weeks after the plague first struck, all but four people on the station were dead. The Cybermen were responsible as part of their plan to destroy Voga. The Doctor defeated them.

? 2877 - THE ROBOTS OF DEATH[510] -> By the late twenty-ninth century, robots had become so advanced that some people found themselves greatly unhinged by the robots' inhuman body language. Psychologists christened this 'Grimwade's Syndrome', or 'robophobia'.

Vehicles called Stormminers ventured out on two-year missions into a hundred million mile expanse of desert. Sand blown up in storms was sucked into the Stormminers' scoops, which sifted out the lucrative substances such as zelanite, keefan and lucanol. The water supplies for the Stormminers' eight-man crew was totally recycled once a month, but the crew lived in relative luxury. Most of the work was done for them by robots: around a hundred Dums, capable of only the simplest task; a couple dozen Vocs, more sophisticated; and one Super-Voc co-ordinating them.

One Stormminer, commanded by Uvanov, witnessed a string of murders instigated by Taren Capel, a madman obsessed with freeing the robots from servitude. A robot killed Capel, and only three of the crew - Uvanov, Pool and Toos - survived the slaughter.

Uvanov's Storm Miner mined the deserts of of Iapetus, the second moon of Saturn.[511]

? 2878 - THE POWER OF KROLL[512] -> The Sons of Earth Movement claimed that colonising planets was a mistake. They demanded a return to Earth, but most of its members had never been to the homeworld, which was now suffering major famines.

A classified project, a methane-catalysing refinery, was set up on the third moon of Delta Magna. Two hundred tons of compressed protein were produced every day by extracting material from the marshlands, and sent to Magna by unmanned rockets. It was claimed that the Sons of Earth were supplying gas-operated projectile weapons to the native Swampies on this moon, and that the group was employing the services of the notorious gun-runner Rohm-Dutt. The truth was that Thawn, an official at the refinery, was supplying the Swampies with faulty weapons as an excuse to wipe them out.

A squid creature on this moon had consumed the Fifth Segment of the Key to Time, and grown to a monstrous size. The Swampies regarded it as their god, Kroll. Thawn's plan was uncovered and he was killed. The Doctor and Romana recovered the Fifth Segment, which ended Kroll's power. Kroll had been the source of the refinery's compressed protein, and the facility was left useless upon the creature's reversion.

Earth colonised Dramos, located between the secondary and tertiary spiral arms of the galaxy. Dramos Port became an important trading post.[513] The Doctor and Jo visited the home planet of the Pakha and discovered that an ancient Diadem contained a being that made them aggressive. The diadem was lost when the Doctor cast it into a ravine.[514]

---

511 *Legacy*, although this is contradicted by *Corpse Marker*. In real life, Iapetus isn't large enough to have a desert the size of the one referred to in *The Robots in Death*.

512 Dating *The Power of Kroll* - Kroll manifests "every couple of centuries" according to the Doctor, and this is his fourth manifestation, suggesting it is at least eight hundred years since Delta Magna was colonised. *The Terrestrial Index* set the story in the "52nd Century", *The TARDIS Logs* "c.3000 AD".

513 "Centuries" before *Burning Heart* (p4).

514 'Many hundreds of years' before *Legacy*.

515 Dating *The Caves of Androzani* - There is no indication of dating on-screen. Sharaz Jek seems worried when it appears that the Doctor and Peri are from Earth, suggesting it has political influence. The machine pistols suggest a colonial setting, but Sirius society is long-established; there seems to be an interstellar economy and the androids are highly advanced, so I favour placing this a little later. The Spectrox supplies must be so limited as to have little long-term effect on the human race, explaining why it is not referred to in any other story.

516 Dating *Corpse Marker* - This is a sequel to *The Robots of Death*, and happens an unspecified number of "years" afterward.

BLAKES 7: *Corpse Marker*, a sequel to *The Robots of Death*, features Carnell - a character who also appeared in the *Blakes 7* episode *Weapon* (Chris Boucher wrote all three stories).

This opens a can of worms, as it suggests that *Blakes 7* and *Doctor Who* occur in the same universe, which is just about possible. It's never established in which century *Blakes 7* takes place, and the original proposal stated only that it was 'the third century of the second calendar'. The only real indication was that the Wanderer spacecraft (in the *Blakes 7* story *Killer*, written by Robert Holmes) were the first into deep space "700 years" before Blake's era. In *Doctor Who* terms, that would set *Blakes 7* in the twenty-eighth or twenty-ninth century.

The future history of *Blakes 7* is pretty basic - humanity has colonised many planets and most of those are under the control of the fascist Federation. While never stated in the series itself, publicity for the show (and subsequent guides to the series) said that there was a series of atomic wars across the galaxy several hundred years before Blake's time, and the Federation was founded in the aftermath. By coincidence, this fits quite neatly with the *Doctor Who* timeline, and the atomic war might be the Dalek / Galactic Wars of the twenty-sixth century. As might be expected, not every detail matches perfectly, but the oppressive Earth Empire of *Doctor Who* is not wildly different from the Terran Federation seen in *Blakes 7*. The symbol worn by the Earth expedition in *Death to the Daleks* (authored by Terry Nation, who created *Blakes 7* and wrote a fair amount of it) is the symbol of the Federation in *Blakes 7*, turned ninety degrees.

The audio *Three's a Crowd*, which roughly dates to this era, mentions a Federation and uses *Blakes 7* tele-

? 2884 - THE CAVES OF ANDROZANI[515] **->** Spectrox was 'the most valuable substance in the universe'. At the recommended dose of .3 of a centilitre a day, spectrox could halt the ageing process and double lifespans. There was some evidence that with a sufficient quantity of the substance, a human might live forever.

Spectrox was refined from the nests of the bats of Androzani Minor, a dangerous process carried out by androids. Supplies of spectrox were halted when the scientist Sharaz Jek and his androids rebelled against Androzani Major. The Praesidium sent a taskforce to apprehend Jek and they captured the refinery, but Jek removed the supplies of spectrox. After six months, and with the Doctor's help, the supplies were destroyed in a mudburst - a tidal flood of primeval mud.

? 2887 - CORPSE MARKER[516] **->** In Kaldor City, the lowly-born Uvanov was promoted to being a topmaster of the Company, but this failed to sit well with members of the elite classes on the Company Board. They asked the psycho-strategist Carnell to devise a means by which they could secure their power. Carnell's scheme entailed use of new generation of cyborg-robots, which had been secretly created. The cyborgs proved uncontrollable and went on the rampage, killing many prominent citizens. The Doctor destroyed the cyborgs, and Carnell supplied Uvanov with blackmail information against members of the Board. Uvanov quickly attained the top position of Firstmaster.

The Kaldor City audio series starts around four years after Corpse Marker.

c 2890 - GRIMM REALITY[517] **->** Titan had whale ranches and was being terraformed. Space mining was big business, with prospectors looking for rare particles such as strange matter, squarks and Hydrogen 3. Zero Rad Day was celebrated on Earth.

The Doctor, Anji and Fitz landed on the planet Albert as the salvage ship *Bonadventure* entered orbit. The Doctor realised that the laws of physics on the planet operated much like the rules of a fairy tale. The planet was alive and had absorbed the memory banks of a crashed Earth ship, then modelled itself as a world of fairy tales. The Doctor collected up various 'wishing boxes', which contained the

spawn of a nearby white hole. One of the insectoid Vuim used the great powers of the white hole to cure his race of a wasting disease, which seeded the white hole's spawn into a gap between realities to gestate. The parent white hole left and life on Albert returned to normal.

c 2890 (May) - TEN LITTLE ALIENS[518] **->** Earth was exporting its poor at this point and levying repressive taxes. Those born on Earth had legal and social advantages over off-worlders. Alien planets were renamed after places on Earth. The Earth military was run by Pentagon Central, and included the Pauper Fleet, the Royal Escort and the Peacekeepers. The Japanese Belt was trying to develop teleportation.

An Anti-Terror Elite squad from Earth landed on a planetoid for an exercise and discovered a Schirr building there, with a murdered group of Schirr terrorists inside. The Doctor, Ben and Polly arrived, and the Doctor realised that Nadina Haunt, the human squad's leader, was a Schirr sympathiser who thought she was leading her men into an ambush.

The complex launched itself towards the Morphiean Quadrant. The Schirr terrorists, the Ten Strong, revived. They wanted to ally with a renegade faction of the Morphiean race, and topple the Earth Empire. The Doctor managed to resist the Ten-Strong's spells and annihilate them. The Morphiean authorities dealt with their renegades, ending the Morphiean Quadrant's conflict with humanity.

In 2891, the Daleks destroyed the planet of the Anthaurk, a reptilian race. The Anthaurk occupied Kaillor in the Minerva System and renamed it New Anthaur. The native Izrekt were massacred. The other planets declared war.

On the 16 Lannasirn, following the Anthaurk defeat, the Treaty of Yquatine was signed. The Minerva Space Alliance was formed when the system declared independence from Earth. The Anthaurks began the Century of Waiting, secretly rebuilding their arsenal. For a century, other races flocked to the Minerva System, including the Ixtricite (a crystal race combining 'the Krotons, the Rhotons and the something-else-ons'). The Adamanteans and the Ogri colonised Adamantine. Around 2900, the Vargeld family became prominent in the politics of the system.[519]

---

port sound effects.

517 Dating *Grimm Reality* - The mining companies were active 'a hundred or a hundred and ten years' ago, in the 2780s.

518 Dating *Ten Little Aliens* - It is clearly the subjugation phase of the Earth Empire. An e-zine written somewhat prior to these events (p15), with biographies of

Haunt's troopers, is dated '23.5.90', presumably meaning 23rd May, 2890.

519 *The Fall of Yquatine* (p30, p43).

Decline and Fall

By the beginning of the thirtieth century, the Empire had become utterly corrupt. Planetary Governors, such as the one on Solos, would routinely oppress the native races of the planet.[520] Humans were often little more than 'work units', fit only for manning factories or mines where using humanoid robots was uneconomic. Alien races across the galaxy, such as the Mogarians, resented Earth's exploitation of their planets but could do little. Humanity was "going through the universe like a plague of interplanetary locusts". Mogar, in the Perseus Arm of the Galaxy, was a rich source of rare metals such as vionesium. Although Earth assured the Mogarians that they only required limited mining concessions, they were soon strip-mining the planet, and the shipments to Earth received Grade One security.[521]

Every native animal species died out except humanity and the rat.[522] The humans of Earth in the thirtieth century had no appendix or wisdom teeth, and most racial differences had been smoothed out in the general population.[523] Humans had a lifespan of around one hundred and forty years.[524] Suspensor pools were fashionable in the Earth Empire.[525] In the thirtieth century, the Cybermen built a time capsule, but a test flight left them stranded in Jersey in 1940.[526]

In 2905, Chris Cwej's father graduated from the Academy. He served in the Adjudication Service, as his ancestors had for centuries, until 2971.[527] **Nerva Beacon completed its mission at Voga. The space station remained operational for many centuries afterward.**[528]

The Overcity Era

The pollution levels on the surface of Earth reached such a level that the population was forced to live in vast sky cities. Around 2945, the Wars of Acquisition fought by the Empire reached Earth itself. The Overcities were built over the battle-torn Earth using a new form of cheap and effective null-gravity. They floated around a kilometre from the surface, supported on stilts and by null-grav beams.

Half the Earth's population, everyone that could afford it, lived in the Overcities and Seacities. The wealthier you were, the higher the levels that you were allowed to access. Earth's surface became the Undertown: a flooded, ruined landscape. The Vigilant belt of defence space stations proved invaluable at repelling alien attacks, and within ten years the front had shifted so far away from Earth that humanity had almost forgotten they were taking place.

After a few years of austerity, Earth benefited from a technological and economic upsurge. It was "a time of peace and prosperity: well, for the peaceful and prosper-

---

520 *The Mutants*

521 *Terror of the Vervoids*

522 *Just War* (p143), although we see bears and wolves in *The Ice Warriors*, and hear of a variety of animal specimens in *The Ark in Space*. Pigs and dogs survive until at least the year 5000 AD (judging by *The Talons of Weng-Chiang* and *The Invisible Enemy*), there are sheep and spiders on the colony ship sent to Metebelis III in *Planet of the Spiders*, Europa is well stocked with animal life in *Managra*, and the Ark (in *The Ark*) contains a thriving jungle environment complete with an elephant and tropical birds.

523 *Death and Diplomacy* (p16).

524 *Just War*

525 'Fifty years' before Roz's time. *The Also People* (p10).

526 *Illegal Alien* (p152).

THE THIRTIETH CENTURY: While I don't think that the Earth was ravaged by solar flares at this time (see *The Ark in Space*), the Doctor's description of a "highly compartmentalised" Earth society of the thirtieth century in *The Ark in Space* matches similar descriptions of Earth in stories set at this time. Earth is "grey" in *The Mutants* and "highly organised" in *Terror of the Vervoids* Part Four. We learn of food shortages in *Terror of the Vervoids*.

In terms of the New Adventures, this is Cwej and Forrester's native time, and we meet them there in *Original Sin* - a story that ties in quite closely with *The*

Mutants (Solos is even mentioned on p318). Roz returns and dies in her native time in *So Vile a Sin*.

We first learn of the decline of the Earth Empire and the Overcities in *The Mutants*, although in that story the Solos native Ky calls them "sky cities" and claims they were built because "the air is too poisonous", not because of the wars.

527 *Original Sin* (p160-161).

528 Nerva Beacon has a "thirty year assignment" according to Stevenson in *Revenge of the Cybermen*, so it ought to be decommissioned around 2915. We see the Beacon again in *The Ark in Space*.

529 *The Mutants*

530 *Original Sin*

531 According to a discussion document about Roz and Cwej prepared by Andy Lane for the New Adventures authors. She is in her early forties when she joins the Doctor (*Original Sin*). *The Also People* adds that Roz's clan name is "Inyathi," which means buffalo.

532 "Some" Mendeb years before *Independence Day*.

533 *Original Sin* (p127). Her graduation was 'twenty three years' before meeting the Doctor, according to *So Vile a Sin* (p293), she'd had 'thirty years as an enforcer' in *Zamper*, 'twenty five years' in *The Also People* (p46), and 'over twenty years' in *Just War*. Her graduation in 2955 was mentioned in *GodEngine* (p175).

534 Dating *Independence Day* - It's 'four hundred years' ous, at least". Earth was a cosmopolitan place, with races such as Alpha Centauri, Arcturans, Foamasi, and Thrillip living in the lower areas of the Overcities, although aliens were treated as second-class citizens. Earth at this time had a human population of thirty billion, with almost as many robot workers. The data protection act was modified in 2945 to reflect the changes in technology and society.

Over the generations a semi-feudal system had developed. A Baron was responsible for sections of an Overcity, typically controlling a few hundred levels. A Viscount ran the whole city (an area the size of an old nation state); a Count or Countess was responsible for ten Cities (equivalent to a continent). Earth, and each of the other planets, was ruled by a Marquis or Marquessa. The solar system and its Environs were under the authority of its Lord Protector, the Duke Marmion. The Divine Empress ruled over the whole of the Earth Empire, in which thousands of suns never set, and which stretched across half the galaxy. Few on Earth knew that the Empress was Centcomp - the computer network that ran the solar system - setting judicial sentences, running navigational and library databases, co-ordinating virtually every aspect of life.[530]

Roslyn Sarah Forrester was born in 1935.[531] The Doctor and Jamie arrived at an automatic communications center on Mendeb Two's equator. The two of them pocketed the main communications relay device as a reminder that they should re-visit the area, but this altered history. Without the device, Mendeb Two's disparate settlements were unable to pool their resources and skills, and thus failed to match technological developments on Mendeb Three.[532]

Roz Forrester joined the Adjudicator service, against the wishes of her aristocratic family, in 2950.[533]

c 2950 - INDEPENDENCE DAY[534] -> The Mendeb colonies regressed to a feudal, agricultural society without the advanced technology from the corporations. On Mendeb Three, the tiny region of Gonfallon declared itself a duchy, and came to dominate the planet within a generation.

Military commander Kedin Ashar - the Duke of Jerrissar - helped King Vethran rise to power. Vethran enslaved Mendeb Two, using the drug SS10 to brainwash the populace into submission, but became increasingly tyrannical. Ashar launched a revolt against Vethran, and the Doctor and Ace, hoping to atone for the Doctor's previous error in hindering Mendeb Two's development, helped Ashar achieve victory. Ashar formally ended the slave trade and ordered reparations be made to Mendeb Two.

c 2950 - MASTER[535] -> The Doctor brokered a deal with Death, having come to recognize the entity's hold over the Master. Their agreement was that the Master would remain outside of Death's purview for ten years, and live his days as a contented man. At the end of that time, the Doctor was required to kill his old friend.

The physically scarred Master consequently turned up in the colony of Perfugium with no memory of his past. He came to be known as "John Smith," settled into a happy life and became a physician. Smith inherited, from a former patient named Wolstonecroft, a house that was purportedly cursed.

In Perfugium, a serial killer slaughtered eleven prostitutes and an ordinary teenage girl. Green was the colour of death in the colony, and the bodies were found wrapped in green blankets.

On the tenth anniversary of John Smith's arrival, his friends - the Adjudicator Victor Schaeffer and his wife Jacqueline - gathered at Smith's house to celebrate his "birthday." Their festivities were interrupted by the Doctor, who begrudgingly admitted that Smith's previous identity was the Master. Victor was exposed as the serial killer and further murdered his wife - who was secretly in love with Smith - and Death appeared onhand.

The Doctor and Death amended their deal so Smith could choose whether he wanted to become evil again. Death presented Smith with the option of either killing Victor before he slew Jacqueline, an act that would retroactively save Smith's beloved but make him Death's agent again, or refraining from action and thus saving his benevolent personality. Death expelled the Doctor from Perfugium before he could learn of Smith's decision.

Christopher Rodamonte Cwej was born on 5th September, 2954, in Spaceport Nine Overcity.[536] In 2957, Roz Forrester was squired to Fenn Martle. She would be his partner for fifteen years, and he would save her life on five occasions.[537]

The Black Dalek and the Renegade Dalek Faction may have used the Time Controller to hide from Davros a trillion miles from Earth in the mid-2960s.[538]

after the Galactic Wars (p22), which would place it in the mid-thirtieth century.
535 Dating *Master* - Perfugium is a colony, part of a human empire, ruled by an Empress where Adjudicators enforce the law; so the story is set during the Earth Empire period.
536 According to Andy Lane's Discussion Document about Roz and Cwej, and confirmed in *Head Games*

(p205). The month and day in *The Room with No Doors* (p20).
537 *Original Sin* (p32, p219).
538 This takes the Doctor's remark to the Black Dalek in *Remembrance of the Daleks* that the Daleks are "a thousand years" from home literally, although it's fairly clear the statement is rhetorical.

? 2965 - THE SPACE MUSEUM[539] -> The TARDIS jumped a time track and the Doctor, Ian, Barbara and Vicki found their future selves on exhibit in the Space Museum of the Morok Empire, located on Xeros. The Moroks had executed the adult population of the planet and set the children to work as slaves. The temporal anomaly ended, and the travellers came under risk of the future they'd glimpsed. Vicki incited revolution among some Xeron rebels, and the time travellers made their escape once the Moroks were overpowered.

The Morok Empire collapsed thanks to human intervention, with criminal gangs like the Morok Nostra filling the power vacuum.[540]

? 2966 - THE EVIL OF THE DALEKS[541] -> The Dalek Emperor made plans to capitalise on the difference between the Daleks and humanity. The Daleks were unable to make this distinction on their own, and so the Emperor hatched an elaborate trap in three timezones for their old enemy, the Doctor. The Daleks tricked the Doctor into believing that they wished to become more human. He was all too willing to educate the Daleks about the 'Human Factor', highlighting the difference between the two races: humans were not blindly obedient and showed mercy to their enemies. However, as the Emperor planned, this merely enabled the distillation of the 'Dalek Factor'. The Emperor planned to instill this into all humans throughout the galaxy, forcing them to become Daleks, but the Doctor managed to 'humanise' a number of Daleks.

Civil war broke out between the 'Human' and 'Dalek' factions. Every Dalek in the galaxy had been recalled to Skaro in preparation for the conquest of humanity, and in the ensuing battle they were all wiped out. The Emperor was exterminated by his own kind. The Doctor named this the 'final end' of the Daleks, but even as he said it, it was clear there were survivors.

From the year 3000 to the year 3500, Earth knew of no Dalek activity in the galaxy.[542] During the 2970s, anti-magnetic cohesion was developed.[543] The Landsknecthe - Earth's official security force - fought the Aspenal Campaign in 2970. The Doctor, Chris and Roz helped the Jithra repel the Jeopards, but the Earth Empire conquered both Jithra and Jeopardy. The Jithra were wiped out, but a few hundred thousand Jeopards survived. Meanwhile, Roz's sister, Leabie Forrester, began plotting to

---

539 *Dating The Space Museum* - There's no date given in the story itself. However, it must fall somewhere before the collapse of the Morok Empire in Roz's time (mentioned in *The Death of Art*), and after the Moroks capture a 'banded' Dalek (ie: one with the 'bands' seen in *The Daleks* and *The Dalek Invasion of Earth*, not the 'slatted' ones seen in all subsequent appearances). This date is arbitrary.
540 *The Death of Art*
541 Dating *The Evil of the Daleks* - There is no date given for the Skaro sequences in the scripts. The Doctor murmurs that this is "the final end" of the Daleks, and most fans have taken this statement at face value when they come to date the story. However, a line cut from the camera script of *Day of the Daleks* stated that the Daleks survived the civil war and that the human-ized Daleks were defeated. At the end of this story, as the Doctor makes his declaration, the picture cuts to a seemingly dead Dalek twitching into life.

Taking what we're told at face value, this story has to be set before the destruction of Skaro in *Remembrance of the Daleks*. The *Terrestrial Index* set *The Evil of the Daleks* "a century or so" after *The Daleks' Master Plan*. John Peel and Terry Nation "agreed that *The Evil of the Daleks* was the final story" (*The Frame* #7), but did so before *Remembrance of the Daleks* was written. Peel's novelisation of *The Evil of the Daleks* is set around the year 5000. 'A History of the Daleks' in *DWM* #77 claimed that *The Evil of the Daleks* is set around "7500 AD".

In *Matrix* #45, Mark Jones suggested that the Hand of Omega is sent into Davros' future, thousands of years after Dalek History ends.

In *Mission to the Unknown,* Cory states that the Daleks have not been active in the galaxy "for a thousand years", although later it transpires that they did in fact begin conquering territory five hundred years before. I suggest that the civil war in *The Evil of the Daleks* is not the "final end" of the Daleks, but it does represent a severe defeat, one that removes them from the Milky Way for five hundred years.
542 *The Daleks' Master Plan*
543 *Carnival of Monsters,* "a thousand years" after Jo's time.
544 *So Vile a Sin* (p10, p182).
545 *The Also People* (p101).
546 *Eternity Weeps*
547 *Happy Endings*
548 Dating *Original Sin* - The Doctor tells us that this is the "thirtieth century" (p23). Although we are told at one point that "2955" was "four years" ago (p86), the year appears to be 2975 - this ties in with the birthdates established for Cwej and Forrester in the Discussion Document, and the fact that Cwej's father graduated "seventy years" before, in "oh-five".
549 *The Sorcerer's Apprentice* (p17).
550 *So Vile a Sin*
551 'Six' years before *So Vile a Sin*.
552 *Hope*
553 Dating *So Vile a Sin* - The date is given (p25).

usurp the Empress.[544]

The Earth's oceans were heavily polluted in the thirtieth century.[545]

Humanity and the Silurians were working together by this time.[546] The Doctor hired two Silurian musicians, Jacquilian and Sanki, to play at Benny's wedding.[547]

2975 - ORIGINAL SIN[548] **->** In the early 2970s, mankind fought a short but brutal war with the Hith, a sluglike race. The Empire annexed Hithis and terraformed it. The Hith were displaced, becoming servants and menial workers on hundreds of worlds. They adopted names to denote their displaced status, such as Powerless Friendless and Homeless Forsaken Betrayed and Alone.

The last Wars of Acquisition ended shortly afterward, when Sense-Sphere finally capitulated. The Earth Empire now stretched across half the galaxy.

Soon after the Hith pacification, Roz Forrester saw a man kill a Ditz. When he denied it, she ate his ident and arrested him for perjury and not having valid ID. The incident entered Adjudicator folklore. A year later, Forrester killed her partner Fenn Martle when she discovered he had betrayed the Adjudication Service and was on the payroll of Tobias Vaughn. She attended Martle's funeral, and shortly afterward the Birastrop Doc Dantalion wiped her memories of Martle's death, replacing them with false memories that the Falardi had killed him.

Christopher Cwej graduated from the Academy in 2974. During his training on Ponten IV he had achieved some of the highest marksmanship and piloting scores ever recorded. Cwej's first assignment was a traffic detail. A year later, he was squired to Roslyn Forrester.

The very same day, serious riots started throughout the Empire, particularly on Earth itself. Insurance claims were estimated at five hundred trillion Imperial schillings, a total that would bankrupt the First Galactic Bank. Worst of all, it was revealed that the Adjudication Service was rife with corruption. The riots had been sparked by the release of icaron particles from a Hith battleship, the *Skel'-Ske*, which had been captured by INITEC corporation and kept in hyperspace in Overcity Five.

When the source of the radiation was destroyed, it was clear that the Empire was collapsing. At the time of the rioting on Earth, the Rim World Alliance had applied to leave the Empire. Over the years, all the major corporations had moved from Earth to the outer Rim planets. An Imperial Landsknecht flotilla was sent to pacify them. Rioting also began on Allis Five, Heaven, Murtaugh, and Riggs Alpha. Colony worlds took the opportunity to rebel, stretching the resources of the Landsknecht to their limit.

The Doctor again encountered the now-robotic Tobias Vaughn, leading to a conflict in which Vaughn was decapitated. The Doctor used Vaughn's brain crystal to repair the Cwej family's food irradiator.

The corrupt head of the Adjudicators, Rashid, feared exposure. She decried Roz Forrester and Chris Cwej as rogue Adjudicators, and placed a death sentence on their heads. Roz and Chris departed with the Doctor and Bernice.

At this time, Armstrong Transolar Aerospace were building Starhopper craft on Empire City, Tycho and Luna.[549] The Empire conquered the Ogron homeworld of Orestes, one of the moons of gas giant Clytemnestra, in the Agamemnon System. When humans begin engineering pygmy Ogrons, a native uprising started that would last six years.

While searching for secret Ogron bases, the Imperial ship *Redoubtable* discovered the Nexus on the moon Iphigenia. This was a Gallifreyan device that could alter reality, and drove the expedition insane.[550]

Roz was declared legally dead in 2976. Leabie created a clone of Roz, Thandiwe, to raise as her own daughter.[551] Humberto de Silvestre was born 31st December, 2978. Heavy pollution levels on Earth made him sickly, but his computer skills meant he received medical grants.[552]

2982 - SO VILE A SIN[553] **->** A demilitarised zone existed between the Empires of Earth and the Sontarans. The planet Tara was part of the Empire, and the importance of the nobility had been diminished.

The Doctor, Roz and Chris arrived in this time zone, investigating the source of a signal that was awakening Gallifreyan N-forms. Roz discovered an N-form at the Fury colony on planet Aegistus, the Agamemnon System, but crushed it under a slab of dwarf star alloy. Meanwhile, the Doctor found that the moon Cassandra was actually an ancient TARDIS, wounded during the war with the Vampires, and that its distress signal was waking N-forms. The Doctor programmed the TARDIS to self-destruct, destroying the moon.

Back on Earth, the Doctor euthanised Empress Helen I at her request. He was arrested for regicide. The Empress' death sparked civil war and widespread rioting. The psionic Brotherhood launched a brutal attack on the Forresters' palace on Io, killing a dozen Forresters. The casualties included Roz's niece and nephew, Somezi and Mantsebo.

Abu ibn Walid, actually a pawn of the Brotherhood, was crowned Emperor. He offered Roz the office of Pontifex Saecularis, head of the Order of Adjudicators. Roz's sister Leabie Forrester, with army and Unitatus backing, instigated a rebellion against Walid's rule. Her forces attacked Mars on 26 August. The Battle of Achebe Gorge started. Roz defected to Leabie's side and was appointed the rank of Colonel.

The Doctor and Cwej were captured by the Grandmaster, a psychic gestalt that hoped to use the reality-altering Nexus. The Doctor defeated the Grandmaster's plan, and the dozens of bodies that contained parts of the Grandmaster's persona were either killed or banished to alternate timelines.

Roz lost her life leading a ground assault on the Emperor's palace on Callisto. The death of the Grandmaster left the Emperor lifeless, and Leabie Forrester was declared Empress. The Doctor suffered a heart attack at Roz's burial. A year later, the Doctor, Cwej, Benny, and Jason attended to Roz's final funeral rites.

House Forrester had recently resurrected the long-extinct African elephant.

In 2983, Kimber met Hallett while he was investigating granary shortages on Stella Stora. The Doctor visited this timezone a number of times. On one occasion before Mel joined him, he involved Captain Travers in a "web of mayhem and intrigue", although the Doctor did save Travers' ship. On other visits, the Doctor met Investigator Hallett and visited the planet Mogar.[554]

2986 (16th April) - TERROR OF THE VERVOIDS[555]
-> Professor Sarah Lasky planned to breed intelligent plants, Vervoids, that would hopefully make robots obsolete. Vervoids bred and grew rapidly, plus were quick to learn and cheap to maintain. For an undisclosed reason, the Vervoids also had a poisonous spike. A consortium was ready to exploit the creatures, but as the Vervoids were being transported back to Earth in the intergalactic liner *Hyperion III*, they went on the rampage and killed a number of the passengers and crew, including Lasky. The Doctor's intervention resulted in every example of the species being wiped out using the mineral vionesium, which accelerated their growth cycle.

The ruling Council on Earth came to realise that Earth was "exhausted... politically, economically, bio-logically finished", "fighting for its survival" and was "grey and misty" with "grey cities linked by grey highways across grey deserts... slag, ash, clinker". Earth's air was so polluted that the entire population now had to live in the vast sky cities if they wanted to breathe.

By this point, Earth couldn't afford an Empire any longer. By the end of the thirtieth century, most planets in the Earth Empire had achieved some form of independence from the homeworld.[556] These were "the declining years of Earth's planetary empire".[557]

As the Earth Empire went into the process of collapse, countless planets were cut off and abandoned.[558] The Earth Empress granted Eta Centauri 6 the status of a Duchy Royal with the name of Tractis. Humans had committed genocide there during the Empire period, because the natives refused to allow the mineral exploitation of their planet or the growing of narcotic crops. The Silurian governor of the planet, Menarc, tried to establish an elected council there, but human colonists formed a separatist party and assassinated key politicians. The decaying Empire tried to restore order, leading to a conflict that killed hundreds of thousands. The Doctor commented that matters would improve for Tractis after that.[559]

Human colonists discovered Selonart.[560] The Daleks used time corridors to establish hibernation units on many planets such as Kar-Charrat. The Daleks would only activate when a time traveller entered range, and the Daleks hoped this gambit would help them gain access to the Kar-Charrat Library.[561]

c 2990 - THE MUTANTS[562] -> One of the last planets to gain independence from Earth was Solos. The native Solonians staged organised resistance, but the Marshal of the planet resisted reform for many years. From his Skybase in orbit above Solos, the Marshal had been conducting experiments on the Solonian atmosphere, attempting to render it more suitable for humans.

---

554 *Terror of the Vervoids.* The implication being that these unrecorded adventures took place in the Doctor's future, between the end of his Trial and his encounter with the Vervoids.
555 Dating *Terror of the Vervoids* - The Doctor tells the court that this is "Earth year 2986". A monitor readout suggests it is "April 16".
556 *The Mutants*
557 *Frontier in Space*
558 *Burning Heart, The Ultimate Treasure*
559 *Genocide* (p274-275).
560 'Seventy years' before *The Infinity Race.*
561 'One thousand two hundred and seventy years' before *The Genocide Machine.*
562 Dating *The Mutants* - The Doctor tells Jo that they have been sent to "the thirtieth century". The story must

take place many years after *Original Sin*, where events are set into motion that will eventually mean the Empire's collapse. *The Programme Guide* set the story slightly later ("c.3100"); *Timelink* in 2971.
563 Dating *The Fall of Yquatine* - The date is given (p43, p150).
564 Dating *Superior Beings* - The year is given (p108).
565 *The Dark Path*
566 *Placebo Effect*
567 *Hope*
568 'A thousand years' before *The Book of the Still.*
569 'A few years' before *Festival of Death.*
570 Dating *The Space Age* - The year is given (p216). The people there think it is 2019.
571 Dating *Festival of Death* - The year is given (p115, p116, p194).

When the Solonians began mutating into insect-like creatures, the Marshal ordered the "Mutts" destroyed.

An Independence Conference was arranged between the Solonian leaders and the "Overlords" from Earth, with Solos to be declared independent. The Administrator was assassinated at the meeting, and martial law was declared instead. The Doctor arrived at this time and met Professor Sondergaard, a scientist who had been investigating the history of Solos for many years. Sondergaard had discovered that every five hundred years, the Solonians underwent a radioactive metamorphosis - meaning that the process that was transforming the population into Mutts and altering the atmosphere was seasonal. Earth helped Solos to discover the true form of the mutation, then left the planet alone.

2992 - THE FALL OF YQUATINE[563] -> The Doctor attended the inauguration of Stefan Vargeld, who defeated the unpopular Ignatiev to win the Presidency of Yqatine. Four years later, the Doctor returned just as sentient gas creatures named the Omnethoth, constructed millions of years ago as a weapon to conquer the universe, awoke from dormancy and devastated the planet with searing gas bombs. The reptilian Anthaurk attempted to capitalize on this and seize Yquatine space, but the Doctor's companion Compassion engaged her Chameleon Circuit and impersonated Vargeld, helping to sue for peace. The Doctor mentally reprogrammed the Omnethoth as peaceful cloud-like beings, but a vengeful Vargeld, in retribution for Yquatine's devastation, destroyed the Omnethoth with ionization weapons.

2994 - SUPERIOR BEINGS[564] -> The Doctor and Peri were caught when the fox-like Valethske invaded a pleasure planet, Eknur 4. The invaders were looking for the homeworld of their gods. The Valethske put Peri into suspended animation aboard their ship and departed. The Doctor calculated its next arrival point, in a century's time, and left to rendezvous with Peri then.

Eknur 4 was one of the Wonders of the Universe, and a utopian society given over to hedonism.

At the turn of the thirty-first century, an Imperial Navy force was sent out to seek out alien technology that might help shore up the Earth Empire. They discovered the planet Darkheart and colonised it. They remained isolated for three and a half centuries, but came to discover a device that they also named the Darkheart, and which was built from Chronovore technology. The Chronovores had designed the device to beam healing energy to their remote, injured members, but the colonists adapted it to alter morphic fields. Properly tuned, the Darkheart could transform all alien species into human beings.[565]

From around the year 3000, the Foamasi began gaining in power and reputation across the galaxy.[566] A Sun City teenager hacked Earth's TacNet, causing a meltdown that killed thousands on the East Coast of Australia. Humberto de Silvestre was wounded by this, and only saved when he was grafted with experimental liquid computers. He became the cyborg Silver. In 3006, aliens invaded Earth, overrunning America and taking control of Washington. The government used experimental time machines to send agents to fetch help - Agent Grey was sent to the past, Agent Silver to the far future.[567]

Legends of *The Book of the Still* begin circulating around this time. Unknown parties had developed this artefact as a means by which stranded time travellers could summon help by writing their name in it. Copies of *The Book of the Still*, made from invulnerable taffeta, found their way to various points in time and space, including the planet Lebenswelt in the year 4009.[568]

Documentary maker Harken Batt was discredited when he used actors in an expose of organised crime.[569]

3012 - THE SPACE AGE[570] -> The Doctor, Fitz and Compassion arrived on an asteroid that contained a reconstruction of a futuristic city. The inhabitants - rival members of the Mods and Rockers gangs - had been spirited there from 1965 by a benevolent alien named the Maker. However, the gangs had fallen into continued bloodshed for nineteen years. The Maker, imprisoned by the Mods and compelled to make weapons, had instigated the city's dissolution. Other Makers arrived, liberated their colleague and caused the Mods and Rockers to stand down. The Makers offered the humans a choice: return to 1965 as their younger selves with no memories of these events, or join a futuristic society in 3012. The humans made their decisions, and the Doctor's party departed.

3012 - FESTIVAL OF DEATH[571] -> Against objections from the major religions, Dr Koel Paddox - the galaxy's leading necrologist - opened the Necroport. This housed a machine in which tourists could be temporarily killed and experience the "Beautiful Death", which was touted as the "thrill to end a lifetime". It was located at the G-Lock ship's graveyard in the Teredekethon-Murgatroyd hyperspatial conduit, and swiftly attracted visitors such as the alien Hoopy.

The Doctor and Romana arrived to find that tourists experiencing the Beautiful Death were becoming savage zombies. The Repulsion had temporally swapped the tourists with survivors of the *Cerberus* disaster in 2815. The tourists went into the Repulsions' realm, and the *Cerberus* survivors were endowed with pieces of the Repulsion's essence - the Repulsion hoped this would let it fully manifest in our reality. The Doctor and Romana trapped the Repulsion's essence in ERIC, the G-Lock's central computer, then destroyed it. The Necroport exploded and the zombies expired.

The G-Lock was evacuated and the hyperspace tunnel in which it was located collapsed, eradicating the station. The Arboretan race went extinct as a result of Paddox's experiments. Paddox attempted to reincarnate into his younger self and prevent his parents' deaths, but this trapped him in a recurring loop of his lifetime in which he could only observe, not act.

The Proxima Century All Blacks did the double in 3012. Pratifoon Wabster had their first number one in the same year. The Doctor visited the colony of Puxatawnee, and deemed it a very happy and prosperous place.[572] The planets Emindar and Nimos started a series of minor wars that would run for over a century.[573]

c 3025 - THE SORCERER'S APPRENTICE[574] ->

Although many remained patriotic and a new Empress was crowned, it was clear that the Empire was collapsing. The Landsknechte Corps had fallen, and the newly-independent human worlds were now building vessels of their own. On the medieval world of Avalon, some natives were becoming more proficient at tapping the ancient nanobot system to generate "magic". The Doctor, Ian, Barbara and Susan arrived on the planet as various "sorcerers" sought to gain further power. A magical battle ensued, but the Doctor had his allies place an Avalonian control device - "Merlin's Helm" - on the head of a reptilian cephlie, a native of the planet. The Helm restored the cephlies, but they elected to destroy themselves and the nanobot system. This ended "magic use" on the planet.

= ? 3050 - THE INFINITY RACE[575] ->

Sabbath attempted to harness the infinity forces on the planet Selonart in a parallel universe. Selonart served as host to the Trans-Global Selonart Regatta, which took place every five Earth years. The Doctor joined the fourteenth Regatta, defeating Sabbath's plan. Sabbath had released the Warlocks of Demigest to assist with his scheme, but the Doctor used time crystals formed on Selonart to erase the Warlocks' presence from the universe.

The Greer colonies and Proxima Centauri were part of the Earth Empire. There was civil war on Cygnus, where the rebels refused to give up their plesiosaur farms. The Imperial Security Service covered all humanity, including the Empire, the Bronstein Union of Socialist Systems, Mikron Conglomerates, Proudhon Confederation and the Western Hub Consortium.

3060 to 3090 - FLIP-FLOP[576] ->

The planet Puxatawnee had two timelines.

= 1) The Slithergees arrived around Christmas, 3060, and demanded a moon to inhabit. President Mary Bailey was apparently killed by her secretary, who was allegedly a Slithergee agent. In truth, she was assassinated by beings from another timeline, who feared she would cave in to the Slithergees. There was an uprising, and warfare against the Slithergees left Puxatawnee a heavily damaged, radioactive wasteland. Christmas Day was renamed

---

572 *Flip-Flop*

573 *Vanderdeken's Children*

574 Dating *The Sorcerer's Apprentice* - The TARDIS crew discover a spaceship built in "2976" (p17), which leads the Doctor to suggest this is the "end of the thirtieth century" (p33, p48). We learn that the colony was founded in 2145 (p203), 846 (Avalonian?) years ago (p33), making it the year 2991. Later, though, we learn that the "city riots" seen in *Original Sin* were "fifty years ago" (p156), so it must be nearer 3025.

575 Dating *The Infinity Race* - There's an Earth Empire, but ruled by an Emperor, not an Empress, so it has to be set after *So Vile a Sin*. This presumes that history in the parallel universe in which *The Infinity Race* occurs is roughly comparable to our own.

576 Dating *Flip-Flop* - The dates are given.

577 "Eighteen years" before *The Ribos Operation*.

578 Dating *The Ultimate Treasure* - Rovan Cartovall disappeared in 1936 BC, which was 'five thousand years ago' (p37).

579 Dating *Palace of the Red Sun* - The journalist Dexel

Dynes appeared in *The Ultimate Treasure* and remembers Peri from that story, which he describes as a 'few years' ago (p39).

580 Dating *The Ribos Operation* - A date for the story is not given on-screen. While my date is arbitrary, Ribos is close to the Magellanic Clouds, suggesting that humans have developed at least some level of intergalactic travel. Lofficier placed the story in "the late 26th century", apparently confusing the Cyrrhenic Alliance with the force established to fight the Cybermen in *Earthshock*. *Timelink* says 3010.

Retribution Day. Thirty years later, Professor Capra built a time machine to change history by sending agents back to kill the President's secretary. The time machine overloaded, destroying the planet.

= 2) President Bailey survived thanks to the time travellers' intervention, and yielded to the Slithergee demands. Thirty years later, the aliens had dominated the planet, and any resistance was seen as 'hate crime'. In this timeline, Capra built a mind peeler to interrogate people, not a time machine. Rebels forced the Doctor to take them back in time, hoping to assassinate Bailey before she capitulated to the Slithergees.

Around 3060, The Cyrrehenic Alliance fought a series of Frontier Wars. The Graff Vynda-K led two legions of his men for a year in the Freytus Labyrinth, and also fought on Skarne and Crestus Minor. He was an unstable, temperamental man, though, and upon returning home he discovered that his people had allowed his half-brother to take the throne. The High Court of the Cyrrhenic Empire rejected the Graff's claim for restitution, and he spent eighteen years plotting his revenge.[577]

c 3064 - THE ULTIMATE TREASURE[578] -> The Doctor and Peri arrived at the Astroville Seven trading post. A dying merchant provided them with galactic co-ordinates purporting to pinpoint the treasure of Rovan Cartovall, the emperor of Centros who once ruled fifty star systems. His treasury was worth the equivalent of 64,000,000,000,000 stellar credits. The co-ordinates led to the planet Gelsandor, where some telepaths set a variety of challenges for any who wanted Cartovall's treasure. The Doctor and Peri found themselves in competition against a number of criminals, and the treasure was revealed to be the infinite possibilities of life, as represented by the puzzles themselves.

c 3068 - PALACE OF THE RED SUN[579] -> The warlord Glavis Judd had risen to power on his homeworld of Zalcrossar, and expanded his military might to create a Protectorate of twenty star systems. His forces sought to subjugate the planet Esselven, but King Hathold and his family sealed the Keys to Esselven, an irreplaceable set of documents and protocols, in an impenetrable vault that would only open for their DNA. Without the Keys, Esselven society would degenerate and become useless to Judd.

The royals fled and established the Summer and Winter Palace residences on "Esselven Minor," a planetoid orbiting a white dwarf star. However, the white dwarf's gravity, in conjunction with the planetoid's mass and the royals' planetary defence shield, started altering space-time in the area.

Time within the shield accelerated faster than time in the outside universe.

Judd spent a year tracking the royals and landed on the planetoid in search of them. Due to the fast-time effect, he wasn't seen again for 500 years. Judd never appointed a successor, and his Protectorate collapsed in his absence.

? 3078 - THE RIBOS OPERATION[580] -> The rare mineral Jethrik was now used to power ships such as Pontenese-built battleships. Communication across the galaxy was via hypercable, and highly trained mercenaries, the Schlangi, were available for hire.

Located three light centuries from the Magellanic Clouds, the Cyrrhenic Alliance included the planets Cyrrhenis Minima (co-ordinates 4180), Leviathia and Stapros, as well as the protectorate of Ribos (co-ordinates 4940) in the Constellation of Skythra, 116 parsecs from Cyrrhenis Minima.

The Doctor, Romana and K9 arrived on Ribos looking for the First Segment of the Key to Time. They meet Garron, a con-man from Hackney Wick, who was forced to leave Earth after his attempt to sell Sydney Opera House to the Arabs backfired. Garron's exploits included a successful scheme to sell the planet Mirabilis Minor to three different, unsuspecting clients.

Aware of the Graff Vynda-K's thirst for revenge and need for a powerbase, Garron proposed to sell him the planet Ribos for the sum of ten million Opeks. Garron boosted the Graff's interest by forging a survey suggesting that the planet was rich in Jethrik. Garron's lump of genuine Jethrik, used to con the Graff, was the first segment of the Key.

The Doctor defeated the Graff, leading to the Graff's demise, and outsmarted Garron to obtain the first segment.

In the late thirty-first century, people from the Overcities began to recolonise the surface of the Earth. One group, later known as the Concocters, created Europa: a bizarre and eclectic fusion of historical periods built on the site of Europe. There were three Switzias, four Rhines, six Danubes and dozens of black forests. Each Dominion represented a different period between the fourteenth and early twentieth history. So, for example, there were five Britannias - Gloriana, Regency, Victoriana, Edwardiana and Perfidia.

The undead - the descendants of the vampires Jake and Madeline - dwelt in Transylvania. Fictional and historical characters, named Reprises, were cloned. This enabled the people from the Overcities to jostle with the likes of Byron, Casanova, Crowley, Emily Bronte and the Four Musketeers.

The Vatican, a vast floating city equipped with psychotronic technology, was built to impose order on Europa (as the true papal seat had moved to Betelgeuse by this time).

The entire Concoction was masterminded by the Persona, a being formed from the merging of the Jacobean dramatist Pearson and the ancient Mimic.[581]

c 3094 - SUPERIOR BEINGS[582] -> The Doctor arrived on a garden planet, anticipating the arrival of the Valethske with Peri as their captive. Mindless giant beetles - the remaining physical forms of the Khorlthochloi - dominated the planet. The Doctor rescued Peri and the Valethske discovered the beetles were the last remains of their former gods. The Valethske ship bombarded the planet from orbit, wiping out the Khorlthochoi. Veek, the Valethske leader, realised the futility of his mission and departed for home with his crew.

? 3100 - WARMONGER[583] -> The planet Karn had gained a reputation as a place of healing, presumably due to the presence of the Sisterhood's Elixir of Life, and a medical association constructed a neutral facility there named the Hospice. The scientist Mehendri Solon served as the facility's Surgeon-General. The fifth Doctor suddenly arrived one day with a severely wounded Peri, who had been injured by a flying predator, to procure Solon's surgical skills.

Solon adeptly healed the Doctor's companion. However, the deposed Gallifreyan President Morbius pooled mercenaries and space pirates from many worlds to assault Karn, hoping to gain the Sisterhood's Elixir. The Sisterhood repelled Morbius' attack, but his forces conquered many planets. The Time Lords covertly manipulated events to form an Alliance, led by "the Supremo," to counter Morbius' ambitions. The Alliance defeated most of Morbius' forces, and he suffered a final defeat on Karn when troops from Fangoria interceded.

Morbius was sentenced to execution, but Solon, his disciple, removed Morbius' brain before his body was atomized. The Hospice was disbanded and Karn was left to the Sisterhood. Solon remained on Karn with Morbius' brain.

The seeds of the Galactic Federation were sown during the first third of the thirty-second century, as the Space Powers of the Milky Way began forging links and alliances. Over the course of the first half of the millennium, the various Alliances began to forge links with one another and alien races. These groups drifted closer and closer together until the Galactic Federation was formed. Virtually the entire civilised galaxy was involved to some degree or another.[584]

? 3120 - THE BRAIN OF MORBIUS[585] -> **Karn was a graveyard of spaceships, with Mutt, Dravidian and**

---

581 *Managra*

582 Dating *Superior Beings* - It's 'over five hundred years' after 2594 (p108).

583 Dating *Warmonger* - The story is a prequel to *The Brain of Morbius*, set when Solon was a young, renowned surgeon.

584 *Legacy*, expanding on *The Curse of Peladon* and *The Monster of Peladon*. *Warmonger* sees a huge Alliance between many alien races, and talk of a 'United Planets Organisation' being formed.

585 Dating *The Brain of Morbius* - The Doctor informs Sarah Jane that they are "considerably after" her time. If the Mutt at the beginning of the story originated on Solos, that might affect story dating. *The TARDIS Logs* suggested "3047", *Apocrypha* gave a date of "6246 AD". *The Terrestrial Index* supposed that the "Morbius Crisis" takes place around "10,000 AD". The original version of this chronology set the story around the time of *Mindwarp*. *Timelink* says "2973", and *Warmonger* - the prequel to the story - seems roughly to concur.

586 *Timewyrm: Genesys* (p217).

587 Dating *Vanderdeken's Children* - The year is given (p3). The Galactic Federation exists, although neither Emindar nor Nimos are members.

588 *Burning Heart*. This happened when Mora Valdez, who is 21 (p15), was 'five years old'.

589 Dating *Burning Heart* - The year is given (p20).

590 *Lucifer Rising*. An excommunicated Knight of Oberon, Orcini, appears in *Revelation of the Daleks*. The suggestion that the order was based on the moon of Uranus was first postulated in the Virgin edition of this book, and confirmed in *GodEngine*.

591 'Thirty generations' before *Bang-Bang-A-Boom*.

592 Dating *Managra* - The Doctor sets the co-ordinates for "Shalonar - AD 3278", and the TARDIS lands in the same timezone, but the wrong location (p26). Later Byron states that he was created "in the middle of the thirty-third century" (p113).

593 Dating *Real Time* - It is 'millennia' since the creation of the Cybermen, and the Cybermen are thought to be extinct. The story is set after *Sword of Orion*. The online notes name the planet as Chronos, but the name isn't used in the story.

594 *Dust Breeding*, 'in the thirty-third century'.

595 Dating *The Dalek Factor* - In *Planet of the Daleks*, the Thal space missions against their arch-enemies seem relatively recent. Here, there have been search and destroy missions against the Daleks for "eight centuries" (p17). The lull in Dalek activity ties in with the one noted in *The Daleks' Master Plan*. If the Daleks truly were wiped out in *The Parting of the Ways*, then this 'unspecified' Doctor would seem to be either the eighth after *The Gallifrey Chronicles* or the ninth before *Rose*.

Birastrop vessels all coming to grief. Solon built a hybrid creature from the victims of these crashes and installed Morbius' brain into it, but the Time Lords sent the Doctor to prevent Morbius from escaping. A mindbending contest with the Doctor drove Morbius mad, and the Sisterhood killed his physical form.

In the thirty-second century, Earth made contact with the descendants of Utnapishtim's people.[586]

3123 - VANDERDEKEN'S CHILDREN[587] -> The Doctor and Sam arrived at a derelict structure floating in space - the product of a closed time loop - which was claimed by the warring Emindians and Nimosians. A hyperspace tunnel led to twenty years in the future, when the two planets had wiped each other out. The Doctor was unable to prevent the war, but he managed to save one of the ships and send it a thousand years into the future, where it recolonised Emindar.

In 3158, the Rensec IX catastrophe took place when the planet's inhabited underground caverns were destroyed due to seismic activity caused by Puerto Lumina, the planetary satellite. The survivors were shipped, en masse, to the decommissioned, dormant staging-post facilities of Puerto Lumina. A combination of faulty life support and a ham-fisted attempt to chemically sterilise the survivors there left a hundred thousand civilians dead.[588]

3174 - BURNING HEART[589] -> The population of Earth was rebuilding following the destruction of the Overcities. Across the galaxy, trade, culture and civil liberties suffered as humanity retrenched. On Dramos, a satellite of the gas giant Titania, the Church of Adjudication was becoming ever more draconian. Millions reacted by joining the extremist Human First group, which advocated the genocide of all aliens. White Fire served as the inner core of this group.

The Doctor and Peri arrived on Dramos at this time, and conflict broke out between the Adjudicators and White Fire's forces. The Node of Titania, an area similar to Jupiter's Red Spot, was alive and had been increasing hostilities in its attempts to communicate. The sentience of the Node was allowed to merge with OBERON, the Adjudicators' central computer. The conflict and xenophobia diminished, and the Adjudicators recruited more non-humans into their ranks.

The Sontarans and Cybermen had both recently tried to introduce more individuality into‿ their species. The Sontaran attempt created disunity, and some of their ranks were banished.

As Earth went through its Empire and Federation phases, the fortunes of the Guild of Adjudicators waxed and waned. Eventually, they became unnecessary. A thousand forms of local justice had sprung up. Every planet had its own laws and police. The universe had passed the Guild by, leaving it nothing to adjudicate. The Guild degenerated into a reclusive order of assassins known as the Knights of the Grand Order of Oberon, dreaming of past glories and crusades for truth. The organization was based on the moon of Uranus.[590]

Gholos attacked the pastoral planet Angvia, beginning a conflict that would last thirty generations. Both sides violated the Tenebros IV peace treaty in the name of their cause.[591]

3278 - MANAGRA[592] -> For centuries, the Nicodemus Principle had prevented a Reprise from becoming the Pope of Europa. But in 3278, Cardinal Richelieu, a Reprise, assassinated Pope Lucian and attempted to succeed him. He faced opposition from the Dominoes, a secret organisation stretching across the Dominions. Behind the scenes, the Persona attempted to seize control of Europa. Persona was destroyed along with Europa's Globe Theatre, but Richelieu succeeded in becoming Pope Designate.

3286 - REAL TIME[593] -> Three survey teams went missing on the desert planet Chronos, and the Doctor and Evelyn accompanied a follow-up group there to investigate. They discovered that an absent alien race had equipped a temple of sorts with a time machine. The time traveller Goddard, hailing from 1951, warned the Doctor that events in this era would precipitate the Cybermen conquering Earth in the twentieth century. The Cybermen of the future captured a techno-virus that Goddard carried, and reverse-engineered it into a virus capable of turning living beings into cybernetic ones. The CyberController of the future infected Evelyn with this virus. The Doctor triggered a temporal wave that aged the Cybermen of the future to death, whereupon he and Evelyn departed, unsuspectingly, for 1927.

The Doctor rescued the Rembrandt painting *The Night Watch* from the Reichmuseum in Amsterdam shortly before the facility burned down.[594]

c 3340 - THE DALEK FACTOR[595] -> Thal Search-Destroy squads continued to hunt down the Daleks, but it had been two generations since any significant contact had been made. On an unnamed planet, the Daleks worked to implant the Dalek Factor (or 'Dalek-heart') into all other lifeforms. The Dalek-hearted life on their test planet considered itself superior to the original Daleks, forcing them to quarantine the planet.

The Daleks successfully imprisoned the Doctor on this planet.

The Galactic Federation

Around the turn of the thirty-fifth century, nearly three hundred years after the first steps towards confederation, the Headquarters of the Galactic Federation on Io were officially opened and **the Federation (or Galactic) Charter was signed. Founding members included Earth, Alpha Centauri,** Draconia, New **Mars and Arcturus. At this point in history, Earth was regarded as "remote and unattractive". It was ruled by an aristocracy, "in a democratic sort of way". The Federation prevented armed conflicts, and even the Martians renounced violence (except in self-defence). Under the terms of the Galactic Articles of Peace (paragraph 59, subsection 2), the Federation couldn't override local laws or interfere in local affairs (except in exceptional circumstances), and was hampered by a need for unanimity between members when taking action.**[596]

c 3400 - THE DARK PATH[597] **->** The Adjudicators had become the Arbiters, the judicial service of the Federation. The Federation Chair was located on Alpha Centauri. The Federation included the Veltrochni, Terileptils, Draconians and Xarax.

The Federation ship *Piri Reis* reached the lost colony of Darkheart just as temporal distortion attracted both the Doctor's TARDIS and that of the renegade Time Lord Koschei and his companion Ailla. The Doctor and Koshei found the Darkheart device, which the colonists were using to make alien beings human.

Koshei accidentally killed Ailla and became stricken with grief. He became increasingly intent on hoarding power, and eradicated the planet Terileptus as a necessary means of testing the Darkheart's destructive power. Ailla regenerated, and Koshei became even more isolated upon realizing that she had spied on him for the High Council of the Time Lords. The Doctor stopped Koshei's thirst for power by programming the Darkheart to turn the system's star into a black hole. The colonists evacuated aboard the *Piri Reis*, but Koshei went missing when the black hole consumed his TARDIS.

> = These events happened in the Inferno universe, but in a different form that allowed Koschei and Ailla to continue their travels.[598]

? 3417 - THE MENAGERIE[599] **->** Over the centuries, the Knights of Kuabris had prevented scientific discovery on their planet, and discouraged historical research. They came to be led by Zaitabor, who was unaware that he was

---

596 *The Curse of Peladon* and its two sequels - *The Monster of Peladon* and the New Adventure *Legacy* - are set at the time of a Galactic Federation. The date of its foundation is given in *Legacy* (p164); the words are those of Alpha Centauri and the Doctor from *The Curse of Peladon*.

The justice machines named the Megara also follow "The Galactic Charter" in *The Stones of Blood*, and they are from 2000 BC. Many other stories refer to "Intergalactic Law", "Intergalactic Distress Signals" and so on - there are clearly certain established standards and conventions that apply across the galaxy, although who sets and enforces them is unclear.

597 Dating *The Dark Path* - There is no exact date, but the Galactic Federation exists (p3) and it is over 'three hundred and fifty years' after the turn of the thirty-first century (p175) which was 'nearly half a millennium ago' (p178), which all suggests it's set in the thirty-fifth century. Terileptus is the homeworld of the Terileptils, as seen in *The Visitation*.

598 *The Face of the Enemy*

599 Dating *The Menagerie* - It is "centuries" (p67) after Project Mecrim was initiated in 2416. The Doctor suggests that it happened "a millennium or three" (p126) and "hundreds, perhaps thousands of years ago" (p102).

600 Dating *Terminus* - Once again, an arbitrary date. The date from the Virgin edition of this chronology was adopted by *Asylum*, which is set in 3488, 'six years' later.

The Terrestrial Index saw Terminus Inc. as one of the "various corporations" fought by the Doctor in the late "25th century". The FASA Role-playing game gave the date as "4637 AD". *Timelink* doesn't assume that the characters are human and sets it in 1983.

601 Dating *Asylum* - The year is given. It is "six years" since *Terminus*.

602 'Five hundred years' before *The Book of the Still*.

603 *Mission to the Unknown, The Daleks' Master Plan*. The Daleks occupy Skaro at this time, and according to Marc Cory, they haven't been heard from for five hundred years before this point.

604 Dating *The Sirens of Time* - The date is given.

605 Dating *Palace of the Red Sun* - It is five hundred years after the previous part of the story.

606 The contest in *Bang-Bang-A-Boom* is the 308th.

607 "Twelve generations" before *Head Games* (p15).

608 *A Device of Death*. There's a discussion of the history on p31. No date is given in the novel, but Kambril has been in charge for 'eighteen years' by the time of the novel (p90).

609 *Davros*

an android. Zaitabor hoped to purge his city of corruption and revived some Mecrim, who initiated a slaughter. The Doctor arranged to detonate the city's reactor, which killed Zaitabor and the Mecrim. The Knights fell from power, and negotiations between the planet's various races were arranged.

? 3482 - TERMINUS[600] **->** Passenger liners travelled the universe and sometimes fell victim to raiders, often those combat-trained by Colonel Periera.

Lazars' Disease swept the universe, spreading fear and superstition even among those in the rich sectors. Sufferers were sent secretly to Terminus, a vast structure in the exact centre of the known universe. The station was run by Terminus Incorporated, who extracted massive profits from the operation. The facility was manned by slave workers, the Vanir, who were kept loyal by their need for the drug Hydromel. The Lazars were either killed or cured by a massive burst of radiation from Terminus' engines.

Nyssa of Traken and the Garm, one of the original crew of Terminus, planned to reform the station by introducing proper diagnoses and controlled treatment. Nyssa proposed creating an improved version of Hydromel that would break the Vanir's dependency on the company.

3488 - ASYLUM[601] **->** Nyssa developed a vaccine for Lazar's Disease and travelled the galaxy until it was eradicated. Full of optimism, she discovered there were many other pandemic problems such as war, famine and disease. She worked to relieve suffering, including periods spent as a nurse on Brallis and airlifting food into Exanos.

When Exanos was destroyed in a nuclear war, Nyssa established herself in a peaceful system and became a university teacher specializing in technography, the study of writings about science. As part of this, she studied the works of Roger Bacon. The Doctor met Nyssa while tracking an anomaly in space-time, and discovered discrepancies in her recollection of Bacon. This was evidence of alien interference with the timeline. When the Doctor departed for the thirteenth century, Nyssa stowed aboard. After restoring history to its true course, the Doctor brought Nyssa home.

The planet Lebenswelt sold its entire mineral wealth to Galactinational. Now immeasurably rich, the population dedicated themselves to decadence.[602]

The Daleks returned to Earth's galaxy. Over the next five hundred years, they gained control of more than seventy planets in the ninth galactic system and forty in the constellation of Miros. They were, once again, based on their home planet of Skaro. The Daleks were the only race known to have broken the time barrier,

although Trantis had tried in the past without success. Dalek technology was the most advanced in the universe.[603]

= 3562 - THE SIRENS OF TIME[604] **->** The Knights of Velyshaa fought Earth, but their First Empire fell. Thanks to the seventh Doctor, though, their leader Sancroff escaped to establish the Second Empire. Capturing a Temperon, the Knights built time machines and successfully attacked the Time Lords, although the Knights' bodies had become withered and parasitic. They used Time Lord flesh to maintain themselves.

The fifth, sixth and seventh Doctors joined forces to defeat the Knights. History was restored and Sancroff was executed.

& 3568 - PALACE OF THE RED SUN[605] **->** The Doctor and Peri arrived on Esselven Minor to find time running faster within the planetoid's defence screen than without. The warlord Glavis Judd landed on the planet, intent on capturing the fugitive Esselven royals. The Doctor tricked Judd into thinking that everyone on the planetoid, including the royals' real-life descendents, were holographic projections. Judd departed, but the Doctor corrected the errant defence shield and brought the planetoid back into synch with the rest of the universe. This caused Judd to emerge in normal space 500 years after he'd departed, and after the royals had re-settled Esselven. The royals failed to recognize Judd as the genuine article and, per policy regarding people claiming to be the great warlord, threw him in an asylum.

The first annual Intergalactic Song Contest was held.[606] Around 3700, the planet Detrios lost its sun and the population moved underground. With each generation, the skin of the human inhabitants grew more pale. The Detrian lizard people started a war against the human Ruling Family.[607]

In the Adelphine cluster on the galactic rim, relations between the humans of the Landor Alliance and the Averon Union were strained. Within four years, this became a full-scale war. The Landor Alliance constructed Deepcity, a weapons research station on an asteroid. The Averons attacked Landor, but they were driven back. The Landorans destroyed Averon, but suffered ninety percent casualties themselves. There was a period of civil war across the cluster. Barris Kambril took control of Deepcity, and told the workers there that Landor was destroyed to better motivate them.[608]

Galactic corporation TransAlliedInc was formed in the thirty-eighth century.[609]

c 3788 / = c 3788 - INTERFERENCE[610] **->** The planet Dust, a former Earth colony on the Dead Frontier on the edge of the galaxy, was cut off for centuries. Cattlemen there organised into vigilante gangs called Clansmen.

IM Foreman's travelling show arrived briefly on Dust, distorting space-time in the area. Faction Paradox was planning to use a biodata virus to make Dust a world of paradox. A group from the Remote crashed on Dust around this time, and founded the settlement Anathema II from the remains of their ship. Fitz had risen through the ranks of Faction Paradox and become Father Kreiner. He sought revenge against the Doctor.

IM Foreman released his final incarnation, the elemental Number Thirteen, to eliminate the Remote. Father Kreiner was lost to the Time Vortex. Foreman's first twelve incarnations were killed, displaced to early Gallifrey and underwent regeneration. Number Thirteen was convinced to merge with Dust's biosphere, whereupon Foreman became integrated with the entire planet. Dust was renamed Foreman's World.

= The third Doctor was shot and regenerated, a paradox as he was meant to die on Metebelis III. From this point, the Doctor was infected by the Faction's biodata virus.

On Foreman's World, the now-female IM Foreman created a bottle universe, and she was surprised when its inhabitants soon built their own bottle universe. Time Lords arrived to acquire the bottle, hoping to use it as a potential refuge in the coming future War. Foreman didn't give them an immediate answer. The eighth Doctor arrived, wanting answers about his visit to Dust. He learned that Father Kreiner was trapped in the bottle universe. After the Doctor left, Foreman discovered that the bottle universe had also vanished.

? 3800 - A DEVICE OF DEATH[611] **->** The Doctor, Sarah and Harry arrived at the Adelphine cluster. The Doctor lost his memory, but gradually pieced together enough to reveal Barris Kambril's lies to the workers at the Deepcity weapons research station. The synthonic robots developed here would play a part in the demise of the Daleks.

The Dark Peaks Lodge of the Foamasi was founded, devoted to restoring their home planet of Liasica to its former glory and seizing control of the Federation.[612] **For countless centuries, the people of the primitive planet Peladon had worshipped the creature Aggedor. The planet turned away from war and violence** under King Sherak, **but remained isolated.** In 3864, a Federation shuttlecraft crashed on Peladon after falling foul of an ion storm en route to the base at Analyas VII. The Pels rescued one of the survivors, Princess Ellua of Europa. **The Earthwoman married the King,** Kellian, within a year. Six months after that, she had persuaded him to apply for

---

610 Dating *Interference* - It's the 'thirty-eighth century' (p306) and 'several centuries' after *The Monster of Peladon*. The Foreman / bottle universe story occurs an unspecified time after the main events on Dust

611 Dating *A Device of Death* - No date is given, but this is a time of isolated Earth colonies, and it's fifteen hundred years since Landor was colonised. The implication that the robots are the Movellans, seen in *Destiny of the Daleks*, would seem to contradict *War of the Daleks*.

612 "Two centuries" before *Placebo Effect*.

613 *The Curse of Peladon*, with much elaboration given in *Legacy* - a book that incorporates some details from *The Curse of Peladon* novelisation.

614 *Neverland*. The Sensorian Era was mentioned but not defined in the *Doctor Who* TV Movie.

615 Dating *The Curse of Peladon* - There is absolutely no dating evidence on-screen. The story takes place at a time when Earth is "remote", has interstellar travel and an aristocratic government. Although the Federation seems to be capable of intergalactic travel at the time of *The Monster of Peladon*, Gary Russell suggested in the New Adventure *Legacy* that Galaxy Five was a mere "terrorist organisation" (p27). *Legacy* is set "a century" after *The Curse of Peladon*.

Remarkably, given the lack of on-screen information, there has been fan consensus about the dating of this story and its sequel: *The Programme Guide* set the story in "c.3500", and made the fair assumption that the Federation succeeded the collapsed Earth Empire. *The Terrestrial Index* revised this slightly to "about 3700". *The TARDIS Logs* suggests "3716". *Timelink* suggests "3225".

616 *The Invisible Enemy*. Clones are seen or referred to before this date in a number of stories such as *Heritage*, *Trading Futures*, *Project: Lazarus*, *The Also People* and *So Vile a Sin*. Professor Marius distinguishes between the Kilbracken Technique, which instantly creates a "sort of three-dimensional photocopy", and a true clone that would take "years" to produce. *Heritage* also suggests cloning keeps periodically falling into disuse, whereupon another scientist will come forward and claim to have perfected the science for the "first" time.

617 Dating *The Monster of Peladon* - Sarah guesses that it is "fifty years" after the Doctor's first visit, and this is later confirmed by other people, including the Doctor, Thalira and Alpha Centauri.

618 Dating *The Blue Angel* - No date is given, but the ship serves the Federation and is en route to Peladon.

619 Dating *Bang-Bang-A-Boom* - No date is given, but the story is set in the Federation period.

620 *War of the Daleks*

621 *Legacy*. We learn that the Vogans were "ultimately self-destructive" and that the Cybermen eventually set-

Federation membership. Their son was born a year later. **He was named Peladon, and was destined to become king.** [613]

This era was known to the Time Lords as the Sensorian Era.[614]

& 3885 - THE CURSE OF PELADON[615] ->
The **Preliminary Assessment Team arrived at King Peladon's court to see if Peladon was suitable for Federation membership. As they landed, the spirit of Aggedor was abroad. It killed Chancellor Torbis, one of the chief advocates of Federation membership. This was revealed as a plot brewed between the High Priest of Aggedor, Hepesh, and the delegate from Arcturus. If Peladon was kept from Federation membership, then Arcturus would be granted the mineral rights to the planet. Arcturus was killed while attempting to assassinate one of the delegates, while Aggedor himself killed Hepesh. Peladon was granted Federation membership.**

The first human clone was created in 3922 using the Kilbracken holograph-cloning technique. The process was unreliable and the longest a clone ever lived was 10 minutes, 55 seconds. Most serious scientists thought of it as "a circus trick of no practical value".[616]

& 3935 - THE MONSTER OF PELADON[617] ->
When Federation scientists surveyed Peladon, they discovered that planet was rich in trisilicate: a mineral previously only found on Mars, and which was the basis of Federation technology. Electronic circuitry, heat shields, inert microcell fibres and radionic crystals all used the mineral. Duralinium was still used as armourplating.

King Peladon died and was replaced by his daughter, the child Thalira. As she grew up, Federation mining engineers came to her world. Although Thalira's people were resistant to change, advanced technology such as the sonic lance was gradually introduced to Peladon.

The Federation was subject to a vicious and unprovoked attack from Galaxy Five, who refused to negotiate. The Federation armed for war, with Martian shock troops being mobilised. Peladon's trisilicate supplies would prove crucial in this struggle. The planet was still prone to superstition, however, and when the spirit of Aggedor began to walk once more, killing miners that used the advanced technology, many saw it as a sign that Peladon should leave the Federation. For a time, production in the mines halted.

The murders were the work of a breakaway faction of Martians, led by Azaxyr, who were working for Galaxy Five. When the plot was uncovered, Galaxy Five quickly sued for peace.

c 3935 - THE BLUE ANGEL[618] ->
The Doctor, Fitz and Compassion arrived on the Federation ship *Nepotist*, which was en route to Peladon. The crew discovered the Valcean City of Glass had become connected to the Federation through space-time corridors. As the glass city was located within the Enclase, a pocket universe within the larger Obverse, the Federation feared this could destablise the region.

The Doctor joined the Federation mission to meet the Glass Men, and also met Daedalus, a giant jade elephant, who planned to make war with the Federation. Daedalus had opened up forty-three space-time corridors from the Enclave to planets such as Telosa, Skaro, Wertherkund and Sonturak. The *Nepotist* launched a pre-emptive strike with sonic cannons, shattering the Glass Men, but was counterattacked by the Sahmbekarts, a race of lizards. The *Nepotist* crashed near the Valcean city, and the people of the Obverse rushed to defend their territory. The Doctor attempted to intervene, but Iris Wildthyme tricked him into leaving the area. The Doctor would never know how the situation was resolved.

? 3950 - BANG-BANG-A-BOOM![619] ->
The 308th Intergalactic Song Contest was broadcast to over a quinquillion homes across the universe. Contestants included the Angvia of the Hearth of Celsitor (*My Love is as Limitless as a Black Hole, and I'm Pulling You Over the Event Horizon*), Architects of Algol (*Don't Push Your Tentacle Too Far*), the Breebles, the Cissadian Cephalopods, Cyrene, the Freznixx of Braal and Maaga 29 of Drahva (*Clone Love*). The jury included a Martian. Earth's 'national' anthem at this time was 'I Will Survive'.

The matriarchal warlords of Angvia and the transcendental gestalt Gholos had been feuding for thirty generations. A peace conference between the two was supposedly being held on Achilles 4, but this was a feint for the real conference, which was taking place at the Song Contest on the Dark Space 8 station. A Gholos nationalist tried to disrupt the proceedings, but both sides sued for peace.

Earth discovered and surveyed the planet Antalin.[620] In the mid-fortieth century, a 'Cyber-fad' swept the Federation. The Martian archaeologist Rhukk proved that both Telos and New Mondas had been destroyed, meaning the Cyber Race had been eradicated. The public were briefly fascinated by the Cybermen, and documentary holovid crews went to the dead worlds of Voga and Telos.[621]

Zephon became all-powerful in his own galaxy, the Fifth, when he defeated Fisar and the Embodiment Gris, both of which had tried to depose him. The Daleks recruited Zephon to their Master Plan, and he secured the support of the rulers of two further galaxies, Celation and Beaus. The conspiracy also included

Trantis, Master of the Tenth Galaxy (the largest of the Outer Galaxies), Gearon, Malpha, Sentreal and Warrien.

Around 3950, Mavic Chen became the Guardian of the Solar System, ruling over the forty billion people living on Earth, Venus, Mars, Jupiter and the Moon colonies from his complex in Central City. At this time, the prison planet Desperus was set up to house the most dangerous criminals in the Solar System.

Shortly afterward, the Daleks contacted Chen. They needed taranium, "the rarest mineral in the universe", and which was found only on Uranus. If Chen could supply the material, the Daleks would make him ruler of the entire Galaxy. He agreed, and set up a secret mining operation shortly afterward.

The population of the Solar System knew nothing of this, and many showed an almost religious devotion to Chen. His reputation was enhanced in 3975, when all the planets of the Solar System signed a non-aggression pact. For the next twenty-five years, they lived in peace under the Guardianship, and the Solar System - though "only part of one galaxy" - now had a status that was "exceptional ... it had influences far outside its own sphere". It was hoped that by following Chen's example, peace would spread throughout the universe.[622]

Zephon overthrew the Embodiment of Gris in 3932 and Mavic Chen was elected Guardian of the Solar System in 3950.[623] Around 3970, the Hiinds overthrew the Mufls. The Church of the Way Forward was established by Reverend Lukas, who preached that marriage between alien species was unholy.[624] In 3972, Sirius-One-Bee University Press published Albrecht's *Of Finders and Seekers - a users guide to being lost in time*.[625]

= Circa 3979, emaciated, grotesque beings named the Unnoticed had constructed a Tent City, made from invulnerable taffeta, on the photosphere of Earth's sun and set about breeding a colony of human time sensitives there. Uncertain as to their origins, the Unnoticed used the time sensitives to keep watch for time distortion and time travellers - wary that contact with such phenomena could somehow avert their own creation. The human Carmodi Litian was born as one of the Unnoticed's senstives and served for fifteen years before being left for dead on the planet Porconine. She swore revenge against her former masters.[626]

Carrington Corp built the leisure planet Micawber's World between Pluto and Cassius around 3984.[627]

c 3985 - LEGACY[628] **->** The Federation fought a number of wars to secure its position and to protect democratic regimes. GFTV-3 covered the main news stories of this era: atrocities on the Nematodian Border, the android warriors of Orion, slavery on Rigellon and Operation Galactic Storm. The Martian Star Fleet built the deep space cruiser *Bruk*, one of the largest vessels the galaxy had ever seen, and it helped enforce law throughout the galaxy.

With its trisilicate mines exhausted, Peladon faced a choice between becoming a tourist resort or leaving the Federation altogether. The question remained unaddressed while Queen Thalira ruled, but she died in a space shuttle accident. Within four years of her death, her successor King Tarrol applied to leave the Federation, suggesting that Peladon ought to try and find its own solutions to its problems. His choice had perhaps been made easier by the car-

---

tled on a "New Mondas", as they wished to do in *Silver Nemesis*. However, this second homeworld has also been destroyed by the time of *Legacy*. The Cybermen survive to appear in *The Crystal Bucephalus*.

622 In *The Daleks' Master Plan*, Mavic Chen seems to have been Guardian for a very long time. He says, when accused of stealing the taranium, "Why should I arrange that fifty years be spent secretly mining to acquire this mineral..." (implying that he has been actively involved with the plot for half a century). Then again, he is the newest member of the conspiracy, named the "most recent ally". John Peel's novelisation, loosely based on the original scripts, claims that the crime rate on Earth soared fifty or sixty years before *The Daleks' Master Plan* [3940-3950] as the population increased. Mavic Chen was elected and set up the prison colony on Desperus. This scene does not appear in the broadcast version (it is replaced by a line which William Hartnell delivers as "The Daleks will stop at any-

thing to stop us.").

The non-aggression pact is referred to in *The Daleks' Master Plan*. This perhaps suggests that planets in the Solar System were in conflict before this time, and Chen's hope that peace will spread throughout the universe implies that much of known space is at war. A short scene in the New Adventure *Legacy* suggests that Chen did not become Guardian until much later.

623 *Neverland*. The overthrown entity is referred to as 'the Embodiment Gris' in *The Daleks' Master Plan*, but as 'the Embodiment *of* Gris' in *The Dying Days* and this story.

624 *Placebo Effect*

625 *The Book of the Still*

626 Carmodi was born as one of the Unnoticed's sensitives thirty years before *The Book of the Still*. At the end of that novel, she paradoxically averts the creation of the Unnoticed, making it debatable whether these events occurred in the proper history or not.

nage caused when an ancient weapon, the Pakhar Diadem, was tracked to his world. The Diadem was blasted out of space by the *Bruk* and went missing.

Tarrol's decision probably saved Peladon - had the planet remained in the Federation, it would almost certainly have been targeted by the Daleks thirty years later during the Dalek War.

3985 - THEATRE OF WAR[629] **->** The colony of Heletia was founded by a group of actors wanting to stage the greatest dramas of the universe. Society on Heletia was confined to one small area of the own planet, but nonetheless became an expansionist power and fought a war with the Rippeareans. The Heletians believed that only races with a sophisticated theatre were truly civilised. Following the death of their leader, the Exec, the Heletians sued for peace.

By this point, Stanoff Osterling's play *The Good Soldiers* had been lost.

The artificial star of Tir Na Nog was due to run out of fuel around this time.[630]

3999 (July) - PLACEBO EFFECT[631] **->** The Doctor and Sam attended the wedding of his former companions Stacey Townsend and Ssard on Micawber's World. Stacey and Ssard had settled in this timezone two years ago after leaving the Doctor. The Church of the Way Forward, who opposed interspecies weddings, crashed the ceremony but order was restored.

Micawber's World was hosting the Olympic Games, and scientist Miles Mason was secretly infecting athletes with Wirrn eggs disguised as performance enhancing drugs. The Wirrn hatched, and the Space Security Service was called in to contain the situation. The Doctor found the Wirrn Queen and destroyed her, although one group of Wirrn escaped to Andromeda. The Olympic Games continued.

Earth at this time had a Royal Family. King Garth had just died; Queen Bodicha was in mourning but the rest of the world was glad to see the back of him. His heir was Prince Artemis, Duke of Auckland. Some humans on Earth, but few offworlders, followed the tenants of Christianity. There were 1362 races in the Federation's database, but the Time Lords weren't one of them. The Foamasi were members of the Federation.

The Doctor, Fitz and Compassion tried to find a way into the Obverse in the Wandering Museum of the Verifiably Phantasmagoric, also known as the Museum of Things That Don't Exist.[632]

The Daleks' Master Plan

c 4000 - MISSION TO THE UNKNOWN[633] ->

"This is Marc Cory, Special Security Agent, reporting from the planet Kembel. The Daleks are planning the complete destruction of our galaxy together with powers of the Outer Galaxies. A war party is being assemb—"

In the year 4000, Chen attended an Intergalactic Conference in Andromeda. The Outer Galaxies and the Daleks held a council at the same time, sending Trantis to Andromeda to allay suspicion. The Space Security Service (SSS) and the UN Deep Space Force had been monitoring Dalek activity for five hundred years, and they were to prove vital in discovering the Daleks' scheme.

On the planet Kembel, SSS agent Marc Cory learned

---

627 "Fifteen years" before *Placebo Effect*.

628 Dating *Legacy* - The dating of this book is problematic. It has to be set after "3948", when a couple of the fictional reference texts cited were written (p37). The Doctor says that it is "the thirty-ninth century" (p55) and later narrows this down to the "mid-thirty-ninth century give or take a decade" (p84) [c.3850]. The novel is set "one hundred years" after *The Curse of Peladon* (p106), at a time when "young" Mavic Chen is still a minor official and Amazonia, who first appeared at the end of *The Curse of Peladon*, is the Guardian of the Solar System (p237) [so before 3950]. It is "thirty years" before a Dalek War that might well be *The Daleks' Master Plan* (p299) [therefore 3970] and "six hundred years" after *The Ice Warriors* (p89) [therefore 3600, favouring the dating of that story as 3000]. The book takes place a couple of months before *Theatre of War*,

and as that book is definitely set in 3985, I have adopted this last date.

629 Dating *Theatre of War* - The book is set soon after *Legacy* in "3985" (p1), a fact confirmed by Benny's diary ("Date: 3985, or something close", p21), and the TARDIS' Time Path indicator (p81).

630 'Two thousand years' after *Cat's Cradle: Witch Mark* (p247).

631 Dating *Placebo Effect* - The date is given. *Placebo Effect* states that Christianity is still practised on Earth in 3999, but Sara Kingdom - hailing from the year 4000 - hasn't heard of Christmas in *The Daleks' Master Plan*. Historically, not every version of Christianity has placed an emphasis on Christmas, though

632 *The Taking of Planet 5* (p13).

633 Dating *Mission to the Unknown* - The story is set shortly before *The Daleks' Master Plan*.

that the Daleks and their allies were preparing for conquest. Cory was exterminated, but not before recording a warning.

4000 - THE DALEKS' MASTER PLAN[634] -> Shortly after concluding a mineral agreement with the Fourth Galaxy, Mavic Chen left Earth for a short holiday, or so he told the news service Channel 403. In reality, his Spar 740 spaceship headed through ultraspace to Kembel, the Daleks' secret base. There, he met the delegates from the Outer Galaxies for the first time, and presented the Daleks with a full emm of taranium - enough to power their Time Destructor, a device capable of accelerating time.

Space Security Agents were sent to investigate the disappearance of Marc Cory. One of them, Bret Vyon, allied with the Doctor and his companions. They stole the taranium and also absconded with Chen's ship. The group reached Central City on Earth, where Vyon was killed by Sara Kingdom - his sister and a fellow SSS agent - who believed him a traitor. She came to side with the Doctor against Chen.

Pursued by Chen's own security forces and other Space Security Agents, the Doctor and Steven broke into a research facility. They were transported with Sara across the galaxy, via an experimental teleportation system, to the planet Mira - the home of invisible monsters named the Visians. Mira was close to Kembel and the group returned to the Daleks' base. They fled through time and space in the TARDIS, with the Daleks in pursuit.

Chen was ready to doublecross the Daleks, and had special forces on Venus ready to occupy Kembel.

Eventually the Daleks re-captured the taranium, and they exterminated their allies - including Chen - in readiness for universal domination. They had assembled the 'greatest war force ever assembled'. However, the Doctor activated the Daleks' Time Destructor, which destroyed their army and transformed the surface of Kembel from lush jungle to barren desert in seconds. Sara helped the Doctor in this endeavour and was aged to death. The universe was safe once more.

Earth was under totalitarian rule. Humans were 'bred', and told not to question orders. Christmas was not celebrated or even remembered.

4000 - HEAD GAMES[635] -> On the sunless Detrios, an anomaly feeding off energy from the Land of Fiction had become "the Miracle", a replacement source of heat and light for the planet. The unstable anomaly threatened the entire universe, so the Doctor, Roz, Chris and Bernice sought to close it with force-field generators. This nullified the Miracle, but some rebels on Detrios imposed order and the inhabitants there sought alternative methods of survival without a sun.

SSS agent Dryn Faber investigated the planet Antalin and discovered Daleks there.[636] Earth was involved in a number of wars on the frontier of Earthspace. The Daleks massacred the colonists on a mining outpost.[637]

4009 - THE BOOK OF THE STILL[638] -> About this time, TimeCorp offered its employees the plus of completing their workday, then temporally returning to the morning for family time. Participating TimeCorp workers aged a third faster than their families every day, but got to spend

---

634 Dating *The Daleks' Master Plan* - The date "4000" is established by Chen. The draft script for *Twelve Part Dalek Story* set it in "1,000,000 AD".
635 Dating *Head Games* - The date is given.
636 *War of the Daleks*. Not long after the death of an SSS agent called Marc, presumably Marc Cory from *Mission to the Unknown*. This throws the dating scheme of the book out, as Antalin is the planet the Daleks will disguise as Skaro to be destroyed. But that, according to Peel, will happen *before* this.
637 *Storm Harvest*
638 Dating *The Book of the Still* - It's '4009' (p57).
639 "Thirty years after" *Legacy* (p299), and possibly intended as a reference to events of or following *The Daleks' Master Plan*.
640 *The Crystal Bucephalus*
641 *Prime Time*. Reg Gurney has been in space corps for 'thirty years'.
642 *Emotional Chemistry*
643 'Thirty years ago' in *The Mutant Phase*.

644 'Twenty years' before *The Apocalypse Element*.
645 Dating *The Mutant Phase* - No date is given, but the first of the stories set in the period of the *Dalek Empire* series, *The Genocide Machine*, is set after this in 4256.
646 Dating *The Genocide Machine* - There's no date in the story, but in *Invasion of the Daleks* (Part One of the *Dalek Empire* series), the war between the Knights of Velyshaa and Earth (mentioned in *The Sirens of Time* as ending in 3562) was 'centuries ago'. Skaro exists at this time. The Big Finish website gives it a date of 4256.
647 Dating *The Apocalypse Element* - This is another story set around the time of the *Dalek Empire* audios.
648 Dating *Storm Harvest* - No date is given. Reg Gurney, an engineer and spy on Coralee, spent thirty years in the Space Corps and fought in the Dalek Wars, supporting that dating. There's a reference to London not existing for five thousand years.
649 Dating *Dust Breeding* - It is 'several centuries' in Ace's future, in Earth's colonial period and after the Dalek Wars. Bev Tarrant is also present, and for her, it is

more time with their loved ones.

The temporal expert Albrecht managed to retroactively wipe himself from existence, but his diaries survived in a reality pocket. His theories gave rise to the condition "Albrecht's Ennui," which affected temporally displaced people who went a few years without time travel.

The highly affluent, distant planet Lebenswelt settled into a state of hedonism and decay, as nobody would voluntarily travel so far to perform menial tasks. The IntroInductions escort service on Lebenswelt used illegal fast-acting memory acids to make kidnapped humans fall in love with their clients. Lebenswelt also became home to the Museum of Locks (*Das Museum der Verriegelungen*), which almost incidentally guarded a copy of *The Book of the Still*.

> = In 4009, the Unnoticed desired to examine the *Book* because it mentioned their Tent City on the photosphere of Earth's sun. The Doctor, Fitz and Anji arrived on Lebenswelt, and the Doctor discovered that the Unnoticed were the product of a closed time loop. By touching the time sensitive Carmodi, the Doctor accidentally caused the time loop to unleash waves of "soft Time", which consequently mutated IntroInductions founders Darlow, Gimcrack and Svadhisthana into a twisted gestalt creature that would give rise to the Unnoticed. When the newly created gestalt made contact with the Unnoticed, it simultaneously destroyed the Unnoticed and flung the gestalt back in time to become the Unnoticed.
>
> Shortly afterward, Carmodi departed with the *Book* and retroactively planted a bomb aboard the Unnoticed's spaceship, thus prematurely destroying them and averting the closed time loop altogether.

Around 4015, a massive Dalek War split the Federation. Upon the war's completion, the organisation was forced to re-evaluate itself.[639] Mavic Chen's descendants eventually ended democracy in the Federation. The Chen Dynasty of Federation Emperors ruled for thousands of years.[640] The Colonial Marines raided Dalek strongholds in the 4020s.[641] Kinzhal, a future general of the Icelandic Alliance, earned medals in the forty-second century.[642]

> = Daleks infected with wasp DNA mutated into a swarm of invulnerable, giant wasp-like creatures and devastated Earth, draining the planet of all minerals and nutrients. The colony planets were unable to help and all attempts to recolonise ended in starvation.[643]

Unique minerals on Etra Prime draw the attention of over fifty galactic powers, including the Daleks and the Time Lords. The Daleks removed the planet, along with a team of researchers and President Romana, from spacetime. A galactic war was only narrowly averted.[644]

> **= c 4250 - THE MUTANT PHASE**[645] **->** The mindless, wasp-like "Mutant Phase" Daleks assaulted Skaro, prompting the Emperor Dalek to order the Doctor and Nyssa to travel back to 2158 and prevent the Mutant Phase's creation. The Emperor Dalek self-destructed Skaro, but downloaded his consciousness into the Thal Ganatus and accompanied the TARDIS crew.

4256 - THE GENOCIDE MACHINE[646] **->** The Doctor and Ace visited the library of Kar-Charrat. The chief librarian, Elgin, had built a wetworks research facility that stored the sum of universal knowledge in liquid form. To accomplish this, Elgin had enslaved nearly the entire Kar-Charrat race, using their drop-sized bodies as data storage units.

Dormant Daleks on the planet revived and attacked. They gained access to the library by duplicating Ace, and all but destroyed the library in their quest for its data. The Doctor defeated them with the help of a 'collector', Bev Tarrant, who was planning a heist. The library was left in ruin.

c 4256 - THE APOCALYPSE ELEMENT[647] **->** The Doctor and Evelyn landed on Archetryx as a Time Treaty was being signed. The missing planet Etra Prime suddenly re-appeared on a collision course with Archetryx. The Daleks were hoping to wipe out the conference. Romana escaped her captors on Etra Prime. The Doctor, Romana and Evelyn went to Gallifrey as the planetary collision took place and the Daleks instigated an epic attack. The Daleks destroyed the galaxy of Seriphia with the Apocalypse Element, generating a million new worlds there. The Daleks set about reshaping Seriphia in their image.

The Dalek Empire spin-off audios are set after this point.

c 4260 - STORM HARVEST[648] **-** The inhabitants of the waterworld Coralee had developed the Krill - vicious, aquatic humanoids with razor-sharp teeth - as instruments of war. The Krill wiped out their own creators, then entered hibernation. The Dreekans later colonised the planet, despite the legends of great danger there. They offer private islands for sale to the super-rich. The Krill awakened and were defeated by the Doctor and Ace. Nonetheless, some Krill survived as eggs in a nearby asteroid field.

c 4260 - DUST BREEDING[649] **->** The Master brought the Warp Core, an energy creature contained in Edvard Munch's painting *The Scream*, to the planet Duchamp 331, a refuelling station off the main space lanes. It served as home to technicians and a small colony of artists. The Master sought to seed the Warp Core's energy into the dust on Duchamp 331, then goad it into action against its ancient enemies, the Krill. This would have put a planet-sized weapon at the Master's disposal.

The Doctor and Ace defeated the Master, and the surface of Duchamp 331 was caught in an inferno that destroyed the Warp Core.

& 4261 - PRIME TIME[650] **->** The Doctor and Ace investigated the activities of Channel 400 on Blinni-Gaar, only to become part of the station's programming. Meanwhile, the Master landed on Scrantek and made a deal with the Fleshsmiths, a race that harvested other races to continue their existence. The Master and Fleshsmiths hoped to use the Channel 400 broadcasts to transport 150 billion viewers into the Fleshsmiths' body banks as raw material. The Doctor tricked the Fleshsmiths by letting them analyse a clone of himself, which broke down and released a molecular contagion. The toxin cascaded through the Scrantek network and reduced the Fleshsmiths to ooze. Channel 400 was disgraced and taken off the air.

Prior to its demise, the network tormented Ace with images from the past of her "future" tombstone. The Doctor falsely convinced Ace that the images were faked. Without her knowledge, he went back in time and dug up her corpse for clues as to how she died.

In 4338, Turlough was the guest of Wilhelm, König of the Wine Lords of Chardon.[651] The railway network was reestablished in Europe.[652]

The Davros Era[653]

? 4500 - DESTINY OF THE DALEKS[654] **->** The Daleks encountered a new threat: the Movellans, a race of humanoid androids from system 4X-Alpha-4. The Daleks were forced to abandon all operations elsewhere in the galaxy, including Skaro, and mobilise a huge battlefleet. The mighty Dalek and Movellan fleets faced each other in space, their battlecomputers calcu-

lating the moment of optimum advantage. This created an instant stalemate, and not a shot was fired for centuries. The vast Dalek Fleet was kept completely occupied, except for the occasional raiding mission on Outer Planets such as Kantria for slave workers, or on the starships of Earth's Deep Space Fleet.

The Daleks realised that their dependence on logic made it impossible for them to win a war against another logical machine race. Their battlecomputers suggested that they should turn to their creator, Davros, for help. The Supreme Dalek dispatched a force to Skaro to recover Davros from the ruins of the Kaled Bunker. Mining operations started up, and the Daleks discovered their creator, who had survived in suspended animation for centuries.

A Movellan party was sent to Skaro to investigate Dalek operations. As they arrived, the Daleks' slaves broke free, helped by the Doctor and Romana. Before a Dalek ship could arrive from Supreme Command, the slaves had overpowered the Movellans and defeated the small Dalek force. Davros was captured by the human force, who returned to Earth in the Movellan ship.

Before this time, Arcturus won the Galactic Olympic games, with Betelgeuse coming a close second. The economy of Algol was subject to irreversible inflation.

The Movellans were built by the Daleks, and the entire war was faked as part of their plan to prevent the destruction of Skaro.[655] **Human authorities put Davros on trial. Humanity had abandoned the death penalty, so Davros was placed in suspended animation aboard a prison station in deep space. While Davros slept, humanity discovered a cure for Becks Syndrome.**

Without Davros' help, the Daleks were helpless. They lost the war when the Movellans released a virus that only affected Dalek tissue. Weakened, the Daleks were forced to rely on hired mercenaries and Duplicates - conditioned clones produced by their genetic experiments, and generated from humans snatched from many timezones.[656]

Following another Dalek War with humanity, the Daleks were not active in the galaxy for a century.[657]

---

after *The Genocide Machine*.

650 Dating *Prime Time* - It is a year after *Storm Harvest*.

651 *The Crystal Bucephalus* (p42).

652 'Centuries' before *Emotional Chemistry*.

653 See The Davros Era sidebar.

654 Dating *Destiny of the Daleks* - The Daleks and Movellans have been locked in stalemate for "centuries". At this point, the Daleks are feared, highly

advanced and have a vast war fleet which operates as their command base. In *Resurrection of the Daleks*, it is made clear that there is deadlock between the Movellans and the Daleks' computers, not the Daleks themselves.

655 According to *War of the Daleks*

656 *Resurrection of the Daleks*

657 Before *Davros*.

THE DAVROS ERA: Four consecutive Dalek TV stories (*Destiny of the Daleks, Resurrection of the Daleks, Revelation of the Daleks* and *Remembrance of the Daleks*) form a linked series in which the creator of the Daleks, Davros (first seen in *Genesis of the Daleks*), is revived. In due course, he's captured and imprisoned by Earth before re-engineering the Daleks and gradually taking control over his creations. The series ends with the ultimate destruction of the Daleks' home planet of Skaro, although the novel *War of the Daleks*, set shortly after *Remembrance of the Daleks*, significantly reinterpreted those events.

Three Big Finish audios are set in gaps between the television stories, and act as bridges between them - *Resurrection of the Daleks* is followed by *Davros*, *Revelation of the Daleks* is followed by *The Juggernauts* and *Remembrance of the Daleks* by *Terror Firma*. Here, for the sake of convenience, I refer to the events of these stories as "the Davros Era" - a term that is never used in any of the stories themselves.

It is never stated exactly when the Davros Era is set, although it is clearly far in Earth's future.

The key story here is *Remembrance of the Daleks*. Before *Remembrance*, it was widely felt that *The Evil of the Daleks* really was, as the Doctor said, 'the final end' of the Daleks (even though the story ended with a single Dalek twitching into life, and the draft script *of Day of the Daleks* explained that the Daleks had survived their civil war). *Remembrance of the Daleks* changed that, by ending with the destruction of Skaro. Clearly, taking *Remembrance of the Daleks* at face value, it - and by implication the rest of the Davros Era - has to happen after *The Evil of the Daleks* (the climax of which was set on Skaro).

Even before that, the first two editions of *The Programme Guide* set *Destiny of the Daleks* "c.4500" (as did the earlier versions of this chronology and *Timelink*). Following *The Programme Guide*'s lead, the script of *Resurrection of the Daleks* referred to the year as 4590, although that's not established on-screen.

There have been other attempts to place it. *The Terrestrial Index* took the Doctor's speech to the Black Dalek in *Remembrance of the Daleks* that the Daleks are "a thousand years" from home literally, and respectively set the stories in "as the 27th century began", "towards the end of the 27th century", "as the 28th century began" and "about 2960". *The TARDIS Logs* chose "8740 AD" for *Destiny of the Daleks*. Ben Aaronovitch's novelisation of *Remembrance of the Daleks* and his introduction to the *Abslom Daak - Dalek Killer* graphic album had extracts from a history book, *The Children of Davros*, that was published in "4065" - apparently well after *Remembrance of the Daleks*.

John Peel's *The Official Doctor Who & the Daleks Book* - written with Terry Nation's approval - offers a complete Dalek timeline, although it stresses it's not 'definitive' and could change in the light of a new story (p209), and it was written *before Remembrance of the Daleks* was broadcast. In Peel's version, *Genesis of the Daleks* comes first, followed by *The Daleks* [c.1564], there are Dalek survivors in the Kaled Bunker and after five hundred years they emerge and force the Thals to flee Skaro. The Daleks discover space travel after about a hundred years, and launch *The Dalek Invasion of Earth* [2164]. The Dalek Wars begin, after several hundred years of Dalek preparation, leading to *Frontier in Space* and *Planet of the Daleks* [2540]. The Daleks developed time travel, as seen in *The Chase*. The Daleks and Mechonoids fought the Mechon Wars, and one Dalek capsule from that conflict ends up crashing on Vulcan where it is unearthed in *The Power of the Daleks* ['several centuries' after 2010]. The Daleks went back in time to reinvade Earth (*Day of the Daleks*). The Daleks were then attacked by the Movellans (*Destiny of the Daleks*) and the two races were deadlocked for 'decades'.

Ninety years later followed *Resurrection of the Daleks* (by which time Earth and Draconia had defeated the Movellans). The Daleks exploited a space plague (*Death to the Daleks*). Davros had survived, but was captured by the Daleks at the end of *Revelation of the Daleks*, and he was taken to Skaro and executed. Weakened, the Daleks needed allies to conquer the galaxy, as seen in *The Dalek Master Plan* [4000]. This led to the Dalek Wars, that lasted 'the next couple of centuries' after which the Emperor Dalek initiated the events *of The Evil of the Daleks* [c 4200], which ended in a civil war that wiped out the entire Dalek race, once and for all.

No firm dates for the Davros Era are given, but working backwards, this timeline would seem to place *Destiny of the Daleks* somewhere in the thirty-ninth century.

War of the Daleks, also written by Peel, attempted to reverse the destruction of Skaro in *Remembrance of the Daleks*, and - unsurprisingly - it broadly follows the timeline in Peel's earlier book. Ironically, though, it undermines the case for setting the Davros Era before 4000 - first, the SSS explore Antalin (the planet the Daleks trick the Doctor into destroying instead of Skaro) after the events of *The Daleks' Master Plan*. Secondly, for the Dalek plan to work, the Doctor has to think Skaro was destroyed in *Remembrance of the Daleks*, and he wouldn't if he knew it still existed in the year 4000. (Lawrence Miles has suggested that while the Daleks report to Skaro in *The Daleks' Master Plan*, the Doctor doesn't *see* them doing that, so he might not realise they do.)

Some fans have speculated that the Daleks might move to "New Skaro" after *Remembrance of the Daleks*, but no evidence exists for this on-screen, and on the occasions when we see Skaro it is clearly the same world.

In two New Adventures by Andy Lane (*Lucifer Rising, Original Sin*) we discover that the Guild of Adjudicators

continued on page 239...

On Riften-5, the fifth Doctor saw archives of genetic tests on Daleks after the War of Sharpened Hearts.[658]

& 4590 - RESURRECTION OF THE DALEKS[659] **->** One Supreme Dalek came up with an audacious plan that would strengthen the Daleks' position. Davros would be released from prison, and use his scientific genius and understanding of the Daleks to find an antidote for the Movellan virus. Dalek Duplicate technology would be used to strike on twentieth century Earth, while a second group, composed of Duplicate versions of the Doctor and his companions, would assassinate the High Council of Gallifrey. The plan totally failed.

Once Davros was released, he attempted to usurp control of the Dalek army and completely re-engineer the race. This met from resistance from those loyal to the Supreme Dalek, and the two factions began fighting. The Duplicates rebelled, destroying the prison station. The resulting explosion destroyed the Dalek battlecruiser. Davros escaped.

The war with the Movellans didn't take place, as it was part of a Dalek trick to prevent Skaro's destruction.[660] The parents of Geoff, who was later a member of Davros' science team, died in the Kensington disaster of '97.[661]

c 4600 - DAVROS[662] **->** Arnold Baines, head of the TAI corporation (which sold everything from foodstuffs to recreational narcotics to laser cannons), tracked down Davros' body. The Doctor arrived in time to see Davros revived. Baines hired both the Doctor and Davros to develop business strategies to help mankind spread to other galaxies. Davros secretly developed a computer model that could accurately predict the galactic stock market. With it, he planned to destroy capitalism and replace it with a system that placed the entire galaxy's economy on a permanent war footing. He launched a coup against Baines, but the Doctor and Baines survived his assassination attempt. Davros escaped in Baines' spacecraft with a hostage, Kim, who killed herself - allowing the Doctor to crash the ship. The Doctor suspected that Davros survived.

Collectors were looking for Dalek regalia at this time. Some historians, like Lorraine Baines, offered revisionist histories where the Daleks were seen as victims, not aggressors, and Davros was hailed as a visionary. The Treaty of Parlagon prevented individuals from having nuclear weapons. There was famine in the galaxy, virtually every available planet of which had been colonised by humanity.

The Daleks reoccupied Skaro, and a new Supreme Dalek came to power. The Daleks developed bio-

658 *Christmas on a Rational Planet.* No date is given, but Riften-5 was the home planet of Lytton according to *Attack of the Cybermen,* and this is (presumably) his home timezone. *Attack of the Cybermen* ends with the Doctor saying he misjudged Lytton, yet they didn't meet at all in *Resurrection of the Daleks* (unless you count Lytton shooting at the Doctor) and they barely meet in *Attack of the Cybermen.*

If we wanted to fix that, we could theorise that the Doctor met Lytton - from his perspective - between the two stories (it would be before *Resurrection of the Daleks* for Lytton). Lytton calls the people of 1985 'our ancestors' in *Attack of the Cybermen,* so Riften-5 is a human colony planet.

659 Dating *Resurrection of the Daleks* - This is the sequel to *Destiny of the Daleks.* Davros says he has been imprisoned for "ninety years". According to some reports, the rehearsal script set the story in 4590, which would follow the date established in *The Programme Guide.* This date also appears in *The Encyclopaedia of the Worlds of Doctor Who.*

660 According to *War of the Daleks.*

661 *The Juggernauts*

662 Dating *Davros* - *Davros* is set after *Resurrection of the Daleks.* It's never explicitly stated that it occurs between that story and *Revelation of the Daleks,* but the Big Finish website places it between *The Two Doctors* and *Timelash.* TAI was formed 'back in the thirty-eighth

century'.

663 Skaro has been abandoned for "centuries" before *Destiny of the Daleks,* but the Supreme Dalek is based there in *Revelation of the Daleks.* We see a bio-mechanoid in *Remembrance of the Daleks* - presumably the Daleks haven't developed the technology when they lose the war with the Movellans. Although, according to *War of the Daleks,* the Movellan War was a ruse.

664 Dating *Revelation of the Daleks* - This story is set an unspecified amount of time after *Resurrection of the Daleks.* It has been long enough for Davros to gain a galaxy-wide reputation and build a new army of Daleks. The galaxy is ruled by a human President and faces famine.

665 Dating *The Juggernauts* - This story is set an unspecified amount of time after *Revelation of the Daleks.* It's said that Davros crash-landed 716 days prior to this story, but there's no indication of the duration of time in a day on Lethe.

666 Dating *Remembrance of the Daleks* - This story is the sequel to *Revelation of the Daleks,* and again there is no indication how long it has been since the previous story. Davros has completely revamped the Daleks and their technology, which was presumably a fairly lengthy process.

667 Dating *War of the Daleks* - It's "about thirty years" after *Remembrance of the Daleks.* Davros' appearance in *Terror Firma* seemingly contradicts this story. However, mechanoid computers that interfaced with human brains to provide the Daleks with raw creativity, and they began to reassert their power.[663]

? 4615 - REVELATION OF THE DALEKS[664] ->

The galaxy was now ruled by a human President and was becoming overpopulated, with famine a problem on worlds across known space. Tranquil Repose on Necros has been established for some time by now as a resting place for the dead of the galaxy - literally, as they were kept in suspended animation there until whatever killed them was cured by medical science. The "rock and roll years" of twentieth century Earth were extremely popular. The DJ's grandfather purchased some genuine records from Earth on a visit there.

Davros went into hiding on Necros and formed an alliance with Kara, a local businesswoman. Davros took control of Tranquil Repose, and secretly began to break down the corpses there into a foodstuff. This ended famine across the galaxy, and Davros gained a reputation as "the Great Healer". Kara discovered that Davros was also growing a new army of genetically re-engineered Daleks from the corpses, and planned to use them to take effective control of her company. She hired Orcini, an excommunicated member of the Grand Order of Oberon, to assassinate Davros.

Like the Daleks before him, Davros had been keeping track of the Doctor's movements. When one of the Doctor's friends, the agronomist Arthur Stengos, died, Davros prepared for the Doctor to attend the funeral. Orcini and the Doctor thwarted Davros' plans, although Orcini died in the process, and the Daleks were summoned from Skaro to capture their creator. The Doctor suggested that protein from a commonplace purple flower could alleviate the famine.

? 4620 - THE JUGGERNAUTS[665] ->

Davros crashed on the planet Lethe, where mining engineers excavated a group of Mechonoids. Davros attempted to build an army of Mechonoids (re-named "the Juggernauts") that incorporated human tissue, but the grey Daleks tracked him down. The Doctor and Mel sabotaged the Juggernaut production lines, and Davros' body was severely injured in the fighting. His life-support chair self-destructed, which obliterated the colony, the grey Daleks and the Juggernauts, although the colonists themselves evacuated. Earth had by now passed mandatory organ donation laws.

? 4663 - REMEMBRANCE OF THE DALEKS[666] ->

Upon returning to Skaro, Davros usurped control from the Supreme Dalek and declared himself an Emperor Dalek. With his body now wasted, Davros was reduced

...continued from page 237

eventually becomes the Grand Order of Oberon referred to in *Revelation of the Daleks*, yet the Adjudicators are still active in *Original Sin*, so *Revelation of the Daleks* must take place well after the thirtieth century.

The Daleks' Master Plan established that the Daleks hadn't been a force in Earth's galaxy for a thousand years (and in one of the scenes where 'galaxy' seems to mean 'galaxy', not 'solar system'). This - and perhaps the presence of the Galactic Federation - would seem to rule out the Davros Era taking place between 3000 and 4000. (Humans from the time of *Destiny*, *Resurrection* and *Revelation* all know and fear the Daleks, and see them as an active threat.) The Daleks have been deadlocked for 'centuries' with the Movellans before *Destiny of the Daleks* (tellingly, Peel has to reduce this to 'decades' in his timeline). The preminence of the Earth Empire in the centuries before 3000 seems incompatible with the idea the Daleks are a major galactic power. I think *Destiny of the Daleks* has to be set at least 'centuries' after 4000. As we know the *Dalek Empire* series is set in the first half of the millennium, the case for *The Programme Guide's* 4600 AD date, while not indisputable, is certainly persuasive.

to little more than a disembodied head. He fashioned a new casing for himself. Most Daleks supported Davros, who genetically re-engineered the race and oversaw a complete revamp of Dalek technology. These 'Imperial Daleks' were given new cream and gold livery, improved weapons, sensor plates and eyestalks. As always, some Daleks dissented: this 'Renegade Dalek' faction followed the Black Dalek and fled Skaro using a Time Controller.

Both factions had discovered the existence of the Hand of Omega, a powerful Gallifreyan device capable of manipulating stars. They converged to its location on Earth in 1963. There, Davros acquired the Hand of Omega, but he was unable to control the device. On the Doctor's instructions, it travelled to Skaro in Davros' native time and made its sun go supernova, obliterating the planet. Davros escaped, but his flagship was obliterated and the Dalek homeworld was seemingly destroyed forever.

& 4693 - WAR OF THE DALEKS[667] ->

The Daleks had invaded Earth 'several times' by this point.

The garbage ship *Quetzel* recovered both the Doctor's TARDIS and Davros' escape pod. Thals raided the ship, and Delani, the Thal commander, asked Davros to reengineer his race to defeat the Daleks. Davros' reactivation alerted the Daleks, and the Doctor, Sam and Davros were taken to Skaro ... which the Doctor had thought destroyed. The Dalek Prime explained that the Daleks had learned of Skaro's destruction beforehand and plotted to prevent it.

The Daleks had previously taken the dormant Davros

from Skaro, and placed him in ruins on Antalin, which were designed to look like Skaro. The planet was then bathed in radioactivity. The Daleks then faked the Movellan War using their own robot servants, fooling Davros into believing they needed his help, but Davros escaped and triggered a civil war. He took the Hand of Omega, which destroyed *Antalin* rather than Skaro. The Daleks' real homeplanet survived.

Now, the Dalek Prime planned to draw the Daleks who supported Davros out into the open and destroy them. The Doctor made a seemingly easy escape in the Thal ship - then discovered a Dalek factory in the hold. He jettisoned it back in time, where it crashed on Vulcan.

Daleks loyal to Davros attempted to rescue him, but the Dalek Prime's forces prevailed. Davros was supposedly placed in a dispersion chamber and vapourised.

Davros randomly encountered the Doctor and his companions, the librarian Samson and his sister Gemma Griffen. A vengeful Davros overpowered the Doctor and - desiring to strip the Time Lord of everything he held dear - erased the Doctor's memories of his companions. Davros mentally conditioned Samson and Gemma to accompany him back to Earth, then embarked on a scheme to turn it

into a new Dalek homeworld. Samson was allowed to live with his mother, Harriet Griffen, in Folkestone.[668]

& 4703 - TERROR FIRMA[669] -> On Earth, Davros and his Daleks encountered the Doctor, Charley and C'rizz upon their return from the Divergent Universe. Davros believed that his Daleks had turned Earth into a "new Dalek homeworld" and converted eight billion humans into Daleks; however, the Daleks were actually operating to their own agenda while Davros was mutating into an Emperor Dalek. Davros hoped the Doctor would end his suffering and gave him a genocidal virus, hoping he would use it to end Davros' life. But the Doctor instead used the threat of the virus to make the Daleks abandon Earth. The Emperor Dalek persona completely erased Davros' own, and the Daleks left with their new leader.

Gemma Griffen was 'lost' in the conflict. Her brother Samson regained his memories of the Doctor, but continued living on Earth.

The metamorphic Collectors were galactic scavengers who entirely lacked the ability to discern the value or relevance of an item - essentially, they amassed junk. The Collectors' hyperwobble-drives and psychonomic shield-

---

War of the Daleks has a built-in loophole in that the Dalek working the controls of Davros' dispersion chamber is one of his loyalists. The Dalek in question is ordered to purge the chamber's memory core to prevent Davros being reconstituted later, so it's highly probable that it simply fakes the purge and restores Davros in secret.

WAS SKARO DESTROYED?: The 'retcon' in *War of the Daleks* that saw the destruction of Skaro reversed proved controversial with fans. A couple of references in later BBC Books suggested that Skaro had been destroyed, after all. *Unnatural History* stated that the Doctor tricked the Daleks into tangling their timelines so much their history collapsed; *The Infinity Doctors* that Skaro suffered more than one destruction. *Doctor Who - The Movie* (after *Remembrance of the Daleks* in the Doctor's own timeline) opened on Skaro, but it could have been a point in its history before it was destroyed. The 2005 TV series never stated that Skaro had been destroyed in the Time War (Russell T Davies' essay in the *2006 Doctor Who Annual* does name it and says it's now 'ruins', though).

There are a number of get-out clauses in *War of the Daleks* itself - the events aren't seen, only reported. Internal dating seems confused, and Antalin appears after it's meant to have been destroyed. There are pieces of contradictory information elsewhere - the origins of the Movellans in the book contradict their implied beginnings in *A Device of Death*, for example.

668 Years rather than decades before *Terror Firma*. The

presence of Samson and Gemma's mother suggests that this is their native time zone.

669 Dating *Terror Firma* - No specific date is given, but it is obviously after *Remembrance of the Daleks*, and a gap of some measure (Davros mentions 'years of solitude') is required after the novel *War of the Daleks*. *Terror Firma* doesn't acknowledge *War of the Daleks*, but the two are not irreconcilable. Neither Davros nor the Doctor here mention events from *War of the Daleks*, but as Davros' mental health is clearly eroding throughout this audio, it's entirely possible that the Daleks have altered his memories or that he's simply too far gone to remember. In fact, as the Daleks are obviously fooling Davros into thinking that he's in charge, it suits their plans if he forgets about Skaro and believes he's gaining revenge against the Doctor by "turning Earth" into a new Dalek homeworld. The eighth Doctor doesn't recall events in *War of the Daleks* because they've yet to occur in his lifetime. (This actually supports the notion that the McGann audios pre-date most of the novel range and his journeys with Samantha Jones.) It's also worth noting that we are only told the Daleks have converted eight billion humans; we don't see it, and it might be another lie.

Big Finish says that Davros *does not* become the Emperor Dalek seen in *The Parting of the Ways*.

670 *Heart of TARDIS*

671 *Trading Futures*. Magnus Greel feared Time Agents tracking him down in *The Talons of Weng-Chiang*. In the original, unbroadcast version of *An Unearthly Child*, the ing meant that no culture's defences could stand against them. The Daleks pretended that their planet had been destroyed to avoid being attacked by the Collectors.[670]

The Time Agents

The forty-ninth century was an era of unparalleled peace and prosperity on Earth. Advanced ubertronic devices existed. Earth developed time travel using transduction beams, but Time Agents strictly regulated the proliferation of the technology. Time travel had other uses: the film archivist Jaxa recovered all the lost films and television programmes. Thirty years before her native time, the Moon was terraformed. Sabbath press-ganged Jaxa into his service following a failed time-jump on her part.[671]

Under the auspices of the Great World Computer, human civilisation was more efficiently run than ever. But Earth regularly suffered massive famines. An artificial food was created on Earth that solved the problem. On the land once used to grow food, up-to-date living units were built to house the ever-increasing population. The amount of plants on the planet was reduced to an absolute minimum, and all plant life on Earth became extinct.[672]

A thousand murders took place on the worlds of the Nepotism of Vaal in the fiftieth century. The Memeovore had made the population think their loved ones are impostors. The Doctor would visit and see them establish a universal brotherhood.[673]

The Filipino Protectorate was established on Earth by 4993. Technology at the time included binoculars that could see through walls and read lips.[674] Professor Marius registered K9 as a data patent on 3rd October, 4998.[675] K9 was not Y5K compliant.[676]

5000 - THE INVISIBLE ENEMY[677] -> Five thousand AD was "the Year of the Great Breakout", when humanity "went leapfrogging across the galaxy like a tidal wave". To prepare the way, the Space Exploration Programme was instigated in the late fiftieth century, and a huge methane/oxygen refinery was set up on Titan. On asteroid K4067, the centre for Alien Biomorphology (the Bi-Al Foundation) treated extraterrestrial diseases, as well as tending those who were injured in space. Regular shuttle runs were set up between the planets of the solar system and "good for nothing" spaceniks also travelled the cosmos.

Photon beam weapons were in common use, as were visiphones. Sophisticated robots and computers were built. The native language of the time was Finglish, a form of phonetic English.

The Nucleus of the Swarm, a space-borne entity, attempted to replicate itself across the universe. It mentally compelled some humans to adapt the methane refinery on Titan into a breeding ground, but was destroyed before it could reproduce.

Doctor said he was from the forty-ninth century.

672 In the century before *The Ice Warriors*.

673 *The Taking of Planet 5* (p222).

674 *Interference*. The Doctor has a pair of those binoculars, likely acquired when he was with the Filipino army (mentioned in *The Talons of Weng-Chiang*).

675 *The English Way of Death*

676 *The Gallifrey Chronicles*

677 Dating *The Invisible Enemy* - The Doctor states that it is the year "5000, the year of the Great Breakout" and implies that the human race has not yet left the Solar System. This contradicts virtually every other story set in the future - indeed, *The Invisible Enemy* would fit very neatly into this timeline about the year 2100.

The Breakout might be to other *galaxies*, and this is supported by the audio *Davros*, which has humanity poised to dominate the whole galaxy and eager to expand. Alternatively, perhaps a big section of humanity wants to leave because they've had enough of the Ice Age, lack of scientific progress, threat of World War and genocidal dictators we hear are on Earth in *The Talons of Weng-Chiang*. If so, no-one mentions it in *The Invisible Enemy*, and Marius' main concern with returning to Earth is that he has too much stuff to take home.

Looking more closely at the history of Earth since the collapse of the Earth Empire around the year 3000, it's clear that there are many human colonies - but there's no evidence that Earth has any political influence on them. While it's a major player on the galactic political stage, Earth's civilisation does seem to be confined to the solar system in *The Daleks' Master Plan*, the Peladon stories and the Davros Era stories (which even following the Peel timeline would fall between 3000 and 5000). Earth maintains a military capable of (small) missions across the galaxy, but the fact that it's ignorant of massive Dalek conquests in *The Daleks' Master Plan* - even the fact that Earth needs to name a fleet as 'the Deep Space Fleet' in *Destiny of the Daleks* and finds it hard to fund or reinforce Davros' prison station in *Resurrection of the Daleks* - suggests that Earth doesn't dominate the galaxy. In *The Talons of Weng-Chiang*, we learn that Earth's in a technological cul-de-sac.

In short, it actually ties in with other stories that human civilisation is confined to Earth's solar system for a couple of millennia before 5000, by which time it's ripe for a 'breakout', a new wave of colonisation.

The Gallifrey Chronicles gives the story the 'relative date one-one-one-five-zero-zero-zero'. *The TARDIS Logs* offered the date "4778".

The Second Ice Age

? 5000 - THE ICE WARRIORS[678] ->

"And then suddenly one year, there was no spring. Even then it wasn't understood, not until the ice caps began to advance."

On Earth, the Second Ice Age had begun. Glaciers rapidly spread across every continent, displacing tens of billions of people to the Equatorial regions. Scientists attempted to come up with a theory that might account for the ice flow. They quickly ruled out a number of the possibilities: a reversal of the Earth's magnetic field, interstellar clouds obscuring the sun's rays, an excessive burst of sunspot activity and a severe shift of the Earth's angle of rotation. They came to realise that the extinction of Earth's plant life had dramatically reduced the carbon dioxide levels in the lower atmosphere, leading to severe heat loss across the world. Scientists tried to reverse the flow of ice, installing Ioniser Bases at strategic points across the globe: Britannicus Base in Europe, and complexes in America, Australasia, South Africa and Asia. These were all co-ordinated by the Great World Computer.

Many refused to leave their homelands and became scavengers. Before long, everywhere on Earth apart from the equatorial areas was an Arctic wasteland, home to wolves and bears. When captured, scavengers were registered and sent to the African Rehabilitation Centres. Scientists remained behind to measure the flow of the ice with movement probes.

Varga the Ice Warrior, who had been trapped in the glacier since the First Ice Age, was revived. He excavated his ship and crew, but was defeated by the Doctor, Jamie and Victoria before he could use sonic weapons to destroy Brittanicus Base.

In the Ice Age around the year five thousand, Findecker's discovery of the double-nexus particle had sent human technology into a cul-de-sac. Humans nonetheless developed limited psychic techniques such as the ability to read and influence the weak-minded. The Ice Age affected the Earth once more, and various Alliances governed the world.

The Peking Homunculus, an automaton with the cerebral cortex of a pig, assassinated the commissioner of the Icelandic Alliance and almost precipitated World War Six. The Supreme Alliance came to power, and horrific war crimes were committed. The Alliance

---

678 Dating *The Ice Warriors* - The date of this story is never given on-screen. Base leader Clent says that if the glaciers advance, then "five thousand years of history" will be wiped out. If he's referring to Brittanicus Base, a Georgian house, this would make the date about 6800 AD. If he is referring to human or European history, the date becomes more vague. It has to be set well over a century in the future, because the world has been run by the Great World Computer for that long. In *The Talons of Weng-Chiang*, the Doctor talks of "the Ice Age about the year five thousand".

An article in the *Radio Times* at the time of broadcast stated that the year is "3000 AD", and almost every other fan chronology used to follow that lead. The first edition of *The Making of Doctor Who* said that the Doctor travels "3000 years" into the future after *The Abominable Snowmen*, making the date 4935 AD. *The Dark Path* and *Legacy* both allude to the date of this story as being 3000 AD (p63 and p89 respectively). The earlier versions of this chronology did the same.

Timelink and *About Time*, though, settle on 5000, making the connection between the ice age mentioned in *The Talons of Weng-Chiang*. This does certainly seem to be a neater solution than proposing two ice ages in quick succession - particularly when there are a fair few stories set on Earth around 3000 which don't seem to be affected by an ice age. Occam's Razor doesn't always work on fictional timelines, and can be wielded too liberally, but it seems sensible to invoke it here.

One peculiarity is that the Martians have only been buried for "centuries", although it is also made clear that they have been buried since the First Ice Age, when mastadons roamed the Earth. *The Terrestrial Index* and *Legacy* (p90) both suggest that the Ice Age began as a result of "solar flares" (presumably in an attempt to link it with Earth's evacuation in *The Ark in Space*).

One problem is that later stories would establish the Martians as a significant presence in the future, which would make the humans' ignorance of them in this story notable - mankind has apparently forgotten about the Martians who were fellow members of the Galactic Federation in the Peladon stories.

THE SECOND ICE AGE: When base leader Clent explains the historical background to *The Ice Warriors*, he implies that the Ice Age began a century ago, but people are still being evacuated from England during the story, suggesting that glaciation is a more recent phenomenon. It would seem that although the global temperature drop is a direct result of the destruction of plant life, its consequences weren't felt immediately.

The present scientific consensus, of course, is that destroying the forests would cause global *warming* because of the resulting rise in carbon dioxide levels. However, this didn't gain widespread awareness until the 1970s; when *The Ice Warriors* was produced in the 1960s, the idea that the Earth might undergo global cooling was given more credence.

679 *The Talons of Weng-Chiang*. This happened "about

was finally defeated by the Filipino Army at the Battle of Reykjavik.

Magnus Greel - the Alliance's Minister of Justice, and the infamous Butcher of Brisbane - had performed terrible scientific experiments on one hundred thousand prisoners in an attempt to discover time travel and immortality. He escaped to the nineteenth century using a beam of zygma energy, and feared Time Agents would pursue him.[679]

The Doctor witnessed the sonic massacres in Brisbane.[680] Greel's path through time was deflected when his zygma beam hit the TARDIS.[681]

5000 - EMOTIONAL CHEMISTRY[682] -> Magnus Greel had been a Chinese national, part of the PacBloc regime. The PacBloc used anti-matter shells against opposing armies, but not on population centres, and deployed Stepperiders and Locust aircraft. The Alliance forces used Thor battle tanks and Fenrir reconnaissance tanks. An Alliance division commanded by Razum Kinzhal stormed Greel's fortress and secured his Zygma technology. Using this, Kinzhal developed transit belts that let his agents roam time and secure possessions formerly owned by Kinzhal's beloved, Dusha.

Hostilities had increased between the PacBloc - led by one of Greel's lieutenants, Karsen Mogushestvo - and the Icelandic Alliance. The strategies of the Alliance's Lord General Razum Kinzhal devastated the PacBloc's air force. Kinzhal's forces further eliminated Mogushestvo's troops in Sverdlovsk, and overran Omsk.

Formerly a being known as a Magellan, Kinzhal sought to reunite with his other half, the nineteenth century Russian noblewoman Dusha. The Doctor realized that such an act would obliterate Earth as the Magellan recorporalized. Kinzhal's assistant, Angel Malenkaya, was mortally wounded protecting Kinzhal from an assassination attempt and offered herself as a host. The Doctor used the Misl Vremya device in 2024 to link this era with 1812, and

thereby transferred Dusha's soul into Angel's body. Reuinted with his love, Kinzhal set about reorganizing his temporal paratroopers into operatives that would guard the past from temporal interference.

As part of these events, Trix stole a psionic weapon that Kinzhal had developed using enemy technology. However, she was forced to abandon it.

This era was the native time of Time Agents Kala, Jode and Fatboy; the Doctor met them in Marpling in 1932. They could time travel using a temporal transduction beam.[683]

Jack Harkness was a Time Agent in the fifty-first century. He awoke one morning while still in the Time Agents' employ and found two years of his memories were missing. He eventually acquired a Chula warship and took up trying to con his former colleagues. Jack came to own a sonic blaster / cannon / disruptor, fitted with digital removal and rewind, and which was made at the weapons factories at Villengard. The Doctor visited the weapons factories, leading to an incident where the main reactor went critical. The summer groves of Villengard, which produced bananas, took to growing in the factories' place.

By this point, humanity had spread out across half the galaxy, and had commenced 'dancing' with many species.[684] The fifty-first century was the era of the time traveller Chronodev, who was known to the Onihr.[685] The Taklarian Empire began a program of selective breeding to create a master race.[686]

Olleril was colonised. Governed by the principles laid down in the ancient records *The Collins Guide to the Twentieth Century*, *One of Us* by Hugo Young, *The Manufacture of Consent* and *The Smash Hits Yearbook*, it developed an eccentric, unworkable political and economic system that was an almost exact copy of the United Kingdom in the twentieth century. The cult of Luminus managed the planet in secret.[687]

---

the year five thousand" according to the Doctor; "the fifty-first" century according to Greel. Presumably it is after *The Invisible Enemy* - it's a little odd that the Doctor and Leela are involved in events of the year 5000 in two near-consecutive stories (only *Horror of Fang Rock* is between them) without any link being made between the two. The Doctor says he was with the Filipino army during their final advance. Note that World War Six is *averted* at this time, not fought, as some sources state.
680 *The Hollow Men*, in the "fifty-first century".
681 *The Shadows of Weng-Chiang*
682 Dating *Emotional Chemistry* - The date is given in the blurb (and is clearly tied in with *The Talons of Weng-Chiang*). This book seems to show Kinzhal founding the Time Agents, but such operatives are clearly active

before this, as Greel would hardly worry in *Talons* about 'Time Agents' following him if the group didn't already exist. More likely, Kinzhal centralizes the freelance Time Agents' operations and augments their time-travel technology. The psionic weapon that Trix loses is presumably the one that surfaces in *Eater of Wasps*.
683 *Eater of Wasps*. The trio hails from 'three thousand years' after 1932, but I have rounded up as they're dispatched after the psionic device lost in 5000; it's unclear if Kala's group is affiliated with Kinzahl or not.
684 *The Empty Child* and *The Doctor Dances*. The latter states Jack is from the fifty-first century.
685 *Trading Futures*
686 'A thousand years' before *City at World's End*.
687 "597" years before *Tragedy Day* (p97).

? 5433 - PLANET OF THE SPIDERS[688] -> An Earth ship came out of its time jump without power and crashed on Metebelis III. Some humans, a few sheep and a handful of spiders survived the crash. The spiders found their way to the cave of the Blue Crystals, and the energies there mutated them, making them grow and boosting their intelligence and psychic abilities. The 'Eight-Legs' came to dominate the planet, harvesting the human population as cattle. The Eight-Legs were ruthless - they wiped out two hundred and sixty-nine villagers, the entire population of Skorda, when they tried to resist.

Four hundred and thirty-three years after the crash, the Spiders set up a psychic bridge with a Tibetan monastery on twentieth century Earth. They plotted to travel back in time to conquer their homeworld, but were defeated. Their leader, the 'Great One', had planned to gain further power by completing the crystal lattice of the cave, but an energy backlash killed her.

c 5433 - THE EIGHT DOCTORS[689] -> The humans on Metebelis III hunted down the spiders. The seventh Doctor visited the planet and was caught by a giant spider. The eighth Doctor rescued him.

Along the Eastern edge of the galaxy, there was political upheaval for a thousand years. Many human colony worlds such as Pyka, Marlex, Dalverius, Pantorus and Shaggra warred with each other, and the galaxy's monetary system was in almost permanent crisis. In the fifty-fourth century, a consortium of industrialists attempted to solve the problem. Eventually they built Zamper: a neutral planet, snug in its own mini-universe, that would supply state-of-the-art battleships to all sides.

The only way to the planet was through a hyperspace gate controlled by Zamper itself, and the planet was completely self-contained to keep its designs secret. In four hundred and seventy three years of operation, Zamper became rich and maintained a balance of power in East Galaxy. The operation was completely smooth, averaging one minor technical failure every two hundred years.[690]

Sabalom Glitz stole a Tzun data core from the reptilian Veltrochni. He sold it to Niccolo Mandell, an agent of the Vandor Prime government.[691]

? 5595 - MISSION: IMPRACTICAL[692] -> Ten years later, the Veltrochni threatened to make war against Vandor Prime over the Tzun data core that Sabalom Glitz had stolen. The data core was the last surviving information cache from the Tzun Empire, and contained blueprints on how to construct Tzun Stormblades. Vandor Prime head of security Niccolo Mandell, hoping to sell the data core himself, coerced the Doctor, Frobisher and Glitz into retrieving the device from an orbital facility.

Glitz's associate Dibber died in a crossfire, but the Doctor purged the data core of its more dangerous infor-

---

688 Dating *Planet of the Spiders* - The colony ship that crashes on Metebelis III has intergalactic capability, as Metebelis is in the Acteon Galaxy. *The Terrestrial Index* claimed that the colony ship was "lost during the early days of the 22nd century", dating *Planet of the Spiders* itself as "c.2530". *The TARDIS Logs* suggested "4256", *Timelink* "3415".

689 Dating *The Eight Doctors* - This happens at some point in the aftermath of *Planet of the Spiders*.

690 *Zamper*

691 About ten years before *Mission: Impractical*.

692 Dating *Mission: Impractical* - It is 'a couple of million years' before *The Trial of a Time Lord* (p56). Ernie McCartney from *Tragedy Day* is mentioned (p215), setting this around the same time as that book. This would not appear, from the other stories featuring Glitz, to be his native timezone. We might conclude that he has ended up somehow either acquiring time travel or been brought here by a time traveller.

693 Dating *Tragedy Day* - There is no indication of the date in the book, although the colony planet Pantorus is mentioned here (p83) and in *Zamper* (p57), perhaps suggesting they are set around the same time.

694 *The Highest Science*

695 *Synthespians*[TM]

696 'Thousands of years' after *Asylum*. No date given,

and this is an arbitrary placing.

697 "Five thousand years" before *The Crystal Bucephalus* (p114).

698 'Two hundred and seventy years' before *Half-Life*.

699 Dating *Combat Rock* - There's no date given, although cigarettes were banned on the colonies 'hundreds of years ago'. There are smokers in *Resurrection of the Daleks*, but of course a smoking ban can be lifted and ignored, so it's hardly firm evidence that this story is set after that. My date is arbitrary, but I've linked it to the Christian colonists of Espero.

The date of the Earth-Indoni war is unspecified, but Jenggel's current political climate seems to stem from its fallout, suggesting a shorter rather than longer span of time since it occurred. The Indoni subjugated the Papul, and the Christian missionaries arrived, some "30 rainseasons" before the novel takes place.

700 *Heritage*. Cole's grandmother fights in it.

701 Dating *Zamper* - It is "the sixtieth century" (p77). Earth appears to be populated at this time.

702 'Twenty' (p8) and 'ten' (p18) years before *Heritage*.

703 Three years before *Heritage* (p56).

704 Dating *Heritage* - Each chapter in the book has a precise date and time.

mation and returned it to the Veltrochni. Vandor Prime authorities arrested Mandell. Glitz continued travelling in his *Nosferatu*.

? 5597 - TRAGEDY DAY[693] -> On the Earth colony Olleril, the precocious boy genius Crispin, leader of the secret society of Luminus, sought to gain mental control of the population, and to pattern everyone after characters from the show *Martha and Arthur*. Meanwhile, the immortal Friars of Pangloss hired the arachnid mutant Ernie "Eight Legs" McCartney, the most feared assassin in the Seventh Quadrant, to retrieve a cursed piece of red glass that the Doctor had acquired. The Doctor thwarted Crispin's plans, and Crispin died when the Luminus submarine *Gargantuan* was destroyed. Ravenous Slaag creatures consumed McCartney. The Friars were disrupted by an anti-matter burst, and flung powerless into the Time Vortex.

In 5665, the Chelonians launched an attack on the human colony Vaagon, but the Chelonians' tanks vanished mysteriously before they could complete their conquest, transported by a Fortean Flicker to the twenty-seventh century. Believing themselves blessed by divine intervention, the colonists were quite unprepared when the Chelonians reinvaded several generations later and wiped out the colony.[694]

In 5720, archaeologists discovered the remains of a Khorlthochloi starship.[695] The militaristic Narbrab conquered an alien civilization. The survivors, hosted in Ikshar host bodies, were banished in a solar-powered ship and arrived in London, 1346.[696]

Around 5764, a Dalek civil war became so serious that the Time Lords intervened.[697] Espero was colonised by mostly African and Asian humans with a shared Christian faith. The colonists hoped to escape the influence of the Eurozone and America, and bought the planet from the Homeworld Corporation. Renouncing technology, the colony hit problems when it proved all but impossible to extract the planet's natural resources and, with nothing to offer in trade, Espero quickly became isolated from the rest of the galaxy. Religious schisms led to the Almost War.[698]

? 5800 - COMBAT ROCK[699] -> Earth won a war against the Indoni, making the planet Jenggel an Earth colony. The Indoni subsequently invaded the rival Papul people, forcing the Papul leaders to vote for 'integration'. Tourism swelled amid the new political climate, with visitors arriving to experience the "primitive" Papul culture. The corrupt President Sabit of the Indoni kept most of the profits for himself. Christian missionaries arrived to minister to the Papul. Twentieth century icons such as *Winnie the Pooh*, *Wind in the Willows* and Leatherface horror films were in use in pop culture.

On Jenggel, a sentient organism contained in a purple fungus from the Papul swamps possessed a Papul named Kepennis. As the mysterious "Krallik", the organism-Kepennis founded the OPG, a Papul resistance movement. Some eight rainseasons later, Kepennis rigged Papul mumis to kill tourists and Indoni soldiers by spitting snakes, furthering an atmosphere of anarchy. The Doctor, Jamie and Victoria arrived onhand, and the Doctor ingested some of the fungus himself, enabling him to mentally nullify the organism within Kepennis. A cannibalistic Papul tribe took Kepennis away to consume him as punishment, and a mercenary with a bit of a noble streak killed Sabit.

There was a Cyber War in the late sixtieth century.[700]

c 5995 - ZAMPER[701] -> There was revolution on Chelonia, where the peaceful forces of Little Sister overthrew Big Mother. This initiated a cultural reformation that saw the warlike race transformed into the galaxy's foremost flower-arrangers. Forty years later, many Chelonians hankered for the old blood-and-glory days, and Big Mother's fleet headed for Zamper to purchase a powerful Series 336c Delta-Spiral Sun Blaster - a ship whose effectiveness had been demonstrated in the Sprox civil war and the skirmishes of Pancoza. It was capable of withstanding neutronic ray blasts of up to an intensity of sixty blarks. With such a ship, power could have been wrested back from Little Sister, but the Chelonians discovered that the Zamps - slug-like creatures used to build the ships on the planet - had dreams of conquest and were building their own battleship. In a variation of the Diemlisch manoeuvre (first used in the third Wobesq-Majjina war), the Chelonian fleet destroyed itself in order to seal the gate between Zamper and the rest of the universe.

Colonists established a colony on Heritage. Ten years later, a company at Galactic Central developed a way of synthesising Thydonium, instantly putting mining colonies such as Heritage out of business. Melanie Bush and her husband Ben Heyworth settled on the impoverished Heritage sometime afterward.[702]

Years later on Heritage, the geneticist Wakeling successfully cloned a raven, naming her Arabella.[703]

6048 (6th August) - HERITAGE[704] -> Menopause had become extremely rare. Undergoing the condition, Melanie Bush Heyworth asked Wakeling for a genetic solution to the problem. Wakeling's treatment seemingly led to Mel and her husband Ben conceiving a child named Sweetness, but the Heyworths discovered that Wakeling had violated their wishes by cloning Sweetness from Mel. A subsequent argument between Wakeling and Mel led to his striking her with a genetic sequencer, killing her.

The Heritage residents overlooked Wakeling's act of murder, believing his experiments could restore prosperity to the hard-up colony. Ben Heyworth's attempt to seek justice by alerting off-world authorities was discovered. Wakeling further persuaded the townfolk to favour his experiments, and the locals tore Ben to pieces with their bare hands before torching his house. Wakeling took Sweetness into his own home.

A shuttlecraft arrived on Heritage - the first in years - and two visitors wanted to see the Heyworths, causing quite a stir. The buried memories of the Heyworths' deaths began to surface among the locals. One of visitors, the Doctor, gatecrashed an interstellar video conference and revealed Wakeling as a murderer, destroying the man's chance to reveal his success at cloning. Wakeling and two other inhabitants subsequently fell to their deaths when some of the old mineshafts collapsed under them. Cole, the Heritage town barman, adopted Sweetness.

c 6050 - HALF-LIFE[705] -> Two races, the parasitic Makers and the Oon, had by now been at war for centuries. The organic spaceship Tain, a Maker construct, sought to escape his bloody role and tried to escape the war. However, the Oon infected Tain with a Trojan program that assaulted his consciousness. Tain crashed onto the planet Espero, and his personality remained in conflict.

The Trojan program, unable to fully dominate Tain, generated a distress signal to alert the Oon to its situation. The Doctor, Fitz and Trix received the signal and arrived on Espero to help. Tain panicked upon the TARDIS' arrival, thinking it heralded the Oon's arrival, and unleashed its ultimate weapon: a wavefront designed to gradually disintegrate and reconstitute a planet under Tain's control. The internal struggle between Tain and the Trojan program interrupted the wavefront's effects, throwing it into chaos. The Doctor helped Tain purge the Trogan program and

end the wavefront. Tain prepared to leave Espero afterward.

The Imperial family on Espero was composed of Imperator Tannalis, age 120, his wife Alinti and children Javill and Sensimi. Javill's mind was erased by a Oon neural-rubber, which forced him, age 23, to mentally remature.

High Catholic doctrine came to forbid use of matter transmitters, stating it was impossible to teleport a soul.

The last colonist left Heritage in 6057. None of the ex-colonists ever discussed their reasons for departing.[706] On 8th December, 6064, former Heritage colonist Lee Marks, now head of the Ellershaw Foundation, died in a fire deliberately set at his home.[707] A grown-up Sweetness Cole penned an autobiography entitled *First of a New Breed*.[708]

On the desert planet Chronos, a race of beings built a time machine. This enabled them to travel into their world's future, when it had become a water planet and was far more habitable.In the distant future, only a handful of Cybermen survived. They fled to the water world Chronos and exterminated the beings who lived there, acquiring their time machine in the process. The Cybermen used it to travel back to 3286, but a temporal blast from that era surged here and aged them to death.[709]

The Solar Flares and the Evacuation of Earth

The Earth was ruled by the World Executive. Earth at this time was technically advanced, with advanced suspended animation techniques, fission guns and power supplied via solar stacks and granavox turbines.

Scientists monitoring the Sun predicted a series of massive solar flares: within only a matter of years, the

---

705 Dating *Half-Life* - This story is set after *Heritage*, as there are references to that story.
706 *Heritage* (p227).
707 *Heritage* (p279).
708 Years after *Heritage*.
709 *Real Time*. No date given. The CyberController in this era is an alternate history version of Evelyn Smythe.
710 *The Ark in Space*
THE SOLAR FLARES: The solar flares ravage the Earth "thousands of years" after the thirtieth century (*Revenge of the Cybermen*). Judging by information in the TV series, the last recorded human activity on Earth for millions of years is in the fifty-first century (*The Talons of Weng-Chiang, The Invisible Enemy*). The books push this forward by about a thousand years, to around 6000. I speculate that the Solar Flares occur relatively soon after this time.

The first edition of *The Programme Guide* claimed that Earth was only evacuated between "c.2800" and "c.2900", the second suggested dates between "c.2900" and "c.4300". *The Terrestrial Index* attempted to rationalise the statement that the Ark was built in the "thirtieth century", stating that Nerva was built, but then the Solar Flares "abated", Nerva was not informed and the population of Nerva went on to recolonise Ravolox "between 15,000 and 20,000" (as seen in *The Mysterious Planet*). This contradicts the date for *The Mysterious Planet* established on-screen and would represent a rather implausible oversight on behalf of the Earth's authorities. The book's supposition that the Solar Flares caused the Ice Age we see in *The Ice Warriors* (a theory repeated in *Legacy*) is specifically ruled out by dialogue in *The Ice Warriors*.

Earth's surface would be ravaged and virtually all life would be wiped out. It would be five thousand years before the planet would be habitable again.

The High Minister and the Earth Council began working on humanity's salvation. Carefully screened humans, the Star Pioneers, were sent out in vast colony ships to places such as Colony 9 and Andromeda. Nerva was converted into an Ark housing the cream of humanity, some one hundred thousand people, who were placed in suspended animation along with samples of animal and plant life. The Ark also contained the sum of human knowledge stored on microfilm.

The rest of humanity took to Thermic Shelters, knowing that they wouldn't survive. When the Solar Flares came, every living thing on the Earth perished.

A group of Star Pioneers reached Andromeda and encountered the Wirrn, a race of parasitic insects who lived in the depths of space, visiting worlds only to breed.[710]

? 6000 - DREAMTIME[711] -> Facing a catastrophic natural disaster, evacuation coordinators herded the people onto Phoenix lifeships that departed for space. In Australia, a guru named Baiame sought an alternative and hoped to channel the Dreaming - a collective force, derived from the minds and dreams of humanity - to influence matter. Baiame wanted to lift the Uluru, a sacred bluff, and its people into space under protection of a Dreaming-generated force field. The Doctor traversed the Dreaming and arrived from thousands of years in the future. Baiame acceded to the Doctor's request that he extend his sphere of protection a few miles and include settlers in the surrounding vicinity. The Uluru lifted off from Earth with its people and sped into space, and the Doctor returned to the future.

After a thousand years, the Star Pioneers had destroyed all the Wirrn breeding grounds, making Andromeda suitable for colonisation. One Wirrn Queen survived and travelled through space towards the Earth. After thousands of years, she reached the Nerva Beacon, and although the station's automatic defences killed her. Before her death, the Queen damaged the systems that would have revived the humans, and laid her eggs within one of the sleeping Nerva engineers.[712]

---

711 Dating *Dreamtime* - Simon Forward scripted this story with the intent of it occurring during the time of the World Zones Authority in the 21st century, but nothing in the story itself supports this, and it's obviously during the evacuation at the time of the solar flares. The alternative is to judge the "past" segments as part of the Dreaming and inherently unreliable, in which case dating becomes even murkier. Forward concedes that the Galyari Korshal in *Dreamtime* isn't the character of the same name in the Benny audio *The Bone of Contention* (even if Steffan Rhodri voices both parts); the Galyari are long-lived, but traditionally hand down some names through the generations.

THE ABANDONMENT OF EARTH: Earth is completely evacuated six times that we know of: for "ten thousand years" between the time of the Solar Flares and *The Sontaran Experiment* (c.5000-c.15,000 AD); for at least three thousand five hundred years before (and an unknown amount of time after) *Birthright* (c.18,500 AD-?); a line cut from the rehearsal script but retained in the *Planet of Evil* novelisation reveals that "The Tellurian planet [Earth] has been uninhabited since the Third Era" (significantly before 37,166 AD); and for a significant time after the Usurians move the workforce to Pluto before *The Sun Makers* (before c.2,000,000 AD). There is a mass evacuation shortly before Earth plunges into the Sun, seen in *The Ark* and reported in *Frontios*. Finally, Earth was empty at the time of its final destruction, seen in *The End of the World*.

712 *The Ark in Space*. As the colonists are scheduled to revive after "five thousand years" [c.11,000 AD], the Wirrn Queen must arrive on Nerva before that time.

ANDROMEDA: Andromeda is mentioned a number of times in *Doctor Who*, sometimes as a reference to the constellation, other times as the galaxy of the same name. According to the TARDIS Information File entry that the Master fakes in *Castrovalva*, Castrovalva itself is a planet in the Phylox series in Andromeda. There is some evidence that Zanak (*The Pirate Planet*) raided worlds there, as the ground is littered with Andromedan bloodstones. In *The Daleks' Master Plan*, an intergalactic conference was held in Andromeda. In *The Ark in Space*, we learn that Star Pioneers from Earth reached Andromeda and discovered that it was infested with the Wirrn. The two races fought each other or a thousand years, until humanity succeeded in destroying the Wirrn's breeding grounds. Mankind went on to colonise the galaxy, and by the time of *The Mysterious Planet*, the civilisation was established on planets such as Sabalom Glitz's homeworld, Salostopus. At that time, Andromedans capable of building advanced robots and harnessing black light stole Matrix secrets and fled the wrath of the Time Lords. The Doctor considers visiting "the constellation of Andromeda" in *Timelash*. The Doctor took the mer-children to a water planet in the Andromeda Galaxy at the end of *Evolution*. According to Trix in *The Gallifrey Chronicles*, the currency in Andromeda is the Andromedan Euro, although *Dragonfire*, *Legacy* and *Business Unusual* all agree it is the Grotzi in Glitz's time.

While those aboard Nerva slept, human colonies such as Gal Sec carved out an Empire, with bases across half the galaxy. They retained legends of Nerva, "The Lost Colony" from the time of the Expansion, but most didn't believe that such a place really existed. In time, the colonies grew to distrust talk of "Mother Earth".[713]

The New Dark Age

In 6198, the Federation Scientific Executive funded a research project into genetic experimentation. The geneticist Maximillian Arrestis hired a team of consultants to develop the Lazarus Intent, a religion that he hoped would become a moneymaking venture. His 'miracles' were publicised for three years, and his predictions of disasters all came to pass. *The Codex of Lazarus* was published early in the sixty-third century, and for nearly a decade he reaped the financial rewards of being the 'Messiah'.

Not content with this, Arrestis began to sell defence secrets to the Cybermen, Sontarans and Rutans. The Federation was fighting a war with the Sontarans at the time. In 6211, Sontarans launched a stealth attack that wiped much of the Federation DataCore on Io. Three weeks later, an earthshock bomb - sold by the Cybermen to the Sontarans - destroyed Tersurus. This didn't stop the Federation from winning the war. When the Sontaran Emperor suspected that Arrestis had double-crossed him, the traitor was brought to the Sontaran Throneworld and executed. "Lazarus" became a martyr, the saviour of the

galaxy, and it was the Intent of his followers to resurrect him.

Alexhendri Lassiter built a time machine and did rescue Arrestis moments before his death. Later, Arrestis escaped the destruction of the Crystal Bucephalus restaurant by fleeing through time, only to arrive back on Sontara right before his execution, which proceeded as planned.[714]

Around 6976, the Vardans who invaded Earth in 1976 arrived back home. They discovered there had been a revolution, and that the military had lost power.[715]

> = The Doctor and Mel arrived on the Federation planet Marandnias, where the Doctor failed to prevent nuclear warfare. A group of Chronovores and Eternals, grateful for the Doctor's help in the Bophemeral affair, changed history to prevent Maradnias' destruction.[716]

Marandnias would become the centre of the Union.[717] After the great cybernetic massacres of the eighty-fifth century, sentient androids fell out of favour. From this point most robot servants were connected to a central webwork rather than being autonomous.

Eventually civil war broke out in the Galaxy, splitting the Federation into the Confederation, democratic rebels and the Humanic Empire ruled over by the Chen dynasty. Early in the war, Mirabilis had sided with the rebel forces, those opposed to the Emperor. The final battle of the war took place in the Mirabilis System. The democratic forces won, but the Imperial Fleet devastated Mirabilis itself with

---

713 *The Sontaran Experiment*
714 *The Crystal Bucephalus*
715 'Five thousand years' after *No Future*.
716 *The Quantum Archangel*
717 *The Quantum Archangel*. No date is given, but it's before the Federation splits.
718 *The Crystal Bucephalus*
719 *Pyramids of Mars*
720 Dating *Dreamtime* - Some 'thousands of years' have passed since the Uluru departed into space. Simon Forward says it's possible that as much as 10,000 years have elapsed. This date is arbitrary.
721 *The Crystal Bucephalus*
722 *Killing Ground*. The ArcHivists first appeared in the reference book *Cybermen*.
723 *The Quantum Archangel*
724 Dating *The Crystal Bucephalus* - The Doctor claims they are "six or seven centuries into the tenth millennium" (p27), but also says that it is the "108th century" (p40, which is in the *eleventh* millennium). The latter date is correct - elsewhere we learn that "10,663" was in the recent past (p69). Although the novel doesn't specify the exact date, author Craig Hinton assumed that it

was set in the year 10,764 and I have adopted that date.
725 Dating *Synthespians*™ - The events of *The Crystal Bucephalus* were 'several centuries' ago.
726 *The Ark in Space*. Vira notes that scientists had calculated it would be "five thousand years before the biosphere was viable" on Earth after the solar flares. In *The Sontaran Experiment*, we learn that humanity has spread across the galaxy, and that Earth has been habitable for "thousands of years" but has remained abandoned.
727 *The Also People* (p247).
728 According to the Doctor in *The End of the World*. This would seem to fall at the time Earth was thought to be abandoned by humanity following the solar flares. Perhaps the New Roman Empire wasn't based on Earth, or there was a shortlived resettlement of the planet.
729 *The Crystal Bucephalus*
730 *Synthespians*™, elaborating on what we learned in *The Crystal Bucephalus*.
731 *The Crystal Bucephalus*

an atmospheric plasma burst that killed ninety percent of the population. Chen was captured and executed, ending the Chen dynasty.

In the aftermath of the Federation Civil War, the galaxy entered a new dark age in which scientific progress all but ceased. During the ninetieth century, the remnants of the Federation became the Union - a united political entity at peace with the Draconian Republic, the Cyberlord Hegemony and the radioactive remains of the Sontaran Empire. There were two other forces for unity: the Elective, a massive criminal organisation that controlled all criminal activity between New Alexandria and the Perseus Rift; and the Lazarus Intent, a religious organisation which now commanded eight quadrillon people.[718]

After around eight thousand years in the Time Corridor created by the Doctor, Sutekh finally perished at the beginning of the ninetieth century. [719]

? 9,000 - DREAMTIME[720] **->** The Doctor, Ace and Hex arrived at the Uluru as it traveled through space. The people's faith in the Dreaming had weakened, and the Dreaming began absorbing people into itself by turning them into stone. The Doctor accidentally traveled to the time of the solar flares and influenced the Uluru's departure from Earth. He returned and restored the people to normal, whereupon it was hoped that the Dreaming's next attempt to terraform the Uluru would prove more successful.

The Antonine rescue raid on Scultiis in 9381 failed when the natives' electric fields disrupted their weapons. Around the end of the one hundredth century, the Silurian scientists Ethra and Teelis worked on time-travel experiments. The results were published in the March 9978 edition of *Abstract Meanderings in Theoretical Physics*.[721]

The ArcHive studied the history of the universe, and served as vast repositories of knowledge. They had access to time-travel technology.[722] Emperor Brandt and the Cyberlord Hegemony possesed the ArcHive in the hundredth century.[723]

10764 - THE CRYSTAL BUCEPHALUS[724] **->** In 10,753 Alexhendri Lassiter fulfilled on the Lazarus Intent, stabilising a time gate that rescued Lazarus from the Sontaran Throneworld before his death. But the truth about the false Messiah quickly became clear, and Arrestis seized control of the criminal Elective. Meanwhile, Lassiter and his brother Sebastian built the Crystal Bucephalus, a time-travel restaurant on the planet New Alexandria, which sent the galaxy's elite to the finest eating establishments in time and space.

Eleven years later, the Crystal Bucephalus was destroyed. Arrestis was revealed as Lazarus and escaped in a time gate, only to arrive back on Sontara moments before his execution.

Over the next century there was a galactic civil war.

c 11,000 - SYNTHESPIANS™ [725] **->** A fleet of ark ships fled the galactic civil war and passed through an area known as the Great Barrier. Cut off from the rest of the galaxy, the colonists found themselves in an area rich with natural resources. The New Earth Republic was founded, and included such planets as Bel Terra, New Alaska, New California, New Regency, Paxas and Tranicula in the Thomas Exultation (which was noted for its vineyards).

A hundred years later, the Republic was peaceful but boring. A business consortium failed in its bid to restore contact with the rest of the galaxy, but managed to pick up old TV broadcasts from twentieth century Earth. These proved extremely popular and Reef Station One was built to produce new shows such as *As the Worlds Turn*, *Dreams of Tomorrow*, *Executive Desires*, *The Rep*, *Star Traveller: The Motion Picture*, *ReefEnders*, *Liberation Street*, *Confessions of a Monoid* and *This Evening With Phil and Bev*. The people of the Republic become obsessed with television.

A Time Lord force of War-TARDISes launched an attack against the Nestene home planet of Polymos. The mission was commanded by Lord Vansell, and destroyed swarms of energy units. The Nestene Consciousness attempted to relocate to the New Earth Republic. Plastic automata named Synthespians - in reality Autons - had been freely used to perform manual labour in the Republic, and those aboard Reef Station One instigated a slaughter. The Doctor defeated the Nestene Consciousness and its Autons. The Consciousness was trapped in a plastic Replica body, forced to again and again act out the last episode of *Executive Desires*.

The Earth became habitable again. Humanity didn't recolonise its homeworld.[726] Cyberblind released their DTM *Machina ex Machina* in 11265.[727]

The year 12005 was the time of the New Roman Empire.[728] The Union was replaced by the Junta, a military dictatorship that had developed from the Elective.[729]

The Union had previously remained a powerful force in the rest of the galaxy, although humanity was fragmented by civil war lasting centuries. The Union evolved into the Concordance, the Confederation, then the Junta. The Junta was a totalitarian regime ruled by the Chen dynasty. It attempted to invade the New Earth republic several centuries after the Auton incident, but was repelled. The New Earth Republic began intergalactic colonisation efforts, sending sleeper ships to the Wolf-Lundmark-Melotte galaxy and Andromeda.[730]

For a millennium there was barbarism, until a resurgent Confederation overthrew the Junta.[731]

? 15,000 - CITY AT WORLD'S END[732] -> An asteroid hit the moon of Sarath, changing its orbit so that it was now on a collision course with the planet. Ten years later, the Doctor, Ian, Barbara and Susan arrived and found that preparations to build a rocket to evacuate the planet for the nearby Mirath were nearly complete. However, the Sarath leaders, based in the capital city of Arkhaven, had realised that the rocket ship could never fly and were only planning to save five hundred members of the elite.

The Doctor discovered that most of the population had been killed in a recent war and replaced by androids. This was a plot on the part of Monitor, the central computer in Arkhaven, to save itself before the planet's destruction. Monitor was destroyed, and the Doctor and Susan increased the capacity of the true escape rocket to save those they could.

w - The first land battle of the War between the Time Lords and the Enemy was fought on Dronid in the 155th century. It lasted a day, and was utterly devastating. The Time Lords used clockwork bacteria as a weapon. The Time Lords' attempts to cover their tracks after the battle wreaked almost as much harm as the battle itself, and

became known by the inhabitants as 'the Cataclysm'. The Relic, said to be the Doctor's body, was recovered from the planet in 15,414. A misguided Faction Paradox member, Cousin Sanjira, cast the Relic into the Time Vortex and it arrived in the twenty-second century. The Faction made Sanjira murder his younger self as punishment.[733]

Return to Earth

c 16,000 - THE ARK IN SPACE[734] -> The colonists on Nerva were awoken, only to discover that the Wirrn had infested the Ark. The Wirrn were killed, and humanity prepared to reoccupy their homeworld. They intended to restock the planet with plant and animal life and to rebuild human civilisation.

& c 16,000 - THE SONTARAN EXPERIMENT[735] -> Field Major Styre of Sontaran G3 Intelligence conducted a Military Assessment Survey on Earth. The planet had acquired strategic value in the Sontarans' war with the accursed Rutans, and was believed to be devoid of intelligent life. Styre conducted experiments on Gal

---

732 Dating *City at World's End* - This is an arbitrary date, although we are told it is 'thousands of years' after Ian and Barbara's native time.

733 *Alien Bodies*

734 Dating *The Ark in Space* - Harry twice suggests that they are "ten thousand years" after the time of the Solar Flares, and the Doctor confirms this in *The Sontaran Experiment*, which takes place immediately afterwards. *The Terrestrial Index* set the stories between "15,000 and 20,000". *The TARDIS Logs* suggested a date of "28,537". *Cybermen* offered the year "?14714". *The TARDIS Special* gave the date "c.131st Century".

735 Dating *The Sontaran Experiment* - The story immediately follows *The Ark in Space*.

736 Dating *The Eye of the Tyger* - The dating is more than a little confused. The Doctor says this is 'a million and a half years' in Fyne's future (p28), but the blurb says it's the '32nd century'. It's clearly after the solar flares referred to in *The Ark in Space*, so see the dating for that story.

737 *Genesis of the Daleks*. It's a presumption that 'Space Year 17,000' is the same as 17,000AD.

738 Inter Minor is in the Acteon Group, as is Metebelis III (*Carnival of Monsters*), although it is later referred to as the Acteon Galaxy (*The Green Death, Planet of the Spiders*). The Isop Galaxy is the location of Vortis (*The Web Planet, Twilight of the Gods*), the home of the Face of Boe (according to *Bad Wolf*) and possibly the Slitheen ('venom grubs' seen in *The Web Planet* are referred to in *Boom Town*). Artoro and the Anterides are referred to in *Planet of Evil*.

739 Dating *Tomb of Valdemar* - No date is given, but Earth is occupied and humanity has a second galactic empire. This date would slot the story between two points where Earth is abandoned (*The Ark in Space* and *Birthright*), and ties in with the Animus' statement in *The Web Planet* that Earth has 'mastery of space'.

740 'Thousands of years' before *Twilight of the Gods*.

741 'Four thousand years ago' according to *Speed of Flight*.

742 *Birthright*

743 '2347.54 years' before *The Speed of Flight*.

744 Dating *The Web Planet* - The story seems to take place in the future as the Animus craves "Earth's mastery of Space". Bill Strutton's novelisation places it in "20,000", although the Doctor suggests that the TARDIS' "time pointer" might not be working. The New Adventure *Birthright* suggests that Earth is abandoned at this time, but it is established in *The Ark in Space* and *The Sontaran Experiment* that man has spread through the universe.

745 'Over a hundred and fifty years' before *Twilight of the Gods*.

746 Dating *Twilight of the Gods* - This is a sequel to *The Web Planet*. The Animus was defeated 'seventy thousand days ago' (p1), which is a little under one hundred and ninety two years.

747 *Shada*. Chris Parsons' dating of the book gives a figure of "minus twenty thousand years", with time running backwards over the book. This might be a property of the book, rather than an indication it comes from the future.

Sec colonists that he lured to the planet, but the Doctor and Harry Sullivan killed him.

& c 16,000 - THE EYE OF THE TYGER[736] **->** Just after the people aboard Nerva had begun to resettle the Earth, a feline race arrived and helped the reconstruction efforts. Soon, though, some humans turned against the aliens, who left with ten thousand humans to find a new home. They were lured to settle on planets within a black hole by the avatars of their descendants, the Conservers, who existed in the black hole billions of years in the future.

The Dalek War against Venus in Space Year 17,000 was halted by the intervention of a fleet of War Rockets from the planet Hyperon. The rockets were made of a metal completely resistant to Dalek firepower. The Dalek taskforce was completely destroyed.[737]

The Far Future

In the far future, humanity's influence was felt in other galaxies such as Andromeda, Acteon, Isop, Artoro and the Anterides.[738]

? 16,000 - TOMB OF VALDEMAR[739] **->** The Second Empire rose, with its origins on the human colony world of Dephys. The cruel, oppressive Elite ruled it. The Empire fell after a civil war to the New Protectorate, led by the Virgin Lady High Protector, the Civil Matriarch, who had the Elite's palaces destroyed with Immolator Six capsules. A Duke named Paul Neville fled to Terra and became a powerful magician, the head of a cult dedicated to the dark god Valdemar. The Protectorate located Neville, forcing him to flee to the ends of the collapsing Empire. Neville sought the planet Ashkellia, which he believed contained the palace of the Old Ones - Valdemar was the last of their kind.

Neville attempted to resurrect Valdemar through an adolescent psionic named Huvan, but the Doctor and Romana defeated his plans. Huvan nearly punctured the higher dimensions, which could have destroyed the universe, but the Doctor and Romana convinced Huvan that he lacked the maturity for such power. Huvan agreed to erase his memory and assume a new identity on another planet. He became a trapper named Ponch on the planet Janus Forus. Fifteen years later in Huvan's lifetime, Romana returned to help him remember his past. She regenerated at this time.

The New Protectorate lasted around a century or two before burning itself out.

The Gods of Light conducted experiments on Vortis. They replaced the core with a propulsion system, and kidnapped the Menoptra from their home planet.[740]

The Aapex Corporation, based on Mina Fourteen, started a genetics experiment on the planet Nooma to further terraforming and bio-engineering on low-gravity planets. Nooma's sun was an Aapex spaceship, and the planet's artificial "Sky" - actually a sentient being programmed to regulate Nooma's biosphere - formed a protective shell around the planet.

Biology on Nooma became such that humanoids developed in the forest as carnivorous children, but mature males would fight to the death. The winners underwent genetic "Promotion", which entailed their growing wings and joining the flying "naieen", but the losers would reanimate as infertile cadavers named the Dead. The naieen would mate, causing their seed to fall on the forest and bud new children.[741]

Around 18,500, Earth was abandoned once again.[742] The Aapex Corporation went bankrupt. Nooma was abandoned to its own fate.[743]

? 20,000 - THE WEB PLANET[744] **->** The planet Vortis in the Isop Galaxy was the home of the moth-like Menoptra, who worshipped in glorious temples of light and lived in the flower forests. They kept an ant-like race, the Zarbi, as cattle. The planet was invaded by the Animus, an entity that could absorb all forms of energy, and which pulled three planetoids - including the planet Pictos - into orbit around Vortis. Most of the Menoptra fled to Pictos, but the descendants of those that stayed behind slowly devolved into sightless dwarfs, the Optera. The Animus used the Zarbi as soldiers, and had dreams of galactic conquest until the Doctor, Ian, Barbara and Vicki arrived. The Animus was destroyed by the Isop-tope, a Menoptra weapon.

Around 20,040, New Rhumos broke away from Rhumos Prime, which marked the beginning of a lengthy conflict.[745]

c 20,192 - TWILIGHT OF THE GODS[746] **->** After the Animus' defeat, the planet Vortis had wandered into the Rhumos System. Two Rhumon factions, the Imperials and the Republicans, fought for control of the planet. A year later, the Doctor, Jamie and Victoria arrived just as a seed of the first Animus emerged. The Doctor brought the Rhumons and Menoptera together and helped to destroy the new Animus. The Gods of Light who had engineered Vortis agreed to stop interfering in its affairs, and it was hoped that Vortis could peacefully co-exist with its Rhumon neighbors.

Carbon-dating suggested that *The Worshipful and Ancient Law of Gallifrey* was written around 22,000 AD.[747]

c 22,000 - BIRTHRIGHT[748] -> For three thousand four hundred and ninety seven years, the insect-like Charrl had occupied the planet Anthykhon, which was far from the major space lanes. Their vast hive pumped ammonia into the already-depleted atmosphere, the planet's ozone layer had been depleted, the seas had dried up, and the soil was barren. The native life, the Hairies, survived by adapting to this environment.

The Charrl were not savages - indeed they had created over three hundred of the six hundred and ninety-nine wonders of the universe - before coming to this world to escape solar flares on their own planet. The Charrls made contact with Muldwych, a mysterious time-traveller exiled to Anthykhon at this time, and together they attempted to traverse the Great Divide back into the past on Earth. Muldwych came to regret his association with the Charrls and foiled their plans. He remained on Anthykhon in exile. Anthykhon was Earth during one of the several periods when the planet was isolated and forgotten.

c 22,000 - SPEED OF FLIGHT[749] -> The Doctor, Jo and Mike Yates landed on Nooma. The Dead assaulted the planet's artificial sun, working on pre-programmed instructions to seek a means of terminating the Nooma experiment to protect Aapex's trade secrets. The Doctor tapped the sun's databanks and found a message from Aapex granting the citizens of Nooma independence, restoring social order on the planet.

The shafts of the Great Pyramid would align with the constellation of Orion around 23000.[750]

? - THE FACE OF EVIL[751] -> A Mordee colony ship landed on an unnamed world and developed a computer failure. The Doctor helped their descendants by linking the computer to his own mind, but he neglected to remove his personality print from the data core. As a result, the computer became schizophrenic.

Centuries later, the colonists worshipped the computer as Xoanon. It had split them into two groups: the "Sevateem", the savage descendants of Survey Team Six; and the Tesh, formerly the technicians, to whom Xoanon granted psychic powers. Xoanon was thus attempting to breed superhumans, but the Doctor returned and made a reverse transfer, curing the computer's multiple personality disorder. Leela, a warrior of the Sevateem, left with the Doctor.

? - LAST MAN RUNNING[752] -> Class warfare was brewing between the 'firsters' on the First Planet, and the lowly 'toodys' of the Second Planet. An Out System Investigation Group (OIG) was dispatched to a forest plane to look for a toody weapons manufacturer. The OIG team, the Doctor and Leela got caught in a Last Man Running complex, a simulated environment built by the Lentic race to find and clone the ultimate warrior. Leela destroyed the forcefield surrounding the complex, and the OIG bombed it.

37,166 - PLANET OF EVIL[753] -> A Morestran survey team arrived on Zeta Minor, searching for an energy source as their home planet was facing disaster. Zeta Minor was a planet on the edge of the universe, beyond Cygnus A, as distant from the Artoro Galaxy as that is from the Anterides.

---

748 Dating *Birthright* - Ace says she was born "Oh, probably about twenty thousand years ago" (p134), although how she reaches this figure is unclear. It is "year 2959" of the Charrl occupation of Earth (p1) when they start their scheme, which will take "almost five hundred years" (p60), yet curiously it is "year 2497" (p109) when they finish! This is presumably a misprint, and ought to read "3497".
749 Dating *Speed of Flight* - This is 'about twenty thousand years' after Jo's time (p23).
750 'Twenty one thousand years' after *The Sands of Time* (p122).
751 Dating *The Face of Evil* - The story could take place at any point in the far future. The Doctor states in *The Invisible Enemy* that the year 5000 is the time of Leela's ancestors. This story, then, takes place at least ten generations after that - the crew of the colony ship were stranded for 'generations' before the Doctor first helped them, and there have apparently been seven generations since (the Sevateem seem to attack the barrier once a generation, and this is the seventh

attempt). Humans evolve limited psychic powers around the fifty-first century (*The Talons of Weng-Chiang*) and the Tesh have psychic powers, so they might originate after that time, although they probably receive all their abilities from Xoanon's selective breeding programme.

In *The Sun Makers*, the Usurian computer correctly guesses that "Sevateem" is a corruption of "Survey Team", and that Leela comes from a "degenerate, unsupported Tellurian colony" suggesting that there are many such planets known to the Company. *The Terrestrial Index* set the story "several centuries" after the "52nd Century". *The TARDIS Logs* offered the date "4931", *Timelink* "6000".
752 Dating *Last Man Running* - The story could take place at any time in the far future.
753 Dating *Planet of Evil* - While it could be argued that the date "37,166" that appears on the grave marker might use some Morestran scale of dating, the Doctor does state that the TARDIS has overshot contemporary London by "thirty thousand years". *The Dimension Riders*

The Morestran team discovered that a black pool on Zeta Minor was connected to an incomprehensible universe of anti-matter. As a result, it was impossible to remove anything from the planet without incurring the wrath of powerful creatures native to the anti-matter universe. The Doctor and Sarah helped the Morestrans to survive the experience and return home.

The Doctor off-handedly suggested to Professor Sorenson that he explore the energy potential of the kinetic forces involved in planetary movement.

c 39,164 - ZETA MAJOR[754] -> Morestra was abandoned, and the fleet set off on a search for a new home planet. A suitable home was located in the Beta System forty months later, and the city of Archetryx was founded there. The New Church Calendar began and the Sorenson Academy was established.

A hundred years later, work commenced on the Torre del Oro, a structure that would extract energy from planetary motion, but which would take fifteen hundred years to build. The dematerialisation beam was invented after several more centuries. Great Technology Wars were fought as the Cult of Science schismed.

A few years before the Torre del Oro was due to be completed, the Grand Council of Cardinals discovered errors in the equations - the Torre del Oro wouldn't work. To cover up this failure, they dispatched an expedition to extract anti-matter from Zeta Minor, and the Zeta Project was established on the nearby Zeta Major. By that point Morestran territory spanned eighty million light years and contained one thousand four hundred and twenty-seven inhabited star systems, but the energy crisis meant that eight hundred and ninety-two of them, the Outer Systems, were beyond the Empire's reach.

Students of the Sorenson Academy started vanishing, part of the cover up of the Torre del Oro debacle. The Doctor, Tegan and Nysaa arrived at the tower, discovering that it was full of anti-matter. Soon after, anti-matter creatures started a rampage. A State of Crisis was declared and

old political and religious rivalries re-emerged. The Zeta Project was destroyed. The Doctor once again negotiated with the creatures of anti-matter and returned all the plundered material to its original universe.

At this time, a new breed of Zamps should be ready to conquer the universe.[755]

c 50,000 - HEART OF TARDIS[756] -> The Doctor and Romana found and rescued K9, who had become an exhibit at the Collectors' Big Huge and Educational Collection of Old Galactic Stuff.

c 83,000 - THE MALTESE PENGUIN[757] -> Frobisher, the Doctor's shapeshifting companion, briefly returned to his homeworld to resume his occupation as a private investigator. Through a bizarre twist of economics, the mobster Josiah W. Dogbolter was making immense profit on the planet by insuring that no factory actually made anything. Frobisher's ex-wife, the Whifferdill named Francine, manipulated events to display the joke, "You don't have to be crazy to work here, but it helps," on the computer terminals of Dogbolter's employees. This triggered communication and productivity, and ruined Dogbolter's operations. Frobisher resumed travelling with the Doctor.

? 100,000 - INFINITE REQUIEM[758] -> Far in the future, representatives of over seven hundred cultures - including the Monoids, Morestrans, Rakkhins and Rills - used the Pridka Dream Centre. The Pridka were a race of blue-skinned, crested telepaths, and the Centre used their healing skills. At any one time, fifteen thousand individuals would be booked into the Centre, making it a tempting resource for the Sensopaths, a psychic communal mind intent on dominating the physical world.

The malicious Sensopath Shanstra attempted to absorb the Sensopath Jirenal. The benevolent Sensopath Kelzen intervened, and all three of them died.

---

and *Infinite Requiem* both suggest that the Morestrans are not human, which is possible (although they do know of Earth). The Doctor's suggestion to Sorenson leads to events in *Zeta Major*.

754 Dating *Zeta Major* - It is 1998 by the New Church Calendar (p82), and that long since *Planet of Evil*.

755 Forty-two thousand years after *Zamper* (p249).

756 Dating *Heart of TARDIS* - There's no specific date, but it is 'some tens of thousands of years beyond the twentieth century'.

757 Dating *The Maltese Penguin* - No date is given, but this is clearly Frobisher's native time zone, given in the comics as the eighty-second century.

758 Dating *Infinite Requiem* - Events at the Pridka Dream Centre occur "Beyond Common Era of Earth Calendar" (p83), and the presence of Morestrans and Monoids emphasises that this is the far future. This date is arbitrary.

Circa 102,890, the white hole seedling from Albert was supposed to blossom into maturity.[759]

The Daleks were the greatest threat in the universe ... until one day, when they just vanished. Eventually they became mere legends. Unknown to humanity, they had left to fight the Last Great Time War with the Time Lords, a conflict that all but wiped out both races.[760]

The Daleks were part of the history of the First Segment of Time.[761] One Dalek ship, containing the Emperor, survived the Last Great Time War. It arrived at the edge of Earth's solar system, remaining hidden. For centuries, the Daleks would harvest the dregs and unwanted of humanity, building Daleks from their genetic material. The Emperor Dalek meddled in humanity's affairs and sought ways to slow its development. It became convinced it was god, and the Daleks worshipped him.[762]

200,000 - THE LONG GAME[763] -> It was the age of the Fourth Great and Bountiful Human Empire. Earth was at its height: the hub of a domain stretching across a million planets, covered with megacities, possessing five moons and a population of ninety-six billion.

A sandstorm on the New Venus Archipelago left two hundred dead. There were water riots in Glasgow. The Face of Boe was known to the people of Earth, and announced that he was pregnant with a Baby Boemina. The Jagrafess was manipulating humanity by controlling its news media from Satellite Five, which broadcast six hundred channels. This held back humanity's development, and made it fearful of immigrants. The Doctor and Rose defeated the Jagrafess, and the Doctor expected that humanity's development would accelerate back to normal without the its interference.

Adam, a companion of the Doctor and Rose, tried to acquire knowledge from the future and download it to his own time in 2012. The Doctor discovered Adam's intentions and returned him home.

After Satellite Five was put out of commission, the information feed to Earth stopped. The government and economy collapsed. A hundred years of hell ensued.[764] The Great Atlantic Smog Storm started in 200,080. On some days, it wasn't possible to breathe the air. The storm raged for at least twenty years.[765]

---

759 'A hundred millennia' after *Grimm Reality*.

760 'Thousands of years' before *The Parting of the Ways*. It's unclear exactly when this occurs. Captain Jack knows about the Daleks' disappearance, but as he's also a time traveller; it doesn't mean this happened before his native time. It's after 'Space Year 17,000', historically the last recorded reference to the Daleks before *Bad Wolf*.

It's also unclear what this 'vanishing' entails - the Doctor seems amazed that he meets a Dalek in *Dalek*, suggesting that they've been erased from history (would he, for example, have been surprised to meet one around 2164 on Earth, during their invasion?). However, Captain Jack recognises their ships in *Bad Wolf*, and the inhabitants of 200,100 both know the Daleks' name and that they vanished. Perhaps the simplest solution is that the new-style, gold Daleks that make their debut in *Dalek* are 'Time War Era' Daleks, and so none of them should exist after the Time War.

761 *The Ark*

THE SEGMENTS OF TIME: The Commander in *The Ark* states 'Nero, the Trojan Wars, the Daleks ... all that happened in the First Segment of Time'. References in that story to the Tenth and Twenty-Seventh Segments are noted later in this book. *The Well-Mannered War* is set in the Fifty-Eighth.

It's unclear whether a Segment is measured purely mathematically. A 'century' has to mean 'a hundred years'. If a Segment is a fixed period of time, then as *The Ark* is set ten million years in the future, this might sug-

gest fifty-seven equal segments of around 175,000 years).

Equally, the term might mark a specific era with distinct cultural or even physical features (like, say, 'Victorian' or 'Ice Age'). What would mark the beginning or end of a Segment? Would the boundary be formally defined and obvious (like say that of 'the tenth Olympiad', or 'the Leptonic Era'), even if it was open to a degree of interpretation (we can speak of 'the Second World War', even though the exact moment it started and ended depends on which country you're from and how you define terms)?

Timelink offers the theory that as Zentos refers to the 'the Fifty-Seventh Segment of Earth life' and the Commander says 'The Earth also is dying, we have left it for the last time', that Earth has been 'left' before, and each Segment ends with the abandonment of Earth. It's neat and, as noted elsewhere in this book, Earth is certainly totally evacuated more than once. However, *Bad Wolf* and *The Parting of the Ways* have the Daleks active after the first abandonment of Earth, and, if the Commander is right, they were only part of the history of the First Segment.

762 *The Parting of the Ways*. The Controller says the Daleks have been there for 'hundreds and hundreds of years', the Doctor says 'generations', and the Emperor Dalek says 'centuries passed'.

763 Dating *The Long Game* - The Doctor gives the date. It's established in *Bad Wolf* and *The Parting of the Ways* that the Jagrafess was a tool of the Daleks.

200,100 - BAD WOLF / THE PARTING OF THE WAYS[766] -> The Earth was now divided into continents that included Europa, Pacifica, the New American Alliance and Australasia. Default payments were made to Martian Drones. The Great Cobalt Pyramid was built on the remains of the famous Torchwood Institute. The Great Central Ravine was named after the 'ancient' British city of Sheffield. Stella Popbait made hats. There was a penal colony on the Moon. "Jupiter Rising" was a holo-series. The dish gaffabeck had originated on the planet Lucifer. By this point, the Face of Boe was the oldest inhabitant of the Isop Galaxy.

Humanity watched savage game shows such as *Big Brother*, *Call My Bluff* (with real guns), *Countdown* (where the aim was to defuse a bomb), *Ground Force* (contestants were turned to compost), *Wipeout*, *Stars in Your Eyes* (contestants were blinded), *What Not to Wear* (androids mutilated people), *Bear with Me* (contestants lived with a bear) and *The Weakest Link* (overseen by the dreaded Anne Droid). These were produced by the Bad Wolf Corporation, broadcast on ten thousand channels and filmed aboard the former Satellite Five, now called the Game Station.

Losing contestants were apparently vaporised, but in truth were teleported away and secretly converted into Daleks. The ranks of the Emperor Dalek's army swelled. The human, slaved Controller overseeing this operation sought out the Daleks' greatest enemy to help, and transmatted the Doctor, Captain Jack and Rose to the Game Station.

The Doctor discovered the Daleks' machinations, and the Emperor mobilized his forces against Earth. Dalek missiles bombarded many of the continents, with enough force to alter their very shape. The Doctor briefly sent Rose to safety in her native time, but Rose gazed into the heart of the TARDIS and thus became endowed with the power of the Time Vortex. She gained the godlike ability to alter time, and used it to destroy the Emperor and his Daleks. The Doctor sacrificed his life to stop the Vortex energies from consuming Rose, and regenerated as a result. Jack was left behind on the remains of the Game Station.

309,906 - THE WAR GAMES[767] -> A race of alien warlords attempted to raise an army of galactic conquest by programming human soldiers kidnapped from various points in history with stolen Time Lord technology. A renegade Time Lord named the War Chief aided them, and was shot during an uprising engineered by the Doctor, Jamie and Zoe. When the plan was uncovered, the Time Lords erected a forcefield that confined the aliens to their planet. The kidnapped soldiers were returned home, with no awareness of these events. The Time Lords also dematerialised the aliens' leader, the War Lord.

---

764 *Bad Wolf*

765 'Twenty years' before *Bad Wolf*, according to the *Big Brother* contestant Lynda Moss.

766 Dating *Bad Wolf / The Parting of the Ways* - The Doctor says in *Bad Wolf* that 'it's the year two-zero-zero-one-zero-zero', and the opening caption says it is 'one hundred years' after *The Long Game*. Lynda says the Game Station has ten thousand channels, although the Doctor's *Big Brother* game is broadcast on Channel 44,000. Lucifer is (almost certainly) the planet featured in *Lucifer Rising*. It's unclear whether Rose used her power to restore anyone or anything other than Captain Jack - it's not stated that she, for example, resurrected Lynda or anyone else who was killed, or reset the devastated Earth.

THE EARTH EMPIRES: The first Earth Empire lasted from the twenty-sixth century of *Frontier in Space* to the thirtieth of *The Mutants* and has been well documented, particularly in the New Adventures (the Doctor's companion Benny was from the early period, Ace lived in that time zone for several years and his later companions Chris and Roz were from the period when the Empire was starting to collapse).

The Second Empire was named in *Tomb of Valdemar*, and could well be the human empire mentioned in *The Sontaran Experiment*.

There's been no reference specifically to the Third.

The Long Game is set, in theory at least, at the time of The Fourth Great and Bountiful Human Empire, but the Emperor Dalek's machinations appear to alter history, and the apparent obliteration of Earth's continents casts doubt on whether this Empire ever comes to pass. If Rose reset all the actions of the Daleks, Earth's history could be restored to the one the Doctor knows about, but there's no evidence on-screen she did that.

Either way, the overwhelming amount of evidence suggests that Earth survives and continues to have great influence on the universe, at least for billions of years into the future (*The End of the World*). It's probable, then, that there's a fifth and many more Empires after this point.

767 Dating *The War Games* - It is stated that humanity has been killing itself for "half a million years" before this story takes place, which (coincidentally) ties up with the date 309,906 established for the Doctor's first trial (or "Malfeasance Tribunal") in *The Deadly Assassin*. *The TARDIS Logs* suggested a date of "48,063" for this story, *Apocrypha* offered "5950 AD".

The aliens in this story are unnamed on-screen, yet they're referred to as "the War Lords" in *The War Games*

309,906 - THE EIGHT DOCTORS -> The eighth Doctor rescued his second incarnation and encouraged him to summon the Time Lords to deal with the War Lords.[768]

The War Chief was horrifically injured rather than killed. He was sent to the War Lords' home planet, but his regeneration aborted and his new form was disfigured. He allied with the son of the War Chief, and after many years, they broke through the force field the Time Lords had placed around the War Lords' home planet. They revived their dreams of galactic conquest, and decided to concentrate on helping Nazi Germany.[769]

Around 315,000, humans encroached on the territory of the Sulumians in the eighth dimension. The Sulumians began a time travel campaign dedicated to rewriting human history to prevent this.[770] In 365,509, the collapse of a star in NGC4258 destroyed four civilisations. A region of space warps, the Grey Interchange, was created.[771]

= "Half a million years of industrial progress" had left the Earth's surface as "just a chemical slime". The Ancient One, a Haemovore, was the last living creature to inhabit an Earth.[772]

Lady Ruath showed Yarven, the Vampire Messiah, that mankind was destined to become a vampire race. The Haemovores lived in the sea, where they ganged up to hunt whales.[773]

? 802,701 - TIMELASH[774] -> The third Doctor and Jo visited Karfel, preventing a great famine there. The Doctor also reported the scientist Magellan, who had been conducting unethical experiments on the reptilian Morlox, to the praesidium.

Over the next century, an accident with the substance Mustakozene caused Magellan to merge with a Morlox and became the mutated Borad. He took control of Karfel, enforcing discipline with an army of androids and the threat of exile into a time corridor, the Timelash. The Borad planned to provoke a war with neighbouring Bandril as a means of populating the planet with mutated clones of himself. Following the arrival of the Doctor and Peri, the Borad was thrown into the Timelash, ending up in Loch Ness in the twelfth century.

Man fought the Primal Wars in the Tenth Segment of Time. Much scientific knowledge was lost during this period, including the cure for the common cold.[775]

Glitz's Time

The criminal Kane was guilty of systematic acts of violence and extortion with his lover Sana, who killed herself rather than face trial. Kane was exiled from his home planet of Proammon, and sent to the barren planet Svartos. He remained there for three thousand years, slowly building his powerbase and dreaming of a return to his homeworld.

Unknown to Kane, Proammon was destroyed when its star went supernova a thousand years after his exile. Kane operated from the trading post of Iceworld, which was capable of spaceflight. This required the Dragonfire, a source of energy contained within the head of the Dragon - a biomechanoid sent to Svartos to prevent Kane from escaping the planet. Kane remained trapped on Iceworld.[776]

Sabalom Glitz came from Salostopus in Andromeda. He was an habitual jailbird and thief, always on the lookout for a fast grotzi.[777]

---

novelisation by Malcolm Hulke, *The Making of Doctor Who* 1972 edition, the Lofficier *Programme Guide*, and *Timewyrm: Exodus* by Terrance Dicks. They're simply "Aliens" in the 1973 *Radio Times Special*. As both Hulke and Dicks independently use the name "War Lords" in their other work, it has been adopted in this volume to avoid confusion with other unnamed alien races.

WAR ZONES: *The War Games* establishes that the aliens have "ten" zones under their control (this is emphasised by the map we see), including the Control Zone. However, fourteen distinct war zones are referred to, meaning there are at least fifteen zones (the dates in quotes are explicitly given on screen): W.W.I ("1917"), The Roman Zone ("2000 years" before 1917), The Franco-Prussian War (1870-1871), the 30 Years War (1618-1648), The Jacobite Rebellion ("1745"), The English Civil War (1642-1646), The Boer War (1899-1902), The American Civil War ("1862"), Napoleon's advance into Russia ("1812"), The Russo-Japanese War

("1905"), the Boxer Rising (1900), the Crimean War (1853-1856), the Mexican Uprising (1867) and the Greek Zone (c.500 BC).

768 Dating *The Eight Doctors* - This happens during *The War Games*.

769 The War Chief is shot in *The War Games*, and reappears in *Timewyrm: Exodus*.

770 'Three hundred and seventeen thousand years' after 40 BC, according to *The Gallifrey Chronicles*.

771 *The English Way of Death*

772 "Half a million years" after *The Curse of Fenric*. When the Reverend Wainwright asks the Doctor how he knows about the Haemovores' future, the Doctor says "I've seen it". The Ancient Haemovore presumably erased this timeline when it killed Fenric, preventing him from releasing the poison that would start the destruction of life on Earth.

773 *Goth Opera*

774 Dating *Timelash* - No date is given on-screen. I

c 2,000,000 - THE MYSTERIOUS PLANET[778] -> A group of Earth-based Andromedans stole scientific secrets contained in the Matrix of the Time Lords and took shelter on Earth. By order of the High Council, the Magnotron was used to move the Earth and its entire constellation two light years, destroying everyone on the surface. The planet became known as Ravolox. The Andromedans, though, knew that the Time Lords had discovered them and had built a survival chamber. They entered suspended animation, awaiting rescue. The robot recovery mission sent to retrieve the Andromedans missed the Earth in its new location and sped on into the depths of space.

After five hundred years, this survival shelter had become Marb Station, a completely self-contained system. Station guards maintained strict water rationing and population control. The population worshipped "the Immortal" - a being that lived in a citadel within their complex, and which was actually the robot caretaker of the facility, Drathro. The Earth's surface became viable again and served as home to "The Tribe of the Free" - a few primitive humans who had escaped from Marb Station. They worshipped the god Haldron, and killed any space traveller trying to steal his totem, a black light converter made from pure siligtone. They believed their ancestors' space travel had brought down the wrath of their god and caused the solar fireball.

Glitz formed a business partnership with the renegade Time Lord the Master, who knew that Earth had been moved and renamed Ravolox by the High Council. Glitz's accomplice was a young man, Dibber. The Master sent Dibber and Glitz to Ravolox to retrieve the Matrix files.

The Doctor arrived and defeated Drathro, allowing the two communities of humans to make contact.

The Time Lords subsequently restored Earth to its correct location.[779] Thanks to a timestorm engineered by Fenric, Ace arrived on the ice planet of Svartos. Glitz used his ship, the *Nosferatu*, to raid space freighters. He ended up on Svartos with a rotten cargo and a mutinous crew, and tried to sell both to Kane.[780]

c 2,000,000 - DRAGONFIRE[781] -> On the trading colony Iceworld, located on the dark side of Svartos, Kane was assembling an army. He put his soldiers into cryosleep, which robbed their memories of their former life and insured they would serve him without question.

Others chose to serve Kane willingly... Kane, whose natural body temperature was minus 193 Celsius, would burn the Mark of the Sovereign onto the palm of their right hand. One of Kane's officers, Belazs, joined him when she was sixteen and served for twenty years. Kane earned many Crowns trading supplies to space travellers.

Many beings were drawn to Iceworld by the legends of a firebreathing dragon that supposedly lived in the ice tunnels beneath the colony. Kane finally killed the Dragon, his bio-mechanoid jailer, and acquired its Dragonfire power source. The Doctor helped Kane to realize that his homeworld had been destroyed two thousand years ago, which deprived Kane of his revenge. Kane killed himself upon realising this. The Doctor's companion Melanie Bush elected to stay behind on Iceworld, now renamed the *Nosferatu II*, with Sabalom Glitz.

Mel soon left Glitz and attempted to reach Earth. She ended up marooned on the holiday planet Avalone, and spent two years there. She tried to get a lift from Glitz, and planted messages for him in the Galactic Banking

have arbitrarily set it in the same year that the Time Traveller met the Eloi and the Morlocks in H.G. Wells' *The Time Machine*. There is no indication on-screen exactly when the third Doctor visited Karfel; the novelisation suggests it was "at least one hundred years" before this story, during the time of Katz's grandfather.

775 *The Ark*
776 *Dragonfire*
777 *The Mysterious Planet*
778 Dating *The Mysterious Planet* - The Doctor consults his pocket watch and suggests that it is "two million years" after Peri's time. Both the camera script and the novelisation confirm this date. *The Terrestrial Index* attempted to rationalise the various 'ends of the Earth' seen in the series, but in doing so it ignored virtually every date given on-screen. It is claimed, for example, that this story was set "c.14,500". *The TARDIS Special* gave

the date as "two billion" AD, an understandable mishearing of the Doctor's line. *About Time* speculates that this is the same destruction of Earth seen in *The Ark* (the first Doctor was confused about the date) but doesn't explain why Time Lords who would covertly sterilise the Earth to prevent their secrets getting out would not only give humanity notice this would happen, but enough notice to build a giant evacuation ship.

The setting reminds Peri of 'a wet November', perhaps suggesting the month. There's nothing on-screen to suggest this isn't Glitz's native time.
779 *The Eight Doctors*
780 Before *Dragonfire*.
781 Dating *Dragonfire* - No date is given on-screen, but Glitz's presence suggests the story takes place after *The Mysterious Planet*. Iceworld services "twelve galaxies",

Conglomerate's computer system, knowing that the Dragon cypher program she'd made for Glitz would find them. Glitz tried to exploit the open door and lift ten million grotzits from the bank, but he failed - causing officials to trace the intrusion to Mel's terminal. Avalone security caught up with Mel, who ran away to find the evil duplicate Dr Who.[782]

Glitz found a miniscope and briefly met Romana, who was trapped inside. Flavia arrived in a Type 90 TARDIS and returned Romana to Gallifrey.[783]

c 4,000,000 - THE SUN MAKERS[784] -> Earth's mineral wealth was finally exhausted and its people were dying. In return for their labour, the Usurians moved mankind to Mars, which they terraformed. The population was later moved on to Pluto, where six megropolises were built, each with its own artificial sun. However, the Doctor, who the Usurians knew had "a long history of violence and economic subversion", started a rebellion. He imposed a growth tax and rendered the planet uneconomic.

The Doctor took the Cold to Pluto in the far future.[785] Many millions of years in the future, the people of Phryxus established a technocracy in NGC4258 and developed galactic travel using warp capsules in the Grey Interchange. The renegade scientist Zodaal was jailed for experimenting on lesser life forms, and tried to escape using a warp capsule. This failed and he had to reduce himself to a gaseous state to survive. He escaped to the year 1929.[786]

Humanity attempted time-travel experiments during the Twenty-Seventh Segment of Time, but these proved to be a total failure.[787]

The Destruction of Earth

"Fleeing from the imminence of a catastrophic collision with the sun, a group of refugees from the *doomed* planet Earth..."[788]

c 10,000,000 - THE ARK[789] -> In the Fifty-Seventh Segment of Time, ten million years hence, scientists realised that the Earth was falling towards the Sun. With the help of the Monoids, a mysterious race whose own planet had been destroyed in a supernova many years before, humanity constructed a great space vessel. It contained the entire human, Monoid, animal and plant population of the Earth held on microcells in miniaturised form. Audio space research revealed that Refusis II was suitable for colonisation. It would take seven hundred years to reach the new world, and to symbolise the journey and the survival of man, a vast statue of a human carved from gregarian rock was begun.

The ship set out, and the few humans and Monoid servants that remained active - the Guardians - watched the Earth's destruction. Very soon afterward the common cold swept through the vessel, brought by the Doctor's companion Dodo. The Doctor cured the disease using animal membranes.

c 10,000,000 - FRONTIOS[790] -> A vast colony ship containing thousands of people, plus the technology and material capable of rebuilding the whole of human civilisation, was sent to the Veruna System on the distant edge of the universe. Despite being touted as failure-proof, every system on the colony ship failed. The

and Glitz comes from Andromeda, suggesting that intergalactic travel is now routine (and that it's after Andromeda was colonised). According to the novelisation, Svartos is in the "Ninth Galaxy".

Head Games claimed it was 'a few thousand years into the future', at the time of the Galactic Federation. *Head Games* also establishes that Earth is devastated at this time, a reference to *The Mysterious Planet / The Ultimate Foe* (but one that might also support a dating around the time of the solar flares). Assuming it's the same Galactic Federation seen in the Peladon stories, that and the dating of *Mission: Impractical* would seem to agree that Glitz's native time - and so the events of *Dragonfire* - is much earlier than two million years in the future. Glitz is working for the Master in *The Mysterious Planet*, so could have been taken to the far future. However, with absolutely no evidence for this, or for Glitz having his own time machine, it seems better to conclude that he was in his native time in *The*

Mysterious Planet.

782 *Head Games*, which confirms that Glitz is from the period when Earth was moved to become Ravolox.

783 *Goth Opera*

784 Dating *The Sun Makers* - Set unspecified "millions of years in the future" according to contemporary publicity material, but this is never stated explicitly onscreen. Earth has had time to regenerate its mineral wealth, which would suggest the story is set a very long way into the future. *The Programme Guide* failed to reconcile *The Sun Makers* with other stories, claiming that the Company dominated humanity only from "c.2100" to "c.2200" (first edition), or "c.2200" to "c.2300" (second edition). *The Terrestrial Index* suggested that the Earth was abandoned some centuries after the "52nd Century", and recolonised "5000 years" later. *The TARDIS Logs* suggested that the story was set "c.40,000", *Timelink* "25,000".

785 *Time and Relative*. No date is specified, but it's safe ship crashed on Frontios. Most of the crew died in the crash, and many more perished from diseases that spread through the colony immediately afterward.

Captain Revere eventually restored order. For ten years, the survivors planted and harvested crops, stocking up with food. But then meteorite bombardments began, striking the colony with such accuracy to make plain that it was being deliberately targeted. For thirty years the bombardment continued, but that wasn't the worst of it: the earth began swallowing up the dead. Over the years, the number of Retrogrades - people who deserted the colony - swelled.

And then, the earth swallowed Captain Revere while he was investigating the planet's potential mineral wealth. This left his son, Plantagenet, in command. The colony was soon in danger of falling apart.

The Tractators, insect creatures with the power to harness gravity, had arrived on Frontios five hundred years before and were responsible for the colony's setbacks. Under the command of their leader, the Gravis, they had pulled down the colony ship. They had given the colonists ten years to establish themselves, then began the meteorite bombardment. The Tractators had been kidnapping humans to serve as "drivers" for their tunnelling machines. The Gravis hoped to create a tunnel system that would amplify the Tractators' gravity fields and let them pilot Frontios throughout the cosmos.

The Gravis was isolated and transported to the planet Kolkokron. Without their leader, the Tractators were mindless drones, and the survival of the human colony was assured.

After delivering the Gravis to Kolkokron, the Doctor made a side trip to the planet Artaris circa 1001 before returning to Frontios.[791]

c 10,000,700 - THE ARK[792] -> The fever that had swept through the Ark had never fully abated, and it had weakened the humans. Seven hundred years after leaving the Solar System, the Monoids had seized control of the ship, and the statue commemorating the voyage was now of a Monoid. The humans now called the ship "the Ark" after an old Earth legend, but the Monoids kept the Guardians' descendants in check with heat prods.

The Ark arrived at Refusis II and Launcher 14 was sent to the surface. At first there was no sign of life, but it quickly transpired that the native Refusians were invisible giants. Nevertheless, the Monoid leader, named 1, planned to take his race's microcells to the planet. He also intended to destroy the Ark with a bomb planted in the head of the statue, but the Refusians helped to throw the statue overboard, allowing it to explode harmlessly in space. The Refusians allowed the humans and Monoids to live on their world, but only if they promised to live in peace.

Thus, humanity survived the destruction of its homeworld by travelling across the universe and rebuilding human civilisation on distant planets. What happened in the untold billions of years after that was a mystery - any TARDIS attempting to travel further into the future than this exceeded its time parameters, and the Time Lords themselves were unaware of anything beyond this time. "Knowledge has its limits; ours reaches this far and no further".[793]

---

to presume it wasn't when the Company occupied the planet.

786 'Many millions of years' after *The English Way of Death* (p189).

787 *The Ark*. Earth, and a number of races known to Earth - most notably the Daleks - achieved limited success with time travel experiments (one human scientist built a time machine in the nineteenth century, according to *The Evil of the Daleks*), but these have presumably been forgotten by now.

788 *Frontios*

789 Dating *The Ark* - The Commander states that this is "the Fifty-Seventh Segment" of time, which the Doctor instantly calculates to be "ten million years" after Steven and Dodo's time.

790 Dating *Frontios* - According to the Doctor, the story happens "on the outer limits. The TARDIS has drifted too far into the future". The inhabitants of Frontios are among the very last humans, and they have evacu-

ated the Earth in circumstances that sound very similar to those of *The Ark*. While this would seem to dictate that *Frontios* is contemporary with *The Ark*, there is room for debate: no date is given in *Frontios*, there's no explicit link made to the earlier story, the colony ship is of a very different design, there is no sign of the Monoids and neither story refers to other arks. It is difficult to judge the level of technology, as virtually everything is lost in the crash, but it does not seem as advanced as that of *The Ark*.

791 *Excelis Dawns*

792 Dating *The Ark* - The last two episodes of the story take place at the end of the Ark's journey, which occurs "seven hundred years" after the first two episodes.

793 In *Frontios*, a message flashes up on a TARDIS console screen: "Boundary Error - Time Parameters Exceeded". Likewise, in *The Sun Makers*, the Doctor is worried that the TARDIS might have "gone right through the time spiral". This limitation doesn't seem to

The Doctor estimated that dogs would evolve thumbs in around twenty million years time.[794]

The Fifty-Eighth Segment of Time - THE WELL-MANNERED WAR[795] -> In the Fifty-Eighth Segment of Time, human refugees colonised the planet Metralubit. There was peace for two thousand years, but then a planet-wide war suddenly wiped out two-thirds of the population. This had been engineered by the Hive, an evolved gestalt of flies that fed on dead bodies. There were four more such wars at roughly two-thousand-year intervals. The Helducc civilisation emerged from the sixth war, but fell to war in the same way. A new civilisation rose and developed the Femdroids, led by Galatea, to increase male efficiency.

The Black Guardian brought a Chelonian squad from the distant past in a timestorm. The Chelonians claimed the planet Barclow, close to Metalubit, and the two races fought a short war until the Bechet Treaty was signed. Galatea learned the secret of the devastating world wars, evacuated most of the Femdroids to Regus V and plotted to lure the Hive back.

The Doctor, Romana and K9 arrived on Barclow and discovered that the Black Guardian was trying to trick the Doctor into releasing the Hive in the twenty-sixth century, an act that would destroy human history. The Doctor defeated the Guardian by removing himself and Romana from time and space altogether.

This was the end of the Humanian Era.[796]

The Navarino civilisation was the only one to survive the war on its home planet - their culture was based on frivolity, and they were having too good a time to join in the conflict. The Navarinos had time tourism, but paid exhorbitant taxes to the Time Lords for the privilege.[797]

? - DELTA AND THE BANNERMEN[798] -> The Bannermen invaded the home planet of the Chimerons, but the Chimeron Queen escaped to Tollport G715. She joined the Doctor, Mel and a party of Navarinos on a Nostalgia Trips tour to America in the 1950s.

Nostalgia Trips were notorious following an incident with the Glass Eaters of Traal, and true to form, their Hellstrom II cruiser wound up at a holiday camp in Wales by mistake. The Bannermen pursued them back in time.

The Vulgar End of Time - THE ONE DOCTOR[799] -> In the far future, everything had been discovered, everything had been done and technology made everything possible and affordable. It was therefore very boring.

A company on Generios VIII had thrived by exporting furniture, but the company's Assembler robots had wiped out the thirty-million-year-old population thousands of years ago. The Rim World of Abydos had no interesting features whatsoever, and Zynglat 3 boasted a sensory deprivation device. The Skardu-Rosbrix Wars were recent history. The super-computer Mentos spent 33,000 years playing *Super Brain* against a holographic Questioner, even

---

affect the TARDIS in *The Ark* or *The Savages*, or the New Adventures story *Timewyrm: Apocalypse*, which is also set in the distant future. The words quoted are those of the Doctor in *Frontios*. The novelisation of that story makes it clear that "ours" refers to the Time Lords, and that the story is set at the "edge of the Gallifreyan noosphere". It may - or may not - be significant that the Time Lords are unable to travel beyond the time of Earth's destruction.

It is perhaps also significant that in stories set after the destruction of Gallifrey, such as *Father Time, Hope, Sometime Never* and *The End of the World*, the Doctor is capable of travelling much further into the future (although he also seems quite capable of doing so in other stories set before Gallifrey's destruction, such as *Timewyrm: Apocalypse* and *The One Doctor*).

794 *Evolution* (p40).

795 Dating *The Well-Mannered War* - This is 'right at the end of the Humanian era, after the destruction of Earth' (p25) and 'the fifty-eighth segment of time'.

796 *The Well-Mannered War*

ERAS: The Humanian Era was first mentioned in *Doctor Who - The Movie*, which also referred to the

Rassilon Era. The TARDIS console prop for that story also included references to the Peon, Manussan, Sumaron, Kraaiian and Sensorian eras. *Zagreus* adds the Morestran Era to the list.

The Humanian Era includes Earth in 1999, and is presumably a reference to the human race. *The Well-Mannered War* implies that it's simply the Era when humans exist. The Rassilon Era applies to Gallifrey (the 'present' for the Doctor would seem to be 5725.2 in the Rassilon Era, according to the TV movie). *Neverland* specifies that the period around the Federation and Mavic Chen was the Sensorian. The Manussan and Morestran eras are presumably references to the planets from *Snakedance* and *Planet of Evil* respectively. Taking all this at face value, it would seem that eras can overlap each other - the Sensorian and Morestran eras, at least, fall comfortably within the Humanian Era.

797 *Return of the Living Dad*, tying in with the date for *Delta and the Bannermen*.

798 Dating *Delta and the Bannermen* - An entirely arbitrary date. However, Nostalgia Trips is notorious throughout the "five galaxies", suggesting that the story is set in a far future period of intergalactic travel. In when warfare destroyed all other civilization on Generios XIV.

The Doctor was famous in this era for his heroism, and the con man Banto Zame (a native of Osphogus, a planet that was terraformed five thousand years before) impersonated the Doctor to stage "defeats" of alien invasions, then collect rewards from grateful rulers. Banto tried his scheme on Generios I, but a genuine alien spaceship arrived and demanded the Generios System's three greatest treasures as tribute.

The Doctor, Mel and Banto banded together to collect the Mentos super-computer from Generios XIV, furniture Unit ZX419 from Generios VIII, and the largest diamond in existence on Generios XV. The Cylinder accepted the tribute as proof of the Doctor's identity, but mistook Banto for the genuine Time Lord. The Cylinder spirited Banto away to face retribution for a past offence the Doctor had committed against the Cylinder's masters.

(? The Vulgar End of Time) - OMEGA[800] **->** By now, the legend of Omega was widely known. Jolly Chronolidays set up a heritage center in the Sector of Forgotten Souls, where it was believed Omega had detonated a star on behalf of the Time Lords. The center was modeled on Omega's ship, the *Eurydice*.

Omega himself arrived in this time zone and met Sentia, a telepath who became enamoured of him. However, Omega's failed attempt to merge with the Doctor in Amsterdam, 1983, had left him with a copy of the Doctor's memories and a split persona. The "Doctor" aspect of his mind was unaware that he was part of Omega's body. Omega's mental health further deteriorated, and Sentia conspired to return Omega to his anti-matter universe aboard the real *Eurydice*, which was within a dimensional anomaly. The genuine Doctor arrived onhand, Sentia was killed and Omega was yet again cast - along with the *Eurydice* - over the event horizon of a black hole.

Two agents of Gallifrey's Celestial Preservation Agency - Maven and the living TARDIS Glinda - arrived to preserve the Doctor's reputation by insuring that his eradication of the Scintillan race remained secret. They offered Daland, an actor, a job in a Gallifreyan museum.

The End of Time

"A distant point of time, an age of great advancement, peace and prosperity".[801]

= If history had run differently, and Gallifrey had been destroyed at the time of Rassilon, the first time travellers would have evolved a billion years from now. These would have been the Ferutu. They intervened to optimise history, so that the Daleks and CyberHost were both forces for good in a utopian universe. The Doctor tricked the Ferutu into preventing their creation to save our timeline.[802]

Two billion years in the future, the Time Lord Solenti observed how the Dagusan sun ended its lifespan as a main sequence star. The planet's seas consequently evaporated, even as the remaining population retreated to the South Pole.[803]

Three hundred thousand years before the Last of Man, the Doctor negotiated a lasting peace between the Sontarans and the Rutans. By this time, Gallifrey had long fallen. The Sontarans and Rutans undertook the largest demobilisation in the history of the universe.[804]

Dragonfire, Svartos serves "the twelve galaxies", so perhaps it is set later than this story. While only the Daleks had broken the time barrier by 4000 AD (*The Daleks' Master Plan*), the human ship in *Planet of the Spiders* and the Movellan ship in *Destiny of the Daleks* have "time warp capability", and we see a couple of races developing rudimentary time travel around now (Magnus Greel in 5000 AD, the Metebelis Spiders a little later). Such secrets are limited, and are lost by the time of *The Ark*. Murray, the bus driver, says "the 1950s nights back on Navaro were never like this", which implies nostalgia parties rather than that he lived through the 1950s himself. *The Terrestrial Index* set this story "c.15,000".

799 Dating *The One Doctor* - The Doctor expounds on the subject of the Vulgar End of Time at the beginning of the story.

800 Dating *Omega* - The dating is arbitrary, but much about this story resembles the Vulgar End of Time: time travel is now deemed unfashionable rather than unattainable; the exploits of the Doctor, Omega and - generally speaking - the Time Lords are widely renowned, if somewhat erroneously; and the period is one of prosperity, leisure and dullness. The Doctor is said to have accidentally wiped out the thought-based Scintillans while combating space pirates who used telepathically-controlled weapons and ships, but a proper dating for this isn't given.

801 *The Savages*
802 *Cold Fusion*
803 *The Suns of Caresh*
804 *The Infinity Doctors*

5,000,000,000 - THE END OF THE WORLD[805] -> Earth was seen as the cradle of civilisation, and there was not a star in the sky that humanity hadn't touched. Humanity had evolved into new humans, protohumans, digihumans and the humanish. Many other races had evolved from Earth plants and animals.

For years, Earth was preserved by the National Trust, who reversed the process of continental drift (although by this time, Los Angeles was a crevasse and the Arctic was a desert). When the preservation money ran out, many diverse alien races, including the Trees of the Forest of Cheam (descendants of trees from Earth's tropical rainforest), the Moxx of Balhoon, the Adherents of the Repeated Meme, the Face of Boe, the Ambassadors from the City State of Blinding Light and the Doctor and Rose all gathered on Platform One to witness the planet's final destruction.

The last purebred human, Cassandra, plotted to engineer a hostage situation to sue the corporation that ran the Platform. Failing that, she tried to kill the assembled beings, as she had invested heavily in their rivals' companies. Cassandra's plan was defeated, and she was made to pay for her crimes by the Doctor.

The Doctor once speculated that Earth's sun would finally become a supernova in ten thousand million years time. [806]

? - THE SAVAGES[807] -> On one planet, the Elders maintained a utopian civilisation free from material needs. They survived by draining 'life energy' from the savages who lived in the wastelands outside their beautiful city. "The Traveller from Beyond Time", the Doctor, ended this injustice, and his companion Steven Taylor remained behind to rule the civilisation as it renounced barbarism.

Towards the End of the Universe

Many billions of years from now, the universe was cold and almost dead. The suns were exhausted. The last few survivors of the universe huddled around whatever energy sources they could find. [808]

Eight billion years in the future, and humanity was long dead. The Mutter's Spiral had been abandoned by all sentient life. [809] A few ten billions of years in the future, the Conservers existed in a black hole, preserving information there in the face of the universe's death. They engineered their own creation by sending avatars into the past to bring a colony ship to their black hole. The Doctor visited the Conservers. [810]

TIMEWYRM: APOCALYPSE[811] -> Billions of years in the future, the guardians of the universe, even the Time Lords, were long extinct. The people of Kirith (the only planet orbiting a red giant in Galaxy QSO 0046 at the edge of the universe) never grew old or unhappy. For three thousand eight hundred and thirty-three years, the Kirithons had been ruled by the eighty-four Panjistri, who gave them food and technology. For nearly a thousand years, the

805 Dating *The End of the World* - The Doctor tells Rose "this is the year 5.5/apple/26, five billion years in your future".

This story seems to contradict *The Ark* (and, by implication, *Frontios*), which witnessed the destruction of the Earth a mere ten million years in our future, and had a different fate for humanity. The obvious inference to make is that the Earth wasn't completely destroyed in *The Ark*, and the National Trust's renovations were more extensive than the Doctor told Rose.

806 *Colony in Space*. It's possible the Doctor witnessed this for himself. It doesn't contradict *The Ark*, which had Earth crashing into the Sun, not the Sun going supernova, or *The End of the World*, where the Sun merely expands enough to destroy the Earth.

807 Dating *The Savages* - At the end of *The Gunfighters*, the Doctor claims that they have now landed at "a distant point in time" (see the quote above). The Elders have the technology to track the TARDIS, but are not capable of time travel themselves. They declare themselves to be "human".

808 *Timewyrm Apocalypse, The Infinity Doctors, Father* *Time, Hope, The Eye of the Tyger, Sometime Never.*

809 'Eight billion years' after *Cold Fusion*.

810 *The Eye of the Tyger*

811 Dating *Timewyrm: Apocalypse* - The novel is set "several billion years" in the future (p3), "ten billion years" before the end of the universe (p178).

812 *Zagreus*. These facts were presented as part of a simulation, and so may not take place.

813 *The Infinity Doctors, Father Time*

814 *Unnatural History*

815 Dating *Father Time* - The exact timescale is unclear, and is stated to be 'a few million years in the future', 'several million years hence', and 'a million years in the future'. The physical state of the universe, however, suggests it is much later than that.

816 Dating *Hope* - The Doctor pushes the TARDIS to see how far into the future he can take it and the TARDIS goes "too far". This is the same far, far future time period referred to in *The Infinity Doctors* and *Father Time*, which alluded to Silver and this time period (p191).

817 *Sometime Never*

Panjistri performed genetic experiments, forcing the evolution of the Kirithons in an attempt to create a being that had reached the Omega Point: an omniscient, omnipotent entity capable of halting the destruction of the universe. They succeeded in creating a golden sphere of expanding light, but the machine destroyed itself and the Panjistri, knowing that the universe must end.

The Divergents almost emerged into our universe sixty billion years in the future, towards the end of time. Uncle Winky's Wonderland had been moved several times and was situated atop the ruins of Rassilon's lab on Gallifrey. Uncle Winky revived from stasis, but died from his heart condition.[812]

There was a huge disaster that led to galaxies being evacuated and whole sections of the timeline being erased. The Doctor's people were somehow responsible, and the four surviving Time Lords used their great powers to impose control on the rest of the universe. The last Time Lord became the first ever Emperor of the entire Universe, ruling over a divided and broken populace that split into Factions and Houses. These included the Klade, 'goblin shapeshifters' and cybernetic gangsters - the ultimate descendants of the Daleks, Sontarans, Rutans and the Cybermen.

Most of the people of the universe relocated to the Needle, a light-year long structure that was the remains of a TARDIS that had tried to escape the pull of a black hole. The largest building on the Needle was the Librarinth, where all surviving knowledge and art was preserved.[813]

Griffin the Unnaturalist was an inhabitant of the Needle.[814]

FATHER TIME[815] -> The Doctor and two companions visited the planets Galspar and Falkus around this time. The Doctor also fought a robotic tyrant who panicked, accidentally destroyed his own palace and killed his own wife. This robot - who later assumed the identity Mr Gibson to blend in on twentieth century Earth - vowed revenge.

At least some of the Emperor's subjects, such as the Klade - the super-evolved descendants of the Daleks - resented Imperial rule. One Klade senator, the mother of Zevron and Ferran, incited revolution against the Emperor but was assassinated. Zevron stormed the Imperial Palace, killing and scattering all of the Imperial Family. The Emperor was killed. The Emperor's daughter, Miranda, was rescued by her nanny and taken down a time corridor to twentieth century Earth.

Over the years, Zevron tracked down and killed every other member of the Imperial Family. Finally he located Miranda and led the mission to kill her on Earth in the early nineteen-eighties.

When Zevron failed to return, Ferran became Prefect of Faction Klade. Some years later, Ferran received a distress signal from Sallak, Zevron's deputy. Ferran travelled to twentieth century Earth to complete Zevron's mission but failed and returned to his native time.

A team of Ferran's scholars spent fifteen years in the Librarinth, and they eventually pinpointed Miranda's whereabouts. During this time, Ferran also recovered a derelict sentient ship built by the People of the Worldsphere, which he christened the *Supremacy*. The political situation had deteriorated, putting the Houses and Factions at open war, and soon galactic civilisation was on the brink of collapse. Ferran believed Miranda could access sealed sections of the Librarinth and thus give him the power to dominate the other Factions. Using the *Supremacy*, he again set off to the twentieth century.

Miranda and Ferran returned to this time. Convinced she could unite the universe, Miranda was crowned Empress.

The Miranda spin-off comic follows on from these events.

HOPE[816] -> Taking the TARDIS into the far future, the Doctor landed on planet A245, known locally as Endpoint. It was an icy planet with a toxic environment. The TARDIS fell through the frozen crust of an acid sea, and the Doctor asked the cyborg Silver - the warlord of the nearest settlement, Hope - for assistance. In return, the Doctor tracked down a serial killer. Silver was from the far past, the year 3006.

Anji was tempted to use the cloning technology of the far future to recreate her dead boyfriend, Dave, and granted Silver scans of the TARDIS in return for this. The Doctor found survivors from other colonies were murdering the people of Hope to harvest Kallisti, a hormone that could revive more of the colonists from cryo-sleep. Silver found the sleepers and converted them into Silverati: half-synthetic soldiers loyal to him. With his soldiers and the colonists' hypertunnel, Silver attempted to take control of a richer planet. The Doctor exiled Silver and his Silverati to the barren planet A2756.

There were no pure humans left, but human genes survived in a number of races. Apple trees were extinct until Silver cloned one from an apple core that the Doctor gave him. The universe was past the point of sustainable expansion, and the rate of star death had dramatically increased.

Miranda brought the Factions and Houses together and united the people of the universe. She had at least one child, a daughter named Zezanne. Zezanne's father died. The Council of Eight kidnapped Miranda and Zezanne when Zezanne was a teenager.[817]

Event Two

"One mad prophet martyr journeyed too far and saw the Timewyrm. He saw it in a timeline that he could not be sure of, devouring Rassilon or his shade, during the Blue Shift, that time of final conflict when Fenric shall slip his chains and the evil of the worlds shall rebound back on them in war." [818]

100,000,000,000,000,000,000,000,000,000,000 - THE INFINITY DOCTORS[819] -> The Needle had been inhabited for tens of millions of years, but now it was all but abandoned. Ruined cities dotted its surface, and the atmosphere had frozen. The only known survivors were the predator animals named the Maltraffi, mushrooms and four 'knights': Gordel, Willhuff, Pallent and Helios. Each could only remember the future - with less and less to remember each day - and each had his own theory as to their origins. They may have been the last survivors of the Children of Kasterborous, human / Gallifreyan hybrids who intervened in the universe at great cost; superevolved Thals who fled the penultimate destruction of Skaro at the start of the Final Dalek War; members of the People of the Worldsphere, left behind when everyone else transcended reality; or the last High Evolutionaries (Helios might have been Merlin, or his son).

The Doctor arrived from Gallifrey to find the god Ohm, who was trapped in the black hole at one end of the Needle. Two of the Doctor's colleagues, the Magistrate and Larna, were sent in to rescue him when he vanished. Omega emerged from the black hole wearing the Doctor's body, banishing the Magistrate somewhere unknown and taking Larna back to Gallifrey.

Omega sought to attain ultimate power by unleashing the Eye of Harmony. The Doctor had been reunited with his wife as part of these events, but was forced to lose her again. He once more defeated Omega.

The Last Museum stood as a collection of the human race's greatest objects and achievements. It was located at the end of Time, at the exact centre of the universe. The Council of Eight member Soul served at the Museum, disguised as an old man named Singleton.[820]

SOMETIME NEVER[821] -> The Council of Eight existed in the Vortex Palace, right at the end of time. By placing unique crystals at the beginning of time, they mapped out events across the universe, and generated energy from unused potential timelines by correctly predicting the course of events. This energy was stored in Schrodinger Cells. The Council sent apes mutated by the Time Winds ('the Agents of the Council') to ensure their version of history transpired, and also recruited Sabbath to unwittingly work on their behalf. The Council deemed many of the Doctor's companions a threat, as they were touched by his innate ability to influence history, and thus engineered the possible deaths of Sarah Jane Smith, Harry Sullivan, Melanie Bush, Ace and Samantha Jones.

The Council leader, Octan, planned to destroy human history with a starkiller, releasing vast amounts of energy as universal history was rewritten. This energy would paradoxically create the Council of Eight, and in all probability allow them to survive the end of the universe. Octan took Miranda hostage, but she sacrificed herself, allowing the Doctor a free hand to fight them. Octan tried manipulating Sabbath into doing his bidding, but Sabbath killed himself to thwart his former employers. Sabbath's death helped to instigate the destruction of the Vortex Palace.

The Council of Eight perished except for the benevolent Soul and Octan, who journeyed to 1588 in a last-ditch effort to save their plans. The Doctor donated some of his life energy to stabilize Soul's body into his former guise as the old man Singleton. Soul took Octan's starkiller.

The Doctor and his allies departed in the TARDIS, while Soul and Miranda's daughter Zezanne evacuated in the *Jonah*, which arrived in a junkyard in 1963. Beings with a mind toward acquiring the starkiller monitored the *Jonah*'s departure.

Other beings that survived until the last moments of the universe included the Solarii and Korsann's reptilian race.

Our universe was destroyed in the Big Crunch. All matter imploded to a central point, returning to the state from which it was created: "a bright blazing pinprick of sheer energy".[822] The Time Lords referred to the end of the universe as Event Two.[823]

Just as a universe existed before ours, so will another universe be formed from the ashes of ours, and the physical laws there will be very different. This will be the domain of Saraquazel.[824]

---

818 *Timewyrm: Revelation*
819 Dating *The Infinity Doctors* - The date is given (p137). This is 'within a few decades of Event Two' (p130).
820 *Sometime Never*

821 Dating *Sometime Never* - The scene in the Vortex Palace ends with the end of the universe.
822 *Timewyrm: Apocalypse*
823 *The Infinity Doctors*
824 *Millennial Rites*

The history of the Time Lords and their homeworld of Gallifrey was shrouded in mystery. The Time Lords knew little of their own past, and much of what was known was cloaked in uncertainty and self-contradiction. It is extremely difficult to reconcile the various accounts of the origins of the Time Lords. The authorities suppressed politically inconvenient facts, although few Time Lords were very interested in politics anyway.[1]

Gallifreyan history can be divided into two periods: "the Old Time", the semi-legendary foundation of Time Lord society millions of years ago; and "recent history", that which has happened within living memory. (Time Lords, of course, live a long time.)[2]

The Old Time

We have only a few scraps of knowledge about the history of Gallifrey before the discovery of time travel. Gallifrey was the home of "the oldest civilisation in the universe", and had "ten million years of absolute power".[3]

Gallifreyans mastered the use of transmats when the universe was less than half its present size.[4] Time Lords used to speak and write Old High Gallifreyan, now a dead language.[5] Gallifrey means, literally "they that walk in shadows".[6] Gallifrey was in the constellation Kasterborous.[7]

Kasterborous was a mythological figure who was chained to a chariot of silver fire by the gods.[8] **The planet Karn was close to Gallifrey.**[9] Karn was in conjunction with the gas giant Polarfrey.[10]

Gallifreyans were naturally telepathic and could build "living" machinery that was also telepathic.[11] They possessed a 'reflex link', superganglions in their brains that allowed the Time Lord intelligentsia to commune.[12] The Time Lords discovered that they had a 'dark side' of their minds.[13]

Masonry from the Old Time survived, deep beneath the Capitol, into the modern era.[14] Gallifrey had a single moon, Pazithi Gallifreya.[15]

The Dark Days

At the very dawn of Time Lord history were "the Dark Days".[16] This was "the time of Chaos". One of the Doctor's most closely guarded secrets was that he was somehow involved with this period.[17]

> "In the days before Rassilon, my ancestors had tremendous powers which they misused disgracefully. They set up this place, the Death Zone and walled it around with an impenetrable force field. Then they kidnapped other beings and set them down here... even in our most corrupt period, our ancestors never allowed the Cybermen to play the

---

1 In *The Deadly Assassin*, the Time Lords don't know that their power comes from the Eye of Harmony and in both that story and *The Ultimate Foe*, they haven't heard of the Master. In *The Deadly Assassin*, even the Doctor seems unaware of the APC Net, and knows little about Rassilon.
2 The phrase "the Old Time" is first used in *The Deadly Assassin*. Not all Gallifreyans are Time Lords, as the Time Lords are the ruling elite of Gallifrey - the Doctor seems to say in *The Invisible Enemy* that there are only "one thousand" Time Lords. However, the terms "Time Lord" and "Gallifreyan" seem interchangeable for most practical purposes. Likewise, "Time Lord" is used to refer to the Doctor's race even before they master time travel (e.g.: *Remembrance of the Daleks,* where the "Time Lords" have trouble with the prototype of the Hand of Omega). Gallifrey is first named in *The Time Warrior*, although the Time Lords' home planet was called Jewel in the TV Comic strip *Return of the Daleks*.
3 *The Ultimate Foe*
4 *Genesis of the Daleks*
5 *The Five Doctors*
6 *The Pit*
7 *Pyramids of Mars*

8 *Lungbarrow*
9 *The Brain of Morbius*
10 *Lungbarrow*
11 We learn that Susan is telepathic in *The Sensorites*, and it has been stated on a number of occasions that the Doctor (e.g. *The Three Doctors*), the TARDIS (e.g. *The Time Monster*) and all Time Lords (e.g. *The Deadly Assassin*) are telepathic. The Doctor has also stated on a number of occasions that the TARDIS is alive (e.g. *The Five Doctors*), and so is the Nemesis seen in *Silver Nemesis*.
12 *The Invisible Enemy*
13 Omega has a "dark side" to his mind in *The Three Doctors* and the Valeyard [q.v.] represents the Doctor's dark side (*The Ultimate Foe*). In *Falls the Shadow*, the Doctor refers to this as the "Dark Design".
14 *The Deadly Assassin*. Engin says that deep beneath the Capitol there are "vaults and foundations dating from the Old Time".
15 *Cat's Cradle: Time's Crucible, The Infinity Doctors, The Gallifrey Chronicles*
16 *The Five Doctors*
17 *Silver Nemesis*

game - like the Daleks they played too well... old Rassilon put a stop to it in the end. He sealed off the entire zone and forbade the use of the Time Scoop... there are rumours and legends to the contrary. Some say his fellow Time Lords rebelled against his cruelty and locked him in the Tower in eternal sleep." [18]

Gallifreyans were naturally "time sensitive", with a unique understanding of time.[19] The earliest Time Lords discovered dematerialisation theory. [20] Another key discovery was transdimensional engineering.[21] The Time Lords built the Time Vortex, a vast transdimensional spiral encompassing all points in space and time.[22]

The Time Lords' ancestors built the Time Scoop.[23] The Gallifreyans mostly resembled tall, athletic humans. They were truly immortal, barring accidents.[24]

CAT'S CRADLE: TIME'S CRUCIBLE ->

The Pythias, a line of prophetesses who, since the 254th Pythia, rejected technology in favour of magic and superstition, ruled Gallifrey. Time travel was achieved by psychic prophecy, not physical means. The Pythias were guided by the prophesies in *The Book of Future Legends*, and saw their heritage as the Bright Past. The great philosopher Pelatov lived five thousand years before Rassilon.

At the time of the Intuitive Revelation, the age of Rassilon, the barbaric Gallifreyan Empire spread across the universe and encompassed the Pen-Shoza, Jagdagian, Oshakarm, the Star Grellades, Mirphak 2 and the rebellious Aubert Cluster. For aeons, Gallifreyan Heroes such as Ao had fought campaigns against foes such as the Gryffnae, lacustrine Sattisar and the batworms of the asteroid archipelago. The Winter Star was besieged for a century. The great hero Haclav Agusti Prydonius, commander of the Apollaten, defeated the marauding Sphinx of Thule, and was sent to observe a dispute brewing between Ruta III and the Sontara Warburg.

Across the cosmos, the ruling seers were dying: the Sphinx of Thule; the Logistomancer of A32K, foreseer of a cold empire of logic; the Core Sybilline of Klanti; the Sosostris in the West Spiral; The-Nameless-That-Sees-All in the North Constellations. The 508th Pythia became the last of her line. After a visit from a Master Trader of the South, she finally recognised that the veil of Time would soon only be traversed physically, not mentally. She instigated the Time Programme.

The Time Scaphe, the first time vessel and powered by the mental energy of its crew, was launched but vanished. Rassilon and his neo-technologists overthrew the Pythia. As her followers fled to Karn, the Pythia cursed Gallifrey with her dying words: its people became infertile, the colonies began to demand their independence and an Ice Age commenced. The Pythia cast herself into an abyss.

Rassilon lost a daughter to the Pythia's curse. The only good omen was the return of the Time Scaphe. Quennesander Olyesti Pekkary, captain of the Time Scaphe and first son of the House of Fordfarding, was Rassilon's nephew.

---

18 According to the Doctor in *The Five Doctors*.

19 *City of Death, Warriors' Gate, Time and the Rani*.

20 *The Claws of Axos*

21 *The Robots of Death*

22 *Just War*. The Time Vortex was first named in *The Time Monster*.

23 *The Five Doctors*

24 *The Infinity Doctors*

25 *Lungbarrow*

26 *Cat's Cradle: Time's Crucible, Lungbarrow*

27 *Lungbarrow*

28 *Interference*. Rassilon's dissolution of the monasteries presumably accompanies his defeat of the Pythia.

29 Omega first appears in *The Three Doctors* and reappears in *Arc of Infinity, The Infinity Doctors* and *Omega*. The Hand of Omega, his stellar-manipulation device, appears in *Remembrance of the Daleks, Lungbarrow* and *The Infinity Doctors*.

The first reference to Rassilon is in *The Deadly Assassin*; after that he becomes the central figure of Gallifreyan history, referred to in many subsequent stories (the quotes are from the Doctor, in *The Five Doctors* and *Shada* respectively). Both Rassilon and Omega are the legendary founders of Time Lord society, both are "the greatest" of the Doctor's race and supply the energy necessary for time travel. The first time that it is explicitly stated on-screen that they were contemporaries is in *Silver Nemesis*, although earlier in Season Twenty-Five, *Remembrance of the Daleks* attempted to rationalise the two accounts of Time Lord origins. Early *Doctor Who Weekly* issues included a back-up strip written by Alan Moore which was an account of the origins of the Time Lords, and which has been referred to in novels such as *The Infinity Doctors* and *Interference*.

30 *Silver Nemesis*

31 The Other was mentioned or alluded to in countless New and Missing Adventures, his first appearance being in the *Remembrance of the Daleks* novelisation.

32 Engin, *The Deadly Assassin*.

33 *The Infinity Doctors*

34 *The Three Doctors*

35 The Doctor, *Remembrance of the Daleks*.

36 *Omega*. These details hail from Omega's unreliable memories and are highly suspect. The details about Omega committing genocide, certainly, stem from a blending of the Doctor's recollections and are likely to be false.

The family Houses of Gallifrey were sentient and the oldest beings on Gallifrey. They were born at the time of the Intuitive Revelation.[25]

To get around the Pythia's curse of sterility, Rassilon and the Other built Looms capable of weaving Gallifreyans from existing genetic material.[26] Time Lords were born from the Loom fully grown and fully conscious, but needed educating.[27]

A priest on early Gallifrey was driven into the wilderness when Rassilon dissolved the monasteries. While wandering, he happened across all twelve of his future incarnations, who had no memory of how they came to appear together. The priest became known as IM Foreman, and his thirteen incarnations founded a time-travelling carnival. Their caravan was a complex space-time event that would model itself a new shape on each arrival.

Events on Dust in the thirty-eighth century mortally wounded Foreman's incarnations, forcing them to regenerate and causing amnesia. They were flung through time to early Gallifrey for the original Foreman to paradoxically find.[28]

The Mastery of Time

Two Gallifreyans ensured that their people became the Lords of Time: Rassilon and Omega. Rassilon was the "greatest single figure in Time Lord history", yet "no one really knows how extensive his powers were" and he "had powers and secrets that even we don't understand". To this day, the Time Lords revere Omega as their "greatest hero", "one of the greatest of all our race".[29]

Omega, Rassilon and another Time Lord developed Validium, a "living metal" designed to be the last line of defence for Gallifrey.[30] The third Time Lord was known as "the Other" to modern Time Lords.[31]

> "Today we tend to think of Rassilon as the founder of our modern civilisation, but in his own time he was regarded mainly as an engineer and an architect. And, of course, it was long before we turned away from the barren road of technology." [32]

The Time Lord Capitol and Citadel dated from the time of Rassilon and Omega, but in those days they weren't enclosed in a dome. The Citadel was built to withstand a siege, but against what enemy had been lost to history.[33]

Omega was a member of the High Council, the solar engineer who found and created the power source needed for time travel: the energy released by a supernova. He was lost in the explosion, and the Time Lords believed that he had been killed.[34]

> "A long time ago on my home planet of Gallifrey there lived a stellar engineer called Omega. It was Omega who created the supernova that was the initial power source for Gallifreyan time-travel experiments. He left behind him the basis on which Rassilon founded Time lord society... and he left behind the Hand of Omega. The Hand of Omega is the mythical name for Omega's remote stellar manipulator - the device used to customise stars with. And didn't we have trouble with the prototype..." [35]

One version of Omega's history suggested that he was originally an Academy student named Peylix. He theorized that his people could gain mastery of time by exploding a star within the Sector of Lost Souls, but Peylix's tutor, Luvis, deemed this nonsense and awarded him an 'omega' grade - the lowest score attainable. The nickname "Omega" plagued Peylix, but Rassilon's rise to power allowed him to properly implement his theories.

Peylix set out aboard the *Eurydice* to detonate a star, but his colleague Vandekirian warned that the targeted system contained sentient life. Omega proceeded anyway, and Vandekirian - trying to prevent Omega from gaining his handprint for security clearance - destroyed one of his hands in the ship's fusion reactors. Omega cut off Vandekirian's other hand, and used it to launch his stellar manipulator. The star exploded, killing the system's inhabitants. Vandekirian's hand caused an impurity in the fusion reactor and the ship exploded, consigning Omega to a universe of anti-matter.[36]

THE INFINITY DOCTORS -> The Ice Age had led to the collapse of Gallifreyan civilisation, in the time known as the Darkness. Libraries and temples burned. Many Gallifreyans perished. The Loom-born were smaller than the Womb-born and were mortal, but they preserved the Gallifreyan genetic codes.

Nine years after the Pythia's curse, the Elders still treated the Loom-born with disdain, viewing them a temporary solution to a problem. Rassilon and his Consortium gave everyone hope by finding 'the Fragment', the last surviving prophecy that spoke of Rassilon's personal rise and how the Gallifreyans would become the Lords of Time. The Other knew that Rassilon had faked the Fragment.

Rassilon and Omega set out for Qqaba, the only surviving Population III star in the galaxy. There were two Hands of Omega. They would detonate the star, releasing Time Energy that would be syphoned into fuel cells. However, the stasis halo protecting Omega's ship failed as Qqaba went supernova and Omega fell into the black hole that was forming. The crews of the surviving ships were infused with the energies. At the heart of this, Rassilon used the power of the singularity to rewrite the laws of physics across the entire universe. One effect of this, whether Rassilon knew it or not, was that Omega still lived, trapped inside the black hole.

Omega left behind a widow, a Womb-born Gallifreyan who would become known as Patience.

The star Omega detonated was in the Constellation of Ao.[37] Omega had used the sunskipper *Eurydice* to travel to the star he detonated, Jartus. Some scholars at the Omega Heritage Centre (a popular tour destination) think that Rassilon deliberately got rid of Omega, who was more popular.[38]

Two members of a Council of Three - Provost Tepesh (the Prime of the Arcalian chapterhouses) and Lady Ouida, both of them vampires - allied with the Great Mother of a Sisterhood against Rassilon. The Great Mother's assistant was Cassandra, a member of the House of Jade Dreamers. They sought to discover the secrets of Rassilon's Foundry, but the Divergents again threatened to break through at this juncture. The Foundry was firestormed to prevent this, which wiped out the conspirators.[39]

"And Rassilon journeyed into the black void with a great fleet. Within the void no light would shine. And nothing of that outer nature continued in being except that which existed within the Sash of Rassilon. Now Rassilon found the Eye of Harmony which balances all things that they may neither flux, whither nor change their state in any measure, and he caused the Eye to be brought to the world of Gallifrey wherein he sealed this munificence with the Great Key. Then the people rejoiced." [40]

The Gallifreyans successfully concluded the experi-ments, becoming the Time Lords. Mastery of Time required an unimaginably vast energy supply, which Rassilon set about acquiring.[41]

Modern Time Lords believed the Eye of Harmony to be a myth, that and the Sash of Rassilon had merely symbolic importance. In reality, the Sash prevented the wearer from being sucked into a parallel universe. The Eye of Harmony was the nucleus of a black hole, from which all the power of the Time Lords devolved. "Rassilon stabilised all the elements of the black hole and set them in an eternally dynamic equation against the mass of the planet." [42]

The earliest time-travel legends say Rassilon decapitated a Great Beast, took the branching golden tree of its metathalmus and found the First Secret of Chrononambulatory Egress.[43] Rassilon anchored the time-line of the universe, creating one unified history. The Antiverse was created as an equal and opposite reaction to this.[44]

LUNGBARROW -> Nine point six years after Omega was lost, Rassilon was purging anyone opposed to his regime. The Other was disgusted, and tried to get his granddaughter Susan and her nanny Mamlaurea to safety on the planet Tersurus. Susan had coined the term 'TARDIS' to describe the new time ships. The Other then threw himself into the Prime Distributor that fed all the Looms. He knew he would be reborn at some point in Gallifrey's history.

A year later, the Doctor - unknown even to him, the reincarnation of the Other - arrived from the distant future. He found Susan wandering the streets, unable to escape. She recognised him as her grandfather and they left Gallifrey together to explore the universe ...

---

37 *Lungbarrow*
38 *Omega*, an idea supported by *Zagreus*.
39 *Zagreus*. According to a questionable simulation, this occurred after Omega detonated his star. Arata is named as the third member of the Council of Three. The Great Mother belongs to the Sisterhood of Karn, although it isn't mentioned by name. Of all the suspect recreations shown in *Zagreus*, this one is the most dubious due to Tepesh's biased claims, and because he and Ouida, as vampires, would be unlikely to hold such authority in the Gallifreyan echelons for long, if at all.
40 *The Book of the Old Time*, referred to in *The Deadly Assassin*.
41 *The Three Doctors*, *The Deadly Assassin*, *Remembrance of the Daleks*.
42 *The Deadly Assassin*
43 *Heart of TARDIS*
44 *Neverland*
45 *Shada*

46 *Four to Doomsday*
47 *Neverland*
48 *The Deadly Assassin*, *The Invasion of Time*
49 *The Two Doctors*. *Zagreus* further suggests that the Imprimatur also facilitated regeneration, and that Rassilon introduced the limit of twelve regenerations to avoid the problem of degenerating biogenic molecules.
50 *The Five Doctors*
51 *The Invasion of Time*
THE KEY: In *The Deadly Assassin*, the Great Key is "an ebonite rod" that seals the Eye of Harmony within its monolith. By *The Invasion of Time*, that artefact is called "the Rod", and the Great Key is an ordinary-looking mortise key that can power the Demat Gun and has been hidden from the President by successive Chancellors since the time of Rassilon. We might presume that the Chancellor told the President that the Rod *is* the Key, hence the confusion of the two. However, two

The Great Days of Rassilon

As President of the Time Lords, Rassilon ushered in an age of technological and political progress. The phrase "the Great Days of Rassilon" appears in the Gallifreyan book *Our Planet's Story*, which was read by every Time Tot.[45]

Even races such as the Urbankans, who knew nothing of the Time Lords, had legends of Rassilon.[46] Rassilon's exploits were remembered on many planets, whose legends speak of Azaron, Razlon and Ra.[47]

Rassilon was credited with many scientific achievements: He created the Transduction Barriers surrounding Gallifrey. These prevented the unauthorised landing of a TARDIS or similar vehicle. A quantum force-field also existed as a barrier against more conventional threats.[48]

Rassilon introduced the symbiotic nuclei - the "Rassilon Imprimature" - into the genetic make-up of Time Lords, allowing them to fully travel through Time.[49] He also discovered the secret of temporal fission.[50]

Rassilon invented the Demat Gun, a weapon that required the Great Key to function. This weapon was so powerful that the Great Key was hidden from all future Presidents by successive Chancellors.[51] The Time Lord Tribunal could impose the penalty of dematerialisation on other races or individuals, such as the War Lord.[52]

... Of Rassilon

Rassilon was associated with many relics and concepts, all of which had "stupendous power". Many were lost, or their true purpose was unknown.[53]

These included the Sash of Rassilon, the Great Key of Rassilon, Rassilon's Star (the Eye of Harmony) and the Seal of Rassilon.[54] The Sash of Rassilon could alter the biodata of Time Lord President to allow better access to the Matrix. The Doctor, a former President, was affected by it.[55]

The Seal of Rassilon was also known as the omniscate.[56] The pattern for the Seal of Rassilon scrambled the neurosystems of beings from outside our Universe, such as vampires, to ward them off.[57]

Other relics and items included the Wisdom of Rassilon, the Rod of Rassilon ("Rassilon's Rod!" was also a mild Gallifreyan expletive)[58], the Record of Rassilon, the Directive of Rassilon[59], the Tomb or Tower of Rassilon, the Game of Rassilon, the Black Scrolls of Rassilon, the Harp of Rassilon, the Coronet of Rassilon and the Ring of Rassilon.[60]

The music the fifth Doctor played on the Harp of Rassilon was called "Rassilon's Lament".[61] The Rassilon Imprimature[62] mapped Time Lords on to the Vortex.[63] There was also the Key of Rassilon (not the Great Key, but one which allows access to the Matrix)[64] ... the Legacy of Rassilon[65] ... the Horns of Rassilon, also known as the Sign of Rassilon (a magical warding sign)[66] ... Rassilon's Red, Gallifrey's finest vintage wine[67] ... the Runes of Rassilon[68] ... and the Equation of Rassilon which allowed for travel through a time corridor. It "is and isn't" a scientific formula.[69]

The Time Lords signed the Pact (or Treaty) of Rassilon with the Sisterhood of Karn, protecting them in return for the Elixir of Life.[70] Romana learned to dance the Foxtrots of Rassilon, as well as learning the Seven Strictures of Rassilon.[71] The Master destroyed TOM-TIT with a Profane Virus of Rassilon, which was designed to prevent Gallifreyan technology falling into alien hands.[72]

Chancellors we know about - Goth and Borusa - are both in line to be President while (presumably, in Goth's case) knowing the whereabouts of the real Great Key.

In *The Ultimate Foe*, "The Key of Rassilon" allows access to the Matrix through portals such as the Seventh Door, and the Keeper of the Matrix wears it on his robes - this is presumably an entirely different artefact.

52 *The War Games*
53 *Shada*
54 *The Deadly Assassin*
55 *Alien Bodies*
56 *The Infinity Doctors*
57 *Interference*
58 *The Invasion of Time*, *The Androids of Tara*
59 *State of Decay*
60 *The Five Doctors*
61 *Blood Harvest*. He played the Harp in *The Five Doctors*.
62 *The Two Doctors*, spelled that way in the script and novelisation, and in its more usual form as 'Imprimatur' in some of the later books.
63 *Interference*
64 *The Ultimate Foe*
65 *Remembrance of the Daleks*
66 *Timewyrm: Revelation* (p54), *No Future* (p203).
67 *The Eight Doctors*
68 *The Ancestor Cell*
69 *The English Way of Death*
70 *Warmonger*
71 *Tomb of Valdemar*
72 *The Quantum Archangel*

Rassilon as Ruler

Rassilon became President of Gallifrey.[73] Rassilon was the first - and to date only - Lord High President.[74] Rassilon was also a legislator. In his time, five principles were laid down.[75]

The Constitution was drafted. Article Seventeen guaranteed the freedom of political candidates.[76] Only a unanimous vote of the High Council could over-rule the President.[77] Thanks to Rassilon, TARDIS databanks contained 18,348 coded emergency instructions. Older TARDISes (Type 40 and older) had a magnetic card system, the 'Record of Rassilon', which contained emergency instructions regarding the Vampires.[78] The 'Rules Governing Time Lords' were probably drafted at this time.[79]

Article Seven of Gallifreyan Law forbid Time Lords from committing genocide.[80] The death penalty was abolished, except in extreme circumstances such as a threat to Gallifrey or genocide.[81] The prison planet Shada was set up to house the most dangerous criminals in the universe. A key to the facility was encoded in the pages of Rassilon's book, *The Worshipful and Ancient Law of Gallifrey*, which was housed in the Panopticon Archive.[82]

Rassilon decreed that no Time Lord should travel into Gallifrey's past.[83] Rassilon's technology stopped Time Lords from investigating their own futures.[84] Rassilon built the Oubliette of Eternity, which exiled prisoners to the Antiverse. He was known as the Conqueror of Yssgaroth, Overpriest of Drornid, First Earl of Prydon, Patris of the Vortex and Ravager of the Void.[85]

The Eternal Wars

"The myths of Gallifrey talk about nameless horrors infesting our universe that were only defeated through the might of the Time Lords."

Rassilon's experiments created holes in the fabric of space-time, which consequently unleashed monsters from another universe. For over a thousand years, across the cosmos, the Ancient Gallifreyans fought the Eternal Wars against the monsters from another universe. These included the Vampires and the Yssgaroth. The great general Kopyion Liall a Mahajetsu was said to have died during this time, but he'd secretly survived. The Matrix contained no record of this war. When Rassilon overthrew the Pythia, Gallifrey was cursed with a plague from which only a few survived. Some suggested that Rassilon himself released the virus to wipe out all who knew of his mistake - they further claim that Rassilon deliberately sealed Omega in his black hole.[86]

When Rassilon was young, a Vampire army swarmed across the universe. Each Vampire could suck the life out of an entire planet.

"Energy weapons were useless, because the monsters absorbed and transmuted the energy, using it to become stronger. Therefore Rassilon ordered the construction of bowships, swift vessels that fired a mighty bolt of steel that transfixed the monsters through the heart - for only if his heart be utterly

73 *The Invasion of Time.* The Doctor becomes "the first President since Rassilon to hold the Great Key", implying that Rassilon was President.
74 *The Infinity Doctors*
75 *Shada*
76 *The Deadly Assassin*
77 *The Five Doctors*
78 *State of Decay*
79 *The Androids of Tara*
80 *Terror of the Vervoids*
81 *The Brain of Morbius, Arc of Infinity, Terror of the Vervoids.* In *The Invasion of Time*, it's said that unauthorized use of a TARDIS "carries only one penalty," but this isn't definitively stated as execution.
82 *Shada*
83 *Timewyrm: Revelation*
84 *Alien Bodies*
85 *Neverland*
86 *The Pit*
87 *State of Decay*
88 *Damaged Goods*
89 *So Vile a Sin*

90 *Goth Opera*
91 *Zagreus*
92 *Lungbarrow*
93 *The Five Doctors*
94 *Neverland*
95 *The Five Doctors*
96 *The Infinity Doctors*
97 *The Ancestor Cell*
98 *Cat's Cradle: Time's Crucible*
99 We hear a female voice read an extract from the modern translation of *The Book of the Old Time* in *The Deadly Assassin*.
100 The last extant copy of The Black Scrolls of Rassilon is destroyed in *The Five Doctors*.
101 *Goth Opera* (p119).
102 *No Future* (p203).
103 *Timewyrm: Revelation* (p65).
104 *Lungbarrow*
105 *The Infinity Doctors*
106 *The Gallifrey Chronicles*
107 *The Infinity Doctors, The Ancestor Cell*

destroyed will the Vampire die... The Vampire Army: so powerful were the bodies of these great creatures, and so fiercely did they cling to life, that they were impossible to kill, save by the use of bow-ships. Yet slain they all were, and to the last one, by the Lords of Time - the Lords of Time destroying them utterly. However, when the bodies were counted, the King Vampire, mightiest and most malevolent of all, had vanished, even to his shadow, from Time and Space. Hence it is the directive of Rassilon that any Time Lord who comes upon this enemy of our people and of all living things shall use all his efforts to destroy him, even at the cost of his own life..."

This war was so long and so bloody, that afterward the Time Lords renounced violence forever.[87]

Members of the Prydonian and Arcalian chapters crewed the bowships. N-forms were developed to fight vampires by the Patrexes Chapter. N-forms existed in pocket universes and could quickly extrude a vast killing machine onto planets infected by vampirism. They were programmed to kill all life on planets where vampires were detected.[88]

Warships were built to act as carriers for the bowships.[89] A marginal illustration in one book of legends showed a bat overcoming an owl. The owl was a traditional symbol of Rassilon; the bat of the Vampires. Some Gallifreyan heretics to this day worship Rassilon the Vampire, believing the Great Vampire bit Rassilon, and that Rassilon himself became a vampire towards the end of his life.[90]

A powerful rival race would have evolved after the Time Lords, but Rassilon trapped them in a moebius loop. They became known as the Divergents.[91]

Four of the outer worlds built temples to honour Rassilon in his own time.[92] **Rassilon discovered the secret of perpetual regeneration - "timeless, perpetual bodily regeneration - true immortality", but knew that only the power-mad would attempt such a thing. Rassilon had prevented at least four such Time Lords from discovering the secret of true immortality.**[93]

The Neverpeople - a group of exiled Time Lord criminals - falsified legends which stated that Rassilon fought and prevailed against the destroyer Zagreus in the Antiverse, but was entombed in a Zero Cabinet. This was part of the Neverpeople's plan to lure Time Lords into the Antiverse and facilitate their escape.[95]

Upon his death, Rassilon was entombed in the Dark Tower, where he remains to this day in eternal sleep. Legends state that anyone who reaches the Tower and takes the Ring of Rassilon will gain immortality. Gallifreyan children were familiar with the story and learned a nursery rhyme:

"Those to Rassilon's Tower Would Go... Must choose: Above, Between, Below." [95]

There were six vast statues in the Panopticon. These honoured the Founders of Gallifrey. Omega's statue was in the southern corner, Rassilon was opposite. Another statue was that of Apeiron (who wore combat boots). There was a nursery riddle that, when solved, revealed the identity of all six ... although the Doctor couldn't remember all of it:

"Neath Panopticon dome Rassilon faces Omega... But who is the other?... brother." [96]

The six statues represented the six Gallifreyan Colleges.[97] While both Rassilon and Omega were virtually canonised, if not deified, there were no further records of the Other in any of the histories. Speculation says that he left Gallifrey altogether. Legend says that he grew weary of being an all-powerful player at the chess game of the Universe. Instead he longed to be a pawn on the board in the thick of the action.[98]

The Ancient Texts

The Book of the Old Time was the official version of Rassilon's achievements, and a modern transgram had been made of it.[99] The Black Scrolls of Rassilon contained a forbidden account of the same period, including the secrets of Rassilon's power.[100] There were many R.O.O. texts (those dealing with legends of Rassilon, Omega and the Other).[101]

The Red Book of Gallifrey concerned the Dark Time and talked of Rassilon the Ravager, Omega the Fallen and the Other. It also contained magical incantations.[102] The Green and Black Books of Gallifrey discussed legends of the future, including the Timewyrm.[103] There was a book called *The Triumphs of Rassilon*.[104]

There were records known as *The Other Scrolls*.[105] There was a prophecy that the Time Lord who found the lost scrolls of Rassilon will lead Gallifrey from darkness.[106] One book, bound in reptile skin and with an embossed omniscate on the cover, survived until the end of the universe. It contained one last prophecy, which terrified the Doctor when he read it.[107]

Between the Ancient and Modern

The Time Wars were fought in the generation after Rassilon. The Tomb of the Uncertain Soldier in the Capitol honours a Gallifreyan who died during the Time Wars, cancelling out his own timeline for the greater good of Gallifrey. The Time Lords' Oldharbour Clock is the only surviving relic from an alternate universe wiped out in the

Time Wars. Unknown to anyone, the clockwork figures had evolved into the most intelligent beings on the planet.[108] The Doctor said he witnessed Gallifrey's Time Wars first-hand, although the Time Lords wiped the wars from their history books.[109]

The Time Lords time-looped the Fifth Planet, home of the Fendahl, twelve million years ago.[110] When the Gallifreyans were new to space / time exploration, they discovered the inhabited world of Minyos and were worshipped by the population there. In return, they gave technology to the Minyans. The Minyans eventually used nuclear technology to destroy their planet. The Time Lords subsequently renounced intervention in the affairs of other planets.[111]

The Time Lords used their great powers to help the people of Micen Island, in Orion. This led to chemical and biological warfare on the planet. The Time Lords renounced interference, erecting the Temple of the Fourth as a monument. A small number of Time Lords, though, felt the need to atone for past sins, and covertly intervened in the universe's affairs.[112]

Because of their great powers, and their tendency to lead to corruption, Time Lords were discouraged from emotion and affection. They were trained with a series of tests, including a journey to Anima Persis. They were mentored by older Time Lords, but the final judgement on whether an individual can be a Time Lord (and the punishment of any Time Lords who misuse their power) was handled by the mysterious Kingmaker, an ancient crone.[113]

Time Lords appear to have possessed mental blocks that prevented their interfering in history. However, if one of these blocks was broken, the others soon shattered.[114] Three centuries after Rassilon's death, Rassilon's Rampart was built to defend against the lawless Shobogans.[115]

It took fifty generations for TARDISes to become an acceptable form of travel, and another twenty for them to be used to participate in history.[116] Epsilon Delta was a Time Lord from the Ancient Time who gained a double beta in cybernetics. He stole a TARDIS and adopted the name 'the President'. He settled in St Matthew's College, Oxford.[117]

The shanty township of Low Town sprang up at the base of the Capitol Dome, and was settled by normal Gallifreyans, Outsiders and those seeking a life free of the restrictions of Time Lord society. The Capitol once had a Harbour.[118] A suit of armour belonging to Tegorak gathered dust in one storeroom, as did a giant stuffed bird.[119]

Time Lords dabbled at breaching the higher dimensions, but the Dimensional Ethics Committee banned the work.[120] At some point, the Biblioclasm claimed the

108 *The Infinity Doctors*
109 *Heart of TARDIS*
110 *Image of the Fendahl*
111 *Underworld*
112 *Death Comes to Time.* This sounds like a retelling of the Minyan story, or possibly an indication that there were many such mistakes made in Gallifrey's past.
113 *Death Comes to Time*
114 *Time and Relative*
115 *Lungbarrow*
116 *The Ancestor Cell*
117 *The Dimension Riders*
118 *The Eight Doctors, The Infinity Doctors*
119 *The Infinity Doctors*
120 *Tomb of Valdemar*
121 *The Infinity Doctors*
122 *The Infinity Doctors.* The implication is that they would be (or had been?) used against the People of the Worldsphere first seen in *The Also People*.
123 *Divided Loyalties*
124 *The Deadly Assassin*
125 *Matrix*
126 *The Dimension Riders*
127 *Conundrum*
128 *So Vile a Sin*
129 *Millennial Rites*
130 *Christmas on a Rational Planet*
131 *The Mutants*
132 *The Deadly Assassin*
133 *The Leisure Hive*
134 *The Trial of a Time Lord*
135 *Shada*
136 *Mawdryn Undead*
137 *The Stones of Blood*
138 *The Dimension Riders*
139 *Legacy*
140 *The Devil Goblins from Neptune*
141 *A Device of Death*
142 *Managra*
143 *Timewyrm: Genesys*
144 *Damaged Goods*
145 *Cold Fusion*
146 *Goth Opera*
147 *The Crystal Bucephalus*
148 *The Gallifrey Chronicles*
149 *Love and War*
150 *The Eight Doctors*
151 Aliens recognise the Doctor as a Time Lord in *The Time Warrior, The Brain of Morbius, Image of the Fendahl, Underworld, The Invasion of Time, The Ribos Operation, State of Decay, The Keeper of Traken, Earthshock, Mawdryn Undead, Resurrection of the Daleks, Vengeance on Varos, The Two Doctors, Timelash, The Trial of a Time Lord, The Curse of Fenric, Rose, The End of the World* and *Dalek*.
152 *The Two Doctors*

Endless Library. The Watch checked every night to prevent such a thing happening again. A quarter of a million years ago, the Time Lords were afflicted with the Blank Plague. The Time Lords fought military campaigns against Rigel, Gosolus and about a dozen other worlds.[121]

The Time Lords developed the blackstar, a weapon to crack Dyson Spheres.[122] Gallifreyan artefacts included Pandeka's staff and an artefact associated with Helron.[123]

The Matrix

The Time Lords built the Matrix, a form of computer that could - amongst other things - store the minds of dead Time Lords.[124] When the Matrix was young, it began to break down as thousands of Time Lord minds resented their deaths. The Time Lords cleaned the Matrix by isolating its dark part - the Dark Matrix. It was caged and forgotten about beneath the Citadel, sealed with a great key held by the Keeper of the Matrix.[125]

The Garvond was imprisoned for a time in the Gallifreyan Matrix, where it assimilated copies of Time Lord minds, including that of the Doctor. The creature's exact origins were unknown, although by nature it was the embodiment of the evil in the minds in the Matrix. The Garvond wanted to sail the Time Vortex and consume all life. It had several thousand names, all corruptions of the High Gallifreyan term for "of darkest thought".[126]

The Land of Fiction was originally part of the Matrix.[127]

Technological and Scientific Advancement

Gallifreyan technology has been refined, rather than totally reworked, over the last ten million years.[128] A dark science of earlier Time Lords was quantum mnemonics, a reality-altering power that manipulated the basic nature of reality and probability. Quantum mnemonics allowed one to transform the history of a planet or an individual by warping space and time.[129]

The Time Lords used devices called amaranths to rebuild parts of time and space that were damaged in the Time Wars. They were originally built to manipulate black holes.[130] **The Time Lords discovered an indestructible material.**[131] **They learnt to engineer micro-universes. Eventually, they abandoned the barren road of technology.**[132]

They abandoned tachyonics for warp matrix engineering.[133] **They invented the Magnotron. Over time, the Primitive Phases One and Two of the Matrix were relegated to the Archives. Phases Three to Six remain in use.**[134] **They developed Gallifreyan Morse.**[135]

Three thousand years ago, Mawdryn and his followers stole a Metamorphic Symbiosis Regenerator.[136] Two thousand years ago, the Time Lords abandoned interspacial geometry.[137] Some Time Lords such as Epsilon Delta could rehearse various events without altering the true timeline.[138] Time Lords could use Reverse Tachyon-Chronons to move time backwards and forwards, manipulating material so that it wouldn't age.[139]

With great effort, Time Lords used a process called "soul-catching" to absorb a dying Gallifreyan's memories.[140] The Time Lords built the Parachronistic Chamber, deep in the Capitol, to regulate time distortions.[141] Mimesis was a Gallifreyan art in which anything you write came true. It was practiced by a cult that held an annual ritual called "the Thirteenth Night," but the High Council banned the ritual and the art, probably because it was too arcane and unpredictable.[142]

Time Lords' extended lifespans sometimes necessitated that they edit out their more useless memories, storing them electronically or erasing them.[143] An artificial, multidimensional art gallery was located beneath the Capitol.[144]

TARDISes were grown in space, away from Gallifrey, to prevent time pollution. Stattenheim signals could broadcast along Eye of Harmony time contours, so TARDIS remote control worked even from across the Universe.[145] Time Lord technology could retrieve ancestral memories from the blood of virgins. Time Lords could communicate telepathically across the Time Vortex. The poisons in tea couldn't harm them.[146]

Time Lords used 208 language tenses, most of which didn't translate well.[147] The Time Lords used an omegabet, which was better than an alphabet.[148] Castellan Lode, a female, was the greatest literary historian the Time Lords ever had.[149]

A Gallifreyan golden guinea could buy you a few drinks at a bar.[150]

Foreign Policy

Alien races from all periods of recorded time have had dealings with the Time Lords, ranging from those in the ancient past such as the Kastrians and the destroyer Sutekh to those in the far future such as the Usurians. Other races or beings who know something of the Time Lords and Gallifrey (without hearing just of the Doctor or another individual) include the Andromedans, the Bandrils, the Cybermen, the Daleks, the Fendahl, Fenric, the Forest of Cheam, the Guardians, Mawdryn's race, the Mentors, the Minyans, the Nestene, the Sisterhood, the Sontarans, some residents of the Third Zone, the Keeper of Traken, Vampires and the Vardans.

Clearly, the Time Lords visited many worlds in many time periods, even in an official capacity.[151] They also authorised (or prevented) other races' time travel experiments and defended the Laws of Time.[152] Time

Lords observed but didn't interfere.[153] At times they intervened with regards to unauthorized time travel, and could almost be thought of as "galactic ticket inspectors".[154]

They were committed to protecting weaker species, and to preventing aggression against indigenous populations.[155] Time Lords were "forbidden to interfere".[156] The vast majority of Time Lords didn't concern themselves with the universe outside the Capitol, and were more concerned with internal politics.[157]

The Celestial Intervention Agency was concerned with covert intervention.[158] Study of the later Humanian era was forbidden by the Academy as being outside the Gallifreyan sphere of influence.[159]

Political

More Presidents hailed from the Prydonian Chapter than all other chapters combined. Prydonians were viewed as cunning, but claimed they "simply saw a little further ahead than most". They wore scarlet and orange robes. Other chapters included the Arcalians (who wore green) and Patrexes (who wore heliotrope).[160] The Patrexes were aesthetes who saw artistic value in all things, including suffering, but lacked the imagination to be true artists.[161]

The Celestial Intervention Agency evolved from Rassilon's personal guard.[162] At some point, the Time Lords Rungar and Sabjatric were sent to Shada. They remained there.[163] Apart from Rassilon, only President Torkal was ever referred to as 'the Great'.[164] While young, Salyavin learnt how to project his mind into others' and was sentenced to imprisonment in Shada as a result. He escaped, using his powers to erase all knowledge of the prison planet.[165]

Mundat the Third's reputation swung from his being a brutal murderer to a noble warrior - and that's just in the documentaries of the historian Ertikus.[166] In the lifetime of some contemporary Time Lords, President Pandak III ruled for nine hundred years.[167]

Savar tried to rescue Omega from his black hole, but was ambushed by the Time Lord god Ohm. Attempting to escape, Savar's TARDIS was stretched until it became the light-year-long structure called the Needle. Savar fled in an escape capsule, which was intercepted by the I. The I stripped the ship of technology and took Savar's eyes. He was found by the Time Lords, but was utterly insane from the experience. He regenerated, but was a broken man.[168]

The Doctor's TARDIS

The Doctor's TARDIS was known as a Type 40.[170] The Type 40 TT-Capsule was introduced when Salyavin was young.[171] The Type 40 was withdrawn centuries ago and was considered a 'Veteran and Vintage Vehicle'.[172]

---

153 *The War Games*
154 *The Time Warrior*
155 *The Hand of Fear*
156 According to the Cyber Lieutenant in *Earthshock*.
157 *The Deadly Assassin, The Invasion of Time*
158 *The Deadly Assassin*. Fans and recent writers have rationalised away the Time Lords' stated 'non-intervention' and the clear evidence that they have intervened by assuming that it's the secret (and in some stories highly sinister) 'CIA' who are behind the interventions. This builds quite a lot on the one reference in the TV series.
159 *The Well-Mannered War*
160 *The Deadly Assassin*
161 *Damaged Goods*
162 *Lungbarrow*
163 *Shada*
164 *The Ancestor Cell*
165 *Shada*
166 *Omega*
167 *The Deadly Assassin*
    GALLIFREYAN PRESIDENTS: *The Ancestor Cell* says the Doctor was the 407th and 409th President of Gallifrey. *The Gallifrey Chronicles* says that Romana is the 413th. From this, we can extrapolate that the 405th President was the one killed in *The Deadly Assassin* (and almost certainly, in a previous incarnation, the one seen in *The Three Doctors*); the 406th was Greyjan the Sane (*The Ancestor Cell*); the 407th was the Doctor (he was 'inducted' in *The Invasion of Time*); the 408th was Borusa (the President is referred to by the Doctor in *The Ribos Operation*, and he - or more likely the White Guardian posing as him - sends Romana on the quest for the Key to Time. It's *Arc of Infinity* before it's confirmed that Borusa is now President. Borusa regenerates twice more and his reign ends in *The Five Doctors*); the 409th is the Doctor; the 410th is Flavia, the 411th is Niroc, who's corrupt and deposed with the help of the Doctor and Rassilon in *The Eight Doctors*; the 412th is Flavia again, according to *Happy Endings*, which is set soon after Romana is installed as the 413th.
169 Savar is first mentioned in *Seeing I*, but these events take place 'a thousand years' before *The Infinity Doctors*, as far as Savar is concerned. There was a Time Lord called Savar in *The Invasion of Time*.
170 The term was first used in *The Deadly Assassin*.
171 *Shada*
172 *The Pirate Planet*
173 *The Creature from the Pit*
174 In *Time and the Rani*, the Doctor deduces the combination to the Rani's lock is 953, 'my age ... and the Rani's'.

The Early Life of the Doctor

There are a number of seemingly contradictory facts about the Doctor's birth and upbringing.

The Doctor was born under the sign of 'Crossed Computers'.[173] He was born the same year as the Rani.[174] He was one of forty-five cousins from the House of Lungbarrow. Unusually for a Time Lord, he had a belly button, which earned him the nicknames 'Wormhole' and 'Snail'.[175] His Gallifreyan name had thirty-eight syllables.[176]

Irving Braxiatel was a relative of the Doctor, either his brother or one of his Cousins. Braxiatel spent twenty years arranging the Armageddon Convention. After this, he dedicated himself to building the Braxiatel Collection, a repository of universal knowledge and art. Braxiatel collected every book banned by the Catholic Church. Unlike the Doctor, he freely left Gallifrey.[177]

The Doctor was half human on his mother's side.[178] He had a family.[179] He may have had an uncle.[180] As the Doctor let the Master die on Sarn, the Master called out 'Won't you show mercy to your own — '[181]

The Doctor's family owned a home in South Gallifrey.[182] This home was House Lungbarrow, which was perched on the side of Mount Lung, overlooking the Cadonflood river, two days from Rassilon's Rampart.[183] The Doctor doesn't know much about Gallifrey's Southern Hemisphere.[184]

There are a number of seemingly contradictory facts about the Doctor's age.[185]

---

175 *Lungbarrow*, with *The One Doctor* confirming the 'Snail' nickname.

176 *SLEEPY* (p204).

177 The Braxiatel Collection was first mentioned in *City of Death*. We first meet Irving Braxiatel in *Theatre of War*, but he's also present at the Armageddon Convention in *The Empire of Glass*, which occurs first chronologically. He has gone on to be a regular character in the Big Finish Bernice Summerfield books and audios, where Benny currently works for the Braxiatel Collection; and the *Gallifrey* series, which deals with his earlier history. The Benny novel *Tears of the Oracle* strongly suggests that Braxiatel and the Doctor are brothers.

178 *Doctor Who - The Movie*

179 *The Tomb of the Cybermen*, further implied in *The Curse of Fenric* and confirmed in *Father's Day*.

180 *Time and the Rani*. He says, possibly facetiously, 'you should see my uncle'.

181 *Planet of Fire*. The sentence isn't complete, but the next word could well spell out a family relationship (fan speculation over the years has suggested a number of things, usually 'brother' and less usually 'husband').

182 *Planet of the Spiders*

183 *Lungbarrow*

184 *The Scarlet Empress*

185 THE DOCTOR'S AGE: The Doctor's age has been specified a number of times, but he is often vague and contradictory on the subject.

The second Doctor tells Victoria that he is "450" in *The Tomb of the Cybermen*. The Master of the Land of Fiction says he is "ageless" in *The Mind Robber*. (In the draft scripts of *The Power of the Daleks* and *The Underwater Menace*, he was "750".)

The third Doctor claims to have been a scientist for "thousands of years" in both *Doctor Who and the Silurians* and *The Mind of Evil*.

The fourth Doctor says he is "749" in *Planet of Evil*, *The Brain of Morbius* and *The Seeds of Doom*, and "nearly 750" in *Pyramids of Mars*. He is "750" by *The Robots of Death*, 756 (according to him) or 759 (according to Romana) in *The Ribos Operation*, nearly 760 in *Nightmare of Eden*, 750 again in *The Creature from the Pit* and *The Leisure Hive*. (A scripted scene in *The Stones of Blood* showed him celebrating his 751st birthday.)

The sixth Doctor is 900 in *Revelation of the Daleks* and *The Mysterious Planet* Part One, but "over 900" by *Terror of the Vervoids* Part One.

In *Time and the Rani*, both the seventh Doctor and the Rani are "953", and the Doctor has "nine hundred years experience" by *Remembrance of the Daleks*. In the New Adventures, he was around a thousand years old. According to *SLEEPY*, he celebrated his 1000th birthday during *Set Piece*.

The eighth Doctor is 1012 in *Vampire Science* and is twelve hundred by *The Dying Days*. We also know that he resided on Earth for one hundred and eleven years, from 1890-2001, beginning with *The Ancestor Cell* and ending with *Escape Velocity*, although accommodating this depends on where one places *The Dying Days* in the eighth Doctor's lifetime.

The ninth Doctor says he's 900 in *Aliens of London* and *The Doctor Dances*. In response to Rose's question about the problems introducing himself without a real name in *The Empty Child*, he says, 'Nine centuries in, I'm coping'.

From this, we can infer some other dates:

• The Doctor has been operating his TARDIS for 523 years by *The Pirate Planet*, and was 759 in previous story, *The Ribos Operation*. This means that the Doctor left Gallifrey when he was 236.

• The Doctor attended his Tech Course with Drax "450 years" before *The Armageddon Factor*. This would mean he was 309 at the time (implying it was after he left Gallifrey, or that he left and then returned before leaving for the last time).

• Romana is equally inconsistent with her age, and the age difference between her and the Doctor can variously be calculated as 617 or 620 (*The Ribos Operation*), 625 (*City of Death*, *Creature from the Pit*) or 600 (*The Leisure Hive*).

The Doctor's Father

The Doctor remembered 'I'm with my father. We're lying back in the grass... it's a warm Gallifreyan night'.[186] The Doctor's father was taught by the ancient Gallifreyan who would be known as Patience, as his father had been. Many of his generation - such as Savar; Hedin; the Doctor's mentor, Lady Zurvana; the future President (a Chancellor at the time) and Marnal thought they could change the universe.[187]

The Doctor's father was a member of the High Council. He launched a great exploration of the universe, which became known as the Odyssey.[188] On his travels, he met an Earthwoman, the Victorian time traveller Penelope Gate. They married, and had at least one child. The Doctor's father adopted the name Ulysses.[189]

The Doctor's father had many friends and allies from alien planets. He broke protocol by inviting them to his House on Gallifrey. The Doctor's mother owned a Bible from which the Doctor read.

A computer portrait of the Doctor's parents hung on the wall of his quarters on Gallifrey. His father was 'powerfully built with rugged features, a weathered face with dark eyes'. His mother 'a redhead, a little plump'.[190]

One contemporary of the Doctor's father was Marnal, who believed that the Time Lords should intervene to eliminate potential threats to Gallifrey. He became known - dismissively - as a crusader. On one mission, to the Shoal on the edge of Mutter's Spiral, he stumbled across a race of insect creatures that he believed were a threat to Gallifrey. They weren't - until he intervened and changed history. 'Marnal's Error' (meaning that he did not know his enemy) became a Time Lord proverb.[191]

Shortly after the Doctor was born, the Doctor's father was leading a team working on a mysterious Project. Other members included Penelope, Mr Saldaamir and a Time Lady from the relative future, Larna. Some Time Lords (including Marnal and Larna) knew of the Scrolls, recently-discovered prophecies that warned, in Larna's words:

'For millions of years, Gallifrey has existed in isolation. Soon - not imminently, not all at once - there will be a spate of attacks. Omega, the Sontarans, Tannis, Faction Paradox, Varnax, Catavolcus, the Timewyrm. You know some of those names, you will come to know the others. It is very important that Gallifrey survives all these attacks. All things must pass. Gallifrey will fall. But it must fall at precisely the right time. The enemy

186 *Doctor Who - The Movie*

187 *The Infinity Doctors*

188 *Cold Fusion*

189 *The Gallifrey Chronicles*. Penelope Gate first appeared in *The Room with No Doors*.

190 *The Infinity Doctors*

191 *The Infinity Doctors, The Taking of Planet 5, The Gallifrey Chronicles*.

192 *The Gallifrey Chronicles*. The prophecy is a paraphrase of one from an abandoned American pilot script from the nineties. The book shows the Doctor fulfilling the prophecy - assuming the 'lost scrolls of Rassilon' are the Matrix files in his mind. He had already made Last Contact in *The Daleks*, when he made contact with the race that would eventually destroy the Time Lords in the Last Great Time War, as revealed in *Dalek*.

193 *Unnatural History*

194 *The Ghosts of N-Space*

195 *The Eight Doctors*

196 *The Infinity Doctors*

197 *Master*. This account is told as a fable, and so may not be true.

198 *The Time Monster, Planet of the Spiders, State of Decay*

199 *Lungbarrow*

200 *The Five Doctors*

201 *Shada*

202 *Image of the Fendahl*

203 *Black Orchid*

204 *Seasons of Fear*

205 *The Gallifrey Chronicles*

206 *Terror of the Autons, The Deadly Assassin, The Armageddon Factor, The Mark of the Rani.*

207 *The Time Meddler*

208 *The War Games*

209 *Arc of Infinity*

210 *Terror of the Autons*

211 *Divided Loyalties, Neverland*

212 *The Death of Art*

213 *Time and the Rani*

214 *The Five Doctors*

215 *The Armageddon Factor*

216 *The Scarlet Empress*

217 *Verdigris*

218 *Excelis Dawns*

219 *The Deadly Assassin*

220 *Timewyrm: Revelation*

221 *Divided Loyalties*

222 *Lungbarrow*

223 *Cat's Cradle: Time's Crucible*

224 *The Twin Dilemma*

225 *The Time Monster*

226 *Goth Opera*

is unknown to us. It will be until Last Contact is made. If it's destroyed before that, by any of those other enemies, then the consequences ... that is as much as I know.'

Marnal added:

'The President and members of the Supreme Council know the prophecy. They have been told that a Time Lord now living will be central to all these events. That he will find the lost scrolls of Rassilon and lead Gallifrey from darkness.'

To prevent the exposure of the Project, the Doctor's father wiped Marnal's memory and exiled him to Earth in 1883. He took Marnal's TARDIS, a Type 40, from him.[192]

When the Doctor was ten years old, he was caught skinny-dipping with one of his Cousins.[193] The Doctor flew skimmers as a boy on Gallifrey.[194] The Doctor remembers his mother smiling and his father holding him up to see the stars.[195]

The first time the Doctor left Gallifrey was to visit his family's summer house on the other side of the Constellation. While looking up into the night's sky with his mother, he saw a fleet of time ships but never asked where they were going.[196]

An account of the Doctor's boyhood claims that he and the Master grew up together, and played near the river Lethe. A bully, Torvic, menaced the Master, but the Doctor fought back and thereby caused Torvic's death. Death later visited the Doctor in a dream, and sought to take him as her Champion, but the Doctor told her to take the Master instead. This gave rise to the Master becoming Death's Champion, and would motivate the Doctor and the Master to leave Gallifrey.[197]

The Doctor's Education

The Doctor had a mentor who lived up a mountain near his home and taught him to see the beauty in a simple daisy, and to look into his own mind. The mentor told him ghost stories about the Vampires.[198] Satthralope, a member of House Lungbarrow, sacked the hermit because he was a bad influence and too expensive.[199]

The Doctor was interested enough in Gallifreyan history to take the unusual step of learning the dead language of Old High Gallifreyan.[200] **The Doctor admired Salyavin.**[201] **He was frightened by stories of the Fendahl.**[202] **He always wanted to be a train driver.**[203]

The Doctor's mother told him a nursery rhyme about Zagreus, which spoke of people disappearing up paradoxical staircases.[204] When he was an impressionable age, she also told him scary stories about Grandfather Paradox.[205]

The Academy Years

The Doctor was a contemporary of the Master, Runcible, Drax and the Rani.[206] He was 'fifty years before' the Monk.[207] The War Chief and the Doctor recognised each other.[208] The Doctor knew Hedin and Damon.[209] He knew the Time Lord who warned him about the Master.[210]

He was at the Academy with Vansell.[211] The Doctor attended the Rani's raucous 94th birthday party.[212] **The Doctor attended University with the Rani, and his speciality was thermodynamics.**[213]

He attended "the Academy" with the Master.[214] **The Doctor attended a Tech Course with the Class of '92, which included Drax, before he gained his Doctorate.**[215]

Iris Wildthyme claimed to have grown up in a House in southern Gallifrey. It was ruled by Aunts including Baba, her favourite. Iris' mother ran away with an off-worlder. Iris found an abandoned TARDIS in the wilderness and adopted it.[216]

Iris Wildthyme also claims to come from one of the New Towns under the Gallifreyan Capitol. Iris found her TARDIS abandoned in the mountains as a wasted experiment, helping it to learn, feed and evolve. In turn, the bus gave Iris advice. She's been travelling longer than the Doctor.

The Doctor said Iris wasn't a proper Time Lady and that the Time Lords were unsure of her identity.[217] Iris referred to the Doctor's people as "a snobby, over-privileged bunch," possibly suggesting she's not a fully-fledged Time Lord.[218] **The Doctor studied at Prydon Academy (where Borusa taught him).**[219]

Gallifrey's highest peak, Mount Cadon, extended to the fringes of the planet's atmosphere and held the Prydonian Academy far up its slopes. Acolytes there endlessly recanted protocols and procedures. In high towers, special pupils learned dark arts.[220] The Academy was basically a self-contained city annexed to the Gallifreyan Capitol. It took up twenty-eight square miles of Gallifrey's surface.[221]

Lord Cardinal Lenadi led the Prydonian Chapter during the Doctor's time on Gallifrey.[222] Cardinal Borusa wrote a history called *Rassilon the God*.[223] **The Doctor was taught by Azmael.**[224] **He used to build time jammers to disrupt others' experiments.**[225] Ruath and the Doctor staged pranks together - they introduced cats into the Gallifreyan eco-system, altered gravity to make a Panoptican graduation take place in mid-air and electrified Borusa's perigosto stick.[226]

Daring neonates at the Academy played a dangerous game called "Eighth Man Bound". This entailed deliberately putting an 'Initiate' into a state of flux between life or death, enabling them to witness and experience their future regenerations. The term was coined after a student of the Arcalian Chapter who was able to discover the natures of his first seven bodies, but couldn't observe the eighth. A student of the Prydonian Chapter was rumoured to have tied this record.[227]

The Doctor used to play truant so he could down pints of Best Shobogan beer at the Golden Grockle in Low Town. He seethed with anger at the High Council.[228] **The Doctor at this time was called Theta Sigma, his nickname.[229] The Master got a higher grade at Cosmic Science than the Doctor. The Doctor claims he was a late developer.[230]** Cardinal Sendok taught the Doctor and the Master cosmic science.[231]

DIVIDED LOYALTIES -> The Doctor was part of the Deca, a group of ten brilliant students who were activists in favour of more Time Lord intervention. The Deca members were: the Doctor, Koschei (the Master), Mortimus (the Monk), Magnus (the War Chief), Drax, Ushas (the Rani), Vansell (actually a Celestial Intervention Agency spy), Rallon, Millennia and Jelpax.

They were taught by Borusa, Franilla, Sendok and Zass.

It was as part of the Deca that the Doctor learned about the Toymaker. The Doctor, Rallon and Millennia located the Toymaker and were caught up in his games. Rallon and Millennia were apparently killed, and the Doctor was expelled from the Academy on his return to Gallifrey, ordered to spend five hundred years in Records and Traffic Control. He studied for his doctorate in his spare time.

The President at this time was Drall, the Castellan was Rannex. Type 35 TARDISes were in operation, the Doctor used a Type 18 to visit the Toymaker.

Only Jelpax completed his time at the Academy in the conventional manner, the others either went to special projects or vanished. Jelpax went on to work with Borusa.

The Doctor deliberately failed his exams so that people would underestimate him, and to avoid office duty.[232] **The Doctor eventually scraped through the Academy with 51 percent on the second attempt.[233]** The Doctor's poor results were a grave disappointment to his parents.[234]

The Doctor on Gallifrey

The Doctor says he was a pioneer among his people.[235] He built his Ship, and Susan coined the acronym TARDIS.[236]

Before leaving Gallifrey the Doctor was used on a diplomatic mission at least once, when he visited the inauguration of Station Chimera in the Third Zone.[237] Following a campaign by the Doctor, the Time Lords banned miniscopes.[238] The Doctor was a member of the Prydonian Chapter but came to forsake his birthright.[239] When the Doctor was on Gallifrey, Cardinal Lenadi led the Prydonians.[240]

The Doctor's reflex link connected him to the Time Lord intelligentsia.[241] Like all Time Lords, he swore an oath to protect the Law of Gallifrey.[242]

The Doctor was a member of the Supreme Council.[243] He held a powerful position before leaving Gallifrey.[244]

Past Lives

Morbius would later probe the Doctor's mind, and see eight incarnations of the Doctor before the one generally accepted as the 'first' Doctor.[245]

The Doctor's Marriage

The Doctor fell in love with his former nurse and tutor, the Womb-born Gallifreyan who would become known as Patience. She taught him to dance, which he did in front of some house guests including Mr Saldaamir, a pair from Althrace and a yellow-skinned man with red fins.

They married. Savar was one of the guests at the wed-

---

227 According to Professor Thripsted's *Genetic Politics Beyond the Third Zone* in *Christmas on a Rational Planet* (p212-216). The Doctor names himself as "Eighth Man Bound" in *The Dying Days*.
228 *The Eight Doctors*
229 *The Armageddon Factor, The Happiness Patrol*
230 *Terror of the Autons*
231 *The Quantum Archangel*
232 *Lungbarrow*
233 *The Ribos Operation*
234 *The King of Terror*
235 *The Daleks*
236 *The Chase, An Unearthly Child*, although later stories seem to contradict both claims. Some commentators have tried to attribute the Doctor's statement in *The Chase* to mean that he only built his Ship's time-

path detector, not the whole Ship, but this is a rationalisation after-the-fact and not borne out by the scene itself. *Lungbarrow*, at least, supports the notion that Susan created the word TARDIS by claiming she was around when TARDISes were relatively new.
237 *The Two Doctors*
238 *Carnival of Monsters*
239 *The Deadly Assassin*
240 *Lungbarrow*
241 *The Invisible Enemy*
242 *Shada*
243 *Cold Fusion, The Infinity Doctors*
244 *Deadly Reunion*
245 *The Brain of Morbius*
See the Past Lives sidebar.

PAST LIVES: The orthodox view accepted wholesale by most fans is that the Doctor is a Time Lord who can regenerate his body twelve times when it is seriously injured. It's also held that William Hartnell played "the first Doctor" and that by the end of *The Parting of the Ways* the Doctor has regenerated nine times, so that David Tennant is the tenth incarnation of the Time Lord. This version of events is actually established very late in the show's history (the term "regeneration", for example, is not even used until *Planet of the Spiders* at the end of Season Eleven, the word "incarnation" is only used on rare occasions - such as in *The Twin Dilemma* and *The Trial of a Time Lord* (Season Twenty-Three) - and so on).

Only a half a dozen stories refer to the orthodox view: In *The Three Doctors*, the Time Lords claim that the Hartnell Doctor is the "earliest". We learn that the Time Lords are limited to twelve regenerations in *The Deadly Assassin*, a view that is reinforced by *The Keeper of Traken*, *The Five Doctors* and *The Twin Dilemma*. (Although in *The Deadly Assassin*, *The Keeper of Traken* and *The Five Doctors*, we learn that it is indeed possible for a Time Lord to regenerate more than twelve times, and in *The Twin Dilemma*, Azmael initiates a thirteenth regeneration, the strain of which kills him).

It is *Mawdryn Undead* (Season Twenty) before the Doctor explicitly states that he has regenerated four times and has eight regenerations remaining. In *The Five Doctors*, the Hurndall Doctor sees the Davison Doctor and concludes "so there are five of me now" and refers to himself as "the original, you might say". In *Time and the Rani*, the Doctor talks of his "seventh persona". The voiceover at the start of the *Doctor Who* TVM says that the Doctor is "nearing the end of my seventh life".

Despite all this, the commonly used terms such as "first Doctor", "second Doctor" and so on are never used on-screen (and should never be capitalised).

More often, the evidence about the Doctor's past is ambiguous or inconclusive: he seems vague about his age throughout his life, the details varying wildly from story to story, likewise his name, his doctorate and the reasons why he left Gallifrey. In *The Deadly Assassin*, Runcible remarks that the Doctor has had a facelift and the Doctor replies that he has had "several so far" (the original script more specifically said he had done so "three times"). In *The Ultimate Foe*, the Valeyard comes from somewhere between the Doctor's "twelfth and final incarnation" (not the "twelfth and thirteenth"). No unfamiliar Doctors come to light in *The Three Doctors* or *The Five Doctors*, but on two occasions (*Day of the Daleks* and *Resurrection of the Daleks*) an attempt to probe the Doctors mind is abruptly halted just as the William Hartnell incarnation appears on the monitor. In *The Creature from the Pit*, he claims Time Lords have ninety lives, and he's had a hundred and twenty.

There have been a number of hints that incarnation of the Doctor played by William Hartnell was not the first. In the script for *The Destiny of Doctor Who*, the new Doctor confides to his astonished companions that he has "renewed himself" before. In the transmitted version of the story, *The Power of the Daleks*, the line does not appear, but neither is it contradicted. In *The Brain of Morbius*, Morbius succeeds in mentally regressing the Doctor back from his Tom Baker incarnation, through Jon Pertwee, Patrick Troughton and William Hartnell, but this time no-one interrupts and we go on to see a further eight incarnations of the Doctor prior to Hartnell. Morbius shouts - as the sequence of mysterious faces appears on the scanner - "How far Doctor? How long have you lived? Your puny mind is powerless against the strength of Morbius! Back! Back to your beginning! Back!". These are certainly not Morbius' faces (as has occasionally been suggested) or the Doctor's ancestors or his family. Morbius is not deluding himself. The Doctor fails to win the fight and almost dies, only surviving because of the Elixir... it just happens that Morbius' brain casing can't withstand the pressures either.

The production team at the time (who bear a remarkable resemblance to the earlier Doctors, probably because eight of them - Christopher Barry, George Gallacio, Robert Banks Stewart, Phillip Hinchcliffe, Douglas Camfield, Graeme Harper, Robert Holmes and Chris Baker - posed for the photographs used in the sequence), definitely intended the faces to be those of earlier Doctors. Producer Philip Hinchcliffe said: "We tried to get famous actors for the faces of the Doctor. But because no-one would volunteer, we had to use backroom boys. And it is true to say that I attempted to imply that William Hartnell was not the first Doctor".

However we might want to fit this scene into the series' other continuity, or to rationalise it away, taking *The Brain of Morbius* on its own, there's no serious room for doubt that these are pre-Hartnell incarnations of the Doctor. This hasn't stopped fans doubting, of course.

Two stories later, in *The Masque of Mandragora*, the Doctor and Sarah Jane discover "the old control room" that the Doctor claims to have used, although it had never been seen in the television series before.

Cold Fusion features a sequence where the Doctor remembers his past on Gallifrey (p172-173), where he has recently regenerated to resemble the "Camfield Doctor" seen in *The Brain of Morbius*. However, there is a degree of ambiguity as to whether these are the Doctor's own memories.

Lungbarrow states that the Hartnell Doctor was the first and hints, but never explicitly states, that the faces seen in *The Brain of Morbius* are incarnations of the Other, not the Doctor.

ding.[246] The Doctor painted his wife's portrait. As he finished, she told him she was pregnant.[247] They went on to have thirteen children.[248]

Shortly after he regenerated, the Doctor and Patience celebrated the birth of their first grandchild. Their son was a Cardinal and the Doctor sat on the Supreme Council, as his father did before him. The President ordered the Guard to search the Doctor's family home for 'children born of woman'. The Doctor's thirteen children were dragged out and his daughter-in-law's baby was scheduled for termination. The Doctor's whereabouts during this incident were unknown, but there was a warrant for his arrest - he stood accused of 'consorting with aliens'.

The Doctor (in what we would consider his 'first' incarnation) would later travel back in time to this point. He rescued his infant granddaughter and took her to the ancient past. He then got Patience to safety by taking her to an ancient TARDIS. As he did this, the Capitol was burning.[249] Mobs stormed the Panopticon that night.[250]

The Doctor's memories of this trauma were blocked, although by who or what is unclear. He believed his wife had died.[251] It is unclear if the Doctor's father was still on Gallifrey at this point. After this, the Doctor's father may have adopted the name Joyce and relocated to San Francisco on Earth, continuing the Project with Larna and Mr Saldaamir.[252]

The Infinity Doctor

? (=?) (w?) - THE INFINITY DOCTORS -> The Doctor mourned for his dead wife, and even though she died a long time ago, he still lit a new candle every year in her memory. Before this time, he had travelled the universe and returned to Gallifrey. He had defeated and imprisoned Centro, a mechanical being that could warp space.

On Gallifrey, the Doctor served as a tutor who oversaw - amongst others - the brilliant student Larna. He negotiated a final peace between the Sontarans and the Rutans, ending their eternal war. Gallifrey monitored 'the Effect', a reality-altering ripple. The Doctor and his friend the Magistrate went to the end of time to confront the one who was responsible: Omega. The Doctor met his wife Patience, whom Omega had rescued from death, but again lost her. Omega was defeated, but the Magistrate didn't return from this mission. The Doctor did, and had grown restless with Gallifrey.

Voran became President. Larna was charged to travel the universe and clear up after the Effect, a mission that would take two thousand years.

Susan

The Doctor's granddaughter Susan was something of an enigma.

Susan was the Doctor's grand-daughter "and always will be".[254] Susan described her home planet as "quite like Earth, but at night the sky is a burned orange, and the leaves on the trees are bright silver".[255] She knew about the Dark Tower.[256] She was fifteen when she met Ian and Barbara.[257] The other Time Lords never referred to Susan.[258] She coined the name 'TARDIS'.[259]

Susan was born in Gallifrey's recent past. Her grandfather was the Doctor. She was a naturally-born child, an abomination in the eyes of the authorities of Gallifrey. Her mother's fate was unknown. Her father was a Cardinal.[260]

Susan was born in Gallifrey's distant past. Her grandfather was the Other. She was the last naturally-born child on Gallifrey. Her mother died at the moment of her birth, as the Pythia's curse of sterility came into effect. Her father was a warrior.[261]

---

246 *Cold Fusion, The Infinity Doctors*
247 *The Infinity Doctors*
248 *Cold Fusion*
249 *Cold Fusion, The Infinity Doctors.* The Doctor's new incarnation matches the description of the "Camfield Doctor" seen in *The Brain of Morbius*.
250 *The Infinity Doctors*
251 *Cold Fusion*
252 *Unnatural History.* There's also no account of what happened to the Doctor's son and daughter-in-law, or any of the Doctor's other children.
253 Dating *The Infinity Doctors* - The story takes place an unspecified amount of time after Patience disappears, to an unspecified incarnation of the Doctor, at an unspecified point before Gallifrey's destruction (possibly between *The Gallifrey Chronicles* and *Rose*). It's a thousand years since Savar lost his eyes.

254 *An Unearthly Child*, the quote comes from *The Dalek Invasion of Earth.* The Doctor and Susan frequently refer to each other as grandfather and grandchild.
255 *Marco Polo*
256 *The Five Doctors*
257 Barbara says Susan is fifteen in *An Unearthly Child*. In *Marco Polo*, Ping Cho says she is 'in my sixteenth year', and Susan says 'Well, so am I'. So Susan is not far older than she looks, unlike Romana.
258 Susan is never mentioned by any Time Lord, either those on Gallifrey or the various renegades.
259 *An Unearthly Child.* Later stories showed the manual for the Doctor's TARDIS which has the word on the cover, suggesting it was coined long before the Doctor's time. One possible conclusion is that Susan is from an earlier period of Gallifreyan history, and which is indeed what *Lungbarrow* established.

The Doctor Leaves Gallifrey

The exact nature of the Doctor's departure from Gallifrey is still a mystery, and there have been a number of seemingly contradictory accounts of the circumstances in which he left.

LUNGBARROW[262] -> The Doctor worked as a Scrutationary Archivist in the Prydonian Chapterhouse Bureau of Possible Events. His applications for promotion were always turned down.

Consulting the Bench of Matrocians, Quences - the head of the Lungbarrow household - learned that the Doctor would be a huge influence on the future of Gallifrey. He wanted the Doctor to become a Cardinal. The Doctor stormed out of his family home after an argument with Quences about the Doctor's future prospects. With the Doctor no longer regarded as a member of the family, a replacement - Owis - was Loomed to maintain the Family Quota. However, this was illegal and the House was ostracised from Gallifreyan affairs. The Doctor's Cousins were trapped in the House.

The Doctor left an experiment with water-sligs running. A hundred and thirty years, later they broke out.

Quences was the 422nd Kithriarch of Lungbarrow.

The Doctor decided to steal a TARDIS and leave Gallifrey. The Hand of Omega recognised the Doctor was linked to the Other. When the Doctor left Gallifrey, the Hand redirected him to Gallifrey's ancient past.

He was an 'exile', unable to return home.[263] The Doctor 'had reasons of his own' for leaving his home planet.[264] He might have left of his own free will, because he was 'bored' or had 'grown tired of their lifestyle'. He renounced the society of Time Lords. He abandoned his Prydonian birthright.[265] But he has also stated he was 'kicked out' and was 'on the run'.[266]

The following image appears early in the Doctor's memory: "Here was a cowled figure shaking a fist at a dark castle, and in the next picture he was cowering from something huge and fearful. Then he was running." [267]

The Doctor claims to have borrowed rather than stolen the TARDIS.[268] **He wasn't authorised to take it.**[269] **Nor did he own the Ship.**[270]

The TARDIS was a family heirloom.[271] The TARDIS had been taken from Marnal by Ulysses. Marnal's son knew the truth about the Doctor's departure, and told his father what had happened afterwards.[272] The Doctor chose not to take a Type 53 TARDIS.[273]

The authorities thought of him as arrogant.[274] **In addition to the TARDIS, the Doctor took the Hand of Omega, the Validium statue and his granddaughter Susan.**[275]

The Doctor and Susan left home "ages" before they met Ian and Barbara.[276] **Possibly more than fifty years.**[277]

Many other Time Lords were known to have left Gallifrey in the Doctor's lifetime: Azmael left Gallifrey to become Master of Jaconda. The Rani was exiled following illegal experiments on animals, including an incident where genetically re-engineered mice that she had created ate the President's cat and attacked the President himself. She became ruler of Miasimia Goria. The Doctor's mentor left Gallifrey for Earth and became known as K'Anpo.[278]

The Doctor left before the Monk, the War Chief and probably before the Master.[279]

260 *Cold Fusion*

261 *Lungbarrow*

262 Dating *Lungbarrow* - This was 'eight hundred and seventy three years ago'. Given that this is set just before *Doctor Who - The Movie*, and *Vampire Science* states that the Doctor was 1009 when he regenerated, it would make him 136. However, given the contradictions over his age, it is probably best not to rely on this figure. Owis was Loomed 675 years ago.

THE DOCTOR'S FAMILY: Sixteen of the Doctor's forty four Cousins are named in Lungbarrow: Quences, Owis, Glospin, Satthralope, Jobiska, Rynde, Arkhew, Maljamin, Farg, Celesia, Almund, Tugel, Chovor the Various, DeRoosifa, Salpash and Luton. Braxiatel is presumably another.

263 *An Unearthly Child, The Edge of Destruction, The Massacre, The Two Doctors*

264 *The War Games*

265 *The War Games, Resurrection of the Daleks, Pyramids of Mars, The Deadly Assassin*.

266 *The Invisible Enemy, The Five Doctors*

267 *Timewyrm: Revelation* (p48).

268 *Frontier in Space, Logopolis*

269 *The Invasion of Time*

270 *Logopolis, Cold Fusion*

271 *The Infinity Doctors*

272 *The Gallifrey Chronicles*

273 *Lungbarrow*

274 *The Eight Doctors*

275 *Remembrance of the Daleks, Silver Nemesis, An Unearthly Child*.

276 *The Sensorites*

277 *The Time Meddler*. The Doctor says the Monk left their home planet fifty years after he did.

278 *The Twin Dilemma, The Mark of the Rani, Planet of the Spiders* respectively.

279 The Doctor says he comes from 'fifty years earlier' than the Monk in *The Time Meddler*. The War Chief

The Morbius Crisis

The Cult of Morbius was formed in 5725.3, Rassilon Era.[280]

Morbius, the leader of the High Council, proposed that the Time Lords should end their policy of non-interference. When the High Council rejected this, he left Gallifrey and raised an army of conquest, promising them immortality. Devastating several planets on the way, the Cult of Morbius arrived on Karn, home of the Sisterhood. The Time Lords attacked them on Karn, destroying his army. Following a trial, Morbius was vaporised. Solon had removed Morbius' brain before his execution and preserved it.[281]

WARMONGER[282] -> Morbius was deposed by Saran, who became Acting President in his place. Junior Cardinal Borusa assisted Saran. Morbius was exiled from Gallifrey. Adopting the identity General Rombusi, he raised an army of mercenaries using stolen Celestial Intervention Agency funds. These armies came from Darkeen, Fangoria, Martak and Romark. They conquered, among many other worlds, Tanith and the Ogron homeworld. Freedonia joined the General, and conquered nearby Sylvana. The General met the surgeon Solon, who pledged to build an army for him from patched-together corpses.

The fifth Doctor encountered Morbius and travelled to Gallifrey, where he convinced Acting President Saran to act. The Doctor was placed in charge of a large Alliance - an army that included the Draconians, Sontarans, Ice Warriors, Cybermen and Ogrons.

Acting President Saran was almost certainly never elected President.[283]

THE DARK PATH -> Two hundred years after the Doctor last saw Koschei, they met on the Earth colony of Darkheart in the thirty-fourth century. Koschei wanted an ordered universe, but his methods for achieving this became increasingly questionable. He felt betrayed upon realising that his dear companion Ailla was a Time Lord spy, and came into conflict with the Doctor also, which kept him emotionally isolated. Koschei became obsessed with the power of the Darkheart and declared himself the Master.

The Master has had many enemies, and always misses them when they are gone.[284]

Increasing Intervention

THE THREE DOCTORS ->
THE TWO DOCTORS ->
Although the Doctor was now travelling through space and time, the Time Lords still occasionally used him as an agent or messenger. Two incarnations of the Doctor were sent to stop the cosmic energy drain caused by Omega, and the Doctor's second incarnation was also sent to space station Chimera to call a halt to the time travel experiments of Kartz and Reimer.[285]

The Doctor's Exile

THE WAR GAMES / SPEARHEAD FROM SPACE -> In 309,906, the Doctor faced a Malfeasance Tribunal, and the Time Lords found the Doctor guilty of interfering in history. They exiled him to Earth in the twentieth

remembers him leaving his home planet in *The War Games*. The Master is first seen in *Terror of the Autons*.

280 *Neverland*

281 *The Brain of Morbius*

282 Dating *Warmonger* - It is never stated how long ago Morbius ruled Gallifrey in *The Brain of Morbius*. The Doctor recognises Morbius, but Morbius doesn't recognise the Doctor.

In his novelisation of the story, Terrance Dicks states that Morbius came to power after the Doctor left Gallifrey, and that the Doctor heard of Morbius on his travels. In *Warmonger*, also by Dicks, the Doctor (who has travelled into Gallifrey's past) muses that Borusa might be in his first incarnation (p166), and that this is the first time Borusa has met him, almost certainly setting it before the Doctor was born - but this is directly contradicted just a few pages later (p173), when it's made clear that it's after the Doctor stole a TARDIS and has left Gallifrey.

Neverland places it before the Master steals the files

on the Doomsday Weapon. *The Book of the War* (in the *Faction Paradox* series) has what it calls 'the Imperator Presidency' occurring between 870 and 866 years before the War starts, so (almost certainly) after the Doctor left Gallifrey. *Timelink* prefers the idea that Morbius rose after *The Three Doctors*.

283 While everyone is happy to call him 'Lord President' in *Warmonger*, Saran is only Acting President until elections are held (p175). The Doctor thinks of Saran as 'a very minor figure in Time Lord history' (p166), so we can probably infer that he lost the election.

We can also speculate that the President who is elected at this point is the one seen in *The Three Doctors* and (after regenerating) the one assassinated in *The Deadly Assassin*. The Doctor never met the President killed in *The Deadly Assassin*, according to that story, but he had known Saran before originally leaving Gallifrey.

284 *Terror of the Autons*

century timezone, changing his appearance. The Tribunal continued to monitor him.[286]

TERROR OF THE AUTONS -> Around this time, the Master removed Time Lord files containing information about the Doomsday Weapon and the Sea Devils. The Time Lords sent a messenger to warn the Doctor about the Master's imminent arrival on Earth.[287]

The Master stole the plans for the Doomsday Weapon on 5892.9, Rassilon Era.[288]

COLONY IN SPACE / THE CURSE OF PELADON / THE MUTANTS -> The Time Lords sent the Doctor on various missions to other planets and times. These were always crucial points of galactic history, with implications for the entire universe. The Doctor was sent to Uxarieus to prevent the Doomsday Weapon from falling into the hands of the Master; to Peladon to ease the passage of that planet into the Galactic Federation and to prevent galactic war; and to Solos, where the Doctor delivered a message to Ky, the leader of the Solonian independence movement, that allowed him to fulfil his race's evolutionary potential.

THE THREE DOCTORS -> A black hole suddenly drained the cosmic energy of the Time Lords. Unable to power their machinery, the Time Lords called on the Doctor for help. They brought two previous incarnations of the Doctor into the present to try and counteract whatever was draining the power.

Two incarnations of the Doctor travelled into the black hole and arrived in a universe of anti-matter. They discovered that Omega lived, maintaining an entire world with his mental control of a singularity. Omega resented the Time Lords, feeling they had abandoned him. He couldn't leave his domain without it ceasing to exist before he departed, and needed the Doctors' help to leave. But the Doctor learnt that Omega's body had long been destroyed, and that only his will remained. It would be impossible for him to return to the universe of matter.

The Doctors tricked their way back to their TARDIS, apparently destroying Omega in a matter/anti-matter explosion. The power drain ended, and the Time Lords had a new source of energy. In gratitude, the Time Lords lifted the Doctor's exile.

PLANET OF THE DALEKS / GENESIS OF THE DALEKS / THE BRAIN OF MORBIUS -> The Time Lords still called upon the Doctor's services from time to time. At the Doctor's request, the Time Lords piloted the TARDIS to Spiridon, the location of a Dalek army. Later, the Time Lords predicted a time when the Daleks would dominate the universe, and sent the Doctor to prevent the Dalek's creation (or at least slow their development). The Time Lords also apparently sent the TARDIS to Karn to prevent the resurrection of Morbius.

Lord Ferain was head of Allegiance at the Celestial Intervention Agency, and it was he who sent the Doctor to Skaro to prevent the Daleks' creation.[289]

---

285 SEASON 6B: *The Two Doctors*. This looks like a major contradiction of the established facts, as it's made clear in *The War Games* that the Doctor has fled his home planet and is terrified of any contact with the Time Lords. Fans don't seem so worried that the Time Lords also contacted the first and second Doctors in *The Three Doctors*.

One theory that has gained currency since appearing in *The Discontinuity Guide* is that after *The War Games*, the Doctor wasn't regenerated straight away but was reunited with Jamie and Victoria (who is mentioned in *The Two Doctors*) and sent on missions for the Time Lords. Supporting evidence for this is that the second Doctor seems to remember *The War Games* in *The Five Doctors*. It also ties in with *TV Comic*, which had the second Doctor exiled to Earth for a time before he became his third incarnation. Two novels by Terrance Dicks - *Players* and *World Game* - explicitly have sequences that, from the Doctor's point of view, occur during Season 6B.

286 *The War Games*. The event is recalled and dated in *The Deadly Assassin*, the Doctor's exile begins in *Spearhead from Space* (continuing until *The Three Doctors*), and we learn the Tribunal is still monitoring the Doctor in *Terror of the Autons*.

287 *Terror of the Autons*. The files are referred to in *Colony in Space* and *The Sea Devils*. Presumably, although this is never stated, the Master also finds out about many of his other future allies and accomplices from these files.

288 *Neverland*

289 *Lungbarrow*

Romana

Romana was born when the Doctor was between six hundred and six hundred twenty-five.[290] She read *Our Planet's Story* as a Time Tot.[291] For her seventieth birthday, she was given an air-car.[292]

As part of her studies, Romana studied the lifecycle of the Gallifreyan Flutterwing and she eventually graduated from the Academy with a Triple First.[293] Romana was an historian and worked in the Bureau of Ancient Records.[294] She was a Prydonian.[295] When she was sixty, she went to Lake Abydos on holiday with her family. She was an only child, as her brother Rorvan had been consigned to the Oubliette of Eternity and erased from history.[296]

Chancellor Goth visited Tersurus on 6241.11, Rassilon Era.[297]

Faction Paradox was created during a time of cultural crisis on Gallifrey.[298] The Faction set out to be deliberately confrontational. Whereas the Time Lords abhorred time paradoxes, Faction Paradox revelled in them. The Time Lords were immortal, so much of the Faction's iconography - like their skull masks - celebrated death. The relationship between the Time Lord authorities and Faction Paradox was analogous to that of the Catholic Church and satanic cults on Earth.[299]

THE DEADLY ASSASSIN ->

"Through the millennia, the Time Lords of Gallifrey led a life of peace and ordered calm, protected against all threats from lesser civilisations by their great power. But this was to change. Suddenly and terribly, the Time Lords faced the most dangerous crisis in their long history..."

The Doctor received a telepathic message, warning him that the President was going to be assassinated. He returned to his home planet immediately, only to find himself implicated in the assassination. The President had been due to resign anyway after centuries in office, and the murder appeared motiveless.

The Doctor's old enemy, the Master, had lured him back to frame him for the murder. The Master had exhausted his regenerations, and had been found by Chancellor Goth on the planet Tersurus. Although Goth had been favoured to succeed the outgoing President, he discovered that another was to be nominated instead. In return for Goth's help, the Master killed the incumbent President.

The Master wanted full access to various items such as the Sash of Rassilon, as he needed to find a way to prolong his life. He discovered that he might regenerate again if he had a powerful enough source of energy - the Master selected the Eye of Harmony. He believed

290 WHEN WAS ROMANA BORN?: Like the Doctor, Romana doesn't give a consistent account of her age - she's 'nearly 140' in *The Ribos Operation*, '125' in *City of Death* and '150' in *The Leisure Hive*.

Her birth would thus occur between *The Tomb of the Cybermen* and *Pyramids of Mars* - almost exactly halfway between those stories, in the Doctor's personal timeline. Given the continuity of companions and the Doctor's exile to Earth, the only certain gap between those two stories where the Doctor could age three hundred years would be between *The Green Death* and *The Time Warrior*, when the Doctor travels alone in his TARDIS. The UNIT personnel have no idea if the Doctor is away, as far as he is concerned, for decades or centuries at a time. If the Season 6B theory is true, there could be another significant gap there. The probability, then, is that Romana was born while the Doctor was in his third incarnation.

291 *Shada*

292 *The Pirate Planet*

293 *The Ribos Operation*

294 *State of Decay*

295 *The Romance of Crime, The Ancestor Cell.*

296 *Neverland*

297 *Neverland.* This visit is presumably the one that occurred in *Legacy of the Daleks*.

298 *Interference.* The *Faction Paradox* novel line contains more detail about the history of Faction Paradox. Morbius is 'the Imperator', who has his own entry in *The Book of the War.* Morbius' reign was one of the main factors that lead Grandfather Paradox to found House Paradox. Morbius and Grandfather Paradox were close contemporaries, however Lawrence Miles read a draft of this chronology and stated the formation of Faction Paradox 'should come just before *The Deadly Assassin* (or just after *Genesis of the Daleks*) ... It's the long-term effects of the Morbius / Imperator crisis that lead to the rise of the Faction, rather than its direct aftermath ... the point when Gallifrey starts being shaken up by renegades, assassinations and invasions, and mortality suddenly becomes a major issue.'

299 *Alien Bodies, Interference*

300 *Cat's Cradle: Time's Crucible* (p210-211).

301 A different actor plays Borusa in each of his televised appearances (Angus MacKay in *The Deadly Assassin*, John Arnatt in *The Invasion of Time*, Leonard Sachs in *Arc of Infinity* and Philip Latham in *The Five Doctors*).

302 *The Ancestor Cell.* The online Faction Paradox timeline suggests that this Presidency fell between *The Deadly Assassin* and *The Invasion of Time*.

303 *The Ancestor Cell*

the Sash would protect him if he unleashed the Eye's power. The Doctor prevented the Master from destroying Gallifrey, but the Master escaped.

Around this time, the Doctor began to learn more about the Time Lords' ancient past.

"It was a chance encounter with the *Book of the Old Time* that had first nudged the Doctor's own thoughts back towards his world's archae-barbaric past. A suspicion had been born in his mind that before regeneration there had been reincarnation. Some memories might be more than racial inheritance. Nothing lasts that does not change." [300]

Borusa regenerated at some point between this and the Doctor's next visit to Gallifrey. [301]

IMAGE OF THE FENDAHL / UNDERWORLD -> Soon after learning of his planet's past, the Doctor began to encounter survivors from his race's ancient history: the Fendahl and the Minyans.

Greyjan the Sane dabbled with the idea of time paradoxes. His three-year reign was the shortest in Gallifreyan history, and coincided with the relative Earth dates that saw the creation of the Eleven-Day Empire. [302]

THE INVASION OF TIME -> The Doctor was contacted by the Vardans, a race capable of travelling down energy waves, including thought. The Vardans had infiltrated the Matrix, and now wanted to commence a physical invasion of Gallifrey. The Doctor tricked the Vardans, returning the invasion force to their home planet, then time-looping it. The Sontarans had been manipulating the Vardans all along, and attempted to invade Gallifrey themselves. This incursion was also repelled. Leela and K9 elected to stay behind on Gallifrey.

The Doctor was the 407th President. [303] While in the Matrix, the Doctor became aware of the Timewyrm. He sent his future self a warning about it. [304] Leela and Andred, a member of the Chancellery Guard, married soon afterward, but the Doctor was unable to attend the ceremony. [305] Borusa became President and regenerated once again. [306]

The Key to Time

The White Guardian picked Romana to aid the Doctor and recover the six segments of the Key to Time. [307]

A schism in College of Cardinals led to a rival President setting himself up on Drornid. The Time Lords ignored them, and they eventually returned home. [308] Drornid was also known as Dronid. [309]

SHADA -> The Doctor prevented Skraga of Drornid from using the powers of the Time Lord mind criminal Salyavin to impose himself as the 'universal mind'

With the quest for the Key to Time long-completed, the Time Lords recalled Romana. Before she could return, the TARDIS fell through a CVE into E-Space. [310]

STATE OF DECAY -> The Doctor destroyed the Great Vampire, who had survived the war with the Time Lords and fled to E-Space.

ARC OF INFINITY -> Omega had survived, and convinced a member of the High Council, Hedin, that he had been wronged by Gallifrey. With access to a bio-data extract, Omega would be able to bond with a Time Lord, re-entering our universe. Hedin chose the Doctor as Omega's target - when the High Council discovered this, they recalled the Doctor's TARDIS to Gallifrey (only the third time this had been done in the planet's history) and lifted the ban on the death penalty. Killing the Doctor, they believed, would break the renegade's link with our universe. The Doctor survived vaporisation by entering the Matrix, where he discovered Omega's plan. He tracked Omega to Amsterdam, where the renegade's new body proved unstable and disintegrated.

---

304 *Timewyrm: Genesys*
305 We learn of Leela and Andred's marriage in *Arc of Infinity*.
306 In *The Ribos Operation*, the Doctor wishes that he'd thrown the President to the Sontarans, suggesting that Borusa has become President (although the treacherous Kelner apparently survived *The Invasion of Time* and he'd have a strong constitutional case, as the Doctor named him Vice-President). The Doctor was meant to have lost his memory of the Sontaran invasion at the end of *The Invasion of Time*, but clearly did-

n't, or was given some sort of account of it before he left Gallifrey. By *Arc of Infinity*, Borusa is President.
307 *The Ribos Operation*
308 *Shada*. It's unclear when this happened. *The Book of the War* states it was 392 years before the War starts, and 474 years after Morbius' execution.
309 *Alien Bodies*. *The Terrestrial Index* and *The Discontinuity Guide* both mistakenly refer to Drornid as Dronid.
310 *Meglos, Full Circle*

THE FIVE DOCTORS -> Borusa regenerated once more. He had become dissatisfied with ruling Gallifrey. Now he wanted "perpetual regeneration": a secret discovered by Rassilon that allowed true immortality, not simply the vast lifespans granted to other Time Lords. Borusa discovered the ancient Time Scoop machinery and restarted the Game of Rassilon, pitting four incarnations of the Doctor and his old friends against a selection of old enemies. Rassilon gave Borusa the immortality he sought, transforming him into a living statue. Chancellor Flavia declared the Doctor as President, but he left Gallifrey before he could take up office, and appointed Flavia to rule in his stead.

The Doctor was the 409th President.[311] **Type 57 TARDISes were in operation at this time.**[312] Flavia didn't chase the Doctor because she wanted the Presidency for herself. Her reign was one of prosperity.[313]

RESURRECTION OF THE DALEKS -> The Daleks planned to assassinate the High Council of the Time Lords using duplicates of the Doctor and his companions, but the Doctor prevented this.

ATTACK OF THE CYBERMEN -> The Doctor sent a signal to the Time Lords, asking for assistance, when some Cybermen invaded his TARDIS. The Cybermen forced the Doctor to terminate his call for help.[314]

New surveillance methods were developed, increasing the range of information that the Matrix could harvest. The Matrix could now record events that occurred within a certain vicinity of a TARDIS.[315]

The Celestial Intervention Agency worried that the Ravolox Affair would be exposed. They spread rumours that Flavia wasn't legitimately President, and she ordered an election to settle the matter. The Agency fixed the election, installing their supporter, Niroc.[316]

---

311 *The Ancestor Cell*

312 In *Warriors of the Deep*, the Doctor says he should have changed his TARDIS for a Type 57 'when he had the chance'. This could imply that Type 57 is the most advanced model at present, or simply that newer models exist but the Doctor prefers Type 57.

313 *The Eight Doctors*

314 Later in the story, the Doctor suspects that the Time Lords *are* aware of events and have been manipulating him, but this is never confirmed.

315 *The Mysterious Planet*. The Valeyard's "evidence", as displayed throughout *The Trial of a Time Lord*, derives from this feature, although it's unclear if the Doctor's TARDIS was secretly fitted with surveillance gear at some point (his visit to Gallifrey in *Arc of Infinity*, for instance), or if the Ship was incorporated into the system by remote.

316 *The Eight Doctors*

317 THE VALEYARD: It is unclear exactly what the Valeyard is. The Master, who knows a great deal about him, says, "there is some evil in all of us, Doctor, even you. The Valeyard is an amalgamation of the darker sides of your nature, somewhere between your twelfth and final incarnation, and I must say you do not improve with age".

This is rather vague, and it seems that the Valeyard might be a potential future for the Doctor (like those presented to him in *The War Games* or arguably those of Romana in *Destiny of the Daleks*), a projection (like Cho-je in *Planet of the Spiders* or the Watcher in *Logopolis*) or an actual fully-fledged future incarnation (as he was in the original script). The Master seems to have met the Valeyard before, and sees him as a rival (he also says "as I've always know him, the Doctor" - suggesting that the Valeyard would normally refer to himself as "the Doctor" not "the Valeyard").

Whatever the Valeyard is, he doesn't have any qualms about killing his past self - perhaps if the sixth Doctor died, the Valeyard would apparently gain his remaining regenerations by default. His survival at the end of the trial, when we had seen him disseminated (and the Doctor has promised to mend his ways) perhaps suggests that he is something more than just a mere Time Lord.

Note also that the Master says "twelfth and final", not "twelfth and thirteenth" - which, if you squint, leaves open the possibility that the Doctor will survive the end of his regenerative cycle.

The novels and audios have tended to steer clear of the Valeyard - indeed the Writers' Guide for the New Adventures stated, "anything featuring the Valeyard is out - he's a continuity nightmare, and a rather dull villain". Despite this, a number of the novels (particularly *Time of Your Life*, *Head Games* and *Millennial Rites*) have developed the idea first aired in *Love and War* that the Doctor sacrificed his sixth incarnation ("the colourful jester") to create a stronger, more ruthless seventh persona ("Time's Champion"), and who was better equipped to change his destiny. Ironically, books such as *Love and War* and *Head Games* suggest that this internal conflict might well have been the catalyst that brought the Valeyard into being.

The PDAs *Matrix* and *Mission: Impractical* feature the Valeyard, as does the non-canonical audio *He Jests at Scars*.

318 It's difficult to say how much the CIA is operating independently in this story, or to what degree it's sanctioned by the High Council. Presuming the CIA isn't acting totally solo, the High Council that initiated the project is possibly the administration that was overthrown in *The Trial of a Time Lord*.

319 *Lungbarrow*

THE TRIAL OF A TIME LORD / THE ULTIMATE FOE
-> The Doctor discovered that the planet Ravolox was in fact the Earth in the far future, but he didn't know what had moved the planet two light years or, more importantly, why. Despite this, the High Council became worried that the Doctor knew too much, and they brought him to a vast space station. The Doctor at first learned that he was to undergo an impartial enquiry into his activities. He also learnt that as he had neglected his duties, he had been deposed from the Presidency.

The prosecuting council, named the Valeyard, successfully argued that the Doctor was guilty of interference on a grand scale, and the enquiry became a trial. It was revealed that the Doctor's actions on Thoros Beta had threatened the course of universal evolution. The Time Lords had been forced to intervene directly, killing the scientist Crozier, the Mentor Kiv and possibly the Doctor's companion Peri. When the Doctor's own evidence proved that on another occasion he had committed genocide - wiping out the Vervoids to save the Earth - he faced a death sentence.

The Doctor claimed that the Matrix was being tampered with. The Keeper of the Matrix was brought in as an expert witness, but the Master suddenly appeared on the Matrix screen, demonstrating that it was indeed possible to breach the security of the Time Lords' master computer. The Master explained that Andromedans had previously entered the Matrix from their base on Earth and stolen valuable scientific secrets. To protect their position, the High Council had covertly ordered Earth's destruction.

Perhaps the Master's greatest bombshell was the identity of the prosecuting council: the Valeyard was an amalgamation of all that was evil in the Doctor, somewhere between his twelfth and final incarnation.[317] The Master had encountered the Valeyard before, and knew that the High Council had brought him in to frame the Doctor, in return for which the Valeyard would gain the Doctor's remaining regenerations.

When the truth about Ravolox was revealed, popular unrest deposed the High Council. Both the Master and Valeyard moved to take advantage of the situation: the Master planned to take control of Gallifrey, even as the Valeyard attempted to assassinate senior members of the Time Lord hierarchy. Both failed. The Master was trapped by the Limbo Atrophier, a booby trap placed on the Matrix files. The Valeyard was believed destroyed by his own particle disseminator, but he somehow survived. When last seen, he had assumed the guise of the Keeper of the Matrix.

The Doctor suggested that once order was restored, the Inquisitor should run for President.

THE EIGHT DOCTORS -> The eighth Doctor travelled to the time of his trial. He called on Rassilon to briefly free Borusa's noblest incarnation. Borusa deposed the corrupt High Council and arranged honest elections. Flavia was re-elected and restored Earth to its rightful place. Rassilon might have intervened to make the Doctor meet his companion Sam Jones in 1997.

UNREGENERATE![318] -> The High Council foresaw a time when lesser species would develop time travel, and pack the space-time continuum to the bursting point. The Gallifreyan CIA therefore instigated a project to install the sentiences of newly birthed TARDISes into living beings. They hoped the sentiences would operate as CIA agents on their hosts' homeworlds, thwarting the lesser species' endeavors to create time-travel technology. The CIA believed this would prove far more successful than the usual array of spies and brainwashing.

Professor Klyst, a Time Lord, spearheaded the research. Experiments on Daleks were forbidden, but subjects were recruited from at least fifty worlds. Each were offered lifetimes of success if they participated in the research on the day before their deaths. Yet the beings' brains were unable to host the TARDIS sentiences, and many went insane.

The Doctor brought a halt to the operation, helping to destroy the relevant data. One TARDIS sentience stabilized in the human Johannes Rausch. Klyst agreed to host another sentience, thus erasing her own knowledge of the research. The sentiences in Rausch and Klyst transferred another of their number into the Institute where the research was conducted, turning it into a makeshift travel vehicle. They went on the run from the Time Lords, hoping to in time stabilize the other sentiences in their host bodies.

REMEMBRANCE OF THE DALEKS -> Addressing Davros, the Doctor claimed to be "President-Elect of the High Council of Time Lords ... Keeper of the Legacy of Rassilon". Its work done, the Hand of Omega returned to Gallifrey.

Back on Gallifrey, the Hand of Omega missed its creator and tended to hover around the Omega Memorial.[319]

BLOOD HARVEST / GOTH OPERA -> Three Time Lords - Rath (the younger brother of Goth), Elar and Morin - took responsibility for security matters. Most Time Lords considered this a rather lowly position, but the Committee of Three, as they styled themselves, used their office to build their own powerbase. Using their expertise, they planned to kill Rassilon in his Tower and take control of the galaxy. At the time of President Flavia's inauguration, they were defeated by the Doctor, Ace, Benny and Romana.

The three traitors were sentenced to vaporisation. Romana settled back on Gallifrey, and was greeted by Ruathadvorophrenaltid, a Time Lady acquaintance of the Doctor. Ruath planned to be the consort of the Vampire Messiah, and targeted the fifth Doctor. Romana alerted Gallifrey and the Doctor to the threat, and was rewarded with a seat on the High Council.

The Romana Presidency

HAPPY ENDINGS -> Romana was elected President of the Time Lords, beating the previous Madame President by 53 to 47 percent in the elections, and won the support of the Interventionist movement. She promised an end to isolationism and to open an embassy with the Tharils. Very soon after her election, she investigated a Fortean Flicker which the Master was exploiting. He had stolen the Loom of Rassilon's Mouse, which could build monsters. The Master was defeated and the Loom retrieved, but he escaped Gallifreyan custody.

Romana was the 413th President.[320]
The Carnival Queen affected rationality throughout the universe. On Gallifrey, Grandfather Paradox, 'voodoo priest of the House of Lungbarrow', escaped his prison when the Lady President had a fit and released three hundred prisoners from their prison asteroid. Six hundred Time Lords claimed to be the ghost of Morbius, and the planet's automatic defences activated.[321]

Grandfather Paradox removed his arm, as the Time Lords had branded it. Soon, he would remove himself from history. With its leader free, Faction Paradox would grow in size and influence.[322]

LUNGBARROW -> The Doctor returned to his ancestral home of Lungbarrow. He was accused of murdering Quences, the head of the household. The Doctor was badly beaten and incapacitated by his family, who blamed him for all their woes. Innocet - one of the Doctor's Cousins - joined Ace, Leela, Chris Cwej and Romana in reviving him. They learned the Doctor contained the genetic codes of the Other.

The Doctor deduced that another Cousin, Glospin, had briefly regenerated to look like the Doctor and thus framed him for Quences' murder. Quences' mind was in Badger, the House's robot servant. The House itself committed suicide, throwing itself from the mountain it rested upon. Romana ordered a new House built for the Cousins.

The Doctor's companion, Chris Cwej, decided to stay on Gallifrey and work as an agent for the President. He was given a time ring. Leela discovered she was pregnant. The Dromeians and Arcalians objected to Romana's interventionist policies. She was given a gift by the Chairman of Argolis and opened an Embassy with Karn.

The Celestial Intervention Agency sent the Doctor to recover the Master's remains from Skaro.

The further adventures of Chris Cwej appear in Virgin's Bernice Summerfield New Adventures, and then the Faction Paradox series.

Romana and a research team went missing when the planetoid Etra Prime vanished on 6776.7, Rassilon Era. An interim President was appointed in Romana's absence.[323]

= THE SIRENS OF TIME[324] **->** The Knights of Velyshaa seized control of the Gallifreyan Capitol. They were exploiting time disturbances using a captured Temperon, an animal that could release particles capable of disrupting time. The fifth, sixth and seventh Doctors restored established history and the conquest of Gallifrey never happened. The Temperon sacrificed itself to forever hold in check the Sirens of Time, extra-dimensional creatures that fed off time distortion.

Type 70 TARDISes were in operation at this time.

320 *The Gallifrey Chronicles*
321 *Christmas on a Rational Planet.* No date given in the *Doctor Who* books, but it's '151' years before the War starts, according to *The Book of the War*.
322 *Christmas on a Rational Planet, Alien Bodies, Interference.*
323 *Neverland*
324 The story takes place during the interim Presidency, in the seventh Doctor's 'current' Gallifrey.
325 *Neverland*
326 Dating *Death Comes to Time* - While there are discrepancies, *Death Comes to Time* shares a number of features with the timeline of the later New Adventures - the Time Lords are more openly interventionist, and Ace is training up as a Time Lord. While *Lungbarrow* is clearly meant to lead straight into *Doctor Who - The Movie*, there are other stories set in the 'gap', such as *Excelis Decays* and *Master*. Ace is a lot older than she was in the New Adventures (her last appearance is in *Lungbarrow*). As with events in *Death Comes to Time* that occur in the Present Day section, the canonicity of these details is highly debatable. Fans are free to incorporate this story or ignore it.
327 *Neverland*
328 *Neverland.* The date was given earlier in the story as 6978.5, but this is clearly a fluffed line, given the other recent dates.
329 *Terror Firma*

THE APOCALYPSE ELEMENT -> Twenty time-active races met on Archetryx for a summit, but the planetoid Etra Prime reappeared. Based on Etra Prime, the Daleks were working on 'the Apocalypse Element' - a substance capable of shredding the raw fabric of space-time in an unstoppable reaction. The Daleks attacked Archetryx and stole components needed to finish making the Element.

Romana had been imprisoned on Etra Prime for twenty years. She escaped as the Daleks, using a Monan Host time ship as a Trojan horse, attacked Gallifrey. The Daleks detonated the Apocalypse Element in the Seriphia Galaxy. As was part of their plan, the Daleks sacrificed those of their number on Gallifrey to reinforce the Eye of Harmony's power. The Eye contained the Element's destruction to Seriphia, which was restructured to create millions of new worlds for the Daleks.

The Daleks killed the interim President of Gallifrey, and Romana was restored to the Presidency.

The Dalek invasion was in 6796.8, Rassilon Era. The Dalek Fleet was time-looped in 6798.2.[325]

DEATH COMES TO TIME[326] **->** A new generation of Time Lords was far more open to the idea of intervention. Among them was the Minister of Chance, and he met with the Doctor to discuss intergalactic crises. One such matter emerged when the Time Lords Antinor and Valentine were killed on Earth. Meanwhile, Ace trained to be a Time Lord under Casmus. Events climaxed on the twenty-first century Earth.

DOCTOR WHO - THE MOVIE -> The Doctor recovered the Master's remains from Skaro, and was heading for Gallifrey in 5725.2, Rassilon Era. The Master sabotaged the TARDIS, forcing a landing in San Francisco, 1999, but was later lost to the TARDIS' Eye of Harmony.

NEVERLAND -> President Romana allied the Time Lords with the Warpsmiths of Phaedon and the Monan Host.

A warfleet of TARDISes pursued the Doctor and Charley, who decided it was time to resolve the paradox of her existence (as she had been saved from dying in the *R-101* crash). The two of them were taken to a Time Station.

President Romana and Vansell warned that the structure of space and time was on the verge of collapse. They believed that Charley had attracted Anti-Time particles from the Antiverse, which was disrupting the universal balance. The Time Lords adapted the Station to pass into the Antiverse to investigate. The Doctor discovered Rassilon's TARDIS, the size of a planetoid, with a surface populated by 'Neverpeople'. Rassilon's casket was there. Vansell fell under the sway of the Neverpeople, who were actually exiled Time Lord criminals.

The Doctor realised that the Neverpeople had travelled to our universe and spread rumours throughout time of Zagreus, hoping to tempt the Time Lords here. The casket didn't contain Rassilon, but rather a mass of Anti-time sufficient to destabilise the universe. Vansell sacrificed his life, but was unable to prevent the Time Station, with the casket onboard, from reaching Gallifrey. The Doctor surrounded the Station with his TARDIS. The Station exploded, but the TARDIS contained the Anti-Time. However, the Doctor was saturated with Anti-Time energy ... which split his personality and made him the destroyer Zagreus.

> = In the Matrix, the Doctor saw a possible future where Gallifrey had been attacked and Romana was the Imperiatrix responsible for the genocide of the Daleks.[327]

This occurred in 6798.3, Rassilon Era.[328]

ZAGREUS -> The Anti-Time-infected Doctor became Zagreus, and a revived Rassilon sought to use him as a weapon against the Divergents. "Zagreus" objected to being manipulated and cast Rassilon through a portal into the Divergents' timeline. The TARDIS helped the Doctor stabilize his true persona and he departed for a Divergent Universe, fearing that by remaining, he would risk the Anti-Time within him allowing Zagreus to again take control. Charley accompanied the Doctor on his journey.

THE NEXT LIFE -> Rassilon was caught in a recurring time loop, and his identity began slipping away. The Zagreus persona was separated from the Doctor and took on female form, but learned "she" was destined to remain in the Divergent Universe for at least twenty to thirty millennia. The purged Doctor returned to our universe with Charley and their new companion C'rizz. They immediately came into conflict with Davros and the Daleks.[329]

The Big Finish Gallifrey mini-series takes place during Romana's Presidency, before her second regeneration.

Eve of the War

ALIEN BODIES / INTERFERENCE / THE TAKING OF PLANET 5 -> Although Time Lords were unable to see into their own future, the eighth Doctor found evidence that the Time Lords would fight a War across time and space against an unknown Enemy. This War involved exotic weapons and such shifts in the timeline, reality cause and effect as to make it all but impossible to determine any firm details. The broad sweep of events became apparent among the fragmentary evidence, however, and it was bleak news for Gallifrey.

Romana regenerated for the second time. Her third incarnation became increasingly concerned - perhaps even paranoid - about the prospect of the War.[330] Some Time Lords tried to acquire a bottle universe from IM Foreman, hoping to flee into it when the Enemy attacked.[331]

THE SHADOWS OF AVALON -> President Romana now put the survival of the Time Lords over more ethical considerations. While she was concerned with the dispute with the People of the Worldsphere, Romana was aware that the War with the unknown Enemy would soon be upon Gallifrey.

Learning that the Doctor's companion, Compassion, was mutating into a TARDIS thanks to her contact with future technology, Romana sent Interventionist agents Cavis and Gandar to capture her. Romana planned to force Compassion to breed with other TARDISes. Compassion made her transformation into a TARDIS, but the Doctor rescued her and they fled the Time Lord authorities.

Until Compassion, the most advanced TARDIS was the Type 98.[332]

THE ANCESTOR CELL / THE GALLIFREY CHRONI-CLES -> As the War approached, Gallifreyan society was starting to fray at the edges and many Time Lords were becoming superstitious. Time Lords succumbed to the cults of Ferisix, Thrayke, Sabjatric, Rungar, the Pythian Heresy, Klade and the legend of Cuwirti.

A vast Edifice materialised over Gallifrey. This was the Doctor's original TARDIS, which was drawing energy from IM Foreman's leaking bottle universe.

On Gallifrey, many Time Lords had fallen under the sway of Faction Paradox. They summoned the dead President, Greyjan the Sane, who infected the Matrix with Faction Paradox virus. Faction Paradox arrived in force to occupy Gallifrey, led by Grandfather Paradox.

The Enemy was revealed as evolved ancestor cells - primeval lifeforms that have been mutated and empowered by the leaking bottle universe. The Enemy now launched its first strike on Gallifrey, destroying the TARDIS berths.

Faced with the choice of either submitting to Faction Paradox or escaping, the Doctor instead used the remaining energy of the Edifice to destroy Gallifrey. Faction Paradox was wiped out, and the annihilation was so complete that it destroyed the entire constellation of Kasterborous, creating disturbances in space and time that prevented any further time travel to or from Gallifrey.

The Doctor and Compassion downloaded the entire contents of the Matrix into the Doctor's brain. Compassion sent the Doctor and his TARDIS, which had been all but destroyed, to Earth to recover. She left with Nivet, a technician.

The destruction of Gallifrey thus prevented ...

---

330 *The Shadows of Avalon*

331 *Interference*

332 *The Book of the War* specifies that Compassion becomes a Type 102 TARDIS.

333 THE WAR: *Alien Bodies* introduced the future War and the Enemy (neither of which were capitalised at that point). Further details were added in subsequent books, principally *Interference*, *The Taking of Planet 5*, *The Shadows of Avalon* and *The Ancestor Cell*.

The Doctor destroyed Gallifrey in *The Ancestor Cell*, in large part to avert the War. At that point, all the events of the War ceased to be the 'real' future of the *Doctor Who* universe.

A great many more details about the war are revealed in the *Faction Paradox* series. This book will confine itself, as far as possible, to information given in the *Doctor Who* novels. There's also the caveat that, by definition, it's difficult to establish facts or the sequence of events of a time war.

334 *Alien Bodies*. No date given in the novels, but this was t w e n t y years before the War started, according to *The Book of the War*.

WHEN DID THE WAR START?: There's no indication in the *Doctor Who* books exactly when the War was due to start relative to the Doctor. The War began one hun-

dred and fifty-one years after Grandfather Paradox escaped his prison, according to *The Book of the War*. That escape occurred in *Christmas on a Rational Planet*, shortly after Romana became President. Romana celebrates her one hundred and fiftieth year as President in *The Ancestor Cell*, meaning the War is now imminent.

335 *The Ancestor Cell*

336 *Alien Bodies*

337 *The Ancestor Cell*

338 *Alien Bodies*

339 *Interference*

340 *Alien Bodies*

341 *Interference*

342 Subsequent events would suggest the clone was of the Master.

343 *The Taking of Planet 5*

344 *Alien Bodies*

345 *The Taking of Planet 5*

The War[333]

Realising that the Enemy could erase them from history, some Celestial Intervention Agency members tried to remove themselves from the universe as a means of defence. They became conceptual beings named the Celestis. They operated from a realm called Mictlan, and influenced universal affairs with a network of agents.[334]

The Enemy struck Gallifrey, completely destroying it. Aware this attack was coming, the Time Lords broke their oldest laws, travelling back in time to assault their Enemy before they were attacked.[335]

Early in the War, the Enemy succeeded in wiping out the most powerful Gallifreyan artefacts like the Demat Gun and the Sash of Rassilon. Many secrets and pieces of bio-data were lost. Those that survived became extremely valuable, and much sought-after, as they could be adapted into weapons.

The first land battle of the War was fought on Dronid in the 155th century. The Doctor was thought to have died on Dronid. His body was recovered, and its unique biodata would make it perhaps the most valuable artefact in the universe. The Doctor had agreed to donate his body to the Celestis in return for their non-intervention on Dronid.[336]

Every battle was fought and then refought, as the losing side retroactively attempted to reverse the result. Eventually, time collapsed in the vicinity and the fighting would move elsewhere.

The Time Lords began searching their own future for advanced weapons to be used in the War.[337] The Enemy learned how to build conceptual entities such as the anarchitects, beings capable of rearranging architecture.

Qixotl met the Doctor and saw him escape the Antiridean organ-eaters.[338]

Faction Paradox grew corrupt and started trading weapons and time travel. The Time Lord authorities moved to wipe them out as they would a virus. In 2596, the Time Lords destroyed the Earth colony Ordifica because of its contact with Faction Paradox.[339]

The Time Lords allied themselves with the Gabrielideans. The Time Lords had a military training ground on Gallifrey XII. The latest model TARDISes were the Type 103s, which were sentient and could take the form of people.[340]

ALIEN BODIES -> As some of the Celestis began switching sides, the War began tipping in favour of the Enemy. The Doctor's dead body - the Relic - was auctioned by Mr Qixotl. The Celestis won by giving Qixotl a new body when his original one was fatally wounded. The Doctor tricked the Celestis and stole the Relic. He took it to Quiescia, then destroyed it with a thermosystron bomb.

The Time Lords quickly moved to occupy or control millions of planets. They created the Ogron Lords, shock troops with the ability to time travel.[341]

INTERFERENCE -> The Time Lords were losing the War. They had a last resort - a weapon designed to destroy Earth, which would not only destroy the Enemy's homeworld but collapse the entire web of time. The ship was dispatched at sub-light speeds, and was due to arrive at Earth in 1996. Fitz became Father Kreiner of Faction Paradox and hunted down Time Lords, including the Master and the Rani. One of these was actually a clone.[342]

The Time Lords created at least nine duplicate Gallifreys, in case the Enemy destroyed the original. Not even the President knew which was the 'real' one. One of the Gallifreys was destroyed in the Battle of Mutter's Cluster. Gallifrey VIII was an industrial planet with vast Looms pouring out soldiers.[343] There was a Gallifrey XII.[344]

Time Lords were force-regenerated into physical forms engineered to fight. Fifteen out of a thousand Time Lords survived each combat mission. There were distinct Waves of warfare, with gaps between them allowing the Time Lords to Loom more soldiers. Only those from the First Wave resembled humans. The Time Lords suffered heavy losses in the Third Zone during the Fifth Wave.

The War President was a man with a pointed beard that had grown white with age, and who wore black robes. Any gathering of around a dozen TARDISes would attract an Enemy attack. The Time Lords used Parallel Cannons that created holes to other, more hostile, parts of the universe and unleashed the forces there.

The Enemy detonated the star of the planet Delphon, causing a significant rout of the Time Lords.[345]

THE TAKING OF PLANET 5 -> The Time Lords planned to smash a fleet of War TARDISes against the barriers around the Fifth Planet, hoping to free the Fendahl for use against the Enemy. The Doctor, Fitz and Compassion discovered the plot, and Compassion tried to save the War TARDISes. The barrier was destroyed, but the Fendahl had been wiped out by the Fendahl Predator - a Memovore creature that had evolved the ability to destroy concepts. The Fendahl Predator was drawn to Mictlan and destroyed the Celestis before the Doctor banished it.

THE ANCESTOR CELL / THE GALLIFREY CHRONICLES -> Faction Paradox had gone from being a secret society to an army, led by Grandfather Paradox, the future self none of us hope to become. As well as a new rank of initiate - the Uncles, leather-clad assassins - there was now an armoured infantry, known as skulltroopers, and their shadow weapons had evolved so that they resembled guns. Although they were experienced at fighting Time Lords,

Faction Paradox was not the Enemy.

Now they travelled two hundred and ninety-seven years into their own past to launch an invasion of Gallifrey. This would be the event that would lead to both the Faction conquering Gallifrey, and - three minutes seven seconds later - their total destruction and the annihilation of the War timeline.

Aided by Compassion, the Doctor had downloaded the entire contents of the Matrix - the memories of almost every Time Lord who had ever lived - into his own mind. They survived in a supercompressed form that left no room for the Doctor's own memories. Compassion apparently took the Doctor's memories, although for what purpose remains a mystery. Compassion dropped the amnesiac Doctor off in the late nineteenth century.

After Gallifrey

When his travels through time and space resumed, the Doctor met a man in the eighteenth century who resembled the Master and said the following:

"There are only four of us left now, you know. Four of us in all the universe." [346]

Without the Time Lords controlling the proliferation of time travel, many races attempted to gain mastery of time, often by acquiring Gallifreyan artefacts. Without the Time Lords to enforce the laws of time, magic started to seep back into the universe.[347]

THE GALLIFREY CHRONICLES -> Marnal regenerated and automatically regained his memories. He soon discovered the Doctor had destroyed Gallifrey and lured him to Earth to punish him.

The Doctor and Marnal came to realise that the Doctor's mind contained the contents of the Matrix and the memories of all the Time Lords. Marnal died saving the Doctor, convinced that the Doctor should dedicate himself to the task of building a New Gallifrey. The Doctor despatched K9 to track down Compassion.

It would appear that the Doctor succeeded in building a new Gallifrey. His memories certainly returned. The next we learn of Time Lord history is ...

The Last Great Time War

The Doctor's home planet was destroyed in the Last Great Time War, 'a war between the Daleks and the Time Lords with the whole of creation at stake'.

Many planets, such as those of the Nestene and the Gelth, were affected. This was a time war that was invisible to 'smaller' species, but was devastating to 'the higher forms'. The Doctor destroyed the entire Dalek race, and their million-strong war fleet. The Time Lords - save for the Doctor - also perished. The Doctor instigated this destruction, referred to as an 'inferno'. He 'watched them burn'.

The Doctor survived, as did a single Dalek that fell through time to the early twenty-first century, and the Emperor Dalek's flagship that limped to the solar system 'centuries' before the year 200,000.

Time was more fragile without the Time Lords to protect it, and some of the rules governing time were suspended.[348]

---

346 FOUR: *The Infinity Doctors* (p213) first mentioned 'four names' as the four people that Rassilon had ordered killed as a threat to Gallifrey, with Omega and the Doctor specified as two of the four. The above quote comes from *The Adventuress of Henrietta Street* (p231). In *The Gallifrey Chronicles*, the four survivors are described as 'A man with a sallow face and small, pointed black beard, who wore a blue rosette; a young woman with long blonde hair in an extraordinary piece of haute couture; a tall man with a bent nose wearing a cravat and holding a pair of dice; the Doctor himself with close-cropped hair, sitting on an ornate throne, a new-born baby girl in his arms' - intended, but not named, as the Master; Iris Wildthyme (or possibly Romana); the Minister of Chance from *Death Comes to Time*; the Doctor (possibly the Doctor from *The Infinity Doctors*, or in his role as the Emperor of the Universe, father of Miranda, mentioned in *Father Time*).

347 The books from *Father Time* to *Sometime Never* often showed races with either time travel or magical abilities.

348 *Rose, The End of the World, The Unquiet Dead, Dalek, Father's Day, Bad Wolf, The Parting of the Ways.* The *2006 Doctor Who Annual* contains a short account of the Time War written by Russell T Davies, which links the story to *Lungbarrow* and *The Apocalypse Element*, mentions the Deathsmiths of Goth (from the *DWM* back-up strip *Black Legacy*) and adds the information that the Animus (*The Web Planet*) and the Eternals (*Enlightenment*) were caught in the fighting. This is the only place related to the 2005 series that names Gallifrey as the Doctor's destroyed home planet, and says Skaro was also in 'ruins' by the end - a reference that would seem to support the claim in *War of the Daleks* that Skaro wasn't destroyed in *Remembrance of the Daleks*.

There is no indication whether it was the eighth or ninth Doctor who fought in the Last Great Time War, or whether he regenerated during (as a result of?) events during the War. The Dalek in *Dalek* seems to respond to the Doctor's name rather than because he recognises his appearance. Many fans have speculated that the Doctor has recently regenerated in *Rose*, as he seems unfamiliar with his reflection. The consensus seems to be that it's the eighth Doctor who fought the Time War and that its climax somehow triggered the regeneration - although there's no evidence that's the case, and it seems clear from Clive's website in *Rose* that the ninth Doctor's an established incarnation.

ONLY ONE DESTRUCTION OF GALLIFREY?: The intention of both the creative team behind the EDAs and the new series producer Russell T Davies is that the destruction of Gallifrey seen in *The Ancestor Cell* and the destruction of Gallifrey reported in the new series are entirely separate events. As the Doctor destroys Gallifrey once while preventing the Enemy and Faction Paradox from taking control of his homeworld, then (presumably after rebuilding Gallifrey, as he pledges to do at the end of *The Gallifrey Chronicles*) he destroys Gallifrey again in a great war with the Daleks, it would seem clear these are indeed mutually exclusive. Russell

Davies likened it, in a *DWM* column, to the two World Wars humanity fought in quick succession.

But could Gallifrey have been destroyed just once? The Doctor certainly experiences the destruction of Gallifrey twice, in two different contexts. But this doesn't rule out it being the same *event*. If there was only one destruction of Gallifrey, he and his future self would have to be present, and both culpable.

Surprisingly, this already fits what we know from *The Ancestor Cell* - the Doctor's future self, Grandfather Paradox was there. Moreover, this future eighth Doctor fits everything we know about the Doctor who fought the Time War: fighting a vast time war has scarred him, made him lose his faith in humanity, made him a little callous. In *The Gallifrey Chronicles* recap of the end of *The Ancestor Cell*, Grandfather Paradox even wears a leather coat. As for the destruction of Gallifrey - the Doctor's description in *Dalek*, 'I watched it happen ... I made it happen ... I tried to stop it' is a neat summary of his actions in *The Ancestor Cell*.

If this theory is true, the Doctor's memories of the War are conflicted because he was *literally* fighting his (earlier) self over 'pulling the lever' that destroyed Gallifrey. So it's *Grandfather Paradox* who has fought the Last Great Time War, the Daleks, the Nestenes and so on. He goes back to *The Ancestor Cell* having done all that, confronts his earlier self ... who then outsmarts him by blowing up Gallifrey. Following this defeat, it's Grandfather Paradox who regenerates into Eccleston (growing his arm back in the process).

For this to be the case, it involves the introduction of the tiniest bit of extra information: the War that's being fought in the future has the Daleks in it and at some point they make a decisive move on Gallifrey. What the 'current' eighth Doctor doesn't know - but which his future self does - is that, in the future, the War's going so badly that the Daleks are heading for Gallifrey. The Daleks were ruled out as 'the Enemy' in *Alien Bodies*, but they don't need to be for this theory to work - they just need to be capable of hitting the Time Lords hard.

There are a number of stories without the references needed to place them in any meaningful relation to the rest of universal history.

Some (such as *The Celestial Toymaker*) take place in a reality that is completely detached from the universe's timeline. Some, such as the E-Space Trilogy (*Full Circle* to *Warriors' Gate*) and the Divergent Universe Series (the Big Finish audios *Scherzo* to *The Next Life*), take place in locations clearly outside the universe's physical boundaries.

A number of stories simply fail to provide (or aren't interested in providing) more evidence beyond the fact that they occur "on an alien planet in the future". Given the entire duration of human development into space, this isn't particularly helpful, presuming the humanoids featured in the story are human in the first place. Without more clues as to how such stories relate to human history or another documented event, a proper dating is impossible. A story such as *Anachrophobia* looks for all the world like placement on the timeline should be attainable, but the evidence (or lack thereof) says otherwise.

The following stories are among those that defy a proper dating. The TV stories are listed in broadcast order; the books and audios are listed alphabetically.

TV Stories

The Edge of Destruction
The Keys of Marinus
The Chase (the sequence on Aridius - although it has to take place after the Daleks launch their time machine, as the Doctor and companions see that on the time-space visualiser, which can only see into the past)
Galaxy 4
The Daleks' Master Plan (the sequences on Tigus and the ice planet)
The Celestial Toymaker
The Dominators (at a time when the Dominators control 'ten galaxies')
The Mind Robber
The Krotons
Carnival of Monsters
The Ribos Operation (the White Guardian sequence)
The Armageddon Factor
The Creature from the Pit
The Horns of Nimon
Full Circle
State of Decay
Warriors' Gate
Castrovalva (the non-Earth sequences)
Snakedance
Enlightenment
The Five Doctors (the first Doctor's kidnap and the Eye of Orion sequences)

Time and the Rani (the Rani wants to take Earth 'back' to the Cretaceous, which suggests it's after that)
The Greatest Show in the Galaxy

Novels, Audios and Novellas

Anachrophobia
Arrangements for War
Axis of Insanity, The
Beltempest
Caedroia
Citadel of Dreams
Coldheart
Creatures of Beauty
Creed of the Kromon, The
Crooked World, The
Dark Flame, The
Dreams of Empire
Eight Doctors, The (the Eye of Orion sequence)
Embrace the Darkness
Faith Stealer
Frontier Worlds
Her Final Flight
Holy Terror, The
... Ish
Kursaal
Last of the Titans
Last, The
Match of the Day
Natural History of Fear, The
Nekromanteia
Next Life, The
Nightdreamers
No Place Like Home
Parallel 59
Scarlet Empress, The
Scherzo
Shell Shock
Sirens of Time, The (sixth Doctor segment)
Sky Pirates!
Twilight Kingdom, The

The following is a list of useful resources for anyone interested in the 'fictional facts' of Doctor Who.

The Making of Doctor Who. (Malcolm Hulke and Terrance Dicks: first edition Piccolo/Pan Books, April 1972; second edition Target/Tandem Books, November 1976) - The earliest source of dates, often direct from BBC material.

Dr Who Special. (ed. David Driver, Jack Lundin: BBC, November 1973) - The tenth anniversary *Radio Times* special, including many previously unpublished story details. This magazine perpetuated the 'incorrect' story titles, used by many fans.

The Doctor Who Programme Guide. (Jean-Marc Lofficier: first edition [2 vols] WH Allen, May 1981, second edition [2 Vols] Target/WH Allen, October 1981, second edition has separate volume titles 'The Programmes' and 'What's What and Who's Who') **Doctor Who - The Programme Guide.** (Jean-Marc Lofficier: third edition Target/WH Allen, December 1989) **Doctor Who - The Terrestrial Index.** (Jean-Marc Lofficier: Target/Virgin Publishing, November 1991) **Doctor Who - The Universal Databank.** (Jean-Marc Lofficier: Doctor Who Books/Virgin Publishing, November 1992) **Doctor Who Programme Guide.** (Jean-Marc Lofficier: fourth edition Doctor Who Books/Virgin Publishing, June 1994) - The standard reference work, with most fans owning a copy of at least one of these books. A good starting point.

Doctor Who Monthly. (Marvel Comics Ltd.) - Richard Landen wrote a series of pseudohistories in the twentieth anniversary year: Issues 75-83 (April 1983 - December 1983) featured *The TARDIS Logs*, a list of TARDIS landings riddled with annoying little errors; issue 77 had a more concise list *Travels with the Doctor*, and a good attempt at 'A History of the Daleks'; 'A History of the Cybermen' (issue 83, with Michael Daniels) and *Shades of Piccolo* (UNIT history, issue 80) were both sensible, simple treatments of potential minefields.

The Doctor Who Role Playing Game. (FASA Corporation [US], 1985; Supplements published 1985-6) - Various dates, including much invented for the game's purposes.

Doctor Who. (Marvel Comics Group [US]) - A series of pseudohistories written by Patrick Daniel O'Neill covering 'A Probable History of the Daleks' (issue 9, June 1985), 'A Probable History of the Cybermen' (issue 10, July 1985) and 'The Master Log' Parts I and II (issues 14, 15,

November, December 1985). Enthusiastic but ill-researched.

The Doctor Who File. (Peter Haining: WH Allen, September 1986) - Pages 223 to 228 contain a table listing the Doctor's adventures and where / when they took place.

Encyclopedia of the Worlds of Doctor Who. (David Saunders: Piccadilly/Knight Press 1986, 1989, 1990) - An A-Z of the series with many entries giving dates.

The Official Doctor Who & the Daleks Book. (John Peel & Terry Nation: St Martin's Press [US], April 1989) - Dalek history, including various other sources (comic strips etc). Approved by Terry Nation.

In-Vision 11: UNIT Special. (CMS, December 1988) - Includes *Down to Earth*, a history of UNIT, by Garry Bradbury. Each issue of *In-Vision* is a comprehensive analysis of an individual story, and the magazine is an indispensable reference work.

Doctor Who - Cybermen. (David Banks, with Andrew Skilleter, Adrian Rigelsford and Jan Vincent-Rudzki: Who Dares, November 1988; Virgin Publishing, September 1990) - Comprehensive, if elaborate, history of the Cybermen. The first, and still best, reference book of its kind.

Doctor Who Magazine. (Marvel Comics Ltd) - issue 174: *The TARDIS Special* (June 12th 1991) features 'Journies' by Andrew Pixley, a superbly researched list of every landing made by the TARDIS. Issue 176 (August 7th 1991) contains an addendum.

The Gallifrey Chronicles. (John Peel: Doctor Who Books/Virgin Publishing, October 1991) - Gallifreyan history and other information. (This isn't the same book as *The Gallifrey Chronicles*, the 2005 EDA).

Doctor Who Magazine Winter Special 1991 - UNIT Exposed. (Marvel Comics Ltd, 28th November, 1991) - Includes an excellent UNIT chronology by John Freeman and Gary Russell, as well as 'UNIT Exposed' by Andrew Dylan.

The Doctor Who Writers' Guide. (Peter Darvill-Evans, Rebecca Levene & Andy Bodle: Virgin Publishing, 1991) - The guidelines for prospective authors of New and Missing Adventures. Includes notes on Gallifreyan history.

Apocrypha. (Adrian Middleton: 1993-95). Fan published chronology drawing together everything the author can get his hands on: comic strips, novelisations, role-playing scenarios and so on.

The Discontinuity Guide. (Paul Cornell, Martin Day and Keith Topping: Virgin Publishing, May 1994) - Survey of the series' continuity and continuity mistakes. Many interesting fan theories, all marked as such.

I, Who vols. 1-3. (Lars Pearson, Mad Norwegian Press, 1999 -) - An ongoing book-by-book and audio-by-audio survey of the novels and BF audios, including spin-offs and detailed breakdowns of the stories.

Timelink (Jon Preddle, TSV Books, 2000) - A massive fan-produced survey of the television series's continuity. With extensive quotes, and a story-by-story breakdown.

Doctor Who - The Legend. (Justin Richards, BBC Books, 2003) - A hardback introduction to *Doctor Who*, with a story-by-story section that lists dates where they are known.

About Time. (Lawrence Miles and Tat Wood, Mad Norwegian Press, 2004 -) - A series of books that place Doctor Who in a cultural context and offer opinions and essays on continuity matters, including some chronological ones like UNIT Dating.

Who's Next. (Mark Clapham, Eddie Robson and Jim Smith, Virgin Publishing, 2005) - A one-volume guide to *Doctor Who* on television, with a breakdown of continuity.

The following timeline serves as a compressed version of the history presented throughout the book. The same symbols apply as before... "c" refers to an approximate dating, "&" is when a story's dating is based on another adventure, "?" amounts to what's largely a guess, "=" denotes a story that occurs partly / fully in an alternate history and "@" signifies the amnesiac Doctor's stay on Earth.

Section 1: Pre-History

The Dawn of Time	Timeless
c 6,000,000,000 BC	Eternity Weeps
c 3,000,000,000 BC	Venusian Lullaby
c 400,000,000 BC	City of Death
c 150,000,000 BC	Hand of Fear, The
140,000,000 BC	Time-Flight
c 65,000,000 BC	Earthshock
Age of the Reptile People	Bloodtide
Birth of the Cybermen	Spare Parts
c 12,000,000 BC	Taking of Planet 5, The
2,579,868 BC	Genocide
c 100,000 BC	Unearthly Child, An
c 100,000 BC	Eight Doctors, The

Section 2: Known History

& 4,000 BC	Davros
? 4,000 BC	Genesis of the Daleks
c 2,700 BC	Timewyrm: Genesys
c 2,650 BC	Daleks' Master Plan, The
c 2,000 BC	Fallen Gods
c 2,000 BC	Sands of Time, The
c 1,500 BC	Time Monster, The
c 1,400 BC	Eye of the Scorpion, The
1,366 BC	Set Piece
c 1,184 BC	The Myth Makers
c 1,000 BC	Primeval
10 BC	State of Change
64 AD	Rescue, The
64	Byzantium!
64	Romans, The
79	Fires of Vulcan, The
= 305	Seasons of Fear
325	Council of Nicaea, The
c 1001	Excelis Dawns
1066	Time Meddler, The
c 1190	Crusade, The
1215	King's Demons, The
1240	Bunker Soldiers
1242	Sanctuary
c 1273	Time Warrior, The
1278	Asylum
1289	Marco Polo

c 1454	Aztecs, The
1485	Sometime Never
1487	Left-Handed Hummingbird, The
c 1492	Masque of Mandragora, The
c 1500	Ghosts of N-Space, The
1505	City of Death
1555	Marian Conspiracy, The
1560	Room With No Doors, The
1572	Massacre, The
1605	Plotters, The
1609	Empire of Glass, The
1626	Church and the Crown, The
1638	Silver Nemesis
1648	Roundheads, The
1666	Visitation, The
1692	Witch Hunters, The
c 1696	Smugglers, The
1702	Phantasmagoria
c 1705	Doctor Who and the Pirates
1746	Highlanders, The / War Games, The
1781/2	Catch-1782
1782/3	Adventuress of Henrietta Street, The
1794	Reign of Terror, The
1798	Set Piece
1799	Christmas on a Rational Planet
1800	Foreign Devils
= 1804	Man in the Velvet Mask, The
= 1806	Seasons of Fear
1812	Emotional Chemistry
c 1813	Mark of the Rani, The
1818	Ghosts of N-Space, The
1827/8	Medicinal Purposes
1835	Bloodtide
= 1843	Reckless Engineering
1863	Empire of Death
1865	Blood and Hope
1865	Eleventh Tiger, The
1866	Evil of the Daleks, The
1869	Unquiet Dead, The
1871	Set Piece
1872	Eye of Heaven
1872	Chase, The
1873	Strange England
1878	Imperial Moon
1880	Evolution
1881	Gunfighters, The
1883	Ghost Light
1885	Timelash
1887	All-Consuming Fire

1888	Pit, The
c 1889	Talons of Weng-Chiang, The
c 1889	@ The Burning
1893	Camera Obscura
1894	Time Zero
1894	Bodysnatchers, The
1896	Sands of Time, The
1897	Death of Art, The
1898	Banquo Legacy, The
1900	Foreign Devils
c 1902	Horror of Fang Rock
1903	Sleep of Reason, The
= 1906	Chimes of Midnight, The
1909	Birthright
1911	Pyramids of Mars
1912	Left-Handed Hummingbird, The
1914	Human Nature
1915	Sirens of Time, The
1915	White Darkness
1915	Players
1916	Wages of Sin, The
1917	Roof of the World, The
1918	@ Casualties of War
1919	Toy Soldiers
c 1921	Daleks' Master Plan, The
1923	Timewyrm: Exodus
1925	Black Orchid
= 1927	Real Time
1929	Blood Harvest
? 1930	Wormery, The
1930	English Way of Death, The
1930	Storm Warning
1930	Seasons of Fear
1933	Eater of Wasps
1934	Eye of the Giant, The
1935	Abominable Snowmen, The
1936	@ Wolfsbane
1936	Players
1937	History 101
1937	Shadow of Weng-Chiang, The
1938	Invaders from Mars
1940	Timewyrm: Exodus
1940	Illegal Alien
1941	Just War
1941	Empty Child, The / Doctor Dances, The
1942	Shadow in the Glass, The
1943	Curse of Fenric, The
1943	@ Turing Test, The
= 1944	Colditz
1944	Deadly Reunion

1944	Shadow in the Glass, The
1944	Autumn Mist
1944/5	Turing Test, The
1945	Shadow in the Glass, The
1947	Dying in the Sun
1949	Cabinet of Light, The
= 1951	Timewyrm: Exodus
1951	@ Endgame
= 1951	Real Time
1952	Amorality Tale
1954	Witch Hunters, The
1957	First Frontier
1958	Bad Therapy
1959	Delta and the Bannermen
= 1959	Loving the Alien
1960	Mad Dogs and Englishmen

Section 3: Present Day

1963	Time and Relative
1963	Taint, The
1963	Ghost Ship
1963	Unearthly Child, The
1963	Remembrance of the Daleks
1963	Who Killed Kennedy
= 1963	Matrix
1963	Winter for the Adept
1964	Land of the Dead, The
c 1964	Planet of Giants
1965	Chase, The
1965	Massacre, The
1965	Salvation
1965	Daleks' Master Plan, The
1966	Chase, The
1966	War Machines, The
1966	Faceless Ones, The
1967	Wonderland
1967	Revolution Man
1968	Nightshade
1969	Revolution Man

UNIT Era

Unit Year -4	Web of Fear, The
Unit Year -4	Left-Handed Hummingbird, The
Unit Year 1	Invasion, The
Unit Year 1	Spearhead from Space
Unit Year 2	Doctor Who and the Silurians
Unit Year 2	Ambassadors of Death, The
Unit Year 2	Inferno
Unit Year 3	Eye of the Giant, The

Unit Year 3	Scales of Injustice, The	1980	Fires of Vulcan, The
Unit Year 3	Devil Goblins from Neptune, The	c 1980	Shada / Five Doctors, The
		c 1980	Shada
Unit Year 3	Terror of the Autons	c 1980	Meglos
Unit Year 3	Mind of Evil, The	c 1980	@ Father Time
Unit Year 3	Deadly Reunion	c 1981	Keeper of Traken, The
Unit Year 4	Claws of Axos, The	1981	Logopolis
Unit Year 4	Colony in Space	1981	Castrovalva
Unit Year 4	Daemons, The	1981	Four to Doomsday
Unit Year 5	Who Killed Kennedy	1981	K9 and Company
Unit Year 5	Day of the Daleks	1981	Blue Box
= Unit Year 5	Face of the Enemy, The	c 1982	Time-Flight
Unit Year 5	Sea Devils, The	1982	Relative Dementias
Unit Year 5	Eight Doctors, The	1982	Living Legend
Unit Year 5	Time Monster, The	c 1983	Arc of Infinity
Unit Year 6	Rags	1983	Mawdryn Undead
Unit Year 6	Verdigris	1983	Turlough and the Earthlink Dilemma
Unit Year 6	Three Doctors, The		
Unit Year 6	Wages of Sin, The	c 1983	Five Doctors, The
Unit Year 6	Suns of Caresh, The	c 1983	Heart of TARDIS
Unit Year 6	Dancing the Code	1983	Return of the Living Dad
Unit Year 6	Last of the Gaderene	1984	Awakening, The
Unit Year 6	Speed of Flight	1984	Resurrection of the Daleks
Unit Year 6	Green Death, The	c 1984	Planet of Fire
Unit Year 6	Deep Blue	1984	Downtime
Unit Year 7	Time Warrior, The	= 1984	Turlough and the Earthlink Dilemma
Unit Year 7	Paradise of Death, The		
Unit Year 7	Invasion of the Dinosaurs	1985	Attack of the Cybermen
Unit Year 7	Five Doctors, The	c 1985	Two Doctors, The
Unit Year 7	Ghosts of N-Space, The	c 1985	Father Time
Unit Year 8	Amorality Tale	c 1986	Harry Sullivan's War
Unit Year 8	Planet of the Spiders	1986	Tenth Planet, The
Unit Year 8	Robot	1987	Damaged Goods
Unit Year 8	Terror of the Zygons	= 1987	Father's Day
= Unit Year 8	Pyramids of Mars	1988	Silver Nemesis
Unit Year 8	Heart of TARDIS	1989	Business Unusual
Unit Year 8	No Future	c 1989	Survival
Unit Year 8	Android Invasion, The	1989	@ Father Time
Unit Year 8	Seeds of Doom, The	c 1990	Cat's Cradle: Time's Crucible
Unit Year 8	Pescatons, The	1992	Timewyrm: Revelation
Unit Year 8	Hand of Fear, The	c 1992	Cat's Cradle: Witch Mark
		= 1993	Blood Heat

The Non-UNIT 70s

		1993	Left-Handed Humming-bird, The
c 1970	Underwater Menace, The	= 1993	Conundrum
c 1975	Fury From the Deep	1993	Dimension Riders, The
1976	Vampire Science	1993	Goth Opera
c 1977	Image of the Fendahl	1993	Instruments of Darkness
c 1978	Pirate Planet, The	1994	Land of the Dead, The
c 1978	Stones of Blood, The	1994	Invasion of the Cat-People
1979	City of Death	c 1995	Downtime
c 1980	Leisure Hive, The	1996	Interference
1980	City of the Dead, The	1996	Chase, The

1996	Sands of Time, The
1997	Rapture, The
c 1997	Battlefield
1997	Dying Days, The
1997	Eight Doctors, The
1997	Bullet Time
1997	Vampire Science
c 1997	Pit, The
1997	Infinite Requiem
1998	System Shock
c 1998	Option Lock
1999	King of Terror, The
1999	Dominion
1999/2000	Millennial Rites
1999/2000	Doctor Who - The Movie
2000	Millennium Shock
c 2000	Marian Conspiracy, The
c 2000	Spectre of Lanyon Moor, The
c 2000	Project: Twilight
c 2000	Grave Matter
c 2000	Imperial Moon
c 2000	Excelis Rising
2001	Shadow in the Glass, The
2001	@ Escape Velocity
2001	Head Games
c/= 2001	Psi-ence Fiction
2002	Unnatural History
c 2002	Ratings War, The
c 2002	Fearmonger, The
c 2002	Drift
2002	Time Zero
= 2003	Domino Effect, The
= 2003	Reckless Engineering
= 2003	Last Resort, The
c 2003	Timeless
2003	Eternity Weeps
c 2003	Rip Tide
2003	Quantum Archangel, The
2003	Minuet in Hell
c 2003	Scream of the Shalka
c 2003	Hollow Men, The
2003	Shadow in the Glass, The
= 2003	Jubilee
c 2003	Falls the Shadow
2003	Catch-1782
2004	Sometime Never
2004	Tomorrow Windows, The
c 2004	Sleep of Reason, The
2004	Project: Lazarus
c 2004	Algebra of Ice, The
c 2004	City of the Dead, The
c 2004	Deadstone Memorial, The

2005	Rose
c 2005	Death Comes to Time
2005	Gallifrey Chronicles, The

Section 4: The Future

c 2005	Red Dawn
2006	Aliens of London / World War Three
2006	Boom Town
2006	Parting of the Ways, The
2006	Iceberg
c 2007	Cat's Cradle: Warhead
2010	Happy Endings
2012	Shadows of Avalon, The
2012	Dalek
2012	Long Game, The
2012	Christmas on a Rational Planet
2013	Death and Diplomacy
c 2016	Trading Futures
? 2017	Enemy of the World, The
2020	Power of the Daleks, The
2021	Harvest, The
2024	Emotional Chemistry
2030	Warchild
? 2044	Seeds of Death, The
c 2050	Time of the Daleks, The
? 2068	Wheel in Space, The / War Games, The
2069	Alien Bodies
2070	Moonbase, The
2074	Mad Dogs and Englishmen
2080	Loups-Garoux
c 2084	Warriors of the Deep
2096	Indestructible Man
c 2100	Paradise Towers
= 2108	Genocide
c 2109	Transit
2116	Nightmare of Eden
2130	Face-Eater, The
2135	Space Pirates, The
2146	Murder Game, The
2148	St. Anthony's Fire
c 2157	Lucifer Rising
2157	GodEngine
= 2158	Mutant Phase, The
c 2167	Dalek Invasion of Earth, The
= 2172	Day of the Daleks
2191	Time of Your Life
2191	Killing Ground
& 2199	Legacy of the Daleks
& 2202	Longest Day

& 2202	Dreamstone Moon		2587	Return of the Living Dad
c 2202	Seeing I		c 2590	Demontage
2204	Final Sanction, The		2592	Cold Fusion
& 2205	Seeing I		2593	Dying Days, The
2211	Janus Conjunction, The		? 2600	Death to the Daleks
? 2225	Year of Intelligent Tigers, The		2673	Shadowmind
2227	SLEEPY		c 2675	Sandman, The
? 2230	Frayed		2680	Highest Science, The
2257	SLEEPY		c 2764	Sensorites, The
? 2263	Daleks, The		? 2782	Kinda
? 2265	Chase, The		c 2799	Companion Piece
c 2285	Vengeance on Varos		c 2800	Earthworld
2290	Leisure Hive, The		2815	Festival of Death
2294	Stones of Venice, The		2847	Dark Progeny
c 2295	Whispers of Terror		c 2850	Three's a Crowd
c 2301	Excelis Decays		? 2875	Revenge of the Cybermen
? 2305	Slow Empire, The		? 2877	Robots of Death, The
? 2310	Twin Dilemma, The		? 2878	Power of Kroll, The
? 2366	Macra Terror, The		? 2884	Caves of Androzani, The
2371	Lords of the Storm		? 2887	Corpse Marker
2376	Shakedown		c 2890	Grimm Reality
c 2378	Androids of Tara, The		c 2890	Ten Little Aliens
2379	Mindwarp		c 2950	Independence Day
c 2380	Romance of Crime, The		c 2950	Master
& 2381	Dimension Riders, The		? 2965	Space Museum, The
2382	Fear of the Dark		? 2966	Evil of the Daleks, The
? 2385	Slipback		2975	Original Sin
2387	Infinite Requiem		2982	So Vile a Sin
? 2388	Happiness Patrol, The		2986	Terror of the Vervoids
2400	Pit, The		c 2990	Mutants, The
? 2405	Vanishing Point		2992	Fall of Yquatine, The
2408	Divided Loyalties		2994	Superior Beings
2472	Colony in Space		3012	Space Age, The
c 2484	Game, The		3012	Festival of Death
c 2486	Tomb of the Cybermen, The		c 3025	Sorcerer's Apprentice
			?/= 3050	Infinity Race, The
c 2493	Rescue, The		3060-3090	Flip-Flop
c 2495	Set Piece		c 3064	Ultimate Treasure, The
2503	Sword of Orion		c 3068	Palace of the Red Sun
c 2505	To the Slaughter		? 3078	Ribos Operation, The
? 2515	Parasite		c 3094	Superior Beings
2526	Earthshock		? 3100	Warmonger
? 2530	Attack of the Cybermen		? 3200	Brain of Morbius, The
2534	Colony of Lies, The		3123	Vanderdeken's Children
c 2540	Frontier in Space		3174	Burning Heart
& 2540	Planet of the Daleks		3278	Managra
c 2547	Return of the Living Dad		3286	Real Time
c 2550	Catastrophea		c 3340	Dalek Factor, The
2570	Love and War		c 3400	Dark Path, The
& 2573	Deceit		? 3417	Menagerie, The
? 2575	Human Nature		? 3482	Terminus
c 2585	Also People, The		3488	Asylum
			= 3562	Sirens of Time, The

& 3568	Palace of the Red Sun		?	Last Man Running
c/= 3788	Interference		37,166	Planet of Evil
? 3800	Device of Death, A		c 39,164	Zeta Major
& 3885	Curse of Peladon, The		c 50,000	Heart of TARDIS
& 3935	Monster of Peladon, The		c 83,000	Maltese Penguin, The
c 3935	Blue Angel, The		? 100,000	Infinite Requiem, The
? 3950	Bang-Bang-A-Boom!		200,000	Long Game, The
c 3985	Legacy		200,100	Bad Wolf / Parting of the Ways, The
3985	Theatre of War			
3999	Placebo Effect		309,906	War Games, The
c 4000	Mission to the Unknown		309,906	Eight Doctors, The
4000	Daleks' Master Plan, The		? 802,701	Timelash
4000	Head Games		c 2,000,000	Mysterious Planet, The
4009	Book of the Still, The		c 2,000,000	Dragonfire
c/= 4250	Mutant Phase, The		c 4,000,000	Sun Makers, The
4256	Genocide Machine, The		c 10,000,000	Ark, The
c 4256	Apocalypse Element, The		c 10,000,000	Frontios
c 4260	Storm Harvest		c 10,000,700	Ark, The
c 4260	Dust Breeding		58th Segment of Time	Well-Mannered War, The
& 4261	Prime Time		?	Delta and the Bannermen
? 4500	Destiny of the Daleks		Vulgar End of Time	One Doctor, The
& 4590	Resurrection of the Daleks		? Vulgar End of Time	Omega
c 4600	Davros		5,000,000,000	End of the World, The
? 4615	Revelation of the Daleks		?	Savages, The
? 4620	Juggernauts, The		Near-End of the Universe	Timewyrm: Apocalypse
? 4663	Remembrance of the Daleks		Near-End of the Universe	Father Time
& 4693	War of the Daleks		Near-End of the Universe	Hope
& 4703	Terror Firma		100,000,000,000,000,	Infinity Doctors, The
5000	Invisible Enemy, The		000,000,000,000,000,000	
? 5000	Ice Warriors, The		Event Two	Sometime Never
5000	Emotional Chemistry			
? 5433	Planet of the Spiders			
c 5433	Eight Doctors, The			
? 5595	Mission: Impractical			
? 5597	Tragedy Day			
? 5800	Combat Rock			
c 5995	Zamper			
? 6000	Dreamtime			
6048	Heritage			
c 6050	Half-Life			
? 9000	Dreamtime			
10,764	Crystal Bucephalus, The			
c 11,000	Synthespians™			
? 15,000	City at World's End			
c 16,000	Ark in Space, The			
c & 16,000	Sontaran Experiment, The			
c & 16,000	Eye of the Tiger, The			
? 16,000	Tomb of Valdemar, The			
? 20,000	Web Planet, The			
c 20,192	Twilight of the Gods			
c 22,000	Birthright			
c 22,000	Speed of Flight			
?	Face of Evil, The			

Section 5: Gallifrey

The Dark Days

	Cat's Cradle: Time's Crucible

The Mastery of Time

	Infinity Doctors, The
	Lungbarrow

The Doctor

	Divided Loyalties
	Lungbarrow

The Infinity Doctor

	Infinity Doctors, The

Gallifrey

Warmonger
Three Doctors, The
Two Doctors, The

The Doctor's Exile

War Games, The
Spearhead from Space
Terror of the Autons
Colony in Space
Curse of Peladon, The
Mutants, The
Three Doctors, The

Gallifrey

Planet of the Daleks
Genesis of the Daleks
Brain of Morbius, The
Deadly Assassin, The
Image of the Fendahl
Underworld
Invasion of Time, The
Shada
State of Decay
Arc of Infinity
Five Doctors, The
Resurrection of the Daleks
Attack of the Cybermen
Trial of a Time Lord, The /
Ultimate Foe, The
Eight Doctors, The
Unregenerate!
Remembrance of the Daleks
Blood Harvest
Goth Opera

The Romana Presidency

Happy Endings
Lungbarrow
Sirens of Time, The
Apocalypse Element, The
Death Comes to Time
Doctor Who - The Movie
Neverland
Zagreus
Next Life, The

Eve of the War

Alien Bodies
Interference
Taking of Planet Five, The
Shadows of Avalon, The
Ancestor Cell, The
Gallifrey Chronicles, The

The War (AKA The War in Heaven)

Alien Bodies
Intererence
Taking of Planet Five, The
Ancestor Cell, The
Gallifrey Chronicles, The

After Gallifrey

Gallifrey Chronicles, The

The Last Great Time War

Bold numbers indicate main story entries for each adventure (the same information is found in the Table of Contents). Plain-text numbers indicate a story reference in the footnotes.

NTRODUCING THE ALL-N
introducing the all-new novel...
the all-new novel...

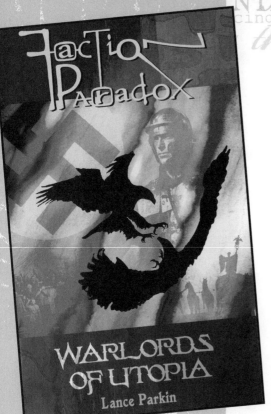

introducing the all-new novel...

Faction Paradox

WARLORDS OF UTOPIA

Adolf Hitler, the Gaol.

In the exact centre of the island was a tower.

It was an ugly concrete stump four storeys high, a brutalist version of a medieval keep. There were tiny slits for windows. There wasn't a door. Around the tower, thorns and weeds had grown into a jungle. The tower held one prisoner.

Surrounding it was an electric fence. And the guards. Millions of strong men and women with the bodies they should have had, unmarked by armband or tattoo, allowed to grow up and grow old. Proud people, many with names like Goldberg, Cohen and Weinstein. Men and women who would never forgive. Men and women who lived in the vast, beautiful community that surrounded the tower, keeping him awake with their laughter, their music, the smell of their food, the sight of their clothes, the sound of their language and their prayers and the cries of their babies. They felt they had a duty to be here. They had always been free to leave, but few had.

On Resurrection Day itself, some had realised that as everyone who had ever lived was in the City, then *he* was here. It had taken longer to hunt him down. Few knew where he'd been found, how he'd been leading his life. Had he tried to disguise himself? Had he proclaimed his name and tried to rally supporters? It didn't matter. He had been brought here, his identity had been confirmed and he had been thrown in the tower that had been prepared for him.

Some of those living in sight of the tower had wondered if they were protecting him from the people of the City, not protecting the City from him. And it was true: the City - the glorious, colourful, polymorphous, diverse City, with uncounted races of people living side by side - was the ultimate negation of the prisoner's creed. The vast, vast majority people of the City didn't care who he was and couldn't comprehend his beliefs, let alone be swayed by his rhetoric. Individuals who'd killed, or wanted to kill, many more people than he had remained at liberty and found themselves powerless. Had imprisoning him marked out as special? Such things were argued about, but the prisoner remained in his tower.

Every day bought requests from individuals, organisations and national groupings who had come up with some way to harm him within the protocols of the City. There were also representations from his supporters, or from civil liberties groups, concerned that his imprisonment was vigilante justice or that no attempt was being made to rehabilitate him. There were historians and psychologists and journalists who wanted to interview him. There were those that just wanted to gawp at or prod the man they'd heard so much about. All of them were turned away.

One man had come here in person. An old Roman, in light armour.

The clerk, a pretty girl with dark hair and eyes, greeted him.

'Your name?'

'Marcus Americanius Scriptor.'

While she dialled up his records and waited for them to appear on her screen, she asked: 'He's after your time. You're a historian?'

'I was,' the old man said. 'May I see him?'

'The prisoner isn't allowed visitors, or to communicate with the outside world. He is allowed to read, but not to write. Oh, that's odd. Your record isn't coming up.'

'It wouldn't.' The Roman didn't elaborate.

He looked out over the city to the tower. The young woman was struck by how solemn his face was. Most people who came all the way out here were sightseers, sensation seekers. Even some of the gaolers treated the prisoner with levity. Mocking him, belittling him.

'Don't you ever want to let him loose?' he asked, finally. 'Let him wander the streets, let his words be drowned out. On another world he was an indifferent, anonymous painter.'

'It sounds like you know that for certain,' she said, before checking herself. 'To answer the question: no. He stays here.'

'I met him,' the Roman told her. 'On a number of occasions.'

She frowned.

'A long story,' he told her. 'I suppose I'm concerned that you torture yourselves by having that monster in your midst.'

The woman had heard many people say such a thing.

'Not a monster. A human being.'

'But the only human being you've locked away for all eternity.'

'The wardens have ruled that he will be freed,' she told him.

Americanius Scriptor seemed surprised. 'When?'

'First he must serve his sentence, then he will be released.'

'When?' he asked again.

'In six million lifetimes,' she told him.

Marcus Americanius Scriptor smiled.

'I'll be waiting for him,' he told her. He turned and headed back to the docks.

OUT NOW. Retail Price: $17.95

1150 46th Street
Des Moines, Iowa 50311
info@madnorwegian.com

www.madnorwegian.com

POLICE PUBLIC CALL BOX

OPEN THE DOOR TO
A NEW DIMENSION

www.galaxy4.co.uk

CREDITS

LANCE PARKIN has written a fair few novels, non-fiction books and edited the diary of Amanda Dingle, a former workmate. He was a storyline writer on UK soap *Emmerdale* for a couple of years, wrote a biography of Alan Moore, authored *Miranda* - a creator-owned science fiction comic - and wrote *Doctor Who* novels such as *The Dying Days*, *The Infinity Doctors* and *Trading Futures*.

Recent projects include *Dark Matter* (co-written with Mark Jones), a guide to the writer Phillip Pullman; a comic that's a hush-hush revamp of a character you've all heard of and the last of the BBC Books' regular Eighth Doctor adventures, *The Gallifrey Chronicles*, which features an evil talking mule. He also wrote *Warlords of Utopia* for Mad Norwegian's *Faction Paradox* series.

Mad Norwegian Press

Publisher / Editor-in-Chief
Lars Pearson

Copy Editor
Steve Manfred

Interior/Cover Design
Christa Dickson

Cover Art
Sandy Gardner

Associate Editor / Index
Dave Gartner

Associate Editor (AHistory)
Graeme Burk

Associate Editors (MNP)
Milo Burke
Marc Eby
Val Sowell
Joshua Wilson

Technical Support
Michael O'Nele
Robert Moriarity

The Publisher Would Like to Thank...
Bill Albert, Jeremy Bement, John and Heather Innis and everyone at the United Network of Iowan Time Lords; Lawrence Miles, Robert Smith?, Shaun Lyon, Tony and Missy Clifton, Michael and Amy Tax, Bill and Mandy Vadbunker.

mad norwegian press

1150 46th St
Des Moines, IA 50311
info@madnorwegian.com
www.madnorwegian.com